Four Galt Novels

Four Galt Novels

Annals of the Parish
The Ayrshire Legatees
The Provost
The Entail

John Galt

with an introduction by
Ian Campbell

Kennedy & Boyd

Kennedy & Boyd
an imprint of
Zeticula Ltd
Unit 13
196 Rose Street
Edinburgh
EH2 4AT
Scotland.

http://www.kennedyandboyd.co.uk
admin@kennedyandboyd.co.uk

Annals of the Parish first published in 1821.
The Ayrshire Legatees first published in 1820.
The Provost first published in 1822.
The Entail first published in 1823

Cover image derived from an engraving by J. Swan, from a drawing by J. Fleming, 1830.

First published in this edition 2015
Introduction Copyright © Ian Campbell 2001, 2015

ISBN 978-1-84921-147-5

Contents

Introduction

I

This edition was developed from a previous collection published in 2001 by the Saltire Society in Edinburgh, to whom grateful thanks are offered. That edition brought together *Annals of the Parish, The Ayrshire Legatees* and *The Provost*, and to those characteristic and very successful shorter Scottish novels is now added *The Entail*, a full-length masterpiece already republished by Kennedy & Boyd in 2007, but now added to those others with a new introduction. Galt's output was copious and frequently little short of brilliant: of *The Provost* no less a critic than Coleridge was to write "This and 'the Entail' would alone suffice to place Galt in the first rank of contemporary Novellists – and second only to Sir W. Scot [sic] in technique"[1]. In this collection, the longer work has been deliberately placed after the Scottish briefer ones to give the reader an opportunity to appreciate the extent of Galt's talent as he develops his comic and constructional abilities to handle a longer plot, a larger cast of characters – and a splendid palette of language[2]. But first, the original three titles.

II

It has taken a long time for John Galt to emerge from the shadow he created for himself with his most successful work, *Annals of the Parish* (1821), the supposed autobiography of a country minister whose fifty years in Dalmailing cover the momentous decades of war and revolution from 1760 to 1810. But the Reverend Micah Balwhidder is a deceptive figure, and the white-haired stereotype, sitting in his study in retirement to tell the story of his life, is very far from being the whole of John Galt's intention in writing the *Annals* and still less a reflection of Galt himself. His success has been hard to live down. Galt the local historian, Galt the Scottish painter of a rural idyll, Galt the genial satirist, Galt the regretful describer of a vanishing Scotland—all true, all most successfully achieved, all partial. The real John Galt, at last, is a little more visible.

But to go back to the other Galt, the stereotype, to the picture of Mr Balwhidder in the Autumn of his days in the study, looking back over a vanished Scotland—it would be very misleading to brush that Galt aside simply because the reality was more complicated. It may overlay that Galt, but that too was part of his experience: the *Annals*, he was to confirm, did not arise exactly from experience but they incorporated memory and historical event and personage, they incorporated the memory of real

---

1 Quoted by Keith M. Costain in "Mind-Forg'd Manacles: *The Entail* as Romantic Comedy", *John Galt 1779-1979* ed. C. A. Whatley (Edinburgh, Ramsay Head, 1979), 164-194 (165). For an interesting brief note on Galt's developing attitude to genre, see Ian A. Gordon's introduction to *John Galt, Selected Short Stories* (Edinburgh, Scottish Academic Press, 1977), viii-ix. Coleridge's comments on Galt (on his copy of *The Provost*, now in the British Library) are transcribed in I. A. Gordon's edition of *The Provost* (London, Oxford UP, 1973), xv.

2 On this see J Derrick McClure "Scots and English in *Annals of the Parish* and *The Provost*" in Whatley (cited above), 195-210. See also A. M. Scriven's introduction to *The Entail* (Glasgow, Kennedy & Boyd, 2007) p. ix discussing "oral performance" in the novel.

places and real changes in a real Scotland. The choice of 1760-1810 could hardly have been better. At the outset of the *Annals*, Scotland seems timeless. Dalmailing is a rural centre, poor, hard-working, intensely centred on its church. How else could we explain a riot over the choice of Balwhidder as minister, 'imposed' by the local landowner rather than chosen by democratic ballot? It is noteworthy that Balwhidder does not need, in his early diaries, to discuss the attendance figures in a Church doubtless always full, where his public utterances would probably hit the whole community, where his political and social attitudes, no matter how naive or under-informed, would be accepted as gospel.

Dalmailing is to be transformed in Galt's hands, rather than in Balwhidder's. For Galt begins to emerge himself, however much we focus on the kindly minister: the minister is a front, a spokesman, a voice, but never the totality of the book. The reader always retains an ironic distance from the minister, noting his kindliness, his generosity, his Christian mission and his many likeable human qualities: noting also his naive attempts to disguise his passion for Mrs Malcolm, his snobbery, his timidity, his rustic self-satisfaction, his readiness to enjoy the world's good things, his entire unfitness to keep up with a world changing too fast for him to understand—and one which in any case he hardly tries to keep up with.

The entire narrative method of Galt's *Annals*—and his *Ayrshire Legatees* (1820)—is to create this double reading from the outset, keep it up, and maintain in the narrative what Coleridge called 'the perfect irony of self-delusion' which allows the character in the book to believe the implied reader will accept the narrative at face value—while the reader sees something bigger, something different, something perhaps the character in the book would much rather keep quiet. Like Provost Pawkie in *The Provost*, like the central character of *The Member*, Mr Balwhidder of *Annals of the Parish* thinks he is in control. It is, after all, his book, his annals of his parish. Because he has chosen to spend all his adult life there, with infrequent and uncomfortable excursions to Glasgow and Edinburgh, Balwhidder thinks himself on safe territory in Dalmailing. Looked up to at the outset as an imposed minister who convinces and wins over his flock by the devotion of his ministry, he metamorphoses during fifty years' work at the centre of the parish into the white-haired patriarch who is offered an assistant in 1809 (though he pawkily sees no need for it, when he can hold forth half an hour longer on any topic than he could in his younger days) and accepts, reluctantly, the inevitable in 1810 and retires, his memory failing, his physical infirmity consoled by the third Mrs Balwhidder whom he prudently chooses to care for him in his declining years. This has been his world, and he has built up a central consciousness of it despite the rapidly accelerating change he chronicles towards the end of the eighteenth century, and the bewildering years of the Napoleonic Wars which opened the nineteenth. Whatever happens in the outside world—dangerous and murderous when it comes close to home and kills Charlie Malcolm—Dalmailing is safe, secure, unchangingly Scottish.

Is it? To Balwhidder, perhaps. He lets slips little hints of change: the local landowner Lord Eglesham, who had the power to impose a minister in 1760 and was the unquestioned authority and source of local power and change in 1760, has long since disappeared. Mr Cayenne the mill owner had become a much more important figure, though even he has risen and had his day during Mr Balwhidder's long ministry.

Significantly, there is no Mr Cayenne, no single figure with whom Balwhidder can identify, or argue with, towards the end of his description of Dalmailing. Lord Eglesham was distant but approachable: Cayenne irritable but human: but the enemies the Church faces in 1810 are impersonal, and do not yield to the simple approaches and remedies of 1760 and the Divinity Hall of Glasgow College. In a telling passage, Balwhidder notices a falling-off in the attendances at Church of the young weavers, and summons them to the Manse. The ironies are rich: while the weavers are summoned (and come, out of deference to a minister plainly out of touch with their world which he never once describes nor apparently visits for first-hand experience of a growing part of his parish) the interview is a disaster, for the weavers run circles round Balwhidder, and use his arguments as 'the light sayings of a vain man'. His arguments, he proudly tells us, are those he was taught in the 1750s in Glasgow, a different world from that of the new industrial poor of the 1780s, who (as it turns out in the diary for 1790) not only know more than the minister, but even subscribe from their miserable wages to take a daily London newspaper to keep up with events in France. The ironic contrast could hardly be more skilfully pointed up by Galt. The parish minister, revered in earlier years as source of all information, sacred and secular, has been completely sidelined in a new world where harder, fresher news is available—at a price—quite outside the Church and its institutions. Balwhidder himself, though he gives us the information on which we can build this picture— his breathless description of a bookshop stuffed with nicknacks, though he hardly mentions the books and the newspaper—cannot see how far he is out of step with his times. It apparently does not cross his mind to buy a newspaper himself, to catch up with events, to try to appeal to the new underclass of his parish, to read some new Divinity to freshen his discourses. Not he. He tells us about the bookshop, and we ironically deduce the rest.

The real Galt is coming closer. Galt is the product of that little secure world of Dalmailing in mid-century, albeit from the slightly more cosmopolitan Port Glasgow and Greenock area, in touch with a mighty trading route from the Clyde to the industrial heartlands of England and beyond, a young man fired by ambition which took him through education to enterprise, to a business career as writer and as entrepreneur and manager in England and Scotland, and very widely in Canada, to success and to financial ruin, to literary fame and to literary disillusion. While he had an insider's knowledge of rural Dalmailing, he had by 1821 an outsider's awareness that there was a larger world beyond, and an ironist's ability to play off the limitations of the people in his novels against the wider knowledge his readers brought. *Annals of the Parish* was published in 1821, by which time the revolution in Dalmailing was finished, indeed was old hat. The new industrial proletariat were an established fact, the wars had given travel and wider knowledge to a whole generation, and the kirks were fast emptying from that secure position they had enjoyed when Balwhidder was placed in 1760. The Cayennes and the Egleshams had had their day, and Britain increasingly was run by the impersonal, the centralised forces which subtly displace in Galt's narrative the face-to-face contact with aristocrat and local mill owner which had sufficed for Dalmailing in the previous century. No longer can the Kirk Session and its modest coffers handle small problems of local poverty and distress: no longer can a single Mrs Malcolm, fallen on hard times but scratching a modest living, stand out by her exceptional nature. Dalmailing is part of the larger world, for better or worse, and perhaps the greatest part of Galt's description of that process is Balwhidder's failure to recognise it.

The Galt of the wider world is very much present in the plot of his first success, *The Ayrshire Legatees* which is reprinted along with the *Annals* and *The Provost* in this volume. Here, with a vengeance, is a book about the wider world, dawning slowly on people who come from a secure smaller one, on people who simultaneously want it and fear it, their fortunes reflected in a wonderful series of letters which not only go back to their sleepy parish of Garnock (not a thousand miles from Dalmailing) but are read aloud there by session clerk and schoolmaster, seamstress and gossip, young and old, sophisticated and apparently clodhopper. From the moment Dr Pringle and his country family learn of their inheritance and resolve to leave their country Manse a while and venture to London, Galt has the scene set for a masterly investigation of what he had himself lived, and what the Scotland of his time was learning to live with—the fact of a larger world outside, the dubious pleasure of learning about that world, the fate of the old when the new intrudes and presents a more attractive face. Balwhidder took refuge, all too often, from that world by pretending it could not exist, and considering the plot of *Annals* (in which he visits the cities hardly at all, and cannot get home fast enough) that was easy for him. In *The Ayrshire Legatees* this will not be so simple. The epistolary novel begins with the Doctor's fearful leaving of his parish, and ends with his triumphant return, enriched, emboldened, his innocence a little lost, the tell-tale signs of the new coach and the newly-Englished manner and dress betraying the sophisticate. Pringle has seen the outside world that Balwhidder feared to encounter: he has gained something compared with Balwhidder (something more, that is, than the cool £100, 000 of his inheritance). But he has lost something too.

Balwhidder remains, pretty well to the end of his novel, a loveable and delightful man, quaint, 'pawky', picturesque in his appearance, shameless in his sexist assumptions and his businesslike approach to choosing a wife. He could only survive in this character, through the turbulent second half of the eighteenth century, by being cut off from the mainstream of change, and we accept this without demur from the ironic position we enjoy as modern readers. But Pringle thinks himself better informed than someone like Balwhidder, and he has higher ambitions for himself and his family. Balwhidder certainly wants the best for his family-placing his son in business even drags him to Glasgow—but no inheritance makes him move in the circles of the aristocracy and the royal family in London. He does not mix, as Pringle does, with rich lawyers like Argent, nor with the upwardly mobile Captain Sabre with his eyes fixed on Pringle's daughter, as much no doubt for her looks as for the enormous dowry she would bring. Balwhidder's three wives apparently show little ambition to move beyond Dalmailing, even though his second one transforms the quiet Manse to a hive of industry. In *The Ayrshire Legatees* people move on: even Mrs Pringle, though she is very much against London and its ways, learns from London and even reluctantly admits that some of its ways are better than Garnock's. Though her frugal habits persist even after her elevation to financial riches—she tosses bawbees to the children from the returning coach, less extravagant than her husband's pennies—she consents to the buying of richer clothes and London goods for their return to Garnock.

Two very strong points are made by Galt in the concluding part of *The Ayrshire Legatees* which would not have been in place in the *Annals*. One concerns the younger generation, people like himself who grow up in Scotland and move on, driven partly by ambition and partly by the need to leave a much-loved Scotland in search of work or career prospects. In *The Ayrshire Legatees* the younger generation cannot wait to get rid of their Scottish background. While Balwhidder's children naturally get on in the world, they seem happy with their parents' solid Christian values, and respect the provincial setting they came from. Not so the repellent Andrew and Rachel Pringle. As soon as they can, they cut the tie and use their new-found riches to start a new life, as far from their Garnock roots as they can. Andrew enters the world of parliamentary politics (and we know from *The Member* a how little respect Galt felt for that line of work) and Rachel marries into fashionable English society, her affected and sentimental letters to Garnock not hiding for a moment her satisfaction at moving onward and upward. Nor does Garnock, for a moment, fail to see through the affectation and politeness of the younger Pringles' letters; after all, they have known Andrew and Rachel all their lives.

The other point concerns their parents. That the minister and his wife feel their roots are in Garnock, and that (give or take a new coach and a new coat) their obvious path is the path back home, is in many ways admirable, but Galt shrewdly points our attention at the assistant minister, Mr Snodgrass, left in charge during Pringle's absence, a well-travelled and able young man who has not only seen more of the world than Garnock, but is more up to date than even his senior colleague—he surreptitiously is reading Scott, for instance, in a village where the activity would be anathema to many of the older and more strait-laced. Andrew Pringle recognises Snodgrass's qualities, but only to say he is sorry that they are wasted in a place like Garnock. All the more credit to Andrew Pringle's father, then, that the old Doctor is able to see Garnock with new eyes, and himself with new eyes, after London. Unlike his fashionable children, he does not slip on a ready-made identity from English society; he wants to retain his Scottishness, but not blindly. Almost his first act on reaching home is to check that the parish is in good order: but after that he loses no time in preparing to step aside, and hand the parish over to the younger and more flexible hands of Mr Snodgrass while he and Mrs Pringle retire to a new life as laird and lady in a nearby country house, fallen vacant by good timing. Galt's affectionate satire is spot-on in describing the first Sunday service after their return.

And some little change had taken place during his absence in his visible equipage. His stockings, which were wont to be of worsted, had undergone a translation into silk; his waistcoat, instead of the venerable Presbyterian flap-covers to the pockets, which were of Johnsonian magnitude, was become plain—his coat, in all times single-breasted, with no collar, still, however, maintained its ancient characteristics; instead, however, of the former bright black cast-horn, the buttons were covered with cloth. But the chief alteration was discernible in the furniture of the head. He had exchanged the simplicity of his own respectable grey hairs for the cauliflower hoariness of a PARRISH wig, on which he wore a broad-brimmed hat, turned up a little at each side behind, in a portentous manner, indicatory of Episcopalian predilections. This, however, was not justified by any alteration in his principles, being merely an innocent variation of fashion, the natural result of a Doctor of Divinity buying a hat and wig in London.

The moment that the Doctor made his appearance, his greeting and salutation was quite delightful; it was that of a father returned to his children, and a king to his people.

Of course Galt is hinting at all kinds of things here, the genuine slip towards the Episcopalian, the manner of the king to his people, the not very unconscious imitation of Dr Johnson. But the parish receives him with affectionate respect, as they receive his wife rustling in her London clothes with a new veneration 'neither unobserved nor unappreciated by that acute and perspicacious lady'. Nothing has changed, everything has changed. The Moneypennies estate is bought by Dr Pringle 'as a great bargain', but 'It was not on account of the advantageous nature of the purchase that our friend valued this acquisition, but entirely because it was situated in his own parish, and part of the lands marching with the Glebe'. No doubt. Pringle has the sense to move out of Manse and pulpit, for a few months in London has changed him beyond moving back to his much-loved earlier self. The inside of the man is as changed as the outside coat and wig.

The outside of Garnock has changed, too, as little details in Galt's description confirm. When the Pringles' coach comes into the village from London, Galt pointedly contrasts the welcome of the older poor people—who reverently doff their bonnets to the minister—with that of the younger workers, with their 'green aprons and thin yellow faces', products of a new weaving factory generation who look on with 'a melancholy smile', pleased enough to see their minister back, but quite without the older generation's instinctive reverence. The position is exactly the same as in Balwhidder's Dalmailing, where the older minister has lost that enormous part of his congregation who either have given up church-going, or prefer the livelier service in Cayenneville. But while Balwhidder cannot comprehend the notion, Pringle does something about it: he stands aside for a younger man who has a chance to be minister to a mixed parish like the one Garnock has become.

More than any other of his books, *The Ayrshire Legatees* catches the paradoxical nature of Galt's Scottishness, since it never ceases to juxtapose the world of the traveller, the man of business, the Scot of the world, with the never-to-be-forgotten roots of the Scottish character and the Scottish imagination. Galt was a product of both, and while his bodily existence was to be one of strenuous travel and effort—and bitter disappointment when his Canadian business went sour and he was recalled in disgrace by his employers—his mental existence was very much one of exercise of the memory, recreating a vanishing Scotland, one remembered far away, one reconstructed from gossip and local history, one imagined by comparing the here and now of the 1820s—the aftermath of an enormous war, the still ongoing industrial revolution, the country revolutionised by transport and trade—with sleepy Garnock and Dalmailing.

'A certain distance', he wrote in his *Autobiography*, 'in all limning is necessary to enable an artist to contemplate, in the most picturesque point of view, the objects he would represent'. Galt argues for the advantage of having been away, of not having been too close to the Scotland he depicts in these books. 'The vraisemblance of my pictures ought to have been regarded as a proof that I could not have been very intimately near those things which I have chosen to depict; although in all of them there may be a bringing together of homogenous circumstances, so obvious, that the mere mirroring of the mind is not their sole merit ...' In a much-quoted passage Galt rebukes people for taking his *Annals* as literal autobiography: 'to myself it has ever been a kind of treatise on the history of society in the west of Scotland during the reign of King George the Third; and when it was written, I had no idea it would ever have been received as a novel, Fables are often a better way of illustrating philosophical truths than abstract reasoning; and in this class of composition I would place the *Annals of the Parish*; but the public consider it as a novel, and it is of no use to think of altering the impression with which it has been received'. Galt acknowledged some of the characters were recognisably linked to 'real' people, but denied his readers the pleasure of source hunting, holding that his creations were 'things of which the originals are, or were, actually in nature, but brought together into composition by art'. And there it has to remain.

The Provost (1822) represents for Galt a subtle but successful modification of the technique he used for Balwhidder and the *Annals*. Where the minister is too unworldly (it seems) to keep up with events, relying on a combination of innocence and occasional country cunning to get through the tumultuous years of his time in Dalmailing, Provost Pawkie is almost—but not quite—too clever for his own good. He certainly has the wider vision Balwhidder so lamentably lacks: in chapter 23 he reflects that "I have lived long enough to remark, that if we judge of past events by present motives, and do not try to enter into the spirit of the age when they took place, and to see them with the eyes with which they were really seen, we shall conceit many things to be of a bad and wicked character, that were not thought so harshly of by those who witnessed them". But a wider vision? Obliquely, this is an *apologia* for the events before and after, an excuse for what might have seemed at the time (rouping a field of potatoes at an outrageous price to make a quick profit) almost excusable, but in retrospect is jobbing of the worst kind.

Galt was a well-travelled man of affairs, and he knew that jobbing was rife in the public affairs of the world he lived in. Later, in Canada, he was to come against (and be hurt by) the corporate politics of the company for which he worked in Ontario. In novels like *The Member* he played openly on the public's perception that politicians were crooks, and that they sought public office to line their pockets. Pawkie is not without such ambition, and his provostries certainly coincide with (as he would complacently put it) an augmentation of his worldly affairs. Sometimes, this is no doubt his own hard work and native shrewdness in cultivating his business. At others, he lets us know, more or less, it is the outcome of a deliberate scheme, to take a lucrative office into his own hands, to arrange public money should be spent in a way which suits his own interest, to form a strategic alliance which—not necessarily at once—will be to his benefit.

Pawkie most endearingly illustrates the truth of Coleridge's insight that Galt is master of the unconscious self-betrayal of a character by his memoirs. Pawkie is keenly aware of public opinion, and of changes in public opinion: in chapter 28 he tells us quite openly that "the peremptory will of authority was no longer sufficient for the rule of mankind", and a public figure must have more "deference to public opinion". Quite so. But he also lets slip his utter defiance of public opinion in his own interest, never more so than in his slipping in and out of office, best of all when he finally retires and arranges everything as he would like it, right down to the address of congratulation which crowns his years of service. The "levity and indiscretion of a young man" (chapter 44) gives way to the gravity of the experienced politician, and *The Provost* becomes the most entertaining balancing act between changing times—for here they change as much as in the *Annals*—and a changing narrator who is gaining experience as well as authority and worldly goods. But through it all the confidentiality of narrator and audience is maintained, and while Pawkie obviously courts his audience's good opinion, he continually lets slip the odd detail which betrays his vanity, his self-regard and his ambition. In *The Provost* Galt continues the deftness with which he captures the change in the Scotland he had himself lived through. The roads are widened and surfaced, public lands enclosed, the relation of the local to the urban and central government continually reinforced, the Church and local government see their power change and, ultimately, wane. But the false centre is Pawkie's self-conceit. He sees the change, and thinks himself master and choreographer. We see past him, round him, at the Scotland which is being redefined round the limits of Pawkie's experience.

One thing this volume should do, forcibly, is undermine the impression sometimes given that Galt is a novelist of the kailyard, clinging profitably but exploitatively to a vanished Scotland and representing that Scotland as the one, true picture to an audience eager to be deceived into believing in a Dalmailing or a Garnock, still there, still waiting to be discovered. Galt's fiction, as shown in this volume, combines highly profitable writing with a sharp-eyed recognition of the inevitability of change in Scotland. Balwhidder's clinging to the past and all its values is, ultimately, futile: Cayenneville grows without him, the church empties, the world of the 1760s is far away indeed when white-haired old Balwhidder sits down in 1810 to write his memoirs. And everything about Pringle's visit to London shows the futility of coming back to Garnock and pretending that nothing has changed. That the Pringles came back, loyal to their roots, yet made a new life for themselves in which the real change they had experienced—and recognised in their homely village—could be assimilated, is Galt's message to his Scottish readers. The annals of his parish are annals of change: the legacy of a trip to London is not retreat to comforting familiarity, but the bitter-sweet recognition that there is no going back. Rather, like Galt himself, his characters learn to adapt and live with the new world. He gives his readers the pleasure of the old world and all its distinctive Scottish character: but the future lies not in burying one's head in the past, but in learning to live with the present. Galt's message to his readers, Scots and non-Scots, is as relevant today as it was in the 1820s when his novels raised him to the rank of best-seller. *Annals of the Parish*, *The Ayrshire Legatees* and *The Provost* as they are read, will only enhance his reputation in the twenty-first century.

III

Galt wrote to the publisher William Blackwood on 23 June 1822, reporting on his progress with writing *The Entail*, and he made a point which the novel bore out; "It has taken full possession of my fancy and I always know that when I am myself interested I do not fail in the effort. . . I am anxious to make arrangements for spending three months in Scotland, where I may be enabled to add to my vernacular vocabulary"[3].

---

3 John Galt, *The Entail* ed. Ian A Gordon, (London, Oxford UP, 1970), 370.

That Scottish vocabulary is one of *The Entail*'s main claims to fame as Galt populates South West Scotland with authentic speakers who counterpoint the English of the interpolated narrative, and who emphasise in their contrast with younger and English-speaking Scots the changes which Galt picked up in his earlier fiction. Just as Andrew Pringle in *The Ayrshire Legatees* shows little trace of his parents' unforced command of Scots, and the visiting younger ministers in Balwhidder's pulpit disturb him with their English ways, so *The Entail* charts the rapid change of register in spoken speech, deliberately sampling at each generation the process of change, and anchoring all with the splendid creation of the Leddy Grippy who sees no need to change, and uses the Scots of her earlier years without hesitation or apology, dipping in and out of Biblical phraseology with entire naturalness and illogic.

"'Come awa, Bell Fatherlans,' said she, 'come away, and sit down. O this is a most uncertain world—nothing in it has stability;—the winds blow—the waters run—the grass grows—the snow falls—the day flieth away unto the uttermost parts of the sea, and the night hideth her head in the morning cloud, and perisheth for evermore. Many a lesson we get—many a warning to set our thoughts on things above; but we're ay sinking, sinking, sinking, as the sparks fly upward.—Bell, Bell, we're a' like thorns crackling under a kail-pot.'"

Less sententiously but just as seriously, she offers advice on marriage:

"'And what for no? I'm sure Beenie's fortune will be a better bargain than a landless lad like you can hope for at ony other hand.'
'True, but I'll never marry for money.'
'And what will ye marry for, then?' exclaimed the Leddy. 'Tak my word o' experience for't, my man,—a warm downseat's o' far mair consequence in matrimony than the silly low o' love; and think what a bonny business your father and mother made o' their gentle-shepherding. But, Jamie, what's the reason ye'll no tak Beenie?—there maun surely be some because for sic unnaturality?'

The Leddy, as critics have agreed, is a comic masterpiece: to quote Roderick Watson, Galt "uses a denser dialect than Scott allowed himself – amounting to a *tour de force* in the case of Lady Grippy in *The Entail*"[4]: Ian A. Gordon, one of Galt's best critics, describes *The Entail* as "a linguistic triumph"[5].

The Entail is more than skilful Scots. For one thing, it covers in its sweep generations of change in Glasgow and its countryside and shows, through generation of change, how Scotland was in an upheaval that neither provost nor country minister could comprehend. Alan Riach has written that "The tension between industrial commerce and rural hinterland is brilliantly realised in both the narrative and texture of the novel, as it moves between Glasgow and the Ayrshire countryside, with reference to the Muirkirk iron works, the merchants of Glasgow, the city's theatre world and

---

4 Roderick Watson, *The Literature of Scotland* (second edition, Houndmills, Palgrave Macmillan, 2007), 2:294.
5 *The Entail* (n. 3 above) p. xv.

the different characters of the two principal cities"[6]. Galt repeatedly contrasts the narrow perspective of human plotting and human greed with the larger forces of change which no individual, no single generation fully understands. The narrow and selfish ambition which was the motivation behind the entail in the first place is long overtaken by events which could hardly have been anticipated – births, details, marriage, misunderstanding, and brooding over all the operations of the law.

Galt had himself reason to know that the law could frustrate human planning and in *The Entail* he offers a striking set of analyses of how the law operates for good and ill. Ian Duncan has remarked in an acute essay that "The entrepreneurial, indeed opportunistic, impulse of Galt's literary career determines its strikingly fitful and uneven contours"[7]. The remark applies to the sometimes fitful texture of *The Entail*, though Keith Costain has defended the novel against critics who see in the second half a diminution of quality[8]. Claud's entrepreneurial urge indeed would have been something Galt could relate to his own early life and his self-made success: the Leddy's relentless pursuit of what she sees as the right, or the defensible, also something he will have encountered in his own dealings with publishers and business people.

What most of all in *The Entail* succeeds is the sweep of generations driven by that initial perverted decision to favour one son over another, and the working out of what became a family curse, its malign influence almost but not quite cancelled by a deathbed realisation, its application monitored by a surprisingly sympathetic lawyer character, and everywhere human planning coming against the seemingly random operation of fate.

Galt himself wrote that "We see every day around us men who are influenced by impulses which they cannot control, who are driven into new circumstances by what is called good or bad luck, without any exercise of their own faculties, nay, often against the conclusions of their understandings; and others, who are equally subject to the dictates of reason"[9]. The achievement of *The Entail* is to draw from his own hectic life-experience, with the various successes and failures implicit in Ian Duncan's description, a plot which he managed at some length while balancing the tension of plot resolution, the development of character, and the fine balance of humour and seriousness which is achieved above all by The Leddy. "O this is a most uncertain world—nothing in it has stability", she may complain, but she is unconsciously presenting the reader with Galt's picture of that rapidly changing Scotland he so deftly conjures in all the books reprinted here.

---

6   Alan Riach, "The Literature of Industrialisation" in *The Edinburgh History of Scottish Literature* (Edinburgh, Edinburgh UP, 2007), 2: 236-7. Galt contrasted the two cities brilliantly in the squib *The Gathering of the West*, which coincided with George IV's royal 1822 visit.

7   Ian Duncan, "Altered States: Galt, Serial Fiction, and the Romantic Miscellany" in *John Galt: Observations and Conjectures on Literature, History and Society* ed. Regina Hewitt (Lewisburg, Bucknell University Press, 2012), 53-71 (53)

8   Mind-Forg'd Manacles": see fn. 1 above.

9   *The Literary Life, and Miscellanies, of John Galt* (Edinburgh, Blackwood, 1834) 2:199.

Further reading

Ian A Gordon's splendid introductions to the Oxford University Press editions remain an excellent starting point, as does his *John Galt, the Life of a Writer* (Edinburgh, Oliver & Boyd, 1972). Gordon's edition of *The Entail* (Oxford, OUP 1970) has a particularly interesting appendix (p. 365) on the modifications made to the 1842 text of the novel by the publishers when it was re-issued, badly interfering with Galt's skilful rendering of colloquial Scots. Paul H. Scott has a fine précis of the novel in *John Galt* (Scottish Writers Series), (Edinburgh, Scottish Academic Press, 1985), 64-9. The recent histories of Scottish literature demonstrate a growing awareness of Galt's importance, taking him seriously as variously social critic, linguistic experimenter, realist portrayer of country life – far from the supposition that he was in any way one of the kailyard school in advance of its time. A sampling of recent critical thinking on Galt is to be found in *John Galt: Observations and Conjectures on Literature, History and Society* ed. Regina Hewitt (Lewisburg, Bucknell University Press, 2012).

Annals of the Parish

Introduction

In the same year, and on the same day of the same month, that his Sacred Majesty King George, the third of the name, came to his crown and kingdom, I was placed and settled as the minister of Dalmailing. When about a week thereafter this was known in the parish, it was thought a wonderful thing, and everybody spoke of me and the new king as united in our trusts and temporalities, marvelling how the same should come to pass, and thinking the hand of Providence was in it, and that surely we were preordained to fade and flourish in fellowship together; which has really been the case, for, in the same season that his Most Excellent Majesty, as he was very properly styled in the proclamations for the general fasts and thanksgivings, was set by as a precious vessel which had received a crack or a flaw, and could only be serviceable in the way of an ornament, I was obliged, by reason of age and the growing infirmities of my recollection, to consent to the earnest entreaties of the Session, and to accept of Mr Amos to be my helper. I was long reluctant to do so, but the great respect that my people had for me, and the love that I bore towards them, over and above the sign that was given to me in the removal of the royal candlestick from its place, worked upon my heart and understanding, and I could not stand out. So, on the last Sabbath of the year 1810, I preached my last sermon, and it was a moving discourse. There were few dry eyes in the kirk that day, for I had been with the aged from the beginning—the young considered me as their natural pastor—and my bidding them all farewell was, as when of old among the heathen, an idol was taken away by the hands of the enemy.

At the close of the worship, and before the blessing, I addressed them in a fatherly manner, and although the kirk was fuller than ever I saw it before, the fall of a pin might have been heard—at the conclusion there was a sobbing and much sorrow. I said:

'My dear friends, I have now finished my work among you for ever. I have often spoken to you from this place the words of truth and holiness, and, had it been in poor frail human nature to practise the advice and counselling that I have given in this pulpit to you, there would not need to be any cause for sorrow on this occasion—the close and latter end of my ministry. But, nevertheless, I have no reason to complain, and it will be my duty to testify, in that place where I hope we are all one day to meet again, that I found you a docile and a tractable flock, far more than at first I could have expected. There are among you still a few, but with grey heads and feeble hands now, that can remember the great opposition that was made to my placing, and the stout part they themselves took in the burly, because I was appointed by the patron; but they have lived to see the error of their way, and to know that preaching is the smallest portion of the duties of a faithful minister. I may not, my dear friends, have applied my talent in the pulpit so effectually as perhaps I might have done, considering the gifts that it pleased God to give me in that way, and the education that I had in the Orthodox University of Glasgow, as it was in the time of my youth, nor can I say that, in the works of peacemaking and charity, I have done all that I should have done.

But I have done my best, studying no interest but the good that was to rise according to the faith in Christ Jesus.

'To my young friends I would, as a parting word, say, Look to the lives and conversation of your parents—they were plain, honest, and devout Christians, fearing God and honouring the king. They believed the Bible was the word of God, and when they practised its precepts, they found, by the good that came from them, that it was truly so. They bore in mind the tribulation and persecution of their forefathers for righteousness' sake, and were thankful for the quiet and protection of the government in their day and generation. Their land was tilled with industry, and they ate the bread of carefulness with a contented spirit, and, verily, they had the reward of well-doing even in this world, for they beheld on all sides the blessing of God upon the nation, and the tree growing, and the plough going, where the banner of the oppressor was planted of old, and the war-horse trampled in the blood of martyrs. Reflect on this, my young friends, and know, that the best part of a Christian's duty in this world of much evil, is to thole and suffer with resignation, as lang as it is possible for human nature to do. I do not counsel passive obedience; that is a doctrine that the Church of Scotland can never abide; but the divine right of resistance, which, in the days of her trouble, she so bravely asserted against popish and prelatic usurpations, was never resorted to till the attempt was made to remove the ark of the tabernacle from her. I therefore counsel you, my young friends, no to lend your ears to those that trumpet forth their hypothetical politics, but to believe that the laws of the land are administered with a good intent, till in your own homes and dwellings ye feel the presence of the oppressor—then, and not till then, are ye free to gird your loins for battle—and woe to him, and woe to the land where that is come to, if the sword be sheathed till the wrong be redressed.

'As for you, my old companions, many changes have we seen in our day, but the change that we ourselves are soon to undergo will be the greatest of all. We have seen our bairns grow to manhood—we have seen the beauty of youth pass away—we have felt our backs become unable for the burthen, and our right hand forget its cunning. Our eyes have become dim, and our heads grey—we are now tottering with short and feckless steps towards the grave; and some, that should have been here this day, are bed-rid, lying, as it were, at the gates of death, like Lazarus at the threshold of the rich man's door, full of ails and sores, and having no enjoyment but in the hope that is in hereafter. What can I say to you but farewell! Our work is done—we are weary and worn out, and in need of rest—may the rest of the blessed be our portion! -and, in the sleep that all must sleep, beneath the cold blanket of the kirkyard grass, and on that clay pillow where we must shortly lay our heads, may we have pleasant dreams, till we are awakened to partake of the everlasting banquet of the saints in glory.'

When I had finished, there was for some time a great solemnity throughout the kirk, and, before giving the blessing, I sat down to compose myself, for my heart was big, and my spirit oppressed with sadness.

As I left the pulpit, all the elders stood on the steps to hand me down, and the tear was in every eye, and they helped me into the session—house; but I could not speak to them, nor them to me. Then Mr Dalziel, who was always a composed and sedate man, said a few words of prayer, and I was comforted therewith, and rose to go home to the manse; but in the churchyard all the congregation was assembled, young and old, and they made a lane for me to the back-yett that opened into the manse-garden. Some of them put out their hands and touched me as I passed, followed by the elders, and some of them wept. It was as if I was passing away, and to be no more—verily, it was the reward of my ministry—a faithful account of which, year by year, I now sit down, in the evening of my days, to make up, to the end that I may bear witness to the work of a beneficent Providence, even in the narrow sphere of my parish, and the concerns of that flock of which it was His most gracious pleasure to make me the unworthy shepherd.

Chapter 1

Year 1760

The placing of Mr Balwhidder—The resistance of the parishioners—Mrs Malcolm, the widow—Mr Balwhidder's marriage .

The Ann. Dom. one thousand seven hundred and sixty was remarkable for three things in the parish of Dalmailing. First and foremost, there was my placing; then the coming of Mrs. Malcolm with her five children to settle among us; and next, my marriage upon my own cousin, Miss Betty Lanshaw, by which the account of this year naturally divides itself into three heads or portions.

First, of the placing. It was a great affair; for I was put in by the patron, and the people knew nothing whatsoever of me, and their hearts were stirred into strife on the occasion, and they did all that lay within the compass of their power to keep me out, insomuch, that there was obliged to be a guard of soldiers to protect the presbytery; and it was a thing that made my heart grieve when I heard the drum beating and the fife playing as we were going to the kirk. The people were really mad and vicious, and flung dirt upon us as we passed, and reviled us all, and held out the finger of scorn at me; but I endured it with a resigned spirit, compassionating their wilfulness and blindness. Poor old Mr. Kilfuddy of the Braehill got such a clash of glar on the side of his face, that his eye was almost extinguished.

When we got to the kirk door, it was found to be nailed up, so as by no possibility to be opened. The sergeant of the soldiers wanted to break it, but I was afraid that the heritors would grudge and complain of the expense of a new door, and I supplicated him to let it be as it was; we were, therefore, obliged to go in by a window, and the crowd followed us, in the most unreverent manner, making the Lord's house like an inn on a fair day, with their grievous yellyhooing. During the time of the psalm and the sermon, they behaved themselves better, but when the induction came on, their clamour was dreadful; and Thomas Thorl, the weaver, a pious zealot in that time, he got up and protested, and said, 'Verily, verily, I say unto you, he that entereth not by the door into the sheepfold, but climbeth up some other way, the same is a thief and a robber.' And I thought I would have a hard and sore time of it with such an outstrapolous people. Mr. Given, that was then the minister of Lugton, was a jocose man, and would have his joke even at a solemnity. When the laying of the hands upon me was a-doing, he could not get near enough to put on his, but he stretched out his staff and touched my head, and said, to the great diversion of the rest, 'This will do well enough, timber to timber,' but it was an unfriendly saying of Mr Given, considering the time and the place, and the temper of my people.

After the ceremony, we then got out at the window, and it was a heavy day to me, but we went to the manse, and there we had an excellent dinner, which Mrs Watts of the new inns of Irville prepared at my request, and sent her chaise-driver to serve, for he was likewise her waiter, she having then but one chaise, and that no often called for.

But, although my people received me in this unruly manner, I was resolved to cultivate civility among them; and therefore, the very next morning I began a round of visitations; but oh, it was a steep brae that I had to climb, and it needed a stout heart. For I found the doors in some places barred against me; in others, the bairns, when they saw me coming, ran crying to their mothers, 'Here's the feckless Mess-John'; and then when I went in into the houses, their parents would no ask me to sit down, but with a scornful way, said, 'Honest man, what's your pleasure here?' Nevertheless, I walked about from door to door, like a dejected beggar, till I got the almous deed of a civil reception, and who would have thought it, from no less a person than the same Thomas Thorl that was so bitter against me in the kirk on the foregoing day.

Thomas was standing at the door with his green duffle apron and his red Kilmarnock nightcap—I mind him as well as if it was but yesterday—and he had seen me going from house to house, and in what manner I was rejected, and his bowels were moved, and he said to me in a kind manner, 'Come in, sir, and ease yoursel'; this will never do, the clergy are God's gorbies, and for their Master's sake it behoves us to respect them. There was no ane in the whole parish mair against you than mysel', but this early visitation is a sympton of grace that I couldna have expectit from a bird out the nest of patronage.' I thanked Thomas, and went in with him, and we had some solid conversation together, and I told him that it was not so much the pastor's duty to feed the flock, as to herd them well; and that although there might be some abler with the head than me, there wasna a he within the bounds of Scotland more willing to watch the fold by night and by day. And Thomas said he had not heard a mair sound observe for some time, and that if I held to that doctrine in the poopit, it wouldna be lang till I would work a change.

'I was mindit,' quoth he, 'never to set my foot within the kirk door while you were there; but to testify, and no to condemn without a trial, I'll be there next Lord's day, and egg my neighbours to be likewise, so ye'll no have to preach just to the bare walls and the laird's family.'

I have now to speak of the coming of Mrs Malcolm. She was the widow of a Clyde shipmaster, that was lost at sea with his vessel. She was a genty body, calm and methodical. From morning to night she sat at her wheel, spinning the finest lint, which suited well with her pale hands. She never changed her widow's weeds, and she was aye as if she had just been ta'en out of a bandbox. The tear was aften in her e'e when the bairns were at the school; but when they came home, her spirit was lighted up with gladness, although, poor woman, she had many a time very little to give them. They were, however, wonderful well-bred things, and took with thankfulness whatever she set before them, for they knew that their father, the bread-winner, was away, and that she had to work sore for their bit and drap. I daresay, the only vexation that ever she had from any of them, on their own account, was when Charlie, the eldest laddie, had won fourpence at pitch and toss at the school, which he brought home with a proud heart to his mother. I happened to be daunrin' by at the time, and just looked in at the door to say gude-night:

It was a sad sight. There was she sitting with the silent tear on her cheek, and Charlie greeting as if he had done a great fault, and the other four looking on with sorrowful faces. Never, I am sure, did Charlie Malcolm gamble after that night. I often wondered what brought Mrs. Malcolm to our clachan, instead of going to a populous town, where she might have taken up a huxtry-shop, as she was but of a silly constitution, the which would have been better for her than spinning from morning to far in the night, as if she was in verity drawing the thread of life. But it was, no doubt, from an honest pride to hide her poverty; for when her daughter Effie was ill with the measles—the poor lassie was very ill—nobody thought she could come through, and when she did get the turn, she was for many a day a heavy handful;—our Session being rich, and nobody on it but cripple Tammy Daidles, that was at that time known through all the country-side for begging on a horse, I thought it my duty to call upon Mrs Malcolm in a sympathising way, and offer her some assistance, but she refused it.

'No, sir,' said she, 'I canna take help from the poor's-box, although it's very true that I am in great need; for it might hereafter be cast up to my bairns, whom it may please God to restore to better circumstances when I am no to see't; but I would fain borrow five pounds, and if, sir, you will write to Mr Maitland, that is now the Lord Provost of Glasgow, and tell him that Marion Shaw would be obliged to him for the lend of that soom, I think he will not fail to send it.' I wrote the letter that night to Provost Maitland, and, by the retour of the post, I got an answer, with twenty pounds for Mrs Malcolm, saying, 'that it was with sorrow he heard so small a trifle could be serviceable.' When I took the letter and the money, which was in a bank-bill, she said, 'This is just like himsel'.' She then told me, that Mr Maitland had been a gentleman's son of the east country, but driven out of his father's house, when a laddie, by his step-mother; and that he had served as a servant lad with her father, who was the Laird of Yillcogie, but ran through his estate, and left her, his only daughter, in little better than beggary with her auntie, the mother of Captain Malcolm, her husband that was. Provost Maitland in his servitude had ta'en a notion of her, and when he recovered his patrimony, and had become a great Glasgow merchant, on hearing how she was left by her father, he offered to marry her, but she had promised herself to her cousin the captain, whose widow she was. He then married a rich lady, and in time grew, as he was, Lord Provost of the City; but his letter with the twenty pounds to me, showed that he had not forgotten his first love. It was a short, but a well-written letter, in a fair hand of write, containing much of the true gentleman; and Mrs Malcolm said, 'Who knows but out of the regard he once had for their mother, he may do something for my five helpless orphans.' Thirdly, upon the subject of taking my cousin, Miss Betty Lanshaw, for my first wife, I have little to say. It was more out of a compassionate habitual affection, than the passion of love. We were brought up by our grandmother in the same house, and it was a thing spoken of from the beginning, that Betty and me were to be married. So when she heard that the Laird of Breadland had given me the presentation of Dalmailing, she began to prepare for the wedding. And as soon as the placing was well over, and the manse in order, I gaed to Ayr, where she was, and we were quietly married, and came home in a chaise, bringing with us her little brother Andrew, that died in the East Indies, and he lived and was brought up by us.

Now, this is all, I think, that happened in that year worthy of being mentioned, except that at the Sacrament, when old Mr Kilfuddy was preaching in the tent, it came on such a thunder-plump, that there was not a single soul staid in the kirkyard to hear him; for the which he was greatly mortified, and never after came to our preachings.

Chapter 2

Year 1761

The great increase in smuggling—Mr Balwhidder disperses a tea—drinking party of gossips—He records the virtues of Nanse Banks, the schoolmistress—The servant of a military man, who had been prisoner in France, comes to the parish, and opens a dancing-school.

It was in this year that the great smuggling trade corrupted all the west coast, especially the Laigh Lands about the Troon and the Loans. The tea was going like the chaff, the brandy like well-water, and the wastrie of all things was terrible. There was nothing minded but the riding of cadgers by day, and excisemen by night—and battles between the smugglers and the king's men, both by sea and land. There was a continual drunkenness and debauchery; and our Session, that was but on the lip of this whirlpool of iniquity, had an awful time o't. I did all that was in the power of nature to keep my people from the contagion ; I preached sixteen times from the text, Render to Cesar the things that are Cesar's. I visited, and I exhorted; I warned, and I prophesied; I told them that, although the money came in like sclate stones, it would go like the snow off the dyke. But for all I could do, the evil got in among us, and we had no less than three contested bastard bairns upon our hands at one time, which was a thing never heard of in a parish of the shire of Ayr, since the Reformation. Two of the bairns, after no small sifting and searching, we got fathered at last; but the third, that was by Meg Glaiks, and given to one Rab Rickerton, was utterly refused, though the fact was not denied; but he was a termagant fellow, and snappit his fingers at the elders. The next day he listed in the Scotch Greys, who were then quartered at Ayr, and we never heard more of him, but thought he had been slain in battle, till one of the parish, about three years since, went up to London to lift a legacy from a cousin, that died among the Hindoos; when he was walking about, seeing the curiosities, and among others Chelsea Hospital, he happened to speak to some of the invalids, who found out from his tongue that he was a Scotchman; and speaking to the invalids, one of them, a very old man, with a grey bead, and a leg of timber, inquired what part of Scotland he was come from; and when he mentioned my parish, the invalid gave a great shout, and said he was from the same place himself; and who should this old man be, but the very identical Rab Rickerton, that was art and part in Meg Glaiks' disowned bairn. Then they had a long converse together, and he had come through many hardships, but had turned out a good soldier; and so, in his old days, was an indoor pensioner, and very comfortable; and he said that he had, to be sure, spent his youth in the devil's service, and his manhood in the king's, but his old age was given to that of his Maker, which I was blithe and thankful to hear; and he inquired about many a one in the parish, the blooming and the green of his time, but they were all dead and buried; and he had a contrite and penitent spirit, and read his Bible every day, delighting most in the Book of Joshua, the Chronicles and the Kings.

Before this year, the drinking of tea was little known in the parish, saving among a few of the heritors' houses on a Sabbath evening, but now it became very rife, yet the commoner sort did not like to let it be known that they were taking to the new luxury, especially the elderly women, who, for that reason, had their ploys in outhouses and byplaces, just as the witches lang syne had their sinful possets and galravitchings; and they made their tea for common in the pint-stoup, and drank it out of caps and luggies, for there were but few among them that had cups and saucers. Well do I remember one night in harvest, in this very year, as I was taking my twilight dauner aneath the hedge along the back side of Thomas Thorl's yard, meditating on the goodness of Providence, and looking at the sheafs of victual on the field, that I heard his wife, and two three other carlins, with their bohea in the inside of the hedge, and no doubt but it had a lacing of the conek,[1] for they were all cracking like pen-guns. But I gave them a sign by a loud host, that Providence sees all, and it skailed the bike; for I heard them, like guilty creatures, whispering and gathering up their truck-pots and trenchers, and cowering away home.

It was in this year that Patrick Dilworth (he had been schoolmaster of the parish from the time, as his wife said, of Anna Regina, and before the Rexes came to the crown) was disabled by a paralytic, and the heritors, grudging the cost of another schoolmaster as long as he lived, would not allow the Session to get his place supplied, which was a wrong thing, I must say of them; for the children of the parishioners were obliged, therefore, to go to the neighbouring towns for their schooling, and the custom was to take a piece of bread and cheese in their pockets for dinner, and to return in the evening always voracious for more, the long walk helping the natural crave of their young appetites. In this way Mrs Malcolm's two eldest laddies, Charlie and Robert, were wont to go to Irville, and it was soon seen that they kept themselves aloof from the other callans in the clachan, and had a genteeler turn than the grulshy bairns of the cotters. Her bit lassies, Kate and Effie, were better off; for some years before, Nanse Banks had taken up a teaching in a garret-room of a house, at the corner where John Bayne has biggit the sclate-house for his grocery-shop. Nanse learnt them reading and working stockings, and how to sew the semplar, for twal-pennies a week. She was a patient creature, well cut out for her calling, with bleer eyn, a pale face, and a long neck, but meek and contented withal, tholing the dule of this world with a Christian submission of the spirit; and her garret-room was a cordial of cleanliness, for she made the scholars set the house in order, time and time about, every morning; and it was a common remark for many a day, that the lassies who had been at Nanse Banks's school were always well spoken of, both for their civility, and the trigness of their houses, when they were afterwards married. In short, I do not know, that in all the long epoch of my ministry, any individual body did more to improve the ways of the parishioners, in their domestic concerns, than did that worthy and innocent, creature, Nanse Banks, the schoolmistress; and she was a great loss when she was

---

1 Cogniac

removed, as it is to be hoped, to a better world; but anent this I shall have to speak more at large hereafter.

It was in this year that my patron, the Laird of Breadland, departed this life, and I preached his funeral-sermon; but he was none beloved in the parish, for my people never forgave him for putting me upon them, although they began to be more on a familiar footing with myself. This was partly owing to my first wife, Betty Lanshaw, who was an active through-going woman, and wonderfu' useful to many of the cotters' wives at their lying-in; and when a death happened among them, her helping hand, and anything we had at the manse, was never wanting; and I went about myself to the bed-sides of the frail, leaving no stone unturned to win the affections of my people, which, by the blessing of the Lord, in process of time, was brought to a bearing.

But a thing happened in this year, which deserves to be recorded, as manifesting what effect the smuggling was beginning to take in the morals of the country-side. One Mr Macskipnish, of Highland parentage, who had been a *valet-de-chambre* with a major in the campaigns, and taken a prisoner with him by the French, he having come home in a cartel, took up a dancing-school at Irville, the which art he had learnt in the genteelest fashion, in the mode of Paris, at the French Court. Such a thing as a dancing-school had never, in the memory of man, been known in our country-side; and there was such a sound about the steps and cotillions of Mr Macskipnish, that every lad and lass, that could spare time and siller, went to him, to the great neglect of their work. The very bairns on the loan, instead of their wonted play, gaed linking and louping in the steps of Mr Macskipnish, who was, to be sure, a great curiosity, with long spindle legs, his breast shot out like a duck's, and his head powdered and frizzled up like a tappit-hen. He was, indeed, the proudest peacock that could be seen, and he had a ring on his finger, and when he came to drink his tea at the Breadland, he brought no hat on his head, but a droll cockit thing under his arm, which, he said, was after the manner of the courtiers at the petty suppers of one Madam Pompadour, who was at that time the concubine of the French king.

I do not recollect any other remarkable thing that happened in this year. The harvest was very abundant, and the meal so cheap, that it caused a great defect in my stipend, so that I was obligated to postpone the purchase of a mahogany scrutoire for my study, as I had intended. But I had not the heart to complain of this; on the contrary, I rejoiced thereat, for what made me want my scrutoire till another year, had carried blitheness into the hearth of the cotter, and made the widow's heart sing with joy; and I would have been an unnatural creature, had I not joined in the universal gladness, because plenty did abound.

Chapter 3

Year 1762

Havoc produced by the small-pox—Charles Malcolm is sent off a cabinboy, on a voyage to Virginia—Mizy Spaewell dies on Hallowe'en—Tea begins to be admitted at the manse, but the minister continues to carry his authority against smuggling.

The third year of my ministry was long held in remembrance for several very memorable things. William Byres of the Loanhead had a cow that calved two calves at one calving; Mrs. Byres, the same year, had twins, male and female; and there was such a crop on his fields, testifying that the Lord never sends a mouth into the world without providing meat for it. But what was thought a very daunting sign of something, happened on the Sacrament Sabbath at the conclusion of the action sermon, when I had made a very suitable discourse. The day was tempestuous, and the wind blew with such a pith and birr, that I thought it would have twirled the trees in the kirkyard out by the roots, and, blowing in this manner, it tirled the thack from the rigging of the manse stable; and the same blast that did that, took down the lead that was on the kirk-roof, which hurled on; as I was saying, at the conclusion of the action sermon, with such a dreadful sound, as the like was never heard, and all the congregation thought that it betokened a mutation to me. However, nothing particular happened to me; but the small-pox came in among the weans of the parish, and the smashing that it made of the poor bits o' bairns was indeed woeful.

One Sabbath, when the pestilence was raging, I preached a sermon about Rachel weeping for her children, which Thomas Thorl, who was surely a great judge of good preaching, said, 'was a monument of divinity whilk searched the heart of many a parent that day'; a thing I was well pleased to hear, for Thomas, as I have related at length, was the most zealous champion against my getting the parish; but, from this time, I set him down in my mind for the next vacancy among the elders. Worthy man! it was not permitted him to arrive at that honour. In the fall of that year he took an income in his legs, and could no go about, and was laid up for the remainder of his days, a perfect Lazarus, by the fireside. But he was well supported in his affliction. In due season, when it pleased HIM that alone can give and take, to pluck him from this life, as the fruit ripened and ready for the gathering, his death, to all that knew him, was a gentle dispensation, for truly he had been in sore trouble.

It was in this year that Charlie Malcolm, Mrs Malcolm's eldest son, was sent to be a cabin-boy in the obanno trader, a three-masted ship, that sailed between Port-Glasgow and Virginia in America. She was commanded by Captain Dickie, an Irville man; for at that time the Clyde was supplied with the best sailors from our coast, the coal trade with Ireland being a better trade for bringing up good mariners than the long voyages in the open sea; which was the reason, as I often heard said, why the Clyde shipping got so many of their men from our country-side. The going to sea of Charlie Malcolm was, on divers accounts, a very remarkable thing to us all, for he was the first that ever went from our parish, in the memory of man, to be a sailor, and everybody was concerned at it, and some thought it was a great venture of his mother to let him, his father having been lost at sea. But what could the forlorn widow do? She had five weans, and little to give them; and, as she herself said, he was aye in the hand of his Maker, go where he might, and the will of God would be done, in spite of all earthly wiles and devices to the contrary.

On the Monday morning, when Charlie was to go away to meet the Irville carrier on the road, we were all up, and I walked by myself from the manse into the clachan to bid him farewell, and I met him just coming from his mother's door, as blithe as a bee, in his sailor's dress, with a stick, and a bundle tied in a Barcelona silk handkerchief hanging o'er his shoulder, and his two little brothers were with him, and his sisters, Kate and Effie, looking out from the door all begreeten; but his mother was in the house, praying to the Lord to protect her orphan, as she afterwards told me. All the weans of the clachan were gathered at the kirkyard yett to see him pass, and they gave him three great shouts as he was going by; and everybody was at their doors, and said something encouraging to him; but there was a great laugh when auld Mizy Spaewell came hirpling with her bachle in her hand, and flung it after him for gude luck. Mizy had a wonderful faith in freats, and was just an oracle of sagacity at expounding dreams, and bodes of every sort and description—besides, she was reckoned one of the best howdies in her day; but by this time she was grown frail and feckless, and she died the same year on Hallowe'en, which made everybody wonder, that it should have so fallen out for her to die on Hallowe'en.

Shortly after the departure of Charlie Malcolm, the Lady of Breadland, with her three daughters, removed to Edinburgh, where the young laird, that had been my pupil, was learning to be an advocate, and the Breadland House was set to Major Gilchrist, a nabob from India; but he was a narrow ailing man, and his maiden-sister, Miss Girzie, was the scrimpetest creature that could be; so that, in their hands, all the pretty policy of the Breadlands, that had cost a power of money to the old laird, that was my patron, fell into decay and disorder; and the bonny yew trees, that were cut into the shape of peacocks, soon grew out of all shape, and are now doleful monuments of the major's tack, and that of Lady Skim-milk, as Miss Girzie Gilchrist, his sister, was nicknamed by every ane that kent her.

But it was not so much on account of the neglect of the Breadland, that the incoming of Major Gilchrist was to be deplored. The old men, that had a light labour in keeping the policy in order, were thrown out of bread, and could do little; and the poor women, that whiles got a bit and a drap from the kitchen of the family, soon felt the change, so that by little and little, we were obligated to give help from the Session; insomuch, that before the end of the year, I was necessitated to preach a discourse on almsgiving, specially for the benefit of our own poor, a thing never before known in the parish.

But one good thing came from the Gilchrists to Mrs Malcolm. Miss Girzie, whom they called Lady Skim-milk, had been in a very penurious way as a seamstress, in the Gorbals of Glasgow, while her brother was making the fortune in India, and she was a clever needlewoman—none better, as it was said; and she having some things to make, took Kate Malcolm to help her in the coarse work; and Kate, being a nimble and birky thing, was so useful to the lady, and the complaining man the major, that they invited her to stay with them at the Breadland for the winter, where, although she was holden to her seam from morning to night, her food lightened the hand of her mother, who, for the first time since her coming into the parish, found the penny for the day's dark more than was needed for the meal-basin; and the tea-drinking was beginning to spread more openly, insomuch, that, by the advice of the first Mrs Balwhidder, Mrs Malcolm took in tea to sell, and in this way was enabled to eke something to the small profits of her wheel. Thus the tide, that had been so long ebbing to her, began to turn; and here I am bound in truth to say, that although I never could abide the smuggling, both on its own account, and the evils that grew therefrom to the country-side, I lost some of my dislike to the tea, after Mrs Malcolm began to traffic in it, and we then had it for our breakfast in the morning at the manse, as well as in the afternoon. But what I thought most of it for, was, that it did no harm to the head of the drinkers, which was not always the case with the possets that were in fashion before. There is no meeting now in the summer evenings, as I remember often happened in my younger days, with decent ladies coming home with red faces, tozy and cosh from a posset masking; so, both for its temperance, and on account of Mrs Malcolm's sale, I refrained from the November in this year to preach against tea; but I never lifted the weight of my displeasure from off the smuggling trade, until it was utterly put down by the strong hand of government.

There was no other thing of note in this year, saving only that I planted in the garden the big pear tree, which had the two great branches that we call the Adam and Eve. I got the plant, then a sapling, from Mr Graft, that was Lord Eglesham's head-gardener; and he said it was, as indeed all the parish now knows well, a most juicy sweet pear, such as was not known in Scotland, till my lord brought down the father plant from the king's garden in London, in the forty-five, when he went up to testify his loyalty to the House of Hanover.

Chapter 4

Year 1763

*Charles Malcolm's return from sea—Kate Malcolm is taken to live with Lady
Malcolm—Death of the first Mrs Balwhidder.*

The Ann. Dom. 1763, was, in many a respect, a memorable year, both in public and in private. The king granted peace to the French, and Charlie Malcolm, that went to sea in the *Tobacco* trader, came home to see his mother. The ship, after being at America, had gone down to Jamaica, an island in the West Indies, with a cargo of live lumber, as Charlie told me himself, and had come home with more than a hundred and fifty hoggits of sugar, and sixty-three puncheons full of rum; for she was, by all accounts, a stately galley, and almost two hundred tons in the burden, being the largest vessel then sailing from the creditable town of Port-Glasgow. Charlie was not expected; and his coming was a great thing to us all, so I will mention the whole particulars.

One evening, towards the gloaming, as I was taking my walk of meditation, I saw a brisk sailor laddie coming towards me. He had a pretty green parrot, sitting on a bundle, tied in a Barcelona silk handkerchief, which he carried with a stick over his shoulder, and in this bundle was a wonderful big nut, such as no one in our parish had ever seen. It was called a cocker-nut. This blithe callant was Charlie Malcolm, who had come all the way that day his leaful lane, on his own legs from Greenock, where the *Tobacco* trader was then 'livering her cargo. I told him how his mother, and his brothers, and his sisters were all in good health, and went to convoy him home; and as we were going along, he told me many curious things, and he gave me six beautiful yellow limes, that he had brought in his pouch all the way across the seas, for me to make a bowl of punch with, and I thought more of them than if they had been golden guineas, it was so mindful of the laddie.

When we got to the door of his mother's house, she was sitting at the fireside, with her three other bairns at their bread and milk, Kate being then with Lady Skim-milk, at the Breadland, sewing. It was between the day and dark, when the shuttle stands still till the lamp is lighted. But such a shout of joy and thankfulness as rose from that hearth when Charlie went in! The very parrot, ye would have thought, was a participator, for the beast gied a skraik that made my whole head din; and the neighbours came flying and flocking to see what was the matter, for it was the first parrot ever seen within the bounds of the parish, and some thought it was but a foreign hawk, with a yellow head and green feathers.

In the midst of all this, Effie Malcolm had run off to the Breadland for her sister Kate, and the two lassies came flying breathless, with Miss Girzie Gilchrist, the Lady Skim-milk, pursuing them like desperation, or a griffon, down the avenue; for Kate, in her hurry, had flung down her seam, a new printed gown, that she was helping to make, and it had fallen into a boyne of milk that was ready for the creaming, by which ensued a double misfortune to Miss Girzie, the gown being not only ruined, but licking up the cream. For this, poor Kate was not allowed ever to set her face in the Breadland again.

When Charlie Malcolm had staid about a week with his mother, he returned to his birth in the *Tobacco* trade; and shortly after his brother Robert was likewise sent to serve his time to the sea, with an owner that was master of his own bark, in the coal trade at Irville. Kate, who was really a surprising lassie for her years, was taken off her mother's hands by the old Lady Macadam, that lived in her jointure house, which is now the Cross Keys Inns. Her Ladyship was a woman of high-breeding, her husband having been a great general, and knighted by the king for his exploits; but she was lame, and could not move about in her dining-room without help, so hearing from the first Mrs Balwhidder how Kate had done such an unatonable deed to Miss Girzie Gilchrist, she sent for Kate, and finding her sharp and apt, she took her to live with her as a companion. This was a vast advantage, for the lady was versed in all manner of accomplishments, and could read and speak French, with more ease than any professor at that time in the College of Glasgow; and she had learnt to sew flowers on satin, either in a nunnery abroad, or in a boarding-school in England, and took pleasure in teaching Kate all she knew, and how to behave herself like a lady.

In the summer of this year, old Mr Patrick Dilworth, that had so long been doited with the paralytics, died, and it was a great relief to my people, for the heritors could no longer refuse to get a proper schoolmaster; so we took on trial Mr Lorimore, who has ever since the year after, with so much credit to himself, and usefulness to the parish, been schoolmaster, session-clerk, and precentor—a man of great mildness and extraordinary particularity. He was then a very young man, and some objection was made on account of his youth, to his being session-clerk, especially as the smuggling immorality still gave us much trouble in the making up of irregular marriages; but his discretion was greater than could have been hoped for from his years; and after a twelve-month's probation in the capacity of schoolmaster, he was installed in all the offices that had belonged to his predecessor, old Mr Patrick Dilworth that was. But the most memorable thing that befell among my people this year, was the burning of the lint-mill on the Lugton Water, which happened, of all the days of the year, on the very self-same day that Miss Girzie Gilchrist, better known as Lady Skim-milk, hired the chaise from Mrs. Watts of the New Inns of Irville, to go with her brother the major to consult the faculty in Edinburgh concerning his complaints. For, as the chaise was coming by the mill, William Huckle, the miller that was, came flying out of the mill like a demented man, crying fire!—and it was the driver that brought the melancholy tidings to the clachan—and melancholy they were; for the mill was utterly destroyed, and in it not a little of all that year's crop of lint in our parish. The first Mrs Balwhidder lost upwards of twelve stone, which we had raised on the glebe with no small pains, watering it in the drouth, as it was intended for sarking to ourselves, and sheets and napery. A great loss indeed it was, and the vexation thereof had a visible effect on Mrs Balwhidder's health, which from the spring had been in a dwining way. But for it, I think she might have wrestled through the winter; however, it was ordered otherwise, and she was removed from mine to Abraham's bosom on Christmas day, and buried on Hogmanae, for it was thought uncanny to have a dead corpse in the house on the New Year's day. She was a worthy woman, studying with all her capacity to win the hearts of my people towards me—in the which good work she prospered greatly; so that when she died, there was not a single soul in the parish that was not contented with both my walk and conversation. Nothing could be more peaceable than the way we lived together. Her brother Andrew, a fine lad, I had sent to the College at Glasgow, at my own cost, and when he came out to the burial, he staid with me a month, for the manse after her decease was very dull, and it was during this visit that he gave me an inkling of his wish to go out to India as a cadet, but the transactions anent that fall within the scope of another year—as well as what relates to her headstone, and the epitaph in metre, which I indited myself thereon; John Truel, the mason, carving the same, as may be seen in the kirkyard, where it wants a little reparation and setting upright, having settled the wrong way when the second Mrs Balwhidder was laid by her side. But I must not here enter upon an anticipation.

Chapter 5

Year 1764

He gets a headstone for Mrs Balwhidder, and writes an epitaph for it—He is afflicted with melancholy, and thinks of writing a book—Nichol Snipe the gamekeeper's device when reproved in church.

This year well deserved the name of the monumental year in our parish; for the young Laird of the Breadland, that had been my pupil, being learning to be an advocate among the faculty in Edinburgh, with his lady mother, who had removed thither with the young ladies her daughters, for the benefit of education, sent out to be put up in the kirk, under the loft over the family vault, an elegant marble headstone, with an epitaph engraven thereon, in fair Latin, setting forth many excellent qualities which the old laird, my patron that was, the inditer thereof, said he possessed. I say the inditer, because it could no have been the young laird himself, although he got the credit o't on the stone, for he was nae daub in my aught at the Latin or any other language. However, he might improve himself at Edinburgh, where a' manner of genteel things were then to be got at an easy rate, and doubtless, the young laird got a probationer at the College to write the epitaph; but I have often wondered sin' syne, how he came to make it in Latin, for assuredly his dead parent, if he could have seen it, could not have read a single word o't, notwithstanding it was so vaunty about his virtues, and other civil and hospitable qualifications.

The coming of the laird's monumental stone had a great effect on me, then in a state of deep despondency for the loss of the first Mrs Balwhidder; and I thought I could not do a better thing, just by way of diversion in my heavy sorrow, than to get a well-shapen headstone made for her—which, as I have hinted at in the record of the last year, was done and set up. But a headstone without an epitaph is no better than a body without the breath of life in't; and so it behoved me to make a posey for the monument, the which I conned and pondered upon for many days. I thought as Mrs Balwhidder, worthy woman as she was, did not understand the Latin tongue, it would not do to put on what I had to say in that language, as the laird had done—nor indeed would it have been easy, as I found upon the experimenting, to tell what I had to tell in Latin, which is naturally a crabbed language, and very difficult to write properly. I therefore, after mentioning her age and the dates of her birth and departure, composed in sedate poetry, the following epitaph, which may yet be seen on the tombstone.

EPITAPH

'A lovely Christian, spouse, and friend, Pleasant in life, and at her end.
A pale consumption dealt the blow
That laid her here, with dust below.
Sore was the cough that shook her frame;
That cough her patience did proclaim-
And as she drew her latest breath,
She said, "The Lord is sweet in death."
O pious reader, standing by,
Learn like this gentle one to die.
The grass doth grow and fade away,
And time runs out by night and day;
The King of Terrors has command
To strike us with his dart in hand.
Go where we will by flood or field,
He will pursue and make us yield.
But though to him we must resign
The vesture of our part divine,
There is a jewel in our trust,
That will not perish in the dust,
A pearl of price, a precious gem,
Ordain'd for Jesus' diadem;
Therefore be holy while you can,
And think upon the doom of man.
Repent in time and sin no more,
That when the strife of life is o'er,
On wings of love your soul may rise,
To dwell with angels in the skies,

Where psalms are sung eternally,
And martyrs ne'er again shall die;
But with the saints still bask in bliss,
And drink the cup of blessedness.'

This was greatly thought of at the time, and Mr Lorimore, who had a nerve for poesy himself in his younger years, was of opinion that it was so much to the purpose and suitable withal, that he made his scholars write it out for their examination copies, at the reading whereof before the heritors, when the examination of the school came round, the tear came into my eye, and every one present sympathised with me in my great affliction for the loss of the first Mrs Balwhidder.

Andrew Lanshaw, as I have recorded, having come from the Glasgow College to the burial of his sister, my wife that was, staid with me a month to keep me company; and staying with me, he was a great cordial, for the weather was wet and sleety, and the nights were stormy, so that I could go little out, and few of the elders came in, they being at that time old men in a feckless condition, not at all qualified to warsle with the blasts of winter. But when Andrew left me to go back to his classes, I was eirie and lonesome, and but for the getting of the monument ready, which was a blessed entertainment to me in those dreary nights, with consulting anent the shape of it with John Truel, and meditating on the verse for the epitaph, I might have gone altogether demented. However, it pleased HIM, who is the surety of the sinner, to help me through the Slough of Despond, and to set my feet on firm land, establishing my way thereon.

But the work of the monument, and the epitaph, could not endure for a constancy, and after it was done, I was again in great danger of sinking into the hypochonderies a second time. However, I was enabled to fight with my affliction, and by and by, as the spring began to open her green lattice, and to set out her flower-pots to the sunshine, and the time of the singing of birds was come, I became more composed, and like myself, so I often walked in the fields, and held communion with nature, and wondered at the mysteries thereof.

On one of these occasions, as I was sauntering along the edge of Eglesham Wood, looking at the industrious bee going from flower to flower, and the idle butterfly, that layeth up no store, but perisheth ere it is winter, I felt as it were a spirit from on high descending upon me, a throb at my heart, and a thrill in my brain, and I was transported out of myself, and seized with the notion of writing a book—but what it should be about, I could not settle to my satisfaction: sometimes I thought of an orthodox poem, like *Paradise Lost* by John Milton, wherein I proposed to treat more at large of Original Sin, and the great mystery of Redemption; at others, I fancied that a correct treatise on the efficacy of Free Grace would be more taking; but although I made divers beginnings in both subjects, some new thought ever came into my head, and the whole summer passed away and nothing was done. I therefore postponed my design of writing a book till the winter, when I would have the benefit of the long nights. Before that, however, I had other things of more importance to think about: my servant lasses, having no eye of a mistress over them, wastered everything at such a rate, and made such a galravitching in the house, that, long before the end of the year, the year's stipend was all spent, and I did not know what to do. At lang and length I mustered courage to send for Mr Auld, who was then living, and an elder. He was a douce and discreet man, fair and well-doing in the world, and had a better handful of strong common sense than many even of the heritors. So I told him how I was situated, and conferred with him, and he advised me, for my own sake, to look out for another wife as soon as decency would allow, which he thought might very properly be after the turn of the year, by which time the first Mrs Balwhidder would be dead more than twelve months; and when I mentioned my design to write a book, he said (and he was a man of good discretion) that the doing of the book was a thing that would keep, but wasterful servants were a growing evil; so, upon his counselling, I resolved not to meddle with the book till I was married again, but employ the interim, between then and the turn of the year, in looking out for a prudent woman to be my second wife, strictly intending, as I did perform, not to mint a word about my choice, if I made one, till the whole twelve months and a day, from the date of the first Mrs Balwhidder's interment, had run out.

In this the hand of Providence was very visible, and lucky for me it was that I had sent for Mr Auld when I did send, as the very week following, a sound began to spread in the parish, that one of my lassies had got herself with bairn, which was an awful thing to think had happened in the house of her master, and that master a minister of the Gospel. Some there were, for backbiting appertaineth to all conditions, that jaloused and wondered if I had not a finger in the pye; which, when Mr Auld heard, he bestirred himself in such a manful and godly way in my defence, as silenced the clash, telling that I was utterly incapable of any such thing, being a man of a guileless heart, and a spiritual simplicity, that would be ornamental in a child. We then had the latheron summoned before the Session, and was not long of making her confess that the father was Nichol Snipe, Lord Glencairn's gamekeeper; and both her and Nichol were obligated to stand in the kirk, but Nichol was a graceless reprobate, for he came with two coats, one buttoned behind him, and another buttoned before him, and two wigs of my lord's, lent him by the valet-de-chamer; the one over his face, and the other in the right way; and he stood with his face to the church wall. When I saw him from the pu'pit, I said to him, 'Nichol, you must turn your face towards me!' At the which, he turned round to be sure, but there he presented the same show as his back. I was confounded, and did not know what to say, but cried out, with a voice of anger, 'Nichol, Nichol! if ye had been a' back, ye would nae hae been there this day'; which had such an effect on the whole congregation, that the poor fellow suffered afterwards more derision, than if I had rebuked him in the manner prescribed by the Session.

This affair, with the previous advice of Mr Auld, was, however, a warning to me, that no pastor of his parish should be long without a helpmate. Accordingly, as soon as the year was out, I set myself earnestly about the search for one, but as the particulars fall properly within the scope and chronicle of the next year, I must reserve them for it; and I do not recollect that anything more particular befell in this, excepting that William Mutchkins, the father of Mr Mutchkins, the great spirit-dealer in Glasgow, set up a change-house in the clachan, which was the first in the parish, and which, if I could have helped,) it would have been the last; for it was opening a howf to all manner of wickedness, and was an immediate get and offspring of the smuggling trade, against which I had so set my countenance. But William Mutchkins himself was a respectable man, and no house could be better ordered than his change. At a stated hour he made family worship, for he brought up his children in the fear of God and the Christian religion; and although the house was full, he would go into the customers, and ask them if they would want anything for half an hour, for that he was going to make exercise with his family; and many a wayfaring traveller has joined in the prayer. There is no such thing, I fear, nowadays, of publicans entertaining travellers in this manner.

Chapter 6

Year 1765

Establishment of a whisky distillery—He is again married to Miss Lizy Kibbock—
Her industry in the dairy—Her example diffuses a spirit of industry throughout
the parish.

As there was little in the last year that concerned the parish, but only myself, so in this the like fortune continued; and saving a rise in the price of barley, occasioned, as was thought, by the establishment of a house for brewing whisky in a neighbouring parish, it could not be said that my people were exposed to the mutations and influences of the stars which ruled in the seasons of Ann. Dom. 1765. In the winter there was a dearth of fuel, such as has not been since; for when the spring loosened the bonds of the ice, three new coal-heughs were shanked in the Douray Moor, and ever since there has been a great plenty of that necessary article. Truly, it is very wonderful to see how things come round; when the talk was about the shanking of their heughs, and a paper to get folk to take shares in them, was carried through the circumjacent parishes, it was thought a gawk's errand; but no sooner was the coal reached, but up sprung such a traffic, that it was a God-send to the parish, and the opening of a trade and commerce that has, to use an old bye-word, brought gold in gowpins amang us. From that time my stipend has been on the regular increase, and therefore I think that the incoming of the heritors must have been in like manner augmented.

Soon after this, the time was drawing near for my second marriage. I had placed my affections, with due consideration, on Miss Lizy Kibbock, the well-brought-up daughter of Mr Joseph Kibbock of the Gorbyholm, who was the first that made a speculation in the farming way in Ayrshire, and whose cheese were of such an excellent quality, that they have, under the name of Delap cheese, spread far and wide over the civilised world. Miss Lizy and me were married on the 29th day of April, with some inconvenience to both sides, on account of the dread that we had of being married in May, for it is said,

'Of the marriages in May,
The bairns die of a decay.'

However, married we were, and we hired the Irville chaise, and with Miss Jenny her sister, and Becky Cairns her niece, who sat on a portmanty at our feet, we went on a pleasure jaunt to Glasgow, where we bought a miracle of useful things for the manse, that neither the first Mrs Balwhidder nor me ever thought of; but the second Mrs Balwhidder that was, had a geni for management, and it was extraordinary what she could go through. Well may I speak of her with commendations, for she was the bee that made my honey, although at first things did not go so clear with us. For she found the manse rookit and herrit, and there was such a supply of plenishing of all sort wanted, that I thought myself ruined and undone by her care and industry. There was such a buying of wool to make blankets, with a booming of the meikle wheel to spin the same, and such birring of the little wheel for sheets and napery, that the manse was for many a day like an organ kist. Then we had milk cows, and the calves to bring up, and a kirning of butter, and a making of cheese; in short, I was almost by myself with the jangle and din, which prevented me from writing a book as I had proposed, and I for a time thought of the peaceful and kindly nature of the first Mrs Balwhidder with a sigh; but the outcoming was soon manifest. The second Mrs Balwhidder sent her butter on the market-days to Irville, and her cheese from time to time to Glasgow, to Mrs Firlot, that kept the huxtry in the Saltmarket, and they were both so well made, that our dairy was just a coining of money, insomuch, that after the first year, we had the whole tot of my stipend to put untouched into the bank.

But I must say, that although we were thus making siller like sclate stones, I was not satisfied in my own mind that I had got the manse merely to be a factory of butter and cheese, and to breed up veal calves for the slaughter; so I spoke to the second Mrs Balwhidder, and pointed out to her what I thought the error of our way; but she had been so ingrained with the profitable management of cows and grumphies in her father's house, that she could not desist, at the which I was greatly grieved. By and by, however, I began to discern that there was something as good in her example as the giving of alms to the poor folk. For all the wives of the parish were stirred up by it into a wonderful thrift, and nothing was heard of in every house, but of quiltings and wabs to weave; insomuch, that before many years came round, there was not a better-stocked parish, with blankets and napery, than mine was, within the bounds of Scotland.

It was about the Michaelmas of this year that Mrs Malcolm opened her shop, which she did chiefly on the advice of Mrs Balwhidder, who said it was far better to allow a little profit on the different haberdasheries that might be wanted, than to send to the neighbouring towns an end's errand on purpose for them, none of the lasses that were so sent ever thinking of making less than a day's play on every such occasion. In a word, it is not to be told how the second Mrs Balwhidder, my wife, showed the value of flying time, even to the concerns of this world, and was the mean of giving a life and energy to the housewifery of the parish, that has made many a one beek his shins in comfort, that would otherwise have had but a cold coal to blow at. Indeed, Mr Kibbock, her father, was a man beyond the common, and had an insight of things, by which he was enabled to draw profit and advantage, where others could only see risk and detriment. He planted mounts of fir-trees on the bleak and barren tops of the hills of his farm, the which everybody, and I among the rest, considered as a thrashing of the water, and raising of bells. But as his tack ran his trees grew, and the plantations supplied him with stabs to make stake and rice between his fields, which soon gave them a trig and orderly appearance, such as had never before been seen in the west country; and his example has, in this matter, been so followed, that I have heard travellers say, who have been in foreign countries, that the shire of Ayr, for its bonny round green plantings on the tops of the hills, is above comparison either with Italy or Switzerland, where the hills are, as it were, in a state of nature.

Upon the whole, this was a busy year in the parish, and the seeds of many great improvements were laid. The king's road, which then ran through the Vennel, was mended; but it was not till some years after, as I shall record by and by, that the trust road, as it was called, was made, the which had the effect of turning the town inside out.

Before I conclude, it is proper to mention that the kirk-bell, which had to this time, from time immemorial, hung on an ash-tree, was one stormy night cast down by the breaking of the branch, which was the cause of the heritors agreeing to build the steeple. The clock was a mortification to the parish from the Lady Breadland, when she died some years after.

Chapter 7

Year 1766

The burning of the Breadland—A new bell, and also a steeple—Nanse Birrel found drowned in a well—The parish troubled with wild Irishmen.

It was in this Ann. Dom. that the great calamity happened, the which took place on a Sabbath evening in the month of February. Mrs Balwhidder had just infused or masket the tea, and we were set round the fireside to spend the night in an orderly and religious manner, along with Mr and Mrs Petticrew, who were on a friendly visitation to the manse, the mistress being full cousin to Mrs Balwhidder. Sitting, as I was saying, at our tea, one of the servant lasses came into the room with a sort of a panic laugh, and said,

'What are ye all doing there when the Breadland's in a low?' 'The Breadland in a low!' cried I. 'Oh, ay,' cried she; 'bleezing at the windows and the rigging, and out at the turn, like a killogie.' Upon the which, we all went to the door, and there, to be sure, we did see that the Breadland was burning, the flames crackling high out o'er the trees, and the sparks flying like a comet's tail in the firmament.

Seeing this sight, I said to Mr Petticrew that, in the strength of the Lord, I would go and see what could be done, for it was as plain as the sun in the heavens, that the ancient place of the Breadlands would be destroyed; whereupon he accorded to go with me, and we walked at a lively course to the spot, and the people from all quarters were pouring in, and it was an awsome scene. But the burning of the house, and the droves of the multitude, were nothing to what we saw when we got forenent the place. There was the rafters crackling, the flames raging, the servants running, some with bedding, some with looking-glasses, and others with chamber utensils, as little likely to be fuel to the fire, but all testifications to the confusion and alarm. Then there was a shout, 'Whar's Miss Girzie? whar's the major?' The major, poor man, soon cast up, lying upon a feather-bed, ill with his complaints, in the garden; but Lady Skim-milk was nowhere to be found. At last, a figure was seen in the upper flat, pursued by the flames, and that was Miss Girzie. Oh! it was a terrible sight to look at her in that jeopardy at the window, with her gold watch in the one hand and the silver teapot in the other, skreighing like desperation for a ladder and help. But before a ladder or help could be found, the floor sunk down, and the roof fell in, and poor Miss Girzie, with her idols, perished in the burning. It was a dreadful business; I think to this hour, how I saw her at the window, how the fire came in behind her, and claught her like a fiery Belzebub, and bore her into perdition before our eyes. The next morning the atomy of the body was found among the rubbish, with a piece of metal in what had been each of its hands, no doubt the gold watch and the silver teapot. Such was the end of Miss Girzie, and the Breadland, which the young laird, my pupil that was, by growing a resident at Edinburgh, never rebuilt. It was burnt to the very ground, nothing was spared but what the servants in the first flaught gathered up in a hurry and ran with, but no one could tell how the major, who was then, as it was thought by the faculty, past the power of nature to recover, got out of the house, and was laid on the feather-bed in the garden. However, he never got the better of that night, and before Whitsunday he was dead too, and buried beside his sister's bones at the south side of the kirkyard dyke, where his cousin's son, that was his heir, erected the handsome monument, with the three urns and weeping cherubims, bearing witness to the great valour of the major among the Hindoos, as well as other commendable virtues, for which, as the epitaph says, he was universally esteemed and beloved by all who knew him, in his public and private capacity.

But although the burning of the Breadland House was justly called the great calamity, on account of what happened to Miss Girzie, with her gold watch and silver teapot, yet, as Providence never fails to bring good out of evil, it turned out a catastrophe that proved advantageous to the parish; for the laird, instead of thinking to build it up, was advised to let the policy out as a farm, and the tack was taken by Mr Coulter, than whom there had been no such man in the agriculturing line among us before, not even excepting Mr Kibbock of the Gorbyholm, my father-in-law that was. Of the stabling, Mr Coulter made a comfortable dwelling-house, and having rugget out the evergreens and other unprofitable plants, saving the twa ancient yew-trees which the near-begun major and his sister had left to go to ruin about the mansion-house, he turned all to production, and it was wonderful what an increase he made the land bring forth. He was from far beyond Edinburgh, and had got his insight among the Lothian farmers, so that he knew what crop should follow another, and nothing could surpass the regularity of his rigs and furrows. Well do I remember the admiration that I had, when, in a fine sunny morning of the first spring after he took the Breadland, I saw his braird on what had been the cows' grass, as even and pretty as if it had been worked and stripped in the loom with a shuttle. Truly, when I look back at the example he set, and when I think on the method and dexterity of his management, I must say, that his coming to the parish was a great God-send, and tended to do far more for the benefit of my people, than if the young laird had rebuilded the Breadland House in a fashionable style, as was at one time spoken of.

But the year of the great calamity was memorable for another thing. In the December foregoing, the wind blew, as I have recorded in the chronicle of the last year, and broke down the bough of the tree, whereon the kirk-bell had hung from the time, as was supposed, of the Persecution, before the bringing over of King William.

Mr Kibbock, my father-in-law then that was, being a man of a discerning spirit, when he heard of the unfortunate fall of the bell, advised me to get the heritors to big a steeple, but which, when I thought of the expense, I was afraid to do. He, however, having a great skill in the heart of man, gave me no rest on the subject, but told me, that if I allowed the time to go by, till the heritors were used to come to the kirk without a bell, I would get no steeple at all. I often wondered what made Mr Kibbock so fond of a steeple, which is a thing that I never could see a good reason for, saving that it is an ecclesiastical adjunct, like the gown and bands. However, he set me on to get a steeple proposed, and after no little argol-bargling with the heritors, it was agreed to. This was chiefly owing to the instrumentality of Lady Moneyplack, who in that winter was much subjected to the rheumatics, she having one cold and raw Sunday morning, there being no bell to announce the time, come half an hour too soon to the kirk, made her bestir herself to get an interest awakened among the heritors in behalf of a steeple.

But when the steeple was built, a new contention arose. It was thought that the bell, which had been used in the ash-tree, would not do in a stone and lime fabric, so, after great agitation among the heritors, it was resolved to sell the old bell to a foundry in Glasgow, and buy a new bell suitable to the steeple, which was a very comely fabric. The buying of the new bell led to other considerations, and the old Lady Breadland, being at the time in a decaying condition, and making her will, she left a mortification to the parish, as I have intimated, to get a clock, so that, by the time the steeple was finished, and the bell put up, the Lady Breadland's legacy came to be implemented, according to the ordination of the testatrix.

Of the casualties that happened in this year, I should not forget to put down, as a thing for remembrance, that an aged woman, one Nanse Birrel, a distillator of herbs, and well skilled in the healing of sores, who had a great repute among the quarriers and colliers,—she having gone to the physic well in the sandy hills to draw water, was found with her feet uppermost in the well by some of the bairns of Mr Lorimore's school; and there was a great debate whether Nanse had fallen in by accident head-foremost, or, in a temptation, thrown herself in that position, with her feet sticking up to the evil one; for Nanse was a curious discontented blear-eyed woman, and it was only with great ado that I could get the people keepit from calling her a witchwife.

I should likewise place on record, that the first ass that had ever been seen in this part of the country came in the course of this year with a gang of tinklers, that made horn-spoons and mended bellows. Where they came from never was well made out, but being a blackaviced crew, they were generally thought to be Egyptians. They tarried about a week among us, living in tents, with their little ones squattling among the litter; and one of the older men of them set and tempered to me two razors, that were as good as nothing, but which he made better than when they were new.

Shortly after, but I am not quite sure whether it was in the end of this year or the beginning of the next, although I have a notion that it was in this, there came over from Ireland a troop of wild Irish, seeking for work, as they said, but they made free quarters, for they herrit the roosts of the clachan, and cutted the throat of a sow of ours, the carcase of which they no doubt intended to steal, but something came over them, and it was found lying at the back-side of the manse, to the great vexation of

Mrs Balwhidder, for she had set her mind on a clecking of pigs, and only waited for the China boar, that had been brought down from London by Lord Eglesham, to mend the breed of pork—a profitable commodity that her father, Mr Kibbock, cultivated for the Glasgow market. The destruction of our sow, under such circumstances, was therefore held to be a great crime and cruelty, and it had the effect to raise up such a spirit in the clachan that the Irish were obligated to decamp; and they set out for Glasgow, where one of them was afterwards hanged for a fact, but the truth concerning how he did it, I either never heard, or it has passed from my mind, like many other things I should have carefully treasured.

Chapter 8

Year 1767

Lord Eglesham meets with an accident which is the mean of getting the parish a new road—I preach for the benefit of Nanse Banks, the schoolmistress reduced to poverty.

All things in our parish were now beginning to shoot up into a great prosperity. The spirit of farming began to get the upper hand of the spirit of smuggling, and the coal-heughs that had been opened in the Douray now brought a pour of money among us. In the manse, the thrift and frugality of the second Mrs Balwhidder throve exceedingly, so that we could save the whole stipend for the bank.

The king's highway, as I have related in the foregoing, ran through the Vennel, which was a narrow and a crooked street, with many big stones here and there, and every now and then, both in the spring and the fall, a gathering of middens for the fields, insomuch that the coal carts from the Dowray Moor were often reested in the middle of the causeway, and on more than one occasion some of them laired altogether in the middens, and others of them broke down. Great complaint was made by the carters anent these difficulties, and there was for many a day a talk and sound of an alteration and amendment, but nothing was fulfilled in the matter till the month of March in this year, when the Lord Eglesham was coming from London to see the new lands that he had bought in our parish. His lordship was a man of a genteel spirit, and very fond of his horses, which were the most beautiful creatures of their kind that had been seen in all the country-side. Coming, as I was noting, to see his new lands, he was obliged to pass through the clachan one day, when all the middens were gathered out reeking and sappy in the middle of the causeway. Just as his lordship was driving in with his prancing steeds like a Jehu at the one end of the Vennel, a long string of loaded coal carts came in at the other, and there was hardly room for my lord to pass them. What was to be done? his lordship could not turn back, and the coal carts were in no less perplexity. Everybody was out of doors to see and to help, when, in trying to get his lordship's carriage over the top of a midden, the horses gave a sudden loup, and couped the coach, and threw my lord, head-foremost, into the very scent-bottle of the whole commodity, which made him go perfect mad, and he swore like a trooper, that he would get an Act of Parliament to put down the nuisance—the which now ripened in the course of this year into the undertaking of the trust road.

His lordship being in a woeful plight, left the carriage and came to the manse, till his servant went to the castle for a change for him; but he could not wait nor abide himself, so he got the lend of my best suit of clothes, and was wonderful jocose both with Mrs Balwhidder and me, for he was a portly man, and I but a thin body, and it was really a droll curiosity to see his lordship clad in my garments.

Out of this accident grew a sort of a neighbourliness between that Lord Eglesham and me, so that when Andrew Lanshaw, the brother that was of the first Mrs Balwhidder, came to think of going to India, I wrote to my lord for his behoof, and his lordship got him sent out as a cadet, and was extraordinary discreet to Andrew when he went up to London to take his passage, speaking to him of me as if I had been a very saint, which the Searcher of Hearts knows I am far from thinking myself.

But to return to the making of the trust road, which, as I have said, turned the town inside out. It was agreed among the heritors that it should run along the back-side of the south houses; and that there should be steadings fewed off on each side, according to a plan that was laid down, and this being gone into, the town gradually, in the course of years, grew up into that orderliness which makes it now a pattern to the country-side—all which was mainly owing to the accident that befell the Lord Eglesham, which is a clear proof how improvements come about, as it were, by the immediate instigation of Providence, which should make the heart of man humble, and change his eyes of pride and haughtiness into a lowly demeanour.

But although this making of the trust road was surely a great thing for the parish, and of an advantage to my people, we met, in this year, with a loss not to be compensated,—that was the death of Nanse Banks, the schoolmistress. She had been long in a weak and frail state, but, being a methodical creature, still kept on the school, laying the foundation for many a worthy wife and mother. However, about the decline of the year her complaints increased, and she sent for me to consult about her giving up the school; and I went to see her on a Saturday afternoon, when the bit lassies, her scholars, had put the house in order, and gone home till the Monday.

She was sitting in the window-nook reading THE WORD to herself, when I entered, but she closed the book, and put her spectacles in for a mark when she saw me; and, as it was expected I would come, her easy-chair, with a clean cover, had been set out for me by the scholars, by which I discerned that there was something more than common to happen, and so it appeared when I had taken my seat.

'Sir,' said she, 'I hae sent for you on a thing troubles me sairly. I have warsled with poortith in this shed, which it has pleased the Lord to allow me to possess, but my strength is worn out, and I fear I maun yield in the strife'; and she wiped her eye with her apron. I told her, however, to be of good cheer; and then she said, 'that she could no longer thole the din of the school, and that she was weary, and ready to lay herself down to die whenever the Lord was pleased to permit. But,' continued she, 'what can I do without the school; and alas! I can neither work nor want; and I am wae to go on the Session, for I am come of a decent family.' I comforted her, and told her that I thought she had done so much good in the parish that the Session was deep in her debt, and that what they might give her was but a just payment for her service. ' I would rather, however, sir,' said she, 'try first what some of my auld scholars will do, and it was for that I wanted to speak with you. If some of them would but just, from time to time, look in upon me, that I may not die alane; and the little pick and drap that I require would not be hard upon them—I am more sure that in this way their gratitude would be no discredit, than I am of having any claim on the Session.'

As I had always a great respect for an honest pride, I assured her that I would do what she wanted, and accordingly, the very morning after, being Sabbath, I preached a sermon on the helplessness of them that have no help of man, meaning aged single women, living in garret-rooms, whose forlorn state, in the gloaming of life, I made manifest to the hearts and understandings of the congregation, in such a manner that many shed tears, and went away sorrowful.

Having thus roused the feelings of my people, I went round the houses on the Monday morning, and mentioned what I had to say more particularly about poor old Nanse Banks the schoolmistress, and truly I was rejoiced at the condition of the hearts of my people. There was a universal sympathy among them; and it was soon ordered that, what with one and another, her decay should be provided for. But it was not ordained that she should be long heavy on their goodwill. On the Monday the school was given up, and there was nothing but wailing among the bit lassies, the scholars, for getting the vacance, as the poor things said, because the mistress was going to lie down to dee. And, indeed, so it came to pass, for she took to her bed the same afternoon, and, in the course of the week, dwindled away, and slippet out of this howling wilderness into the kingdom of heaven, on the Sabbath following, as quietly as a blessed saint could do.

And here I should mention, that the Lady Macadam, when I told her of Nanse Banks's case, inquired if she was a snuffer, and being answered by me that she was, her ladyship sent her a pretty French enamel box full of Macabaw, a fine snuff that she had in a bottle; and among the Macabaw was found a guinea, at the bottom of the box, after Nanse Banks had departed this life, which was a kind thing of Lady Macadam to do.

About the close of this year there was a great sough of old prophecies, foretelling mutations and adversities, chiefly on account of the canal that was spoken of to join the rivers of the Clyde and the Forth, it being thought an impossible thing to be done; and the Adam and Eve pear-tree in our garden budded out in an awful manner, and had divers flourishes on it at Yule, which was thought an ominous thing, especially as the second Mrs Balwhidder was at the down-lying with my eldest son Gilbert, that is the merchant in Glasgow, but nothing came o't, and the howdie said she had an easy time when the child came into the world, which was on the very last day of the year, to the great satisfaction of me, and of my people, who were wonderful lifted up because their minister had a man-child born unto him.

Chapter 9

Year 1768

Lord Eglesham uses his interest in favour of Charles Malcolm—The finding of a new schoolmistress—Miss Sabrina Hookie gets the place—Change of fashions in the parish.

It's a surprising thing how time flieth away, carrying off our youth and strength, and leaving us nothing but wrinkles and the ails of old age. Gilbert, my son, that is now a corpulent man, and a Glasgow merchant, when I take up my pen to record the memorables of this Ann. Dom., seems to me yet but a suckling in swaddling clothes, mewing and peevish in the arms of his mother, that has been long laid in the cold kirkyard, beside her predecessor, in Abraham's bosom. It is not, however, my design to speak much anent my own affairs, which would be a very improper and uncomely thing, but only of what happened in the parish, this book being for a witness and testimony of my ministry. Therefore, setting out of view both me and mine, I will now resuscitate the concerns of Mrs Malcolm and her children; for, as I think, never was there such a visible preordination seen in the lives of any persons, as was seen in that of this worthy decent woman and her well-doing offspring. Her morning was raw, and a sore blight fell upon her fortunes, but the sun looked out on her mid-day, and her evening closed loun and warm, and the stars of the firmament, that are the eyes of Heaven, beamed, as it were, with gladness when she lay down to sleep the sleep of rest.

Her son Charles was by this time grown up into a stout buirdly lad, and it was expected that before the return of the *Tobacco* trader, he would have been out of his time, and a man afore the mast, which was a great step of preferment, as I heard say by persons skilled in sea-faring concerns. But this was not ordered to happen; for, when the *Tobacco* trader was lying in the harbour of Virginia in the North America, a pressgang, that was in need of men for a man-of-war, came on board, and pressed poor Charles, and sailed away with him on a cruise, nobody, for many a day, could tell where, till I thought of the Lord Eglesham's kindness. His lordship having something to say with the king's government, I wrote to him, telling him who I was, and how jocose he had been when buttoned in my clothes, that he might recollect me, thanking him at the same time for his condescension and patronage to Andrew Lanshaw, in his way to the East Indies. I then slipped in, at the end of the letter, a bit *nota bene* concerning the case of Charles Malcolm, begging his lordship, on account of the poor lad's widow mother, to inquire at the government if they could tell us anything about Charles. In the due course of time, I got a most civil reply from his lordship, stating all about the name of the man-of-war, and where she was; and at the conclusion his lordship said, that I was lucky in having the brother of a Lord of the Admiralty on this occasion for my agent, as otherwise, from the vagueness of my statement, the information might not have been procured; which remark of his lordship was long a great riddle to me, for I could not think what he meant about an agent, till, in the course of the year, we heard that his own brother was concerned in the Admiralty; so that all his lordship meant was only to crack a joke with me, and that he was ever ready and free to do, as shall be related in the sequel, for he was an excellent man.

There being a vacancy for a schoolmistress, it was proposed to Mrs Malcolm, that, under her superintendence, her daughter Kate, that had been learning great artifices in needlework so long with Lady Macadam, should take up the school, and the Session undertook to make good to Kate the sum of five pounds sterling per annum, over and above what the scholars were to pay. But Mrs Malcolm said she had not strength herself to warsle with so many unruly brats, and that Kate, though a fine lassie, was a tempestuous spirit, and might lame some of the bairns in her passion; and that night, Lady Macadam wrote me a very complaining letter, for trying to wile away her companion; but her ladyship was a canary-headed woman, and given to flights and tantrums, having in her youth been a great toast among the quality. It would, however, have saved her from a sore heart had she never thought of keeping Kate Malcolm. For this year her only son, who was learning the art of war at an academy in France, came to pay her, his lady mother, a visit. He was a brisk and light-hearted stripling, and Kate Malcolm was budding into a very rose of beauty; so between them a hankering began, which, for a season, was productive of great heaviness of heart to the poor old cripple lady; indeed, she assured me herself, that all her rheumatics were nothing to the heartache which she suffered in the progress of this business. But that will be more treated of hereafter; suffice it to say for the present, that we have thus recorded how the plan for making Kate Malcolm our schoolmistress came to nought. It pleased however Him, from whom cometh every good and perfect gift, to send at this time among us a Miss Sabrina Hookie, the daughter of old Mr Hookie, who had been schoolmaster in a neighbouring parish. She had gone after his death to live with an auntie in Glasgow, that kept a shop in the Gallowgate. It was thought that the old woman would have left her heir to all her gatherings, and so she would, but alas! our life is but within our lip. Before testament was made, she was carried suddenly off by an apoplectick, an awful monument of the uncertainty of time, and the nearness of eternity, in her own shop, as she was in the very act of weighing out an ounce of snuff to a Professor of the College, as Miss Sabrina herself told me. Being thus destitute, it happened that Miss Sabrina heard of the vacancy in our parish, as it were, just by the cry of a passing bird, for she could not tell how; although I judge myself that William Keckle the elder had a hand in it, as he was at the time in Glasgow; and she wrote me a wonderful well-penned letter, bespeaking the situation, which letter came to hand on the morn following Lady Macadam's stramash to me about Kate Malcolm, and I laid it before the Session the same day; so that by the time her auntie's concern was taken off her hands, she had a home and a howff among us to come to, in the which she lived upwards of thirty years in credit and respect, although some thought she had not the art of her predecessor, and was more uppish in her carriage than befitted the decorum of her vocation. Hers, however, was but a harmless vanity; and, poor woman, she needed all manner of graces to set her out, for she was made up of odds and ends, and had but one good eye, the other being blind, and just like a blue bead; at first she plainly set her cap for Mr. Lorimore, but after ogling and gogling at him every Sunday in the kirk for a whole half year and more, Miss Sabrina desisted in despair.

But the most remarkable thing about her coming into the parish was the change that took place in Christian names among us. Old Mr Hookie, her father, had, from the time he read his Virgil, maintained a sort of intromission with the Nine Muses, by which he was led to baptize her Sabrina, after a name mentioned by John Milton in one of his works. Miss Sabrina began by calling our Jennies, Jessies, and our Nannies, Nancies; alas! I have lived to see even these likewise grow old-fashioned. She had also a taste in the mantua-making line, which she had learnt in Glasgow, and I could date from the very Sabbath of her first appearance in the kirk, a change growing in the garb of the younger lassies, who from that day began to lay aside the silken plaidie over the head, the which had been the pride and bravery of their grandmothers, and instead of the snood, that was so snod and simple, they hided their heads in round-eared bees-cap mutches, made of gauze and catgut, and other curious contrivances of French millendery; all which brought a deal of custom to Miss Sabrina, over and above the incomings and Candlemas offerings of the school; insomuch, that she saved money, and in the course of three years had ten pounds to put in the bank.

At the time, these alterations and revolutions in the parish were thought a great advantage; but now when I look back upon them, as a traveller on the hill over the road he has passed, I have my doubts. For with wealth come wants, like a troop of clamorous beggars at the heels of a generous man, and it's hard to tell wherein the benefit of improvement in a country parish consists, especially to those who live by the sweat of their brow. But it is not for me to make reflections, my task and duty is to note the changes of time and habitudes.

Chapter 10

Year 1769

A toad found in the heart of a stone—Robert Malcolm, who had been at sea,
returns from a northern voyage—Kate Malcolm's clandestine correspondence with
Lady Macadam's son.

I have my doubts whether it was in the beginning of this year, or in the end of the last, that a very extraordinary thing came to light in the parish; but howsoever that may be, there is nothing more certain than the fact, which it is my duty to record. I have mentioned already how it was that the toll, or trust road, was set agoing, on account of the Lord Eglesham's tumbling on the midden in the Vennel. Well, it happened to one of the labouring men, in breaking the stones to make metal for the new road, that he broke a stone that was both a large and remarkable, and in the heart of it, which was boss, there was found a living creature, that jumped out the moment it saw the light of heaven, to the great terrification of the man, who could think it was nothing but an evil spirit that had been imprisoned therein for a time. The man came to me like a demented creature, and the whole clachan gathered out, young and old, and I went at their head, to see what the miracle could be, for the man said it was a fiery dragon, spuing smoke and flames. But when we came to the spot, it was just a yird toad, and the laddie weans nevelled it to death with stones, before I could persuade them to give over. Since then I have read of such things coming to light in the *Scots Magazine*, a very valuable book.

Soon after the affair of 'the wee deil in the stane,' as it was called, a sough reached us that the Americas were seized with the rebellious spirit of the ten tribes, and were snapping their fingers in the face of the king's government. The news came on a Saturday night, for we had no newspapers in those days, and was brought by Robin Modiwort, that fetched the letters from the Irville post. Thomas Fullarton (he has been dead many a day) kept the grocery-shop in Irville, and he had been in at Glasgow, as was his yearly custom, to settle his accounts, and to buy a hogshead of tobacco, with sugar and other spiceries; and being in Glasgow, Thomas was told by the merchant of a great rise in tobacco, that had happened by reason of the contumacity of the plantations, and it was thought that blood would be spilt before things were ended, for that the king and Parliament were in a great passion with them. But as Charles Malcolm, in the king's ship, was the only one belonging to the parish that was likely to be art and part in the business, we were in a manner little troubled at the time with this first gasp of the monster of war, who, for our sins, was ordained to swallow up and devour so many of our fellow-subjects, before he was bound again in the chains of mercy and peace.

I had, in the meantime, written a letter to the Lord Eglesham to get Charles Malcolm out of the clutches of the press-gang in the man-of-war; and about a month after, his lordship sent me an answer, wherein was inclosed a letter from the captain of the ship, saying, that Charles Malcolm was so good a man, that he was reluctant to part with him, and that Charles himself was well contented to remain aboard. Anent which, his lordship said to me, that he had written back to the captain to make a midshipman of Charles, and that he would take him under his own protection, which was great joy on two accounts to us all, especially to his mother; first, to hear that Charles was a good man, although in years still but a youth; and secondly, that my lord had of his own free will taken him under the wing of his patronage.

But the sweet of this world is never to be enjoyed without some of the sour. The coal bark between Irville and Belfast, in which Robert Malcolm, the second son of his mother, was serving his time to be a sailor, got a charter, as it was called, to go with to Norway for deals, which grieved Mrs Malcolm to the very heart, for there was then no short cut by the canal, as now is, between the rivers of the Forth and Clyde, but every ship was obligated to go far away round by the Orkneys, which, although a voyage in the summer not overly dangerous, there being long days and short nights then, yet in the winter it was far otherwise, many vessels being frozen up in the Baltic till the spring; and there was a story told at the time, of an Irville bark coming home in the dead of the year, that lost her way altogether, and was supposed to have sailed north into utter darkness, for she was never more heard of; and many an awful thing was said of what the auld mariners about the shore thought concerning the crew of that misfortunate vessel. However, Mrs Malcolm was a woman of great faith, and having placed her reliance on Him who is the orphant's stay and widow's trust, she resigned her bairn into his hands, with a religious submission to His pleasure, though the mother's tear of weak human nature was on her cheek and in her e'e. And her faith was well rewarded, for the vessel brought him safe home, and he had seen such a world of things, that it was just to read a story-book to hear him tell of Elsineur and Gottenburgh, and other fine and great places that we had never heard of till that time; and he brought me a bottle of Riga balsam, which for healing cuts was just miraculous, besides a clear bottle of Rososolus for his mother, a spirit which for cordiality could not be told; for though since that time we have had many a sort of Dantzick cordial, I have in never tasted any to compare with Robin Malcolm's Rososolus. The Lady Macadam, who had a knowledge of such things, declared it was the best of the best sort; for Mrs Malcolm sent her ladyship some of it in a doctor's bottle, as well as to Mrs Balwhidder, who was then at the down-lying with our daughter Janet—a woman now in the married state, that makes a most excellent wife, having been brought up with great pains, and well educated, as I shall have to record by and by.

About the Christmas of this year, Lady Macadam's son having been perfected in the art of war at a school in France, had, with the help of his mother's friends, and his father's fame, got a stand of colours in the Royal Scots regiment; he came to show himself in his regimentals to his lady mother, like a dutiful son, as he certainly was. It happened that he was in the kirk in his scarlets and gold, on the same Sunday that Robert Malcolm came home from the long voyage to Norway for deals; and I thought when I saw the soldier and the sailor from the pulpit, that it was an omen of war among our harmless country folks, like swords and cannon amidst ploughs and sickles, coming upon us, and I became laden in spirit, and had a most weighty prayer upon the occasion, which was long after remembered, many thinking, when the American war broke out, that I had been gifted with a glimmering of prophecy on that day.

It was during this visit to his lady mother, that young Laird Macadam settled the correspondence with Kate Malcolm, which, in the process of time, caused us all so much trouble; for it was a clandestine concern, but the time is not yet ripe for me to speak of it more at large. I should however mention, before concluding this annal, that Mrs Malcolm herself was this winter brought to death's door by a terrible host that came on her in the kirk, by taking a kittling in her throat. It was a terrification to hear her sometimes; but she got the better of it in the spring, and was more herself thereafter than she had been for years before; and her daughter Effie, or Euphemia, as she was called by Miss Sabrina, the schoolmistress, was growing up to be a gleg and clever quean; she was, indeed, such a spirit in her way, that the folks called her Spunkie; while her son William, that was the youngest of the five, was making a wonderful proficiency with Mr Lorimore. He was indeed a douce, well-doing laddie, of a composed nature; insomuch that the master said he was surely chosen for the ministry. In short, the more I think on what befell this family, and of the great meekness and Christian worth of the parent, I verily believe there never could have been in any parish such a manifestation of the truth, that they who put their trust in the Lord are sure of having a friend that will never forsake them.

Chapter 11

Year 1770

This year a happy and tranquil one—Lord Eglesham establishes a fair in the village—The show of punch appears for the first time in the parish.

This blessed Ann. Dom. was one of the Sabbaths of my ministry; when I look back upon it, all is quiet and good order; the darkest cloud of the smuggling had passed over, at least from my people, and the rumours of rebellion in America were but like the distant sound of the bars of Ayr. We sat, as it were, in a lown and pleasant place, beholding our prosperity, like the apple-tree adorned with her garlands of flourishes, in the first fair mornings of the spring, when the birds were returning thanks to their Maker for the coming again of the seed-time, and the busy bee goeth forth from her cell, to gather honey from the flowers of the field, and the broom of the hill, and the blue-bells and gowans, which Nature, with a gracious and a gentle hand, scatters in the valley, as she walketh forth in her beauty, to testify to the goodness of the Father of all mercies.

Both at the spring and the harvest sacraments, the weather was as that which is in Paradise; there was a glad composure in all hearts, and the minds of men were softened towards each other. The number of communicants was greater than had been known for many years, and the tables were filled by the pious from many a neighbouring parish; those of my hearers who had opposed my placing declared openly for a testimony of satisfaction and holy thankfulness, that the tent, so surrounded as it was on both occasions, was a sight they never had expected to see. I was, to be sure, assisted by some of the best divines then in the land, but I had not been a sluggard myself in the vineyard.

Often, when I think on this year, so fruitful in pleasant intimacies, has the thought come into my mind, that as the Lord blesses the earth from time to time with a harvest of more than the usual increase, so, in like manner, he is sometimes for a season pleased to pour into the breasts of mankind a larger portion of goodwill and charity, disposing them to love one another, to be kindly to all creatures, and filled with the delight of thankfulness to himself, which is the greatest of blessings.

It was in this year that the Earl of Eglesham ordered the fair to be established in the village; and it was a day of wonderful festivity to all the bairns, and lads and lassies, for miles round. I think, indeed, that there has never been such a fair as the first since; for although we have more mountebanks and Merry-andrews now, and richer cargoes of groceries and packman's stands, yet there has been a falling off in the light-hearted daffing, while the hobble-shows in the change-houses have been awfully augmented. It was on this occasion that Punch's opera was first seen in our country-side, and surely never was there such a funny curiosity; for although Mr Punch himself was but a timber idol, he was as droll as a true living thing, and napped with his head so comical; but oh he was a sorrowful contumacious captain, and it was just a sport to see how he rampaged, and triumphed, and sang. For months after, the laddie weans did nothing but squeak and sing like Punch. In short, a blithe spirit was among us throughout this year, and the briefness of the chronicle bears witness to the innocency of the time.

Chapter 12

Year 1771

The nature of Lady Macadam's amusements—She intercepts letters from her son to Kate Malcolm.

It was in this year that my troubles with Lady Macadam's affair began. She was a woman, as I have by hint here and there intimated, of a prelatic disposition, seeking all things her own way, and not overly scrupulous about the means, which I take to be the true humour of prelacy. She was come of a high episcopal race in the east country, where sound doctrine had been long but little heard, and she considered the comely humility of a presbyter as the wickedness of hypocrisy; so that, saving in the way of neighbourly visitation, there was no sincere communion between us. Nevertheless, with all her vagaries, she had the element of a kindly spirit, that would sometimes kythe in actions of charity, that showed symptoms of a true Christian grace, had it been properly cultivated; but her morals had been greatly neglected in her youth, and she would waste her precious time in the long winter nights, playing at the cards with her visitors; in the which thriftless and sinful pastime, she was at great pains to instruct Kate Malcolm, which I was grieved to understand. What, however, I most misliked in her ladyship was a lightness and juvenility of behaviour altogether unbecoming her years, for she was far past threescore, having been long married without children. Her son, the soldier officer, came so late, that it was thought she would have been taken up as an evidence in the Douglas cause. She was, to be sure, crippled with the rheumatics, and no doubt the time hung heavy on her hands; but the best friends of recreation and sport must allow, that an old woman, sitting whole hours jingling with that paralytic chattel a spinet, was not a natural object! What then could be said for her singing Italian songs, and getting all the newest from Vauxhall in London, a boxful at a time, with new novel-books, and trinkum-trankum flowers and feathers, and sweetmeats, sent to her by a lady of the blood royal of Paris? As for the music, she was at great pains to instruct Kate, which, with the other things she taught, were sufficient, as my lady said herself, to qualify poor Kate for a duchess or a governess, in either of which capacities, her ladyship assured Mrs Malcolm, she would do honour to her instructor, meaning her own self; but I must come to the point anent the affair.

One evening, early in the month of January, as I was sitting by myself in my closet studying the Scots Magazine which I well remember the new number had come but that very night, Mrs Balwhidder being at the time busy with the lasses in the kitchen, and superintending, as her custom was, for she was a clever woman, a great wool-spinning we then had, both little wheel and meikle wheel, for stockings and blankets-sitting, as I was saying, in the study, with the fire well gathered up, for a night's reflection, a prodigious knocking came to the door, by which the book was almost startled out of my hand, and all the wheels in the house were silenced at once. This was her ladyship's flunkey, to beg me to go to her, whom he described as in a state of desperation. Christianity required that I should obey the summons; so, with what haste I could, thinking that perhaps, as she had been low-spirited for some time about the young laird's going to the Indies, she might have got a cast of grace, and been wakened in despair to the state of darkness in which she had so long lived, I made as few steps of the road between the manse and her house as it was in my ability to do.

On reaching the door, I found a great light in the house-candles burning upstairs and downstairs, and a sough of something extraordinar going on. I went into the dining-room, where her ladyship was wont to sit; but she was not there—only Kate Malcolm all alone, busily picking bits of paper from the carpet. When she looked up, I saw that her eyes were red with weeping, and I was alarmed, and said, 'Katy, my dear, I hope there is no danger?' Upon which the poor lassie rose, and flinging herself in a chair, covered her face with her hands, and wept bitterly.

'What is the old fool doing with the wench?' cried a sharp angry voice from the drawing-room—'why does not he come to me?' It was the voice of Lady Macadam herself, and she meant me. So I went to her; but, oh, she was in a far different state from what I had hoped. The pride of this world had got the upper hand of her, and was playing dreadful antics with her understanding. There was she, painted like a Jezebel, with gum-flowers on her head, as was her custom every afternoon, sitting on a settee, for she was lame, and in her hand she held a letter. 'Sir,' said she, as I came into the room, 'I want you to go instantly to that young fellow, your clerk (meaning Mr Lorimore, the schoolmaster, who was likewise session-clerk and precentor), and tell him I will give him a couple of hundred pounds to marry Miss Malcolm without delay, and undertake to procure him a living from some of my friends.'

'Softly, my lady, you must first tell me the meaning of all this haste of kindness,' said I, in my calm methodical manner. At the which she began to cry and sob like a petted bairn, and to bewail her ruin, and the dishonour of her family. I was surprised, and beginning to be confounded, at length out it came. The flunkie had that night brought two London letters from the Irville post, and Kate Malcolm being out of the way when he came home, he took them both in to her ladyship on the silver server, as was his custom; and her ladyship, not jealousing that Kate could have a correspondence with London, thought both the letters were for herself, for they were franked, so, as it happened, she opened the one that was for Kate, and this, too, from the young laird, her own son. She could not believe her eyes when she saw the first words in his hand of write, and she read, and she better read, till she read all the letter, by which she came to know that Kate and her darling were trysted, and that this was not the first love-letter which had passed between them. She therefore tore it in pieces, and sent for me, and screamed for Kate; in short, went, as it were, off at the head, and was neither to bind nor to hold on account of this intrigue, as she in her wrath stigmatised the innocent gallanting of poor Kate and the young laird.

I listened in patience to all she had to say anent the discovery, and offered her the very best advice; but she derided my judgment, and because I would not speak outright to Mr Lorimore, and get him to marry Kate off-hand, she bade me good-night with an air, and sent for him herself. He, however, was on the brink of marriage with his present worthy helpmate, and declined her ladyship's proposals, which angered her still more. But although there was surely a great lack of discretion in all this, and her ladyship was entirely overcome with her passion, she would not part with Kate, nor allow her to quit the house with me, but made her sup with her as usual that night, calling her sometimes a perfidious baggage, and at other times, forgetting her delirium, speaking to her as kindly as ever. At night Kate as usual helped her ladyship into her bed (this she told me with tears in her eyes next morning), and when Lady Macadam, as was her wont, bent to kiss her for good-night, she suddenly recollected 'the intrigue,' and gave Kate such a slap on the side of the head, as quite dislocated for a time the intellects of the poor young lassie. Next morning Kate was solemnly advised never to write again to the laird, while the lady wrote him a letter, which, she said, would be as good as a birch to the breech of the boy. Nothing therefore, for some time, indeed throughout the year, came of this matter, but her ladyship, when Mrs Balwhidder soon after called on her, said that I was a nose of wax, and that she never would speak to me again, which surely was not a polite thing to say to Mrs Balwhidder, my second wife.

This stramash was the first time that I had interposed in the family concerns of my people, for it was against my nature to make or meddle with private actions, saving only such as in course of nature came before the Session; but I was not satisfied with the principles of Lady Macadam, and I began to be weary about Kate Malcolm's situation with her ladyship, whose ways of thinking I saw were not to be depended on, especially in those things wherein her pride and vanity were concerned. But the time ran on—the butterflies and the blossoms were succeeded by the leaves and the fruit, and nothing of a particular nature further molested the general tranquillity of this year; about the end of which there came on a sudden frost after a tack of wet weather. The roads were just a sheet of ice, like a frozen river; insomuch, that the coal-carts could not work; and one of our cows (Mrs Balwhidder said, after the accident, it was our best, but it was not so much thought of before) fell in coming from the glebe to the byre, and broke its two hinder legs, which obligated us to kill it, in order to put the beast out of pain. As this happened after we had salted our mart, it occasioned us to have a double crop of puddings, and such a show of hams in the kitchen as was a marvel to our visitors to see.

Chapter 13

Year 1772

The detection of Mr Heckletext's guilt—He threatens to prosecute the elders for defamation—The Muscovy duck gets an operation performed on it.

On New Year's night, this year, a thing happened, which, in its own nature, was a trifle, but it turned out as a mustard-seed that grows into a great tree. One of the elders, who has long been dead and gone, came to the manse about a fact that was found out in the clachan, and after we had discoursed on it some time, he rose to take his departure. I went with him to the door with the candle in my hand—it was a clear frosty night, with a sharp wind, and the moment I opened the door, the blast blew out the candle, so that I heedlessly, with the candlestick in my hand, walked with him to the yett without my hat, by which I took a sore cold in my head, that brought on a dreadful toothache; insomuch, that I was obligated to go into Irville to get the tooth drawn, and this caused my face to swell to such a fright, that on the Sabbath day I could not preach to my people. There was, however, at that time, a young man, one Mr Heckletext, tutor in Sir Hugh Montgomerie's family, and who had shortly before been licenced. Finding that I would not be able to preach myself, I sent to him, and begged he would officiate for me, which he very pleasantly consented to do, being, like all the young clergy, thirsting to show his light to the world. 'Twixt the fore and afternoon's worship, he took his check of dinner at the manse, and I could not but say that he seemed both discreet and sincere. Judge, however, what was brewing, when the same night Mr Lorimore came and told me, that Mr Heckletext was the suspected person anent the fact, that had been instrumental in the hand of a chastising Providence, to afflict me with the toothache, in order, as it afterwards came to pass, to bring the hidden hypocrisy of the ungodly preacher to light. It seems that the donsie lassie who was in fault had gone to the kirk in the afternoon, and seeing who was in the pulpit, where she expected to see me, was seized with the hystericks, and taken with her crying on the spot, the which being untimely, proved the death of both mother and bairn before the thing was properly laid to the father's charge.

This caused a great uproar in the parish. I was sorely blamed to let such a man as Mr Heckletext go up into my pulpit, although I was as ignorant of his offences as the innocent child that perished; and, in an unguarded hour, to pacify some of the elders, who were just distracted about the disgrace, I consented to have him called before the Session. He obeyed the call, and in a manner that I will never forget, for he was a sorrow of sin and audacity, and demanded to know why and for what reason he was summoned. I told him the whole affair in my calm and moderate way, but it was oil cast upon a burning coal. He flamed up in a terrible passion, threepit at the elders that they had no proof whatever of his having had any trafficking in the business, which was the case, for it was only a notion, the poor deceased lassie never having made a disclosure; called them libellous conspirators against his character, which was his only fortune, and concluded by threatening to punish them, though he exempted me from the injury which their slanderous insinuations had done to his prospects in life. We were all terrified, and allowed him to go away without uttering a word; and sure enough he did bring a plea in the courts of Edinburgh against Mr Lorimore and the elders for damages, laid at a great sum.

What might have been the consequence, no one can tell; but soon after he married Sir Hugh's housekeeper, and went with her into Edinburgh, where he took up a school, and before the trial came on—that is to say, within three months of the day that I myself married them—Mrs Heckletext was delivered of a thriving lad bairn, which would have been a witness for the elders, had the worst come to the worst. This was, indeed, we all thought, a joyous deliverance to the parish, and it was a lesson to me never to allow any preacher to mount my pulpit unless I knew something of his moral character.

In other respects, this year passed very peaceably in the parish; there was a visible increase of worldly circumstances, and the hedges which had been planted along the toll-road began to put forth their branches, and to give new notions of orderliness and beauty to the farmers. Mrs Malcolm heard from time to time from her son Charles, on board the man-of-war the *Avenger* where he was midshipman, and he had found a friend in the captain, that was just a father to him. Her second son Robert, being out of his time at Irville, went to the Clyde to look for a berth, and was hired to go to Jamaica, in a ship called the rooper. He was a lad of greater sobriety of nature than Charles; douce, honest, and faithful; and when he came home, though he brought no limes to me to make punch, like his brother, he brought a Muscovy duck to Lady Macadam, who had, as I have related, in a manner educated his sister Kate. That duck was the first of the kind we had ever seen, and many thought it was of the goose species, only with short bowly legs. It was however, a tractable and homely beast, and after some confabulation, as my lady herself told Mrs Balwhidder, it was received into fellowship by her other ducks and poultry. It is not, however, so much on account of the rarity of the creature, that I have introduced it here, as for the purpose of relating a wonderful operation that was performed on it by Miss Sabrina, the schoolmistress.

There happened to be a sack of beans in our stable, and Lady Macadam's hens and fowls, which were not overly fed at home, through the inattention of her servants, being great stravaggers for their meat, in passing the door, went in to pick, and the Muscovy seeing a hole in the bean-sack, dabbled out a crap-full before she was disturbed. The beans swelled on the poor bird's stomach, and her crap bellied out like the kyte of a Glasgow magistrate, until it was just a sight to be seen with its head back on its shoulders. The bairns of the clachan followed it up and down, crying, the lady's muckle jock's aye growing bigger, till every heart was wae for the creature. Some thought it was afflicted with a tympathy, and others, that it was the natural way for such like ducks to deck their young. In short, we were all concerned, and my lady having a great opinion of Miss Sabrina's skill, had a consultation with her on the case, at which Miss Sabrina advised, that what she called the Cesarian operation should be tried, which she herself performed accordingly, by opening the creature's crap, and taking out as many beans as filled a mutchkin stoup, after which she sewed it up, and the Muscovy went its way to the water-side, and began to swim, and was as jocund as ever; insomuch, that in three days after it was quite cured of all the consequences of its surfeit. I had at one time a notion to send an account of this to the *Scots Magazine* but something always came in the way to prevent me; so that it has been reserved for a place in this chronicle, being, after Mr Heckletext's affair, the most memorable thing in our history of this year.

Chapter 14

Year 1773

The new schoolhouse—Lord Eglesham comes down to he castle—I refuse to go and dine there on Sunday, but go on Monday, and meet with an English dean.

In this Ann. Dom. there was something like a plea getting to a head, between the Session and some of the heritors, about a new schoolhouse; the thatch having been torn from the rigging of the old one by a blast of wind, on the first Monday of February, by which a great snow-storm got admission, and the school was rendered utterly uninhabitable. The smaller sort of lairds were very willing to come into the plan with an extra contribution, because they respected the master, and their bairns were at the school; but the gentlemen who had tutors in their own houses were not so manageable, and some of them even went so far as to say, that the kirk being only wanted on Sunday, would do very well for a school all the rest of the week, which was a very profane way of speaking, and I was resolved to set myself against any such thing, and to labour according to the power and efficacy of my station to get a new school built.

Many a meeting the Session had on the subject, and the heritors debated and discussed, and revised their proceedings, and still no money for the needful work was forthcoming. Whereupon it happened one morning, as I was rummaging in my scrutoire, that I laid my hand on the Lord Eglesham's letter anent Charles Malcolm, and it was put into my head at that moment, that if I was to write his lordship, who was the greatest heritor, and owned now the major part of the parish, that by his help and influence, I might be an instrument to the building of a comfortable new school; accordingly I sat down and wrote my lord all about the accident, and the state of the schoolhouse, and the divisions and seditions among the heritors, and sent the letter to him at London by the post the same day, without saying a word to any living soul on the subject.

This in me was an advised thought, for, by the return of post, his lordship, with his own hand, in a most kind manner, authorised me to say that he would build a new school at his own cost, and bade me go over and consult about it with his steward, at the castle, to whom he had written by the same post the necessary instructions. Nothing could exceed the gladness which the news gave to the whole parish, and none said more in behalf of his lordship's bounty and liberality than the heritors; especially those gentry who grudged the undertaking, when it was thought that it would have to come out of their own pock-nook.

In the course of the summer, just as the roof was closing in of the schoolhouse, my lord came to the castle with a great company, and was not there a day till he sent for me to come over on the next Sunday to dine with him; but I sent him word that I could not do so, for it would be a transgression of the Sabbath, which made him send his own gentleman to make his apology for having taken so great a liberty with me, and to beg me to come on the Monday, which I accordingly did, and nothing could be better than the discretion with which I was used. There was a vast company of English ladies and gentlemen, and his lordship, in a most jocose manner, told them all how he had fallen on the midden, and how I had clad him in my clothes, and there was a wonder of laughing and diversion; but the most particular thing in the company was a large round-faced man, with a wig, that was a dignitary in some great Episcopalian church in London, who was extraordinary condescending towards me, drinking wine with me at the table, and saying weighty sentences in a fine style of language, about the becoming grace of simplicity and innocence of heart, in the clergy of all denominations of Christians, which I was pleased to hear; for really he had a proud red countenance, and I could not have thought he was so mortified to humility within, had I not heard with what sincerity he delivered himself, and seen how much reverence and attention was paid to him by all present, particularly by my lord's chaplain, who was a pious and pleasant young divine, though educated at Oxford for the Episcopalian persuasion.

One day soon after, as I was sitting in my closet conning a sermon for the next Sunday, I was surprised by a visit from the dean, as the dignitary was called. He had come, he said, to wait on me as rector of the parish, for so it seems they call a pastor in England, and to say, that, if it was agreeable, he would take a family dinner with us before he let the castle. I could make no objection to this kindness, but said I hoped my lord would come with him, and that we would do our best to entertain them with all suitable hospitality. About an hour or so after he had returned to the castle, one of the flunkies brought a letter from his lordship to say, that not only he would come with the dean, but that they would bring his other guests with them, and that, as they could only drink London wine, the butler would send me a hamper in the morning, assured, as he was pleased to say, that Mrs Balwhidder would otherwise provide good cheer.

This notification, however, was a great trouble to my wife, who was only used to manufacture the produce of our glebe and yard to a profitable purpose, and not used to the treatment of deans and lords, and other persons of quality. However, she was determined to stretch a point on this occasion, and we had, as all present declared, a charming dinner; for fortunately one of the sows had a litter of pigs a few days before, and, in addition to a goose, that is but a boss bird, we had a roasted pig, with an apple in its mouth, which was just a curiosity to see; and my lord called it a tythe pig, but I told him it was one of Mrs Balwhidder's own clecking, which saying of mine made no little sport when expounded to the dean.

But, och how! this was the last happy summer that we had for many a year in the parish; and an omen of the dule that ensued, was in a sacrilegious theft that a daft woman, Jenny Gaffaw, and her idiot daughter, did in the kirk, by tearing off and stealing the green serge lining of my lord's pew, to make, as they said, a hap for their shoulders in the cold weather-saving, however, the sin, we paid no attention at the time to the mischief and tribulation that so unheard-of a trespass boded to us all. It took place about Yule, when the weather was cold and frosty, and poor Jenny was not very able to go about seeking her meat as usual. The deed, however, was mainly done by her daughter, who, when brought before me, said, 'her poor mother's back had mair need of claes than the kirk-boards,' which was so true a thing, that I could not punish her, but wrote anent it to my lord, who not only overlooked the offence, but sent orders to the servants at the castle to be kind to the poor woman, and the natural, her daughter.

Chapter 15

Year 1774

The murder of Jean Glaikit—The young Laird Macadam comes down and marries Kate Malcolm—The ceremony performed by me, and I am commissioned to break the matter to Lady Macadam—Her behaviour.

When I look back on this year, and compare what happened therein with the things that had gone before, I am grieved to the heart, and pressed down with an afflicted spirit. We had, as may be read, trials and tribulations in the days that were past, and in the rank and boisterous times of the smuggling there was much sin and blemish among us, but nothing so dark and awful as what fell out in the course of this unhappy year. The evil omen of daft Jenny Gaffaw, and her daughter's sacrilege, had soon a bloody verification.

About the beginning of the month of March in this year, the war in America was kindling so fast that the government was obligated to sent soldiers over the sea, in the hope to quell the rebellious temper of the plantations, and a party of a regiment that was quartered at Ayr was ordered to march to Greenock, to be there shipped off. The men were wild and wicked profligates, without the fear of the Lord before their eyes, and some of them had drawn up with light women in Ayr, who followed them on their march. This the soldiers did not like, not wishing to be troubled with such gear in America; so the women, when they got the length of Kilmarnock, were ordered to retreat, and go home, which they all did, but one Jean Glaikit, who persisted in her intent to follow her jo, Patrick O'Neil, a Catholic Irish corporal. The man did, as he said, all in his capacity to persuade her to return, but she was a contumacious limmer, and would not listen to reason, so that, in passing along our toll-road, from less to more, the miserable wretches fell out, and fought, and the soldier put an end to her, with a hasty knock on the head with his firelock, and marched on after his comrades.

The body of the woman was, about half an hour after, found by the scholars of Mr Lorimore's school, who had got the play to see the marching, and to hear the drums of the soldiers. Dreadful was the shout and the cry throughout the parish at this foul work. Some of the farmer lads followed the soldiers on horseback, and others ran to Sir Hugh, who was a justice of the peace, for his advice. Such a day as that was!

However, the murderer was taken, and, with his arms tied behind him with a cord, he was brought back to the parish, where he confessed before Sir Hugh the deed, and how it happened. He was then put in a cart, and being well guarded by six of the lads, was taken to Ayr jail.

It was not long after this that the murderer was brought to trial, and, being found guilty on his own confession, he was sentenced to be executed, and his body to be hung in chains near the spot where the deed was done. I thought that all in the parish would have run to desperation with horror when the news of this came, and I wrote immediately to the Lord Eglesham to get this done away by the merciful power of the government, which he did to our great solace and relief.

In the autumn, the young Laird Macadam, being ordered with his regiment for the Americas, got leave from the king to come and see his lady-mother, before his departure. But it was not to see her only, as will presently appear.

Knowing how much her ladyship was averse to the notion he had of Kate Malcolm, he did not write of his coming, lest she would send Kate out of the way, but came in upon them at a late hour, as they were wasting their precious time, as was the nightly wont of my lady, with a pack of cards; and so far was she from being pleased to see him, that no sooner did she behold his face, but like a tap of tow, she kindled upon both him and Kate, and ordered them out of her sight and house. The young folk had discretion: Kate went home to her mother, and the laird came to the manse, and begged us to take him in. He then told me what had happened, and that having bought a captain's commission, he was resolved to marry Kate, and hoped I would perform the ceremony, if her mother would consent. 'As for mine,' said he, 'she will never agree; but, when the thing is done, her pardon will not be difficult to get, for, with all her whims and caprice, she is generous and affectionate.' In short, he so wiled and beguiled me, that I consented to marry them, if Mrs Malcolm was agreeable. 'I will not disobey my mother,' said he, 'by asking her consent, which I know she will refuse ; and, therefore, the sooner it is done the better.' So we then stepped over to Mrs Malcolm's house, where we found that saintly woman, with Kate and Effie, and Willie, sitting peacefully at their fireside, preparing to read their Bibles for the night. When we went in and when I saw Kate, that was so ladylike there with the decent humility of her parent's dwelling, I could not but think she was destined for a better station; and when I looked at the captain, a handsome youth, I thought surely their marriage is made in Heaven; and so I said to Mrs Malcolm, who after a time consented, and likewise agreed that her daughter should go with the captain to America, for her faith and trust in the goodness of Providence was great and boundless, striving, as it were, to be even with its tender mercies. Accordingly, the captain's man was sent to bid the chaise wait that had taken him to the lady's, and the marriage was sanctified by me before we left Mrs Malcolm's. No doubt, they ought to have been proclaimed three several Sabbaths, but I satisfied the Session, at our first meeting, on account of the necessity of the case. The young couple went in the chaise travelling to Glasgow, authorising me to break the matter to Lady Macadam, which was a sore task, but I was spared from the performance. For her ladyship had come to herself, and thinking on her own rashness in sending away Kate and the captain in the way she had done, she was like one by herself; all the servants were scattered out and abroad in quest of the lovers, and some of them, seeing the chaise drive from Mrs Malcolm's door, with them in it, and me coming out, jealoused what had been done, and told their mistress outright of the marriage, which was to her like a clap of thunder; insomuch that she flung herself back in her settee, and was beating and drumming with her heels on the floor, like a madwoman in Bedlam, when I entered the room. For some time she took no notice of me, but continued her din; but, by and by, she began to turn her eyes in fiery glances upon me, till I was terrified lest she would fly at me with her claws in her fury. At last she stopped all at once, and, in a calm voice, said, 'But it cannot now be helped, where are the vagabonds?' 'They are gone,' replied I. 'Gone?' cried she, 'gone where?' 'To America, I suppose,' was my answer; upon which she again threw herself back in the settee, and began again to drum and beat with her feet as before. But not to dwell on small particularities, let it suffice to say, that she sent her coachman on one of her coach horses, which being old and stiff, did not overtake the fugitives till they were in their bed at Kilmarnock, where they stopped that night; but when they came back to the lady's in the morning, she was as cagey and meikle taken up with them, as if they had gotten her full consent and privilege to marry from the first. Thus was the first of Mrs Malcolm's children well and creditably settled. I have only now to conclude with observing that my son Gilbert was seized with the small-pox about the beginning of December, and was blinded by them for seventeen days; for the inoculation was not in practice yet among us, saving only in the genteel families, that went into Edinburgh for the education of their children, where it was performed by the faculty there.

Chapter 16

Year 1775

Captain Macadam provides a house and an annuity for old Mrs Malcolm—Miss Betty Wudrife brings from Edinburgh new-fashioned silk mantle, but refuses to give the pattern to old Lady Macadam—Her revenge.

The regular course of nature is calm and orderly, and tempests and troubles are but lapses from the accustomed sobriety with which Providence works out the destined end of all things. From Yule till Pace-Monday there had been a gradual subsidence of our personal and parochial tribulations, and the spring, though late, set in bright and beautiful, and was accompanied with the spirit of contentment, so that, excepting the great concern that we all began to take in the American rebellion, especially on account of Charles Malcolm that was in the man-of-war, and of Captain Macadam that had married Kate, we had throughout the better half of the year but little molestation of any sort. I should, however, note the upshot of the marriage.

By some cause that I do not recollect, if I ever had it properly told, the regiment wherein the captain had bought his commission was not sent to the plantations, but only over to Ireland, by which the captain and his lady were allowed to prolong their stay in the parish with his mother, and he, coming of age, while he was among us, in making a settlement on his wife, bought the house at the braehead, which was then just built by Thomas Shivers the mason, and he gave that house, with a judicious income, to Mrs Malcolm, telling her that it was not becoming, he having it in his power to do the contrary, that she should any longer be dependent on her own industry. For this the young man got a name like a sweet odour in all the country-side; but that whimsical and prelatic lady his mother just went out of all bounds, and played such pranks, for an old woman, as cannot be told. To her daughter-in-law, however, she was wonderful kind; and in fitting her out for going with the captain to Dublin, it was extraordinary to hear what a paraphernalia she provided her with. But who could have thought that in this kindness a sore trial was brewing for me!

It happened that Miss Betty Wudrife, the daughter of an heritor, had been on a visit to some of her friends in Edinburgh; and, being in at Edinburgh, she came out with a fine mantle, decked and adorned with many a ribbon-knot, such as had never been seen in the parish. The Lady Macadam, hearing of this grand mantle, sent to beg Miss Betty to lend it to her, to make a copy for young Mrs Macadam. But Miss Betty was so vogie with her gay mantle, that she sent back word, it would be making it o'er common; which so nettled the old courtly lady, that she vowed revenge, and said the mantle would not be long seen on Miss Betty. Nobody knew the meaning of her words ; but she sent privately for Miss Sabrina, the schoolmistress, who was aye proud of being invited to my lady's, where she went on the Sabbath night to drink tea, and read Thomson's *Seasons* and Hervey's *Meditations* on for her ladyship's recreation. Between the two, a secret plot was laid against Miss Betty and her Edinburgh mantle; and Miss Sabrina, in a very treacherous manner, for the which I afterwards chided her severely, went to Miss Betty, and got a sight of the mantle, and how it was made, and all about it, at until she was in a capacity to make another like it; by which in my lady and her, from old silk and satin *negligées* which her ladyship had worn at the French court, made up two mantles of the self-same fashion as Miss Betty's, and, if possible, more sumptuously garnished, but in a flagrant fool way. On the Sunday morning after, her ladyship sent for Jenny Gaffaw, and her daft daughter Meg, and showed them the mantles, and said she would give them half-a-crown if they would go with them to the kirk, and take their place on the bench beside the elders, and after worship, walk home before Miss Betty Wudrife. The two poor natural things were just transported with the sight of such bravery, and needed no other bribe; so, over their bits of ragged duds, they put on the pageantry, and walked away to the kirk like peacocks, and took their place on the bench, to the great diversion of the whole congregation.

I had no suspicion of this, and had prepared an affecting discourse about the horrors of war, in which I touched, with a tender hand, on the troubles that threatened families and kindred in America; but all the time I was preaching, doing my best, and expatiating till the tears came into my eyes, I could not divine what was the cause of the inattention of my people. But the two vain haverels were on the bench under me, and I could not see them; where they sat, spreading their feathers and picking their wings, stroking down and setting right their finery, with such an air as no living soul could see and withstand; while every eye in the kirk was now on them, and now at Miss Betty Wudrife, who was in a worse situation than if she had been on the stool of repentance.

Greatly grieved with the little heed that was paid to my discourse, I left the pulpit with a heavy heart; but when I came out into the kirkyard, and saw the two antics linking like ladies, and aye keeping in the way before Miss Betty, and looking back and around in their pride and admiration, with high heads and a wonderful pomp, I was really overcome, and could not keep my gravity, but laughed loud out among the graves, and in the face of all my people, who, seeing how I was vanquished in that unguarded moment by my enemy, made a universal and most unreverent breach of all decorum, at which Miss Betty, who had been the cause of all, ran into the first open door, and almost fainted away with mortification.

This affair was regarded by the elders as a sinful trespass on the orderliness that was needful in the Lord's house, and they called on me at the manse that night, and said it would be a guilty connivance, if I did not rebuke and admonish Lady Macadam of the evil of her way; for they had questioned daft Jenny, and had got at the bottom of the whole plot and mischief. But I, who knew her ladyship's light way, would fain have had the elders to overlook it, rather than expose myself to her tantrums; but they considered the thing as a great scandal, so I was obligated to conform to their wishes. I might, however, have as well stayed at home, for her ladyship was in one of her jocose humours when I went to speak to her on the subject; and it was so far from my power to make a proper impression on her of the enormity that had been committed, that she made me laugh, in spite of my reason, at the fantastical drollery of her malicious prank on Miss Betty Wudrife.

It, however, did not end here; for the Session knowing that it was profitless to speak to the daft mother and daughter, who had been the instruments, gave orders to Willy Howking, the betheral, not to let them again so far into the kirk, and Willy, having scarcely more sense than them both, thought proper to keep them out next Sunday altogether. They twa said nothing at the time, but the adversary was busy with them; for, on the Wednesday following, there being a meeting of the Synod at Ayr, to my utter amazement, the mother and daughter made their appearance there in all their finery, and raised a complaint against me and the Session, for debarring them from church privileges. No stage play could have produced such an effect; I was perfectly dumbfoundered, and every member of the Synod might have been tied with a straw, they were so overcome with this new device of that endless woman, when bent on provocation—the Lady Macadam; in whom the saying was verified, that old folk are twice bairns, for in such plays, pranks, and projects, she was as play-rife as a very lassie at her sampler, and this is but a swatch to what lengths she would go. The complaint was dismissed, by which the Session and me were assoilzied; but I'll never forget till the day of my death what I suffered on that occasion, to be so put to the wall by two born idiots.

Chapter 17

Year 1776

A recruiting party comes to Irville—Thomas Wilson and some others enlist— Charles Malcolm's return.

It belongs to the chroniclers of the realm, to describe the damage and detriment which fell on the power and prosperity of the kingdom, by reason of the rebellion that was fired into open war against the name and authority of the king in the plantations of America; for my task is to describe what happened within the narrow bound of the pasturage of the Lord's flock, of which, in His bounty and mercy, He made me the humble, willing, but alas! the weak and ineffectual shepherd.

About the month of February, a recruiting party came to our neighbour town of Irville, to beat up for men to be soldiers against the rebels; and thus the battle was brought, as it were, to our gates, for the very first man that took on with them was one Thomas Wilson, a cotter in our clachan, who, up to that time, had been a decent and creditable character. He was at first a farmer lad, but had forgathered with a doited tawpy, whom he married, and had offspring three or four. For some time it was noticed that he had a down and thoughtful look, that his cleeding was growing bare, and that his wife kept an untrig house, which, it was feared by many, was the cause of Thomas going o'er often to the change-house; he was, in short, during the greater part of the winter, evidently a man foregone in the pleasures of this world, which made all that knew him compassionate his situation.

No doubt, it was his household ills that burdened him past bearing, and made him go into Irville, when he heard of the recruiting, and take on to be a soldier. Such a wally-wallying as the news of this caused at every door; for the redcoats,—from the persecuting days, when the black-cuffs rampaged through the country,—soldiers that fought for hire, were held in dread and as a horror among us, and terrible were the stories that were told of their cruelty and sinfulness; indeed, there had not been wanting in our own time a sample of what they were, as witness the murder of Jean Glaikit by Patrick O'Neil, the Irish corporal, anent which I have treated at large in the memorables of the year 1774.

A meeting of the Session was forthwith held; for here was Thomas Wilson's wife and all his weans, an awful cess, thrown upon the parish; and it was settled outright among us that Mr Docken, who was then an elder, but is since dead, a worthy man, with a soft tongue and a pleasing manner, should go to Irville, and get Thomas, if possible, released from the recruiters. But it was all in vain, the serjeant would not listen to him, for Thomas was a strapping lad; nor would the poor infatuated man himself agree to go back, but cursed like a cadger, and swore that if he staid any longer among his plagues, he would commit some rash act; so we were saddled with his family, which was the first taste and preeing of what war is when it comes into our hearths, and among the breadwinners.

The evil, however, did not stop here. Thomas, when he was dressed out in the king's clothes, came over to see his bairns, and take a farewell of his friends, and he looked so gallant, that the very next market-day another lad of the parish listed with him; but he was a ramplor, roving sort of a creature, and, upon the whole, it was thought he did well for the parish when he went to serve the king.

The listing was a catching distemper. Before the summer was over, other three of the farming lads went off with the drum, and there was a wailing in the parish, which made me preach a touching discourse. I likened the parish to a widow woman with a small family, sitting in their cottage by the fireside, herself spinning with an eydent wheel, ettling her best to get them a bit and a brat, and the poor weans all canty about the hearthstane—the little ones at their playocks, and the elder at their tasks—the callans working with hooks and lines to catch them a meal of fish in the morning—and the lassies working stockings to sell at the next Marymas fair. And then I likened war to a calamity coming among them—the callans drowned at their fishing—the lassies led to a misdoing—and the feckless wee bairns laid on the bed of sickness, and their poor forlorn mother sitting by herself at the embers of a cauldrife fire; her tow done, and no a bodle to buy more; dropping a silent and salt tear for her babies, and thinking of days that war gone, and, like Rachel weeping for her children, she would not be comforted. With this I concluded, for my own heart filled full with the thought, and there was a deep sob in the church, verily, it was Rachel weeping for her children.

In the latter end of the year, the man-of-war, with Charles Malcolm in her, came to the Tail of the Bank at Greenock, to press men as it was thought, and Charles got leave from his captain to come and see his mother; and he brought with him Mr Howard, another midshipman, the son of a great Parliament man in London, which, as we had tasted the sorrow, gave us some insight into the pomp of war. Charles was now grown up into a fine young man, rattling, light-hearted, and just a cordial of gladness, and his companion was every bit like him. They were dressed in their fine gold-laced garbs, and nobody knew Charles when he came to the clachan, but all wondered, for they were on horseback, and rode to the house where his mother lived when he went away, but which was then occupied by Miss Sabrina and her school. Miss Sabrina had never seen Charles, but she had heard of him, and when he inquired for his mother, she guessed who he was, and showed him the way to the new house that the captain had bought for her. Miss Sabrina, who was a little overly perjink at times, behaved herself on this occasion with a true spirit, and gave her lassies the play immediately, so that the news of Charles's return was spread by them like wild-fire, and there was a wonderful joy in the whole town. When Charles had seen his mother, and his sister Effie, with that douce and well-mannered lad William, his brother, for of their meeting I cannot speak, not being present, he then came with his friend to see me at the manse, and was most jocose with me, and in a way of great pleasance, got Mrs Balwhidder to ask his friend to sleep at the manse. In short, we had just a ploy the whole two days they staid with us, and I got leave from Lord Eglesham's steward to let them shoot on my lord's land, and I believe every laddie wean in the parish attended them to the field. As for old Lady Macadam, Charles being, as she said, a near relation, and she having likewise some knowledge of his comrade's family, she was just in her element with them, though they were but youths, for she was a woman naturally of a fantastical, and, as I have narrated, given to comical devices and pranks to a degree. She made for them a ball, to which she invited all the bonniest lassies, far and near, in the parish, and was out of the body with mirth, and had a fiddler from Irville; and it was thought by those that were there, that had she not been crippled with the rheumatics, she would have danced herself. But I was concerned to hear both Charles and his friend, like hungry hawks, rejoicing at the prospect of the war, hoping thereby, as soon as their midship term was out, to be made lieutenants; saving this, there was no allay in the happiness they brought with them to the parish, and it was a delight to see how auld and young of all degrees made of Charles, for we were proud of him, and none more than myself, though he began to take liberties with me, calling me old governor; it was, however, in a warm-hearted manner, only I did not like it when any of the elders heard. As for his mother, she deported herself like a saint on the occasion. There was a temperance in the pleasure of her heart, and in her thankfulness, that is past the compass of words to describe. Even Lady Macadam, who never could think a serious thought all her days, said, in her wild way, that the gods had bestowed more care in the making of Mrs Malcolm's temper, than on the bodies and souls of all the saints in the calendar. On the Sunday the strangers attended divine worship, and I preached a sermon purposely for them, and enlarged at great length and fulness on how David overcame Goliath; and they both told me that they had never heard such a good discourse, but I do not think they were great judges of preachings. How, indeed, could Mr Howard know anything of sound doctrine, being educated, as he told me, at Eton school, a prelatic establishment. Nevertheless, he was a fine lad, and though a little given to frolic and diversion, he had a principle of integrity, that afterwards kithed into much virtue; for, during this visit, he took a notion of Effie Malcolm, and the lassie of him, then a sprightly and blooming creature, fair to look upon, and blithe to see; and he kept up a correspondence with her till the war was over, when, being a captain of a frigate, he came down among us, and they were married by me, as shall be related in its proper place.

Chapter 18

Year 1777

Old Widow Mirkland—Bloody accounts of the war—He gets a newspaper—Great flood.

This may well be called the year of the heavy heart, for we had sad tidings of the lads that went away as soldiers to America. First, there was a boding in the minds of all their friends that they were never to see them more, and their sadness, like a mist spreading from the waters and covering the fields, darkened the spirit of the neighbours. Secondly, a sound was bruited about, that the king's forces would have a hot and a sore struggle before the rebels were put down, if they were ever put down. Then came the cruel truth of all that the poor lads' friends had feared; but it is fit and proper that I should relate at length, under their several heads, the sorrows and afflictions as they came to pass.

One evening, as I was taking my walk alone, meditating my discourse for the next Sabbath—it was shortly after Candlemas—it was a fine clear frosty evening, just as the sun was setting. Taking my walk alone, and thinking of the dreadfulness of Almighty Power, and how that if it was not tempered and restrained by infinite goodness, and wisdom, and mercy, the miserable sinner man, and all things that live, would be in a woeful state, I drew near the beild where old Widow Mirkland lived by herself who was grandmother to Jock Hempy, the ramplor lad that was the second who took on for a soldier. I did not mind of this at the time, but passing the house, I heard the croon, as it were, of a laden soul, busy with the Lord, and, not to disturb the holy workings of grace, I paused, and listened. It was old Mizy Mirkland herself, sitting at the gable of the house, looking at the sun setting in all his glory behind the Arran hills; but she was not praying—only moaning to herself,—an oozing out, as it might be called, of the spirit from her heart, then grievously oppressed with sorrow, and heavy bodements of grey hairs and poverty.

'Yonder it slips awa',' she was saying, 'and my poor bairn, that's o'er the seas in America, is maybe looking on its bright face, thinking of his hame, and aiblins of me, that did my best to breed him up in the fear of the Lord; but I couldna warsle wi' what was ordained. Ay, Jock! as ye look at the sun gaun down, as many a time, when ye were a wee innocent laddie at my knee here, I hae bade ye look at him as a type of your Maker, you will hae a sore heart; for ye hae left me in my need, when ye should hae been near at hand to help me, for the hard labour and industry with which I brought you up. But it's the Lord's will,—blessed be the name of the Lord, that makes us to thole the tribulations of this world, and will reward us, through the mediation of Jesus, hereafter.' She wept bitterly as she said this, for her heart was tried, but the blessing of a religious contentment was shed upon her; and I stepped up to her, and asked about her concerns, for, saving as a parishioner, and a decent old woman, I knew little of her. Brief was her story, but it was one of misfortune. 'But I will not complain,' she said, 'of the measure that has been meted unto me. I was left myself an orphan; when I grew up, and was married to my gudeman, I had known but scant and want. Our days of felicity were few, and he was ta'en awa' from me shortly after my Mary was born—a wailing baby, and a widow's heart, was a' he left me. I nursed her with my salt tears, and bred her in straits, but the favour of God was with us, and she grew up to womanhood, as lovely as the rose, and as blameless as the lily. In her time she was married to a farming lad; there never was a brawer pair in the kirk, than on that day when they gaed there first as man and wife. My heart was proud, and it pleased the Lord to chastise my pride—to nip my happiness even in the bud. The very next day he got his arm crushed. It never got well again, and he fell into a decay, and died in the winter, leaving my Mary far on in the road to be a mother.

'When her time drew near, we both happened to be working in the yard. She was delving to plant potatoes, and I told her it would do her hurt, but she was eager to provide something, as she said, for what might happen. Oh, it was an ill-omened word. The same night her trouble came on, and before the morning she was a cauld corpse, and another wee wee fatherless baby was greeting at my bosom. It was him that's noo awa' in America. He grew up to be a fine bairn, with a warm heart, but a light head, and, wanting the rein of a father's power upon him, was no sae douce as I could have wished; but he was no man's foe save his own. I thought, and hoped, as he grew to years of discretion, he would have sobered, and been a consolation to my old age; but he's gone, and he'll never come back—disappointment is my portion in this world, and I have no hope; while I can do, I will seek no help, but threescore and fifteen can do little, and a small ail is a great evil to an aged woman who has but the distaff for her breadwinner.'

I did all that I could to bid her be of good cheer, but the comfort of a hopeful spirit was dead within her; and she told me, that by many tokens she was assured her bairn was already slain. 'Thrice,' said she, ' I have seen his wraith. The first time he was in the pride of his young manhood, the next he was pale and wan, with a bloody and a gashy wound in his side, and the third time there was a smoke, and when it cleared away, I saw him in a grave, with neither winding-sheet nor coffin.'

The tale of this pious and resigned spirit dwelt in mine ear, and when I went home, Mrs Balwhidder thought that I had met with an o'ercome, and was very uneasy; so she got the tea soon ready to make me better, but scarcely had we tasted the first cup when a loud lamentation was heard in the kitchen. This was from that tawpy the wife of Thomas Wilson, with her three weans. They had been seeking their meat among the farmer houses, and, in coming home, forgathered on the road with the Glasgow carrier, who told them that news had come in the *London Gazette* of a battle, in which the regiment that Thomas had listed in was engaged, and had suffered loss both in rank and file; none doubting that their head was in the number of the slain, the whole family grat aloud, and came to the manse, bewailing him as no more; and it afterwards turned out to be the case, making it plain to me that there is a far-seeing discernment in the spirit, that reaches beyond the scope of our incarnate senses.

But the weight of the war did not end with these afflictions; for, instead of the sorrow that the listing caused, and the anxiety after, and the grief of the bloody tidings, operating as wholesome admonition to our young men, the natural perversity of the human heart was more and more manifested. A wonderful interest was raised among us all to hear of what was going on in the world, insomuch, that I myself was no longer contented with the relation of the news of the month in the *Scots Magazine*, but joined with my father-in-law, Mr Kibbock, to get a newspaper twice a week from Edinburgh. As for Lady Macadam, who being naturally an impatient woman, she had one sent to her three times a week from London, so that we had something fresh five times every week; and the old papers were lent out to the families who had friends in the wars. This was done on my suggestion, hoping it would make all content with their peaceable lot, but dominion for a time had been given to the power of contrariness, and it had quite an opposite effect. It begot a curiosity, egging on to enterprise, and, greatly to my sorrow, three of the brawest lads in the parish, or in any parish, all in one day took on with a party of the Scots Greys that were then lying in Ayr; and nothing would satisfy the callans at Mr Lorimore's school, but, instead of their innocent plays with girs and shintys, and sicklike, they must go ranking like soldiers, and fight sham-fights in bodies. In short, things grew to a perfect hostility, for a swarm of weans came out from the schools of Irville on a Saturday afternoon, and, forgathering with ours, they had a battle with stones on the toll-road, such as was dreadful to hear of, for many a one got a mark that day he will take to the grave with him.

It was not, however, by accidents of the field only, that we were afflicted; those of the flood, too, were sent likewise against us. In the month of October, when the corn was yet in the holms, and on the cold land by the river-side, the water of Irville swelled to a great speat, from bank to brae, sweeping all before it, and roaring, in its might, like an agent of divine displeasure sent forth to punish the inhabitants of the earth. The loss of the victual was a thing reparable, and those that suffered did not greatly complain; for, in other respects, their harvest had been plenteous; but the river, in its fury, not content with overflowing the lands, burst through the sandy hills with a raging force, and a riving asunder of the solid ground, as when the fountains of the great deep were broken up. All in the parish was afoot, and on the hills, some weeping and wringing their hands not knowing what would happen, when they beheld the landmarks of the waters deserted, and the river breaking away through the country, like the warhorse set loose in his pasture, and glorying in his might. By this change in the way and channel of the river, all the mills in our parish were left more than half a mile from dam or lade; and the farmers through the whole winter, till the new mills were built, had to travel through a heavy road with their victual, which was a great grievance, and added not a little to the afflictions of this unhappy year, which to me were flat without a particularity, by the death of a full cousin of Mrs Balwhidder, my first wife; she was grievously burnt by looting over a candle. Her mutch, which was of the high structure then in vogue, took fire, and being fastened with corking pins to a great toupee, it could not be got off until she had sustained a deadly injury, of which, after lingering long, she was kindly eased by her removal from trouble. This sore accident was to me a matter of deep concern and cogitation; but as it happened in Tarbolton, and no in our parish, I have only alluded to it to show, that when my people were chastised by the hand of Providence, their pastor was not spared, but had a drop from the same vial.

Chapter 19

Year 1778

Revival of the smuggling trade—Betty and Janet Pawkie, and Robin Bicker, an exciseman, come to the parish—Their doings—Robin is succeeded by Mungo Argyle—Lord Eglesham assists William Malcolm.

This year was as the shadow of the bygane; there was less actual suffering, but what we came through cast a gloom among us, and we did not get up our spirits till the spring was far advanced; the corn was in the ear, and the sun far towards midsummer height, before there was any regular show of gladness in the parish.

It was clear to me that the wars were not to be soon over, for I noticed, in the course of this year, that there was a greater christening of lad bairns than had ever been in any year during my incumbency; and grave and wise persons, observant of the signs of the times, said, that it had been long held as a sure prognostication of war, when the births of male children outnumbered that of females.

Our chief misfortune in this year was a revival of that wicked mother of many mischiefs, the smuggling trade, which concerned me greatly; but it was not allowed to it to make anything like a permanent stay among us, though in some of the neighbouring parishes its ravages, both in morals and property, were very distressing, and many a mailing was sold to pay for the triumphs of the cutters and gaugers; for the Government was by this time grown more eager, and the war caused the king's ships to be out and about, which increased the trouble of the smugglers, whose wits in their turn were thereby much sharpened.

After Mrs Malcolm, by the settlement of Captain Macadam, had given up her dealing, two maiden-women, that were sisters, Betty and Janet Pawkie, came in among us from Ayr, where they had friends in league with some of the laigh land folk, that carried on the contraband with the Isle of Man, which was the very eye of the smuggling. They took up the tea-selling, which Mrs Malcolm had dropped, and did business on a larger scale, having a general huxtry, with parliament-cakes, and candles, and pin-cushions, as well as other groceries, in their window. Whether they had any contraband dealings, or were only back-bitten, I cannot take it upon me to say, but it was jealoused in the parish, that the meal in the sacks, that came to their door at night, and was sent to the Glasgow market in the morning, was not made of corn. They were, however, decent women, both sedate and orderly; the eldest, Betty Pawkie, was of a manly stature, and had a long beard, which made her have a coarse look, but she was, nevertheless, a worthy, well-doing creature, and at her death she left ten pounds to the poor of the parish, as may be seen in the mortification board that the Session put up in the kirk as a testification and an example.

Shortly after the revival of the smuggling, an exciseman was put among us, and the first was Robin Bicker, a very civil lad, that had been a flunkie with Sir Hugh Montgomerie, when he was a residenter in Edinburgh, before the old Sir Hugh's death. He was a queer fellow, and had a coothy way of getting in about folk, the which was very serviceable to him in his vocation; nor was he overly gleg, but when a job was ill done, and he was obliged to notice it, he would often break out on the smugglers for being so stupid, so that for an excise-man he was wonderful well liked, and did not object to a waught of brandy at a time, when the auld wives ca'd it well-water. It happened, however, that some unneighbourly person sent him notice of a decking of tea chests, or brandy kegs, at which both Jenny and Betty Pawkie were the howdies. Robin could not but therefore enter their house; however, before going in, he just cried at the door to somebody on the road, so as to let the twa industrious lassies hear he was at hand. They were not slack in closing the trance-door, and putting stoups and stools behind it, so as to cause trouble, and give time before anybody could get in. They then emptied their chaff-bed, and filled the tikeing with tea, and Betty went in on the top, covering herself with the blanket, and graining like a woman in labour. It was thought that Robin Bicker himself would not have been overly particular in searching the house, considering there was a woman seemingly in the dead thraws; but a sorner, an incomer from the east country, and that hung about the change-house as a divor hostler, that would rather gang a day's journey in the dark than turn a spade in daylight, came to him as he stood at the door, and went in with him to see the sport. Robin, for some reason, could not bid him go away, and both Betty and Janet were sure he was in the plot against them; indeed, it was always thought he was an informer, and no doubt he was something not canny, for he had a down look.

It was some time before the doorway was cleared of the stoups and stools, and Jenny was in great concern, and flustered, as she said, for her poor sister, who was taken with a heart-cholic. 'I'm sorry for her,' said Robin, 'but I'll be as quiet as possible'; and so he searched all the house, but found nothing, at the which his companion, the divor east-country hostler, swore an oath that could not be misunderstood, so, without more ado, but as all thought against the grain, Robin went up to sympathise with Betty in the bed, whose groans were loud and vehement. 'Let me feel your pulse,' said Robin, and he looted down as she put forth her arm from aneath the clothes, and laying his hand on the bed, cried, 'Hey! what's this? this is a costly filling.' Upon which Betty jumpet up quite recovered, and Jenny fell to the wailing and railing, while the hostler from the east country took the bed of tea on his back, to carry it to the change-house, till a cart was gotten to take it into the custom-house at Irville.

Betty Pawkie being thus suddenly cured, and grudging the lose of property, took a knife in her hand, and as the divor was crossing the burn at the stepping-stones that lead to the back of the change-house, she ran after him, and ripped up the tikeing, and sent all the tea floating away on the burn, which was thought a brave action of Betty, and the story not a little helped to lighten our melancholy meditations.

Robin Bicker was soon after this affair removed to another district, and we got in his place one Mungo Argyle, who was as proud as a provost, being come of Highland parentage. Black was the hour he came among my people, for he was needy and greedy, and rode on the top of his commission. Of all the manifold ills in the train of smuggling, surely the excisemen are the worst, and the setting of this rabiator over us was a severe judgment for our sins. But he suffered for't, and peace be with him in the grave, where the wicked cease from troubling.

Willie Malcolm, the youngest son of his mother, had by this time learnt all that Mr Lorimore, the schoolmaster, could teach, and as it was evidenced to everybody, by his mild manners and saintliness of demeanour, that he was a chosen vessel, his mother longed to fulfil his own wish, which was doubtless the natural working of the act of grace that had been shed upon him; but she had not the wherewithal to send him to the College of Glasgow, where he was desirous to study, and her just pride would not allow her to cess his brother-in-law, the Captain Macadam, whom, I should now mention, was raised, in the end of this year, as we read in the newspapers, to be a major. I thought her in this somewhat unreasonable, for she would not be persuaded to let me write to the captain; but when I reflected on the good that Willie Malcolm might in time do as a preacher, I said nothing more to her, but indited a letter to the Lord Eglesham, setting forth the lad's parts, telling who he was and all about his mother's scruples; and, by the retour of the post from London, his lordship sent me an order on his steward, to pay me twenty pounds towards equipping my *protégé*, as he called Willie, with a promise to pay for his education, which was such a great thing for his lordship to do off-hand on my recommendation, that it won him much affection throughout the country-side; and folk began to wonder, rehearsing the great things, as was said, that I had gotten my lord at different times, and on divers occasions, to do, which had a vast of influence among my brethren of the presbytery, and they grew into a state of greater cordiality with me, looking on me as a man having authority; but I was none thereat lifted up, for not being gifted with the power of a kirk-filling eloquence, I was but little sought for at sacraments and fasts, and solemn days, which was doubtless well ordained, for I had no motive to seek fame in foreign pulpits, but was left to walk in the paths of simplicity within my own parish. To eschew evil myself; and to teach others to do the same, I thought the main duties of the pastoral office, and with a sincere heart endeavoured what in me lay to perform them with meekness, sobriety, and a spirit wakeful to the inroads of sin and Satan. But oh the sordidness of human nature!—The kindness of the Lord Eglesham's own disposition was ascribed to my influence, and many a dry answer I was obliged to give to applicants that would have me trouble his lordship, as if I had a claim upon him. In the ensuing year, the notion of my cordiality with him came to a great head, and brought about an event that could not have been forethought by me as a thing within the compass of possibility to bring to pass.

Chapter 20

Year 1779

He goes to Edinburgh to attend the General Assembly—Preaches before the Commissioner.

I was named in this year for the General Assembly, and Mrs Balwhidder, by her continual thrift, having made our purse able to stand a shake against the wind, we resolved to go into Edinburgh in a creditable manner. Accordingly, in conjunct with Mrs Dalrymple, the lady of a major of that name, we hired the Irville chaise, and we put up in Glasgow at the Black Boy, where we staid all night. Next morning by seven o'clock we got into the fly coach for the capital of Scotland, which we reached after a heavy journey, about the same hour in the evening, and put up at the public where it stopped, till the next day; for really both me and Mrs Balwhidder were worn out with the undertaking, and found a cup of tea a vast refreshment.

Betimes, in the morning, having taken our breakfast, we got a caddy to guide us and our wallise to Widow McVicar's, at the head of the Covenanters' Close. She was a relation to my first wife, Betty Lanshaw, my own full cousin that was, and we had advised her, by course of post, of our coming, and intendment to lodge with her, as uncos and strangers. But Mrs McVicar kept a cloth shop, and sold plaidings and flannels, besides Yorkshire superfines, and was used to the sudden incoming of strangers, especially visitants, both from the West and the North Highlands, and was withal a gawsy furthy woman, taking great pleasure in hospitality and every sort of kindliness and discretion. She would not allow of such a thing as our being lodgers in her house, but was so cagey to see us, and to have it in her power to be civil to a minister, as she was pleased to say, of such repute, that nothing less would content her, but that we must live upon her, and partake of all the best that could be gotten for us within the walls of 'the gude town.'

When we found ourselves so comfortable, Mrs Balwhidder and me waited on my patron's family, that was, the young ladies, and the laird, who had been my pupil, but was now an advocate high in the law. They likewise were kind also. In short, everybody in Edinburgh were in a manner wearisome kind, and we could scarcely find time to see the Castle and the palace of Holyrood House, and that more sanctified place, where the Maccabeus of the Kirk of Scotland, John Knox, was wont to live.

Upon my introduction to his Grace the Commissioner, I was delighted and surprised to find the Lord Eglesham at the levee, and his lordship was so glad on seeing me, that he made me more kenspeckle than I could have wished to have been in his Grace's presence; for, owing to the same, I was required to preach before his Grace, upon a jocose recommendation of his lordship; the which gave me great concern, and daunted me, so that in the interim I was almost bereft of all peace and studious composure of mind. Fain would I have eschewed the honour that was thus thrust upon me, but both my wife and Mrs McVicar were just lifted out of themselves with the thought.

When the day came, I thought all things in this world were loosened from their hold, and that the sure and steadfast earth itself was grown coggly beneath my feet, as I mounted the pulpit. With what sincerity I prayed for help that day, and never stood man more in need of it, for through all my prayer the congregation was so watchful and still, doubtless to note if my doctrine was orthodox, that the beating of my heart might have been heard to the uttermost corners of the kirk.

I had chosen as my text, from Second Samuel, xixth chapter, and 35th verse, these words—'Can I hear any more the voice of singing men and singing women? wherefore then should thy servant be yet a burden to the king?' And hardly had I with a trembling voice read the words, when I perceived an awful stir in the congregation, for all applied the words to the state of the Church, and the appointment of his Grace the Commissioner. Having paused after giving out the text, the same fearful and critical silence again ensued, and every eye was so fixed upon me, that I was for a time deprived of courage to look about; but Heaven was pleased to compassionate my infirmity, and as I proceeded, I began to warm as in my own pulpit. I described the gorgeous Babylonian harlot riding forth in her chariots of gold and silver, with trampling steeds, and a hurricane of followers, drunk with the cup of abominations, all shouting with revelry, and glorying in her triumph, treading down in their career those precious pearls, the saints and martyrs, into the mire beneath their swinish feet. 'Before her you may behold Wantonness playing the tinkling cymbal, Insolence beating the drum, and Pride blowing the trumpet. Every vice is there with his emblems, and the seller of pardons, with his crucifix and triple crown, is distributing his largess of perdition. The voices of men shout to set wide the gates, to give entrance to the Queen of nations, and the gates are set wide, and they all enter. The avenging gates close on them—they are all shut up in hell.'

There was a sough in the kirk as I said these words, for the vision I described seemed to be passing before me as I spoke, and I felt as if I had witnessed the everlasting destruction of Antichrist, and the worshippers of the beast. But soon recovering myself; I said, in a soft and gentle manner,

'Look at yon lovely creature in virgin-raiment, with the Bible in her hand. See how mildly she walks along, giving alms to the poor as she passes on towards the door of that lowly dwelling. Let us follow her in. She takes her seat in the chair at the bedside of the poor old dying sinner, and as he tosses in the height of penitence and despair, she reads to him the promise of the Saviour, "This night thou shalt be with me in Paradise"; and he embraces her with transports, and falling back on his pillow, calmly closes his eyes in peace. She is the true religion; and when I see what she can do even in the last moments of the guilty, well may we exclaim, when we think of the symbols and pageantry of the departed superstition, Can I hear any more the voice of singing men and singing women? No; let us cling to the simplicity of the Truth that is now established in our native land.'

At the conclusion of this clause of my discourse, the congregation, which had been all so still and so solemn, never coughing, as was often the case among my people, gave a great rustle, changing their positions, by which I was almost overcome; however, I took heart, and ventured on, and pointed out, that with our Bible and an orthodox priesthood, we stood in no need of the king's authority, however bound we were in temporal things to respect it, and I showed this at some length, crying out, in the words of my text, 'Wherefore then should thy servant be yet a burden to the king?' in the saying of which I happened to turn my eyes towards his Grace the Commissioner, as he sat on the throne, and I thought his countenance was troubled, which made me add, that he might not think I meant him any offence, That the King of the Church was one before whom the great, and the wise, and the good,—all doomed and sentenced convicts—implore his mercy. 'It is true,' said I, 'that in the days of his tribulation he was wounded for our iniquities, and died to save us; but, at his death, his greatness was proclaimed by the quick and the dead. There was sorrow, and there was wonder, and there was rage, and there was remorse; but there was no shame there—none blushed on that day at that sight but yon glorious luminary.' The congregation rose and looked round, as the sun that I pointed at shone in at the window. I was disconcerted by their movement, and my spirit was spent, so that I could say no more.

When I came down from the pulpit, there was a great pressing in of acquaintance and ministers, who lauded me exceedingly; but I thought it could be only in derision, therefore I slipped home to Mrs McVicar's as fast as I could.

Mrs McVicar, who was a clever, hearing-all sort of a neighbour, said my sermon was greatly thought of, and that I had surprised everybody; but I was fearful there was something of jocularity at the bottom of this, for she was a flaunty woman, and liked well to give a good-humoured jibe or jeer. However, his Grace the Commissioner was very thankful for the discourse, and complimented me on what he called my apostolical earnestness; but he was a courteous man, and I could not trust to him, especially as my Lord Eglesham had told me in secrecy before—it's true, it was in his gallanting way,—that, in speaking of the king's servant as I had done, I had rather gone beyond the bounds of modern moderation. Altogether, I found neither pleasure nor profit in what was thought so great an honour, but longed for the privacy of my own narrow pasture and little flock.

It was in this visit to Edinburgh that Mrs Balwhidder bought her silver teapot, and other ornamental articles; but this was not done, as she assured me, in a vain spirit of bravery, which I could not have abided, but because it was well known, that tea draws better in a silver pot, and drinks pleasanter in a china cup, than out of any other kind of cup or teapot.

By the time I got home to the manse, I had been three whole weeks and five days absent, which was more than all my absences together, from the time of my placing, and my people were glowing with satisfaction when they saw us driving in a Glasgow chaise through the clachan to the manse.

The rest of the year was merely a quiet succession of small incidents, none of which are worthy of notation, though they were all severally, no doubt, of aught somewhere, as they took up both time and place in the coming to pass, and nothing comes to pass without helping onwards to some great end; each particular little thing that happens in the world, being a seed sown by the hand of Providence to yield an increase, which increase is destined, in its turn, to minister to some higher purpose, until at last the issue affects the whole earth. There is nothing in all the world that doth not advance the cause of goodness; no, not even the sins of the wicked, though, through the dim casement of her mortal tabernacle, the soul of man cannot discern the method thereof.

Chapter 21

Year 1780

Lord George Gordon—Report of an illumination.

This was, among ourselves, another year of few events. A sound, it is true, came among us of a design on the part of the government in London to bring back the old harlotry of papistry; but we spent our time in the lea of the hedge, and the lown of the hill. Some there were that a panic seized upon, when they heard of Lord George Gordon, that zealous Protestant, being committed to the Tower; but for my part, I had no terror upon me, for I saw all things around me going forward improving, and I said to myself, it is not so when Providence permits scathe and sorrow to fall upon a nation. Civil troubles, and the casting down of thrones, is always forewarned by want and poverty striking the people. What I have, therefore, chiefly to record as the memorables of this year are things of small import,—the main of which are, that some of the neighbouring lairds, taking example by Mr Kibbock, my father-in-law that was, began in this fall to plant the tops of their hills with mounts of fir-trees; and Mungo Argyle, the exciseman, just herried the poor smugglers to death, and made a power of prize-money, which, however, had not the wonted effect of riches; for it brought him no honour, and he lived in the parish like a leper, or any other kind of excommunicated person.

But I should not forget a most droll thing that took place with Jenny Gaffaw and her daughter. They had been missed from the parish for some days, and folk began to be uneasy about what could have become of the two silly creatures; till one night, at the dead hour, a strange light was seen beaming and burning at the window of the bit hole where they lived. It was first observed by Lady Macadam, who never went to bed at any Christian hour, but sat up reading her new French novels and play-books with Miss Sabrina, the schoolmistress. She gave the alarm, thinking that such a great and continuous light from a lone house, where never candle had been seen before, could be nothing less than the flame of a burning. And sending Miss Sabrina and the servants to see what was the matter, they beheld daft Jenny, and her as daft daughter, with a score of candle doups (Heaven only knows where they got them!) placed in the window, and the twa fools dancing, and linking, and admiring before the door. 'What's all this about, Jenny?' said Miss Sabrina. 'Awa' wi' you, awa' wi' you—ye wicked pope, ye whore of Babylon. Isna it for the glory of God and the Protestant religion? d'ye think I will be a pope as long as light can put out darkness?' And with that the mother and daughter began again to leap and dance as madly as before. It seems that poor Jenny having heard of the luminations that were lighted up through the country, on the ending of the Popish Bill, had, with Meg, travelled by themselves into Glasgow, where they had gathered or begged a stock of candles, and coming back under the cloud of night, had surprised and alarmed the whole clachan by lighting up their window in the manner that I have described. Poor Miss Sabrina, at Jenny's uncivil salutation, went back to my lady with her heart full, and would fain have had the idiots brought to task before the Session for what they had said to her. But I would not hear tell of such a thing, for which Miss Sabrina owed me a grudge, that was not soon given up.

At the same time, I was grieved to see the testimonies of joyfulness for a holy victory brought into such disrepute by the ill-timed demonstrations of the two irreclaimable naturals, that had not a true conception of the cause for which they were triumphing.

Chapter 22

Year 1781

Argyle, the exciseman, grows a gentleman—Lord Eglesham's concubine—His death—The parish children afflicted with the measles.

If the two last years passed o'er the heads of me and my people without any manifest dolour, which is a great thing to say for so long a period in this world, we had our own trials and tribulations, in the one of which I have now to make mention. Mungo Argyle, the exciseman, waxing rich, grew proud and petulant, and would have ruled the country-side with a rod of iron. Nothing less would serve him than a fine horse to ride on, and a world of other conveniences and luxuries, as if he had been on an equality with gentlemen. And he bought a grand gun, which was called a fowling-piece; and he had two pointer dogs, the like of which had not been seen in the parish since the planting of the Eglesham Wood on the moorland, which was four years before I got the call. Everybody said the man was fey, and truly, when I remarked him so gallant and gay on the Sabbath at the kirk, and noted his glowing face and gleg e'en, I thought at times there was something no canny about him. It was indeed clear to be seen, that the man was hurried out of himself but nobody could have thought that the death he was to dree would have been what it was.

About the end of summer my Lord Eglesham came to the castle, bringing with him an English madam, that was his Miss. Some days after he came down from London, as he was riding past the manse, his lordship stopped to inquire for my health, and I went to the door to speak to him. I thought that he did not meet me with that blithe countenance he was wont, and in going away, he said with a blush, '1 fear I dare not ask you to come to the castle.' I had heard of his concubine, and I said, 'In saying so, my lord, you show a spark of grace, for it would not become me to see what I have heard; and I am surprised, my lord, you will not rather take a lady of your own.' He looked kindly, but confused, saying, he did not know where to get one; so seeing his shame, and not wishing to put him out of conceit entirely with himself, I replied, 'Na, na, my lord, there's nobody will believe that, for there never was a silly Jock, but there was as silly a Jenny,' at which he laughed heartily, and rode away. But I know not what was in't, I was troubled in mind about him, and thought, as he was riding away, that I would never see him again; and sure enough it so happened, for the next day, being airing in his coach with Miss Spangle, the lady he had brought, he happened to see Mungo Argyle with his dogs and his gun, and my lord being as particular about his game as the other was about boxes of tea and kegs of brandy, he jumped out of the carriage, and ran to take the gun. Words passed, and the exciseman shot my lord. Never shall I forget that day; such riding, such running, the whole country-side afoot; but the same night my lord breathed his last, and the mad and wild reprobate that did the deed was taken up and sent off to Edinburgh. This was a woeful riddance of that oppressor, for my lord was a good landlord and a kind-hearted man; and albeit, though a little thoughtless, was aye ready to make his power, when the way was pointed out, minister to good works. The whole parish mourned for him, and there was not a sorer heart in all its bounds than my own. Never was such a sight seen as his burial: The whole country-side was there, and all as solemn as if they had been assembled in the valley of Jehoshaphat in the latter day. The hedges where the funeral was to pass were clad with weans, like bunches of hips and haws, and the kirkyard was as if all its own dead were risen. Never, do I think, was such a multitude gathered together. Some thought there could not be less than three thousand grown men, besides women and children. Scarcely was this great public calamity past, for it could be reckoned no less, when one Saturday afternoon, as Miss Sabrina, the schoolmistress, was dining with Lady Macadam, her ladyship was stricken with the paralytics, and her face so thrown in the course of a few minutes, that Miss Sabrina came flying to the manse for the help and advice of Mrs Balwhidder. A doctor was gotten with all speed by express, but her lady-ship was smitten beyond the reach of medicine. She lived, however, some time after; but oh, she was such an object, that it was a grief to see her. She could only mutter when she tried to speak, and was as helpless as a baby. Though she never liked me, nor could I say there was many things in her demeanour that pleased me, yet she was a free-handed woman to the needful, and when she died she was more missed than it was thought she could have been.

Shortly after her funeral, which was managed by a gentleman sent from her friends in Edinburgh, that I wrote to about her condition, the major, her son, with his lady, Kate Malcolm, and two pretty bairns, came and stayed in her house for a time, and they were a great happiness to us all, both in the way of drinking tea, and sometimes taking a bit dinner, their only mother now, the worthy and pious Mrs Malcolm, being regularly of the company.

Before the end of the year, I should mention that the fortune of Mrs Malcolm's family got another shove upwards, by the promotion of her second son, Robert Malcolm, who, being grown an expert and careful mariner, was made captain of a grand ship, whereof Provost Maitland of Glasgow, that was kind to his mother in her distresses, was the owner. But that douce lad Willie, her youngest son, who was at the University of Glasgow, under the Lord Eglesham's patronage, was like to have suffered a blight; however, Major Macadam, when I spoke to him anent the young man's loss of his patron, said, with a pleasant generosity, he should not be stickit; and, accordingly, he made up, as far as money could, for the loss of his lordship, but there was none that made up for the great power and influence, which, I have no doubt, the earl would have exerted in his behalf when he was ripened for the church. So that, although in time William came out a sound and heart-searching preacher, he was long obliged, like many another unfriended saint, to cultivate sand, and wash Ethiopians in the shape of an east-country gentleman's camstrairy weans; than which, as he wrote me himself there cannot be on earth a greater trial of temper. However, in the end he was rewarded, and is not only now a placed minister, but a doctor of divinity.

The death of Lady Macadam was followed by another parochial misfortune, for, considering the time when it happened, we could count it as nothing less: Auld Thomas Howkings, the betherel, fell sick, and died in the course of a week's illness, about the end of November, and the measles coming at that time upon the parish, there was such a smashery of the poor weans as had not been known for an age; insomuch, that James Banes, the lad who was Thomas Howkings's helper, rose in open rebellion against the Session, during his superior's illness, and we were constrained to augment his pay, and to promise him the place, if Thomas did not recover, which it was then thought he could not do. On the day this happened, there were three dead children in the clachan, and a panic and consternation spread about the burial of them, when James Banes's insurrection was known, which made both me and the Session glad to hush up the affair, that the heart of the public might have no more than the sufferings of individuals to hurt it. Thus ended a year, on many accounts, heavy to be remembered.

Chapter 23

Year 1782

News of the victory over the French fleet—He has to inform Mrs Malcolm of the death of her son Charles in the engagement.

Although I have not been particular in noticing it, from time to time there had been an occasional going off, at fairs and on market-days, of the lads of the parish as soldiers, and when Captain Malcolm got the command of his ship, no less than four young men sailed with him from the clachan; so that we were deeper and deeper interested in the proceedings of the doleful war that was raging in the plantations. By one post we heard of no less than three brave fellows belonging to us being slain in one battle, for which there was a loud and general lamentation.

Shortly after this, I got a letter from Charles Malcolm, a very pretty letter it indeed was; he had heard of my Lord Eglesham's murder, and grieved for the loss, both because his lordship was a good man, and because he had been such a friend to him and his family. 'But,' said Charles, 'the best way that I can show my gratitude for his patronage is to prove myself a good officer to my king and country.' Which I thought a brave sentiment, and was pleased thereat; for somehow Charles, from the time he brought me the limes to make a bowl of punch, in his pocket from Jamaica, had built a nest of affection in my heart. But, oh! the wicked wastry of life in war. In less than a month after, the news came of a victory over the French fleet, and by the same post I got a letter from Mr Howard, that was the midshipman who came to see us with Charles, telling me that poor Charles had been mortally wounded in the action, and had afterwards died of his wounds. 'He was a hero in the engagement,' said Mr Howard, 'and he died as a good and a brave man should.' These tidings gave me one of the sorest hearts I ever suffered, and it was long before I could gather fortitude to disclose the tidings to poor Charles's mother. But the callants of the school had heard of the victory, and were going shouting about, and had set the steeple bell a-ringing, by which Mrs Malcolm heard the news; and knowing that Charles's ship was with the fleet, she came over to the manse in great anxiety, to hear the particulars, somebody telling her that there had been a foreign letter to me by the postman.

When I saw her I could not speak, but looked at her in pity, and the tear fleeing up into my eyes, she guessed what had happened. After giving a deep and sore sigh, she inquired, 'How did he behave? I hope well, for he was aye a gallant laddie!'—and then she wept very bitterly. However, glowing calmer, I read to her the letter, and when I had done, she begged me to give it to her to keep, saying, 'It's all that I have now left of my pretty boy; but it's mair precious to me than the wealth of the Indies'; and she begged me to return thanks to the Lord, for all the comforts and manifold mercies with which her lot had been blessed, since the hour she put her trust in Him alone, and that was when she was left a penniless widow, with her five fatherless bairns.

It was just an edification of the spirit, to see the Christian resignation of this worthy woman. Mrs Balwhidder was confounded, and said, there was more sorrow in seeing the deep grief of her fortitude than tongue could tell.

Having taken a glass of wine with her, I walked out to conduct her to her own house, but in the way we met with a severe trial. All the weans were out parading with napkins and kail-blades on sticks, rejoicing and triumphing in the glad tidings of victory. But when they saw me and Mrs Malcolm coming slowly along, they guessed what had happened, and threw away their banners of joy; and, standing all up in a row, with silence and sadness, along the kirkyard wall as we passed, showed an instinct of compassion that penetrated to my very soul. The poor mother burst into fresh affliction, and some of the bairns into an audible weeping; and, taking one another by the hand, they followed us to her door, like mourners at a funeral. Never was such a sight seen in any town before. The neighbours came to look at it, as we walked along, and the men turned aside to hide their faces, while the mothers pressed their babies fondlier to their bosoms, and watered their innocent faces with their tears.

I prepared a suitable sermon, taking as the words of my text, 'Howl, ye ships of Tarshish, for your strength is laid waste.' But when I saw around me so many of my people, clad in complimentary mourning for the gallant Charles Malcolm, and that even poor daft Jenny Gaffaw, and her daughter, had on an old black ribbon; and when I thought of him, the spirited laddie, coming home from Jamaica, with his parrot on his shoulder, and his limes for me, my heart filled full, and I was obliged to sit down in the pulpit, and drop a tear.

After a pause, and the Lord having vouchsafed to compose me, I rose up, and gave out that anthem of triumph, the 124th Psalm; the singing of which brought the congregation round to themselves; but still I felt that I could not preach as I had meant to do, therefore I only said a few words of prayer, and singing another psalm, dismissed the congregation.

Chapter 24

Year 1783

Janet Gaffaw's death and burial.

This was another Sabbath year of my ministry. It has left me nothing to record, but a silent increase of prosperity in the parish. I myself had now in the bank more than a thousand pounds, and everything was thriving around. My two bairns, Gilbert, that is now the merchant in Glasgow, was grown into a sturdy ramplor laddie, and Janet, that is married upon Dr Kittleword, the minister of Swappington, was as fine a lassie for her years as the eye of a parent could desire to see.

Shortly after the news of the peace, an event at which all gave themselves up to joy, a thing happened among us that at the time caused much talk; but although very dreadful was yet not so serious, somehow or other, as such an awsome doing should have been. Poor Jenny Gaffaw happened to take a heavy cold, and soon thereafter died. Meg went about from house to house, begging dead-clothes, and got the body straighted in a wonderful decent manner, with a plate of earth and salt placed upon it—an admonitory type of mortality and eternal life that has ill-advisedly gone out of fashion. When I heard of this, I could not but go to see how a creature that was not thought possessed of a grain of understanding could have done so much herself. On entering the door, I beheld Meg sitting with two or three of the neighbouring kimmers, and the corpse laid out on a bed. 'Come awa', sir,' said Meg, 'this is an altered house; they're gane that keepit it bein; but, sir, we maun a' come to this—we mann pay the debt o' nature—death is a grim creditor, and a doctor but brittle bail when the hour of reckoning's at han'! What a pity it is, mother, that you're now dead, for here's the minister come to see you. Oh, sir, but she would have had a proud heart to see you in her dwelling, for she had a genteel turn, and would not let me, her only daughter, mess or mell wi' the lathron lasses of the clachan. Ay, ay, she brought me up with care, and edicated me for a lady; nae coarse wark darkened my lily-white hands. But I mann work now, I maun dree the penalty of man.'

Having stopped some time, listening to the curious maunnering of Meg, I rose to come away, but she laid her hand on my arm, saying, 'No, sir, ye mann taste before ye gang! My mother had aye plenty in her life, nor shall her latter day be needy.'

Accordingly, Meg, with all the due formality common on such occasions, produced a bottle of water, and a dram glass, which she filled and tasted, was a consternation to everybody how the daft creature had learnt all the ceremonies, which she performed in a manner past the power of pen to describe, making the solemnity of death, by her strange mockery, a kind of merriment, that was more painful than sorrow; but some spirits are gifted with a faculty of observation, that, by the strength of a little fancy, enables them to make a wonderful and truth-like semblance of things and events which they never saw, and poor Meg seemed to have this gift.

The same night the Session having provided a coffin, the body was put in, and removed to Mr Mutchkin's brew-house, where the lads and lassies kept the late-wake.

Saving this, the year flowed in a calm, and we floated on in the stream of time towards the great ocean of eternity, like ducks and geese in the river's tide, that are carried down without being sensible of the speed of the current. Alas! we have not wings like them, to fly back to the place we set out from.

Chapter 25

Year 1784

A year of sunshine and pleasantness.

I have ever thought that this was a bright year, truly an Ann. Dom., for in it many of the lads came home that had listed to be soldiers; and Mr Howard, that was the midshipman, being now a captain of a man-of-war, came down from England and married Effie Malcolm, and took her up with him to London, where she wrote to her mother, that she found his family people of great note, and more kind to her than she could write. By this time, also, Major Macadam was made a colonel, and lived with his lady in Edinburgh, where they were much respected by the genteeler classes, Mrs Macadam being considered a great unco among them for all manner of ladylike ornaments, she having been taught every sort of perfection in that way by the old lady, who was educated at the court of France, and was, from her birth, a person of quality. In this year, also, Captain Malcolm, her brother, married a daughter of a Glasgow merchant, so that Mrs Malcolm, in her declining years, had the prospect of a bright setting; but nothing could change the sober Christianity of her settled mind; and although she was strongly invited, both by the Macadams and the Howards, to see their felicity, she ever declined the same, saying—'No! I have been long out of the world, or rather, I have never been in it; my ways are not as theirs; and although I ken their hearts would be glad to be kind to me, I might fash their servants, or their friends might think me unlike other folk, by which, instead of causing pleasure, mortification might ensue; so I will remain in my own house, trusting that when they can spare the time, they will come and see me.'

There was a spirit of true wisdom in this resolution, for it required a forbearance that in weaker minds would have relaxed; but though a person of a most slender and delicate frame of body, she was a Judith in fortitude, and in all the fortune that seemed now smiling upon her, she never was lifted up, but bore always that pale and meek look, which gave a saintliness to her endeavours in the days of her suffering and poverty.

But when we enjoy most, we have least to tell. I look back on this year as on a sunny spot in the valley, amidst the shadows of the clouds of time; and I have nothing to record, save the remembrance of welcomings and weddings, and a meeting of bairns and parents, that the wars and the waters had long raged between. Contentment within the bosom lent a livelier grace to the countenance of Nature, and everybody said, that in this year the hedges were statelier trees adorned with a richer coronal of leaves and blossoms. All things were animated with the gladness of thankfulness, and testified to the goodness of their Maker.

Chapter 26

Year 1785

Mr Cayenne comes to the parish—A passionate character—his outrageous behaviour at the Session-house.

Well may we say, in the pious words of my old friend and neighbour, the Reverend Mr Keekie of Loupinton, that the world is such a wheel-carriage, that it might very properly be called the WHIRL'D. This reflection was brought home to me in a very striking manner, while I was preparing a discourse for my people, to be preached on the anniversary day of my placing, in which I took a view of what had passed in the parish during the five-and-twenty years that I had been, by the grace of God, the pastor thereof. The bairns, that were bairns when I came among my people, were ripened unto parents, and a new generation was swelling in the bud around me. But it is what happened that I have to give an account of.

This year the Lady Macadam's jointure-house that was, having been long without a tenant, a Mr Cayenne and his family, American loyalists, came and took it, and settled among us for a time. His wife was a clever woman, and they had two daughters, Miss Virginia and Miss Carolina; but he was himself an etter-cap, a perfect spunkie of passion, as ever was known in town or country. His wife had a terrible time o't with him, and yet the unhappy man had a great share of common sense, and, saving the exploits of his unmanageable temper, was an honest and creditable gentleman. Of his humour we soon had a sample, as I shall relate at length all about it.

Shortly after he came to the parish, Mrs Balwhidder and me waited upon the family, to pay our respects, and Mr Cayenne, in a free and hearty manner, insisted on us staying to dinner. His wife, I could see, was not satisfied with this, not being, as I discerned afterwards, prepared to give an entertainment to strangers; however, we fell into the misfortune of staying, and nothing could exceed the happiness of Mr Cayenne. I thought him one of the blithest bodies I had ever seen, and had no notion that he was such a tap of tow as in the sequel he proved himself.

As there was something extra to prepare, the dinner was a little longer of being on the table than usual, at which, he began to fash, and every now and then took a turn up and down the room, with his hands behind his back, giving a short melancholious whistle. At length the dinner was served, but it was more scanty than he had expected, and this upset his good-humour altogether. Scarcely had I asked the blessing when he began to storm at his blackamoor servant, who was, however, used to his way, and did his work without minding him; but by some neglect there was no mustard down, which Mr Cayenne called for in the voice of a tempest, and one of the servant lassies came in with the pot, trembling. It happened that, as it had not been used for a day or two before, the lid was clagged, and, as it were, glewed in, so that Mr Cayenne could not get it out, which put him quite wud, and he attempted to fling it at Samba, the black lad's head, but it stottit against the wall, and the lid flying open, the whole mustard flew in his own face, which made him a sight not to be spoken of. However it calmed him; but really, as I had never seen such a man before, I could not but consider the accident as a providential reproof, and trembled to think what greater evil might fall out in the hands of a man so left to himself in the intemperance of passion.

But the worst thing about Mr Cayenne was his meddling with matters in which he had no concern, for he had a most irksome nature, and could not be at rest, so that he was truly a thorn in our side. Among other of his strange doings, was the part he took in the proceedings of the Session, with which he had as little to do, in a manner, as the man in the moon; but having no business on his hands, he attended every sederunt, and from less to more, having no self-government, he began to give his opinion in our deliberations; and often bred us trouble, by causing strife to arise.

It happened, as the time of the summer occasion was drawing near, that it behoved us to make arrangements about the assistance; and upon the suggestion of the elders, to which I paid always the greatest deference, I invited Mr Keekie of Loupinton, who was a sound preacher, and a great expounder of the kittle parts of the Old Testament, being a man well versed in the Hebrew and etymologies, for which he was much reverenced by the old people that delighted to search the Scriptures. I had also written to Mr Sprose of Annock, a preacher of another sort, being a vehement and powerful thresher of the word, making the chaff and vain babbling of corrupt commentators to fly from his hand. He was not, however, so well liked, as he wanted that connect method which is needful to the enforcing of doctrine. But he had never been among us, and it was thought it would be a godly treat to the parish to let the people hear him. Besides Mr Sprose, Mr Waikle of Gowanry, a quiet hewer-out of the image of holiness in the heart, was likewise invited, all in addition to our old stoops from the adjacent parishes.

None of these three preachers were in any estimation with Mr Cayenne, who had only heard each of them once; and he happening to be present in the Session-house at the time, inquired how we had settled. I thought this not a very orderly question, but I gave him a civil answer, saying, that Mr Keekie of Loupinton would preach on the morning of the fast-day, Mr Sprose of Annock in the afternoon, and Mr Waikle of Gowanry on the Saturday. Never shall I or the elders, while the breath of life is in our bodies, forget the reply. Mr Cayenne struck the table like a clap of thunder, and cried, 'Mr Keekie of Loupinton, and Mr Sprose of Annock, and Mr Waikle of Gowanry, and all such trash, may go to—and be—!' and out of the house he bounced, like a hand-ball stotting on a stone.

The elders and me were confounded, and for some time we could not speak, but looked at each other, doubtful if our ears heard aright. At long and length I came to myself, and, in the strength of God, took my place at the table, and said, this was an outrageous impiety not to be borne, which all the elders agreed to; and we thereupon came to a resolve, which I dictated myself wherein we debarred Mr Cayenne from ever after entering, unless summoned, the Session-house, the which resolve we directed the Session-clerk to send to him direct, and thus we vindicated the insulted privileges of the church.

Mr Cayenne had cooled before he got home, and our paper coming to him in his appeased blood, he immediately came to the manse, and made a contrite apology for his hasty temper, which I reported, in due time and form, to the Session, and there the matter ended. But here was an example plain to be seen of the truth of the old proverb, that as one door shuts another opens; for scarcely were we in quietness by the decease of that old light-headed woman, the Lady Macadam, till a full equivalent for her was given in this hot and fiery Mr Cayenne.

Chapter 27

Year 1786

Repairs required for the manse—By the sagacious management of Mr Kibbock, the heritors are made to give a new manse altogether—They begin, however, to look upon me with a grudge, which provokes me to claim an augmentation, which I obtain.

From the day of my settlement, I had resolved, in order to win the affections of my people, and to promote unison among the heritors, to be of as little expense to the parish as possible; but by this time the manse had fallen into a sore state of decay—the doors were wormed on the hinges—the casements of the windows chattered all the winter, like the teeth of a person perishing with cold, so that we had no comfort in the house; by which, at the urgent instigations of Mrs Balwhidder, I was obligated to represent our situation to the Session. I would rather, having so much saved money in the bank, paid the needful repairs myself than have done this, but she said it would be a rank injustice to our own family; and her father, Mr Kibbock, who was very long-headed, with more than a common man's portion of understanding, pointed out to me, that as my life was but in my lip, it would be a wrong thing towards whomsoever was ordained to be my successor, to use the heritors to the custom of the minister paying for the reparations of the manse, as it might happen he might not be so well able to afford it as me. So in a manner, by their persuasion, and the constraint of the justice of the case, I made a report of the infirmities both of doors and windows, as well as of the rotten state of the floors, which were constantly in want of cobbling. Over and above all, I told them of the sarking of the roof, which was as frush as a puddock stool; insomuch, that in every blast, some of the pins lost their grip, and the slates came hurling off.

The heritors were accordingly convened, and, after some deliberation, they proposed that the house should be seen to, and white-washed and painted; and I thought this might do, for I saw they were terrified at the expense of a thorough repair; but when I went home and repeated to Mrs Balwhidder what had been said at the meeting, and my thankfulness at getting the heritors' consent to do so much, she was excessively angry, and told me that all the painting and white-washing in the world would avail nothing, for that the house was as a sepulchre full of rottenness; and she sent for Mr Kibbock, her father, to confer with him on the way of getting the matter put to rights.

Mr Kibbock came, and hearing of what had passed, pondered for some time, and then said, 'All was very right! The minister (meaning me) has just to get tradesmen to look at the house, and write out their opinion of what it needs. There will be plaster to mend; so, before painting, he will get a plasterer. There will be a slater wanted; he has just to get a slater's estimate, and a wright's, and so forth, and when all is done, he will lay them before the Session and the heritors, who, no doubt, will direct the reparations to go forward.'

This was very pawkie counselling of Mr Kibbock, and I did not see through it at the time, but did as he recommended, and took all the different estimates, when they came in, to the Session. The elders commended my prudence exceedingly for so doing, before going to work; and one of them asked me what the amount of the whole would be, but I had not cast it up. Some of the heritors thought that a hundred pounds would be sufficient for the outlay, but judge of our consternation, when, in counting up all the, sums of the different estimates together, we found them well on towards a thousand pounds. 'Better big a new house at once than do this!' cried all the elders, by which I then perceived the draughtiness of Mr Kibbock's advice. Accordingly, another meeting of the heritors was summoned, and after a great deal of controversy, it was agreed that a new manse should be erected; and, shortly after, we contracted with Thomas Trowel, the mason, to build one for six hundred pounds, with all the requisite appurtenances, by which a clear gain was saved to the parish, by the foresight of Mr Kibbock, to the amount of nearly four hundred pounds. But the heritors did not mean to have allowed the sort of repair that his plan comprehended.

He was, however, a far forecasting man, the like of him for natural parts not being in our country-side, and nobody could get the whip-hand of him, either in a bargain or an improvement, when he once was sensible of the advantage. He was, indeed, a blessing to the shire, both by his example as a farmer, and by his sound and discreet advice in the contentions of his neighbours, being a man, as was a saying among the commonality, 'wiser than the law and the fifteen lords of Edinburgh.'

The building of the new manse occasioned a heavy cess on the heritors, which made them overly ready to pick holes in the coats of me and the elders; so that, out of my forbearance and delicacy in time past, grew a lordliness on their part, that was an ill return for the years that I had endured no little inconveniency for their sake. It was not in my heart or principles to harm the hair of a dog; but when I discerned the austerity with which they were disposed to treat their minister, I bethought me, that, for the preservation of what was due to the establishment and the upholding of the decent administration of religion, I ought to set my face against the sordid intolerance by which they were actuated. This notion I weighed well before divulging it to any person, but when I had assured myself as to the rectitude thereof, I rode over one day to Mr Kibbock's, and broke my mind to him about claiming out of the teinds an augmentation of my stipend, not because I needed it, but in case, after me, some bare and hungry gorbie of the Lord should be sent upon the parish, in no such condition to plea with the heritors as I was. Mr Kibbock highly approved of my intent, and by his help, after much tribulation, I got an augmentation, both in glebe and income; and to mark my reason for what I did, I took upon me to keep and clothe the wives and orphans of the parish who lost their breadwinners in the American war. But for all that, the heritors spoke of me as an avaricious Jew, and made the hard-won fruits of Mrs Balwhidder's great thrift and good management a matter of reproach against me. Few of them would come to the church, but stayed away, to the detriment of their own souls hereafter, in order, as they thought, to punish me; so that, in the course of this year there was a visible decay of the sense of religion among the better orders of the parish, and, as will be seen in the sequel, their evil example infected the minds of many of the rising generation.

It was in this year that Mr Cayenne bought the mailing of the Wheatrigs, but did not begin to build his house till the following spring; for being ill to please with a plan, he fell out with the builders, and on one occasion got into such a passion with Mr Trowel, the mason, that he struck him a blow in the face, for which he was obligated to make atonement. It was thought the matter would have been carried before the Lords; but, by the mediation of Mr Kibbock, with my helping hand, a reconciliation was brought about, Mr Cayenne indemnifying the mason with a sum of money to say no more anent it; after which, he employed him to build his house, a thing that no man could have thought possible, who reflected on the enmity between them.

Chapter 28

Year 1787

Lady Macadam's house is changed into an inn—The making of jelly becomes common in the parish—Meg Gaffaw is present at a payment of victual—Her behaviour.

There had been, as I have frequently observed, a visible improvement going on in the parish. From the time of the making of the toll-road, every new house that was built in the clachan was built along that road. Among other changes thereby caused, the Lady Macadam's jointure-house that was, which stood in a pleasant parterre, inclosed within a stone wall and an iron gate, having a pillar with a pine-apple head on each side, came to be in the middle of the town. While Mr Cayenne inhabited the same, it was maintained in good order, but on his flitting to his own new house on the Wheatrigs, the parterre was soon overrun with weeds, and it began to wear the look of a waste place. Robert Toddy, who then kept the change-house, and who had from the lady's death rented the coach-house for stabling, in this juncture thought of it for an inn; so he set his own house to Thomas Treddles, the weaver, whose son, William, is now the great Glasgow manufacturer, that has cotton mills and steam-engines; and took 'the Place,' as it was called, and had a fine sign, THE CROSS KEYS, painted and put up in golden characters, by which it became one of the most noted inns anywhere to be seen; and the civility of Mrs Toddy was commended by all strangers. But although this transmutation from a change-house to an inn was a vast amendment, in a manner, to the parish, there was little amendment of manners thereby, for the farmer lads began to hold dancings and other riotous proceedings there, and to bring, as it were, the evil practices of towns into the heart of the country. All sort of licence was allowed as to drink and hours, and the edifying example of Mr Mutchkins, and his pious family, was no longer held up to the imitation of the wayfaring man.

Saving the mutation of 'the Place' into an inn, nothing very remarkable happened in this year. We got into our new manse about the middle of March, but it was rather damp, being new plastered, and it caused me to have a severe attack of the rheumatics in the fall of the year.

I should not, in my notations, forget to mark a new luxury that got in among the commonality at this time. By the opening of new roads, and the traffic thereon with carts and carriers, and by our young men that were sailors going to the Clyde, and sailing to Jamaica and the West Indies, heaps of sugar and coffee-beans were brought home, while many, among the kail-stocks and cabbages in their yards, had planted grozet and berry bushes; which two things happening together, the fashion to make jam and jelly, which hitherto had been only known in the kitchens and confectionaries of the gentry, came to be introduced into the clachan. All this, however, was not without a plausible pretext, for it was found that jelly was an excellent medicine for a sore throat, and jam a remedy as good as London candy for a cough, or a cold, or a shortness of breath. I could not, however, say, that this gave me so much concern as the smuggling trade, only it occasioned a great fasherie to Mrs Balwhidder; for, in the berry time, there was no end to the borrowing of her brass pan, to make jelly and jam, till Mrs Toddy, of the Cross Keys, bought one, which, in its turn, came into request, and saved ours.

It was in the Martinmas quarter of this year that I got the first payment of my augmentation. Having no desire to rip up old sores, I shall say no more anent it, the worst being anticipated in my chronicle of the last year; but there was a thing happened in the payment that occasioned a vexation at the time of a very disagreeable nature. Daft Meg Gaffaw, who, from the tragical death of her mother, was a privileged subject, used to come to the manse on the Saturdays for a meal of meat; and it so fell out, that as, by some neglect of mine, no steps had been taken to regulate the disposal of the victual that constituted the means of the augmentation, some of the heritors, in an ungracious temper, sent what they called the tythe-boll (the Lord knows it was not the fiftieth) to the manse, where I had no place to put it. This fell out on a Saturday night, when I was busy with my sermon, thinking not of silver or gold, but of much better; so that I was greatly molested and disturbed thereby. Daft Meg, who sat by the kitchen chimlay-lug hearing a', said nothing for a time, but when she saw how Mrs Balwhidder and me were put to, she cried out with a loud voice, like a soul under the inspiration of prophecy—'When the widow's creuse had filled all the vessels in the house, the Lord stopped the increase; verily, verily, I say unto you, if your barns be filled, and your girnel-kists can hold no more, seek till ye shall find the tume basins of the poor, and therein pour the corn, and the oil, and the wine of your abundance; so shall ye be blessed of the Lord.' The which words I took for an admonition, and directing the sacks to be brought into the dining-room, and other chambers of the manse, I sent off the heritors' servants, that had done me this prejudice, with an unexpected thankfulness. But this, as I afterwards was informed, both them and their masters attributed to the greedy grasp of avarice, with which they considered me as misled; and having said so, nothing could exceed their mortification on Monday, when they heard (for they were of those who had deserted the kirk) that I had given by the precentor notice to every widow in the parish that was in need, to come to the manse, and she would receive her portion of the partitioning of the augmentation. Thus, without any offence on my part, saving the strictness of justice, was a division made between me and the heritors; but the people were with me; and my own conscience was with me, and though the fronts of the lofts and the pews of the heritors were but thinly filled, I trusted that a good time was coming, when the gentry would see the error of their way. So I bent the head of resignation to the Lord, and, assisted by the wisdom of Mr Kibbock, adhered to the course I had adopted; but at the close of the year, my heart was sorrowful for the schism, and my prayer on Hogmanay was one of great bitterness of soul, that such an evil had come to pass.

Chapter 29

Year 1788

A cotton-mill is built—The new spirit which it introduces among the people.

It had been often remarked by ingenious men, that the Brawl burn, which ran through the parish, though a small, was yet a rapid stream, and had a wonderful capability for damming, and to turn mills. From the time that the Irville water deserted its channel this brook grew into repute, and several mills and dams had been erected on its course. In this year a proposal came from Glasgow to build a cotton-mill on its banks, beneath the Witch-linn, which being on a corner of the Wheatrig, the property of Mr Cayenne, he not only consented thereto, but took a part in the profit or loss therein; and, being a man of great activity, though we thought him, for many a day, a serpent plague sent upon the parish, he proved thereby one of our greatest benefactors. The cotton-mill was built, and a spacious fabric it was—nothing like it had been seen before in our day and generation—and, for the people that were brought to work in it, a new town was built in the vicinity, which Mr Cayenne, the same being founded on his land, called Cayenneville, the name of the plantation in Virginia that had been taken from him by the rebellious Americans. From that day Fortune was lavish of her favours upon him; his property swelled, and grew in the most extraordinary manner, and the whole country-side was stirring with a new life. For, when the mill was set agoing, he got weavers of muslin established in Cayenneville; and shortly after, but that did not take place till the year following, he brought women all the way from the neighbourhood of Manchester in England, to teach the lassie bairns in our old clachan tambouring.

Some of the ancient families, in their turreted houses, were not pleased with this innovation, especially when they saw the handsome dwellings that were built for the weavers of the mills, and the unstinted hand that supplied the wealth required for the carrying on of the business. It sank their pride into insignificance, and many of them would almost rather have wanted the rise that took place in the value of their lands, than have seen this incoming of what they called o'er-sea speculation. But, saving the building of the cotton-mill, and the beginning of Cayenneville, nothing more memorable happened in this year, still it was nevertheless a year of a great activity. The minds of men were excited to new enterprises; a new genius, as it were, had descended upon the earth, and there was an erect and outlooking spirit abroad that was not to be satisfied with the taciturn regularity of ancient affairs. Even Miss Sabrina Hookie, the schoolmistress, though now waned from her meridian, was touched with the enlivening rod, and set herself to learn and to teach tambouring, in such a manner as to supersede by precept and example that old time-honoured functionary, as she herself called it, the spinning-wheel, proving, as she did one night, to Mr Kibbock and me, that, if more money could be made by a woman tambouring than by spinning, it was better for her to tambour than to spin.

But, in the midst of all this commercing and manufacturing, I began to discover signs of decay in the wonted simplicity of our country ways. Among the cotton-spinners and muslin-weavers of Cayenneville, were several unsatisfied and ambitious spirits, who clubbed together, and got a London newspaper to the Cross Keys, where they were nightly in the habit of meeting and debating about the affairs of the French, which were then gathering towards a head. They were represented to me as lads by common in capacity, but with unsettled notions of religion. They were, however, quiet and orderly, and some of them since, at Glasgow, Paisley, and Manchester, even, I am told, in London, have grown into a topping way.

It seems they did not like my manner of preaching, and on that account absented themselves from public worship; which, when I heard, I sent for some of them, to convince them of their error with regard to the truth of divers points of doctrine; but they confounded me with their objections, and used my arguments, which were the old and orthodox proven opinions of the Divinity Hall, as if they had been the light sayings of a vain man. So that I was troubled, fearing that some change would ensue to my people, who had hitherto lived amidst the boughs and branches of the gospel unmolested by the fowler's snare, and I set myself to watch narrowly, and with a vigilant eye, what would come to pass.

There was a visible increase among us of worldly prosperity in the course of this year; insomuch, that some of the farmers, who were in the custom of taking their vendibles to the neighbouring towns on the Tuesdays, the Wednesdays, and Fridays, were led to open a market on the Saturdays in our own clachan, the which proved a great convenience. But I cannot take it upon me to say whether this can be said to have well begun in the present Ann. Dom., although I know that in the summer of the ensuing year it was grown into a settled custom; which I well recollect by the Macadams coming with their bairns to see Mrs Malcolm their mother suddenly on a Saturday afternoon; on which occasion me and Mrs Balwhidder were invited to dine with them, and Mrs Malcolm bought in the market for the dinner that day both mutton and fowls, such as twenty years before could not have been got for love or money on such a pinch. Besides, she had two bottles of red and white wine from the Cross Keys, luxuries which, saving in the Breadland House in its best days, could not have been had in the whole parish, but must have been brought from a borough town; for Eglesham Castle is not within the bounds of Dalmailing, and my observe does not apply to the stock and stores of that honourable mansion, but only to the dwellings of our own heritors, who were in general straitened in their circumstances, partly with upsetting, and partly by the eating rust of family pride, which hurt the edge of many a clever fellow among them, that would have done well in the way of trade, but sunk into divors for the sake of their genteelity.

Chapter 30

Year 1789

William Malcolm comes to the parish and preaches – The opinions upon his sermon.

This I have always reflected upon as one of our blessed years. It was not remarkable for any extraordinary occurrence, but there was a hopefulness in the minds of men, and a planning of new undertakings, of which, whatever may be the upshot, the devising is ever rich in the cheerful anticipations of good.

Another new line of road was planned, for a shorter cut to the cotton-mill, from the main road to Glasgow, and a public-house was opened in Cayenneville; the latter, however, was not an event that gave me much satisfaction, but it was a convenience to the inhabitants, and the carriers that brought the cotton-bags and took away the yarn twice a week, needed a place of refreshment. And there was a stage-coach set up thrice every week from Ayr, that passed through the town, by which it was possible to travel to Glasgow between breakfast and dinner time, a thing that could not, when I came to the parish, have been thought within the compass of man. This stage-coach I thought one of the greatest conveniences that had been established among us; and it enabled Mrs Balwhidder to send a basket of her fresh butter into the Glasgow market, by which, in the spring and the fall of the year, she got a great price, for the Glasgow merchants are fond of excellent eatables, and the payment was aye ready money—Tam Whirlit the driver paying for the one basket when he took up the other. In this year William Malcolm, the youngest son of the widow, having been some time a tutor in a family in the east country, came to see his mother, as indeed he had done every year from the time he went to the College, but this occasion was made remarkable by his preaching in my pulpit. His old acquaintance were curious to hear him, and I myself had a sort of a wish likewise, being desirous to know how far he was orthodox; so I thought fit, on the suggestion of one of the elders, to ask him to preach one day for me, which, after some fleeching, he consented to do. I think, however, there was a true modesty in his diffidence, although his reason was a weak one, being lest he might not satisfy his mother, who had as yet never heard him. Accordingly, on the Sabbath after, he did preach, and the kirk was well packed, and I was not one of the least attentive of the congregation. His sermon assuredly was well put together, and there was nothing to object to in his doctrine; but the elderly people thought his language rather too Englified, which I thought likewise, for I never could abide that the plain auld Kirk of Scotland, with her sober presbyterian simplicity, should borrow, either in word or in deed, from the language of the prelatic hierarchy of England. Nevertheless, the younger part of the congregation were loud in his praise, saying, there had not been heard before such a style of language in our side of the country. As for Mrs Malcolm, his mother, when I spoke to her anent the same, she said but little, expressing only her hope that his example would be worthy of his precepts; so that, upon the whole, it was a satisfaction to us all that he was likely to prove a stoop and upholding pillar to the Kirk of Scotland. And his mother had the satisfaction, before she died, to see him a placed minister, and his name among the authors of his country; for he published at Edinburgh a volume of Moral Essays, of which he sent me a pretty bound copy, and they were greatly creditable to his pen, though lacking somewhat of that birr and smeddum that is the juice and flavour of books of that sort.

Chapter 31

Year 1790

A bookseller's shop is set up among the houses of the weavers at Cayenneville.

The features of this Ann. Dom. partook of the character of its predecessor. Several new houses were added to the clachan; Cayenneville was spreading out with weavers' shops, and growing up fast into a town. In some respects it got the start of ours, for one day, when I was going to dine with Mr Cayenne, at Wheatrig House, not a little to my amazement, did I behold a bookseller's shop opened there, with sticks of red and black wax, pouncet-boxes, pens, pocket-books, and new publications, in the window, such as the like of was only to be seen in cities and borough towns. And it was lighted at night by a patent lamp, which shed a wonderful beam, burning oil, and having no smoke. The man sold likewise perfumery, powder-puffs, trinkets, and Dublin dolls, besides penknives, Castile soap, and walking-sticks, together with a prodigy of other luxuries too tedious to mention.

Upon conversing with the man, for I was enchanted to go into this phenomenon, for as no less could I regard it, he told me that he had a correspondence with London, and could get me down any book published there within the same month in which it came out, and he showed me divers of the newest come out, of which I did not read even in the Scots Magazine, till more than three months after, although I had till then always considered that work as most interesting for its early intelligence. But what I was most surprised to hear, was that he took in a daily London newspaper for the spinners and weavers, who paid him a penny a week apiece for the same; they being all greatly taken up with what, at the time, was going on in France. This bookseller in the end, however, proved a whawp in our nest, for he was in league with some of the English reformers, and when the story took wind three years after, concerning the plots and treasons of the Corresponding Societies and democrats, he was fain to make a moonlight flitting, leaving his wife for a time to manage his affairs. I could not, however, think any ill of the man notwithstanding; for he had very correct notions of right and justice, in a political sense, and when he came into the parish he was as orderly and well-behaved as any other body; and conduct is a test that I have always found as good for a man's principles as professions. Nor, at the time of which I am speaking, was there any of that dread or fear of reforming the government that has since been occasioned by the wild and wasteful hand which the French employed in their Revolution. But, among other improvements, I should mention that a Dr Marigold came and settled in Cayenneville, a small, round, happy-tempered man, whose funny stories were far better liked than his drugs. There was a doubt among some of the weavers if he was a skilful Esculapian, and this doubt led to their holding out an inducement to another medical man, Dr Tanzey, to settle there likewise, by which it grew into a saying, that at Cayenneville there was a doctor for health as well as sickness. For Dr Marigold was one of the best hands in the country at a pleasant punch-bowl, while Dr Tanzey had all the requisite knowledge of the faculty for the bedside.

It was in this year, that the hour-plate and hand on the kirk-steeple were renewed, as indeed may yet be seen by the date, though it be again greatly in want of fresh gilding; for it was by my advice that the figures of the Ann. Dom. were placed one in each corner. In this year, likewise, the bridge over the Brawl burn was built, a great convenience, in the winter time, to the parishioners that lived on the north side for when there happened to be a speat on the Sunday, it kept them from the kirk, but I did not find that the bridge mended the matter, till after the conclusion of the war against the democrats, and the beginning of that which we are now waging with Boney, their child and champion. It is, indeed, wonderful to think of the occultation of grace that was taking place about this time, throughout the whole bound of Christendom; for I could mark a visible darkness of infidelity spreading in the corner of the vineyard committed to my keeping, and a falling away of the vines from their wonted props and confidence in the truths of Revelation. But I said nothing. I knew that the faith could not be lost, and that it would be found purer and purer the more it was tried; and this I have lived to see, many now being zealous members of the church, that were abundantly lukewarm at the period of which I am now speaking.

Chapter 32

Year 1791

I place my son Gilbert in a counting house at Glasgow—My observations on Glasgow—On my return I preach against the vanity of riches, and begin to be taken for a black neb.

In the spring of this year, I took my son Gilbert into Glasgow, to place him in a counting-house. As he had no inclination for any of the learned professions, and not having been there from the time when I was sent to the General Assembly, I cannot express my astonishment at the great improvements, surpassing far all that was done in our part of the country, which I thought was not to be paralleled. When I came afterwards to reflect on my simplicity in this, it was clear to me that we should not judge of the rest of the world by what we see going on around ourselves, but walk abroad into other parts, and thereby enlarge our sphere of observation, as well as ripen our judgment of things.

But although there was no doubt a great and visible increase of the city, loftier buildings on all sides, and streets that spread their arms far into the embraces of the country, I thought the looks of the population were impaired, and that there was a greater proportion of long white faces in the Trongate, than when I attended the Divinity class. These, I was told, were the weavers and others concerned in the cotton trade, which I could well believe, for they were very like in their looks to the men of Cayenneville; but from living in a crowded town, and not breathing a wholesome country air between their tasks, they had a stronger cast of unhealthy melancholy. I was, therefore, very glad that Providence had placed in my hand the pastoral staff of a country parish, for it cut me to the heart to see so many young men, in the rising prime of life, already in the arms of a pale consumption. 'if, therefore,' said I to Mrs Balwhidder, when I returned home to the manse, 'we live, as it were, within the narrow circle of ignorance, we are spared from the pain of knowing many an evil; and, surely, in much knowledge, there is sadness of heart.'

But the main effect of this was to make me do all in my power to keep my people contented with their lowly estate; for in that same spirit of improvement, which was so busy everywhere, I could discern something like a shadow, that showed it was not altogether of that pure advantage, which avarice led all so eagerly to believe. Accordingly, I began a series of sermons on the evil and vanity of riches, and, for the most part of the year, pointed out in what manner they led the possessor to indulge in sinful luxuries, and how heart, making it evident, that the rich man was liable to forget his unmerited obligations to God, and to oppress the laborious and the needful when he required their services.

Little did I imagine, in thus striving to keep aloof the ravenous wolf Ambition from my guileless flock, that I was giving cause for many to think me an enemy to the king and government, and a perverter of Christianity, to suit levelling doctrines. But so it was. Many of the heritors considered me a black-neb, though I knew it not, but went on in the course of my duty, thinking only how best to preserve peace on earth, and goodwill towards men. I saw, however, an altered manner in the deportment of several, with whom I had long lived in friendly terms. It was not marked enough to make me inquire the cause, but sufficiently plain to affect my ease of mind. Accordingly, about the end of this year, I fell into a dull way: my spirit was subdued, and at times I was aweary of the day, and longed for the night, when I might close my eyes in peaceful slumbers. I missed my son Gilbert, who had been a companion to me in the long nights, while his mother was busy with the lasses, and their ceaseless wheels and cardings, in the kitchen. Often could I have found it in my heart to have banned that never-ceasing industry, and to tell Mrs Balwhidder, that the married state was made for something else than to make napery, and beetle blankets; but it was her happiness to keep all at work, and she had no pleasure in any other way of life, so I sat many a night by the fireside with resignation ; sometimes in the study, and sometimes in the parlour, and, as I was doing nothing, Mrs Balwhidder said it was needless to light the candle. Our daughter Janet was in this time at a boarding-school in Ayr, so that I was really a most solitary married man.

Chapter 33

Year 1792

Troubled with low spirits—Accidental meeting with Mr Cayenne, who endeavours to remove the prejudices entertained against me.

When the spring in this year began to brighten on the brae, the cloud of dulness, that had darkened and oppressed me all the winter, somewhat melted away, and I could now and then joke again at the never-ending toil and trouble of that busiest of all bees, the second Mrs Balwhidder. But still I was far from being right, a small matter affected me, and I was overly given to walking by myself, and musing on things that I could tell nothing about—my thoughts were just the rack of a dream without form, and driving witlessly as the smoke that mounteth up, and is lost in the airy heights of the sky.

Heeding little of what was going on in the clachan, and taking no interest in the concerns of anybody, I would have been contented to die, but I had no ail about me. An accident, however, fell out, that, by calling on me for an effort, had the blessed influence of clearing my vapours almost entirely away.

One morning, as I was walking on the sunny side of the road, where the footpath was in the next year made to the cotton-mill, I fell in with Mr. Cayenne, who was seemingly much fashed—a small matter could do that at any time; and he came up to me with a red face and an angry eye. It was not my intent to speak to him, for I was grown loth to enter into conversation with anybody, so I bowed and passed on. 'What,' cried Mr Cayenne, 'and will you not speak to me?' I turned round, and said meekly, 'Mr Cayenne, I have no objections to speak to you; but having nothing particular to say, it did not seem necessary just now.'

He looked at me like a gled, and in a minute exclaimed, 'Mad, by Jupiter! as mad as a March hare!' He then entered into conversation with me, and said, that he had noticed me an altered man, and was just so far on his way to the manse, to inquire what had befallen me So, from less to more, we entered into the marrow of my case; and I told him how I had observed the estranged countenances of some of the heritors; at which he swore an oath, that they were a parcel of the damn'dest boobies in the country, and told me how they had taken it into their heads that I was a leveller. 'But I know you better,' said Mr Cayenne, 'and have stood up for you as an honest conscientious man, though I don't much like your humdrum preaching. However, let that pass; I insist upon your dining with me to-day, when some of these arrant fools are to be with us, and the devil's in't, if I don't make you friends with them.'

I did not think Mr Cayenne, however, very well qualified for a peacemaker, but, nevertheless, I consented to go; and having thus got an inkling of the cause of that cold back-turning which had distressed me so much, I made such an effort to remove the error that was entertained against me, that some of the heritors, before we separated, shook me by the hands with the cordiality of renewed friendship; and, as if to make amends for past neglect, there was no end to their invitations to dinner, which had the effect of putting me again on my mettle, and removing the thick and muddy melancholious humour out of my blood.

But what confirmed my cure, was the coming home of my daughter Janet from the Ayr boarding-school, where she had learnt to play on the spinet, and was become a conversible lassie, with a competent knowledge, for a woman, of geography and history; so that when her mother was busy with the wearyful booming wheel, she entertained me sometimes with a tune, and sometimes with her tongue, which made the winter nights fly cantily by.

Whether it was owing to the malady of my imagination, throughout the greatest part of this year, or that really nothing particular did happen to interest me, I cannot say, but it is very remarkable that I have nothing remarkable to record—farther, than that I was at the expense myself of getting the manse rough cast, and the window cheeks painted, with roans put up, rather than apply to the heritors; for they were always sorely fashed when called upon for outlay.

Chapter 34

Year 1793

I dream a remarkable dream, and reach a sermon in consequence applying to the events of the times—Two democratical weaver lads brought before Mr Cayenne, as justice of peace.

On the first night of this year I dreamt a very remarkable dream, which, when I now recall to mind, at this distance of time, I cannot but think that there was a cast of prophecy in it. I thought that I stood on the tower of an old popish kirk, looking out at the window upon the kirkyard, where I beheld ancient tombs, with effigies and coats of arms on the wall thereof, and a great gate at the one side, and a door that led into a dark and dismal vault at the other. I thought all the dead, that were lying in the common graves, rose out of their coffins; at the same time, from the old and grand monuments, with the effigies and coats of arms, came the great men, and the kings of the earth with crowns on their heads, and globes and sceptres in their hands.

I stood wondering what was to ensue, when presently I heard the noise of drums and trumpets, and anon I beheld an army with banners entering in at the gate; upon which the kings and the great men came also forth in their power and array, and a dreadful battle was foughten; but the multitude, that had risen from the common graves, stood afar off, and were but lookers-on.

The kings and their host were utterly discomfited. They were driven within the doors of their monuments, their coats of arms were broken off, and their effigies cast down, and the victors triumphed over them with the flourishes of trumpets and the waving of banners. But while I looked, the vision was changed, and I then beheld a wide and a dreary waste, and afar off the steeples of a great city, and a tower in the midst, like the tower of Babel, and on it I could discern written in characters of fire, 'Public Opinion.' While I was pondering at the same, I heard a great shout, and presently the conquerors made their appearance, coming over the desolate moor. They were going in great pride and might towards the city, but an awful burning rose, afar as it were in the darkness, and the flames stood like a tower of fire that reached unto the heavens. And I saw a dreadful hand and an arm stretched from out of the cloud, and in its hold was a besom made of the hail and the storm, and it swept the fugitives like dust; and in their place I saw the churchyard, as it were, cleared and spread around, the graves closed, and the ancient tombs, with their coats of arms and their effigies of stone, all as they were in the beginning. I then awoke, and behold it was a dream.

This vision perplexed me for many days, and when the news came that the King of France was beheaded by the hands of his people, I received, as it were, a token in confirmation of the vision that had been disclosed to me in my sleep, and I preached a discourse on the same, and against the French Revolution, that was thought one of the greatest and soundest sermons that I had ever delivered in my pulpit.

On the Monday following, Mr Cayenne, who had been some time before appointed a justice of the peace, came over from Wheatrig House to the Cross Keys, where he sent for me and divers other respectable inhabitants of the clachan, and told us that he was to have a sad business, for a warrant was out to bring before him two democratic weaver lads, on a suspicion of high treason. Scarcely were the words uttered, when they were brought in, and he began to ask them how they dared to think of dividing, with their liberty and equality of principles, his and every other man's property in the country. The men answered him in a calm manner, and told him they sought no man's property, but only their own natural rights; upon which he called them traitors and reformers. They denied they were traitors, but confessed they were reformers, and said they knew not how that should be imputed to them as a fault, for that the greatest men of all times had been reformers,—'Was not,' they said, 'our Lord Jesus Christ a reformer?' 'And what the devil did He make of it?' cried Mr Cayenne, bursting with passion; 'was He not crucified?' I thought, when I heard these words, that the pillars of the earth sunk beneath me, and that the roof of the house was carried away in a whirlwind. The drums of my ears crackit, blue starns danced before my sight, and I was fain to leave the house and hie me home to the manse, where I sat down in my study, like a stupified creature awaiting what would betide. Nothing, however, was found against the weaver lads; but I never from that day could look on Mr Cayenne as a Christian, though surely he was a true government man.

Soon after this affair there was a pleasant re-edification of a gospel-spirit among the heritors, especially when they heard how I had handled the regicides of France; and on the following Sunday, I had the comfortable satisfaction to see many a gentleman in their pews, that had not been for years within a kirk door. The democrats, who took a world of trouble to misrepresent the actions of the gentry, insinuated that all this was not from any new sense of grace, but in fear of their being reported as suspected persons to the king's government. But I could not think so, and considered their renewal of communion with the church as a swearing of allegiance to the King of kings, against that host of French atheists, who had torn the mort-cloth from the coffin, and made it a banner, with which they were gone forth to war against the Lamb. The whole year was, however, spent in great uneasiness, and the proclamation of the war was followed by an appalling stop in trade. We heard of nothing but failures on all hands, and among others that grieved me, was that of Mr Maitland of Glasgow, who had befriended Mrs Malcolm in the days of her affliction, and gave her son Robert his fine ship. It was a sore thing to hear of so many breakings, especially of old respected merchants like him, who had been a Lord Provost, and was far declined into the afternoon of life. He did not, however, long survive the mutation of his fortune, but bending his aged head in sorrow, sunk down beneath the stroke to rise no more.

Chapter 35

Year 1794

The condition of the parish, as divided into government men and Jacobins—I endeavour to prevent Christian charity from being forgotten in the phraseology of utility and philanthropy.

This year had opened into all the leafiness of midsummer before anything memorable happened in the parish, further than that the sad division of my people into government men and Jacobins was perfected. This calamity, for I never could consider such heart-burning among neighbours as anything less than a very heavy calamity, was assuredly occasioned by faults on both sides, but it must be confessed that the gentry did nothing to win the commonality from the errors of their way. A little more condescension on their part would not have made things worse, and might have made them better; but pride interposed, and caused them to think that any show of affability from them would be construed by the democrats into a terror of their power. While the democrats were no less to blame; for hearing how their compeers were thriving in France, and demolishing every obstacle to their ascendency, they were crouse and really insolent, evidencing none of that temperance in prosperity that proves the possessors worthy of their good fortune.

As for me, my duty in these circumstances was plain and simple. The Christian religion was attempted to be brought into disrepute; the rising generation were taught to jibe at its holiest ordinances; and the kirk was more frequented as a place to while away the time on a rainy Sunday, than for any insight of the admonitions and revelations in the sacred book. Knowing this, I perceived that it would be of no effect to handle much the mysteries of the faith; but as there was at the time a bruit and a sound about universal benevolence, philanthropy, utility, and all the other disguises with which an infidel philosophy appropriated to itself the charity, brotherly love, and well-doing inculcated by our holy religion, I set myself to task upon these heads, and thought it no robbery to use a little of the stratagem employed against Christ's Kingdom, to promote the interests thereof in the hearts and understandings of those whose ears would have been sealed against me had I attempted to expound higher things. Accordingly on one day it was my practice to show what the nature of Christian charity was, comparing it to the light and warmth of the sun that shines impartially on the just and the unjust-showing that man, without the sense of it as a duty, was as the beasts that perish, and that every feeling of his nature was intimately selfish, but that when actuated by this divine impulse, he rose out of himself and became as a god, zealous to abate the sufferings of all things that live. And on the next day, I demonstrated that the new benevolence which had come so much into vogue was but another version of this Christian virtue. In like manner I dealt with brotherly love, bringing it home to the business and bosoms of my hearers, that the Christianity of it was neither enlarged nor bettered by being baptized with the Greek name of philanthropy. With well-doing, however, I went more roundly to work. I told my people that I thought they had more sense than to secede from Christianity to become Utilitarians, for that it would be a confession of ignorance of the faith they deserted, seeing that it was the main duty inculcated by our religion to do all in morals and manners to which the new-fangled doctrine of utility pretended.

These discourses, which I continued for some time, had no great effect on the men; but, being prepared in a familiar household manner, they took the fancies of the young women, which was to me an assurance that the seed I had planted would in time shoot forth; for I reasoned with myself, that if the gudemen of the immediate generation should continue free-thinkers, their wives will take care that those of the next shall not lack that spunk of grace; so I was cheered under that obscurity which fell upon Christianity at this time, with a vista beyond, in which I saw, as it were, the children unborn, walking on the bright green, and in the unclouded splendour of the faith.

But, what with the decay of trade, and the temptation of the king's bounty, and over all, the witlessness that was in the spirit of man at this time, the number that enlisted in the course of the year from the parish was prodigious. In one week no less than three weavers and two cotton-spinners went over to Ayr, and took the bounty for the Royal Artillery. But I could not help remarking to myself, that the people were grown so used to changes and extraordinary adventures, that the single enlistment of Thomas Wilson, at the beginning of the American war, occasioned a far greater grief and work among us, than all the swarms that went off week after week in the months of November and December of this year.

Chapter 36

Year 1795

A recruiting party visits the town—After them, players—then preaching quakers—
The progress of philosophy among the weavers.

The present Ann. Dom. was ushered in with an event that I had never dreaded to see in my day, in our once sober and religious country parish. The number of lads that had gone over to Ayr to be soldiers from among the spinners and weavers of Cayenneville had been so great, that the government got note of it, and sent a recruiting party to be quartered in the town; for the term clachan was beginning by this time to wear out of fashion; indeed the place itself was outgrowing the fitness of that title. Never shall I forget the dunt that the first tap of the drum gied to my heart as I was sitting on Hansel Monday by myself at the parlour fireside, Mrs Balwhidder being throng with the lasses looking out a washing, and my daughter at Ayr, spending a few days with her old comrades of the boarding-school. I thought it was the enemy, and then anon the sound of the fife came shrill to the ear; for the night was lown and peaceful. My wife and all the lasses came flying in upon me, crying all, in the name of Heaven, what could it be? by which I was obligated to put on my big coat, and, with my hat and staff go out to inquire. The whole town was aloof, the aged at the doors in clusters, and the bairns following the tattoo, as it was called, and at every doubling beat of the drum, shouting as if they had been in the face of their foemen. Mr Archibald Dozendale, one of my elders, was saying to several persons around him, just as I came up, 'Hech, sirs! but the battle draws near our gates,' upon which there was a heavy sigh from all that heard him; and then they told me of the serjeant's business, and we had a serious communing together anent the same. But while we were thus standing discoursing on the causeway, Mrs Balwhidder and the servant lasses could thole no longer, but in a troop came in quest of me to hear what was doing. In short, it was a night both of sorrow and anxiety. Mr Dozendale walked back to the manse with us, and we had a sober tumbler of toddy together, marvelling exceedingly where these fearful portents and changes would stop, both of us being of opinion that the end of the world was drawing nearer and nearer.

Whether it was, however, that the lads belonging to the place did not like to show themselves with the enlistment cockades among their acquaintance, or that there was any other reason, I cannot take it upon me to say, but certain it is, the recruiting party came no speed, and in consequence were removed about the end of March.

Another thing happened in this year, too remarkable for me to neglect to put on record, as it strangely and strikingly marked the rapid revolutions that were going on. in the month of August, at the time of the fair, a gang of play-actors came, and hired Thomas Thacklan's barn for their enactments. They were the first of that clanjamfrey who had ever been in the parish, and there was a wonderful excitement caused by the rumours concerning them. Their first performance was Douglas Tragedy, and the Gentle She herd; and the general opinion was, that the lad who played Norval in the play, and Patie in the farce, was an English lord's son, who had run away from his parents, rather than marry an old cracket lady, with a great portion. But, whatever truth there might be in this notion, certain it is the whole pack was in a state of perfect beggary; and yet, for all that, they not only in their parts, as I was told, laughed most heartily, but made others do the same; for I was constrained to let my daughter go to see them, with some of her acquaintance, and she gave me such an account of what they did, that I thought I would have liked to have gotten a keek at them myself. At the same time, I must own this was a sinful curiosity, and I stifled it to the best of my ability. Among other plays that they did was one called Macbeth and the Witches, which the Miss Cayennes had seen performed in London, when they were there in the winter time, with their father, for three months, seeing the world, after coming from the boarding-school. But it was no more like the true play of Shakespeare the poet, according to their account, than a duddy betherel set up to fright the sparrows from the pease is like a living gentleman. The hungry players, instead of behaving like guests at the royal banquet, were voracious on the needful feast of bread, and the strong ale, that served for wine in decanters; but the greatest sport of all was about a kail-pot that acted the part of a cauldron, and which should have sunk with thunder and lightning into the earth; however, it did quite as well, for it made its exit, as Miss Virginia said, by walking quietly off, being pulled by a string fastened to one of its feet. No scene of the play was so much applauded as this one; and the actor who did the part of King Macbeth made a most polite bow of thankfulness to the audience, for the approbation with which they had received the performance of the pot.

We had likewise, shortly after the omnes exeunt of the players, an exhibition of a different sort in the same barn. This was by two English quakers, and a quaker lady, tanners from Kendal, who had been at Ayr on some leather business, where they preached, but made no proselytes. The travellers were all three in a whisky, drawn by one of the best-ordered horses, as the hostler at the Cross Keys told me, ever seen. They came to the inn to their dinner, and, meaning to stay all night, sent round to let it be known that they would hold a meeting in friend Thacklan's barn; but Thomas denied they were either kith or kin to him; this, however, was their way of speaking.

In the evening, owing to the notice, a great congregation was assembled in the barn, and I myself, along with Mr Archibald Dozendale, went there likewise, to keep the people in awe; for we feared the strangers might be jeered and insulted. The three were seated aloft on a high stage prepared on purpose, with two mares and scaffold-deals, borrowed from Mr Trowel the mason. They sat long, and silent; but at last the spirit moved the woman, and she rose and delivered a very sensible exposition of Christianity. I was really surprised to hear such sound doctrine; and Mr Dozendale said, justly, that it was more to the purpose than some that my younger brethren from Edinburgh endeavoured to teach. So, that those who went to laugh at the sincere simplicity of the pious quakers were rebuked by a very edifying discourse on the moral duties of a Christian's life.

Upon the whole, however, this, to the best of my recollection, was another unsatisfactory year. In this we were doubtless brought more into the world, but we had a greater variety of temptation set before us, and there was still jealousy and estrangement in the dispositions of the gentry and the lower orders, particularly the manufacturers. I cannot say, indeed, that there was any increase of corruption among the rural portion of my people; for their vocation calling them to work apart, in the purity of the free air of heaven, they were kept uncontaminated by that seditious infection which fevered the minds of the sedentary weavers, and working like flatulence the stomachs of the cotton-spinners, sent up into their heads vain and diseased fume of infidel philosophy.

Chapter 37

Year 1796

Death of second Mrs Balwhidder—look out for a third, and fix upon Mrs Nugent,
a widow—Particulars of the courtship.

The prosperity of fortune is like the blossoms of spring, or the golden hue of the evening cloud. It delighteth the spirit, and passeth away.

In the month of February my second wife was gathered to Lord. She had been very ill for some time with an income in her side, which no medicine could remove. I had the best doctors in the country-side to her, but their skill was of no avail, their opinions being that her ail was caused by an internal abscess, for which physic has provided no cure. Her death was to me a great sorrow, for she was a most excellent wife, industrious to a degree, and managed everything with so brisk a hand, that nothing went wrong that she put it to.

With her I had grown richer than any other minister in the presbytery; but above all, she was the mother of my bairns, which gave her a double claim upon me.

I laid her by the side of my first love, Betty Lanshaw, my own cousin that was, and I inscribed her name upon the same headstone; but time had drained my poetical vein, and I have not yet been able to indite an epitaph on her merits and virtues, for she had an eminent share of both. Her greatest fault—the best have their faults—was an over-earnestness to gather gear; in the doing of which I thought she sometimes sacrificed the comforts of a pleasant fireside, for she was never in her element but when she was keeping the servants eydent at their work. But, if by this she subtracted something from the quietude that was most consonant to my nature, she has left cause, both in bank and bond, for me and her bairns to bless her great household activity.

She was not long deposited in her place of rest till I had occasion to find her loss. All my things were kept by her in a most perjink and excellent order, but they soon fell into an amazing confusion, for, as she often said to me, I had a turn for heedlessness; insomuch that although my daughter Janet was grown up, and able to keep the house, I saw that it would be necessary, as soon as decency would allow, for me to take another wife. I was moved to this chiefly by foreseeing that my daughter would in time be married, and taken away from me, but more on account of the servant lasses, who grew out of all bounds, verifying the proverb, 'Well kens the mouse when the cat's out of the house.' Besides this, I was now far down in the vale of years, and could not expect to be long without feeling some of the penalties of old age, although I was still a hail and sound man. It therefore behoved me to look in time for a helpmate to tend me in my approaching infirmities.

Upon this important concern I reflected, as I may say, in the watches of the night, and, considering the circumstances of my situation, I saw it would not do for me to look out for an overly young woman, nor yet would it do for one of my ways to take an elderly maiden, ladies of that sort being liable to possess strong-set particularities. I therefore resolved that my choice should lie among widows of a discreet age; and I had a glimmer in my mind of speaking to Mrs Malcolm, but when I reflected on the saintly steadiness of her character, I was satisfied it would be of no use to think of her.

Accordingly I bent my brows, and looked towards Irville, which is an abundant trone for widows and other single women; and I fixed my purpose on Mrs Nugent, the relic of a Professor in the University of Glasgow, both because she was a well-bred woman, without any children to plea about the interest of my own two, and likewise because she was held in great estimation by all who knew her, as a lady of a Christian principle.

It was some time in the summer, however, before I made up my mind to speak to her on the subject; but one afternoon, in the month of August, I resolved to do so, and with that intent, walked leisurely over to Irville, and after calling on the Rev Dr Dinwiddie, the minister, I stepped in, as if by chance, to Mrs Nugent's. I could see that she was a little surprised at my visit; however, she treated me with every possible civility, and her servant lass bringing in the tea things, in a most orderly manner, as punctually as the clock was striking, she invited me to sit still and drink my tea with her; which I did, being none displeased to get such encouragement. However, I said nothing that time, but returned to the manse, very well content with what I had observed, which made me fain to repeat my visit. So, in the course of the week, taking Janet, my daughter, with me, we walked over in the forenoon, and called at Mrs Nugent's first, before going to any other house; and Janet saying, as we came out to go to the minister's, that she thought Mrs Nugent an agreeable woman, I determined to knock the nail on the head without further delay.

Accordingly I invited the minister and his wife to dine with us on the Thursday following; and before leaving the town, I made Janet, while the minister and me were handling a subject, as a sort of thing of common civility, go to Mrs Nugent, and invite her also. Dr Dinwiddie was a gleg man, of a jocose nature; and he, guessing something of what I was ettling at, was very mirthful with me, but I kept my own counsel till a meet season.

On the Thursday, the company as invited came, and nothing extraordinary was seen, but in cutting up and helping a hen, Dr Dinwiddie put one wing on Mrs Nugent's plate, and the other wing on my plate, and said, there have been greater miracles than these two wings flying together, which was a sharp joke that caused no little merriment, at the expense of Mrs Nugent and me. I, however, to show that I was none daunted, laid a leg also on her plate, and took another on my own, saying, in the words of the Reverend Doctor, there have been greater miracles than that these two legs should lie in the same nest, which was thought a very clever come off; and at the same time, I gave Mrs Nugent a kindly nip on her sonsy arm, which was breaking the ice in as pleasant a way as could be. In short, before anything passed between ourselves on the subject, we were set down for a trysted pair; and this being the case, we were married as soon as a twelvemonth and a day had passed from the death of the second Mrs Balwhidder; and neither of us have had occasion to rue the bargain. It is, however, but a piece of justice due to my second wife to say, that this was not a little owing to her good management; for she had left such a well-plenished house, that her successor said we had nothing to do but to contribute to one another's happiness.

In this year nothing more memorable happened in the parish, saving that the cotton-mill dam burst, about the time of the Lammas flood, and the waters went forth like a deluge of destruction, carrying off much victual, and causing a vast of damage to the mills that are lower down the stream. It was just a prodigy to see how calmly Mr Cayenne acted on that occasion; for being at other times as crabbed as a wud terrier, folk were afraid to tell him till he came out himself in the morning and saw the devastation; at the sight of which he gave only a shrill whistle, and began to laugh at the idea of the men fearing to take him the news, as if he had not fortune and philosophy enough, as he called it, to withstand much greater misfortunes.

Chapter 38

Year 1797

Mr Henry Melcomb comes to the parish to see his uncle, Mr Cayenne—From some jocular behaviour on his part, Meg Gaffaw falls in love with him—The sad result of the adventure when he is married.

When I have seen in my walks the irrational creatures of God, the birds and the beasts, governed by a kindly instinct in attendance on their young, often has it come into my head that love and charity, far more than reason or justice, formed the tie that holds the world, with all its jarring wants and woes, in social dependence and obligation together; and in this year a strong verification of the soundness of this notion was exemplified in the conduct of the poor haverel lassie, Meg Gaffaw, whose naturality on the occasion of her mother's death I have related at length in this chronicle.

In the course of the summer, Mr Henry Melcomb, who was a nephew to Mr Cayenne, came down from England to see his uncle. He had just completed his education at the College of Christ Church, in Oxford, and was the most perfect young gentleman that had ever been seen in this part of the country.

In his appearance he was a very paragon, with a fine manly countenance, frank-hearted, blithe, and, in many points of character, very like my old friend the Lord Eglesham who was shot. Indeed, in some respects, he was even above his lordship, for he had a great turn at ready wit, and could joke and banter in a most agreeable manner. He came very often to the manse to see me, and took great pleasure in my company, and really used a freedom that was so droll, I could scarcely keep my composity and decorum with him. Among others that shared in his attention was daft Meg Gaffaw, whom he had forgathered with one day in coming to see me, and after conversing with her for some time, he handed her, as she told me herself, over the kirk stile, like a lady of high degree, and came with her to the manse door linking by the arm.

From the ill-timed daffin of that hour, poor Meg fell deep in love with Mr Melcomb, and it was just a play-acting to see the arts and antics she put in practice to win his attention. In her garb she had never any sense of a proper propriety, but went about the country asking for shapings of silks and satins, with which she patched her duds, calling them by the divers names of robes and *negligées*. All hitherto, however, had been moderation compared to the daffadile of vanity which she was now seen, when she had searched, as she said, to the bottom of her coffer. I cannot take it upon me to describe her, but she kithed in such a variety of cuffs and ruffles, feathers, old gum-flowers, painted paper knots, ribbons, and furs, and laces, and went about gecking and simpering with an old fan in her hand, that it was not in the power of nature to look at her with sobriety.

Her first appearance in this masquerading was at the kirk on the Sunday following her adventure with Mr Melcomb, and it was with a sore difficulty that I could keep my eyes off her, even in prayer; and when the kirk skailed, she walked before him, spreading all her grandeur to catch his eye in such a manner as had not been seen or heard of since the prank that Lady Macadam played Miss Betty Wudrife.

Any other but Mr Melcomb would have been provoked by the fool's folly, but he humoured her wit, and, to the amazement of the whole people, presented her his hand, and allemanded her along in a manner that should not have been seen in any street out of a king's court, and far less on the Lord's day. But alas! this sport did not last long. Mr Melcomb had come from England to be married to his cousin, Miss Virginia Cayenne, and poor daft Meg never heard of it till the banns for their purpose of marriage was read out by Mr Lorimore on the Sabbath after. The words were scarcely out of his mouth, when the simple and innocent natural gave a loud shriek, that terrified the whole congregation, and ran out of the kirk demented. There was no more finery for poor Meg; but she went and sat opposite to the windows of Mr Cayenne's house, where Mr Melcomb was, with clasped hands and beseeching eyes, like a monumental statue in alabaster, and no entreaty could drive her away. Mr Melcomb sent her money, and the bride many a fine thing, but Meg flung them from her, and clasped her hands again, and still sat. Mr Cayenne would have let loose the house-dog on her, but was not permitted.

In the evening it began to rain, and they thought that and the coming darkness would drive her away, but when the servants looked out before barring the doors, there she was in the same posture. I was to perform the marriage ceremony at seven o'clock in the morning, for the young pair were to go that night to Edinburgh; and when I went, there was Meg sitting looking at the windows with her hands clasped. When she saw me she gave a shrill cry, and took me by the hand, and wised me to go back, crying out in a heart-breaking voice, 'Oh, sir! No yet—no yet! He'll maybe draw back and think of a far truer bride.' I was wae for her, and very angry with the servants for laughing at the fond folly of the ill-less thing.

When the marriage was over, and the carriage at the door, the bridegroom handed in the bride. Poor Meg saw this, and jumping up from where she sat, was at his side like a spirit, as he was stepping in, and taking him by the hand, she looked in his face so piteously, that every heart was sorrowful, for she could say nothing. When he pulled away his hand, and the door was shut, she stood as if she had been charmed to the spot, and saw the chaise drive away. All that were about the door then spoke to her, but she heard us not. At last she gave a deep sigh, and the water coming into her eye, she said, 'The worm—the worm is my bonny bridegroom, and Jenny with the many-feet my bridal maid. The mill-dam water's the wine o' the wedding, and the clay and the clod shall be my bedding. A lang night is meet for a bridal, but none shall be langer than mine.' In saying which words, she fled from among us, with heels like the wind. The servants pursued, but long before they could stop her, she was past redemption in the deepest plumb of the cotton-mill dam.

Few deaths had for many a day happened in the parish to cause so much sorrow as that of this poor silly creature. She was a sort of household familiar among us, and there was much like the inner side of wisdom in the pattern of her sayings, many of which are still preserved as proverbs.

Chapter 39

Year 1798

*A dearth—Mr Cayenne takes measures to mitigate the evil—He receives kindly
some Irish refugees—His daughter's marriage.*

This was one of the heaviest years in the whole course of my ministry. The spring was
slow of coming, and cold and wet when it did come; the dibs were full, the roads foul,
and the ground that should have been dry at the seed-time was as claggy as clay and
clung to the harrow. The labour of man and beast was thereby augmented, and all nature
being in a state of sluggish indisposition, it was evident to every eye of experience that
there would be a great disappointment to the hopes of the husbandman.

Foreseeing this I gathered the opinion of all the most sagacious of my parishioners,
and consulted with them for a provision against the evil day, and we spoke to Mr
Cayenne on the subject, for he had a talent by common in matters of mercantile
management. It was amazing, considering his hot temper, with what patience he heard
the grounds of our apprehension, and how he questioned and sifted the experience of
the old farmers, till he was thoroughly convinced that all similar seed times were ever
followed by a short crop. He then said , that he would prove himself a better friend
to the parish than he was thought. Accordingly, as he afterwards told me himself, he
wrote off that very night to his correspondents in America to buy for his account all
the wheat and flour they could get, and ship it to arrive early in the fall; and he bought
up likewise in countries round the Baltic great store of victual, and he brought in two
cargoes to Irville on purpose for the parish, against the time of need, making for the
occasion a girnel of one of the warehouses of the cotton-mill.

The event came to pass as had been foretold; the harvest fell short, and Mr Cayenne's
cargoes from America and the Baltic came home in due season, by which he made a
terrible power of money, clearing thousands on thousands by post after post—making
more profit, as he said himself, in the course of one month, he believed, than ever
was made by any individual within the kingdom of Scotland in the course of a year.
He said, however, that he might have made more if he had bought up the corn at
home, but being convinced by us that there would be a scarcity, he thought it his
duty as an honest man to draw from the stores and granaries of foreign countries, by
which he was sure he would serve his country, and be abundantly rewarded. In short,
we all reckoned him another Joseph when he opened his girnels at the cotton-mill,
and after distributing a liberal portion to the poor and needy, selling the remainder
at an easy rate to the generality of the people. Some of the neighbouring parishes,
however, were angry that he would not serve them likewise, and called him a wicked
and extortionate forestaller; but he made it plain to the meanest capacity that if he did
not circumscribe his dispensation to our own bounds it would be as nothing. So that,
although he brought a wonderful prosperity in by the cotton-mill, and a plenteous
supply of corn in a time of famine, doing more in these things for the people than all
the other heritors had done from the beginning of time, he was much reviled; even
his bounty was little esteemed by my people, because he took a moderate profit on
what he sold to them. Perhaps, however, these prejudices might be partly owing to

their dislike of his hasty temper, at least I am willing to think so, for it would grieve me if they were really ungrateful for a benefit that made the pressure of the time lie but lightly on them.

The alarm of the Irish rebellion in this year was likewise another source of affliction to us, for many of the gentry coming over in great straits, especially ladies and their children, and some of them in the hurry of their flight having but little ready money, were very ill off. Some four or five families came to the Cross Keys in this situation, and the conduct of Mr Cayenne to them was most exemplary. He remembered his own haste with his family from Virginia, when the Americans rebelled; and immediately on hearing of these Irish refugees, he waited on them with his wife and daughter, supplied them with money, invited them to his house, made ploys to keep up their spirits, while the other gentry stood back till they knew something of the strangers.

Among these destitute ladies was a Mrs Desmond and her two daughters, a woman of a most august presence, being indeed more like one ordained to reign over a kingdom, than for household purposes. The Miss Desmonds were only entering their teens, but they also had no ordinary stamp upon them. What made this party the more particular, was on account of Mr Desmond, who was supposed to be a united man with the rebels, and it was known his son was deep in their plots; yet although this was all told to Mr Cayenne by some of the other Irish ladies who were of the loyal connection, it made no difference with him, but, on the contrary, he acted as if he thought the Desmonds the most of all the refugees entitled to his hospitable civilities. This was a wonderment to our strait-laced narrow lairds, as there was not a man of such strict government principles in the whole country-side as Mr. Cayenne: but he said he carried his political principles only to the camp and the council. 'To the hospital and the prison,' said he, 'I take those of a man'—which was almost a Christian doctrine, and from that declaration Mr Cayenne and me began again to draw a little more cordially together; although he had still a very imperfect sense of religion, which I attributed to his being born in America, where even as yet, I am told, they have but a scanty sprinkling of grace.

But before concluding this year, I should tell the upshot of the visitation of the Irish, although it did not take place until some time after the peace with France.

In the putting down of the rebels Mr Desmond and his son made their escape to Paris, where they staid till the Treaty was signed, by which, for several years after the return to Ireland of the grand lady and her daughters, as Mrs Desmond was called by our commonality, we heard nothing of them. The other refugees repaid Mr Cayenne his money with thankfulness, and on their restoration to their homes, could not sufficiently express their sense of his kindness. But the silence and seeming ingratitude of the Desmonds vexed him; and he could not abide to hear the Irish rebellion mentioned without flying into a passion against the rebels, which everybody knew was owing to the ill return he had received from that family. However, one afternoon, just about half an hour before his wonted dinner hour, a grand equipage, with four horses and outriders, stopped at his door, and who was in it but Mrs Desmond and an elderly man, and a young gentleman with an aspect like a lord. It was her husband and son. They had come from Ireland in all their state on purpose to repay with interest the money Mr Cayenne had counted so long lost, and to express in person the perpetual obligation which he had conferred upon the Desmond family, in all time coming. The lady then told him that she had been so straitened in helping the poor ladies that it was not in her power to make repayment till Desmond, as she called her husband, came home; and not choosing to assign the true reason, lest it might cause trouble, she rather submitted to be suspected of ingratitude than do an improper thing.

Mr Cayenne was transported with this unexpected return, and a friendship grew up between the families which was afterwards cemented into relationship by the marriage of the young Desmond with Miss Caroline Cayenne. Some in the parish objected to this match, Mrs. Desmond being a papist; but as Miss Caroline had received an Episcopalian education, I thought it of no consequence, and married them after their family chaplain from Ireland, as a young couple, both by beauty and fortune, well matched, and deserving of all conjugal felicity.

Chapter 40

Year 1799

My daughter's marriage—Her large portion—Mrs Malcolm's death.

There are but two things to make me remember this year; the first was the marriage of my daughter Janet with the Reverend Dr Kittleword of Swappington, a match in every way commendable, and on the advice of the third Mrs Balwhidder, I settled a thousand pounds down, and promised five hundred more at my own death, if I died before my spouse, and a thousand at her death, if she survived me; which was the greatest portion ever minister's daughter had in our country-side. In this year, likewise, I advanced fifteen hundred pounds for my son in a concern in Glasgow,—all was the gathering of that indefatigable engine of industry the second Mrs Balwhidder, whose talents her successor said were a wonder, when she considered the circumstances in which I had been left at her death, and made out of a narrow stipend.

The other memorable was the death of Mrs Malcolm. If ever there was a saint on this earth she was surely one. She had been for some time bedfast, having all her days from the date of her widowhood been a tender woman; but no change made any alteration on the Christian contentment of her mind. She bore adversity with an honest pride, she toiled in the day of penury and affliction with thankfulness for her earnings, although ever so little. She bent her head to the Lord in resignation when her first-born fell in battle; nor was she puffed up with vanity when her daughters were married, as it was said, so far above their degree, though they showed it was but into their proper sphere by their demeanour after. She lived to see her second son, the captain, rise into affluence, married, and with a thriving young family; and she had the very great satisfaction, on the last day she was able to go to church, to see her youngest son the clergyman standing in my pulpit, a doctor of divinity, and the placed minister of a richer parish than mine. Well indeed might she have said on that day, 'Lord, let thy servant depart in peace, for mine eyes have seen thy salvation.'

For some time it had been manifest to all who saw her that her latter end was drawing nigh; and therefore, as I had kept up a correspondence with her daughters, Mrs Macadam and Mrs Howard, I wrote them a particular account of case, which brought them to the clachan. They both came their own carriages, for Colonel Macadam was now a general, and had succeeded to a great property by an English uncle, his mother's brother; and Captain Howard, by the death of his father, was also a man, as it was said, with a lord's living. Robert Malcolm, her son the captain, was in the West Indies at the time, but his wife came on the first summons, as did William the minister.

They all arrived about four o'clock in the afternoon, and at seven a message came for me and Mrs Balwhidder to go over to them, which we did, and found the strangers seated by the heavenly patient's bedside. On my entering she turned her eyes towards me and said, 'Bear witness, sir, that I die thankful for an extraordinary portion of temporal mercies. The heart of my youth was withered like the leaf that is seared with the lightning, but in my children I have received a great indemnification for the sorrows of that trial.' She then requested me to pray, saying, 'No, let it be a thanksgiving. My term is out, and I have nothing more to hope or fear from the good or evil of this world. But I have had much to make me grateful; therefore, sir, return thanks for the time I have been spared, for the goodness granted so long unto me, and the gentle hand with which the way from this world is smoothed for my passing.' There was something so sweet and consolatory in way she said this, that although it moved all present to tears, they were tears without the wonted bitterness of grief. Accordingly, I knelt down and did as she had required, and there was a great stillness while I prayed; at the conclusion we looked to the bed, but the spirit had in the meantime departed, and there was nothing remaining but the clay tenement.

It was expected by the parish, considering the vast affluence of the daughters, that there would have been a grand funeral, and Mrs Howard thought it was necessary; but her sister, who had from her youth upward a superior discernment of propriety, said, 'No, as my mother has lived so shall be her end.' Accordingly, everybody of any respect in the clachan was invited to the funeral; but none of the gentry, saving only such as had been numbered among the acquaintance of the deceased. But Mr Cayenne came unbidden, saying to me, that although he did not know Mrs Malcolm personally, he had often heard she was an amiable woman, and therefore he thought it a proper compliment to her family, who were out of the parish, to show in what respect she was held among us; for he was a man that would take his own way, and do what he thought was right, heedless alike of blame or approbation.

If, however, the funeral was plain, though respectable, the ladies distributed a liberal sum among the poor families; but before they went away, a silent token of their mother's virtue came to light, which was at once a source of sorrow and pleasure. Mrs Malcolm was first well provided by the Macadams, afterwards the Howards settled on her an equal annuity, by which she spent her latter days in great comfort. Many a year before, she had repaid Provost Maitland the money he sent her in the day of her utmost distress, and at this period he was long dead, having died of a broken heart at the time of his failure. From that time his widow and her daughters had been in very straitened circumstances, but unknown to all but herself and HIM from whom nothing is hid, Mrs Malcolm from time to time had sent them, in a blank letter, an occasional note to the young ladies to buy a gown. After her death, a bank bill for a sum of money, her own savings, was found in her scrutoire, with a note of her own writing pinned to the same, stating, that the amount being more than she had needed for herself, belonged of right to those who had so generously provided for her, but as they were not in want of such a trifle, it would be a token of respect to her memory, if they would give the bill to Mrs Maitland and her daughters, which was done with a most glad alacrity; and, in the doing of it, the private kindness was brought to light.

Thus ended the history of Mrs Malcolm, as connected with our Parish Annals. Her house was sold, and is the same now inhabited by the mill-wright, Mr Periffery, and a neat house it still is, for the possessor is an Englishman, and the English have an uncommon taste for snod houses and trim gardens; but, at the time it was built, there was not a better in the town, though it's now but of the second class. Yearly we hear both from Mrs Macadam and her sister, with a five-pound note from each to the poor of the parish, as a token of their remembrance; but they are far off, and were anything ailing me, I suppose the gift will not be continued. As for Captain Malcolm, he has proved, in many ways, a friend to such of our young men as have gone to sea. He has now left it off himself; and settled at London, where he latterly sailed from, and I understand is in a great way as a ship-owner. These things I have thought it fitting to record, and will now resume my historical narration.

Chapter 41

Year 1800

Return of an inclination towards political tranquillity—Death of the Schoolmistress.

The same quietude and regularity that marked the progress of the last year continued throughout the whole of this. We sowed and reaped in tranquillity, though the sough of distant war came heavily from a distance. The cotton- mill did well for the company, and there was a sobriety in the minds of the spinners and weavers, which showed that the crisis of their political distemperature was over;—there was something more of the old prudence in men s reflections; and it was plain to me that the elements of reconciliation were coming together throughout the world. The conflagration of the French Revolution was indeed not extinguished, but it was evidently burning out, and their old reverence for the Grand Monarque was beginning to revive among them, though they only called him a Consul. Upon the king's fast I preached on this subject; and when the peace was concluded, I got great credit for my foresight, but there was no merit in't. I had only lived longer than the most of those around me, and had been all my days a close observer of the signs of the times; so that what was lightly called prophecy and prediction, were but a probability that experience had taught me to discern.

In the affairs of the parish, the most remarkable generality (for we had no particular catastrophe) was a great death of old people in the spring. Among others, Miss Sabrina, the schoolmistress, paid the debt of nature, but we could now better spare her than we did her predecessor; for at Cayenneville there was a broken manufacturer's wife, an excellent teacher, and a genteel and modernised woman, who took the better order of children; and Miss Sabrina having been long frail (for she was never stout), a decent and discreet carlin, Mrs McCaffie, the widow of a custom-house officer, that was a native of the parish, set up another for plainer work. Her opposition, Miss Sabrina did not mind, but she was sorely displeased at the interloping of Mrs Pirn at Cayenneville, and some said it helped to kill her—of that, however, I am not so certain, for Dr Tanzey had told me in the winter, that he thought the sharp winds in March would blow out her candle, as it was burnt to the snuff; accordingly she took her departure from this life, on the twenty-fifth day of that month, after there had, for some days prior, been a most cold and piercing east wind.

Miss Sabrina, who was always an oddity and aping grandeur, it was found, had made a will, leaving her gatherings to her favourites, with all regular formality. To one she bequeathed a gown, to another this, and a third that, and to me, a pair of black silk stockings. I was amazed when I heard this; but judge what I felt, when a pair of old marrow-less stockings, darned in the heel, and not whole enough in the legs to make a pair of mittens to Mrs Balwhidder, were delivered to me by her executor Mr Caption, the lawyer. Saving, however, this kind of flummery, Miss Sabrina was a harmless creature, and could quote poetry in discourse more glibly than texts of Scripture—her father having spared no pains on her mind; as for her body, it could not be mended; but that was not her fault.

After her death, the Session held a consultation, and we agreed to give the same salary that Miss Sabrina enjoyed to Mrs McCaffie; which angered Mr Cayenne, who thought it should have been given to the headmistress; and it made him give Mrs Pirn, out of his own pocket, double the sum. But we considered that the parish funds were for the poor of the parish, and therefore it was our duty to provide for the instruction of the poor children. Saving, therefore, those few notations, I have nothing further to say concerning the topics and progress of this Ann. Dom.

Chapter 42

Year 1801

An account of Colin Mavis, who becomes a poet.

It is often to me very curious food for meditation, that as the parish increased in population, there should have been less cause for matter to record. Things that in former days would have occasioned great discourse and cogitation are forgotten, with the day in which they happen; and there is no longer that searching into personalities which was so much in vogue during the first epoch of my ministry, which I reckon the period before the American war; nor has there been any such germinal changes among us, as those which took place in the second epoch, counting backward from the building of the cotton-mill that gave rise to the town of Cayenneville. But still we were not, even at this era, of which this Ann. Dom. is the beginning, without occasional personality, or an event that deserved to be called a germinal.

Some years before, I had noted among the callans at Mr Lorimore's school, a long soople laddie, who, like all bairns that grow fast and tall, had but little smeddum. He could not be called a dolt, for he was observant and thoughtful, and given to asking sagacious questions; but there was a sleepiness about him, especially in the kirk, and he gave, as the master said, but little application to his lessons, so that folk thought he would turn out a sort of gaunt-at-the-door, more mindful of meat than work. He was, however, a good-natured lad; and, when I was taking my solitary walks of meditation, I sometimes fell in with him, sitting alone on the brae by the water-side, and sometimes lying on the grass, with his hands under his head, on the sunny green knolls where Mr Cylindar, the English engineer belonging to the cotton-work, has built the bonny house that he calls Diryhill Cottage. This was when Colin Mavis was a laddie at the school, and when I spoke to him, I was surprised at the discretion of his answers, so that gradually I began to think and say, that there was more about Colin than the neighbours knew. Nothing however, for many a day, came out to his advantage; so that his mother, who was by this time a widow woman, did not well know what to do with him, and folk pitied her heavy handful of such a droud.

By and by, however, it happened that one of the young clerks at the cotton-mill shattered his right-hand thumb by a gun bursting; and, being no longer able to write, was sent into the army to be an ensign, which caused a vacancy in the office; and, through the help of Mr Cayenne, I got Colin Mavis into the place, where, to the surprise of everybody, he proved a wonderful eydent and active lad, and, from less to more, has come at the head of all the clerks, and deep in the confidentials of his employers. But although this was a great satisfaction to me, and to the widow woman his mother, it somehow was not so much so to the rest of the parish, who seemed, as it were, angry that poor Colin had not proved himself such a dolt as they had expected and foretold.

Among other ways that Colin had of spending his leisure, was that of playing music on an instrument, in which it was said he made a wonderful proficiency; but being long and thin, and of a delicate habit of body, he was obligated to refrain from this recreation; so he betook himself to books, and from reading, he began to try writing; but, as this was done in a corner, nobody jealoused what he was about, till one evening in this year, he came to the manse, and asked a word in private with me. I thought that perhaps he had fallen in with a lass and was come to consult me anent matrimony; but when we were by ourselves, in my study, he took out of his pocket a number of the *Scots Magazine* and said, 'Sir, you have been long pleased to notice me more than any other body, and when I got this, I could not refrain from bringing it to let you see't. Ye maun ken, sir, that I have been long in secret given to trying my hand at rhyme, and, wishing to ascertain what others thought of my power in that way, I sent, by the post, twa three verses to the *Scots Magazine* and they have not only inserted them, but placed them in the body of the book, in such a way, that I kenna what to think.' So I looked at the magazine, and read his verses, which were certainly very well made verses, for one who had no regular education. But I said to him, as the Greenock magistrates said to John Wilson, the author of *Clyde* when they stipulated with him to give up the art, that poem-making was a profane and unprofitable trade, and he would do well to turn his talent to something of more solidity, which he promised to do; but he has since put out a book, whereby he has angered all those that had foretold he would be a do-nae-gude. Thus has our parish walked sidy for sidy with all the national improvements, having an author of its own, and getting a literary character in the ancient and famous republic of letters.

Chapter 43

Year 1802

The political condition of the world felt in the private concerns of individuals –
Mr Cayenne comes to ask my advice, and acts according to it

'Experience teaches fools,' was the first moral apothegm that I wrote in small text, when learning to write at the school, and I have ever since thought it was a very sensible reflection. For assuredly, as year after year has flown away on the swift wings of time, I have found my experience mellowing, and my discernment improving; by which I have, in the afternoon of life, been enabled to foresee what kings and nations would do, by the symptoms manifested within the bounds of the society around me. Therefore, at the beginning of the spring in this Ann. Dom. , I had misgivings at the heart, a fluttering in thoughts, and altogether a strange uneasiness as to the stability of the peace and harmony that was supposed to be founded upon a stedfast foundation between us and the French people. What my fears principally took their rise from was a sort of compliancy, on the part of those in power and authority, to cultivate the old relations and parts between them and the commonalty. It did not appear to me that this proceeded from any known or decided event, for I read the papers at this period daily, but from some general dread and fear, that was begotten, like a vapour, out of the fermentation of all sorts of opinions; most people of any sagacity, thinking that the state of things in France being so much of an antic, poetical, and play-actor-like guise, that it would never obtain that respect, far less that reverence from the world, which is necessary to the maintenance of all beneficial government. The consequence of this was a great distrust between man and man, and an aching restlessness among those who had their bread to bake in the world. Persons possessing the power to provide for their kindred, forcing them, as it were, down the throats of those who were dependent on them in business, a bitter morsel.

But the pith of these remarks chiefly applies to the manufacturing concerns of the new town of Cayenneville, for in the clachan we lived in the lea of the dike, and were more taken up with our own natural rural affairs, and the markets for victual, than the craft of merchandise. The only man interested in business, who walked in a steady manner at his old pace, though he sometimes was seen, being of a spunkie temper, grinding the teeth of vexation, was Mr Cayenne himself. One day, however, he came to me at the manse. 'Doctor,' says he, for so he always called me, 'I want your advice. I never choose to trouble others with my private affairs, but there are times when the word of an honest man may do good. I need not tell you, that when I declared myself a Royalist in America, it was at a considerable sacrifice. I have, however, nothing to complain of against government on that score, but I think it damn'd hard that those personal connections, whose interests I preserved, to the detriment of my own, should, in my old age, make such an ungrateful return. By the steps I took prior to quitting America, I saved the property of a great mercantile concern in London. In return for that, they took a share with me, and for me, in the cotton-mill; and being here on the spot as manager, I have both made and saved them money. I have, no doubt, bettered my own fortune in the meantime. Would you believe it, doctor, they have written a letter to me, saying, that they wish to provide for a relation, and requiring me to give up to him a portion of my share in the concern—a pretty sort of providing this, at another man's expense. But I'll be damn'd if I do any such thing. If they want to provide for their friend, let them do so from themselves, and not at my cost. What is your opinion?'

This appeared to me a very weighty concern, and not being versed in mercantile dealing, I did not well know what to say; but I reflected for some time, and then I replied, 'As far, Mr Cayenne, as my observation has gone in this world, I think that the giffs and the gaffs nearly balance one another; and when they do not, there is a moral defect on the failing side. If a man long gives his labour to his employer, and is paid for that labour, it might be said that both are equal, but I say no. For it's in human nature to be prompt to change; and the employer, having always more in his power than his servant or agent, it seems to me a clear case, that in the course of a number of years, the master of the old servant is the obligated of the two; and, therefore, I say, in the first place, in your case there is no tie or claim, by which you may, in a moral sense, be called upon to submit to the dictates of your London correspondents; but there is a reason, in the nature of the thing and case, by which you may ask a favour from them. So, the advice I would give you would be this, write an answer to their letter, and tell them, that you have no objection to the taking in of a new partner, but you think it would be proper to revise all the copartnery, especially as you have, considering the manner in which you have advanced the business, been of opinion that your share should be considerably enlarged.'

I thought Mr Cayenne would have louped out of his skin with mirth at this notion, and being a prompt man, he sat down at my scrutoire, and answered the letter which gave him so much uneasiness. No notice was taken of it for some time; but, in the course of a month, he was informed, that it was not considered expedient at that time to make any change in the Company. I thought the old man was gone by himself when he got this letter. He came over instantly in his chariot, from the cotton-mill office to the manse, and swore an oath, by some dreadful name, that I was a Solomon. However, I only mention this to show how experience had instructed me, and as a sample of that sinister provisioning of friends that was going on in the world at this time-all owing, as I do verily believe, to the uncertain state of governments and national affairs.

Besides these generalities, I observed another thing working to effect—mankind read more, and the spirit of reflection and reasoning was more awake than at any time within my remembrance. Not only was there a handsome bookseller's shop in Cayenneville, with a London newspaper daily, but magazines, and reviews, and other new publications.

Till this year, when a chaise was wanted, we had to send to Irville; but Mr Toddy of the Cross Keys being in at Glasgow, he bought an excellent one at the second hand, a portion of the effects of a broken merchant, by which, from that period, we had one of our own; and it proved a great convenience, for I, who never but twice in my life before hired that kind of commodity, had it thrice during the summer, for a bit jaunt with Mrs Balwhidder, to divers places and curiosities in the county, that I had not seen before, by which our ideas were greatly enlarged; indeed, I have always had a partiality for travelling, as one of the best means of opening the faculty of the mind, and giving clear and correct notions of men and things.

Chapter 44

Year 1803

Fear of an invasion—Raising of volunteers in the parish—The young ladies embroider a stand of colours for the regiment.

During the tempestuous times that ensued, from the death of the King of France, by the hands of the executioner, in 1793, there had been a political schism among my people that often made me very uneasy. The folk belonging to the cotton-mill, and the muslin-weavers in Cayenneville, were afflicted with the itch of Jacobinism, but those of the village were staunch and true to king and country; and some of the heritors were desirous to make volunteers of the young men of them, in case of anything like the French anarchy and confusion rising on the side of the manufacturers. I, however, set myself, at that time, against this, for I foresaw that the French business was but a fever which would soon pass off but no man could tell the consequence of putting arms in the hands of neighbour against neighbour, though it was but in the way of policy.

But when Bonaparte gathered his host fornent the English coast, and the government at London were in terror of their lives for an invasion, all in the country saw that there was danger, and I was not backward in sounding the trumpet to battle. For a time, however, there was a diffidence among us somewhere. The gentry had a distrust of the manufacturers, and the farming lads were wud with impatience, that those who should be their leaders would not come forth. I, knowing this, prepared a sermon suitable to the occasion, giving out from the pulpit myself the Sabbath before preaching it, that it was my intent on the next Lord's day to deliver a religious and political exhortation on the present posture of public affairs. This drew a vast congregation of all ranks.

I trow that the stoor had no peace in the stuffing of the pulpit in that day, and the effect was very great and speedy, for next morning the weavers and cotton-mill folk held a meeting, and they, being skilled in the ways of committees and associating together, had certain resolutions prepared, by which a select few was appointed to take an enrolment of all willing in the parish to serve as volunteers in defence of their king and country, and to concert with certain gentlemen named therein, about the formation of a corps, of which, it was an understood thing, the said gentlemen were to be the officers. The whole of this business was managed with the height of discretion, and the weavers, and spinners, and farming lads vied with one another who should be first on the list. But that which the most surprised me, was the wonderful sagacity of the committee in naming the gentlemen that should be the officers. I could not have made a better choice myself, for they were the best built, the best bred, and the best natured in the parish. In short, when I saw the bravery that was in my people, and the spirit of wisdom by which it was directed, I said in my heart, The Lord of Hosts is with us, and the adversary shall not prevail.

The number of valiant men which at that time placed themselves around the banners of their country was so great, that the government would not accept of all who offered; so, like as in other parishes, we were obligated to make a selection, which was likewise done in a most judicious manner, all men above a certain age being reserved for the defence of the parish, in the day when the young might be called to England, to fight the enemy.

When the corps was formed, and the officers named, they made me their chaplain, and Dr Marigold their doctor. He was a little man with a big belly, and was as crouse as a bantam cock; but it was not thought he could do so well in field exercises, on which account he was made the doctor, although he had no repute in that capacity, in comparison with Dr Tanzey, who was not however liked, being a stiff-mannered man, with a sharp temper.

All things having come to a proper head, the young ladies of the parish resolved to present the corps with a stand of colours, which they embroidered themselves, and a day was fixed for the presentation of the same. Never was such a day seen in Dalmailing. The sun shone brightly on that scene of bravery and grandeur, and far and near the country folk came flocking in, and we had the regimental band of music hired from the soldiers that were in Ayr barracks. The very first sound o't made the hair on my old grey head to prickle up, and my blood to rise and glow, as if youth was coming again into my veins.

Sir Hugh Montgomery was the commandant, and he came in all the glory of war, on his best horse, and marched at the head of the men, to the green-head. The doctor and me were the rearguard: not being able, on account of my age, and his fatness, to walk so fast as the quick-step of the corps. On the field we took our place in front, near Sir Hugh and the ladies with the colours; and, after some salutations, according to the fashion of the army, Sir Hugh made a speech to the men, and then Miss Maria Montgomery came forward, with her sister. Miss Eliza, and the other ladies, and the banners were unfurled all glittering with gold, and the king's arms in needlework Miss Maria then made a speech, which she had got by heart but she was so agitated, that it was said she forgot the best part of it; how ever, it was very well considering. When this was done, I then stepped forward, and laying my hat on the ground, every man and boy taking off theirs, I said a prayer, which I had conned most carefully, and which I thought the most suitable I could devise, in unison with Christian principles, which are averse to the shedding of blood; and I particularly dwelt upon some of the specialities of our situation.

When I had concluded, the volunteers gave three great shouts, and the multitude answered them to the same tune, and all the instruments of music sounded, making such a bruit, as could not be surpassed for grandeur—a long and very circumstantial account of all which may be read in the newspapers of that time.

The volunteers, at the word of command, then showed us the way they were to fight with the French, in the doing of which a sad disaster happened; for when they were charging bayonets, they came towards us like a flood, and all the spectators ran, and I ran, and the doctor ran, but being laden with his belly, he could not run fast enough, so he lay down, and being just before me at the time, I tumbled over him, and such a shout of laughter shook the field as was never heard.

When the fatigues of the day were at an end, we marched to the cotton-mill, where, in one of the warehouses, a vast table was spread, and a dinner, prepared at Mr Cayenne's own expense, sent in from the Cross Keys, and the whole corps, with many of the gentry of the neighbourhood, dined with great jollity, the band of music playing beautiful airs all the time. At night, there was a universal dance, gentle and semple mingled together. All which made it plain to me, that the Lord, by this unison of spirit, had decreed our national preservation; but I kept this in my own breast, lest it might have the effect to relax the vigilance of the kingdom. And I should note, that Colin Mavis, the poetical lad, of whom I have spoken in another part, made a song for this occasion, that was very mightily thought of, having in it a nerve of valiant genius, that kindled the very souls of those that heard it.

Chapter 45

Year 1804

The session agrees that church censures shall be commuted with fines—Our parish has an opportunity of seeing a turtle, which is sent to Mr Cayenne—Some fears of popery—Also about a preacher of universal redemption—Report of a French ship appearing in the west, which sets the volunteers astir.

In conformity with the altered fashions of the age, in this year the Session came to an understanding with me, that we should not inflict the common church censures for such as made themselves liable thereto; but we did not formally promulge our resolution as to this, wishing as long as possible to keep the deterring rod over the heads of the young and thoughtless. Our motive, on the one hand, was the disregard of the manufacturers in Cayenneville, who were, without the breach of truth, an irreligious people, and, on the other, a desire to preserve the ancient and wholesome admonitory and censorian jurisdiction of the minister and elders. We therefore laid it down as a rule to ourselves, that, in the case of transgressions on the part of the inhabitants of the new district of Cayenneville, we should subject them rigorously to a fine; but that for the farming lads, we would put it in their option to pay the fine, or stand in the kirk.

We conformed also in another matter to the times, by consenting to baptize occasionally in private houses. Hitherto it had been a strict rule with me only to baptize from the pulpit. Other parishes, however, had long been in the practice of this relaxation of ancient discipline.

But all this on my part was not done without compunction of spirit; for I was of opinion, that the principle of Presbyterian integrity should have been maintained to the uttermost. Seeing, however, the elders set on an alteration, I distrusted my own judgment, and yielded myself to the considerations that weighed with them; for they were true men, and of a godly honesty, and took the part of the poor in all contentions with the heritors, often to the hazard and damage of their own temporal welfare.

I have now to note a curious thing, not on account of its importance, but to show to what lengths a correspondence had been opened in the parish with the farthest parts of the earth. Mr Cayenne got a turtle-fish sent to him from a Glasgow merchant, and it was living when it came to the Wheatrig House, and was one of the most remarkable beasts that had ever been seen in our country-side. It weighed as much as a well-fed calf, and had three kinds of meat in its body, fish, flesh, and fowl, and it had four water-wings, for they could not be properly called fins; but what was little short of a miracle about the creature, happened after the head was cutted off, when, if a finger was offered to it, it would open its mouth and snap at it, and all this after the carcase was divided for dressing.

Mr Cayenne made a feast on the occasion to many of the neighbouring gentry, to the which I was invited, and we drank lime-punch as we ate the turtle, which, as I understand, is the fashion in practice among the Glasgow West Indy merchants, who are famed as great hands with turtles and lime-punch. But it is a sort of food that I should not like to fare long upon. I was not right the next day; and I have heard it said, that, when eaten too often, it has a tendency to harden the heart and make it crave for greater luxuries.

But the story of the turtle is nothing to that of the Mass, which, with all its mummeries and abominations, was brought into Cayenneville by an Irish priest of the name of Father O'Grady, who was confessor to some of the poor deluded Irish labourers about the new houses and the cotton-mill. How he had the impudence to set up that memento of Satan, the crucifix, within my parish and jurisdiction, was what I never could get to the bottom of; but the soul was shaken within me, when, on the Monday after, one of the elders came to the manse, and told me, that the old dragon of Popery, with its seven heads and ten horns, had been triumphing in Cayenneville on the foregoing Lord's day! I lost no time in convening the Session to see what was to be done; much, however, to my surprise, the elders recommended no step to be taken, but only a zealous endeavour to greater Christian excellence on our part, by which we should put the beast and his worshippers to shame and flight. I am free to confess, that, at the time, I did not think this the wisest counsel which they might have given; for, in the heat of my alarm, I was for attacking the enemy in his camp. But they prudently observed, that the days of religious persecution were past, and it was a comfort to see mankind cherishing any sense of religion at all, after the vehement infidelity that had been sent abroad by the French Republicans; and to this opinion, now that I have had years to sift its wisdom, I own myself a convert and proselyte.

Fortunately, however, for my peace of mind, there proved to be but five Roman Catholics in Cayenneville; and Father O'Grady, not being able to make a living there, packed up his Virgin Marys, saints, and painted Agnuses in a portmanteau, and went off in the Ayr Fly one morning for Glasgow, where I hear he has since met with all the encouragement that might be expected from the ignorant and idolatrous inhabitants of that great city.

Scarcely were we well rid of Father O'Grady, when another interloper entered the parish. He was more dangerous, in the opinion of the Session, than even the Pope of Rome himself; for he came to teach the flagrant heresy of Universal Redemption, a most consolatory doctrine to the sinner that is loth to repent, and who loves to troll his iniquity like a sweet morsel under his tongue. Mr Martin Siftwell, who was the last ta'en on elder, and who had received a liberal and judicious education, and was, moreover, naturally possessed of a quick penetration, observed, in speaking of this new doctrine, that the grossest papist sinner might have some qualms of fear after he had bought the Pope's pardon, and might thereby be led to a reformation of life; but that the doctrine of universal redemption was a bribe to commit sin, the wickedest mortal, according to it, being only liable to a few thousand years, more or less, of suffering, which, compared with eternity, was but a momentary pang, like having a tooth drawn for the toothache. Mr Siftwell is a shrewd and clear-seeing man in points of theology, and I would trust a great deal to what he says, as I have not, at my advanced age, such a mind for the kittle crudities of polemical investigation that I had in my younger years, especially when I was a student in the Divinity Hall of Glasgow.

It will be seen from all I have herein recorded, that, in the course of this year, there was a general resuscitation of religious sentiments; for what happened in my parish was but a type and index to the rest of the world. We had, however, one memorable that must stand by itself; for although neither death nor bloodshed happened, yet was it cause of the fear of both.

A rumour reached us from the Clyde, that a French man-of-war had appeared in a Highland loch, and that all the Greenock volunteers had embarked in merchant-vessels to bring her in for a prize. Our volunteers were just jumping and yowling, like chained dogs, to be at her too; but the colonel, Sir Hugh, would do nothing without orders from his superiors. Mr Cayenne, though an aged man, above seventy, was as bold as a lion, and came forth in the old garb of an American huntsman, like, as I was told, a Robin Hood in the play is; and it was just a sport to see him, feckless man trying to march so crousely with his lean, shaking hands. But the whole affair proved a false alarm, and our men, when they heard it, were as well pleased that they had been constrained to sleep in their warm beds at home, instead of lying on coils of cables, like the gallant Greenock sharp-shooters.

Chapter 46

Year 1805

Retrenchment of the extravagant expenses usual at burials—I use an expedient for putting even the second service out of fashion.

For some time I had meditated a reformation in the parish, and this year I carried the same into effect. I had often noticed with concern, that, out of a mistaken notion of paying respect to the dead, my people were wont to go to great lengths at their burials, and dealt round shortbread and sugar biscuit, with wine and other confections, as if there had been no ha'd in their hands; which straitened many a poor family, making the dispensation of the Lord a heavier temporal calamity than it should naturally have been. Accordingly, on consulting with Mrs Balwhidder, who has a most judicious judgment, it was thought that my interference would go a great way to lighten the evil. I therefore advised with those whose friends were taken from them, not to make that amplitude of preparation which used to be the fashion, nor to continue handing about as long as the folk would take, but only at the very most to go no more than three times round with the service. Objections were made to this, as if it would be thought mean; but I put on a stern visage, and told them, that if they did more I would rise up and rebuke and forbid the extravagance. So three services became the uttermost modicum at all burials. This was doing much, but it was not all that I wished to do.

I considered that the best reformations are those which proceed step by step, and stop at that point where the consent to what has been established becomes general;

and so I governed myself, and therefore interfered no farther; but I was determined to set an example. Accordingly, at the very next draigie, after I partook of one service, I made a bow to the servitors and they passed on, but all before me had partaken of the second service; some, however, of those after me did as I did, so I foresaw that in a quiet canny way I would bring in the fashion of being satisfied with one service. I therefore, from that time, always took my place as near as I possible to the door, where the chief mourner sat, and made a point of nodding away the second service, which has now grown into a custom, to the great advantage of surviving relations.

But in this reforming business I was not altogether pleased with our poet; for he took a pawkie view of my endeavours, and indited a ballad on the subject, in the which he makes a clattering carlin describe what took place, so as to turn a very solemn matter into a kind of derision. When he brought his verse and read it to me, I told him that I thought it was overly natural; for I could not find another term to designate the cause of the dissatisfaction that I had with it; but Mrs Balwhidder said that it might help my plan if it were made public, so upon her advice we got some of Mr Lorimore's best writers to make copies of it for distribution, which was not without fruit and influence. But a sore thing happened at the very next burial. As soon as the nodding away of the second service began, I could see that the gravity of the whole meeting was discomposed, and some of the irreverent young chiels almost broke out into even-down laughter, which vexed me exceedingly. Mrs Balwhidder, howsoever, comforted me by saying, that custom in time would make it familiar, and by and by the thing would pass as a matter of course, until one service would be all that folk would offer; and truly the thing is coming to that, for only two services are now handed round, and the second is regularly nodded by.

Chapter 47

Year 1806

The deathbed behaviour of Mr Cayenne—A schism in the parish, and a subscription to build a meeting-house.

Mr Cayenne of Wheatrig having for several years been in a declining way, partly brought on by the consuming fire of his furious passion, and partly by the decay of old age, sent for me on the evening of the first Sabbath of March in this year. I was surprised at the message, and went to the Wheatrig House directly, where, by the lights in the windows as I gaed up through the policy to the door, I saw something extraordinary was going on. Sambo, the blackamoor servant, opened the door, and without speaking shook his head; for he was an affectionate creature, and as fond of his master as if he had been his own father. By this sign I guessed that the old gentleman was thought to be drawing near his latter end, so I walked softly after Sambo up the stair, and was shown into the chamber where Mr Cayenne, since he had been confined to the house, usually sat. His wife had been dead some years before.

Mr Cayenne was sitting in his easy-chair, with a white cotton night-cap on his head, and a pillow at his shoulders to keep him straight. But his head had fallen down on his breast, and he breathed like a panting baby. His legs were swelled, and his feet rested on a footstool. His face, which was wont to be the colour of a peony rose, was of a yellow hue, with a patch of red on each cheek like a wafer, and his nose was shirpit and sharp, and of an unnatural purple. Death was evidently fighting with Nature for the possession of the body. 'Heaven have mercy on his soul,' said I to myself, as I sat down beside him.

When I had been seated some time, the power was given him to raise his head as it were ajee, and he looked at me with the tail of his eye, which I saw was glittering and glassy. 'Doctor,' for he always called me doctor, though I am not of that degree, 'I am glad to see you,' were his words, uttered with some difficulty.

'How do you find yourself, sir?' I replied in a sympathising manner.

'Damned bad,' said he, as if I had been the cause of his suffering. I was daunted to the very heart to hear him in such an unregenerate state; but after a short pause I addressed myself to him again, saying, that 'I hoped he would soon be more at ease, and he should bear in mind that the Lord chasteneth whom He loveth.'

'The devil take such love,' was his awful answer, which was to me as a blow on the forehead with a mell. However, I was resolved to do my duty to the miserable sinner, let him say what he would. Accordingly, I stooped towards him with my hands on my knees, and said in a compassionate voice, It's very true, sir, that you are in great agony, but the goodness of God is without bound.'

'Curse me if I think so, doctor,' replied the dying uncircumcised Philistine. But he added at whiles, his breathlessness being grievous, and often broken by a sore hiccup, 'I am, however, no saint, as you know, doctor; so I wish you to put in a word for me, doctor; for you know that in these times, doctor, it is the duty of every good subject to die a Christian.'

This was a poor account of the state of his soul, but it was plain I could make no better o't by entering into any religious discourse or controversy with him, he being then in the last gasp; so I knelt down and prayed for him with great sincerity, imploring the Lord, as an awakening sense of grace to the dying man, that it would please Him to lift up, though it were but for the season of a minute, the chastening hand which was laid so heavily upon His aged servant; at which Mr Cayenne, as if indeed the hand had been then lifted, cried out, 'None of that stuff, doctor; you know that I cannot call myself His servant.'

Was ever a minister in his prayer so broken in upon by a perishing sinner! However, I had the weight of a duty upon me, and made no reply, but continued, 'Thou hearest, O Lord! how he confesses his unworthiness. Let not Thy compassion, therefore, be withheld, but verify to him the words that I have spoken in faith, of the boundlessness of Thy goodness, and the infinite multitude of Thy tender mercies. I then calmly, but sadly, sat down, and presently, as if my prayer had been heard, relief was granted; for Mr. Cayenne raised his head, and, giving me a queer look, said, 'That last clause of your petition, doctor, was well put, and I think, too, it has been granted, for I am easier,'—adding, 'I have no doubt, doctor, given much offence in the world, and oftenest when I meant to do good; but I have wilfully injured no man, and as God is my judge, and His goodness, you say, is so great, He may, perhaps, take my soul into His holy keeping.' In saying which words, Mr Cayenne dropped his head upon his breast, his breathing ceased, and he was wafted away out of this world with as little trouble as a blameless baby.

This event soon led to a change among us. In the settling of Mr Cayenne's affairs in the Cotton-mill Company, it was found that he had left such a power of money, that it was needful to the concern, in order that they might settle with the doers under his testament, to take in other partners. By this Mr Speckle came to be a resident in the parish, he having taken up a portion of Mr Cayenne's share. He likewise took a tack of the house and policy of Wheatrig. But although Mr Speckle was a far more conversible man than his predecessor, and had a wonderful plausibility in business, the affairs of the Company did not thrive in his hands. Some said this was owing to his having ower many irons in the fire; others, to the circumstances of the times; in my judgment, however, both helped; but the issue belongs to the events of another year. In the meanwhile, I should here note, that in the course of this current Ann. Dom. it pleased Heaven to visit me with a severe trial, the nature of which I will here record at length—the upshot I will make known hereafter.

From the planting of inhabitants in the cotton-mill town of Cayenneville, or, as the country folk, not used to such langnebbit words, now call it, Canaille, there had come in upon the parish various sectarians among the weavers, some of whom were not satisfied with the Gospel as I preached it, and endeavoured to practise it in my walk and conversation; and they began to speak of building a kirk for themselves, and of getting a minister that would give them the Gospel more to their own ignorant fancies. I was exceedingly wroth and disturbed when the thing was first mentioned to me; and I very earnestly, from the pulpit, next Lord's day, lectured on the growth of new-fangled doctrines; which, however, instead of having the wonted effect of my discourses, set up the theological weavers in a bleeze, and the very Monday following they named a committee to raise money by subscription to build a meeting-house. This was the first overt act of insubordination collectively manifested in the parish; and it was conducted with all that crafty dexterity, with which the infidel and Jacobin spirit of the French Revolution had corrupted the honest simplicity of our good old hameward fashions. In the course of a very short time, the Canaille folk had raised a large sum, and seduced not a few of my people into their schism, by which they were enabled to set about building their kirk; the foundations thereof were not, however, laid till the following year, but their proceedings gave me a het heart, for they were like an open rebellion to my authority, and a contemptuous disregard of that religious allegiance which is due from the flock to the pastor.

On Christmas day the wind broke off the main arm of our Adam and Eve pear-tree, and I grieved for it more as a type and sign of the threatened partition, than on account of the damage, though the fruit was the juiciest in all the countryside.

Chapter 48

Year 1807

Numerous marriages—Account of a pay-wedding, made to set up a shop.

This was a year to me of satisfaction, in many points, for a greater number of my younger flock married in it, than had done for any one of ten years prior. They were chiefly the offspring of the marriages that took place at the close of the American war; and I was pleased to see the duplification of well-doing, as I think marrying is, having always considered the command to increase and multiply, a holy ordinance, which the circumstances of this world but too often interfere to prevent.

It was also made manifest to me, that in this year there was a very general renewal in the hearts of men, of a sense of the utility, even in earthly affairs, of a religious life: in some, I trust it was more than prudence, and really a birth of grace. Whether this was owing to the upshot of the French Revolution, all men being pretty well satisfied in their minds that uproar and rebellion make but an ill way of righting wrongs, or that the swarm of unruly youth, the offspring, as I have said, of the marriages after the American war, had grown sobered from their follies, and saw things in a better light, I cannot take upon me to say. But it was very edifying to me, their minister, to see several lads, who had been both wild and free in their principles, marrying with sobriety, and taking their wives to the kirk, with the comely decorum of heads of families.

But I was now growing old and could go seldomer out among my people than in former days, so that I was less a partaker of their ploys and banquets, either at birth, bridal, or burial. I heard, however, all that went on at them, and I made it a rule, after giving the blessing at the end of the ceremony, to admonish the bride and bridegroom to ca' canny, and join trembling with their mirth. It behoved me on one occasion, however, to break through a rule, that age and frailty had imposed upon me, and to go to the wedding of Tibby Banes, the daughter of the betherel, because she had once been a servant in the manse, besides the obligation upon me from her father's part, both in the kirk and kirkyard. Mrs Balwhidder went with me, for she liked to countenance the pleasantries of my people; and, over and above all, it was a pay-wedding, in order to set up the bridegroom in a shop.

There was, to be sure, a great multitude, gentle and semple, of all denominations, with two fiddles and a bass, and the volunteers' fife and drum, and the jollity that went on was a perfect feast of itself, though the wedding-supper was a prodigy of abundance. The auld carles kecklet with fainness, as they saw the young dancers; and the carlins sat on forms, as mim as May puddocks, with their shawls pinned apart, to show their muslin napkins. But, after supper, when they had got a glass of the punch, their heels showed their mettle, and grannies danced with their oyes, holding out their hands as if they had been spinning with two rocks. I told Colin Mavis, the poet, that an *Infare* was a fine subject for his muse, and soon after he indited an excellent ballad under that title, which he projects to publish with other ditties by subscription; and I have no doubt a liberal and discerning public will give him all manner of encouragement, for that is the food of talent of every kind, and without cheering, no one can say what an author's faculty naturally is.

Chapter 49

Year 1808

Failure of Mr Speckle, the proprietor of the cotton mill—The melancholy end of one of the overseers and his wife.

Through all the wars that have raged from the time of the king's accession to the throne, there has been a gradually coming nearer and nearer to our gates, which is a very alarming thing to think of. In the first, at the time he came to the crown, we suffered nothing. Not one belonging to the parish was engaged in the battles thereof, and the news of victories, before they reached us, which was generally by word of mouth, were old tales. In the American war, as I have related at length, we had an immediate participation, but those that suffered were only a few individuals, and the evil was done at a distance, and reached us not until the worst of its effects were spent. And during the first term of the present just and necessary contest for all that is dear to us as a people, although, by the offswarming of some of the our restless youth, we had our part and portion in common was a with the rest of the Christian world; yet still there was at home a great augmentation of prosperity, and everything had thriven in a surprising manner; somewhat, however, to the detriment of our country simplicity. By the building of the cotton-mill, and the rising up of the new town of Cayenneville, we had intromitted so much with concerns of trade, that we were become a part of the great web of commercial reciprocities, and felt in our corner and extremity every touch or stir that was made on any part of the texture. The consequence of this I have now to relate.

Various rumours had been floating about the business of the cotton manufacturers not being so lucrative as it had been; and Bonaparte, as it is well known, was a perfect limb of Satan against our prosperity, having recourse to the most wicked means and purposes to bring ruin upon us as a nation. His cantrips, in this year, began to have a dreadful effect.

For some time it had been observed in the parish, that Mr Speckle, of the cotton-mill, went very often to Glasgow, and was sometimes off at a few minutes' warning to London, and the neighbours began to guess and wonder at what could be the cause of all this running here, and riding there, as if the littlegude was at his heels. Sober folk augured ill o't; and it was remarked, likewise, that there was a haste and confusion in his mind, which betokened a foretaste of some change of fortune. At last, in the fulness of time, the babe was born.

On a Saturday night, Mr Speckle came out late from Glasgow; on the Sabbath he was with all his family at the kirk, looking as a man that had changed his way of life; and on the Monday, when the spinners went to the mill, they were told that the company had stopped payment. Never did a thunder-clap daunt the heart like this news, for the bread in a moment was snatched from more than a thousand mouths. It was a scene not to be described, to see the cotton-spinners and the weavers, with their wives and children, standing in bands along the road, all looking and speaking as if they had lost a dear friend or parent. For my part, I could not bear the sight, but hid myself in my closet, and prayed to the Lord to mitigate a calamity, which seemed to me past the capacity of man to remedy; for what could our parish fund do in the way of helping a whole town, thus suddenly thrown out of bread.

In the evening, however, I was strengthened, and convened the elders at the manse to consult with them on what was best to be done, for it was well known that the sufferers had made no provision for a sore foot. But all our gathered judgments could determine nothing; and therefore we resolved to wait the issue, not doubting but that HE who sends the night, would bring the day in His good and gracious time, which so fell out. Some of them who had the largest experience of such vicissitudes, immediately began to pack up their ends and their awls, and to hie them into Glasgow and Paisley in quest of employ; but those who trusted to the hopes that Mr Speckle himself still cherished, lingered long, and were obligated to submit to sore distress. After a time, however, it was found that the company was ruined, and the mill being sold for the benefit of the creditors, it was bought by another Glasgow company, who, by getting it a good bargain, and managing well, have it still, and have made it again a blessing to the country. At the time of the stoppage, however, we saw that commercial prosperity, flush as it might be, was but a perishable commodity, and from thence, both by public discourse and private exhortation, I have recommended to the workmen to lay up something for a reverse; and showed that, by doing with their bawbees and pennies, what the great do with their pounds, they might in time get a pose to help them in the day of need. This advice they have followed, and made up a Savings Bank, which is a pillow of comfort to many an industrious head of a family.

But I should not close this account of the disaster that befell Mr Speckle, and the cotton-mill company, without relating a very melancholy case that was the consequence. Among the overseers there was a Mr Dwining, an Englishman from Manchester, where he had seen better days, having had himself there of his own property, once as large a mill, according to report, as the Cayenneville mill. He was certainly a man above the common, and his wife was a lady in every point; but they held themselves by themselves, and shunned all manner of civility, giving up their whole attention to their two little boys, who were really like creatures of a better race than the callans of our clachan.

On the failure of the company, Mr Dwining was observed by those who were present to be particularly distressed: his salary being his all; but he said little, and went thoughtfully home. Some days after he was seen walking by himself with a pale face, a heavy eye, and slow step—all tokens of a sorrowful heart. Soon after he was missed altogether; nobody saw him. The door of his house was however open, and his two pretty boys were as lively as usual, on the green before the door. I happened to pass when they were there, and I asked them how their father and mother were. They said they were still in bed, and would no waken, and the innocent lambs took me by the hand, to make me waken their parents. I know not what was in it, but I trembled from head to foot, and I was led in by the babies, as if I had not the power to resist. Never shall I forget what I saw in that bed.

I found a letter on the table; and I came away, locking the door behind me, and took the lovely prattling orphans home. I could but shake my head and weep, as I gave them to the care of Mrs Balwhidder, and she was terrified but said nothing. I then read the letter. It was to send the bairns to a gentleman, their uncle, in London. Oh it is a terrible tale, but the winding-sheet and the earth is over it. I sent for two of my elders. I related what I had seen. Two coffins were got, and the bodies laid in them; and the next day, with one of the fatherless bairns in each hand, I followed them to the grave, which was dug in that part of the kirkyard where unchristened babies are laid. We durst not take it upon us to do more, but few knew the reason, and some thought it was because the deceased were strangers, and had no regular lair.

I dressed the two bonny orphans in the best mourning at my own cost, and kept them in the manse till we could get an answer from their uncle, to whom I sent their father's letter. It stung him to the quick, and he came down all the way from London, and took the children away himself. Oh he was a vext man when the beautiful bairns, on being told he was their uncle, ran into his arms, and complained that their papa and mamma had slept so long, that they would never waken.

Chapter 50

Year 1809

Opening of a meeting-house—The elders come to the manse, and offer me a helper.

As I come towards the events of these latter days, I am surprised to find myself not at all so distinct in my recollection of them, as in those of the first of my ministry; being apt to confound the things of one occasion with those of another, which Mrs Balwhidder says is an admonishment to me to leave off my writing. But, please God, I will endeavour to fulfil this as I have through life tried, to the best of my capacity, to do every other duty; and with the help of Mrs Balwhidder, who has a very clear understanding, I think I may get through my task in a creditable manner, which is all I aspire after; not writing for a vain world, but only to testify to posterity anent the great changes that have happened in my day and generation—a period which all the best-informed writers say, has not had its match in the history of the world since the beginning of time.

By the failure of the cotton-mill company, whose affairs were not settled till the spring of this year, there was great suffering during the winter; but my people, those that still adhered to the establishment, bore their share of the dispensation with meekness and patience, nor was there wanting edifying monuments of resignation even among the strayvaggers.

On the day that the Canaille Meeting-house was opened, which was in the summer, I was smitten to the heart to see the empty seats that were in my kirk, for all the thoughtless, and some that I had a better opinion of, went to hear the opening discourse. Satan that day had power given to him to buffet me as he did Job of old; and when I looked around and saw the empty seats, my corruption rose, and I forgot myself in the remembering prayer; for when I prayed for all denominations of Christians, and worshippers, and infidels, I could not speak of the schismatics with patience, but entreated the Lord to do with the hobbleshow at Cayenneville as He saw meet in His displeasure, the which, when I came afterwards to think upon, I grieved at with a sore contrition.

In the course of the week following, the elders, in a body, came to me in the manse, and after much commendation of my godly ministry, they said, that seeing I was now growing old, they thought they could not testify their respect for me in a better manner, than by agreeing to get me a helper. But I would not at that time listen to such a proposal, for I felt no falling off in my powers of preaching; on the contrary, I found myself growing better at it, as I was enabled to hold forth, in an easy manner, often a whole half-hour longer than I could do a dozen years before. Therefore nothing was done in this year anent my resignation; but during the winter, Mrs Balwhidder was often grieved, in the bad weather, that I should preach, and, in short, so worked upon my affections, that I began to think it was fitting for me to comply with the advice of my friends. Accordingly, in the course of the winter, the elders began to cast about for a helper, and during the bleak weather in the ensuing spring, several young men spared me from the necessity of preaching. But this relates to the concerns of the next and last year of my ministry. So I will now proceed to give an account of it, very thankful that I have been permitted, in unmolested tranquillity, to bring my history to such a point.

Chapter 51

Year 1810

Conclusion—I repair to the church for the last time—Afterwards receive a silver server from the parishioners—And still continue to marry and baptize.

My tasks are all near a close; and in writing this final record of my ministry, the very sound of my pen admonishes me that my life is a burden on the back of flying Time, that he will soon be obliged to lay down in his great storehouse, the grave. Old age has, indeed, long warned me to prepare for rest, and the darkened windows of my sight show that the night is coming on, while deafness, like a door fast barred, has shut out all the pleasant sounds of this world, and inclosed me, as it were, in a prison, even from the voices of my friends.

I have lived longer than the common lot of man, and I have seen, in my time, many mutations and turnings, and ups and downs, notwithstanding the great spread that has been in our national prosperity. I have beheld them that were flourishing like the green bay trees, made desolate, and their branches scattered. But, in my own estate, I have had a large and liberal experience of goodness.

At the beginning of my ministry I was reviled and rejected, but my honest endeavours to prove a faithful shepherd were blessed from on high, and rewarded with the affection of my flock. Perhaps, in the vanity of doting old age, I thought in this there was a merit due to myself, which made the Lord to send the chastisement of the Canaille schism among my people, for I was then wroth without judgment, and by my heat hastened into an open division the flaw that a more considerate manner might have healed. But I confess my fault, and submit my cheek to the smiter; and now I see that the finger of Wisdom was in that probation, and it was far better that the weavers meddled with the things of God, which they could not change, than with those of the king, which they could only harm. In that matter, however, I was like our gracious monarch in the American war; for though I thereby lost the pastoral allegiance of a portion of my people, in like manner as he did of his American subjects; yet, after the separation, I was enabled so to deport myself, that they showed me many voluntary testimonies of affectionate respect, and which it would be a vainglory in me to rehearse here. One thing I must record, because it is as much to their honour as it is to mine.

When it was known that I was to preach my last sermon, every one of those who had been my hearers, and who had seceded to the Canaille meeting, made it a point that day to be in the parish kirk, and to stand in the crowd, that made a lane of reverence for me to pass from the kirk door to the back-yett of the manse. And shortly after a deputation of all their brethren, with their minister at their head, came to me one morning, and presented to me a server of silver, in token, as they were pleased to say, of their esteem for my blameless life, and the charity that I had practised towards the poor of all sects in the neighbourhood; which is set forth in a wellpenned inscription, written by a weaver lad that works for his daily bread. Such a thing would have been a prodigy at the beginning of my ministry, but the progress of book-learning and education has been wonderful since, and with it has come a spirit of greater liberality than the world knew before, bringing men of adverse principles and doctrines into a more humane communion with each other, showing, that it's by the mollifying influence of knowledge, the time will come to pass, when the tiger of papistry shall lie down with the lamb of reformation, and the vultures of prelacy be as harmless as the presbyterian doves; when the independent, the anabaptist, and every other order and denomination of Christians, not forgetting even those poor wee wrens of the Lord, the burghers and anti-burghers, who will pick from the hand of patronage, and dread no snare.

On the next Sunday, after my farewell discourse, I took the arm of Mrs Balwhidder, and with my cane in my hand, walked to our own pew, where I sat some time, but owing to my deafness, not being able to hear, I have not since gone back to the church. But my people are fond of having their weans still christened by me, and the young folk, such as are of a serious turn, come to be married at my hands, believing, as they say, that there is something good in the blessing of an aged Gospel minister. But even this remnant of my gown I must lay aside, for Mrs Balwhidder is now and then obliged to stop me in my prayers, as I sometimes wander—pronouncing the baptismal blessing upon a bride and bridegroom, talking as if they were already parents. I am thankful, however, that I have been spared with a sound mind to write this book to the end; but it is my last task, and, indeed, really I have no more to say, saving only to wish a blessing on all people from on High, where I soon hope to be, and to meet there all the old and long-departed sheep of my flock, especially the first and second Mrs Balwhidders.

The Ayrshire Legatees

Chapter I

The Departure

On New Year's day Dr Pringle received a letter from India, informing him that his cousin, Colonel Armour, had died at Hydrabad, and left him his residuary legatee. The same post brought other letters on the same subject from the agent of the deceased in London, by which it was evident to the whole family that no time should be lost in looking after their interests in the hands of such brief and abrupt correspondents. 'To say the least of it,' as the Doctor himself sedately remarked, 'considering the greatness of the forthcoming property, Messieurs Richard Argent and Company, of New Broad Street, might have given a notion as to the particulars of the residue.' It was therefore determined that, as soon as the requisite arrangements could be made, the Doctor and Mrs. Pringle should set out for the metropolis, to obtain a speedy settlement with the agents, and, as Rachel had now, to use an expression of her mother's, 'a prospect before her,' that she also should accompany them: Andrew, who had just been called to the Bar, and who had come to the manse to spend a few days after attaining that distinction, modestly suggested, that, considering the various professional points which might be involved in the objects of his father's journey, and considering also the retired life which his father had led in the rural village of Garnock, it might be of importance to have the advantage of legal advice.

Mrs Pringle interrupted this harangue, by saying, 'We see what you would be at, Andrew; ye're just wanting to come with us, and on this occasion I'm no for making step-bairns, so we'll a' gang thegither.'

The Doctor had been for many years the incumbent of Garnock, which is pleasantly situated between Irvine and Kilwinning, and, on account of the benevolence of his disposition, was much beloved by his parishioners. Some of the pawkie among them used indeed to say, in answer to the godly of Kilmarnock, and other admirers of the late great John Russel, of that formerly orthodox town, by whom Dr Pringle's powers as a preacher were held in no particular estimation,—'He kens our pu'pit's frail, and spar'st to save outlay to the heritors.' As for Mrs Pringle, there is not such another minister's wife, both for economy and management, within the jurisdiction of the Synod of Glasgow and Ayr, and to this fact the following letter to Miss Mally Glencairn, a maiden lady residing in the Kirkgate of Irvine, a street that has been likened unto the Kingdom of Heaven, where there is neither marriage nor giving in marriage, will abundantly testify.

LETTER 1
Mrs Pringle to Miss Mally Glencairn

GARNOCK MANSE.

DEAR MISS MALLY—The Doctor has had extraordinar news from India and London, where we are all going, as soon as me and Rachel can get ourselves in order, so

I beg you will go to Bailie Delap's shop, and get swatches of his best black bombaseen, and crape, and muslin, and bring them over to the manse the morn's morning. If you cannot come yourself, and the day should be wat, send Nanny Eydent, the mantua-maker, with them; you'll be sure to send Nanny, onyhow, and I requeesht that, on this okasion, ye'll get the very best the Bailie has, and I'll tell you all about it when you come. You will get, likewise, swatches of mourning print, with the lowest prices. I'll no be so particular about them, as they are for the servan lasses, and there's no need, for all the greatness of God's gifts, that we should be wasterful. Let Mrs Glibbans know, that the Doctor's second cousin, the colonel, that was in the East Indies, is no more;—I am sure she will sympatheese with our loss on this melancholy okasion. Tell her, as I'll no be out till our mournings are made, I would take it kind if she would come over and eate a bit of dinner on Sunday. The Doctor will no preach himself, but there's to be an excellent young man, an acquaintance of Andrew's, that has the repute of being both sound and hellaquaint. But no more at present, and looking for you and Nanny Eydent, with the swatches,—I am, dear Miss Mally, your sinsare friend,

JANET PRINGLE

The Doctor being of opinion that, until they had something in hand from the legacy, they should walk in the paths of moderation, it was resolved to proceed by the coach from Irvine to Greenock, there embark in a steam-boat for Glasgow, and, crossing the country to Edinburgh, take their passage at Leith in one of the smacks for London. But we must let the parties speak for themselves.

LETTER 2
Miss Rachel Pringle to Miss Isabella Tod

GREENOCK

MY DEAR ISABELLA—I know not why the dejection with which I parted from you still hangs upon my heart, and grows heavier as I am drawn farther and farther away. The uncertainty of the future—the dangers of the sea—all combine to sadden my too sensitive spirit. Still, however, I will exert myself, and try to give you some account of our momentous journey.

The morning on which we bade farewell for a time—alas! it was to me as if for ever, to my native shades of Garnock—the weather was cold, bleak, and boisterous, and the waves came rolling in majestic fury towards the shore, when we arrived at the Tontine Inn of Ardrossan. What a monument has the late Earl of Eglinton left there of his public spirit! It should embalm his memory in the hearts of future ages, as I doubt not but in time Ardrossan will become a grand emporium; but the people of Saltcoats, a sordid race, complain that it will be their ruin; and the Paisley subscribers to his lordship's canal grow pale when they think of profit.

The road, after leaving Ardrossan, lies along the shore. The blast came dark from the waters, and the clouds lay piled in every form of grandeur on the lofty peaks of Arran. The view on the right hand is limited to the foot of a range of abrupt mean hills, and on the left it meets the sea—as we were obliged to keep the glasses up, our drive for several miles was objectless and dreary. When we had ascended a hill, leaving Kilbride on the left, we passed under the walls of an ancient tower. What delightful ideas are associated with the sight of such venerable remains of antiquity!

Leaving that lofty relic of our warlike ancestors, we descended again towards the shore. On the one side lay the Cumbra Islands, and Bute, dear to departed royalty. Afar beyond them, in the hoary magnificence of nature, rise the mountains of Argyllshire; the cairns, as my brother says, of a former world. On the other side of the road, we saw the cloistered ruins of the religious house of Southenan, a nunnery in those days of romantic adventure, when to live was to enjoy a poetical element. In such a sweet sequestered retreat, how much more pleasing to the soul it would have been, for you and I, like two captive birds in one cage, to have sung away our hours in innocence, than for me to be thus torn from you by fate, and all on account of that mercenary legacy, perchance the spoils of some unfortunate Hindoo Rajah!

At Largs we halted to change horses, and saw the barrows of those who fell in the great battle. We then continued our journey along the foot of stupendous precipices; and high, sublime, and darkened with the shadow of antiquity, we saw, upon its lofty station, the ancient Castle of Skelmorlie, where the Montgomeries of other days held their gorgeous banquets, and that brave knight who fell at Chevy-Chace came pricking forth on his milk-white steed, as Sir Walter Scott would have described him. But the age of chivalry is past, and the glory of Europe departed for ever!

When we crossed the stream that divides the counties of Ayr and Renfrew, we beheld, in all the apart and consequentiality of pride, the house of Kelly overlooking the social villas of Wemyss Bay. My brother compared it to a sugar hogshead, and them to cotton-bags; for the lofty thane of Kelly is but a West India planter, and the inhabitants of the villas on the shore are Glasgow manufacturers.

To this succeeded a dull drive of about two miles, and then at once we entered the pretty village of Inverkip. A slight snow-shower had given to the landscape a sort of copperplate effect, but still the forms of things, though but sketched, as it were, with China ink, were calculated to produce interesting impressions. After ascending, by a gentle acclivity, into a picturesque and romantic pass, we entered a spacious valley, and, in the course of little more than half an hour, reached this town; the largest, the most populous, and the most superb that I have yet seen. But what are all its warehouses, ships, and smell of tar, and other odoriferous circumstances of fishery and the sea, compared with the green swelling hills, the fragrant bean-fields, and the peaceful groves of my native Garnock!

The people of this town are a very busy and clever race, but much given to litigation. My brother says, that they are the greatest benefactors to the Outer House, and that their lawsuits are the most amusing and profitable before the courts, being less for the purpose of determining what is right than what is lawful. The chambermaid of the inn where we lodge pointed out to me, on the opposite side of the street, a magnificent edifice erected for balls; but the subscribers have resolved not to allow any dancing till it is determined by the Court of Session to whom the seats and chairs belong, as they were brought from another house where the assemblies were formerly held. I have heard a lawsuit compared to a country-dance, in which, after a great bustle and regular confusion, the parties stand still, all tired, just on the spot where they began; but this is the first time that the judges of the land have been called on to decide when a dance may begin.

We arrived too late for the steam-boat, and are obliged to wait till Monday morning; but to-morrow we shall go to church, where I expect to see what sort of creatures the beaux are. The Greenock ladies have a great name for beauty, but those that I have seen are perfect frights. Such of the gentlemen as I have observed passing the windows of the inn may do, but I declare the ladies have nothing of which any woman ought to be proud. Had we known that we ran a risk of not getting a steam-boat, my mother would have provided an introductory letter or two from some of her Irvine friends; but here we are almost entire strangers: my father, however, is acquainted with one of the magistrates, and has gone to see him. I hope he will be civil enough to ask us to his house, for an inn is a shocking place to live in, and my mother is terrified at the expense. My brother, however, has great confidence in our prospects, and orders and directs with a high hand. But my paper is full, and I am compelled to conclude with scarcely room to say how affectionately I am yours,

RACHEL PRINGLE

LETTER 3

The Rev Dr Pringle to Mr Micklewham, Schoolmaster and Session Clerk, Garnock

EDINBURGH

DEAR SIR—We have got this length through many difficulties, both in the travel by land to, and by sea and land from Greenock, where we were obligated, by reason of no conveyance, to stop the Sabbath, but not without edification; for we went to hear Dr Drystour in the forenoon, who had a most weighty sermon on the tenth chapter of Nehemiah. He is surely a great orthodox divine, but rather costive in his delivery. In the afternoon we heard a correct moral lecture on good works, in another church, from Dr Eastlight—a plain man, with a genteel congregation. The same night we took supper with a wealthy family, where we had much pleasant communion together, although the bringing in of the toddy-bowl after supper is a fashion that has a tendency to lengthen the sederunt to unseasonable hours.

On the following morning, by the break of day, we took shipping in the steam-boat for Glasgow. I had misgivings about the engine, which is really a thing of great docility; but saving my concern for the boiler, we all found the place surprising comfortable. The day was bleak and cold; but we had a good fire in a carron grate in the middle of the floor, and books to read, so that both body and mind are therein provided for.

Among the books, I fell in with a History of the Rebellion, anent the hand that an English gentleman of the name of Waverley had in it. I was grieved that I had not time to read it through, for it was wonderful interesting, and far more particular, in many points, than any other account of that affair I have yet met with; but it's no so friendly to Protestant principles as I could have wished. However, if I get my legacy well settled, I will buy the book, and lend it to you on my return, please God, to the manse. We were put on shore at Glasgow by breakfast-time, and there we tarried all day, as I had a power of attorney to get from Miss Jenny Macbride, my cousin, to whom the colonel left the thousand pound legacy. Miss Jenny thought the legacy should have been more, and made some obstacle to signing the power; but both her lawyer and Andrew Pringle, my son, convinced her, that, as it was specified in the testament, she could not help it by standing out; so at long and last Miss Jenny was persuaded to put her name to the paper.

Next day we all four got into a fly coach, and, without damage or detriment, reached this city in good time for dinner in Macgregor's hotel, a remarkable decent inn, next door to one Mr Blackwood, a civil and discreet man in the bookselling line. Really the changes in Edinburgh since I was here, thirty years ago, are not to be told. I am confounded; for although I have both heard and read of the New Town in the Edinburgh Advertiser, and the Scots Magazine, I had no notion of what has come to pass. It's surprising to think wherein the decay of the nation is; for at Greenock I saw nothing but shipping and building; at Glasgow, streets spreading as if they were one of the branches of cotton-spinning; and here, the houses grown up as if they were sown in the seed-time with the corn, by a drill-machine, or dibbled in rigs and furrows like beans and potatoes.

To-morrow, God willing, we embark in a smack at Leith, so that you will not hear from me again till it please HIM to take us in the hollow of His hand to London. In the mean-time, I have only to add, that, when the Session meets, I wish you would speak to the elders, particularly to Mr Craig, no to be overly hard on that poor donsie thing, Meg Milliken, about her bairn; and tell Tam Glen, the father o't, from me, that it would have been a sore heart to that pious woman, his mother, had she been living, to have witnessed such a thing; and therefore I hope and trust, he will yet confess a fault, and own Meg for his wife, though she is but something of a tawpie. However, you need not diminish her to Tam. I hope Mr Snodgrass will give as much satisfaction to the parish as can reasonably be expected in my absence; and I remain, dear sir, your friend and pastor,

ZACHARIAH PRINGLE

Mr Micklewham received the Doctor's letter about an hour before the Session met on the case of Tam Glen and Meg Milliken, and took it with him to the session-house, to read it to the elders before going into the investigation. Such a long and particular letter from the Doctor was, as they all justly remarked, kind and dutiful to his people, and a great pleasure to them.

Mr Daff observed, 'Truly the Doctor's a vera funny man, and wonderfu' jocose about the toddy-bowl.' But Mr Craig said, that 'sic a thing on the Lord's night gi'es me no pleasure; and I am for setting my face against Waverley's History of the Rebellion, whilk I hae heard spoken of among the ungodly, both at Kilwinning and Dalry; and if it has no respect to Protestant principles, I doubt it's but another dose o' the radical poison in a new guise.' Mr Icenor, however, thought that 'the observe on the great Doctor Drystour was very edifying; and that they should see about getting him to help at the summer Occasion.'[1]

While they were thus reviewing, in their way, the first epistle of the Doctor, the betherel came in to say that Meg and Tam were at the door. 'Oh, man,' said Mr Daff, slyly, 'ye shouldna hae left them at the door by themselves.' Mr Craig looked at him austerely, and muttered something about the growing immorality of this backsliding age; but before the smoke of his indignation had kindled into eloquence, the delinquents were admitted. However, as we have nothing to do with the business, we shall leave them to their own deliberations.

1 The administration of the Sacrament.

Chapter 2

The Voyage

On the fourteenth day after the departure of the family from the manse, the Rev Mr Charles Snodgrass, who was appointed to officiate during the absence of the Doctor, received the following letter from his old chum, Mr Andrew Pringle. It would appear that the young advocate is not so solid in the head as some of his elder brethren at the Bar; and therefore many of his flights and observations must be taken with an allowance on the score of his youth.

LETTER 4

Andrew Pringle, Esq , Advocate, to the Rev Charles Snodgrass

LONDON

MY DEAR FRIEND—We have at last reached London, after a stormy passage of seven days. The accommodation in the smacks looks extremely inviting in port, and in fine weather, I doubt not, is confortable, even at sea; but in February, and in such visitations of the powers of the air as we have endured, a balloon must be a far better vehicle than all the vessels that have been constructed for passengers since the time of Noah. In the first place, the waves of the atmosphere cannot be so dangerous as those of the ocean, being but 'thin air'; and I am sure they are not so disagreeable; then the speed of the balloon is so much greater, -and it would puzzle Professor Leslie to demonstrate that its motions are more unsteady; besides, who ever heard of sea-sickness in a balloon? the consideration of which alone would, to any reasonable person actually suffering under the pains of that calamity, be deemed more than an equivalent for all the little fractional difference of danger between the two modes of travelling. I shall henceforth regard it as a fine characteristic trait of our national prudence, that, in their journies to France and Flanders, the Scottish witches always went by air on broomsticks and benweeds, instead of venturing by water in sieves, like those of England. But the English are under the influence of a maritime genius.

When we had got as far up the Thames as Gravesend, the wind and tide came against us, so that the vessel was obliged to anchor, and I availed myself of the circumstance, to induce the family to disembark and go to London by LAND; and I esteem it a fortunate circumstance that we did so, the day, for the season, being uncommonly fine. After we had taken some refreshment, I procured places in a stage-coach for my mother and sister, and, with the Doctor, mounted myself on the outside. My father's old-fashioned notions boggled a little at first to this arrangement, which he thought somewhat derogatory to his ministerial dignity; but his scruples were in the end overruled.

The country in this season is, of course, seen to disadvantage, but still it exhibits beauty enough to convince us what England must be when in leaf. The old gentleman's admiration of the increasing signs of what he called civilisation, as we approached London, became quite eloquent; but the first view of the city from Blackheath (which, by the bye, is a fine common, surrounded with villas and handsome houses) overpowered his faculties, and I shall never forget the impression it made on myself.

The sun was declined towards the horizon; vast masses of dark low-hung clouds were mingled with the smoky canopy, and the dome of St. Paul's, like the enormous idol of some terrible deity, throned amidst the smoke of sacrifices and magnificence, darkness, and mystery, presented altogether an object of vast sublimity. I felt touched with reverence, as if I was indeed approaching the city of THE HUMAN POWERS.

The distant view of Edinburgh is picturesque and romantic, but it affects a lower class of our associations. It is, compared to that of London, what the poem of the Seasons is with respect to Paradise Lost—the castellated descriptions of Walter Scott to the Darkness of Byron—the Sabbath of Grahame to the Robbers of Schiller. In the approach to Edinburgh, leisure and cheerfulness are on the road; large spaces of rural and pastoral nature are spread openly around, and mountains, and seas, and headlands, and vessels passing beyond them, going like those that die, we know not whither, while the sun is bright on their sails, and hope with them; but, in coming to this Babylon, there is an eager haste and a hurrying on from all quarters, towards that stupendous pile of gloom, through which no eye can penetrate; an unceasing sound, like the enginery of an earthquake at work, rolls from the heart of that profound and indefinable obscurity—sometimes a faint and yellow beam of the sun strikes here and there on the vast expanse of edifices; and churches, and holy asylums, are dimly seen lifting up their countless steeples and spires, like so many lightning rods to avert the wrath of Heaven.

The entrance to Edinburgh also awakens feelings of a more pleasing character. The rugged veteran aspect of the Old Town is agreeably contrasted with the bright smooth forehead of the New, and there is not such an overwhelming torrent of animal life, as to make you pause before venturing to stem it; the noises are not so deafening, and the occasional sound of a ballad-singer, or a Highland piper, varies and enriches the discords; but here, a multitudinous assemblage of harsh alarms, of selfish contentions, and of furious carriages, driven by a fierce and insolent race, shatter the very hearing, till you partake of the activity with which all seem as much possessed as if a general apprehension prevailed, that the great clock of Time would strike the doom-hour before their tasks were done. But I must stop, for the postman with his bell, like the betherel of some ancient 'borough's town' summoning to a burial, is in the street, and warns me to conclude.

—Yours,

ANDREW PRINGLE

LETTER 5

The Rev Dr Pringle to Mr Micklewham, Schoolmaster and Session Clerk,
Garnock

LONDON, 49 NORFOLK STREET, STRAND.

DEAR SIR—On the first Sunday forthcoming after the receiving hereof, you will not fail to recollect in the remembering prayer, that we return thanks for our safe arrival in London after a dangerous voyage. Well, indeed, is it ordained that we should pray for those who go down to the sea in ships, and do business on the great deep; for what me and mine have come through is unspeakable, and the hand of Providence was visibly manifested.

On the day of our embarkation at Leith, a fair wind took us onward at a blithe rate for some time; but in the course of that night the bridle of the tempest was slackened, and the curb of the billows loosened, and the ship reeled to and fro like a drunken man, and no one could stand therein. My wife and daughter lay at the point of death; Andrew Pringle, my son, also was prostrated with the grievous affliction; and the very soul within me was as if it would have been cast out of the body.

On the following day the storm abated, and the wind blew favourable; but towards the heel of the evening it again became vehement, and there was no help unto our distress. About midnight, however, it pleased HIM, whose breath is the tempest, to be more sparing with the whip of His displeasure on our poor bark, as she hirpled on in her toilsome journey through the waters; and I was enabled, through His strength, to lift my head from the pillow of sickness, and ascend the deck, where I thought of Noah looking out of the window in the ark, upon the face of the desolate flood, and of Peter walking on the sea; and I said to myself, it matters not where we are, for we can be in no place where Jehovah is not there likewise, whether it be on the waves of the ocean, or the mountain tops, or in the valley and shadow of death.

The third day the wind came contrary, and in the fourth, and the fifth, and the sixth, we were also sorely buffeted; but on the night of the sixth we entered the mouth of the river Thames, and on the morning of the seventh day of our departure, we cast anchor near a town called Gravesend, where, to our exceeding great joy, it pleased HIM, in whom alone there is salvation, to allow us once more to put our foot on the dry land.

When we had partaken of a repast, the first blessed with the blessing of an appetite, from the day of our leaving our native land, we got two vacancies in a stage-coach for my wife and daughter; but with Andrew Pringle, my son, I was obligated to mount aloft on the outside. I had some scruple of conscience about this, for I was afraid of my decorum. I met, however, with nothing but the height of discretion from the other outside passengers, although I jealoused that one of them was a light woman. Really I had no notion that the English were so civilised; they were so well bred, and the very duddiest of them spoke such a fine style of language, that when I looked around on the country, I thought myself in the land of Canaan. But it's extraordinary what a power of drink the coachmen drink, stopping and going into every change-house, and yet behaving themselves with the greatest sobriety. And then they are all so well dressed, which is no doubt owing to the poor rates. I am thinking, however, that for all they cry against them, the poor rates are but a small evil, since they keep the poor folk in such food and raiment, and out of the temptations to thievery; indeed, such a thing as a common beggar is not to be seen in this land, excepting here and there a sorner or a ne'er-do-weel.

When we had got to the outskirts of London, I began to be ashamed of the sin of high places, and would gladly have got into the inside of the coach, for fear of anybody knowing me; but although the multitude of by-goers was like the kirk scailing at the Sacrament, I saw not a kent face, nor one that took the least notice of my situation. At last we got to an inn, called The White Horse, Fetter-Lane, where we hired a hackney to take us to the lodgings provided for us here in Norfolk Street, by Mr Pawkie, the

Scotch solicitor, a friend of Andrew Pringle, my son. Now it was that we began to experience the sharpers of London; for it seems that there are divers Norfolk Streets. Ours was in the Strand (mind that when you direct), not very far from Fetter-Lane; but the hackney driver took us away to one afar off, and when we knocked at the number we thought was ours, we found ourselves at a house that should not be told. I was so mortified, that I did not know what to say; and when Andrew Pringle, my son, rebuked the man for the mistake, he only gave a cunning laugh, and said we should have told him whatna Norfolk Street we wanted. Andrew stormed at this—but I discerned it was all owing to our own inexperience, and put an end to the contention, by telling the man to take us to Norfolk Street in the Strand, which was the direction we had got. But when we got to the door, the coachman was so extortionate, that another hobbleshaw arose. Mrs Pringle had been told that, in such disputes, the best way of getting redress was to take the number of the coach; but, in trying to do so, we found it fastened on, and I thought the hackneyman would have gone by himself with laughter. Andrew, who had not observed what we were doing, when he saw us trying to take off the number, went like one demented, and paid the man, I cannot tell what, to get us out, and into the house, for fear we should have been mobbit.

I have not yet seen the colonel's agents, so can say nothing as to the business of our coming; for, landing at Gravesend, we did not bring our trunks with us, and Andrew has gone to the wharf this morning to get them, and, until we get them, we can go nowhere, which is the occasion of my writing so soon, knowing also how you and the whole parish would be anxious to hear what had become of us; and I remain, dear sir, your friend and pastor,

ZACHARIAH PRINGLE

On Saturday evening, Saunders Dickie, the Irvine postman, suspecting that this letter was from the Doctor, went with it himself on his own feet, to Mr Micklewham, although the distance is more than two miles; but Saunders, in addition to the customary twal pennies on the postage, had a dram for his pains. The next morning being wet, Mr Micklewham had not an opportunity of telling any of the parishioners in the churchyard of the Doctor's safe arrival, so that when he read out the request to return thanks (for he was not only schoolmaster and session-clerk, but also precentor), there was a murmur of pleasure diffused throughout the congregation, and the greatest curiosity was excited to know what the dangers were, from which their worthy pastor and his whole family had so thankfully escaped in their voyage to London; so that, when the service was over, the elders adjourned to the session-house to hear the letter read; and many of the heads of families, and other respectable parishioners, were admitted to the honours of the sitting, who all sympathised, with the greatest sincerity, in the sufferings which their minister and his family had endured. Mr Daff, however, was justly chided by Mr Craig, for rubbing his hands, and giving a sort of sniggering laugh, at the Doctor's sitting on high with a light woman. But even Mr Snodgrass was seen to smile at the incident of taking the number off the coach, the meaning of which none but himself seemed to understand.

When the epistle had been thus duly read, Mr Micklewham promised, for the satisfaction of some of the congregation, that he would get two or three copies made by the best writers in his school, to be handed about the parish, and Mr Icenor remarked, that truly it was a thing to be held in remembrance, for he had not heard of greater tribulation by the waters since the shipwreck of the Apostle Paul.

Chapter 3

The Legacy

Soon after the receipt of the letters which we had the pleasure of communicating in the foregoing chapter, the following was received from Mrs Pringle, and the intelligence it contains is so interesting and important, that we hasten to lay it before our readers

LETTER 6
Mrs Pringle to Miss Mally Glencairn

LONDON

MY DEAR MISS MALLY—You must not expect no particulars from me of our journey; but as Rachel is writing all the calamities that befell us to Bell Tod, you will, no doubt, hear of them. But all is nothing to my losses. I bought from the first hand, Mr Treddles the manufacturer, two pieces of muslin, at Glasgow, such a thing not being to be had on any reasonable terms here, where they get all their fine muslins from Glasgow and Paisley; and in the same bocks with them I packit a small crock of our ain excellent poudered butter, with a delap cheese, for I was told that such commodities are not to be had genuine in London. I likewise had in it a pot of marmlet, which Miss Jenny Macbride gave me at Glasgow, assuring me that it was not only dentice, but a curiosity among the English, and my best new bumbeseen goun in peper. Howsomever, in the nailing of the bocks, which I did carefully with my oun hands, one of the nails gaed in ajee, and broke the pot of marmlet, which, by the jolting of the ship, ruined the muslin, rottened the peper round the goun, which the shivers cut into more than twenty great holes. Over and above all, the crock with the butter was, no one can tell how, crackit, and the pickle lecking out, and mixing with the seerip of the marmlet, spoilt the cheese. In short, at the object I beheld, when the bocks was opened, I could have ta'en to the greeting; but I behaved with more composity on the occasion, than the Doctor thought it was in the power of nature to do. Howsomever, till I get a new goun and other things, I am obliged to be a prisoner; and as the Doctor does not like to go to the counting-house of the agents without me, I know not what is yet to be the consequence of our journey. But it would need to be something; for we pay four guineas and a half a week for our dry lodgings, which is at a degree more than the Doctor's whole stipend. As yet, for the cause of these misfortunes, I can give you no account of London; but there is, as everybody kens, little thrift in their housekeeping. We just buy our tea by the quarter a pound, and our loaf sugar, broken in a peper bag, by the pound, which would be a disgrace to a decent family in Scotland; and when we order dinner, we get no more than just serves, so that we have no cold meat if a stranger were coming by chance, which makes an unco bare house. The servan lasses I cannot abide; they dress better at their wark than ever

I did on an ordinaire week-day at the manse; and this very morning I saw madam, the kitchen lass, mounted on a pair of pattens, washing the plain stenes before the door; na, for that matter, a bare foot is not to be seen within the four walls of London, at the least I have na seen no such thing.

In the way of marketing, things are very good here, and considering, not dear; but all is sold by the licht weight, only the fish are awful; half a guinea for a cod's head, and no bigger than the drouds the cadgers bring from Ayr, at a shilling and eighteenpence apiece.

Tell Miss Nanny Eydent that I have seen none of the fashions as yet; but we are going to the burial of the auld king next week, and I'll write her a particular account how the leddies are dressed; but everybody is in deep mourning. Howsomever I have seen but little, and that only in a manner from the window; but I could not miss the opportunity of a frank that Andrew has got, and as he's waiting for the pen, you must excuse haste. From your sincere friend,

JANET PRINGLE

LETTER 7
Andrew Pringle, Esq , to the Rev Charles Snodgrass

LONDON

MY DEAR FRIEND—It will give you pleasure to hear that my father is likely to get his business speedily settled without any equivocation; and that all those prudential considerations which brought us to London were but the phantasms of our own inexperience. I use the plural, for I really share in the shame of having called in question the high character of the agents: it ought to have been warrantry enough that everything would be fairly adjusted. But I must give you some account of what has taken place, to illustrate our provincialism, and to give you some idea of the way of doing business in London.

After having recovered from the effects, and repaired some of the accidents of our voyage, we yesterday morning sallied forth, the Doctor, my mother, and your humble servant, in a hackney coach, to Broad Street, where the agents have their counting-house, and were ushered into a room among other legatees or clients, waiting for an audience of Mr Argent, the principal of the house.

I know not how it is, that the little personal peculiarities, so amusing to strangers, should be painful when we see them in those whom we love and esteem; but I own to you, that there was a something in the demeanour of the old folks on this occasion, that would have been exceedingly diverting to me, had my filial reverence been less sincere for them.

The establishment of Messrs Argent and Company is of vast extent, and has in it something even of a public magnitude; the number of the clerks, the assiduity of all, and the order that obviously prevails throughout, give at the first sight, an impression that bespeaks respect for the stability and integrity of the concern. When we had been seated about ten minutes, and my father's name taken to Mr Argent, an answer was brought, that he would see us as soon as possible; but we were obliged to wait at least half an hour more. Upon our being at last admitted, Mr Argent received us standing, and in an easy gentlemanly manner said to my father, 'You are the residuary legatee of the late Colonel Armour. I am sorry that you did not apprise me of this visit, that I might have been prepared to give the information you naturally desire; but if you will call here to-morrow at 12 o'clock, I shall then be able to satisfy you on the subject. Your lady, I presume?' he added, turning to my mother;

'Mrs Argent will have the honour of waiting on you; may I therefore beg the favour of your address?' Fortunately I was provided with cards, and having given him one, we found ourselves constrained, as it were, to take our leave. The whole interview did not last two minutes, and I never was less satisfied with myself. The Doctor and my mother were in the greatest anguish; and when we were again seated in the coach, loudly expressed their apprehensions. They were convinced that some stratagem was meditated; they feared that their journey to London would prove as little satisfactory as that of the Wrongheads, and that they had been throwing away good money in building castles in the air.

It had been previously arranged, that we were to return for my sister, and afterwards visit some of the sights; but the clouded visages of her father and mother darkened the very spirit of Rachel, and she largely shared in their fears. This, however, was not the gravest part of the business; for, instead of going to St. Paul's and the Tower as we had intended, my mother declared, that not one farthing would they spend more till they were satisfied that the expenses already incurred were likely to be reimbursed; and a Chancery suit, with all the horrors of wig and gown, floated in spectral haziness before their imagination. We sat down to a frugal meal, and although the remainder of a bottle of wine, saved from the preceding day, hardly afforded a glass apiece, the Doctor absolutely prohibited me from opening another.

This morning, faithful to the hour, we were again in Broad Street, with hearts knit up into the most peremptory courage; and, on being announced, were immediately admitted to Mr Argent. He received us with the same ease as in the first interview, and, after requesting us to be seated (which, by the way, he did not do yesterday, a circumstance that was ominously remarked), he began to talk on indifferent matters. I could see that a question, big with law and fortune, was gathering in the breasts both of the Doctor and my mother, and that they were in a state far from that of the blessed. But one of the clerks, before they had time to express their indignant suspicions, entered with a paper, and Mr Argent, having glanced it over, said to the Doctor—'I congratulate you, sir, on the amount of the colonel's fortune. I was not indeed aware before that he had died so rich. He has left about £120,000; seventy-five thousand of which is in the five per cents; the remainder in India bonds and other securities. The legacies appear to be inconsiderable, so that the residue to you, after paying them and the expenses of Doctors' Commons, will exceed a hundred thousand pounds.'

My father turned his eyes upwards in thankfulness. 'But,' continued Mr Argent, 'before the property can be transferred, it will be necessary for you to provide about four thousand pounds to pay the duty and other requisite expenses.' This was a thunderclap. 'Where can I get such a sum?' exclaimed my father, in a tone of pathetic simplicity. Mr Argent smiled and said, 'We shall manage that for you'; and having in the same moment pulled a bell, a fine young man entered, whom he introduced to us as his son, and desired him to explain what steps it was necessary for the Doctor to take. We accordingly followed Mr Charles Argent to his own room.

Thus, in less time than I have been in writing it, were we put in possession of all the information we required, and found those whom we feared might be interested to withhold the settlement, alert and prompt to assist us.

Mr Charles Argent is naturally more familiar than his father. He has a little dash of pleasantry in his manner, with a shrewd good-humoured fashionable air, that renders him soon an agreeable acquaintance. He entered with singular felicity at once into the character of the Doctor and my mother, and waggishly drolled, as if he did not understand them, in order, I could perceive, to draw out the simplicity of their apprehensions. He quite won the old lady's economical heart, by offering to frank her letters, for he is in Parliament. 'You have probably,' said he slyly, 'friends in the country, to whom you may be desirous of communicating the result of your journey to London; send your letters to me, and I will forward them, and any that you expect may also come under cover to my address, for postage is very expensive.'

As we were taking our leave, after being fully instructed in all the preliminary steps to be taken before the transfers of the funded property can be made, he asked me, in a friendly manner, to dine with him this evening, and I never accepted an invitation with more pleasure. I consider his acquaintance a most agreeable acquisition, and not one of the least of those advantages which this new opulence has put it in my power to attain. The incidents, indeed, of this day, have been all highly gratifying, and the new and brighter phase in which I have seen the mercantile character, as it is connected with the greatness and glory of my country—is in itself equivalent to an accession of useful knowledge. I can no longer wonder at the vast power which the British Government wielded during the late war, when I reflect that the method and promptitude of the house of Messrs Argent and Company is common to all the great commercial concerns from which the statesmen derived, as from so many reservoirs, those immense pecuniary supplies, which enabled them to beggar all the resources of a political despotism, the most unbounded, both in power and principle, of any tyranny that ever existed so long.—Yours, etc.,

ANDREW PRINGLE

Chapter 4

The Town

There was a great tea-drinking held in the Kirkgate of Irvine, at the house of Miss Mally Glencairn; and at that assemblage of rank, beauty, and fashion, among other delicacies of the season, several new-come-home Clyde skippers, roaring from Greenock and Port-Glasgow, were served up—but nothing contributed more to the entertainment of the evening than a proposal, on the part of Miss Mally, that those present who had received letters from the Pringles should read them for the benefit of the company. This was, no doubt, a preconcerted scheme between her and Miss Isabella Tod, to hear what Mr Andrew Pringle had said to his friend Mr Snodgrass, and likewise what the Doctor himself had indited to Mr Micklewham; some rumour having spread of the wonderful escapes and adventures of the family in their journey and voyage to London. Had there not been some prethought of this kind, it was not indeed probable, that both the helper and session-clerk of Garnock could have been there together, in a party, where it was an understood thing, that not only Whist and Catch Honours were to be played, but even obstreperous Birky itself, for the diversion of such of the company as were not used to gambling games. It was in consequence of what took place at this Irvine route, that we were originally led to think of collecting the letters.

LETTER 8
Miss Rachel Pringle to Miss Isabella Tod

LONDON.

MY DEAR BELL—It was my heartfelt intention to keep a regular journal of all our proceedings, from the sad day on which I bade a long adieu to my native shades-and I persevered with a constancy becoming our dear and youthful friendship, in writing down everything that I saw, either rare or beautiful, till the hour of our departure from Leith. In that faithful register of my feelings and reflections as a traveller, I described our embarkation at Greenock, on board the steamboat,—our sailing past Port-Glasgow, an insignificant town, with a steeple;—the stupendous rock of Dumbarton Castle, that Gibraltar of antiquity;—our landing at Glasgow;—my astonishment at the magnificence of that opulent metropolis of the muslin manufacturers; my brother's remark, that the punch-bowls on the roofs of the Infirmary, the Museum, and the Trades Hall, were emblematic of the universal estimation in which that celebrated mixture is held by all ranks and degrees—learned, commercial, and even medical, of the inhabitants;—our arrival at Edinburgh—my emotion on beholding the Castle, and the visionary lake which may be nightly seen from the windows of Princes Street, between the Old and New Town, reflecting the lights of the lofty city beyond—with a thousand other delightful and romantic circumstances, which render it no longer surprising that the Edinburgh folk should be, as they think themselves, the most accomplished people in the world. But, alas! from the moment I placed my foot on board that cruel vessel, of which the very idea is anguish, all thoughts were swallowed up in suffering—swallowed, did I say? Ah, my dear Bell, it was the odious reverse—but imagination alone can do justice to the subject. Not, however, to dwell on what is past, during the whole time of our passage from Leith, I was unable to think, far less to write; and, although there was a handsome young Hussar officer also a passenger, I could not even listen to the elegant compliments which he seemed disposed to offer by way of consolation, when he had got the better of his own sickness. Neither love nor valour can withstand the influence of that sea-demon. The interruption thus occasioned to my observations made me destroy my journal, and I have now to write to you only about London—only about London! What an expression for this human universe, as my brother calls it, as if my weak feminine pen were equal to the stupendous theme!

But, before entering on the subject, let me first satisfy the anxiety of your faithful bosom with respect to my father's legacy. All the accounts, I am happy to tell you, are likely to be amicably settled; but the exact amount is not known as yet, only I can see, by my brother's manner, that it is not less than we expected, and my mother speaks about sending me to a boarding-school to learn accomplishments. Nothing, however, is to be done until something is actually in hand. But what does it all avail to me? Here am I, a solitary being in the midst of this wilderness of mankind, far from your sympathising affection, with the dismal prospect before me of going a second time to school, and without the prospect of enjoying, with my own sweet companions, that light and bounding gaiety we were wont to share, in skipping from tomb to tomb in the breezy churchyard of Irvine, like butterflies in spring flying from flower to flower, as a Wordsworth or a Wilson would express it.

We have got elegant lodgings at present in Norfolk Street, but my brother is trying, with all his address, to get us removed to a more fashionable part of the town, which, if the accounts were once settled, I think will take place; and he proposes to hire a carriage for a whole month. Indeed, he has given hints about the saving that might be made by buying one of our own; but my mother shakes her head, and says,—'Andrew, dinna be carri't.' From all which it is very plain, though they don't allow me to know their secrets, that the legacy is worth the coming for. But to return to the lodgings;— we have what is called a first and second floor, a drawing-room, and three handsome bedchambers. The drawing-room is very elegant; and the carpet is the exact same pattern of the one in the dress-drawing-room of Eglintoun Castle. Our landlady is indeed a lady, and I am surprised how she should think of letting lodgings, for she dresses better, and wears finer lace, than ever I saw in Irvine. But I am interrupted.—I now resume my pen. We have just had a call from Mrs and Miss Argent, the wife and daughter of the colonel's man of business. They seem great people, and came in their own chariot, with two grand footmen behind; but they are pleasant and easy, and the object of their visit was to invite us to a family dinner to-morrow, Sunday. I hope we may become better acquainted; but the two livery servants make such a difference in our degrees, that I fear this is a vain expectation. Miss Argent was, however, very frank, and told me that she was herself only just come to London for the first time since she was a child, having been for the last seven years at a school in the country. I shall, however, be better able to say more about her in my next letter. Do not, however, be afraid that she shall ever supplant you in my heart. No, my dear friend, companion of my days of innocence, -that can never be. But this call from such persons of fashion looks as if the legacy had given us some consideration; so that I think my father and mother may as well let me know at once what my prospects are, that I might show you how disinterestedly and truly I am, my dear Bell, yours,

RACHEL PRINGLE

When Miss Isabella Tod had read the letter, there was a solemn pause for some time—all present knew something, more or less, of the fair writer; but a carriage, a carpet like the best at Eglintoun, a Hussar officer, and two footmen in livery, were phantoms of such high import, that no one could distinctly express the feelings with which the intelligence affected them. It was, however, unanimously agreed, that the Doctor's legacy had every symptom of being equal to what it was at first expected to be, namely, twenty thousand pounds;—a sum which, by some occult or recondite moral influence of the Lottery, is the common maximum, in popular estimation, of any extraordinary and indefinite windfall of fortune. Miss Becky Glibbans, from the purest motives of charity, devoutly wished that poor Rachel might be able to carry her full cup with a steady hand; and the Rev Mr Snodgrass, that so commendable an expression might not lose its edifying effect by any lighter talk, requested Mr Micklewham to read his letter from the Doctor.

LETTER 9
The Rev Z Pringle, D D , to Mr Micklewham, Schoolmaster and Session-Clerk of Garnock

LONDON

DEAR SIR—I have written by the post that will take this to hand, a letter to Banker M———y, at Irvine, concerning some small matters of money that I may stand in need of his opinion anent; and as there is a prospect now of a settlement of the legacy business, I wish you to take a step over to the banker, and he will give you ten pounds, which you will administer to the poor, by putting a twenty-shilling note in the plate on Sunday, as a public testimony from me of thankfulness for the hope that is before us; the other nine pounds you will quietly, and in your own canny way, divide after the following manner letting none of the partakers thereof know from what other hand than the Lord's the help comes, for, indeed, from whom but HIS does any good befall us!

You will give to auld Mizy Eccles ten shillings. She's a careful creature, and it will go as far with her thrift as twenty will do with Effy Hopkirk; so you will give Effy twenty. Mrs Binnacle, who lost her husband, the sailor, last winter, is, I am sure, with her two sickly bairns, very ill off; I would therefore like if you will lend her a note, and ye may put half-a-crown in the hand of each of the poor weans for a playock, for she's a proud spirit, and will bear much before she complain. Thomas Dowy has been long unable to do a turn of work, so you may give him a note too. I promised that donsie body, Willy Shachle, the betherel, that when I got my legacy, he should get a guinea, which would be more to him than if the colonel had died at home, and he had had the howking of his grave; you may therefore, in the meantime, give Willy a crown, and be sure to warn him well no to get fou with it, for I'll be very angry if he does. But what in this matter will need all your skill, is the giving of the remaining five pounds to auld Miss Betty Peerie; being a gentlewoman both by blood and education, she's a very slimmer affair to handle in a doing of this kind. But I am persuaded she's in as great necessity as many that seem far poorer, especially since the muslin flowering has gone so down. Her bits of brats are sairly worn, though she keeps out an apparition of gentility. Now, for all this trouble, I will give you an account of what we have been doing since my last.

When we had gotten ourselves made up in order, we went, with Andrew Pringle, my son, to the counting-house, and had a satisfactory vista of the residue; but it will be some time before things can be settled—indeed, I fear, not for months to come—so that I have been thinking, if the parish was pleased with Mr Snodgrass, it might be my duty to my people to give up to him my stipend, and let him be appointed not only helper, but successor likewise. It would not be right of me to give the manse, both because he's a young and inexperienced man, and cannot, in the course of nature, have got into the way of visiting the sick-beds of the frail, which is the main part of a pastor's duty, and likewise, because I wish to die, as I have lived, among my people. But, when all's settled, I will know better what to do.

When we had got an inkling from Mr Argent of what the colonel has left, — and I do assure you, that money is not to be got, even in the way of legacy, without anxiety,—Mrs Pringle and I consulted together, and resolved that it was our first duty, as a token of our gratitude to the Giver of all Good, to make our first outlay to the poor. So, without saying a word either to Rachel, or to Andrew Pringle, my son, knowing that there was a daily worship in the Church of England, we slipped out of the house by ourselves, and, hiring a hackney conveyance, told the driver thereof to drive us to the high church of St. Paul's. This was out of no respect to the pomp and pride of prelacy, but to Him before whom both pope and presbyter are equal, as they are seen through the merits of Christ Jesus. We had taken a gold guinea in our hand, but there was no broad at the door; and, instead of a venerable elder, lending sanctity to his office by reason of his age, such as we see in the effectual institutions of our own national church—the door was kept by a young man, much more like a writer's whippersnapper-clerk, than one qualified to fill that station, which good King David would have preferred to dwelling in tents of sin. However, we were not come to spy the nakedness of the land, so we went up the outside stairs, and I asked at him for the plate;

'Plate!' says he; 'why, it's on the altar!' I should have known this—the custom of old being to lay the offerings on the altar, but I had forgot; such is the force, you see, of habit, that the Church of England is not so well reformed and purged as ours is from the abominations of the leaven of idolatry. We were then stepping forward, when he said to me, as sharply as if I was going to take an advantage, 'You must pay here.' 'Very well, wherever it is customary,' said I, in a meek manner, and gave him the guinea. Mrs Pringle did the same. 'I cannot give you change,' cried he, with as little decorum as if we had been paying at a playhouse. 'It makes no odds,' said I; 'keep it all.' Whereupon he was so converted by the mammon of iniquity, that he could not be civil enough, he thought-but conducted us in, and showed us the marble monuments, and the French colours that were taken in the war, till the time of worship—nothing could surpass his discretion.

At last the organ began to sound, and we went into the place of worship; but oh, Mr Micklewham, yon is a thin kirk. There was not a hearer forby Mrs Pringle and me, saving and excepting the relics of popery that assisted at the service. What was said, I must, however, in verity confess, was not far from the point. But it's still a comfort to see that prelatical usurpations are on the downfall; no wonder that there is no broad at the door to receive the collection for the poor, when no congregation entereth in. You may, therefore, tell Mr Craig, and it will gladden his heart to hear the tidings, that the great Babylonian madam is now, indeed, but a very little cutty.

On our return home to our lodgings, we found Andrew Pringle, my son, and Rachel, in great consternation about our absence. When we told them that we had been at worship, I saw they were both deeply affected; and I was pleased with my children, the more so, as you know I have had my doubts that Andrew Pringle's principles have not been strengthened by the reading of the Edinburgh Review Nothing more passed at that time, for we were disturbed by a Captain Sabre that came up with us in the smack, calling to see how we were after our journey; and as he was a civil well-bred young man, which I marvel at, considering he's a Hussar dragoon, we took a coach, and went to see the lions, as he said; but, instead of taking us to the Tower of London, as I expected, he ordered the man to drive us round the town. In our way through the city he showed us the Temple Bar, where Lord Kilmarnock's head was placed after the Rebellion, and pointed out the Bank of England and Royal Exchange. He said the steeple of the Exchange was taken down shortly ago—and that the late improvements at the Bank were very grand. I remembered having read in the Edinburgh Advertiser, some years past, that there was a great deal said in Parliament about the state of the Exchange, and the condition of the Bank, which I could never thoroughly understand. And, no doubt, the taking down of an old building, and the building up of a new one so near together, must, in such a crowded city as this, be not only a great detriment to business, but dangerous to the community at large.

After we had driven about for more than two hours, and neither seen lions nor any other curiosity, but only the outside of houses, we returned home, where we found a copperplate card left by Mr Argent, the colonel's agent, with the name of his private dwelling-house. Both me and Mrs Pringle were confounded at the sight of this thing, and could not but think that it prognosticated no good; for we had seen the gentleman himself in the forenoon. Andrew Pringle, my son, could give no satisfactory reason for such an extraordinary manifestation of anxiety to see us; so that, after sitting on thorns at our dinner, I thought that we should see to the bottom of the business. Accordingly, a hackney was summoned to the door, and me and Andrew Pringle, my son, got into it, and told the man to drive to second in the street where Mr Argent lived, and which was the number of his house. The man got up, and away we went; but, after he had driven an awful time, and stopping and inquiring at different places, he said there was no such house as Second's in the street; whereupon Andrew Pringle, my son, asked him what he meant, and the man said that he supposed it was one Second's Hotel, or Coffee house, that we wanted. Now, only think of the craftiness of the ne'er-da-weel; it was with some difficulty that I could get him to understand, that second was just as good as number two; for Andrew Pringle, my son, would not interfere, but lay back in the coach, and was like to split his sides at my confabulating with the hackney man. At long and length we got to the house, and were admitted to Mr Argent, who was sitting by himself in his library reading, with a plate of oranges, and two decanters with wine before him. I explained to him, as well as I could, my surprise and anxiety at seeing his card, at which he smiled, and said, it was merely a sort of practice that had come into fashion of late years, and that, although we had been at his counting. house in the morning, he considered it requisite that he should call on his return from the city. I made the best excuse I could for the mistake; and the servant having placed glasses on the table, we were invited to take wine. But I was grieved to think that so respectable a man should have had the bottles before him by himself, the more especially as he said his wife and daughters had gone to a party, and that he did not much like such sort of things. But for all that, we found him a wonderful conversible man; and Andrew Pringle, my son, having read all the new books put out at Edinburgh, could speak with him on any subject. In the course of conversation they touched upon politick economy, and Andrew Pringle, my son, in speaking about cash in the Bank of England, told him what I had said concerning the alterations of the Royal Exchange steeple, with which Mr Argent seemed greatly pleased, and jocosely proposed as a toast,—'May the country never suffer more from the alterations in the Exchange, than the taking down of the steeple.' But as Mrs Pringle is wanting to send a bit line under the same frank to her cousin, Miss Mally Glencairn, I must draw to a conclusion, assuring you, that I am, dear sir, your sincere friend and pastor,

ZACHARIAH PRINGLE

The impression which this letter made on the auditors of Mr Micklewham was highly favourable to the Doctor—all bore testimony to his benevolence and piety; and Mrs Glibbans expressed, in very loquacious terms, her satisfaction at the neglect to which prelacy was consigned. The only, person who seemed to be affected by other than the most sedate feelings on the occasion was the Rev Mr Snodgrass, who was observed to smile in a very unbecoming manner at some parts of the Doctor's account of his reception at St. Paul's. Indeed, it was apparently with the utmost difficulty that the young clergyman could restrain himself from giving liberty to his risible faculties. It is really surprising how differently the same thing affects different people. 'The Doctor and Mrs. Pringle giving a guinea at the door of St Paul's for the poor need not make folk laugh,' said Mrs Gibbans; 'for is it not written, that whosoever giveth to the poor lendeth to the Lord?' 'True, my dear madam,' replied Mr Snodgrass, 'but the Lord to whom our friends in this case gave their money is the Lord Bishop of London; all the collection made at the doors of St. Paul's Cathedral is, I understand, a perquisite of the Bishop's.' In this the reverend gentleman was not very correctly informed, for, in the first place, it is not a collection, but an exaction; and, in the second place, it is only sanctioned by the Bishop, who allows the inferior clergy to share the gains among themselves. Mrs Glibbans, however, on hearing his explanation, exclaimed, 'Gude be about us!' and pushing back her chair with a bounce, streaking down her gown at the same time with both her hands, added, 'No wonder that a judgment is upon the land, when we hear of money-changers in the temple.' Miss Mally Glencairn, to appease her gathering wrath and holy indignation, said facetiously, 'Na, na, Mrs Glibbans, ye forget, there was nae changing of money there. The man took the whole guineas. But not to make a controversy on the subject, Mr. Snodgrass will now let us hear what Andrew Pringle, "my son," has said to him' :-And the reverend gentleman read the following letter with due circumspection, and in his best manner

LETTER 10
Andrew Pringle, Esq , to the Reverend Charles Snodgrass

MY DEAR FRIEND—I have heard it alleged, as the observation of a great traveller, that the manners of the higher classes of society throughout Christendom are so much alike, that national peculiarities among them are scarcely perceptible. This is not correct; the differences between those of London and Edinburgh are to me very striking. It is not that they talk and perform the little etiquettes of social intercourse differently; for, in these respects, they are apparently as similar as it is possible for imitation to make them; but the difference to which I refer is an indescribable something, which can only be compared to peculiarities of accent. They both speak the same language; perhaps in classical purity of phraseology the fashionable Scotchman is even superior to the Englishman; but there is a flatness of tone in his accent—a lack of what the musicians call expression, which gives a local and provincial effect to his conversation, however, in other respects, learned and intelligent. It is so with his manners; he conducts himself with equal ease, self-possession, and discernment, but the flavour of the metropolitan style is wanting. I have been led to make these remarks by what I noticed in the guests whom I met on Friday at young Argent's. It was a small party, only five strangers; but they seemed to be all particular friends of our host, and yet none of them appeared to be on any terms of intimacy with each other. In Edinburgh, such a party would have been at first a little cold; each of the guests would there have paused to estimate the characters of the several strangers before committing himself with any topic of conversation. But here, the circumstance of being brought together by a mutual friend, produced at once the purest gentlemanly confidence; each, as it were, took it for granted, that the persons whom he had come among were men of education and good-breeding, and, without deeming it at all necessary that he should know something of their respective political and philosophical principles, before venturing to speak on such subjects, discussed frankly, and as things unconnected with party feelings, incidental occurrences which, in Edinburgh, would have been avoided as calculated to awaken animosities.

But the most remarkable feature of the company, small as it was, consisted of the difference in the condition and character of the guests. In Edinburgh the landlord, with the scrupulous care of a herald or genealogist, would, for a party, previously unacquainted with each other, have chosen his guests as nearly as possible from the same rank of life; the London host had paid no respect to any such consideration—all the strangers were as dissimilar in fortune, profession, connections, and politics, as any four men in the class of gentlemen could well be. I never spent a more delightful evening.

The ablest, the most eloquent, and the most elegant man present, without question, was the son of a saddler. No expense had been spared on his education. His father, proud of his talents, had intended him for a seat in Parliament; but Mr. T——— himself prefers the easy enjoyments of private life, and has kept himself aloof from politics and parties. Were I to form an estimate of his qualifications to excel in public speaking, by the clearness and beautiful propriety of his colloquial language, I should conclude that he was still destined to perform a distinguished part. But he is content with the liberty of a private station, as a spectator only, and, perhaps, in that he shows his wisdom; for undoubtedly such men are not cordially received among hereditary statesmen, unless they evince a certain suppleness of principle, such as we have seen in the conduct of more than one political adventurer.

The next in point of effect was young C——— G———. He evidently languished under the influence of indisposition, which, while it added to the natural gentleness of his manners, diminished the impression his accomplishments would otherwise have made. I was greatly struck with the modesty with which he offered his opinions, and could scarcely credit that he was the same individual whose eloquence in Parliament is by many compared even to Mr Canning's, and whose firmness of principle is so universally acknowledged, that no one ever suspects him of being liable to change. You may have heard of his poem 'On the Restoration of Learning in the East,' the most magnificent prize essay that the English Universities have produced for many years. The passage in which he describes the talents, the researches, and learning of Sir William Jones, is worthy of the imagination of Burke; and yet, with all this oriental splendour of fancy, he has the reputation of being a patient and methodical man of business. He looks, however, much more like a poet or a student, than an orator and a statesman; and were statesmen the sort of personages which the spirit of the age attempts to represent them, I, for one, should lament that a young man, possessed of so many amiable qualities, all so tinted with the bright lights of a fine enthusiasm, should ever have been removed from the moon-lighted groves and peaceful cloisters of Magdalen College, to the lamp-smelling passages and factious debates of St. Stephen's Chapel. Mr G—— certainly belongs to that high class of gifted men who, to the honour of the age, have redeemed the literary character from the charge of unfitness for the concerns of public business; and he has shown that talents for affairs of state, connected with class-fellows would have the world to believe. When I contrast the quiet unobtrusive development of Mr G——'s character with that bustling and obstreperous elbowing into notice of some of those to whom the Edinburgh Review owes half its fame, and compare the pure and steady lustre of his elevation, to the rocket-like aberrations and perturbed blaze of their still uncertain course, I cannot but think that we have overrated, if not their ability, at least their wisdom in the management of public affairs.

The third of the party was a little Yorkshire baronet. He was formerly in Parliament, but left it, as he says, on account of its irregularities, and the bad hours it kept. He is a Whig, I understand, in politics, and indeed one might guess as much by looking at him; for I have always remarked, that your Whigs have something odd and particular about them. On making the same sort of remark to Argent, who, by the way, is a high ministerial man, he observed, the thing was not to be wondered at, considering that the Whigs are exceptions to the generality of mankind, which naturally accounts for their being always in the minority. Mr T——, the saddler's son, who overheard us, said slyly, 'That it might be so; but if it be true that the wise are few compared to the multitude of the foolish, things would be better managed by the minority than as they are at present.'

The fourth guest was a stock-broker, a shrewd compound, with all charity be it spoken, of knavery and humour. He is by profession an epicure, but I suspect his accomplishments in that capacity are not very well founded; I would almost say, judging by the evident traces of craft and dissimulation in his physiognomy, that they have been assumed as part of the means of getting into good company, to drive the more earnest trade of money-making. Argent evidently understood his true character, though he treated him with jocular familiarity. I thought it a fine example of the intellectual tact and superiority of T——, that he seemed to view him with dislike and contempt. But I must not give you my reasons for so thinking, as you set no value on my own particular philosophy; besides, my paper tells me, that I have only room left to say, that it would be difficult in Edinburgh to bring such a party together; and yet they affect there to have a metropolitan character. In saying this, I mean only with reference to manners; the methods of behaviour in each of the company were precisely similar—there was no eccentricity, but only that distinct and decided individuality which nature gives, and which no acquired habits can change. Each, however, was the representative of a class; and Edinburgh has no classes exactly of the same kind as those to which they belonged.—Yours truly,

ANDREW PRINGLE

Just as Mr Snodgrass concluded the last sentence, one of the Clyde skippers, who had fallen asleep, gave such an extravagant snore, followed by a groan, that it set the whole company a-laughing, and interrupted the critical strictures which would otherwise have been made on Mr Andrew Pringle's epistle. 'Damn it,' said he, 'I thought myself in a fog, and could not tell whether the land ahead was Plada or the Lady Isle.' Some of the company thought the observation not inapplicable to what they had been hearing.

Miss Isabella Tod then begged that Miss Mally, their hostess, would favour the company with Mrs Pringle's communication. To this request that considerate maiden ornament of the Kirkgate deemed it necessary, by way of preface to the letter, to say, 'Ye a' ken that Mrs Pringle's a managing woman, and ye maunna expect any metaphysical philosophy from her.' In the meantime, having taken the letter from her pocket, and placed her spectacles on that functionary of the face which was destined to wear spectacles, she began as follows

LETTER 11
Mrs Pringle to Miss Mally Glencairn

MY DEAR MISS MALLY—We have been at the counting house, and gotten a sort of a satisfaction; what the upshot may be, I canna take it upon myself to prognosticate; but when the waur comes to the worst, I think that baith Rachel and Andrew will have a nest egg, and the Doctor and me may sleep sound on their account, if the nation doesna break, as the argle-barglers in the House of Parliament have been threatening: for all the cornal's fortune is sunk at present in the pesents. Howsomever, it's our notion, when the legacies are paid off, to lift the money out of the funds, and place it a good interest on hairetable securitie. But ye will hear aften from us, before things come to that, for the delays, and the goings, and the comings in this town of London are past all expreshon.

As yet, we have been to see no fairlies, except going in a coach from one part of the toun to another; but the Doctor and me was at the he-kirk of Saint Paul's for a purpose that I need not tell you, as it was adoing with the right hand what the left should not know. I couldna say that I had there great pleasure, for the preacher was very cauldrife, and read every word, and then there was such a beggary of popish prelacy, that it was compassionate to a Christian to see.

We are to dine at Mr Argent's, the cornal's hadgint, on Sunday, and me and Rachel have been getting something for the okasion. Our landlady, Mrs Sharkly, has recommended us to ane of the most fashionable millinders in London, who keeps a grand shop in Cranburn Alla, and she has brought us arteecles to look at; but I was surprised for I thought them of a very inferior quality, which she said was because they were not made for no costomer, but for the public.

The Argents seem as if they would be discreet people, which, to us who are here in the jaws of jeopardy, would be a great confort—for I am no overly satisfeet with many things. What would ye think of buying coals by the stimpert, for anything that I know, and then setting up the poker afore the ribs, instead of blowing with the bellies to make the fire burn? I was of a pinion that the Englishers were naturally wasterful; but I can ashure you this is no the case at all—and I am beginning to think that the way of leeving from hand to mouth is great frugality, when ye consider that all is left in the logive hands of uncercumseezed servans.

But what gives me the most concern at this time is one Captain Sabre of the Dragoon Hozars, who come up in the smak with us from Leith, and is looking more after our Rachel than I could wish, now that she might set her cap to another sort of object. But he's of a respectit family, and the young lad himself is no to be despisid; howsomever, I never likit officir-men of any description, and yet the thing that makes me look down on the captain is all owing to the cornal, who was an officer of the native poors of India, where the pay must indeed have been extraordinar, for who ever heard either of cornal, or any officer whomsoever, making a hundred thousand pounds in our regiments? no that I say the cornal has left so meikle to us.

Tell Mrs Glibbans that I have not heard of no sound preacher as yet in London—the want of which is no doubt the great cause of the crying sins of the place. What would she think to hear of newspapers selling by tout of horn on the Lord's day? and on the Sabbath night, the change-houses are more throng than on the Saturday! I am told, but as yet I cannot say that I have seen the evil myself with my own eyes, that in the summer time there are tea-gardens, where the tradesmen go to smoke their pipes of tobacco, and to entertain their wives and children, which can be nothing less than a bringing of them to an untimely end. But you will be surprised to hear, that no such thing as whusky is to be had in the public-houses, where they drink only a dead sort of beer; and that a bottle of true jennyinn London porter is rarely to be seen in the whole town—all kinds of piple getting their porter in pewter cans, and a laddie calls for in the morning to take away what has been yoused over night. But what I most miss is the want of creem. The milk here is just skimm, and I doot not, likewise well watered—as for the water, a drink of clear wholesome good water is not within the bounds of London; and truly, now may I say, that I have learnt what the blessing of a cup of cold water is.

Tell Miss Nanny Eydent, that the day of the burial is now settled, when we are going to Windsor Castle to see the precesson-and that, by the end of the wick, she may expect the fashions from me, with all the particulars. Till then, I am, my dear Miss Mally, your friend and well-wisher,

JANET PRINGLE

Noto Beny—Give my kind compliments to Mrs Glibbans, and let her know, that I will, after Sunday, give her an account of the state of the Gospel in London.

Miss Mally paused when she had read the letter, and it was unanimously agreed, that Mrs Pringle gave a more full account of London than either father, son, or daughter.

By this time the night was far advanced, and Mrs Glibbans was rising to go away, apprehensive, as she observed, that they were going to bring 'the carts' into the room. Upon Miss Mally, however, assuring her that no such transgression was meditated, but that she intended to treat them with a bit nice Highland mutton ham, and eggs, of her own laying, that worthy pillar of the Relief Kirk consented to remain.

It was past eleven o'clock when the party broke up; Mr Snodgrass and Mr Micklewham walked home together, and as they were crossing the Red Burn Bridge, at the entrance of Eglintoun Wood,—a place well noted from ancient times for preternatural appearances, Mr Micklewham declared that he thought he heard something purring among the bushes; upon which Mr Snodgrass made a jocose observation, stating, that it could be nothing but the effect of Lord North's strong ale in his head; and we should add, by way of explanation, that the Lord North here spoken of was Willy Grieve, celebrated in Irvine for the strength and flavour of his brewing, and that, in addition to a plentiful supply of his best, Miss Mally had entertained them with tamarind punch, constituting a natural cause adequate to produce all the preternatural purring that terrified the dominie.

Chapter 5

The Royal Funeral

Tam Glen having, in consequence of the exhortations of Mr Micklewham, and the earnest entreaties of Mr Daff, backed by the pious animadversions of the rigidly righteous Mr Craig, confessed a fault, and acknowledged an irregular marriage with Meg Milliken, their child was admitted to church privileges. But before the day of baptism, Mr Daff, who thought Tam had given but sullen symptoms of penitence, said, to put him in better humour with his fate,—'Noo, Tam, since ye hae beguiled us of the infare, we maun mak up for't at the christening; so I'll speak to Mr Snodgrass to bid the Doctor's friens and acquaintance to the ploy, that we may get as meikle amang us as will pay for the bairn's baptismal frock.'

Mr Craig, who was present, and who never lost an opportunity of testifying, as he said, his 'discountenance of the crying iniquity,' remonstrated with Mr Daff on the unchristian nature of the proposal, stigmatising it with good emphasis 'as a sinful nourishing of carnality in his day and generation.' Mr Micklewham, however, interfered, and said, 'It was a matter of weight and concernment, and therefore it behoves you to consult Mr Snodgrass on the fitness of the thing. For if the thing itself is not fit and proper, it cannot expect his countenance; and, on that account, before we reckon on his compliance with what Mr Daff has propounded, we should first learn whether he approves of it at all.' Whereupon the two elders and the session-clerk adjourned to the manse, in which Mr. Snodgrass, during the absence of the incumbent, had taken up his abode.

The heads of the previous conversation were recapitulated by Mr Micklewham, with as much brevity as was consistent with perspicuity; and the matter being duly digested by Mr Snodgrass, that orthodox young man—as Mrs Glibbans denominated him, on hearing him for the first time—declared that the notion of a pay-christening was a benevolent and kind thought: 'For, is not the order to increase and multiply one of the first commands in the Scriptures of truth?' said Mr Snodgrass, addressing himself to Mr Craig. 'Surely, then, when children are brought into the world, a great law of our nature has been fulfilled, and there is cause for rejoicing and gladness! And is it not an obligation imposed upon all Christians, to welcome the stranger, and to feed the hungry, and to clothe the naked; and what greater stranger can there be than a helpless babe? Who more in need of sustenance than the infant, that knows not the way even to its mother's bosom? And whom shall we clothe, if we do not the wailing innocent, that the hand of Providence places in poverty and nakedness before us, to try, as it were, the depth of our Christian principles, and to awaken the sympathy of our humane feelings?'

Mr Craig replied, 'It's a' very true and sound what Mr Snodgrass has observed; but Tam Glen's wean is neither a stranger, nor hungry, nor naked, but a sturdy brat, that has been rinning its lane for mair than sax weeks.'

'Ah!' said Mr Snodgrass familiarly, 'I fear, Mr Craig, ye're a Malthusian in your heart.' The sanctimonious elder was thunderstruck at the word. Of many a various shade and modification of sectarianism he had heard, but the Malthusian heresy was new to his ears, and awful to his conscience, and he begged Mr Snodgrass to tell him in what it chiefly consisted, protesting his innocence of that, and of every erroneous doctrine.

Mr Snodgrass happened to regard the opinions of Malthus on Population as equally contrary to religion and nature, and not at all founded in truth. 'It is evident, that the reproductive principle in the earth and vegetables, and all things and animals which constitute the means of subsistence, is much more vigorous than in man. It may be therefore affirmed, that the multiplication of the means of subsistence is an effect of the multiplication of population, for the one is augmented in quantity, by the skill and care of the other,' said Mr Snodgrass, seizing with avidity this opportunity of stating what he thought on the subject, although his auditors were but the session-clerk, and two elders of a country parish. We cannot pursue the train of his argument, but we should do injustice to the philosophy of Malthus, if we suppressed the observation which Mr Daff made at the conclusion. 'Gude safe's!' said the good-natured elder, 'if it's true that we breed faster than the Lord provides for us, we maun drown the poor folks' weans like kittlings.'

'Na, na!' exclaimed Mr Craig, 'ye're a' out, neighbour; I see now the utility of church-censures.' 'True!' said Mr Micklewham; 'and the ordination of the stool of repentance, the horrors of which, in the opinion of the fifteen Lords at Edinburgh, palliated child-murder, is doubtless a Malthusian institution.' But Mr Snodgrass put an end to the controversy, by fixing a day for the christening, and telling he would do his best to procure a good collection, according to the benevolent suggestion of Mr Daff. To this cause we are indebted for the next series of the Pringle correspondence; for, on the day appointed, Miss Mally Glencairn, Miss Isabella Tod, Mrs Glibbans and her daughter Becky, with Miss Nanny Eydent, together with other friends of the minister's family, dined at the manse, and the conversation being chiefly about the concerns of the family, the letters were produced and read.

LETTER 12
Andrew Pringle, Esq , to the Rev Charles Snodgrass

WINDSOR, CASTLE-INN

MY DEAR FRIEND—I have all my life been strangely susceptible of pleasing impressions from public spectacles where great crowds are assembled. This, perhaps, you say, is but another way of confessing, that, like the common vulgar, I am fond of sights and shows. It may be so, but it is not from the pageants that I derive my enjoyment. A multitude, in fact, is to me as it were a strain of music, which, with an irresistible and magical influence, calls up from unknown abyss of the feelings new combinations of fancy which, though vague and obscure, as those nebulae of light that astronomers have supposed to be the rudiments of unformed stars, afterwards become distinct and brilliant acquisitions. In a crowd, I am like the somnambulist in the highest degree of the luminous crisis, when it is said a new world is unfolded to his contemplation, wherein all things have an intimate affinity with the state of man, and yet bear no resemblance to the objects that address themselves to his corporeal faculties. This delightful experience, as it may be called, I have enjoyed this evening, to an exquisite degree, at the funeral of the king; but, although the whole succession of incidents is indelibly imprinted on my recollection, I am still so much affected by the emotion excited, as to be incapable of conveying to you any intelligible description of what I saw. It was indeed a scene witnessed through the medium of the feelings, and the effect partakes of the nature of a dream.

I was within the walls of an ancient castle,

> *So old as if they had for ever stood,*
> *So strong as if they would for ever stand,*

and it was almost midnight. The towers, like the vast spectres of departed ages, raised their embattled heads to the skies, monumental witnesses of the strength and antiquity of a great monarchy. A prodigious multitude filled the courts of that venerable edifice, surrounding on all sides a dark embossed structure, the sarcophagus, as it seemed to me at the moment, of the heroism of chivalry.

'A change came o'er the spirit of my dream,' and I beheld the scene suddenly illuminated, and the blaze of torches, the glimmering of arms, and warriors and horses, while a mosaic of human faces covered like a pavement the courts. A deep low under sound pealed from a distance; in the same moment, a trumpet answered with a single mournful note from the stateliest and darkest portion of the fabric, and it was whispered in every ear, 'It is coming.' Then an awful cadence of solemn music, that affected the heart like silence, was heard at intervals, and a numerous retinue of grave and venerable men,

> *The fathers of their time,*
> *Those mighty master spirits, that withstood*
> *The fall of monarchies, and high upheld*
> *Their country's standard, glorious in the storm,*

passed slowly before me, bearing the emblems and trophies of a king. They were as a series of great historical events, and I beheld behind them, following and followed, an awful and indistinct image, like the vision of Job. It moved on, and I could not discern the form thereof but there were honours and heraldries, and sorrow, and silence, and I heard the stir of a profound homage performing within the breasts of all the witnesses. But I must not indulge myself farther on this subject. I cannot hope to excite in you the emotions with which I was so profoundly affected. In the visible objects of the funeral of George the Third there was but little magnificence; all its sublimity was derived from the trains of thought and currents of feeling, which the sight of so many illustrious characters, surrounded by circumstances associated with the greatness and antiquity of the kingdom, was necessarily calculated to call forth. In this respect, however, it was perhaps the sublimest spectacle ever witnessed in this island; and I am sure, that I cannot live so long as ever again to behold another, that will equally interest me to the same depth and extent.—Yours,

ANDREW PRINGLE

We should ill perform the part of faithful historians, did we omit to record the sentiments expressed by the company on this occasion. Mrs Glibbans, whose knowledge of the points of orthodoxy had not their equal in the three adjacent parishes, roundly declared, that Mr Andrew Pringle's letter was nothing but a peesemeal of clishmaclavers; that there was no sense in it; and that it was just like the writer, a canary idiot, a touch here and a touch there, without anything to in the shape of cordiality or satisfaction.

Miss Isabella Tod answered this objection with that sweetness of manner and virgin diffidence, which so well becomes a youthful member of the establishment, controverting the dogmas of a stoop of the Relief persuasion, by saying, that she thought Mr Andrew had shown a fine sensibility. 'What is sensibility without judgment,' cried her adversary, 'but a thrashing in the water, and a raising of bells? Couldna the fallow, without a' his parleyvoos, have said, that such and such was the case, and that the Lord giveth and the Lord taketh away ? -but his clouds, and his spectres, and his visions of Job!—Oh, an he would but think like Job!—Oh, an he would but think like the patient man!—and was obliged to claut his flesh with a bit of a broken crock, we might have some hope of repentance unto life. But Andrew Pringle, he's a gone dick; I never had comfort or expectation of the free-thinker, since I heard that he was infected with the blue and yellow calamity of the Edinburgh Review; in which, I am credibly told, it is set forth, that women have nae souls, but only a gut, and a gaw, and a gizzard, like a pigeon-dove, or a raven-crow, or any other outcast and abominated quadruped.' Here Miss Mally Glencairn interposed her effectual mediation, and said, 'It is very true that Andrew deals in the diplomatics of obscurity; but it's well known that he has a nerve for genius, and that, in his own way, he kens the loan from the crown of the causeway, as well as the duck does the midden from the adle dib.' To this proverb, which we never heard before, a learned friend, whom we consulted on the subject, has enabled us to state, that middens were formerly of great magnitude, and often of no less antiquity in the west of Scotland; in so much, that the Trongate of Glasgow owes all its spacious grandeur to them. It being within the recollection of persons yet living, that the said magnificent street was at one time an open road, or highway, leading to the Trone, or market-cross, with thatched houses on each side, such as may still be seen in the pure and immaculate royal borough of Rutherglen; and that before each house stood a luxuriant midden, by the removal of which, in the progress of modern degeneracy, the stately architecture of Argyle Street was formed. But not to insist at too great a length on such topics of antiquarian lore, we shall now insert Dr Pringle's account of the funeral, and which, patly enough, follows our digression concerning the middens and magnificence of Glasgow, as it contains an authentic anecdote of a manufacturer from that city, drinking champaign at the king's dirgie.

LETTER 13
The Rev Z Pringle D D to Mr Micklewham, Schoolmaster and Session Clerk of Garnock

LONDON

DEAR SIR—I have received your letter, and it is a great pleasure to me to hear that my people were all so much concerned at our distress in the Leith smack; but what gave me the most contentment was the repentance of Tam Glen. I hope, poor fellow, he will prove a good husband; but I have my doubts; for the wife has really but a small share of common sense, and no married man can do well unless his wife will let him. I am, however, not overly pleased with Mr Craig on the occasion, for he should have considered frail human nature, and accepted of poor Tam's confession of a fault, and allowed the bairn to be baptized without any more ado. I think honest Mr Daff has acted like himself and I trust and hope there will be a great gathering at the christening, and, that my mite may not be wanting, you will slip in a guinea note when the dish goes round, but in such a manner, that it may not be jealoused from whose hand it comes.

Since my last letter, we have been very thrang in the way of seeing the curiosities of London; but I must go on regular, and tell you all, which, I think, it is my duty to do, that you may let my people know. First, then, we have been at Windsor Castle, to see the king lying in state, and, afterwards, his interment; and sorry am I to say, it was not a sight that could satisfy any godly mind on such an occasion. We went in a coach of our own, by ourselves, and found the town of Windsor like a cried fair. We were then directed to the Castle gate, where a terrible crowd was gathered together; and we had not been long in that crowd, till a pocket-picker, as I thought, cutted off the tail of my coat, with my pocketbook in my pocket, which I never missed at the time. But it seems the coat tail was found, and a policeman got it, and held it up on the end of his stick, and cried, whose pocket is this? showing the book that was therein in his hand. I was confounded to see my pocket-book there, and could scarcely believe my own eyes; but Mrs. Pringle knew it at the first glance, and said, 'It's my gudeman's'; at the which, there was a great shout of derision among the multitude, and we would baith have then been glad to disown the pocketbook, but it was returned to us, I may almost say, against our will; but the scorners, when they saw our confusion, behaved with great civility towards us, so that we got into the Castle-yard with no other damage than the loss of the flap of my coat tail.

Being in the Castle-yard, we followed the crowd into another gate, and up a stair, and saw the king lying in state, which was a very dismal sight—and I thought of Solomon in all his glory, when I saw the coffin, and the mutes, and the mourners; and reflecting on the long infirmity of mind of the good old king, I said to myself, in the words of the book of Job, 'Doth not their excellency which is in them go away? they die even without wisdom!' When we had seen the sight, we came out of the Castle, and went to an inn to get a chack of dinner; but there was such a crowd, that no resting-place could for a time be found for us. Gentle and semple were there, all mingled, and no respect of persons; only there was, at a table nigh unto ours, a fat Glasgow manufacturer, who ordered a bottle of champaign wine, and did all he could in the drinking of it by himself, to show that he was a man in well-doing circumstances. While he was talking over his wine, a great peer of the realm, with a star on his breast, came into the room, and ordered a glass of brandy and water; and I could see, when he saw the Glasgow manufacturer drinking champaign wine on that occasion, that he greatly marvelled thereat.

When we had taken our dinner, we went out to walk and see the town of Windsor; but there was such a mob of coaches going and coming, and men and horses, that we left the streets, and went to inspect the king's policy, which is of great compass, but in a careless order, though it costs a world of money to keep it up. Afterwards, we went back to the inns, to get tea for Mrs Pringle and her daughter, while Andrew Pringle, my son, was seeing if he could get tickets to buy, to let us into the inside of the Castle, to see the burial-but he came back without luck, and I went out myself, being more experienced in the world, and I saw a gentleman's servant with a ticket in his hand, and I asked him to sell it to me, which the man did with thankfulness, for five shillings, although the price was said to be golden guineas. But as this ticket admitted only one person, it was hard to say what should be done with it when I got back to my family. However, as by this time we were all very much fatigued, I gave it to Andrew Pringle, my son, and Mrs Pringle, and her daughter Rachel, agreed to bide with me in the inns.

Andrew Pringle, my son, having got the ticket, left us sitting, when shortly after in came a nobleman, high in the cabinet, as I think he must have been, and he having politely asked leave to take his tea at our table, because of the great throng in the house, we fell into a conversation together, and he, understanding thereby that I was a minister of the Church of Scotland, said he thought he could help us into a place to see the funeral; so, after he had drank his tea, he took us with him, and got us into the Castle-yard, where we had an excellent place, near to the Glasgow manufacturer that drank the champaign. The drink by this time, however, had got into that poor man's head, and he talked so loud, and so little to the purpose, that the soldiers who were guarding were obliged to make him hold his peace, at which he was not a little nettled, and told the soldiers that he had himself been a soldier, and served the king without pay, having been a volunteer officer. But this had no more effect than to make the soldiers laugh at him, which was not a decent thing at the interment of their master, our most gracious Sovereign that was.

However, in this situation we saw all; and I can assure you it was a very edifying sight; and the people demeaned themselves with so much propriety, that there was no need for any guards at all; indeed, for that matter, of the two, the guards, who had eaten the king's bread, were the only ones there, saving and excepting the Glasgow manufacturer, that manifested an irreverent spirit towards the royal obsequies. But they are men familiar with the king of terrors on the field of battle, and it was not to be expected that their hearts would be daunted like those of others by a doing of a civil character.

When all was over, we returned to the inns, to get our chaise, to go back to London that night, for beds were not to be had for love or money at Windsor, and we reached our temporary home in Norfolk Street about four o'clock in the morning, well satisfied with what we had seen,—but all the meantime I had forgotten the loss of the flap of my coat, which caused no little sport when I came to recollect what a pookit like body I must have been, walking about in the king's policy like a peacock without my tail. But I must conclude, for Mrs Pringle has a letter to put in the frank for Miss Nanny Eydent, which you will send to her by one of your scholars, as it contains information that may be serviceable to Miss Nanny in her business, both as a mantua-maker and a superintendent of the genteeler sort of burials at Irvine and our vicinity. So that this is all from your friend and pastor,

ZACHARIAH PRINGLE

'I think,' said Miss Isabella Tod, as Mr Micklewham finished the reading of the Doctor's epistle, 'that my friend Rachel might have given me some account of the ceremony; but Captain Sabre seems to have been a much more interesting object to her than the pride and pomp to her brother, or even the Glasgow manufacturer to her father.' In saying these words, the young lady took the following letter from her pocket, and was on the point of beginning to read it, when Miss Becky Glibbans exclaimed, 'I had aye my fears that Rachel was but light-headed, and I'll no be surprised to hear more about her and the dragoon or a's done.' Mr Snodgrass looked at Becky, as if he had been afflicted at the moment with unpleasant ideas; and perhaps he would have rebuked the spitefulness of her insinuations, had not her mother sharply snubbed the uncongenial maiden, in terms at least as pungent as any which the reverend gentleman would have employed. 'I'm sure,' replied Miss Becky, pertly, 'I meant no ill; but if Rachel Pringle can write about nothing but this Captain Sabre, she might as well let it alone, and her letter canna be worth the hearing.' 'Upon that,' said the clergyman, 'we can form a judgment when we have heard it, and I beg that Miss Isabella may proceed,'—which she did accordingly.

LETTER 14
Miss Rachel Pringle to Miss Isabella Tod

LONDON

MY DEAR BELL—I take up my pen with a feeling of disappointment such as I never felt before. Yesterday was the day appointed for the funeral of the good old king, and it was agreed that we should go to Windsor, to pour the tribute of our tears upon the royal hearse. Captain Sabre promised to go with us, as he is well acquainted with the town, and the interesting objects around the Castle, so dear to chivalry, and embalmed by the genius of Shakespeare and many a minor bard, and I promised myself a day of unclouded felicity—but the captain was ordered to be on duty,—and the crowd was so rude and riotous, that I had no enjoyment whatever; but, pining with chagrin at the little respect paid by the rabble to the virtues of the departed monarch,

I would fainly have retired into some solemn and sequestered grove, and breathed my sorrows to the listening waste. Nor was the loss of the captain, to explain and illuminate the different baronial circumstances around the Castle, the only thing I had to regret in this ever-memorable excursion—my tender and affectionate mother was so desirous to see everything in the most particular manner, in order that she might give an account of the funeral to Nanny Eydent, that she had no mercy either upon me or my father, but obliged us to go with her to the most difficult and inaccessible places. How vain was all this meritorious assiduity! for of what avail can the ceremonies of a royal funeral be to Miss Nanny, at Irvine, where kings never die, and where, if they did, it is not at all probable that Miss Nanny would be employed to direct their solemn obsequies? As for my brother, he was so entranced with his own enthusiasm, that he paid but little attention to us, which made me the more sensible of the want we suffered from the absence of Captain Sabre. In a word, my dear Bell, never did I pass a more unsatisfactory day, and I wish it blotted for ever from my remembrance. Let it therefore be consigned to the abysses of oblivion, while I recall the more pleasing incidents that have happened since I wrote you last.

On Sunday, according to invitation, as I told you, we dined with the Argents—and were entertained by them in a style at once most splendid, and on the most easy footing. I shall not attempt to describe the consumable materials of the table, but call your attention, my dear friend, to the intellectual portion of the entertainment, a subject much more congenial to your delicate and refined character.

Mrs Argent is a lady of considerable personal magnitude, of an open and affable disposition. In this respect, indeed, she bears a striking resemblance to her nephew, Captain Sabre, with whose relationship to her we were unacquainted before that day. She received us as friends in whom she felt a peculiar interest; for when she heard that my mother had got her dress and mine from Cranbury Alley, she expressed the greatest astonishment, and told us, that it was not at all a place where persons of fashion could expect to be properly served. Nor can I disguise the fact, that the flounced and gorgeous garniture of our dresses was in shocking contrast to the amiable simplicity of hers and the fair Arabella, her daughter, a charming girl, who, notwithstanding the fashionable splendour in which she has been educated, displays a delightful sprightliness of manner, that, I have some notion, has not been altogether lost on the heart of my brother.

When we returned upstairs to the drawing-room, after dinner, Miss Arabella took her harp, and was on the point of favouring us with a Mozart; but her mother, recollecting that we were Presbyterians, thought it might not be agreeable, and she desisted, which I was sinful enough to regret; but my mother was so evidently alarmed at the idea of playing on the harp on a Sunday night, that I suppressed my own wishes, in filial veneration for those of that respected parent. Indeed, fortunate it was that the music was not performed; for, when we returned home, my father remarked with great solemnity, that such a way of passing the Lord's night as we had passed it, would have been a great sin in Scotland.

Captain Sabre, who called on us next morning, was so delighted when he understood that we were acquainted with his aunt, that he lamented he had not happened to know it before, as he would, in that case, have met us there.

He is indeed very attentive, but I assure you that I feel no particular interest about him; for although he is certainly a very handsome young man, he is not such a genius as my brother, and has no literary partialities. But literary accomplishments are, you know, foreign to the military profession, and if the captain has not distinguished himself by cutting up authors in the reviews, he has acquired an honourable medal, by overcoming the enemies of the civilised world at Waterloo.

To-night the playhouses open again, and we are going to the Oratorio, and the captain goes with us, a circumstance which I am the more pleased at, as we are strangers, and he will tell us the names of the performers. My father made some scruple of consenting to be of the party; but when he heard that an Oratorio was a concert of sacred music, he thought it would be only a sinless deviation if he did, so he goes likewise.

The captain, therefore, takes an early dinner with us at five o'clock. Alas! to what changes am I doomed,—that was the tea hour at the manse of Garnock. Oh, when shall I revisit the primitive simplicities of my native scenes again! But neither time nor distance, my dear Bell, can change the affection with which I subscribe myself, ever affectionately, yours,

RACHEL PRINGLE

At the conclusion of this letter, the countenance of Mrs Glibbans was evidently so darkened, that it daunted the company, like an eclipse of the sun, when all nature is saddened. 'What think you, Mr Snodgrass,' said that spirit-stricken lady,—'what think you of this dining on the Lord's day,—this playing on the harp; the carnal Mozarting of that ungodly family, with whom the corrupt human nature of our friends has been chambering?' Mr Snodgrass was at some loss for an answer, and hesitated, but Miss Mally Glencairn relieved him from his embarrassment, by remarking, that 'the harp was a holy instrument,' which somewhat troubled the settled orthodoxy of Mrs Glibbans's visage. 'Had it been an organ,' said Mr Snodgrass, dryly, 'there might have been, perhaps, more reason to doubt; but, as Miss Mally justly remarks, the harp has been used from the days of King David in the performances of sacred music, together with the psalter, the timbrel, the sackbut, and the cymbal.' The wrath of the polemical Deborah of the Relief-Kirk was somewhat appeased by this explanation, and she inquired in a more diffident tone, whether a Mozart was not a metrical paraphrase of the song of Moses after the overthrow of the Egyptians in the Red Sea; 'in which case, I must own,' she observed, 'that the sin and guilt of the thing is less grievous in the sight of HIM before whom all the actions of men are abominations.' Miss Isabella Tod, availing herself of this break in the conversation, turned round to Miss Nanny Eydent, and begged that she would read her letter from Mrs Pringle. We should do injustice, however, to honest worth and patient industry, were we, in thus introducing Miss Nanny to our readers, not to give them some account of her lowly and virtuous character.

Miss Nanny was the eldest of three sisters, the daughters of a shipmaster, who was lost at sea when they were very young; and his all having perished with him, they were indeed, as their mother said, the children of Poverty and Sorrow. By the help of a little credit, the widow contrived, in a small shop, to eke out her days till Nanny was able to assist her. It was the intention of the poor woman to take up a girl's school for reading and knitting, and Nanny was destined to instruct the pupils in that higher branch of accomplishment-the different stitches of the sampler. But about the time that Nanny was advancing to the requisite degree of perfection in chain-steek and pie-holes—indeed had made some progress in the Lord's prayer between two yew trees—tambouring was introduced at Irvine, and Nanny was sent to acquire a competent knowledge of that classic art, honoured by the fair hands of the beautiful Helen and the chaste and domestic Andromache. In this she instructed her sisters; and such was the fruit of their application and constant industry, that her mother abandoned the design of keeping school, and continued to ply her little huxtry in more easy circumstances. The fluctuations of trade in time taught them that it would not be wise to trust to the loom, and accordingly Nanny was at some pains to learn mantua-making; and it was fortunate that she did so—for the tambouring gradually went out of fashion, and the flowering which followed suited less the infirm constitution of poor Nanny. The making of gowns for ordinary occasions led to the making of mournings, and the making of mournings naturally often caused Nanny to be called in at deaths, which, in process of time, promoted her to have the management of burials; and in this line of business she has now a large proportion of the genteelest in Irvine and its vicinity; and in all her various engagements her behaviour has been as blameless and obliging as her assiduity has been uniform; insomuch, that the numerous ladies to whom she is known take a particular pleasure in supplying her with the newest patterns, and earliest information, respecting the varieties and changes of fashions; and to the influence of the same good feelings in the breast of Mrs Pringle, Nanny was indebted for the following letter. How far the information which it contains may be deemed exactly suitable to the circumstances in which Miss Nanny's lot is cast, our readers may judge for themselves; but we are happy to state, that it has proved of no small advantage to her: for since it has been known that she had received a full, true, and particular account, of all manner of London fashions, from so managing and notable a woman as the minister's wife of Garnock, her consideration has been so augmented in the opinion of the neighbouring gentlewomen, that she is not only consulted as to funerals, but is often called in to assist in the decoration and arrangement of wedding-dinners, and other occasions of sumptuous banqueting; by which she is enabled, during the suspension of the flowering trade, to earn a lowly but a respected livelihood.

LETTER 15
Mrs Pringle to Miss Nanny Eydent, Mantua-maker, Seagate Head Irvine

LONDON
DEAR MISS NANNY—Miss Mally Glencairn would tell you all how it happent that I was disabled, by our misfortunes in the ship, from riting to you konserning the London fashons as I promist; for I wantit to be partikylor, and to say nothing but what I saw with my own eyes, that it might be servisable to you in your bizness—so now I will begin with the old king's burial, as you have sometimes okashon to lend a helping hand in that way at Irvine, and nothing could be more genteeler of the kind than a royal obsakew for a patron; but no living sole can give a distink account of this matter, for you know the old king was the father of his piple, and the croud was so great. Howsomever we got into our oun hired shaze at daylight; and when we were

let out at the castel yett of Windsor, we went into the mob, and by and by we got within the castel walls, when great was the lamentation for the purdition of shawls and shoos, and the Doctor's coat pouch was clippit off by a pocket-picker. We then ran to a wicket-gate, and up an old timber-stair with a rope ravel, and then we got to a great pentit chamber called King George's Hall: After that we were allowt to go into another room full of guns and guards, that told us all to be silent: so then we all went like sawlies, holding our tongues in an awful manner, into a dysmal room hung with black cloth, and lighted with dum wax-candles in silver skonses, and men in a row all in mulancholic posters. At length and at last we came to the coffin; but although I was as partikylar as possoble, I could see nothing that I would recommend. As for the interment, there was nothing but even-down wastrie-wax-candles blowing away in the wind, and flunkies as fou as pipers, and an unreverent mob that scarsely could demean themselves with decency as the body was going by; only the Duke of York, who carrit the head, had on no hat, which I think was the newest identical thing in the affair: but really there was nothing that could be recommended. Howsomever I understood that there was no draigie, which was a saving; for the bread and wine for such a multitude would have been a destruction to a lord's living: and this is the only point that the fashon set in the king's feunoral may be follot in Irvine.

Since the burial, we have been to see the play, where the leddies were all in deep murning; but excepting that some had black gum-floors on their heads, I saw leetil for admiration—only that bugles, I can ashure you, are not worn at all this season; and surely this murning must be a vast detrimint to bizness—for where there is no verietie, there can be but leetil to do in your line. But one thing I should not forget, and that is, that in the vera best houses, after tea and coffee after dinner, a cordial dram is handed about; but likewise I could observe, that the fruit is not set on with the cheese, as in our part of the country, but comes, after the cloth is drawn, with the wine; and no such a thing as a punch-bowl is to be heard of within the four walls of London. Howsomever, what I principally notised was, that the tea and coffee is not made by the lady of the house, but out of the room, and brought in without sugar or milk, on servors, every one helping himself, and only plain flimsy loaf and butter is served—no such thing as shortbread, seed-cake, bun, marmlet, or jeelly to be seen, which is an okonomical plan, and well worthy of adaptation in ginteel families with narrow incomes, in Irvine or elsewhere.

But when I tell you what I am now going to say, you will not be surprizt at the great wealth in London. I paid for a bumbeseen gown, not a bit better than the one that was made by you that the sore calamity befell, and no so fine neither, more than three times the price; so you see, Miss Nanny, if you were going to pouse your fortune, you could not do better than pack up your ends and your awls and come to London. But ye're far better at home—for this is not a town for any creditable young woman like you, to live in by herself, and I am wearying to be back, though it's hard to say when the Doctor will get his counts settlet. I wish you, howsomever, to mind the patches for the bed-cover that I was going to patch, for a licht afternoon seam, as the murning for the king will no be so general with you, and the spring fashons will be coming on to help my gathering—so no more at present from your friend and well-wisher,

JANET PRINGLE

Chapter 6

Philosophy and Religion

On Sunday morning, before going to church, Mr Micklewham called at the manse, and said that he wished particularly to speak to Mr Snodgrass. Upon being admitted, he found the young helper engaged at breakfast, with a book lying on his table, very like a volume of a new novel called Ivanhoe in its appearance, but of course it must have been sermons done up in that manner to attract fashionable readers. As soon, however, as Mr Snodgrass saw his visitor, he hastily removed the book, and put it into the table-drawer.

The precentor having taken a seat at the opposite side of the fire, began somewhat diffidently to mention, that he had received a letter from the Doctor, that made him at a loss whether or not he ought to read it to the elders, as usual, after worship, and therefore was desirous of consulting Mr Snodgrass on the subject, for it recorded, among other things, that the Doctor had been at the playhouse, and Mr Micklewham was quite sure that Mr Craig would be neither to bind nor to hold when he heard that, although the transgression was certainly mollified by the nature of the performance. As the clergyman, however, could offer no opinion until he saw the letter, the precentor took it out of his pocket, and Mr Snodgrass found the contents as follows

LETTER 16

The Rev Z Pringle D D. , to Mr Micklewham, Schoolmaster and Session-Clerk
Garnock.

LONDON.

DEAR SIR—You will recollect that, about twenty years ago, there was a great sound throughout all the West that a playhouse in Glasgow had been converted into a tabernacle of religion. I remember it was glad tidings to our ears in the parish of Garnock; and that Mr Craig, who had just been ta'en on for an elder that fall, was for having a thanksgiving-day on the account thereof holding it to be a signal manifestation of a new birth in the of-old-godly town of Glasgow, which had become slack in the way of well-doing, and the church therein lukewarm, like that of Laodicea. It was then said, as I well remember, that when the Tabernacle was opened, there had not been seen, since the Kaimslang wark, such a congregation as was there assembled, which was a great proof that it's the matter handled, and not the place, that maketh pure; so that when you and the elders hear that I have been at the theatre of Drury Lane, in London, you must not think that I was there to see a carnal stage play, whether tragical or comical, or that I would so far demean myself and my cloth, as to be a witness to the chambering and wantonness of ne'er-du-weel play-actors. No, Mr Micklewham, what I went to see was an Oratorio, a most edifying exercise of psalmody and prayer, under the management of a pious gentleman, of the name of Sir George Smart, who is, as I am informed, at the greatest pains to instruct the exhibitioners, they being, for the most part, before they get into his hands, poor uncultivated creatures, from Italy, France, and Germany, and other atheistical and popish countries.

They first sung a hymn together very decently, and really with as much civilised harmony as could be expected from novices; indeed so well, that I thought them almost as melodious as your own singing class of the trades lads from Kilwinning. Then there was one Mr Braham, a Jewish proselyte, that was set forth to show us a specimen of his proficiency. In the praying part, what he said was no objectionable as to the matter; but he drawled in his manner to such a pitch, that I thought he would have broken out into an even-down song, as I sometimes think of yourself when you spin out the last word in reading out the line in a warm summer afternoon. In the hymn by himself, he did better; he was, however, sometimes like to lose the tune, but the people gave him great encouragement when he got back again. Upon the whole, I had no notion that there was any such Christianity in practice among the Londoners, and I am happy to tell you, that the house was very well filled, and the congregation wonderful attentive. No doubt that excellent man, Mr W———, has a hand in these public strainings after grace, but he was not there that night; for I have seen him; and surely at the sight I could not but say to myself that it's beyond the compass of the understanding of man to see what great things Providence worketh with small means, for Mr W——— is a small creature. When I beheld his diminutive stature, and thought of what he had achieved for the poor negroes and others in the house of bondage, I said to myself, that here the hand of Wisdom is visible, for the load of perishable mortality is laid lightly on his spirit, by which it is enabled to clap its wings and crow so crously on the dunghill top of this world; yea even in the House of Parliament.

I was taken last Thursday morning to breakfast with him in his house at Kensington, by an East India man, who is likewise surely a great saint. It was a heart-healing meeting of many of the godly, which he holds weekly in the season; and we had such a warsle of the spirit among us that the like cannot be told. I was called upon to pray, and a worthy gentleman said, when I was done, that he never had met with more apostolic simplicity- indeed, I could see with the tail of my eye, while I was praying, that the chief saint himself was listening with a curious pleasant satisfaction.

As for our doings here anent the legacy, things are going forward in the regular manner; but the expense is terrible, and I have been obliged to take up money on account; but, as it was freely given by the agents, I am in hopes all will end well; for, considering that we are but strangers to them, they would not have assisted us in this matter had they not been sure of the means of payment in their own hands.

The people of London are surprising kind to us; we need not, if we thought proper ourselves, eat a dinner in our own lodgings; but it would ill become me, at my time of life, and with the character for sobriety that I have maintained, to show an example in my latter days of riotous living; therefore, Mrs Pringle, and her daughter, and me, have made a point of going nowhere three times in the week; but as for Andrew Pringle, my son, he has forgathered with some acquaintance, and I fancy we will be obliged to let him take the length of his tether for a while. But not altogether without a curb neither, for the agent's son, young Mr Argent, had almost persuaded him to become a member of Parliament, which he said he could get him made, for more than a thousand pounds less than the common price—the state of the new king's health having lowered the commodity of seats. But this I would by no means hear of; he is not yet come to years of discretion enough to sit in council; and, moreover, he has not been tried; and no man, till he has out of doors shown something of what he is, should be entitled to power and honour within. Mrs Pringle, however, thought he might do as well as young Dunure; but Andrew Pringle, my son, has not the solidity of head that Mr K———dy has, and is over free and outspoken, and cannot take such pains to make his little go a great way, like that well-behaved young gentleman. But you will be grieved to hear that Mr K———dy is in opposition to the government; and truly I am at a loss to understand how a man of Whig principles can be an adversary to the House of Hanover. But I never meddled much in politick affairs, except at this time, when I prohibited Andrew Pringle, my son, from offering to be a member of Parliament, notwithstanding the great bargain that he would have had of the place.

And since we are on public concerns, I should tell you, that I was minded to send you a newspaper at the secondhand, every day when we were done with it. But when we came to inquire, we found that we could get the newspaper for a shilling a week every morning but Sunday, to our breakfast, which was so much cheaper than buying a whole paper, that Mrs Pringle thought it would be a great extravagance; and, indeed, when I came to think of the loss of time a newspaper every day would occasion to my people, I considered it would be very wrong of me to send you any at all. For I do think that honest folks in a far-off country parish should not make or meddle with the things that pertain to government,—the more especially, as it is well known, that there is as much falsehood as truth in newspapers, and they have not the means of testing their statements. Not, however, that I am an advocate for passive obedience; God forbid. On the contrary, if ever the time should come, in my day, of a saint-slaying tyrant attempting to bind the burden of prelatic abominations on our backs, such a blast of the gospel trumpet would be heard in Garnock, as it does not become me to say, but I leave it to you and others, who have experienced my capacity as a soldier of the word so long, to think what it would then be. Meanwhile, I remain, my dear sir, your friend and pastor,

Z. PRINGLE

When Mr Snodgrass had perused this epistle, he paused some time, seemingly in doubt, and then he said to Mr Micklewham, that, considering the view which the Doctor had taken of the matter, and that he had not gone to the play-house for the motives which usually take bad people to such places, he thought there could be no possible harm in reading the letter to the elders, and that Mr Craig, so far from being displeased, would doubtless be exceedingly rejoiced to learn that the playhouses of London were occasionally so well employed as on the night when the Doctor was there. Mr Micklewham then inquired if Mr Snodgrass had heard from Mr Andrew, and was answered in the affirmative; but the letter was not read. Why it was withheld our readers must guess for themselves; but we have been fortunate enough to obtain the following copy.

LETTER 17
Andrew Pringle Esq to the Rev Mr Charles Snodgrass

LONDON
MY DEAR FRIEND—As the season advances, London gradually unfolds, like Nature, all the variety of her powers and pleasures. By the Argents we have been

introduced effectually into society, and have now only to choose our acquaintance among those whom we like best. I should employ another word than choose, for I am convinced that there is no choice in the matter. In his friendships and affections, man is subject to some inscrutable moral law, similar in its effects to what the chemists call affinity. While under the blind influence of this sympathy, we, forsooth, suppose ourselves free agents! But a truce with philosophy.

The amount of the legacy is now ascertained. The stock, however, in which a great part of the money is vested being shut, the transfer to my father cannot be made for some time; and till this is done, my mother cannot be persuaded that we have yet got anything to trust to—an unfortunate notion which renders her very unhappy. The old gentleman himself takes no interest now in the business. He has got his mind at ease by the payment of all the legacies; and having fallen in with some of the members of that political junto, the Saints, who are worldly enough to link, as often as they can, into their association, the powerful by wealth or talent, his whole time is occupied in assisting to promote their humbug; and he has absolutely taken it into his head, that the attention he receives from them for his subscriptions is on account of his eloquence as a preacher, and that hitherto he has been altogether in an error with respect to his own abilities. The effect of this is abundantly amusing; but the source of it is very evident. Like most people who pass a sequestered life, he had formed an exaggerated opinion of public characters; and on seeing them in reality so little superior to the generality of mankind, he imagines that he was all the time nearer to their level than he had ventured to suppose; and the discovery has placed him on the happiest terms with himself. It is impossible that I can respect his manifold excellent qualities and goodness of heart more than I do; but there is an innocency in this simplicity, which, while it often compels me to smile, makes me feel towards him a degree of tenderness, somewhat too familiar for that filial reverence that is due from a son.

Perhaps, however, you will think me scarcely less under the influence of a similar delusion when I tell you, that I have been somehow or other drawn also into an association, not indeed so public or potent as that of the Saints, but equally persevering in the objects for which it has been formed. The drift of the Saints, as far as I can comprehend the matter, is to procure the advancement to political power of men distinguished for the purity of their lives, and the integrity of their conduct; and in that way, I presume, they expect to effect the accomplishment of that blessed epoch, the Millennium, when the Saints are to rule the whole earth. I do not mean to say that this is their decided and determined object; I only infer, that it is the necessary tendency of their proceedings; and I say it with all possible respect and sincerity, that, as a public party, the Saints are not only perhaps the most powerful, but the party which, at present, best deserves power.

The association, however, with which I have happened to become connected, is of a very different description. Their object is, to pass through life with as much pleasure as they can obtain, without doing anything unbecoming the rank of gentlemen, and the character of men of honour. We do not assemble such numerous meetings as the Saints, the Whigs, or the Radicals, nor are our speeches delivered with so much vehemence. We even, I think, tacitly exclude oratory. In a word, our meetings seldom exceed the perfect number of the muses; and our object on these occasions is not so much to deliberate on plans of prospective benefits to mankind, as to enjoy the present time for ourselves, under the temperate inspiration of a well-cooked dinner, flavoured with elegant wine, and just so much of mind as suits the fleeting topics of the day. T———, whom I formerly mentioned, introduced me to this delightful society. The members consist of about fifty gentlemen, who dine occasionally at each other's houses; the company being chiefly selected from the brotherhood, if that term can be applied to a circle of acquaintance, who, without any formal institution of rules, have gradually acquired a consistency that approximates to organisation. But the universe of this vast city contains a plurality of systems; and the one into which I have been attracted may be described as that of the idle intellects. In general society, the members of our party are looked up to as men of taste and refinement, and are received with a degree of deference that bears some resemblance to the respect paid to the hereditary endowment of rank. They consist either of young men who have acquired distinction at college, or gentlemen of fortune who have a relish for intellectual pleasures, free from the acerbities of politics, or the dull formalities which so many of the pious think essential to their religious pretensions. The wealthy furnish the entertainments, which are always in a superior style, and the ingredient of birth is not requisite in the qualifications of a member, although some jealousy is entertained of professional men, and not a little of merchants. T———, to whom I am also indebted for this view of that circle of which he is the brightest ornament, gives a felicitous explanation of the reason. He says, professional men, who are worth anything at all, are always ambitious, and endeavour to make their acquaintance subservient to their own advancement; while merchants are liable to such casualties, that their friends are constantly exposed to the risk of being obliged to sink them below their wonted equality, by granting them favours in times of difficulty, or, what is worse, by refusing to grant them.

I am much indebted to you for the introduction to your friend G———. He is one of us; or rather, he moves in an eccentric sphere of his own, which crosses, I believe, almost all the orbits of all the classed and classifiable systems of London. I found him exactly what you described; and we were on the frankest footing of old friends in the course of the first quarter of an hour. He did me the honour to fancy that I belonged, as a matter of course, to some one of the literary fraternities of Edinburgh, and that I would be curious to see the associations of the learned here. What he said respecting them was highly characteristic of the man. 'They are,' said he, 'the dullest things possible. On my return from abroad, I visited them all, expecting to find something of that easy disengaged mind which constitutes the charm of those of France and Italy. But in London, among those who have a character to keep up, there is such a vigilant circumspection, that I should as soon expect to find nature in the ballets of the Opera-house, as genius at the established haunts of authors, artists, and men of science. Bankes gives, I suppose officially, a public breakfast weekly, and opens his house for conversations on the Sundays. I found at his breakfasts, tea and coffee, with hot rolls, and men of celebrity afraid to speak. At the conversations, there was something even worse. A few plausible talking fellows created a buzz in the room, and the merits of some paltry nick-nack of mechanism or science was discussed. The party consisted undoubtedly of the most eminent men of their respective lines in the world; but they were each and all so apprehensive of having their ideas purloined, that they took the most guarded care never to speak of anything that they deemed of the slightest consequence, or to hazard an opinion that might be called in question. The man who either wishes to augment his knowledge, or to pass his time agreeably, will never expose himself to a repetition of the fastidious exhibitions of engineers and artists who have their talents at market. But such things are among the curiosities of London; and if you have any inclination to under go the initiating mortification of being treated as a young man who may be likely to interfere with their professional interests, I can easily get you introduced.'

I do not know whether to ascribe these strictures of your friend to humour or misanthropy; but they were said without bitterness; indeed much as matters of course, that, at the moment, I could not but feel persuaded they were just. I spoke of them to T———, who says, that undoubtedly G———'s account of the exhibitions is true in substance, but that it is his own sharp-sightedness which causes him to see them so offensively; for that ninety-nine out of the hundred in the world would deem an evening spent at the conversations of Sir Joseph Bankes a very high intellectual treat. G has invited me to dinner, and I expect some amusement; for T———, who is acquainted with him, says, that it is his fault to employ his mind too much on all occasions; and that, in all probability, there will be something, either in the fare or the company, that I shall remember as long as I live. However, you shall hear all about it in my next.—Yours,

ANDREW PRINGLE

On the same Sunday on which Mr Micklewham consulted Mr Snodgrass as to the propriety of reading the Doctor's letter to the elders, the following epistle reached the post-office of Irvine, and was delivered by Saunders Dickie himself, at the door of Mrs Glibbans to her servan lassie, who, as her mistress had gone to the Relief Church, told him, that he would have to come for the postage the morn's morning. 'Oh,' said Saunders, 'there's naething to pay but my ain trouble, for it's frankit; but aiblins the mistress will gie me a bit drappie, and so I'll come betimes i' the morning.

LETTER 18
Mrs Pringle to Mrs Glibbans

LONDON.

MY DEAR MRS GLIBBANS—The breking up of the old Parlament has been the cause why I did not right you before, it having taken it out of my poor to get a frank for my letter till yesterday; and I do ashure you, that I was most extraordinar uneasy at the great delay, wishing much to let you know the decayt state of the Gospel in thir perts, which is the pleasure of your life to study by day, and meditate on in the watches of the night.

There is no want of going to church, and, if that was a sign of grease and peese in the kingdom of Christ, the toun of London might hold a high head in the tabernacles of the faithful and true witnesses. But saving Dr Nichol of Swallo-Street, and Dr Manuel of London-Wall, there is nothing sound in the way of preeching here; and when I tell you that Mr John Cant, your friend, and some other flea-lugged fallows, have set up a Heelon congregation, and got a young man to preach Erse to the English, ye maun think in what a state sinful souls are left in London. But what I have been the most consarned about is the state of the dead. I am no meaning those who are dead in trespasses and sins, but the true dead. Ye will hardly think, that they are buried in a popish-like manner, with prayers, and white gowns, and ministers, and spadefuls of yerd cast upon them, and laid in vaults, like kists of orangers in a grocery seller-and I am told that, after a time, they are taken out when the vaut is shurfeeted, and their bones brunt, if they are no made into lamp-black by a secret wark—which is a clean proof to me that a right doctrine cannot be established in this land—there being so little respec shone to the dead.

The worst point, howsomever, of all is, what is done with the prayers—and I have heard you say, that although there was nothing more to objec to the wonderful Doctor Chammers of Glasgou, that his reading of his sermons was testimony against him in the great controversy of sound doctrine; but what will you say to reading of prayers, and no only reading of prayers, but printed prayers, as if the contreet heart of the sinner had no more to say to the Lord in the hour of fasting. and humiliation, than what a bishop can indite, and a book-seller make profit o'. 'Verily,' as I may say, in a word of scripter; I doobt if the glad tidings of salvation have yet been preeched in this land of London; but the ministers have good stipends, and where the ground is well manured, it may in time bring forth fruit meet for repentance.

There is another thing that behoves me to mention, and that is, that an elder is not to be seen in the churches of London, which is a sore signal that the piple are left to themselves; and in what state the morality can be, you may guess with an eye of pity. But on the Sabbath nights, there is such a going and coming, that it's more like a cried fair than the Lord's night—all sorts of poor people, instead of meditating on their bygane toil and misery of the week, making the Sunday their own day, as if they had not a greater Master to serve on that day, than the earthly man whom they served in the week-days. It is, howsomever, past the poor of nature to tell you of the sinfulness of London; and you may well think what is to be the end of all things, when I ashure you, that there is a newspaper sold every Sabbath morning, and read by those that never look at their Bibles. Our landlady asked us if we would take one; but I thought the Doctor would have fired the house, and you know it is not a small thing that kindles his passion. In short, London is not a place to come to hear the tidings of salvation preeched,—no that I mean to deny that there is not herine more than five righteous persons in it, and I trust the cornal's hagent is one; for if he is not, we are undone, having been obligated to take on already more than a hundred pounds of debt, to the account of our living, and the legacy yet in the dead thraws. But as I mean this for a spiritual letter, I will say no more about the root of all evil, as it is called in the words of truth and holiness; so referring you to what I have told Miss Mally Glencairn about the legacy and other things nearest my heart, I remain, my dear Mrs Glibbans, your fellou Christian and sinner,

JANET PRINGLE

Mrs Glibbans received this letter between the preachings, and it was observed by all her acquaintance during the afternoon service, that she was a laden woman. Instead of standing up at the prayers, as her wont was, she kept her seat, sitting with downcast eyes, and ever and anon her left hand, which was laid over her book on the reading-board of the pew, was raised and allowed to drop with a particular moral emphasis, bespeaking the mournful cogitations of her spirit. On leaving the church, somebody whispered to the minister, that surely Mrs Glibbans had heard some sore news; upon which that meek, mild, and modest good soul hastened towards her, and inquired, with more than his usual kindness, How she was? Her answer was brief and mysterious; and she shook her head in such a manner that showed him all was not right. 'Have you heard lately of your friends the Pringles?' said he, in his sedate manner—'when do they think of leaving London?'

'I wish they may ever get out o't,' was the agitated reply of the afflicted lady.

'I am very sorry to hear you say so,' responded the minister. 'I thought all was in a fair way to an issue of the settlement. I'm very sorry to hear this.'

'Oh, sir,' said the mourner, 'don't think that I am grieved for them and their legacy—filthy lucre—no, sir; but I have had a letter that has made my hair stand on end. Be none surprised if you hear of the earth opening, and London swallowed up, and a voice crying in the wilderness, "Woe, woe."'

The gentle priest was much surprised by this information; it was evident that Mrs Glibbans had received a terrible account of the wickedness of London; and that the weight upon her pious spirit was owing to that cause. He, therefore, accompanied her home, and administered all the consolation he was able to give; assuring her, that it was in the power of Omnipotence to convert the stony heart into one of flesh and tenderness, and to raise the British metropolis out of the a miry clay, and place it on a hill, as a city that could not be hid; which Mrs Glibbans was so thankful to hear, that, as soon as he had left her, she took her tea in a satisfactory frame of mind, and went the same night to Miss Mally Glencairn to hear what Mrs Pringle had said to her. No visit ever happened more opportunely; for just as Mrs Glibbans knocked at the door, Miss Isabella Tod made her appearance. She had also received a letter from Rachel, in which it will be seen that reference was made likewise to Mrs Pringle's epistle to Miss Mally.

LETTER 19
Miss Rachel Pringle to Miss Isabella Tod.

LONDON

MY DEAR BELL—How delusive are the flatteries of fortune! The wealth that has been showered upon us, beyond all our hopes, has brought no pleasure to my heart, and I pour my all unavailing sighs for your absence, when I would communicate the cause of my unhappiness. Captain Sabre has been most assiduous in his attentions, and I must confess to your sympathising bosom, that I do begin to find that he has an interest in mine. But my mother will not listen to his proposals, nor allow me to give him any encouragement, till the fatal legacy is settled. What can be her motive for this, I am unable to divine; for the captain's fortune is far beyond what I could ever have expected without the legacy, and equal to all I could hope for with it. If, therefore, there is any doubt of the legacy being paid, she should allow me to accept him; and if there is none, what can I do better? In the meantime, we are going about seeing the sights; but the general mourning is a great drawback on the splendour of gaiety. It ends, however, next Sunday; and then the ladies, like the spring flowers, will be all in full blossom. I was with the Argents at the opera on Saturday last, and it far surpassed my ideas of grandeur. But the singing was not good—I never could make out the end or the beginning of a song, and it was drowned with the violins; the scenery, however, was lovely; but I must not say a word about the dancers, only that the females behaved in a manner so shocking, that I could scarcely believe it was possible for the delicacy of our sex to do. They are, however, all foreigners, who are, you know, naturally of a licentious character, especially the French women.

We have taken an elegant house in Baker Street, where we go on Monday next, and our own new carriage is to be home in the course of the week. All this, which has been done by the advice of Mrs Argent, gives my mother great uneasiness, in case anything should yet happen to the legacy. My brother; however, who knows the law better than her, only laughs at her fears, and my father has found such a wonderful deal to do in religion here, that he is quite delighted, and is busy from morning to night in writing letters, and giving charitable donations. I am soon to be no less busy, but in another manner. Mrs Argent has advised us to get in accomplished masters for me, so that, as soon as we are removed into our own local habitation, I am to begin with drawing and music, and the foreign languages. I am not, however, to learn much of the piano; Mrs A. thinks it would take up more time than I can now afford; but I am to be cultivated in my singing, and she is to try if the master that taught Miss Stephens has an hour to spare—and to use her influence to persuade him to give it to me, although he only receives pupils for perfectioning, except they belong to families of distinction.

My brother had a hankering to be made a member of Parliament, and got Mr Charles Argent to speak to my father about it, but neither he nor my mother would hear of such a thing, which I was very sorry for, as it would have been so convenient to me for getting franks; and I wonder my mother did not think of that, as she grudges nothing so much as the price of postage. But nothing do I grudge so little, especially when it is a letter from you. Why do you not write me oftener, and tell me what is saying about us, particularly by that spiteful toad, Becky Glibbans, who never could hear of any good happening to her acquaintance, without being as angry as if it was obtained at her own expense?

I do not like Miss Argent so well on acquaintance as I did at first; not that she is not a very fine lassie, but she gives herself such airs at the harp and piano—because she can play every sort of music at the first sight, and sing, by looking at the notes, any song, although she never heard it, which may be very well in a play-actor, or a governess, that has to win her bread by music; but I think the education of a modest young lady might have been better conducted.

Through the civility of the Argents, we have been introduced to a great number of families, and been much invited; but all the parties are so ceremonious, that I am never at my ease, which my brother says is owing to my rustic education, which I cannot understand; for, although the people are finer dressed, and the dinners and rooms grander than what I have seen, either at Irvine or Kilmarnock, the company are no wiser; and I have not met with a single literary character among them. And what are ladies and gentlemen without mind, but a well-dressed mob! It is to mind alone that I am at all disposed to pay the homage of diffidence.

The acquaintance of the Argents are all of the first circle, and we have got an invitation to a route from the Countess of J———y, in consequence of meeting her with them. She is a charming woman, and I anticipate great pleasure. Miss Argent says, however, she is ignorant and presuming; but how is it possible that she can be so, as she was an earl's daughter, and bred up for distinction? Miss Argent may be presuming, but a countess is necessarily above that, at least it would only become a duchess or marchioness to say so. This, however, is not the only occasion in which I have seen the detractive disposition of that young lady, who, with all her simplicity of manners and great accomplishments, is, you will perceive, just like ourselves, rustic as she doubtless thinks our breeding has been.

I have observed that nobody in London inquires about who another is; and that in company every one is treated on an equality, unless when there is some remarkable personal peculiarity, so that one really knows nothing of those whom one meets. But my paper is full, and I must not take another sheet, as my mother has a letter to send in the same frank to Miss Mally Glencairn. Believe me, ever affectionately yours,

RACHEL PRINGLE

The three ladies knew not very well what to make of this letter. They thought there was a change in Rachel's ideas, and that it was not for the better; and Miss Isabella expressed, with a sentiment of sincere sorrow, that the acquisition of fortune seemed to have brought out some unamiable traits in her character, which, perhaps, had she not been exposed to the companions and temptations of the great world, would have slumbered, unfelt by herself, and unknown to her friends.

Mrs Glibbans declared, that it was a waking of original sin, which the iniquity of London was bringing forth, as the heat of summer causes the rosin and sap to issue from the bark of the tree. In the meantime, Miss Mally had opened her letter, of which we subjoin a copy.

LETTER 20

Mrs Pringle to Miss Mally Glencairn

LONDON

DEAR MISS MALLY—I greatly stand in need of your advise and counsel at this time. The Doctor's affair comes on at a fearful slow rate, and the money goes like snow off a dyke. It is not to be told what has been paid for legacy-duty, and no legacy yet in hand; and we have been obligated to lift a whole hundred pounds out of the residue, and what that is to be the Lord only knows. But Miss Jenny Macbride, she has got her thousand pound, all in one bank bill, sent to her; Thomas Bowie, the doctor in Ayr, he has got his five hundred pounds; and auld Nanse Sorrel, that was nurse to the cornal, she has got the first year of her twenty pounds a year; but we have gotten nothing, and I jealouse, that if things go on at this rate, there will be nothing to get; and what will become of us then, after all the trubble and outlay that we have been pot too by this coming to London?

Howsomever, this is the black side of the story; for Mr Charles Argent, in a jocose way, proposed to get Andrew made a Parliament member for three thousand pounds, which he said was cheap; and surely he would not have thought of such a thing, had he not known that Andrew would have the money to pay for't; and, over and above this, Mrs Argent has been recommending Captain Sabre to me for Rachel, and she says he is a stated gentleman, with two thousand pounds rental, and her nephew; and surely she would not think Rachel a match for him, unless she had an inkling from her gudeman of what Rachel's to get. But I have told her that we would think of nothing of the sort till the counts war settled, which she may tell to her gudeman, and if he approves the match, it will make him hasten on the settlement, for really I am growing tired of this London, whar I am just like a fish out of the water. The Englishers are sae obstinate in their own way, that I can get them to do nothing like Christians; and, what is most provoking of all, their ways are very good when you know them; but they have no instink to teach a body how to learn them. Just this very morning, I told the lass to get a jiggot of mutton for the morn's dinner, and she said there was not such a thing to be had in London, and threeppit it till I couldna stand her; and, had it not been that Mr Argent's French servan' man happened to come with a cart, inviting us to a ball, and who understood what a jiggot was, I might have reasoned till the day of doom without redress. As for the Doctor, I declare he's like an enchantit person, for he has falling in with a party of the elect here, as he says, and they have a kilfud yoking every Thursday at the house of Mr W———, where the Doctor has been, and was asked to pray, and did it with great effec, which has made him so up in the buckle, that he does nothing but go to Bible soceeyetis, and mishonary meetings, and cherity sarmons, which cost a poor of money.

But what consarns me more than all is, that the temptations of this vanity fair have turnt the head of Andrew, and he has bought two horses, with an English man-servan', which you know is an eating moth. But how he payt for them, and whar he is to keep them, is past the compass of my understanding. In short, if the legacy does not cast up soon, I see nothing left for us but to leave the world as a legacy to you all, for my heart will be broken—and I often wish that the cornel hadna made us his residees, but only given us a clean soom, like Miss Jenny Macbride, although it had been no more; for, my dear Miss Mally, it does not doo for a woman of my time of life to be taken out of her element, and, instead of looking after her family with a thrifty eye, to be sitting dressed all day seeing the money fleeing like sclate stanes. But what I have to tell is worse than all this; we have been persuaded to take a furnisht house, where we go on Monday; and we are to pay for it, for three months, no less than a hundred and fifty pounds, which is more than the half of the Doctor's whole stipend is, when the meal is twenty-pence the peck; and we are to have three servan' lassies, besides Andrew's man, and the coachman that we have hired altogether for ourselves, having been persuaded to trist a new carriage of our own by the Argents, which I trust the Argents will find money to pay for; and masters are to come in to teach Rachel the fasionable accomplishments, Mrs Argent thinking she was rather old now to be sent to a boarding-school. But what I am to get to do for so many vorashous servants, is dreadful to think, there being no such thing as a wheel within the four walls of London; and, if there was, the Englishers no nothing about spinning. In short, Miss Mally, I am driven dimentit, and I wish I could get the Doctor to come home with me to our manse, and leave all to Andrew and Rachel, with kurators; but, as I said, he's as mickle bye himself as onybody, and says that his candle has been hidden under a bushel at Garnock more than thirty years, which looks as if the poor man was fey; howsomever, he's happy in his delooshon, for if he was afflictit with that forethought and wisdom that I have, I know not what would be the upshot of all this calamity. But we maun hope for the best; and, happen what will, I am, dear Miss Mally, your sincere friend,

JANET PRINGLE

Miss Mally sighed as she concluded, and said, 'Riches do not always bring happiness, and poor Mrs. Pringle would have been far better looking after her cows and her butter, and keeping her lassies at their wark, than with all this galravitching and grandeur.' 'Ah!' added Mrs Glibbans, 'she's now a testifyer to the truth—she's now a testifyer; happy it will be for her if she's enabled to make a sanctified use of the dispensation.'

Chapter 7

Discoveries and Rebellions

One evening as Mr Snodgrass was taking a solitary walk towards Irvine, for the purpose of calling on Miss Mally Glencairn, to inquire what had been her latest accounts from their mutual friends in London, and to read to her a letter, which he had received two days before, from Mr Andrew Pringle, he met, near Eglintoun Gates, that pious woman, Mrs Glibbans, coming to Garnock, brimful of some most extraordinary intelligence. The air was raw and humid, and the ways were deep and foul; she was, however, protected without, and tempered within, against the dangers of both. Over her venerable satin mantle, lined with cat-skin, she wore a scarlet duffle Bath cloak, with which she was wont to attend the tent sermons of the Kilwinning and Dreghorn preachings in cold and inclement weather. Her black silk petticoat was pinned up, that it might not receive injury from the nimble paddling of her short steps in the mire; and she carried her best shoes and stockings in a handkerchief to be changed at the manse, and had fortified her feet for the road in coarse worsted hose, and thick plain-soled leather shoes.

Mr Snodgrass proposed to turn back with her, but she would not permit him. 'No, sir,' said she, 'what I am about you cannot meddle in. You are here but a stranger—come to-day, and gane to-morrow ;—and it does not pertain to you to sift into the doings that have been done before your time. Oh dear; but this is a sad thing—nothing like it since the silencing of McAuly of Greenock. What will the worthy Doctor say when he hears tell o't? Had it fa'n out with that neighering body, James Daff, I wouldna hae car't a snuff of tobacco, but wi' Mr Craig, a man so gifted wi' the power of the Spirit, as I hae often had a delightful experience! Ay, ay, Mr Snodgrass, take heed lest ye fall; we maun all lay it to heart; but I hope the trooper is still within the jurisdiction of church censures. She shouldna be spairt. Nae doubt, the fault lies with her, and it is that I am going to search; yea, as with a lighted candle.' Mr Snodgrass expressed his inability to understand to what Mrs Glibbans alluded, and a very long and interesting disclosure took place, the substance of which may be gathered from the following letter; the immediate and instigating cause of the lady's journey to Garnock being the alarming intelligence which she had that day received of Mr Craig's servant-damsel Betty having, by the style and title of Mrs Craig, sent for Nanse Swaddle, the midwife, to come to her in her own case, which seemed to Mrs Glibbans nothing short of a miracle, Betty having, the very Sunday before, helped the kettle when she drank tea with Mr Craig, and sat at the room door, on a buffet-stool brought from the kitchen, while he performed family worship, to the great solace and edification of his visitor.

LETTER 21
The Rev Z Pringle, D D , to Mr Micklewham, Schoolmaster and Session Clerk, Garnock

DEAR SIR—I have received your letter of the 24th, which has given me a great surprise to hear, that Mr. Craig was married as far back as Christmas, to his own servant lass Betty, and me to know nothing of it, nor you neither, until it was time to be speaking to the midwife. To be sure, Mr Craig, who is an elder, and a very rigid man, in his animadversions on the immoralities that come before the session, must have had his own good reasons for keeping his marriage so long a secret. Tell him, however, from me, that I wish both him and Mrs Craig much joy and felicity; but he should be milder for the future on the thoughtlessness of youth and headstrong passions. Not that I insinuate that there has been any occasion in the conduct of such a godly man to cause a suspicion; but it's wonderful how he was married in December, and I cannot say that I am altogether so proud to hear it as I am at all times of the well-doing of my people. Really the way that Mr Daff has comported himself in this matter is greatly to his credit; and I doubt if the thing had happened with him, that Mr Craig would have sifted with a sharp eye how he came to be married in December, and without bridal and banquet. For my part, I could not have thought it of Mr Craig, but it's done now, and the less we say about it the better; so I think with Mr Daff, that it must be looked over; but when I return, I will speak both to the husband and wife, and not without letting them have an inkling of what I think about their being married in December, which was a great shame, even if there was no sin in it. But I will say no more; for truly, Mr Micklewham, the longer we live in this world, and the farther we go, and the better we know ourselves, the less reason have we to think slightingly of our neighbours; but the more to convince our hearts and understandings, that we are all prone to evil, and desperately wicked. For where does hypocrisy not abound? and I have had my own experience here, that what a man is to the world, and to his own heart, is a very different thing.

In my last letter, I gave you a pleasing notification of the growth, as I thought, of spirituality in this Babylon of deceitfulness, thinking that you and my people would be gladdened with the tidings of the repute and estimation in which your minister was held, and I have dealt largely in the way of public charity. But I doubt that I have been governed by a spirit of ostentation, and not with that lowly-mindedness, without which all almsgiving is but a serving of the altars of Belzebub; for the chastening hand has been laid upon me, but with the kindness and pity which a tender father hath for his dear children.

I was requested by those who come so cordially to me with their subscription papers, for schools and suffering worth, to preach a sermon to get a collection. I have no occasion to tell you, that when I exert myself, what effect I can produce; and I never made so great an exertion before, which in itself was a proof that it was with the two bladders, pomp and vanity, that I had committed myself to swim on the uncertain waters of London; for surely my best exertions were due to my people. But when the Sabbath came upon which I was to hold forth, how were my hopes withered, and my expectations frustrated. Oh, Mr Micklewham, what an inattentive congregation was yonder! many slumbered and slept, and I sowed the words of truth and holiness in vain upon their barren and stoney hearts. There is no true grace among some that I shall not name, for I saw them whispering and smiling like the scorners, and altogether heedless unto the precious things of my discourse, which could not have been the case had they been sincere in their professions, for I never preached more to my own satisfaction on any occasion whatsoever—and, when I return to my own parish, you shall hear what I said, as I will preach the same sermon over again, for I am not going now to print it, as I did once think of doing, and to have dedicated it to Mr W———.

We are going about in an easy way, seeing what is to be seen in the shape of curiosities; but the whole town is in a state of ferment with the election of members to Parliament. I have been to see't, both in the Guildhall and at Covent Garden, and it's a frightful thing to see how the Radicals roar like bulls of Bashan, and put down the speakers in behalf of the government. I hope no harm will come of yon, but I must say, that I prefer our own quiet canny Scotch way at Irvine. Well do I remember, for it happened in the year I was licensed, that the town council, the Lord Eglinton that was shot being then provost, took in the late Thomas Bowet to be a counsellor; and Thomas, not being versed in election matters, yet minding to please his lordship (for, like the rest of the council, he had always a proper veneration for those in power), he, as I was saying, consulted Joseph Boyd the weaver, who was then Dean of Guild, as to the way of voting; whereupon Joseph, who was a discreet man, said to him, 'Ye'll just say as I say, and I'll say what Bailie Shaw says, for he will do what my lord bids him'; which was as peaceful a way of sending up a member to Parliament as could well be devised.

But you know that politics are far from my hand—they belong to the temporalities of the community; and the ministers of peace and goodwill to man should neither make nor meddle with them. I wish, however, that these tumultuous elections were well over, for they have had an effect on the per cents, where our bit legacy is funded; and it would terrify you to hear what we have thereby already lost. We have not, however, lost so much but that I can spare a little to the poor among my people; so you will, in the dry weather, after the seed-time, hire two-three thackers to mend the thack on the roofs of such of the cottars' houses as stand in need of mending, and banker M   y will pay the expense; and I beg you to go to him on receipt hereof, for he has a line for yourself; which you will be sure to accept as a testimony from me for the great trouble that my absence from the parish has given to you among my people, and I am, dear sir, your friend and pastor,

Z. PRINGLE

As Mrs Glibbans would not permit Mr Snodgrass to return with her to the manse, he pursued his journey alone to the Kirkgate of Irvine, where he found Miss

Mally Glencairn on the eve of sitting down to her solitary tea. On seeing her visitor enter, after the first compliments on the state of health and weather were over, she expressed her hopes that he had not drank tea; and, on receiving a negative, which she did not quite expect, as she thought he had been perhaps invited by some of her neighbours, she put in an additional spoonful on his account; and brought from her corner cupboard with the glass door, an ancient French pickle-bottle, in which she had preserved, since the great tea-drinking formerly mentioned, the remainder of the two ounces of carvey, the best, Mrs Nanse bought for that memorable occasion. A short conversation then took place relative to the Pringles; and, while the tea was masking, for Miss Mally said it took a long time to draw, she read to him the following letter:-

LETTER 22
Mrs Pringle to Miss Mally Glencairn

MY DEAR MISS MALLY—Trully, it may be said, that the croun of England is upon the downfal, and surely we are all seething in the pot of revolution, for the scum is mounting uppermost. Last week, no farther gone than on Monday, we came to our new house heer in Baker Street, but it's nather to be bakit nor brewt what I hay sin syne suffert. You no my way, and that I like a been house, but no wastrie, and so I needna tell yoo, that we hay had good diners; to be sure, there was not a meerakle left to fill five baskets every day, but an abundance, with a proper kitchen of breed, to fill the bellies of four dumasticks. Howsomever, lo and behold, what was decking downstairs. On Saturday morning, as we were sitting at our breakfast, the Doctor reading the newspapers, who shoud com intil the room but Andrew's grum, follo't by the rest, to give us warning that they were all going to quat our sairvice, becas they were starvit. I thocht that I would hay fentit cauld deed, but the Doctor, who is a consiederat man, inquairt what made them starve, and then there was such an approbrious cry about cold meet and bare bones, and no beer. It was an evendoun resurrection—a rebellion waur than the forty-five. In short, Miss Mally, to make a leettle of a lang tail, they would have a hot joint day and day about, and a tree of yill to stand on the gauntress for their draw and drink, with a cock and a pail; and we were obligated to evacuate to their terms, and to let them go to their wark with flying colors; so you see how dangerous it is to live among this piple, and their noshans of liberty.

You will see by the newspapers that ther's a lection going on for parliament. It maks my corruption to rise to hear of such doings, and if I was a government as I'm but a woman, I woud put them doon with the strong hand, just to be revenged on the proud stomaks of these het and fou English.

We have gotten our money in the pesents put into our name; but I have had no peese since, for they have fallen in price three eight parts, which is very near a half, and if they go at this rate, where will all our legacy soon be? I have no goo of the pesents; so we are on the look-out for a landed estate, being a shure thing.

Captain Saber is still sneking after Rachel, and if she were awee perfited in her accomplugments, it's no saying what might happen, for he's a fine lad, but she's o'er young to be the heed of a family. Howsomever, the Lord's will maun be done, and if there is to be a match, she'll no have to fight for gentility with a straitent circumstance.

As for Andrew, I wish he was weel settlt, and we have our hopes that he's beginning to draw up with Miss Argent, who will have, no doobt, a great fortune, and is a treasure of a creeture in herself being just as simple as a lamb; but, to be sure, she has had every advantage of edication, being brought up in a most fashonible boarding-school.

I hope you have got the box I sent by the smak, and that you like the patron of the goon. So no more at present, but remains, dear Miss Mally, your sinsaire friend,

JANET PRINGLE

'The box,' said Miss Mally, 'that Mrs. Pringle speaks about came last night. It contains a very handsome present to me and to Miss Bell Tod. The gift to me is from Mrs P. herself, and Miss Bell's from Rachel; but that ettercap, Becky Glibbans, is flying through the town like a spunky, mislikening the one and misca'ing the other: everybody, however, kens that it's only spite that gars her speak. It's a great pity that she cou'dna be brought to a sense of religion like her mother, who, in her younger days, they say, wasna to seek at a clashing.'

Mr Snodgrass expressed his surprise at this account of the faults of that exemplary lady's youth; but he thought of her holy anxiety to sift into the circumstances of Betty, the elder's servant, becoming in one day Mrs Craig, and the same afternoon sending for the midwife, and he prudently made no other comment; for the characters of all preachers were in her hands, and he had the good fortune to stand high in her favour, as a young man of great promise. In order, therefore, to avoid any discussion respecting moral merits, he read the following letter from Andrew Pringle:-

LETTER 23
Andrew Pringle, Esq , to the Reverend Charles Snodgrass

MY DEAR FRIEND—London undoubtedly affords the best and the worst specimens of the British character; but there is a certain townish something about the inhabitants in general, of which I find it extremely difficult to convey any idea. Compared with the English of the country, there is apparently very little difference between them; but still there is a difference, and of no small importance in a moral point of view. The country peculiarity is like the bloom of the plumb, or the down of the peach, which the fingers of infancy cannot touch without injuring; but this felt but not describable quality of the town character, is as the varnish which brings out more vividly the colours of a picture, and which may be freely and even rudely handled. The women, for example, although as chaste in principle as those of any other community, possess none of that innocent untempted simplicity, which is more than half the grace of virtue; many of them, and even young ones too, 'in the first freshness of their virgin beauty,' speak of the conduct and vocation of 'the erring sisters of the sex,' in a manner that often amazes me, and has, in more than one instance, excited unpleasant feelings towards the fair satirists. This moral taint, for I can consider it as nothing less, I have heard defended, but only by men who are supposed to have had a large experience of the world, and who, perhaps, on that account, are not the best judges of female delicacy. 'Every woman,' as Pope says, 'may be at heart a rake'; but it is for the interests of the domestic affections, which are the very elements of virtue, to cherish the notion, that women, as they are physically more delicate than men, are also so morally.

But the absence of delicacy, the bloom of virtue, is not peculiar to the females, it is characteristic of all the varieties of the metropolitan mind. The artifices of the medical quacks are things of universal ridicule; but the sin, though in a less gross form, pervades the whole of that sinister system by which much of the superiority of this vast metropolis is supported. The state of the periodical press, that great organ of political instruction—the unruly tongue of liberty, strikingly confirms the justice of this misanthropic remark.

G——— had the kindness, by way of a treat to me, to collect, the other day, at dinner, some of the most eminent editors of the London journals. I found them men of talent, certainly, and much more men of the world, than 'the cloistered student from his paling lamp'; but I was astonished to find it considered, tacitly, as a sort of maxim among them, that an intermediate party was not bound by any obligation of honour to withhold, farther than his own discretion suggested, any information of which he was the accidental depositary, whatever the consequences might be to his informant, or to those affected by the communication. In a word, they seemed all to care less about what might be true than what would produce effect, and that effect for their own particular advantage. It is impossible to deny, that if interest is made the criterion by which the confidences of social intercourse are to be respected, the persons who admit this doctrine will have but little respect for the use of names, or deem it any reprehensible delinquency to suppress truth, or to blazon falsehood. In a word, man in London is not quite so good a creature as he is out of it. The rivalry of interests is here too intense; it impairs the affections, and occasions speculations both in morals and politics, which, I much suspect, it would puzzle a casuist to prove blameless. Can anything, for example, be more offensive to the calm spectator, than the elections which are now going on? Is it possible that this country, so much smaller in geographical extent than France, and so inferior in natural resources, restricted too by those ties and obligations which were thrown off as fetters by that country during the late war, could have attained, in despite of her, such a lofty pre-eminence—become the foremost of all the world—had it not been governed in a manner congenial to the spirit of the people, and with great practical wisdom? It is absurd to assert, that there are no corruptions in the various modifications by which the affairs of the British empire are administered; but it would be difficult to show, that, in the present state of morals and interests among mankind, corruption is not a necessary evil. I do not mean necessary, as evolved from those morals and interests, but necessary to the management of political trusts. I am afraid, however, to insist on this, as the natural integrity of your own heart, and the dignity of your vocation, will alike induce you to condemn it as Machiavellian. It is, however, an observation forced on me by what I have seen here.

It would be invidious, perhaps, to criticise the different candidates for the representation of London and Westminster very severely. I think it must be granted, that they are as sincere in their professions as their opponents, which at least bleaches away much of that turpitude of which their political conduct is accused by those who are of a different way of thinking. But it is quite evident, at least to me, that no government could exist a week, managed with that subjection to public opinion to which Sir Francis Burdett and Mr Hobhouse apparently submit; and it is no less certain, that no government ought to exist a single day that would act in complete defiance of public opinion.

I was surprised to find Sir Francis Burdett an uncommonly mild and gentlemanly-looking man. I had pictured somehow to my imagination a dark and morose character;

but, on the contrary, in his appearance, deportment, and manner of speaking, he is eminently qualified to attract popular applause. His style of speaking is not particularly oratorical, but he has the art of saying bitter things in a sweet way. In his language, however, although pungent, and sometimes even eloquent, he is singularly incorrect. He cannot utter a sequence of three sentences without violating common grammar in the most atrocious way; and his tropes and figures are so distorted, hashed, and broken—such a patchwork of different patterns, that you are bewildered if you attempt to make them out; but the earnestness of his manner, and a certain fitness of character, in his observations a kind of Shaksperian pithiness, redeem all this. Besides, his manifold blunders of syntax do not offend the taste of those audiences where he is heard with the most approbation.

Hobhouse speaks more correctly, but he lacks in the conciliatory advantages of personal appearance; and his physiognomy, though indicating considerable strength of mind, is not so prepossessing. He is evidently a man of more education than his friend, that is, of more reading, perhaps also of more various observation, but he has less genius. His tact is coarser, and though he speaks with more vehemence, he seldomer touches the sensibilities of his auditors. He may have observed mankind in general more extensively than Sir Francis, but he is far less acquainted with the feelings and associations of the English mind. There is also a wariness about him, which I do not like so well as the imprudent ingenuousness of the baronet. He seems to me to have a cause in hand—Hobhouse versus Existing Circumstances—and that he considers the multitude as the jurors, on whose decision his advancement in life depends. But in this I may be uncharitable. I should, however, think more highly of his sincerity as a patriot, if his stake in the country were greater; and yet I doubt, if his stake were greater, if he is that sort of man who would have cultivated popularity in Westminster. He seems to me to have qualified himself for Parliament as others do for the bar, and that he will probably be considered in the House for some time merely as a political adventurer.

But if he has the talent and prudence requisite to ensure distinction in the line of his profession, the mediocrity of his original condition will reflect honour on his success, should he hereafter acquire influence and consideration as a statesman. Of his literary talents I know you do not think very highly, nor am I inclined to rank the powers of his mind much beyond those of any common well-educated English gentleman. But it will soon be ascertained whether his pretensions to represent Westminster be justified by a sense of conscious superiority, or only prompted by that ambition which overleaps itself.

Of Wood, who was twice Lord Mayor, I know not what to say. There is a queer and wily cast in his pale countenance, that puzzles me exceedingly. In common parlance I would call him an empty vain creature; but when I look at that indescribable spirit, which indicates a strange and out-of-the-way manner of thinking, I humbly confess that he is no common man. He is evidently a person of no intellectual accomplishments; he has neither the language nor the deportment of a gentleman, in the usual understanding of the term; and yet there is something that I would almost call genius about him. It is not cunning, it is not wisdom, it is far from being prudence, and yet it is something as wary as prudence, as effectual as wisdom, and not less sinister than cunning. I would call it intuitive skill, a sort of instinct, by which he is enabled to attain his ends in defiance of a capacity naturally narrow, a judgment that topples with vanity, and an address at once mean and repulsive. To call him a great man, in any possible approximation of the word, would be ridiculous; that he is a good one, will be denied by those who envy his success, or hate his politics; but nothing, save the blindness of fanaticism, can call in question his possession of a rare and singular species of ability, let it be exerted in what cause it may. But my paper is full, and I have only room to subscribe myself faithfully, yours,

A. PRINGLE

'It appears to us,' said Mr Snodgrass, as he folded up the letter to return it to his pocket, 'that the Londoners, with all their advantages of information, are neither purer nor better than their fellow-subjects in the country.' 'As to their betterness,' replied Miss Mally, 'I have a notion that they are far waur; and I hope you do not think that earthly knowledge of any sort has a tendency to make mankind, or womankind either, any better; for was not Solomon, who had more of it than any other man, a type and testification, that knowledge without grace is but vanity?' The young clergyman was somewhat startled at this application of a remark on which he laid no particular stress, and was thankful in his heart that Mrs Glibbans was not present. He was not aware that Miss Mally had an orthodox corn, or bunyan, that could as little bear a touch from the royne-slippers of philosophy, as the inflamed gout of polemical controversy, which had gumfiated every mental joint and member of that zealous prop of the Relief Kirk. This was indeed the tender point of Miss Mally's character; for she was left unplucked on the stalk of single blessedness, owing entirely to a conversation on this very subject with the only lover she ever had, Mr Dalgliesh, formerly helper in the neighbouring parish of Dintonknow. He happened incidentally to observe, that education was requisite to promote the interests of religion. But Miss Mally, on that occasion, jocularly maintained, that education had only a tendency to promote the sale of books. This, Mr Dalgliesh thought, was a sneer at himself, he having some time before unfortunately published a short tract, entitled,

'The moral union of our temporal and eternal interests considered, with respect to the establishment of parochial seminaries,' and which fell still-born from the press. He therefore retorted with some acrimony, until, from less to more, Miss Mally ordered him to keep his distance; upon which he bounced out of the room, and they were never afterwards on speaking terms.

Saving, however, and excepting this particular dogma, Miss Mally was on all other topics as liberal and beneficent as could be expected from a maiden lady, who was obliged to eke out her stinted income with a nimble needle and a close-clipping economy. The conversation with Mr Snodgrass was not, however, lengthened into acrimony; for immediately after the remark which we have noticed, she proposed that they should call on Miss Isabella Tod to see Rachel's letter; indeed, this was rendered necessary by the state of the fire, for after boiling the kettle she had allowed it to fall low. It was her nightly practice after tea to take her evening seam, in a friendly way, to some of her neighbours' houses, by which she saved both coal and candle, while she acquired the news of the day, and was occasionally invited to stay supper.

On their arrival at Mrs Tod's, Miss Isabella understood the purport of their visit, and immediately produced her letter, receiving, at the same time, a perusal of Mr Andrew Pringle's. Mrs Pringle's to Miss Mally she had previously seen.

LETTER 24
Miss Rachel Pringle to Miss Isabella Tod

MY DEAR BELL—Since my last, we have undergone great changes and vicissitudes. Last week we removed to our present house, which is exceedingly handsome and elegantly furnished; and on Saturday there was an insurrection of the servants, on account of my mother not allowing them to have their dinners served up at the usual hour for servants at other genteel houses. We have also had the legacy in the funds transferred to my father, and only now wait the settling of the final accounts, which will yet take some time. On the day that the transfer took place, my mother made me a present of a twenty pound note, to lay out in any way I thought fit, and in so doing, I could not but think of you; I have, therefore, in a box which she is sending to Miss Mally Glencairn, sent you an evening dress from Mrs Bean's, one of the most fashionable and tasteful dressmakers in town, which I hope you will wear with pleasure for my sake. I have got one exactly like it, so that when you see yourself in the glass, you will behold in what state I appeared at Lady———'s route.

Ah! my dear Bell, how much are our expectations disappointed! How often have we, with admiration and longing wonder, read the descriptions in the newspapers of the fashionable parties in this great metropolis, and thought of the Grecian lamps, the ottomans, the promenades, the ornamented floors, the cut glass, the coup d'oeil, and the tout ensemble 'Alas!' as Young the poet says, 'the things unseen do not deceive us.' I have seen more beauty at an Irvine ball, than all the fashionable world could bring to market at my Lady's emporium for the disposal of young ladies, for indeed I can consider it as nothing else.

I went with the Argents. The hall door was open, and filled with the servants in their state liveries; but although the door was open, the porter, as each carriage came up, rung a peal upon the knocker, to announce to all the square the successive arrival of the guests. We were shown upstairs to the drawing-rooms. They were very well, but neither so grand nor so great as I expected. As for the company, it was a suffocating crowd of fat elderly gentlewomen, and misses that stood in need of all the charms of their fortunes. One thing I could notice—for the press was so great, little could be seen—it was, that the old ladies wore rouge. The white satin sleeve of my dress was entirely ruined by coming in contact with a little round, dumpling duchess's cheek—as vulgar a body as could well be. She seemed to me to have spent all her days behind a counter, smirking thankfulness to bawbee customers.

When we had been shown in the drawing-rooms to the men for some time, we then adjourned to the lower apartments, where the refreshments were set out. This, I suppose, is arranged to afford an opportunity to the beaux to be civil to the belles, and thereby to scrape acquaintance with those whom they approve, by assisting them to the delicacies. Altogether, it was a very dull well-dressed affair, and yet I ought to have been in good spirits, for Sir Marmaduke Towier, a great Yorkshire baronet, was most particular in his attentions to me; indeed so much so, that I saw it made poor

Sabre very uneasy. I do not know why it should, for I have given him no positive encouragement to hope for anything; not that I have the least idea that the baronet's attentions were more than commonplace politeness, but he has since called. I cannot, however, say that my vanity is at all flattered by this circumstance. At the same time, there surely could be no harm in Sir Marmaduke making me an offer, for you know I am not bound to accept it. Besides, my father does not like him, and my mother thinks he's a fortune-hunter; but I cannot conceive how that may be, for, on the contrary, he is said to be rather extravagant.

Before we return to Scotland, it is intended that we shall visit some of the watering-places; and, perhaps, if Andrew can manage it with my father, we may even take a trip to Paris. The Doctor himself is not averse to it, but my mother is afraid that a new war may break out, and that we may be detained prisoners. This fantastical fear we shall, however, try to overcome. But I am interrupted. Sir Marmaduke is in the drawing-room, and I am summoned.—Yours truly,

RACHEL PRINGLE

When Mr Snodgrass had read this letter, he paused for a moment, and then said dryly, in handing it to Miss Isabella, 'Miss Pringle is improving in the ways of the world.'

The evening by this time was far advanced, and the young clergyman was not desirous to renew the conversation; he therefore almost immediately took his leave, and walked sedately towards Garnock, debating with himself as he went along, whether Dr Pringle's family were likely to be benefited by their legacy. But he had scarcely passed the minister's carse, when he met with Mrs Glibbans returning. 'Mr Snodgrass! Mr Snodgrass!' cried that ardent matron from her side of the road to the other where he was walking, and he obeyed her call; 'yon's no sic a black story as I thought. Mrs Craig is to be sure far gane, but they were married in December; and it was only because she was his servan' lass that the worthy man didna like to own her at first for his wife. It would have been dreadful had the matter been jealoused at the first. She gaed to Glasgow to see an auntie that she has there, and he gaed in to fetch her out, and it was then the marriage was made up, which I was glad to hear; for, oh, Mr Snodgrass, it would have been an awfu' judgment had a man like Mr Craig turn't out no better than a Tam Pain or a Major Weir. But a's for the best; and Him that has the power of salvation can blot out all our iniquities. So good-night—ye'll have a lang walk.'

Chapter 8

The Queen's Trial

As the spring advanced, the beauty of the country around Garnock was gradually unfolded; the blossom was unclosed, while the church was embraced within the foliage of more umbrageous boughs. The schoolboys from the adjacent villages were, on the Saturday afternoons, frequently seen angling along the banks of the Lugton, which ran clearer beneath the churchyard wall, and the hedge of the minister's glebe; and the evenings were so much lengthened, that the occasional visitors at the manse could prolong their walk after tea. These, however, were less numerous than when the family were at home; but still Mr Snodgrass, when the weather was fine, had no reason to deplore the loneliness of his bachelor's court.

It happened that, one fair and sunny afternoon, Miss Mally Glencairn and Miss Isabella Tod came to the manse. Mrs Glibbans and her daughter Becky were the same day paying their first ceremonious visit, as the matron called it, to Mr and Mrs Craig, with whom the whole party were invited to take tea; and, for lack of more amusing chit-chat, the Reverend young gentleman read to them the last letter which he had received from Mr Andrew Pringle. It was conjured naturally enough out of his pocket, by an observation of Miss Mally's 'Nothing surprises me,' said that amiable maiden lady, 'so much as the health and good-humour of the commonality. It is a joyous refutation of the opinion, that the comfort and happiness of this life depends on the wealth of worldly possessions.'

'It is so,' replied Mr Snodgrass, 'and I do often wonder, when I see the blithe and hearty children of the cottars, frolicking in the abundance of health and hilarity, where the means come from to enable their poor industrious parents to supply their wants.'

'How can you wonder at ony sic things, Mr Snodgrass? Do they not come from on high,' said Mrs Glibbans, 'whence cometh every good and perfect gift? Is there not the flowers of the field, which neither card nor spin, and yet Solomon, in all his glory, was not arrayed like one of these?'

'I was not speaking in a spiritual sense,' interrupted the other, 'but merely made the remark, as introductory to a letter which I have received from Mr Andrew Pringle, respecting some of the ways of living in London.'

Mrs Craig, who had been so recently translated from the kitchen to the parlour, pricked up her ears at this, not doubting that the letter would contain something very grand and wonderful, and exclaimed, 'Gude safe's, let's hear't—I'm unco fond to ken about London, and the king and the queen; but I believe they are baith dead noo.'

Miss Becky Glibbans gave a satirical keckle at this, and showed her superior learning, by explaining to Mrs Craig the unbroken nature of the kingly office. Mr Snodgrass then read as follows:—

LETTER 25
Andrew Pringle, Esq , to the Rev Charles Snodgrass

MY DEAR FRIEND—You are not aware of the task you impose, when you request me to send you some account of the general way of living in London. Unless you come here, and actually experience yourself what I would call the London ache, it is impossible to supply you with any adequate idea of the necessity that exists in this wilderness of mankind, to seek refuge in society, without being over fastidious with respect to the intellectual qualifications of your occasional associates. In a remote desart, the solitary traveller is subject to apprehensions of danger; but still he is the most important thing 'within the circle of that lonely waste'; and the sense of his own dignity enables him to sustain the shock of considerable hazard with spirit and fortitude. But, in London, the feeling of self-importance is totally lost and suppressed in the bosom of a stranger. A painful conviction of insignificance—of nothingness, I may say—is sunk upon his heart, and murmured in his ear by the million, who divide with him that consequence which he unconsciously before supposed he possessed in a general estimate of the world. While elbowing my way through the unknown multitude that flows between Charing Cross and the Royal Exchange, this mortifying sense of my own insignificance has often come upon me with the energy of a pang; and I have thought, that, after all we can say of any man, the effect of the greatest influence of an individual on society at large, is but as that of a pebble thrown into the sea. Mathematically speaking, the undulations which the pebble causes, continue until the whole mass of the ocean has been disturbed to the bottom of its most secret depths and farthest shores; and, perhaps, with equal truth it may be affirmed, that the sentiments of the man of genius are also infinitely propagated; but how soon is the physical impression of the one lost to every sensible perception, and the moral impulse of the other swallowed up from all practical effect.

But though London, in the general, may be justly compared to the vast and restless ocean, or to any other thing that is either sublime, incomprehensible, or affecting, it loses all its influence over the solemn associations of the mind when it is examined in its details. For example, living on the town, as it is slangishly called, the most friendless and isolated condition possible, is yet fraught with an amazing diversity of enjoyment. Thousands of gentlemen, who have survived the relish of active fashionable pursuits, pass their life in that state without tasting the delight of one new sensation. They rise in the morning merely because Nature will not allow them to remain longer in bed. They begin the day without motive or purpose, and close it after having performed the same unvaried round as the most thoroughbred domestic animal that ever dwelt in manse or manor-house. If you ask them at three o'clock where they are to dine, they cannot tell you; but about the wonted dinner-hour, batches of these forlorn bachelors find themselves diurnally congregated, as if by instinct, around a cozy table in some snug coffee-house, where, after inspecting the contents of the bill of fare, they discuss the news of the day, reserving the scandal, by way of dessert, for their wine. Day after day their respective political opinions give rise to keen encounters, but without producing the slightest shade of change in any of their old ingrained and particular sentiments.

Some of their haunts, I mean those frequented by the elderly race, are shabby enough in their appearance and circumstances, except perhaps in the quality of the wine. Everything in them is regulated by an ancient and precise economy, and you perceive, at the first glance, that all is calculated on the principle of the house giving as much for the money as it can possibly afford, without infringing those little etiquettes which persons of gentlemanly habits regard as essentials. At half price the junior members of these unorganised or natural clubs retire to the theatres, while the elder brethren mend their potations till it is time to go home. This seems a very comfortless way of life, but I have no doubt it is the preferred result of a long experience of the world, and that the parties, upon the whole, find it superior, according to their early formed habits of dissipation and gaiety, to the sedate but not more regular course of a domestic circle.

The chief pleasure, however, of living on the town, consists in accidentally falling in with persons whom it might be otherwise difficult to meet in private life. I have several times enjoyed this. The other day I fell in with an old gentleman, evidently a man of some consequence, for he came to the coffee-house in his own carriage. It happened that we were the only guests, and he proposed that we should therefore dine together. In the course of conversation it came out, that he had been familiarly acquainted with Garrick, and had frequented the Literary Club in the days of Johnson and Goldsmith. In his youth, I conceive, he must have been an amusing companion; for his fancy was exceedingly lively, and his manners altogether afforded a very favourable specimen of the old, the gentlemanly school. At an appointed hour his carriage came for him, and we parted, perhaps never to meet again.

Such agreeable incidents, however, are not common, as the frequenters of the coffee-houses are, I think, usually taciturn characters, and averse to conversation. I may, however, be myself in fault. Our countrymen in general, whatever may be their address in improving acquaintance to the promotion of their own interests, have not the best way, in the first instance, of introducing themselves. A raw Scotchman, contrasted with a sharp Londoner, is very inadroit and awkward, be his talents what they may; and I suspect, that even the most brilliant of your old class-fellows have, in their professional visits to this metropolis, had some experience of what I mean.

ANDREW PRINGLE

When Mr Snodgrass paused, and was folding up the letter, Mrs Craig, bending with her hands on her knees, said, emphatically, 'Noo, sir, what think you of that?' He was not, however, quite prepared to give an answer to a question so abruptly propounded, nor indeed did he exactly understand to what particular the lady referred. 'For my part,' she resumed, recovering her previous posture—'for my part, it's a very caldrife way of life to dine every day on coffee; broth and beef would put mair smeddum in the men; they're just a whin auld fogies that Mr Andrew describes, an' no wurth a single woman's pains.' 'Wheesht, wheesht, mistress,' cried Mr Craig; 'ye mauna let your tongue rin awa with your sense in that gait.' 'It has but a light load,' said Miss Becky, whispering Isabella Tod. In this juncture, Mr Micklewham happened to come in, and Mrs Craig, on seeing him, cried out, 'I hope, Mr Micklewham, ye have brought the Doctor's letter. He's such a funny man! and touches off the Londoners to the nines.'

'He's a good man,' said Mrs Glibbans, in a tone calculated to repress the forwardness of Mrs Craig; but Miss Mally Glencairn having in the meanwhile, taken from her pocket an epistle which she had received the preceding day from Mrs Pringle, Mr Snodgrass silenced all controversy on that score by requesting her to proceed with the reading. 'She's a clever woman, Mrs Pringle,' said Mrs Craig, who was resolved to cut a figure in the conversation in her own house. 'She's a discreet woman, and may be as godly, too, as some that make mair wark about the elect.' Whether Mrs Glibbans thought this had any allusion to herself is not susceptible of legal proof; but she turned round and looked at their 'most kind hostess' with a sneer that might almost merit the appellation of a snort. Mrs Craig, however, pacified her, by proposing, 'that, before hearing the letter, they should take a dram of wine, or pree her cherry bounce'— adding, 'our maister likes a been house, and ye a' ken that we are providing for a handling.' The wine was accordingly served, and, in due time, Miss Mally Glencairn edified and instructed the party with the contents of Mrs Pringle's letter.

LETTER 26
Mrs Pringle to Miss Mally Giencairn

DEAR MISS MALLY—You will have heard, by the peppers, of the gret hobbleshow heer aboot the queen's coming over contrary to the will of the nation; and, that the king and parlement are so angry with her, that they are going to put her away by giving to her a bill of divorce. The Doctor, who has been searchin the Scriptures on the okashon, says this is not in their poor, although she was found guilty of the fact; but I tell him, that as the king and parlement of old took upon them to change our religion, I do not see how they will be hampered now by the word of God.

You may well wonder that I have no ritten to you about the king, and what he is like, but we have never got a sight of him at all, whilk is a gret shame, paying so dear as we do for a king, who shurely should be a publik man. But, we have seen her majesty, who stays not far from our house heer in Baker Street, in dry lodgings, which, I am creditably informed, she is obligated to pay for by the week, for nobody will trust her; so you see what it is, Miss Mally, to have a light character. Poor woman, they say she might have been going from door to door, with a staff and a meal pock, but for ane Mr Wood, who is a baillie of London, that has ta'en her by the hand. She's a woman advanced in life, with a short neck, and a pentit face; housomever, that, I suppose, she canno help, being a queen, and obligated to set the fashons to the court, where it is necessar to hide their faces with pent, our Andrew says, that their looks may not betray them—there being no shurer thing than a false-hearted courtier.

But what concerns me the most, in all this, is, that there will be no coronashon till the queen is put out of the way—and nobody can take upon them to say when that will be, as the law is so dootful and endless—which I am verra sorry for, as it was my intent to rite Miss Nanny Eydent a true account of the coronashon, in case there had been any partiklars that might be servisable to her in her bisness.

The Doctor and me, by ourselves, since we have been settlt, go about at our convenience, and have seen far mae farlies than baith Andrew and Rachel, with all the acquaintance they have forgathert with—but you no old heeds canno be expectit on young shouthers, and they have not had the experience of the world that we have had.

The lamps in the streets here are lighted with gauze, and not with crusies, like those that have lately been put up in your toun; and it is brought in pips aneath the ground from the manufactors, which the Doctor and me have been to see—an awful place—and they say as fey to a spark as poother, which made us glad to get out o't when we heard so;—and we have been to see a brew-house, where they mak the London porter, but it is a sight not to be told. In it we saw a barrel, whilk the Doctor said was by gauging bigger than the Irvine muckle kirk, and a masking fat, like a barn for mugnited. But all thae were as nothing to a curiosity of a steam-ingine, that minches minch collops as natural as life—and stuffs the sosogees itself in a manner past the poor of nature to consiv. They have, to be shure, in London, many things to help work—for in our kitchen there is a smoking-jack to roast the meat, that gangs of its oun free will, and the brisker the fire, the faster it runs; but a potatoe-beetle is not to be had within the four walls of London, which is a great want in a house; Mrs Argent never hard of sic a thing.

Me and the Doctor have likewise been in the Houses of Parliament, and the Doctor since has been again to heer the argol-bargoling aboot the queen. But, cepting the king's throne, which is all gold and velvet, with a croun on the top, and stars all round, there was nothing worth the looking at in them baith. Howsomever, I sat in the king's seat, and in the preses chair of the House of Commons, which, you no, is something for me to say; and we have been to see the printing of books, where the very smallest dividual syllib is taken up by itself and made into words by the hand, so as to be quite confounding how it could ever read sense. But there is ane piece of industry and froughgalaty I should not forget, whilk is wives going about with whirl-barrows, selling horses' flesh to the cats and dogs by weight, and the cats and dogs know them very well by their voices. In short, Miss Mally, there is nothing heer that the hand is not turnt to; and there is, I can see, a better order and method really among the Londoners than among our Scotch folks, notwithstanding their advantages of edicashion, but my pepper will hold no more at present, from your true friend,

JANET PRINGLE

There was a considerable diversity of opinion among the commentators on this epistle. Mrs Craig was the first who broke silence, and displayed a great deal of erudition on the minch-collop-engine, and the potatoe-beetle, in which she was interrupted by the indignant Mrs Glibbans, who exclaimed, 'I am surprised to hear you, Mrs Craig, speak of sic baubles, when the word of God's in danger of being controverted by an Act of Parliament. But, Mr Snodgrass, dinna ye think that this painting of the queen's face is a Jezebitical testification against her?' Mr Snodgrass replied, with an unwonted sobriety of manner, and with an emphasis that showed he intended to make some impression on his auditors—'It is impossible to judge correctly of strangers by measuring them according to our own notions of propriety. It has certainly long been a practice in courts to disfigure the beauty of the human countenance with paint; but what, in itself may have been originally assumed for a mask or disguise, may, by usage, have grown into a very harmless custom. I am not, therefore, disposed to attach any criminal importance to the circumstance of her majesty wearing paint. Her late majesty did so herself.' 'I do not say it was criminal,' said Mrs Glibbans; 'I only meant it was sinful, and I think it is.' The accent of authority in which this was said, prevented Mr Snodgrass from offering any reply; and, a brief pause ensuing, Miss Molly Glencairn observed, that it was a surprising thing how the Doctor and Mrs Pringle managed their matters so well. 'Ay,' said Mrs Craig, 'but we a' ken what a manager the mistress is—she's the bee that mak's the hiney—she does not gang bizzing aboot, like a thriftless wasp, through her neighbours' houses.' 'I tell you, Betty, my dear,' cried Mr Craig, 'that you shouldna make comparisons—what's past is gane—and Mrs Glibbans and you maun now be friends.' 'They're a' friends to me that's no faes, and am very glad to see Mrs Glibbans sociable in my house; but she needna hae made sae light of me when she was here before.' And, in saying this, the amiable hostess burst into a loud sob of sorrow, which induced Mr Snodgrass to beg Mr Micklewham to read the Doctor's letter, by which a happy stop was put to the further manifestation of the grudge which Mrs Craig harboured against Mrs Glibbans for the lecture she had received, on what the latter called 'the incarnated effect of a more than Potipharian claught o' the godly Mr Craig.'

LETTER 27
The Rev Z Pringle D. D., to Mr Micklewham, Schoolmaster and Session Clerk of Garnock

DEAR SIR—I had a great satisfaction in hearing that Mr Snodgrass, in my place, prays for the queen on the Lord's Day, which liberty, to do in our national church, is a thing to be upholden with a fearless spirit, even with the spirit of martyrdom, that we may not bow down in Scotland to the prelatic Baal of an order in Council, whereof the Archbishop of Canterbury, that is cousin-german to the Pope of Rome, is art and part. Verily, the sending forth of that order to the General Assembly was treachery to the solemn oath of the new king, whereby he took the vows upon him, conform to the Articles of the Union, to maintain the Church of Scotland as by law established, so that for the Archbishop of Canterbury to meddle therein was a shooting out of the horns of aggressive domination.

I think it is right of me to testify thus much, through you, to the Session, that the elders may stand on their posts to bar all such breaking in of the Episcopalian boar into our corner of the vineyard.

Anent the queen's case and condition, I say nothing; for be she guilty, or be she innocent, we all know that she was born in sin, and brought forth in iniquity—prone to evil, as the sparks fly upwards—and desperately wicked, like you and me, or any other poor Christian sinner, which is reason enough to make us think of her in the remembering prayer.

Since she came over, there has been a wonderful work doing here; and it is thought that the crown will be taken off her head by a strong handling of the Parliament; and really, when I think of the bishops sitting high in the peerage, like owls and rooks in the bartisans of an old tower, I have my fears that they can bode her no good. I have seen them in the House of Lords, clothed in their idolatrous robes; and when I looked at them so proudly placed at the right hand of the king's throne, and on the side of the powerful, egging on, as I saw one of them doing in a whisper, the Lord Liverpool, before he rose to speak against the queen, the blood ran cold in my veins, and I thought of their woeful persecutions of our national church, and prayed inwardly that I might be keepit in the humility of a zealous presbyter, and that the corruption of the frail human nature within me might never be tempted by the pampered whoredoms of prelacy.

Saving the Lord Chancellor, all the other temporal peers were just as they had come in from the crown of the causeway—none of them having a judicial garment, which was a shame; and as for the Chancellor's long robe, it was not so good as my own gown; but he is said to be a very narrow man. What he spoke, however, was no doubt sound law; yet I could observe he has a bad custom of taking the name of God in vain, which I wonder at, considering he has such a kittle conscience, which, on less occasions, causes him often to shed tears.

Mrs Pringle and me, by ourselves, had a fine quiet canny sight of the queen, out of the window of a pastry baxter's shop, opposite to where her majesty stays. She seems to be a plump and jocose little woman; gleg, blithe, and throwgaun for her years, and on an easy footing with the lower orders—coming to the window when they call for her, and becking to them, which is very civil of her, and gets them to take her part against the government.

The baxter in whose shop we saw this told us that her majesty said, on being invited to take her dinner at an inn on the road from Dover, that she would be content with a mutton-chop at the King's Arms in London,[1] which shows that she is a lady of a very hamely disposition. Mrs Pringle thought her not big enough for a queen; but we cannot expect everyone to be like that bright occidental star, Queen Elizabeth, whose effigy we have seen preserved in armour in the Tower of London, and in wax in Westminster Abbey, where they have a living-like likeness of Lord Nelson, in the very identical regimentals that he was killed in. They are both wonderful places, but it costs a power of money to get through them, and all the folk about them think of nothing but money; for when I inquired, with a reverent spirit, seeing around me the tombs of great and famous men, the mighty and wise of their day, what department it was of the Abbey—'It's the eighteenpence department,' said an uncircumcised Philistine, with as little respect as if we had been treading the courts of the darling Dagon.

Our concerns here are now drawing to a close; but before we return, we are going for a short time to a town on the seaside, which they call Brighton. We had a notion of taking a trip to Paris, but that we must leave to Andrew Pringle, my son, and his sister Rachel, if the bit lassie could get a decent gudeman, which maybe will cast up for her before we leave London. Nothing, however, is settled as yet upon that head, so I can say no more at present anent the same.

Since the affair of the sermon, I have withdrawn myself from trafficking so much as I did in the missionary and charitable ploys that are so in vogue with the pious here, which will be all the better for my own people, as I will keep for them what I was giving to the unknown; and it is my design to write a book on almsgiving, to show in what manner that Christian duty may be best fulfilled, which I doubt not will have the effect of opening the eyes of many in London to the true nature of the thing by which I was myself beguiled in this Vanity Fair, like a bird ensnared by the fowler.

I was concerned to hear of poor Mr Witherspoon's accident, in falling from his horse in coming from the Dalmailing occasion. How thankful he must be, that the Lord made his head of a durability to withstand the shock, which might otherwise have fractured his skull. What you say about the promise of the braird gives me pleasure on account of the poor; but what will be done with the farmers and their high rents, if the harvest turn out so abundant? Great reason have I to be thankful that the legacy has put me out of the reverence of my stipend; for when the meal was cheap, I own to you that I felt my carnality grudging the horn of abundance that the Lord was then pouring into the lap of the earth. In short, Mr Micklewham, I doubt it is o'er true with us all, that the less we are tempted, the better we are; so with my sincere prayers that you may be delivered from all evil, and led out of the paths of temptation, whether it is on the highway, or on the footpaths, or beneath the hedges, I remain, dear sir, your friend and pastor,

ZACHARIAH PRINGLE

'The Doctor,' said Mrs Glibbans, as the schoolmaster concluded, 'is there like himself—a true orthodox Christian, standing up for the word, and overflowing with

---

1 The honest Doctor's version of this *bon mot* of her majesty is not quite correct; her expression was 'I mean to take a hop at the King's Head when I get to London.'

charity even for the sinner. But, Mr Snodgrass, I did not ken before that the bishops had a hand in the making of the Acts of the Parliament; I think, Mr Snodgrass, if that be the case, there should be some doubt in Scotland about obeying them. However that may be, sure am I that the queen, though she was a perfect Deliah, has nothing to fear from them; for have we not read in the Book of Martyrs, and other church histories, of their concubines and indulgences, in the papist times, to all manner of carnal iniquity? But if she be that noghty woman that they say'—'Gude safe's,' cried Mrs Craig, 'if she be a noghty woman, awa' wi' her, awa' wi' her—wha kens the cantrips she may play us?'

Here Miss Mally Glencairn interposed, and informed Mrs Craig, that a noghty woman was not, as she seemed to think, a witch wife. 'I am sure,' said Miss Becky Glibbans, 'that Mrs Craig might have known that.' 'Oh, ye're a spiteful deevil,' whispered Miss Mally, with a smile to her; and turning in the same moment to Miss Isabella Tod, begged her to read Miss Pringle's letter—a motion which Mr Snodgrass seconded chiefly to abridge the conversation, during which, though he wore a serene countenance, he often suffered much.

LETTER 28
Miss Rachel Pringle to Miss Isabella Tod

MY DEAR BELL—I am much obliged by your kind expressions for my little present. I hope soon to send you something better, and gloves at the same time; for Sabre has been brought to the point by an alarm for the Yorkshire baronet that I mentioned, as showing symptoms of the tender passion for my fortune. The friends on both sides being satisfied with the match, it will take place as soon as some preliminary arrangements are made. When we are settled, I hope your mother will allow you to come and spend some time with us at our country-seat in Berkshire; and I shall be happy to repay all the expenses of your journey, as a jaunt to England is what your mother would, I know, never consent to pay for.

It is proposed that, immediately after the ceremony, we shall set out for France, accompanied by my brother, where we are to be soon after joined at Paris by some of the Argents, who, I can see, think Andrew worth the catching for Miss. My father and mother will then return to Scotland; but whether the Doctor will continue to keep his parish, or give it up to Mr Snodgrass, will depend greatly on the circumstances in which he finds his parishioners. This is all the domestic intelligence I have got to give, but its importance will make up for other deficiencies.

As to the continuance of our discoveries in London, I know not well what to say. Every day brings something new, but we lose the sense of novelty. Were a fire in the same street where we live, it would no longer alarm me. A few nights ago, as we were sitting in the parlour after supper, the noise of an engine passing startled us all; we ran to the windows—there was haste and torches, and the sound of other engines, and all the horrors of a conflagration reddening the skies. My father sent out the footboy to inquire where it was; and when the boy came back, he made us laugh, by snapping his fingers, and saying the fire was not worth so much—although, upon further inquiry, we learnt that the house in which it originated was burnt to the ground. You see, therefore, how the bustle of this great world hardens the sensibilities, but I trust its influence will never extend to my heart.

The principal topic of conversation at present is about the queen. The Argents, who are our main instructors in the proprieties of London life, say that it would be very vulgar in me to go to look at her, which I am sorry for, as I wish above all things to see a personage so illustrious by birth, and renowned by misfortune. The Doctor and my mother, who are less scrupulous, and who, in consequence, somehow, by themselves, contrive to see, and get into places that are inaccessible to all gentility, have had a full view of her majesty. My father has since become her declared partisan, and my mother too has acquired a leaning likewise towards her side of the question; but neither of them will permit the subject to be spoken of before me, as they consider it detrimental to good morals. I, however, read the newspapers.

What my brother thinks of her majesty's case is not easy to divine; but Sabre is convinced of the queen's guilt, upon some private and authentic information which a friend of his, who has returned from Italy, heard when travelling in that country. This information he has not, however, repeated to me, so that it must be very bad. We shall know all when the trial comes on. In the meantime, his majesty, who has lived in dignified retirement since he came to the throne, has taken up his abode, with rural felicity, in a cottage in Windsor Forest; where he now, contemning all the pomp and follies of his youth, and this metropolis, passes his days amidst his cabbages, like Dioclesian, with innocence and tranquillity, far from the intrigues of courtiers, and insensible to the murmuring waves of the fluctuating populace, that set in with so strong a current towards 'the mob-led queen,' as the divine Shakespeare has so beautifully expressed it.

You ask me about Vauxhall Gardens ;—I have not seen them—they are no longer in fashion—the theatres are quite vulgar—even the opera-house has sunk into a second-rate place of resort. Almack's balls, the Argyle-rooms, and the Philharmonic concerts, are the only public entertainments frequented by people of fashion; and this high superiority they owe entirely to the difficulty of gaining admission. London, as my brother says, is too rich, and grown too luxurious, to have any exclusive place of fashionable resort, where price alone is the obstacle. Hence, the institution of these select aristocratic assemblies. The Philharmonic concerts, however, are rather professional than fashionable entertainments; but everybody is fond of music, and, therefore, everybody, that can be called anybody, is anxious to get tickets to them; and this anxiety has given them a degree of eclat which I am persuaded the performance would never have excited had the tickets been purchasable at any price.

The great thing here is, either to be somebody, or to be patronised by a person that is a somebody; without this, though you were as rich as Croesus, your golden chariots, like the comets of a season, blazing and amazing, would speedily roll away into the obscurity from which they came, and be remembered no more.

At first when we came here, and when the amount of our legacy was first promulgated, we were in a terrible flutter. Andrew became a man of fashion, with all the haste that tailors, and horses, and dinners, could make him. My father, honest man, was equally inspired with lofty ideas, and began a career that promised a liberal benefaction of good things to the poor—and my mother was almost distracted with calculations about laying out the money to the best advantage, and the sum she would allow to be spent. I alone preserved my natural equanimity; and foreseeing the necessity of new accomplishments to suit my altered circumstances, applied myself to the instructions of my masters, with an assiduity that won their applause. The advantages of this I now experience—my brother is sobered from his champaign fumes—my father has found out that charity begins at home—and my mother, though her establishment is enlarged, finds her happiness, notwithstanding the legacy, still lies within the little circle of her household cares. Thus, my dear Bell, have I proved the sweets of a true philosophy; and, unseduced by the blandishments of rank, rejected Sir Marmaduke Towler, and accepted the humbler but more disinterested swain, Captain Sabre, who requests me to send you his compliments, not altogether content that you should occupy so much of the bosom of your affectionate

RACHEL PRINGLE

'Rachel had ay a gude roose of hersel',' said Becky Glibbans, as Miss Isabella concluded. In the same moment, Mr Snodgrass took his leave, saying to Mr Micklewham, that he had something particular to mention to him. 'What can it be about?' inquired Mrs Glibbans at Mr Craig, as soon as the helper and schoolmaster had left the room: 'Do you think it can be concerning the Doctor's resignation of the parish in his favour?' 'I'm sure,' interposed Mrs Craig, before her husband could reply, 'it winna be wi' my gudewill that he shall come in upon us—a pridefu' wight, whose saft words, and a' his politeness, are but lip-deep; na, na, Mrs Glibbans, we maun hae another on the leet forbye him.'

'And wha would ye put on the leet noo, Mrs Craig, you that's sic a judge?' said Mrs Glibbans, with the most ineffable consequentiality.

'I'll be for young Mr Dirlton, who is baith a sappy preacher of the word, and a substantial hand at every kind of civility.'

'Young Dirlton!—young Deevilton!' cried the orthodox Deborah of Irvine; 'a fallow that knows no more of a gospel dispensation than I do of the Arian heresy, which I hold in utter abomination. No, Mrs Craig, you have a godly man for your husband—a sound and true follower; tread ye in his footsteps, and no try to set up yoursel' on points of doctrine. But it's time, Miss Mally, that we were taking the road; Becky and Miss Isabella, make yourselves ready. Noo, Mrs Craig, ye'll no be a stranger; you see I have no been lang of coming to give you my countenance; but, my leddy, ca' canny, it's no easy to carry a fu' cup; ye hae gotten a great gift in your gudeman. Mr Craig, I wish you a good-night; I would fain have stopped for your evening exercise, but Miss Mally was beginning, I saw, to weary—so good-night; and, Mrs Craig, ye'll take tent of what I have said—it's for your gude.' So exeunt Mrs Glibbans, Miss Mally, and the two young ladies. 'Her bark's waur than her bite,' said Mrs Craig, as she returned to her husband, who felt already some of the ourie symptoms of a henpecked destiny.

Chapter 9

The Marriage

Mr Snodgrass was obliged to walk into Irvine one evening, to get rid of a raging tooth, which had tormented him for more than a week. The operation was so delicately and cleverly performed by the surgeon to whom he applied—one of those young medical gentlemen, who, after having been educated for the army or navy, are obliged, in this weak piping time of peace, to glean what practice they can amid their native shades— that the amiable divine found himself in a condition to call on Miss Isabella Tod.

During this visit, Saunders Dickie, the postman, brought a London letter to the door, for Miss Isabella; and Mr Snodgrass having desired the servant to inquire if there were any for him, had the good fortune to get the following from Mr Andrew Pringle

LETTER 29
Andrew Pringle Esq to the Rev Mr Charles Snodgrass

MY DEAR FRIEND—I never receive a letter from you without experiencing a strong emotion of regret, that talents like yours should be wilfully consigned to the sequestered vegetation of a country pastor's life. But we have so often discussed this point, that I shall only offend your delicacy if I now revert to it more particularly. I cannot, however, but remark, that although a private station may be the happiest, a public is the proper sphere of virtue and talent, so clear, superior, and decided as yours. I say this with the more confidence, as I have really, from your letter, obtained a better conception of the queen's case, than from all that I have been able to read and hear upon the subject in London. The rule you lay down is excellent. Public safety is certainly the only principle which can justify mankind in agreeing to observe and enforce penal statutes; and, therefore, I think with you, that unless it could be proved in a very simple manner, that it was requisite for the public safety to institute proceedings against the queen—her sins or indiscretions should have been allowed to remain in the obscurity of her private circle.

I have attended the trial several times. For a judicial proceeding, it seems to me too long—and for a legislative, too technical. Brougham, it is allowed, has displayed even greater talent than was expected; but he is too sharp; he seems to me more anxious to gain a triumph, than to establish truth. I do not like the tone of his proceedings, while I cannot sufficiently admire his dexterity. The style of Denman is more lofty, and impressed with stronger lineaments of sincerity. As for their opponents, I really cannot endure the Attorney-General as an orator; his whole mind consists, as it were, of a number of little hands and claws—each of which holds some scrap or portion of his subject; but you might as well expect to get an idea of the form and character of a tree, by looking at the fallen leaves, the fruit, the seeds, and the blossoms, as anything like a comprehensive view of a subject, from an intellect so constituted as that of Sir Robert Gifford. He is a man of application, but of meagre abilities, and seems never to have read a book of travels in his life. The Solicitor-General is somewhat better; but he is one of those who think a certain artificial gravity requisite to professional consequence; and which renders him somewhat obtuse in the tact of propriety.

Within the bar, the talent is superior to what it is without; and I have been often delighted with the amazing fineness, if I may use the expression, with which the Chancellor discriminates the shades of difference in the various points on which he is called to deliver his opinion. I consider his mind as a curiosity of no ordinary kind. It deceives itself by its own acuteness. The edge is too sharp; and, instead of cutting straight through, it often diverges—alarming his conscience with the dread of doing wrong. This singular subtlety has the effect of impairing the reverence which the endowments and high professional accomplishments of this great man are otherwise calculated to inspire. His eloquence is not effective—it touches no feeling nor affects any passion; but still it affords wonderful displays of a lucid intellect. I can compare it to nothing but a pencil of sunshine; in which, although one sees countless motes flickering and fluctuating, it yet illuminates, and steadily brings into the most satisfactory distinctness, every object on which it directly falls.

Lord Erskine is a character of another class, and whatever difference of opinion may exist with respect to their professional abilities and attainments, it will be allowed by those who contend that Eldon is the better lawyer—that Erskine is the greater genius. Nature herself, with a constellation in her hand, playfully illuminates his path to the temple of reasonable Justice; while Precedence with her guide-book, and Study with a lantern, cautiously show the road in which the Chancellor warily plods his weary way to that of legal Equity. The sedateness of Eldon is so remarkable, that it is difficult to conceive that he was ever young; but Erskine cannot grow old; his spirit is still glowing and flushed with the enthusiasm of youth. When impassioned, his voice acquires a singularly elevated and pathetic accent; and I can easily conceive the irresistible effect he must have had on the minds of a jury, when he was in the vigour of his physical powers, and the case required appeals of tenderness or generosity. As a parliamentary orator, Earl Grey is undoubtedly his superior; but there is something much less popular and conciliating in his manner. His eloquence is heard to most advantage when he is contemptuous; and he is then certainly dignified, ardent, and emphatic; but it is apt, I should think, to impress those who hear him, for the first time, with an idea that he is a very supercilious personage, and this unfavourable impression is liable to be strengthened by the elegant aristocratic languor of his appearance.

I think that you once told me you had some knowledge of the Marquis of Lansdowne, when he was Lord Henry Petty. I can hardly hope that, after an interval of so many years, you will recognise him in the following sketch:—His appearance is much more that of a Whig than Lord Grey—stout and sturdy—but still withal gentlemanly; and there is a pleasing simplicity, with somewhat of good-nature, in the expression of his countenance, that renders him, in a quiescent state, the more agreeable character of the two. He speaks exceedingly well—clear, methodical, and argumentative; but his eloquence, like himself, is not so graceful as it is upon the whole manly; and there is a little tendency to verbosity in his language, as there is to corpulency in his figure; but nothing turgid, while it is entirely free from affectation. The character of respectable is very legibly impressed, in everything about the mind and manner of his lordship. I should, now that I have seen and heard him, be astonished to hear such a man represented as capable of being factious.

I should say something about Lord Liverpool, not only on account of his rank as a minister, but also on account of the talents which have qualified him for that high situation. The greatest objection that I have to him as a speaker, is owing to the loudness of his voice—in other respects, what he does say is well digested. But I do not think that he embraces his subject with so much power and comprehension as some of his opponents; and he has evidently less actual experience of the world. This may doubtless be attributed to his having been almost constantly in office since he came into public life; than which nothing is more detrimental to the unfolding of natural ability, while it induces a sort of artificial talent, connected with forms and technicalities, which, though useful in business, is but of minor consequence in a comparative estimate of moral and intellectual qualities. I am told that in his manner he resembles Mr Pitt; be this, however, as it may, he is evidently a speaker, formed more by habit and imitation, than one whom nature prompts to be eloquent. He lacks that occasional accent of passion, the melody of oratory; and I doubt if, on any occasion, he could at all approximate to that magnificent intrepidity which was admired as one of the noblest characteristics of his master's style.

But all the display of learning and eloquence, and intellectual power and majesty of the House of Lords, shrinks into insignificance when compared with the moral attitude which the people have taken on this occasion. You know how much I have ever admired the attributes of the English national character—that boundless generosity, which can only be compared to the impartial benevolence of the sunshine—that heroic magnanimity, which makes the hand ever ready to succour a fallen foe; and that sublime courage, which rises with the energy of a conflagration roused by a tempest, at every insult or menace of an enemy. The compassionate interest taken by the populace in the future condition of the queen is worthy of this extraordinary people. There may be many among them actuated by what is called the radical spirit; but malignity alone would dare to ascribe the bravery of their compassion to a less noble feeling than that which has placed the kingdom so proudly in the van of all modern nations. There may be an amiable delusion, as my Lord Castlereagh has said, in the popular sentiments with respect to the queen. Upon that, as upon her case, I offer no opinion. It is enough for me to have seen, with the admiration of a worshipper, the manner in which the multitude have espoused her cause. But my paper is filled, and I must conclude. I should, however, mention that my sister's marriage is appointed to take place to-morrow, and that I accompany the happy pair to France.—Yours truly,

ANDREW PRINGLE

'This is a dry letter,' said Mr Snodgrass, and he handed it to Miss Isabella, who, in exchange, presented the one which she had herself at the same time received; but just as Mr Snodgrass was on the point of reading it, Miss Becky Glibbans was announced. 'How lucky this is,' exclaimed Miss Becky, 'to find you both thegither! Now you maun tell me all the particulars; for Miss Mally Glencairn is no in, and her letter lies unopened. I am just gasping to hear how Rachel conducted herself at being married in the kirk before all the folk—married to the hussar captain, too, after all! who would have thought it?'

'How, have you heard of the marriage already?' said Miss Isabella. 'Oh, it's in the newspapers,' replied the amiable inquisitant,—'Like ony tailor or weaver's—a' weddings maun nowadays gang into the papers. The whole toun, by this time, has got it; and I wouldna wonder if Rachel Pringle's marriage ding the queen's divorce out of folk's heads for the next nine days to come. But only to think of her being married in a public kirk. Surely her father would never submit to hae't done by a bishop? And then to put it in the London paper, as if Rachel Pringle had been somebody of distinction. Perhaps it might have been more to the purpose, considering what dragoon officers are, if she had got the doited Doctor, her father, to publish the intended marriage in the papers beforehand.'

'Haud that condumacious tongue of yours,' cried a voice, panting with haste as the door opened, and Mrs Glibbans entered. 'Becky, will you never devawl wi' your backbiting. I wonder frae whom the misleart lassie takes a' this passion of clashing.'

The authority of her parent's tongue silenced Miss Becky, and Mrs Glibbans having seated herself, continued,—'Is it your opinion, Mr Snodgrass, that this marriage can hold good, contracted, as I am told it is mentioned in the papers to hae been, at the horns of the altar of Episcopalian apostasy?'

'I can set you right as to that,' said Miss Isabella. 'Rachel mentions, that, after returning from the church, the Doctor himself performed the ceremony anew, according to the Presbyterian usage.' 'I am glad to hear't, very glad indeed,' said Mrs Glibbans. 'It would have been a judgment—like thing, had a bairn of Dr Pringle's—than whom, although there may be abler, there is not a sounder man in a the West of Scotland—been sacrificed to Moloch, like the victims of prelatic idolatry.'

At this juncture, Miss Mally Glencairn was announced: she entered, holding a letter from Mrs Pringle in her hand, with the seal unbroken. Having heard of the marriage from an acquaintance in the street, she had hurried home, in the well-founded expectation of hearing from her friend and well-wisher, and taking up the letter, which she found on her table, came with all speed to Miss Isabella Tod to commune with her on the tidings.

Never was any confluence of visitors more remarkable than on this occasion. Before Miss Mally had well explained the cause of her abrupt intrusion, Mr Micklewham made his appearance. He had come to Irvine to be measured for a new coat, and meeting by accident with Saunders Dickie, got the Doctor's letter from him, which, after reading, he thought he could do no less than call at Mrs Tod's, to let Miss Isabella know the change which had taken place in the condition of her friend.

Thus were all the correspondents of the Pringles assembled, by the merest chance, like the *dramatis personae* at the end of a play. After a little harmless bantering, it was agreed that Miss Mally should read her communication first—as all the others were previously acquainted with the contents of their respective letters, and Miss Mally read as follows:—

LETTER 30
Mrs Pringle to Miss Mally Glencairn

DEAR MISS MALLY—I hay a cro to pik with you conserning yoor comishon aboot the partickels for your friends. You can hay no noshon what the Doctor and me suffert on the head of the flooring shrubs. We took your Nota Beny as it was spilt, and went from shop to shop enquirin in a most partiklar manner for 'a Gardner's Bell, or the least of all flowering plants'; but sorrow a gardner in the whole tot here in London ever had heard of sic a thing; so we gave the porshoot up in despare. Howsomever, one of Andrew's acquaintance—a decent lad, who is only son to a saddler in a been way, that keeps his own carriage, and his son a coryikel, happent to call, and the Doctor told him what ill socsess we had in our serch for the gardner's bell; upon which he sought a sight of your yepissle, and read it as a thing that was just wonderful for its whorsogroffie; and then he sayid, that looking at the prinsipol of your spilling, he thought we should reed, 'a gardner's bill, or a list of all flooring plants'; whilk being no doot your intent, I have proqurt the same, and it is included heerin. But, Miss Mally, I would advize you to be more exac in your inditing, that no sic torbolashon may hippen on a future okashon.

What I hay to say for the present is, that you will, by a smak, get a bocks of kumoddities, whilk you will destraboot as derekit on every on of them, and you will before have resievit by the post-offis, an account of what has been don. I need say no forther at this time, knowin your discreshon and prooduns, septs that our Rachel and Captain Sabor will, if it pleese the Lord, be off to Parish, by way of Bryton, as man and wife, the morn's morning. What her father the Doctor gives for tocher, what is settlt on her for jontor, I will tell you all aboot when we meet; for it's our dishire noo to lose no tim in retorning to the manse, this being the last of our diplomaticals in London, where we have found the Argents a most discrit family, payin to the last farding the Cornal's legacy, and most seevil, and well bred to us.

As I am naterally gretly okypt with this matteromoneal afair, you cannot expect ony news; but the queen is going on with a dreadful rat, by which the pesents hay falen more than a whole entirr pesent. I wish our fonds were well oot of them, and in yird and stane, which is a constansie. But what is to become of the poor donsie woman, no one can expound. Some think she will be pot in the Toor of London, and her head chappit off; others think she will raise sic a stramash, that she will send the whole government into the air, like peelings of ingons, by a gunpoother plot. But it's my opinion, and I have weighed the matter well in my understanding, that she will hay to fight with sword in hand, be she ill, or be she good. How els can she hop to get the better of more than two hundred lords, as the Doctor, who has seen them, tells me, with princes of the blood-royal, and the prelatic bishops, whom, I need not tell you, are the worst of all.

But the thing I grudge most, is to be so long in Lundon, and no to see the king. Is it not a hard thing to come to London, and no to see the king? I am not pleesed with him, I assure you, becose he does not set himself out to public view, like ony other curiosity, but stays in his palis, they say, like one of the anshent wooden images of idolatry, the which is a great peety, he beeing, as I am told, a beautiful man, and more the gentleman than all the coortiers of his court.

The Doctor has been minting to me that there is an address from Irvine to the queen; and he, being so near a neighbour to your toun, has been thinking to pay his respecs with it, to see her near at hand. But I will say nothing; he may take his own way in matters of gospel and spiritualety; yet I have my scroopols of conshence, how this may not turn out a rebellyon against the king; and I would hay him to sift and see who are at the address, before he pits his han to it. For, if it's a radikol job, as I jealoos it is, what will the Doctor then say? who is an orthodox man, as the world nose.

In the maitre of our dumesticks, no new axsident has cast up; but I have seen such a wonder as could not have been forethocht. Having a washin, I went down to see how the lassies were doing; but judge of my feelings, when I saw them triomphing on the top of pattons, standing upright before the boyns on chairs, rubbin the clothes to juggins between their hands, above the sapples, with their gouns and stays on, and round-eared mutches. What would you think of such a miracle at the washing-house in the Goffields, or the Gallows-knows of Irvine? The cook, howsomever, has shown me a way to make rice-puddings without eggs, by putting in a bit of shoohet, which is as good—and this you will tell Miss Nanny Eydent; likewise, that the most fashionable way of boiling green pis, is to pit a blade of speermint in the pot, which gives a fine flavour. But this is a long letter, and my pepper is done; so no more, but remains your friend and well-wisher,

JANET PRINGLE

'A great legacy, and her dochtir married, in ae journey to London, is doing business,' said Mrs Glibbans, with a sigh, as she looked to her only get, Miss Becky; 'but the Lord's will is to be done in a' thing;—sooner or later something of the same kind will come, I trust, to all our families.' 'Ay,' replied Miss Mally Glencairn, 'marriage is like death—it's what we are a' to come to.'

'I have my doubts of that,' said Miss Becky with a sneer. 'Ye have been lang spair't from it, Miss Mally.'

'Ye're a spiteful puddock; and if the men hae the e'en and lugs they used to hae, gude pity him whose lot is cast with thine, Becky Glibbans,' replied the elderly maiden ornament of the Kirkgate, somewhat tartly.

Here Mr. Snodgrass interposed, and said, he would read to them the letter which Miss Isabella had received from the bride; and without waiting for their concurrence, opened and read as follows:—

LETTER 31
Mrs Sabre to Miss Isabella Tod

MY DEAREST BELL—Rachel Pringle is no more! My heart flutters as I write the fatal words. This morning, at nine o'clock precisely, she was conducted in bridal array to the new church of Mary-le-bone; and there, with ring and book, sacrificed to the Minotaur, Matrimony, who devours so many of our bravest youths and fairest maidens.

My mind is too agitated to allow me to describe the scene. The office of handmaid to the victim, which, in our young simplicity, we had fondly thought one of us would perform for the other, was gracefully sustained by Miss Argent.

On returning from church to my father's residence in Baker Street, where we breakfasted, he declared himself not satisfied with the formalities of the English ritual, and obliged us to undergo a second ceremony from himself, according to the wonted forms of the Scottish Church. All the advantages and pleasures of which, my dear Bell, I hope you will soon enjoy.

But I have no time to enter into particulars. The captain and his lady, by themselves, in their own carriage, set off for Brighton in the course of less than an hour. On Friday they are to be followed by a large party of their friends and relations; and, after spending a few days in that emporium of salt-water pleasures, they embark, accompanied with their beloved brother, Mr Andrew Pringle, for Paris; where they are afterwards to be joined by the Argents. It is our intention to remain about a month in the French capital; whether we shall extend our tour, will depend on subsequent circumstances: in the meantime, however, you will hear frequently from me.

My mother, who has a thousand times during these important transactions wished for the assistance of Nanny Eydent, transmits to Miss Mally Glencairn a box containing all the requisite bridal recognisances for our Irvine friends. I need not say that the best is for the faithful companion of my happiest years. As I had made a vow in my heart that Becky Glibbans should never wear gloves for my marriage, I was averse to sending her any at all, but my mother insisted that no exceptions should be made. I secretly took care, however, to mark a pair for her, so much too large, that I am sure she will never put them on. The asp will be not a little vexed at the disappointment. Adieu for a time, and believe that, although your affectionate Rachel Pringle be gone that way in which she hopes you will soon follow, one not less sincerely attached to you, though it be the first time she has so subscribed herself, remains in

RACHEL SABRE

Before the ladies had time to say a word on the subject, the prudent young clergyman called immediately on Mr Micklewham to read the letter which he had received from the Doctor; and which the worthy dominie did without delay, in that rich and full voice with which he is accustomed to teach his scholars elocution by example.

LETTER 32
The Rev Z Pringle, D. D., to Mr Micklewham, Schoolmaster and Session-Clerk, Garnock

LONDON

DEAR SIR—I have been much longer of replying to your letter of the 3rd of last month, than I ought in civility to have been, but really time, in this town of London, runs at a fast rate, and the day passes before the dark's done. What with Mrs Pringle and her daughter's concernments, anent the marriage to Captain Sabre, and the trouble I felt myself obliged to take in the queen's affair, I assure you, Mr Micklewham, that it's no to be expressed how I have been occupied for the last four weeks. But all things must come to a conclusion in this world. Rachel Pringle is married, and the queen's weary trial is brought to an end—upon the subject and motion of the same, I offer no opinion, for I made it a point never to read the evidence, being resolved to stand by THE WORD from the first, which is clearly and plainly written in the queen's favour, and it does not do in a case of conscience to stand on trifles; putting, therefore, out of consideration the fact libelled, and looking both at the head and the tail of the proceeding, I was of a firm persuasion, that all the sculduddery of the business might have been well spared from the eye of the public, which is of itself sufficiently prone to keek and kook, in every possible way, for a glimpse of a black story; and, therefore, I thought it my duty to stand up in all places against the trafficking that was attempted with a divine institution. And I think, when my people read how their prelatic enemies, the bishops (the heavens defend the poor Church of Scotland from being subjected to the weight of their paws), have been visited with a constipation of the understanding on that point, it must to them be a great satisfaction to know how clear and collected their minister was on this fundamental of society. For it has turned out, as I said to Mrs. Pringle, as well as others, it would do, that a sense of grace and religion would be manifested in some quarter before all was done, by which the devices for an unsanctified repudiation or divorce would be set at nought.

As often as I could, deeming it my duty as a minister of the word and gospel, I got into the House of Lords, and heard the trial; and I cannot think how ever it was expected that justice could be done yonder; for although no man could be more attentive than I was, every time I came away I was more confounded than when I went; and when the trial was done, it seemed to me just to be clearing up for a proper beginning—all which is a proof that there was a foul conspiracy. Indeed, when I saw Duke Hamilton's daughter coming out of the coach with the queen, I never could think after, that a lady of her degree would have countenanced the queen had the matter laid to her charge been as it was said. Not but in any circumstance it behoved a lady of that ancient and royal blood, to be seen beside the queen in such a great historical case as a trial.

I hope, in the part I have taken, my people will be satisfied; but whether they are satisfied or not, my own conscience is content with me. I was in the House of Lords when her majesty came down for the last time, and saw her handed up the stairs by the usher of the black-rod, a little stumpy man, wonderful particular about the rules of the House, insomuch that he was almost angry with me for stopping at the stair-head. The afflicted woman was then in great spirits, and I saw no symptoms of the swelled legs that Lord Lauderdale, that jooking man, spoke about, for she skippit up the steps like a lassie. But my heart was wae for her when all was over, for she came out like an astonished creature, with a wild steadfast look, and a sort of something in the face that was as if the rational spirit had fled away; and she went down to her coach as if she had submitted to be led to a doleful destiny. Then the shouting of the people began, and I saw and shouted too in spite of my decorum, which I marvel at sometimes, thinking it could be nothing less than an involuntary testification of the spirit within me.

Anent the marriage of Rachel Pringle, it may be needful in me to state, for the satisfaction of my people, that although by stress of law we were obligated to conform to the practice of the Episcopalians, by taking out a bishop's license, and going to their church, and vowing, in a pagan fashion, before their altars, which are an abomination to the Lord; yet, when the young folk came home, I made them stand up, and be married again before me, according to all regular marriages in our national Church. For this I had two reasons: first, to satisfy myself that there had been a true and real marriage; and, secondly, to remove the doubt of the former ceremony being sufficient; for marriage being of divine appointment, and the English form and ritual being a thing established by Act of Parliament, which is of human ordination, I was not sure that marriage performed according to a human enactment could be a fulfilment of a divine ordinance. I therefore hope that my people will approve what I have done; and in order that there may be a sympathising with me, you will go over to Banker M———y, and get what he will give you, as ordered by me, and distribute it among the poorest of the parish, according to the best of your discretion, my long absence having taken from me the power of judgment in a matter of this sort. I wish indeed for the glad sympathy of my people, for I think that our Saviour turning water into wine at the wedding, was an example set that we should rejoice and be merry at the fulfilment of one of the great obligations imposed on us as social creatures; and I have ever regarded the unhonoured treatment of a marriage occasion as a thing of evil bodement, betokening heavy hearts and light purses to the lot of the bride and bridegroom. You will hear more from me by and by; in the meantime, all I can say is, that when we have taken our leave of the young folks, who are going to France, it is Mrs Pringle's intent, as well as mine, to turn our horses' heads northward, and make our way with what speed we can, for our own quiet home, among you. So no more at present from your friend and pastor;

Z. PRINGLE

Mrs Tod, the mother of Miss Isabella, a respectable widow lady, who had quiescently joined the company, proposed that they should now drink health, happiness, and all manner of prosperity, to the young couple; and that nothing might be wanting to secure the favourable auspices of good omens to the toast, she desired Miss Isabella to draw fresh bottles of white and red. When all manner of felicity was duly wished in wine to the captain and his lady, the party rose to seek their respective homes. But a bustle at the street-door occasioned a pause. Mrs. Tod inquired the matter; and three or four voices at once replied, that an express had come from Garnock for Nanse Swaddle the midwife, Mrs Craig being taken with her pains. 'Mr Snodgrass,' said Mrs Glibbans, instantly and emphatically, 'ye maun let me go with you, and we can spiritualise on the road; for I hae promis't Mrs Craig to be wi' her at the crying, to see the upshot—so I hope you will come awa.'

It would be impossible in us to suppose, that Mr Snodgrass had any objections to spiritualise with Mrs Glibbans on the road between Irvine and Garnock; but, notwithstanding her urgency, he excused himself from going with her; however, he recommended her to the special care and protection of Mr Micklewham, who was at that time on his legs to return home. 'Oh! Mr Snodgrass,' said the lady, looking slyly, as she adjusted her cloak, at him and Miss Isabella, 'there will be marrying and giving in marriage till the day of judgment.' And with these oracular words she took her departure.

Chapter 10

The Return

On Friday, Miss Mally Glencairn received a brief note from Mrs Pringle, informing her, that she and the Doctor would reach the manse, 'God willing,' in time for tea on Saturday; and begging her, therefore, to go over from Irvine, and see that the house was in order for their reception. This note was written from Glasgow, where they had arrived, in their own carriage, from Carlisle on the preceding day, after encountering, as Mrs Pringle said, 'more hardships and extorshoning than all the dangers of the sea which they met with in the smack of Leith that took them to London.'

As soon as Miss Mally received this intelligence, she went to Miss Isabella Tod, and requested her company for the next day to Garnock, where they arrived betimes to dine with Mr Snodgrass, Mrs Glibbans and her daughter Becky were then on a consolatory visit to Mr Craig. We mentioned in the last chapter, that the crying of Mrs Craig had come on; and that Mrs Glibbans, according to promise, and with the most anxious solicitude, had gone to wait the upshot. The upshot was most melancholy,—Mrs Craig was soon no more;—she was taken, as Mrs Glibbans observed on the occasion, from the earthly arms of her husband, to the spiritual bosom of Abraham, Isaac, and Jacob, which was far better. But the baby survived; so that, what with getting a nurse, and the burial, and all the work and handling that a birth and death in one house at the same time causes, Mr Craig declared, that he could not do without Mrs Glibbans; and she, with all that Christianity by which she was so zealously distinguished, sent for Miss Becky, and took up her abode with him, till it would please Him, without whom there is no comfort, to wipe the eyes of the pious elder. In a word, she staid so long, that a rumour began to spread that Mr Craig would need a wife to look after his bairn; and that Mrs Glibbans was destined to supply the desideratum. Mr Snodgrass, after enjoying his dinner society with Miss Mally and Miss Isabella, thought it necessary to dispatch a courier, in the shape of a barefooted servant lass, to Mr Micklewham, to inform the elders that the Doctor was expected home in time for tea, leaving it to their discretion either to greet his safe return at the manse, or in any other form or manner that would be most agreeable to themselves.

These important news were soon diffused through the clachan. Mr Micklewham dismissed his school an hour before the wonted time, and there was a universal interest and curiosity excited, to see the Doctor coming home in his own coach. All the boys of Garnock assembled at the braehead which commands an extensive view of the Kilmarnock road, the only one from Glasgow that runs through the parish; the wives with their sucklings were seated on the large stones at their respective door-cheeks; while their cats were calmly reclining on the window soles. The lassie weans, like clustering bees, were mounted on the carts that stood before Thomas Birlpenny the vintner's door, churming with anticipated delight; the old men took their stations on the dike that incloses the side of the vintner's kail-yard, and 'a batch of wabster lads,' with green aprons and thin yellow faces, planted themselves at the gable of the malt kiln, where they were wont, when trade was better, to play at the hand-ball; but, poor fellows, since the trade fell off, they have had no heart for the game, and the vintner's half-mutchkin stoups glitter in empty splendour unrequired on the shelf below the brazen sconce above the bracepiece, amidst the idle pewter pepper-boxes, the bright copper tea-kettle, the coffee-pot that has never been in use, and lids of saucepans that have survived their principals,—the wonted ornaments of every trig change-house kitchen.

The season was far advanced; but the sun shone at his setting with a glorious composure, and the birds in the hedges and on the boughs were again gladdened into song. The leaves had fallen thickly, and the stubble-fields were bare, but Autumn, in a many-coloured tartan plaid, was seen still walking with matronly composure in the woodlands, along the brow of the neighbouring hills.

About half-past four o'clock, a movement was seen among the callans at the braehead, and a shout announced that a carriage was in sight. It was answered by a murmuring response of satisfaction from the whole village. In the course of a few minutes the carriage reached the turnpike—it was of the darkest green and the gravest fashion,—a large trunk, covered with Russian matting, and fastened on with cords, prevented from chafing it by knots of straw rope, occupied the front,—behind, other two were fixed in the same manner, the lesser of course uppermost; and deep beyond a pile of light bundles and bandboxes, that occupied a large portion of the interior, the blithe faces of the Doctor and Mrs Pringle were discovered. The boys huzzaed, the Doctor flung them penny-pieces, and the mistress baubees.

As the carriage drove along, the old men on the dike stood up and reverently took off their hats and bonnets. The weaver lads gazed with a melancholy smile; the lassies on the carts clapped their hands with joy; the women on both sides of the street acknowledged the recognising nods; while all the village dogs, surprised by the sound of chariot wheels, came baying and barking forth, and sent off the cats that were so doucely sitting on the window soles, clambering and scampering over the roofs in terror of their lives.

When the carriage reached the manse door, Mr Snodgrass, the two ladies, with Mr Micklewham, and all the elders except Mr Craig, were there ready to receive the travellers. But over this joy of welcoming we must draw a veil; for the first thing that the Doctor did, on entering the parlour and before sitting down, was to return thanks for his safe restoration to his home and people.

The carriage was then unloaded, and as package, bale, box, and bundle were successively brought in, Miss Mally Glencairn expressed her admiration at the great capacity of the chaise. 'Ay,' said Mrs Pringle, 'but you know not what we have suffert for't in coming through among the English taverns on the road; some of them would not take us forward when there was a hill to pass, unless we would take four horses, and every one after another reviled us for having no mercy in loading the carriage like a waggon,—and then the drivers were so gleg and impudent, that it was worse than martyrdom to come with them. Had the Doctor taken my advice, he would have brought our own civil London coachman, whom we hired with his own horses by the job; but he said it behoved us to gi' e our ain fish guts to our ain sea-maws, and that he designed to fee Thomas Birlpenny's hostler for our coachman, being a lad of the parish. This obliged us to post it from London; but, oh! Miss Mally, what an outlay it has been!'

The Doctor, in the meantime, had entered into conversation with the gentlemen, and was inquiring, in the most particular manner, respecting all his parishioners, and expressing his surprise that Mr Craig had not been at the manse with the rest of the elders. 'It does not look well,' said the Doctor. Mr Daff, however, offered the best apology for his absence that could be made. 'He has had a gentle dispensation, sir—Mrs Craig has won awa' out of this sinful world, poor woman, she had a large experience o't; but the bairn's to the fore, and Mrs Glibbans, that has such a cast of grace, has ta'en charge of the house since before the interment. It's thought, considering what's by gane, Mr Craig may do waur than make her mistress, and I hope, sir, your exhortation will no be wanting to egg the honest man to think o't seriously.'

Mr Snodgrass, before delivering the household keys, ordered two bottles of wine, with glasses and biscuit, to be set upon the table, while Mrs Pringle produced from a paper package, that had helped to stuff one of the pockets of the carriage, a piece of rich plum-cake, brought all the way from a confectioner's in Cockspur Street, London, not only for the purpose of being eaten, but, as she said, to let Miss Nanny Eydent pree, in order to direct the Irvine bakers how to bake others like it.

Tea was then brought in; and, as it was making, the Doctor talked aside to the elders, while Mrs Pringle recounted to Miss Mally and Miss Isabella the different incidents of her adventures subsequent to the marriage of Miss Rachel.

'The young folk,' said she, 'having gone to Brighton, we followed them in a few days, for we were told it was a curiosity, and that the king has a palace there, just a warld's wonder! and, truly, Miss Mally, it is certainly not like a house for a creature of this world, but for some Grand Turk or Chinaman. The Doctor said, it put him in mind of Miss Jenny Macbride's sideboard in the Stockwell of Glasgow; where all the pepperboxes, poories, and teapots, punch-bowls, and china-candlesticks of her progenitors are set out for a show, that tells her visitors, they are but seldom put to use. As for the town of Brighton, it's what I would call a gawky piece of London. I could see nothing in it but a wheen idlers, hearing twa lads, at night, crying, "Five, six, seven for a shilling," in the booksellers' shops, with a play-actor lady singing in a corner, because her voice would not do for the players' stage. Therefore, having seen the Captain and Mrs Sabre off to France, we came home to London; but it's not to be told what we had to pay at the hotel where we staid in Brighton. Howsomever, having come back to London, we settled our counts, and, buying a few necessars, we prepared for Scotland,—and here we are. But travelling has surely a fine effect in enlarging the understanding; for both the Doctor and me thought, as we came along, that everything had a smaller and poorer look than when we went away; and I dinna think this room is just what it used to be. What think ye o't, Miss Isabella? How would ye like to spend your days in't?'

Miss Isabella reddened at this question; but Mrs Pringle, who was as prudent as she was observant, affecting not to notice this, turned round to Miss Mally Glencairn, and said softly in her ear,—'Rachel was Bell's confidante, and has told us all about what's going on between her and Mr Snodgrass. We have agreed no to stand in their way, as soon as the Doctor can get a mailing or two to secure his money upon.'

Meantime, the Doctor received from the elders a very satisfactory account of all that had happened among his people, both in and out of the Session, during his absence; and he was vastly pleased to find there had been no inordinate increase of wickedness; at the same time, he was grieved for the condition in which the poor weavers still continued, saying, that among other things of which he had been of late meditating, was the setting up of a lending bank in the parish for the labouring classes, where, when they were out of work, 'bits of loans for a house-rent, or a brat of claes, or sic like, might be granted, to be repaid when trade grew better, and thereby take away the objection that an honest pride had to receiving help from the Session.

Then some lighter general conversation ensued, in which the Doctor gave his worthy counsellors a very jocose description of many of the lesser sort of adventures which he had met with; and the ladies having retired to inspect the great bargains that Mrs Pringle had got, and the splendid additions she had made to her wardrobe, out of what she denominated the dividends of the present portion of the legacy, the Doctor ordered in the second biggest toddy-bowl, the guardevine with the old rum, and told the lassie to see if the tea-kettle was still boiling. 'Ye maun drink our welcome hame,' said he to the elders; 'it would nae otherwise be canny. But I'm sorry Mr Craig has nae come.' At these words the door opened, and the absent elder entered, with a long face and a deep sigh. 'Ha!' cried Mr. Daff 'this is very droll. Speak of the Evil One, and he'll appear';—which words dinted on the heart of Mr Craig, who thought his marriage in December had been the subject of their discourse. The Doctor, however, went up and shook him cordially by the hand, and said, 'Now I take this very kind, Mr Craig; for I could not have expected you, considering ye have got, as I am told, your jo

181

in the house'; at which words the Doctor winked paukily to Mr Daff who rubbed his hands with fainness, and gave a good-humoured sort of keckling laugh. This facetious stroke of policy was a great relief to the afflicted elder, for he saw by it that the Doctor did not mean to trouble him with any inquiries respecting his deceased wife; and, in consequence, he put on a blither face, and really affected to have forgotten her already more than he had done in sincerity.

Thus the night passed in decent temperance and a happy decorum; insomuch, that the elders when they went away, either by the influence of the toddy-bowl, or the Doctor's funny stories about the Englishers, declared that he was an excellent man, and, being none lifted up, was worthy of his rich legacy.

At supper, the party, besides the minister and Mrs Pringle, consisted of the two Irvine ladies, and Mr Snodgrass. Miss Becky Glibbans came in when it was about half over, to express her mother's sorrow at not being able to call that night, 'Mr Craig's bairn having taken an ill turn.' The truth, however, was, that the worthy elder had been rendered somewhat tozy by the minister's toddy, and wanted an opportunity to inform the old lady of the joke that had been played upon him by the Doctor calling her his jo, and to see how she would relish it. So by a little address Miss Becky was sent out of the way, with the excuse we have noticed; at the same time, as the night was rather sharp, it is not to be supposed that she would have been the bearer of any such message, had her own curiosity not enticed her.

During supper the conversation was very lively. Many 'pickant jokes,' as Miss Becky described them, were cracked by the Doctor; but, soon after the table was cleared, he touched Mr Snodgrass on the arm, and, taking up one of the candles, went with him to his study, where he then told him, that Rachel Pringle, now Mrs Sabre, had informed him of a way in which he could do him a service. 'I understand, sir,' said the Doctor, 'that you have a notion of Miss Bell Tod, but that until ye get a kirk there can be no marriage. But the auld horse may die waiting for the new grass; and, therefore, as the Lord has put it in my power to do a good action both to you and my people,—whom I am glad to hear you have pleased so well,—if it can be brought about that you could be made helper and successor, I'll no object to give up to you the whole stipend, and, by and by, maybe the manse to the bargain. But that is if you marry Miss Bell; for it was a promise that Rachel gar't me make to her on her wedding morning. Ye know she was a forcasting lassie, and, I have reason to believe, has said nothing anent this to Miss Bell herself; so that if you have no partiality for Miss Bell, things will just rest on their own footing; but if you have a notion, it must be a satisfaction to you to know this, as it will be a pleasure to me to carry it as soon as possible into effect.' Mr Snodgrass was a good deal agitated; he was taken by surprise, and without words the Doctor might have guessed his sentiments; he, however, frankly confessed that he did entertain a very high opinion of Miss Bell, but that he was not sure if a country parish would exactly suit him. 'Never mind that,' said the Doctor; 'if it does not fit at first, you will get used to it; and if a better casts up, it will be no obstacle.'

The two gentlemen then rejoined the ladies, and, after a short conversation, Miss Becky Glibbans was admonished to depart, by the servants bringing in the Bibles for the worship of the evening. This was usually performed before supper, but, owing to the bowl being on the table, and the company jocose, it had been postponed till all the guests who were not to sleep in the house had departed.

The Sunday morning was fine and bright for the season; the hoar-frost, till about an hour after sunrise, lay white on the grass and tombstones in the churchyard; but before the bell rung for the congregation to assemble, it was exhaled away, and a freshness, that was only known to be autumnal by the fallen and yellow leaves that strewed the church-way path from the ash and plane trees in the avenue, encouraged the spirits to sympathise with the universal cheerfulness of all nature.

The return of the Doctor had been bruited through the parish with so much expedition, that, when the bell rung for public worship, none of those who were in the practice of stopping in the churchyard to talk about the weather were so ignorant as not to have heard of this important fact. In consequence, before the time at which the Doctor was wont to come from the back-gate which opened from the manse-garden into the churchyard, a great majority of his people were assembled to receive him.

At the last jingle of the bell, the back-gate was usually opened, and the Doctor was wont to come forth as punctually as a cuckoo of a clock at the striking of the hour; but a deviation was observed on this occasion. Formerly, Mrs Pringle and the rest of the family came first, and a few minutes were allowed to elapse before the Doctor, laden with grace, made his appearance. But at this time, either because it had been settled that Mr Snodgrass was to officiate, or for some other reason, there was a breach in the observance of this time-honoured custom.

As the ringing of the bell ceased, the gate unclosed, and the Doctor came forth. He was of that easy sort of featherbed corpulency of form that betokens good-nature, and had none of that smooth, red, well-filled protuberancy, which indicates a choleric humour and a testy temper. He was in fact what Mrs Glibbans denominated 'a man of a gausy external.' And some little change had taken place during his absence in his visible equipage. His stockings, which were wont to be of worsted, had undergone a translation into silk; his waistcoat, instead of the venerable Presbyterian flap-covers to the pockets, which were of Johnsonian magnitude, was become plain—his coat in all times single-breasted, with no collar, still, however, maintained its ancient characteristics; instead, however, of the former bright black cast horn, the buttons were covered with cloth. But the chief alteration was discernible in the furniture of the head. He had exchanged the simplicity of his own respectable grey hairs for the cauliflower hoariness of a PARRISH[1] wig, on which he wore a broad-brimmed hat, turned up a little at each side behind, in a portentous manner, indicatory of Episcopalian predilections. This, however, was not justified by any alteration in his principles, being merely an innocent variation of fashion, the natural result of a Doctor of Divinity buying a hat and wig in London.

The moment that the Doctor made his appearance, his greeting and salutation was quite delightful; it was that of a father returned to his children, and a king to his people.

Almost immediately after the Doctor, Mrs Pringle, followed by Miss Mally Glencairn and Miss Isabella Tod, also debouched from the gate, and the assembled females remarked, with no less instinct, the transmutation which she had undergone. She was dressed in a dark blue cloth pelisse, trimmed with a dyed fur, which, as she told Miss Mally, 'looked quite as well as sable, without costing a third of the money.' A

1 See the Edinburgh Review, for an account of our old friend, Dr Parr's wig, and Spital Sermon.

most matronly muff, that, without being of sable, was of an excellent quality, contained her hands; and a very large Leghorn straw bonnet, decorated richly, but far from excess, with a most substantial band and bow of a broad crimson satin ribbon around her head.

If the Doctor was gratified to see his people so gladly thronging around him, Mrs Pringle had no less pleasure also in her thrice-welcome reception. It was an understood thing, that she had been mainly instrumental in enabling the minister to get his great Indian legacy; and in whatever estimation she may have been previously held for her economy and management, she was now looked up to as a personage skilled in the law, and particularly versed in testamentary erudition. Accordingly, in the customary testimonials of homage with which she was saluted in her passage to the church door, there was evidently a sentiment of veneration mingled, such as had never been evinced before, and which was neither unobserved nor unappreciated by that acute and perspicacious lady.

The Doctor himself did not preach, but sat in the minister's pew till Mr Snodgrass had concluded an eloquent and truly an affecting sermon; at the end of which, the Doctor rose and went up into the pulpit, where he publicly returned thanks for the favours and blessings he had obtained during his absence, and for the safety in which he had been restored, after many dangers and tribulations, to the affections of his parishioners.

Such were the principal circumstances that marked the return of the family. In the course of the week after, the estate of Moneypennies being for sale, it was bought for the Doctor as a great bargain. It was not, however, on account of the advantageous nature of the purchase that our friend valued this acquisition, but entirely because it was situated in his own parish, and part of the lands marching with the Glebe.

The previous owner of Moneypennies had built an elegant house on the estate, to which Mrs Pringle is at present actively preparing to remove from the manse; and it is understood, that, as Mr Snodgrass was last week declared helper, and successor to the Doctor, his marriage with Miss Isabella Tod will take place with all convenient expedition. There is also reason to believe, that, as soon as decorum will permit, any scruple which Mrs Glibbans had to a second marriage is now removed, and that she will soon again grace the happy circle of wives by the name of Mrs Craig. Indeed, we are assured that Miss Nanny Eydent is actually at this time employed in making up her wedding garments; for, last week, that worthy and respectable young person was known to have visited Bailie Delap's shop, at a very early hour in the morning, and to have priced many things of a bridal character, besides getting swatches; after which she was seen to go to Mrs Glibbans's house, where she remained a very considerable time, and to return straight therefrom to the shop, and purchase divers of the articles which she had priced and inspected; all of which constitute sufficient grounds for the general opinion in Irvine, that the union of Mr Craig with Mrs Glibbans is a happy event drawing near to consummation.

The Provost

Introduction

During a recent visit to the west Country, among other old friends we paid our respects to Mrs Pawkie, the relict of the Provost of that name, who three several times enjoyed the honour of being chief magistrate in Gudetown. Since the death of her worthy husband, and the comfortable settlement in life of her youngest daughter, Miss Jenny, who was married last year to Mr Caption, writer to the signet, she has been, as she told us herself, "beeking in the lown o' the conquest which the gudeman had, wi' sic an ettling o' pains and industry, gathered for his family."

Our conversation naturally diverged into various topics, and, among others, we discoursed at large on the manifold improvements which had taken place, both in town and country, since we had visited the Royal Burgh. This led the widow, in a complimentary way, to advert to the hand which, it is alleged, we have had in the editing of that most excellent work, entitled, "Annals of the Parish of Dalmailing," intimating, that she had a book in the handwriting of her deceased husband, the Provost, filled with a variety of most curious matter; in her opinion, of far more consequence to the world than any book that we had ever been concerned in putting out.

Considering the veneration in which Mr Pawkie had been through life regarded by his helpmate, we must confess that her eulogium on the merits of his work did not impress us with the most profound persuasion that it was really deserving of much attention. Politeness, however, obliged us to express an earnest desire to see the volume, which, after some little hesitation, was produced. Judge, then, of the nature of our emotions, when, in cursorily turning over a few of the well-penned pages, we found that it far surpassed every thing the lady had said in its praise. Such, indeed, was our surprise, that we could not refrain from openly and at once assuring her, that the delight and satisfaction which it was calculated to afford, rendered it a duty on her part to lose no time in submitting it to the public; and, after lavishing a panegyric on the singular and excellent qualities of the author, which was all most delicious to his widow, we concluded with a delicate insinuation of the pleasure we should enjoy, in being made the humble instrument of introducing to the knowledge of mankind a volume so replete and enriched with the fruits of his practical wisdom. Thus, partly by a judicious administration of flattery, and partly also by solicitation, backed by an indirect proposal to share the profits, we succeeded in persuading Mrs Pawkie to allow us to take the valuable manuscript to Edinburgh, in order to prepare it for publication.

Having obtained possession of the volume, we lost no time till we had made ourselves master of its contents. It appeared to consist of a series of detached notes, which, together, formed something analogous to an historical view of the different important and interesting scenes and affairs the Provost had been personally engaged in during his long magisterial life. We found, however, that the concatenation of the memoranda which he had made of public transactions, was in several places interrupted by the insertion of matter not in the least degree interesting to the nation at large; and that, in arranging the work for the press, it would be requisite and proper to omit many of the notes and much of the record, in order to preserve the historical coherency of the narrative. But in doing this, the text has been retained inviolate, in so much that while we congratulate the world on the addition we are thus enabled to make to the stock of public knowledge, we cannot but felicitate ourselves on the complete and consistent form into which we have so successfully reduced our precious materials; the separation of which, from the dross of personal and private anecdote, was a task of no small difficulty; such, indeed, as the editors only of the autographic memoirs of other great men can duly appreciate.

Chapter I

The Forecast

It must be allowed in the world, that a man who has thrice reached the highest station of life in his line, has a good right to set forth the particulars of the discretion and prudence by which he lifted himself so far above the ordinaries of his day and generation; indeed, the generality of mankind may claim this as a duty; for the conduct of public men, as it has been often wisely said, is a species of public property, and their rules and observances have in all ages been considered things of a national concernment. I have therefore well weighed the importance it may be of to posterity, to know by what means I have thrice been made an instrument to represent the supreme power and authority of Majesty in the royal burgh of Gudetown, and how I deported myself in that honour and dignity, so much to the satisfaction of my superiors in the state and commonwealth of the land, to say little of the great respect in which I was held by the townsfolk, and far less of the terror that I was to evildoers. But not to be over circumstantial, I propose to confine this history of my life to the public portion thereof, on the which account I will take up the beginning at the crisis when I first entered into business, after having served more than a year above my time, with the late Mr Thomas Remnant, than whom there was not a more creditable man in the burgh; and he died in the possession of the functionaries and faculties of town-treasurer, much respected by all acquainted with his orderly and discreet qualities.

Mr Remnant was, in his younger years, when the growth of luxury and prosperity had not come to such a head as it has done since, a tailor that went out to the houses of the adjacent lairds and country gentry, whereby he got an inkling of the policy of the world, that could not have been gathered in any other way by a man of his station and degree of life. In process of time he came to be in a settled way, and when I was bound 'prentice to him, he had three regular journeymen and a cloth shop. It was therefore not so much for learning the tailoring, as to get an insight in the conformity between the traffic of the shop and the board that I was bound to him, being destined by my parents for the profession appertaining to the former, and to conjoin thereto something of the mercery and haberdashery: my uncle, that had been a sutler in the army along with General Wolfe, who made a conquest of Quebec, having left me a legacy of three hundred pounds because I was called after him, the which legacy was a consideration for to set me up in due season in some genteel business.

Accordingly, as I have narrated, when I had passed a year over my 'prenticeship with Mr Remnant, I took up the corner shop at the Cross, facing the Tolbooth; and having had it adorned in a befitting manner, about a month before the summer fair thereafter, I opened it on that day, with an excellent assortment of goods, the best, both for taste and variety, that had ever been seen in the burgh of Gudetown; and the winter following, finding by my books that I was in a way to do so, I married my wife: she was daughter to Mrs Broderip, who kept the head inn in Irville, and by whose death, in the fall of the next year, we got a nest egg, that, without a vain pretension, I may say we have not failed to lay upon, and clock to some purpose.

Being thus settled in a shop and in life, I soon found that I had a part to perform in the public world; but I looked warily about me before casting my nets, and therefore I laid myself out rather to be entreated than to ask; for I had often heard Mr Remnant observe, that the nature of man could not abide to see a neighbour taking place and preferment of his own accord. I therefore assumed a coothy and obliging demeanour towards my customers and the community in general; and sometimes even with the very beggars I found a jocose saying as well received as a bawbee, although naturally I dinna think I was ever what could be called a funny man, but only just as ye would say a thought ajee in that way. Howsever, I soon became, both by habit and repute, a man of popularity in the town, in so much that it was a shrewd saying of old James Alpha, the bookseller, that "mair gude jokes were cracked ilka day in James Pawkie's shop, than in Thomas Curl, the barber's, on a Saturday night."

Chapter 2

A Kithing

I could plainly discern that the prudent conduct which I had adopted towards the public was gradually growing into effect. Disputative neighbours made me their referee, and I became, as it were, an oracle that was better than the law, in so much that I settled their controversies without the expense that attends the same. But what convinced me more than any other thing that the line I pursued was verging towards a satisfactory result, was, that the elderly folk that came into the shop to talk over the news of the day, and to rehearse the diverse uncos, both of a national and a domestic nature, used to call me bailie and my lord; the which jocular derision was as a symptom and foretaste within their spirits of what I was ordained to be. Thus was I encouraged, by little and little, together with a sharp remarking of the inclination and bent of men's minds, to entertain the hope and assurance of rising to the top of all the town, as this book maketh manifest, and the incidents thereof will certificate.

Nothing particular, however, came to pass, till my wife lay in of her second bairn, our daughter Sarah; at the christening of whom, among divers friends and relations, forbye the minister, we had my father's cousin, Mr Alexander Clues, that was then deacon convener, and a man of great potency in his way, and possessed of an influence in the town-council of which he was well worthy, being a person of good discernment, and well versed in matters appertaining to the guildry. Mr Clues, as we were mellowing over the toddy bowl, said, that by and by the council would be looking to me to fill up the first gap that might happen therein; and Dr Swapkirk, the then minister, who had officiated on the occasion, observed, that it was a thing that, in the course of nature, could not miss to be, for I had all the douce demeanour and sagacity which it behoved a magistrate to possess. But I cannily replied, though I was right contented to hear this, that I had no time for governing, and it would be more for the advantage of the commonwealth to look for the counselling of an older head than mine, happen when a vacancy might in the town-council. In this conjuncture of our discoursing, Mrs Pawkie, my wife, who was sitting by the fireside in her easy chair, with a cod at her head, for she had what was called a sore time o't, said:—"Na, na, gudeman, ye need na be sae mim; everybody kens, and I ken too, that ye're ettling at the magistracy. It's as plain as a pikestaff, gudeman, and I'll no let ye rest if ye dinna mak me a bailie's wife or a' be done"—I was not ill pleased to hear Mrs Pawkie so spiritful; but I replied,' Dinna try to stretch your arm, gudewife, further than your sleeve will let you; we maun ca' canny mony a day yet before we think of dignities." The which speech, in a way of implication, made Deacon Clues to understand that I would not absolutely refuse an honour thrust upon me, while it maintained an outward show of humility and moderation.

There was, however, a gleg old carlin among the gossips then present, one Mrs Sprowl, the widow of a deceased magistrate, and she cried out aloud:—"Deacon Clues, Deacon Clues, I redd you no to believe a word that Mr Pawkie's saying, for that was the very way my friend that's no more laid himself out to be fleeched to tak what he was greenan for; so get him intill the council when ye can: we a' ken he'll be a credit to the place," and "so here's to the health of Bailie Pawkie, that is to be," cried Mrs Sprowl. All present pledged her in the toast, by which we had a wonderful share of diversion. Nothing, however, immediately rose out of this, but it set men's minds abarming and working; so that, before there was any vacancy in the council, I was considered in a manner as the natural successor to the first of the counsellors that might happen to depart this life.

Chapter 3

A Dirgie

In the course of the Summer following the baptism, of which I have rehearsed the particulars in the foregoing chapter, Bailie Mucklehose happened to die, and as he was a man long and well respected, he had a great funeral. All the rooms in his house were filled with company; and it so fell out that, in the confusion, there was neither minister nor elder to give the blessing sent into that wherein I was, by which, when Mr Shavings the wright, with his men, came in with the service of bread and wine as usual, there was a demur, and one after another of those present was asked to say grace; but none of them being exercised in public prayer, all declined, when Mr Shavings said to me, "Mr Pawkie, I hope ye'll no refuse."

I had seen in the process, that not a few of the declinations were more out of the awkward shame of blateness, than any inherent modesty of nature, or diffidence of talent; so, without making a phrase about the matter, I said the grace, and in such a manner that I could see it made an impression. Mr Shavings was at that time deacon of the wrights, and being well pleased with my conduct on this occasion, when he, the same night, met the craft, he spoke of it in a commendable manner; and as I understood thereafter, it was thought by them that the council could not do better than make choice of me to the vacancy. In short, not to spin out the thread of my narration beyond necessity, let it here suffice to be known, that I was chosen into the council, partly by the strong handling of Deacon Shavings, and the instrumentality of other friends and well-wishers, and not a little by the moderation and prudence with which I had been secretly ettling at the honour.

Having thus reached to a seat in the council, I discerned that it behoved me to act with circumspection, in order to gain a discreet dominion over the same, and to rule without being felt, which is the great mystery of policy. With this intent, I, for some time, took no active part in the deliberations, but listened, with the doors of my understanding set wide to the wall, and the windows of my foresight all open; so that, in process of time, I became acquainted with the inner man of the counsellors, and could make a guess, no far short of the probability, as to what they would be at, when they were jooking and wising in a round-about manner to accomplish their own several wills and purposes. I soon thereby discovered, that although it was the custom to deduce reasons from out the interests of the community, for the divers means and measures that they wanted to bring to a bearing for their own particular behoof, yet this was not often very cleverly done, and the cloven foot of self-interest was now and then to be seen aneath the robe of public principle. I had, therefore, but a straightforward course to pursue, in order to overcome all their wiles and devices, the which was to make the interests of the community, in truth and sincerity, the end and object of my study, and never to step aside from it for any immediate speciality of profit to myself. Upon this, I have endeavoured to walk with a constancy of sobriety; and although I have, to a certainty, reaped advantage both in my own person and that of my family, no man living can accuse me of having bent any single thing pertaining to the town and public, from the natural uprightness of its integrity, in order to serve my own private ends.

It was, however, some time before an occasion came to pass, wherein I could bring my knowledge and observations to operate in any effectual manner towards a reformation in the management of the burgh; indeed, I saw that no good could be done until I had subdued the two great factions, into which it may be said the council was then divided; the one party being strong for those of the king's government of ministers, and the other no less vehement on the side of their adversaries. I, therefore, without saying a syllable to any body anent the same, girded myself for the undertaking, and with an earnest spirit put my shoulder to the wheel, and never desisted in my endeavours, till I had got the cart up the brae, and the whole council reduced into a proper state of subjection to the will and pleasure of his majesty, whose deputies and agents I have ever considered all inferior magistrates administering and exercising, as they do, their power and authority in his royal name.

The ways and means, however, by which this was brought to pass, supply matter for another chapter; and after this, it is not my intent to say any thing more concerning my principles and opinions, but only to show forth the course and current of things proceeding out of the affairs, in which I was so called to form a part requiring no small endeavour and diligence.

Chapter 4

The Guildry

When, as related in the foregoing chapter, I had nourished my knowledge of the council into maturity, I began to cast about for the means of exercising the same towards a satisfactory issue. But in this I found a great difficulty, arising from the policy and conduct of Mr Andrew McLucre, who had a sort of infeftment, as may be said, of the office of dean of guild, having for many years been allowed to intromit and manage the same; by which, as was insinuated by his adversaries, no little grist came to his mill. For it had happened from a very ancient date, as far back, I have heard, as the time of Queen Anne, when the union of the kingdoms was brought to a bearing, that the dean of guild among us, for some reason or another, had the upperhand in the setting and granting of tacks of the town lands, in the doing of which it was jealoused that the predecessors of Mr McLucre, no to say an ill word of him, honest man, got their loofs creeshed with something that might be called a grassum, or rather, a gratis gift. It therefore seemed to me that there was a necessity for some reformation in the office, and I foresaw that the same would never be accomplished, unless I could get Mr McLucre wised out of it, and myself appointed his successor. But in this lay the obstacle; for every thing anent the office was, as it were, in his custody, and it was well known that he had an interest in keeping by that which, in vulgar parlance, is called nine points of the law. However, both for the public good and a convenience to myself, I was resolved to get a finger in the dean of guild's fat pie, especially as I foresaw that, in the course of three or four years, some of the best tacks would run out, and it would be a great thing to the magistrate that might have the disposal of the new ones. Therefore, without seeming to have any foresight concerning the lands that were coming on to be out of lease, I set myself to constrain Mr McLucre to give up the guildry, as it were, of his own free-will; and what helped me well to this, was a rumour that came down from London, that there was to be a dissolution of the parliament.

The same day that this news reached the town, I was standing at my shop-door, between dinner and teatime. It was a fine sunny summer afternoon. Standing under the blessed influence of the time by myself at my shop-door, who should I see passing along the crown of the causey, but Mr McLucre himself, and with a countenance knotted with care, little in unison with the sultry indolence of that sunny day.

"Whar awa sae fast, dean o' guild?" quo' I to him; and he stopped his wide stepping, for he was a long spare man, and looting in his gait.

"I'm just," said he, "taking a step to the provost's, to learn the particulars of thir great news—for, as we are to hae the casting vote in the next election, there's no saying the good it may bring to us all gin we manage it wi' discretion."

I reflected the while of a minute before I made any reply, and then I said—"I would hae nae doubt of the matter, Mr McLucre, could it be brought about to get you chosen for the delegate; but I fear, as ye are only dean of guild this year, that's no to be accomplished; and really, without the like of you, our borough, in the contest, may be driven to the wall."

"Contest!" cried the dean of guild, with great eagerness; "wha told you that we are to be contested?"

Nobody had told me, nor at the moment was I sensible of the force of what I said; but, seeing the effect it had on Mr McLucre, I replied—"It does not, perhaps, just now, do for me to be more particular, and I hope what I have said to you will gang no further; but it's a great pity that ye're no even a bailie this year, far less the provost, otherwise I would have great confidence." "Then," said the dean of guild, "you have reason to believe that there is to be a dissolution, and that we are to be contested?"

"Mr McLucre, dinna speer any questions," was my answer, "but look at that and say nothing;" so I pulled out of my pocket a letter that had been franked to me by the earl. The letter was from James Portoport, his lordship's butler, who had been a waiter with Mrs Pawkie's mother, and he was inclosing to me a five-pound note to be given to an auld aunty that was in need. But the dean of guild knew nothing of our correspondence, nor was it required that he should. However, when he saw my lord's franking, he said, "Are the boroughs, then, really and truly to be contested?" "Come into the shop, Mr McLucre," said I sedately; "come in, and hear what I have to say." And he came in, and I shut and barred the half-door, in order that we might not be suddenly interrupted. "You are a man of experience, Mr McLucre," said I, "and have a knowledge of the world, that a young man, like me, would be a fool to pretend to. But I have shown you enough to convince you that I would not be worthy of a trust, were I to answer any improper questions. Ye maun, therefore, gie me some small credit for a little discretion in this matter, while I put a question to yourself.—"Is there no a possibility of getting you made the provost at Michaelmas, or, at the very least, a bailie, to the end that ye might be chosen delegate, it being an unusual thing for any body under the degree of a bailie to be chosen thereto?"

"I have been so long in the guildry," was his thoughtful reply, "that I fear it canna be very well managed without me."

"Mr McLucre," said I, and I took him cordially by the hand, "a thought has just entered my head. Couldna we manage this matter between us? It's true I'm but a novice in public affairs, and with the mystery of the guildry quite unacquaint—if, however, you could be persuaded to allow yourself to be made a bailie, I would, subject to your directions, undertake the office of dean of guild, and all this might be so concerted between us, that nobody would ken the nature of our paction—for, to be plain with you, it's no to be hoped that such a young counsellor as myself can reasonably expect to be raised, so soon as next Michaelmas, to the magistracy, and there is not another in the council that I would like to see chosen delegate at the election but yourself."

Mr McLucre swithered a little at this, fearing to part with the bird he had in hand; but, in the end, he said, that he thought what was proposed no out of the way, and that he would have no objection to be a bailie for the next year, on condition that I would, in the following, let him again be dean of guild, even though he should be called a Michaelmas mare, for it did not so well suit him to be a bailie as to be dean of guild, in which capacity he had been long used.

I guessed in this that he had a vista in view of the tacks and leases that were belyve to fall in, and I said—"Nothing can be more reasonable, Mr McLucre; for the office of dean of guild must be a very fashious one, to folks like me, no skilled in its particularities; and I'm sure I'll be right glad and willing to give it up, when we hae got our present turn served.—But to keep a' things quiet between us, let us no appear till after the election overly thick; indeed, for a season, we maun fight, as it were, under different colours."

Thus was the seed sown of a great reformation in the burgh, the sprouting whereof I purpose to describe in due season.

Chapter 5

The First Contested Election

The sough of the dissolution of Parliament, during the whole of the summer, grew stronger and stronger, and Mr McLucre and me were seemingly pulling at opposite ends of the rope. There was nothing that he proposed in the council but what I set myself against with such bir and vigour, that sometimes he could scarcely keep his temper, even while he was laughing in his sleeve to see how the other members of the corporation were beglammered. At length Michaelmas drew near, when I, to show, as it were, that no ill blood had been bred on my part, notwithstanding our bickerings, proposed in the council that Mr McLucre should be the new bailie; and he on his part, to manifest, in return, that there was as little heart-burning on his, said "he would have no objections; but then he insisted that I should consent to be dean of guild in his stead."

"It's true," said he in the council on that occasion, "that Mr Pawkie is as yet but a greenhorn in the concerns of the burgh: however, he'll never learn younger, and if he'll agree to this, I'll gie him all the help and insight that my experience enables me to afford."

At the first, I pretended that really, as was the truth, I had no knowledge of what were the duties of dean of guild; but aftersome fleeching from the other councillors, I consented to have the office, as it were, forced upon me; so I was made dean of guild, and Mr McLucre the new bailie.

By and by, when the harvest in England was over, the parliament was dissolved, but no candidate started on my lord's interest, as was expected by Mr McLucre, and he began to fret and be dissatisfied that he had ever consented to allow himself to be hoodwinked out of the guildry. However, just three days before the election, and at the dead hour of the night, the sound of chariot wheels and of horsemen was heard in our streets; and this was Mr Galore, the great Indian nabob, that had bought the Beerland estates, and built the grand place that is called Lucknoo House, coming from London, with the influence of the crown on his side, to oppose the old member. He drove straight to Provost Picklan's house, having, as we afterwards found out, been in a secret correspondence with him through the medium of Mrs Picklan, who was conjunct in the business with Miss Nelly, the nabob's maiden sister. Mr McLucre was not a little confounded at this, for he had imagined that I was the agent on behalf of my lord, who was of the government side, so he wist not what to do, in the morning when he came to me, till I said to him briskly—"Ye ken, bailie, that ye're trysted to me, and it's our duty to support the nabob, who is both able and willing, as I have good reason to think, to requite our services in a very grateful manner." This was a cordial to his spirit, and, without more ado, we both of us set to work to get the bailie made the delegate. In this I had nothing in view but the good of my country by pleasuring, as it was my duty, his majesty's government, for I was satisfied with my situation as dean of guild. But the handling required no small slight of skill.

The first thing was, to persuade those that were on the side of the old member to elect Mr McLucre for delegate, he being, as we had concerted, openly declared for that interest, and the benefit to be gotten thereby having, by use and wont, been at an established and regular rate. The next thing was to get some of those that were with me on my lord's side, kept out of the way on the day of choosing the delegate; for we were the strongest, and could easily have returned the provost, but I had no clear notion how it would advantage me to make the provost delegate, as was proposed. I therefore, on the morning of the business, invited three of the council to take their breakfast with me, for the ostensible purpose of going in a body to the council chamber to choose the provost delegate; but when we were at breakfast, John Snakers, my lad in the shop, by my suggestion, warily got a bale of broad cloth so tumbled, as it were by accident, at the door, that it could not be opened; for it bent the key in such a manner in the lock, and crooket the sneck, that without a smith there was no egress, and sorrow a smith was to be had. All were out and around the tolbooth waiting for the upshot of the choosing the delegate. Those that saw me in the mean time, would have thought I had gone demented. I ramped and I stamped; I banned and I bellowed like desperation. My companions, no a bit better, flew fluttering to the windows, like wild birds to the wires of their cage. However, to make a long tale short, Bailie McLucre was, by means of this device, chosen delegate, seemingly against my side. But oh! he was a slee tod, for no sooner was he so chosen, than he began to act for his own behoof and that very afternoon, while both parties were holding their public dinner, he sent round the bell to tell that the potato crop on his back rig was to be sold by way of public roup the same day. There wasna one in the town that had reached the years of discretion, but kent what na sort of potatoes he was going to sell; and I was so disturbed by this open corruption, that I went to him, and expressed my great surprise. Hot words ensued between us; and I told him very plainly that I would have nothing further to say to him or his political profligacy. However, his potatoes were sold, and brought upwards of three guineas the peck, the nabob being the purchaser, who, to show his contentment with the bargain, made Mrs McLucre, and the bailie's three daughters, presents of new gowns and princods, that were not stuffed with wool. In the end, as a natural consequence, Bailie McLucre, as delegate, voted for the Nabob, and the old member was thereby thrown out. But although the government candidate in this manner won the day, yet I was so displeased by the jookerie of the bailie, and the selfish manner by which he had himself reaped all the advantage of the election in the sale of his potatoes, that we had no correspondence on public affairs till long after; so that he never had the face to ask me to give up the guildry, till I resigned it of my own accord after the renewal of the tacks to which I have alluded, by the which renewals, a great increase was effected in the income of the town.

Chapter 6

The Failure of Bailie McLucre

Bailie McLucre, as I have already intimated, was naturally a greedy body, and not being content with the profits of his potatoe rig, soon after the election he set up as an o'er-sea merchant, buying beef and corn by agency in Ireland, and having the same sent to the Glasgow market. For some time, this traffic yielded him a surprising advantage; but the summer does not endure the whole year round, nor was his prosperity ordained to be of a continuance. One mishap befell him after another; cargoes of his corn heated in the vessels, because he would not sell at a losing price, and so entirely perished; and merchants broke, that were in his debt large sums for his beef and provisions. In short, in the course of the third year from the time of the election, he was rookit of every plack he had in the world, and was obligated to take the benefit of the divor's bill, soon after which he went suddenly away from the town, on the pretence of going into Edinburgh, on some business of legality with his wife's brother, with whom he had entered into a plea concerning the moiety of a steading at the town-head. But he did not stop on any such concern there; on the contrary, he was off, and up to London in a trader from Leith, to try if he could get a post in the government by the aid of the nabob, our member; who, by all accounts, was hand and glove with the king's ministers. The upshot of this journey to London was very comical; and when the bailie afterwards came back, and him and me were again on terms of visitation, many a jocose night we spent over the story of the same; for the bailie was a kittle hand at a bowl of toddy; and his adventure was so droll, especially in the way he was wont to rehearse the particulars, that it cannot fail to be an edification to posterity, to read and hear how it happened, and all about it. I may therefore take leave to digress into the circumstantials, by way of lightening for a time the seriousness of the sober and important matter, whereof it is my intent that this book shall be a register and record to future times.

Chapter 7

The Bribe

Mr McLucre, going to London, as I have intimated in the foregoing chapter, remained there, absent from us altogether about the space of six weeks; and when he came home, he was plainly an altered man, being sometimes very jocose, and at other times looking about him as if he had been haunted by some ill thing. Moreover, Mrs Spell, that had the post-office from the decease of her husband, Deacon Spell, told among her kimmers, that surely the bailie had a great correspondence with the king and government, for that scarce a week passed without a letter from him to our member, or a letter from the member to him. This bred no small consideration among us; and I was somehow a thought uneasy thereat, not knowing what the bailie, now that he was out of the guildry, might be saying anent the use and wont that had been practised therein, and never more than in his own time. At length, the babe was born.

One evening, as I was sitting at home, after closing the shop for the night, and conversing concerning the augmentation of our worldly affairs with Mrs Pawkie and the bairns—it was a damp raw night; I mind it just as well as if it had been only yestreen—who should make his appearance at the room door but the bailie himsell and a blithe face he had?

"It's a' settled now," cried he, as he entered with a triumphant voice; "the siller's my ain, and I can keep it in spite of them; I don't value them now a cutty spoon; no, not a dolt; no the worth of that; nor a' their sprose about Newgate and the pillory;"—and he snapped his fingers with an aspect of great courage.

"Hooly, hooly, bailie," said I; "what's a' this for?" and then he replied, taking his seat beside me at the fireside—"The plea with the custom-house folk at London is settled, or rather, there canna be a plea at a', so firm and true is the laws of England on my side, and the liberty of the subject."

All this was Greek and Hebrew to me; but it was plain that the bailie, in his jaunt, had been guilty of some notour thing, wherein the custom-house was concerned, and that he thought all the world was acquaint with the same. However, no to balk him in any communication he might be disposed to make me, I said:—

"What ye say, bailie, is great news, and I wish you meikle joy, for I have had my fears about your situation for some time; but now that the business is brought to such a happy end, I would like to hear all the true particulars of the case; and that your tale and tidings sha'na lack slockening, I'll get in the toddy bowl and the gardevin; and with that, I winket to the mistress to take the bairns to their bed, and bade Jenny Hachle, that was then our fee'd servant lass, to gain the kettle boil. Poor Jenny has long since fallen into a great decay of circumstances, for she was not overly snod and cleanly in her service; and so, in time, wore out the endurance of all the houses and families that fee'd her, till nobody would take her; by which she was in a manner cast on Mrs Pawkie's hands; who, on account of her kindliness towards the bairns in their childhood, has given her a howf among us. But, to go on with what I was rehearsing; the toddy being ordered, and all things on the table, the bailie, when we were quiet by ourselves, began to say—"Ye ken weel, Mr Pawkie, what I did at the 'lection for the member, and how angry ye were yoursel about it, and a' that. But ye were greatly mista'en in thinking that I got ony effectual fee at the time, over and above the honest price of my potatoes; which ye were as free to bid for, had ye liket, as either o' the candidates. I'll no deny, however, that the nabob, before he left the town, made some small presents to my wife and dochter; but that was no fault o' mine. Howsever, when a' was o'er, and I could discern that ye were mindet to keep the guildry, I thought, after the wreck o' my provision concern, I might throw mair bread on the water and not find it, than by a bit jaunt to London to see how my honourable friend, the nabob, was coming on in his place in parliament, as I saw none of his speeches in the newspaper.

"Well, ye see, Mr Pawkie, I gae'd up to London in a trader from Leith; and by the use of a gude Scotch tongue, the whilk was the main substance o' a' the bairns' part o' gear that I inherited from my parents, I found out the nabob's dwelling, in the west end o' the town of London; and finding out the nabob's dwelling, I went and rappit at the door, which a bardy flunkie opened, and speer't what I wantit, as if I was a thing no fit to be lifted off a midden with a pair of iron tongs. Like master, like man, thought I to myself; and thereupon, taking heart no to be put out, I replied to the whipper-snapper—

" 'I'm Bailie McLucre o' Gudetown, and maun hae a word wi' his honour.' The cur lowered his birsses at this, and replied, in a maim ceeveleezed style of language, 'Master is not at home.' But I kent what not at home means in the morning at a gentleman's door in London; so I said, 'Very weel, as I hae had a long walk, I'll e'en rest myself and wait till he come;' and with that, I plumpit down on one of the mahogany chairs in the trance. The lad, seeing that I was na to be jookit, upon this answered me, by saying, he would go and enquire if his master would be at home to me; and the short and the long o't was, that I got at last an audience o' my honourable friend.

" 'Well, Bailie,' said he, 'I'm glad to see you in London,' and a hantle o' ither courtly glammer that's no worth a repetition; and, from less to mair, we proceeded to sift into the matter and end of my coming to ask the help o' his hand to get me a post in the government. But I soon saw, that wi a' the phraseology that lay at his tongue end during the election, about his power and will to serve us, his ain turn ser't, he cared little for me. Howsever, after tarrying some time, and going to him every day, at long and last he got me a tide-waiter's place at the custom-house; a poor hungry situation, no worth the grassum at a new tack of the warst land in the town's aught. But minnows are better than nae fish, and a tide-waiter's place was a step towards a better, if I could have waited. Luckily, however, for me, a flock of fleets and ships frae the East and West Indies came in a' thegither; and there was sic a stress for tide-waiters, that before I was sworn in and tested, I was sent down to a grand ship in the Malabar trade frae China, loaded with tea and other rich commodities; the captain whereof, a discreet man, took me down to the cabin, and gave me a dram of wine, and, when we were by oursels, he said to me—

" 'Mr McLucre, what will you take to shut your eyes for an hour?'

" 'I'll no take a hundred pounds,' was my answer.

" 'I'll make it guineas,' quoth he.

"Surely, thought I, my eyne maun be worth pearls and diamonds to the East India Company; so I answered and said—

" 'Captain, no to argol-bargol about the matter,' (for a' the time, I thought upon how I had not been sworn in;)—'what will ye gie me, if I take away my eyne out of the vessel? '

" 'A thousand pounds,' cried he.

" 'A bargain be't,' said I. I think, however, had I stood out I might hae got mair. But it does na rain thousands of pounds every day; so, to make a long tale short, I got a note of hand on the Bank of England for the sum, and, packing up my ends and my awls, left the ship.

"It was my intent to have come immediately home to Scotland; but the same afternoon, I was summoned by the Board at the Custom-house for deserting my post; and the moment I went before them, they opened upon me like my lord's pack of hounds, and said they would send me to Newgate.

'Cry a' at ance,' quoth I; 'but I'll no gang.' I then told them how I was na sworn, and under no obligation to serve or obey them mair than pleasured mysel'; which set them a' again a barking worse than before; whereupon, seeing no likelihood of an end to their stramash, I turned mysel' round, and, taking the door on my back, left them, and the same night came off on the Fly to Edinburgh. Since syne they have been trying every grip and wile o' the law to punish me as they threatened; but the laws of England are a great protection to the people against arbitrary power; and the letter that I have got to-day frae the nabob, tells me that the commissioners hae abandoned the plea. "

Such was the account and narration that the bailie gave to me of the particulars o' his journey to London; and when he was done, I could not but make a moral reflection or two, on the policy of gentlemen putting themselves on the leet to be members of Parliament; it being a clear and plain thing, that as they are sent up to London for the benefit of the people by whom they are chosen, the people should always take care to get some of that benefit in hand paid down, otherwise they run a great risk of seeing their representatives neglecting their special interests, and treating them as entitled to no particular consideration.

Chapter 8

On the Choosing of a New Minister

The next great handling that we had in the council after the general election, was anent the choice of a minister for the parish. The Rev Dr Swapkirk having had an apoplexy, the magistrates were obligated to get Mr Pittle to be his helper. Whether it was that, by our being used to Mr Pittle, we had ceased to have a right respect for his parts and talents, or that in reality he was but a weak brother, I cannot in conscience take it on me to say; but the certainty is, that when the Doctor departed this life, there was hardly one of the hearers who thought Mr Pittle would ever be their placed minister, and it was as far at first from the unanimous mind of the magistrates, who are the patrons of the parish, as any thing could well be, for he was a man of no smeddum in discourse. In verity, as Mrs Pawkie, my wife, said, his sermons in the warm summer afternoons were just a perfect hushabaa, that no mortal could hearken to without sleeping. Moreover, he had a sorning way with him, that the genteeler sort could na abide, for he was for ever going from house to house about tea-time, to save his ain canister. As for the young ladies, they could na endure him at all, for he had aye the sough and sound of love in his mouth, and a round-about ceremonial of joking concerning the same, that was just a fasherie to them to hear. The commonality, however, were his greatest adversaries; for he was, notwithstanding the spareness of his abilities, a prideful creature, taking no interest in their hamely affairs, and seldom visiting the aged or the sick among them. Shortly, however, before the death of the doctor, Mr Pittle had been very attentive to my wife's full cousin, Miss Lizy Pinkie, I'll no say on account of the legacy of seven hundred pounds left her by an uncle that made his money in foreign parts, and died at Portsmouth of the liver complaint, when he was coming home to enjoy himself and Mrs Pawkie told me, that as soon as Mr Pittle could get a kirk, I needna be surprised if I heard o' a marriage between him and Miss Lizy.

Had I been a sordid and interested man, this news could never have given me the satisfaction it did, for Miss Lizy was very fond of my bairns, and it was thought that Peter would have been her heir; but so far from being concerned at what I heard, I rejoiced thereat, and resolved in secret thought, whenever a vacancy happened, Dr Swapkirk being then fast wearing away, to exert the best of my ability to get the kirk for Mr Pittle, not, however, unless he was previously married to Miss Lizy; for, to speak out, she was beginning to stand in need of a protector, and both me and Mrs Pawkie had our fears that she might outlive her income, and in her old age become a cess upon us. And it couldna be said that this was any groundless fear; for Miss Lizy, living a lonely maiden life by herself, with only a bit lassie to run her errands, and no being naturally of an active or eydent turn, aften wearied, and to keep up her spirits gaed may be now and then, oftener to the gardevin than was just necessar, by which, as we thought, she had a tavert look. Howsever, as Mr Pittle had taken a notion of her, and she pleased his fancy, it was far from our hand to misliken one that was sib to us; on the contrary, it was a duty laid on me by the ties of blood and relationship, to do all in my power to further their mutual affection into matrimonial fruition; and what I did towards that end, is the burden of this current chapter.

Dr Swapkirk, in whom the spark of life was long fading, closed his eyes, and it went utterly out, as to this world, on a Saturday night, between the hours of eleven and twelve. We had that afternoon got an inkling that he was drawing near to his end. At the latest, Mrs Pawkie herself went over to the manse, and stayed till she saw him die. "It was a pleasant end," she said, for he was a godly, patient man; and we were both sorely grieved, though it was a thing for which we had been long prepared; and indeed, to his family and connexions, except for the loss of the stipend, it was a very gentle dispensation, for he had been long a heavy handful, having been for years but, as it were, a breathing lump of mortality, groosy, and oozy, and doozy, his faculties being shut up and locked in by a dumb palsy.

Having had this early intimation of the doctor's removal to a better world, on the Sabbath morning when I went to join the magistrates in the council-chamber, as the usage is, to go to the laft, with the town-officers carrying their halberts before us, according to the ancient custom of all royal burghs, my mind was in a degree prepared to speak to them anent the successor. Little, however, passed at that time, and it so happened that, by some wonder of inspiration, (there were, however, folk that said it was taken out of a book of sermons, by one Barrow an English Divine,) Mr Pittle that forenoon preached a discourse that made an impression, in so much, that on our way back to the council-chamber I said to Provost Vintner, that then was—"Really Mr Pittle seems, if he would exert himself to have a nerve. I could not have thought it was in the power of his capacity to have given us such a sermon."

The provost thought as I did, so I replied—"We canna, I think, do better than keep him among us. It would, indeed, provost, no be doing justice to the young man to pass another over his head." I could see that the provost was na quite sure of what I had been saying; for he replied, that it was a matter that needed consideration. When we separated at the council-chamber, I threw myself in the way of Bailie Weezle, and walked home with him, our talk being on the subject of vacancy; and I rehearsed to him what had passed between me and the provost, saying, that the provost had made no objection to prefer Mr Pittle, which was the truth.

Bailie Weezle was a man no overladen with worldly wisdom, and had been chosen into the council principally on account of being easily managed. In his business, he was originally by trade a baker in Glasgow, where he made a little money, and came to settle among us with his wife, who was a native of the town, and had her relations here. Being therefore an idle man, living on his money, and of a soft and quiet nature, he was for the reason aforesaid chosen into the council, where he always voted on the provost's side; for in controverted questions every one is beholden to take a part, and he thought it was his duty to side with the chief magistrate.

Having convinced the bailie that Mr Pittle had already, as it were, a sort of infeoffment in the kirk, I called in the evening on my old predecessor in the guildry,

Bailie McLucre, who was not a hand to be so easily dealt with; but I knew his inclinations, and therefore I resolved to go roundly to work with him. So I asked him out to take a walk, and led him towards the town-moor, conversing loosely about one thing and another, and touching softly here and there on the vacancy.

When we were well on into the middle of the moor, I stopped, and, looking round me, said, "Bailie, surely it's a great neglec of the magistrates and council to let this braw broad piece of land, so near the town, lie in a state o' nature, and giving pasturage to only twa-three of the poor folk's cows. I wonder you, that's now a rich man, and with eyne worth pearls and diamonds, that ye dinna think of asking a tack of this land; ye might make a great thing o't." The fish nibbled, and told me that he had for sometime entertained a thought on the subject; but he was afraid that I would be overly extortionate. "I wonder to hear you, bailie," said I; "I trust and hope no one will ever find me out of the way of justice; and to convince you that I can do a friendly turn, I'll no objec to gie you a' my influence free gratis, if ye'll gie Mr Pittle a lift into the kirk; for, to be plain with you, the worthy young man, who, as ye heard to-day, is no without an ability, has long been fond of Mrs Pawkie's cousin, Miss Lizy Pinky; and I would fain do all that lies in my power to help on the match." The bailie was well pleased with my frankness, and before returning home we came to a satisfactory understanding; so that the next thing I had to do, was to see Mr Pittle himself on the subject. Accordingly, in the gloaming, I went over to where he stayed: it was with Miss Jenny Killfuddy, an elderly maiden lady, whose father was the minister of Braehill, and the same that is spoken of in the chronicle of Dalmailing, as having had his eye almost put out by a clash of glaur, at the stormy placing of Mr Balwhidder.

"Mr Pittle," said I, as soon as I was in and the door closed. "I'm come to you as a friend; both Mrs Pawkie and me have long discerned that ye have had a look more than common towards our friend, Miss Lizy, and we think it our duty to enquire your intents, before matters gang to greater length."

He looked a little dumfoundered at this salutation, and was at a loss for an answer, so I continued—"If your designs be honourable, and no doubt they are, now's your time; strike while the iron's hot. By the death of the doctor, the kirk's vacant, the town-council have the patronage; and, if ye marry Miss Lizy, my interest and influence shall not be slack in helping you into the poopit." In short, out of what passed that night, on the Monday following Mr Pittle and Miss Lizy were married; and by my dexterity, together with the able help I had in Bailie McLucre, he was in due season placed and settled in the parish; and the next year more than fifty acres of the town-moor were inclosed on a nine hundred and ninety-nine years' tack at an easy rate between me and the bailie, he paying the half of the expense of the ditching and rooting out of the whins; and it was acknowledged by every one that saw it, that there had not been a greater improvement for many years in all the country side. But to the best actions there will be adverse and discontented spirits; and, on this occasion, there were not wanting persons naturally of a disloyal opposition temper, who complained of the inclosure as a usurpation of the rights and property of the poorer burghers. Such revilings, however, are what all persons in authority must suffer; and they had only the effect of making me button my coat, and look out the crooser to the blast.

Chapter 9

An Execution

The attainment of honours and dignities is not enjoyed without a portion of trouble and care, which, like a shadow, follows all temporalities. On the very evening of the same day that I was first chosen to be a bailie, a sore affair came to light, in the discovery that Jean Gaisling had murdered her bastard bairn. She was the daughter of a donsie mother that could gie no name to her gets, of which she had two laddies, besides Jean. The one of them had gone off with the soldiers some time before; the other, a douce well-behaved callan, was in my lord's servitude, as a stable boy at the castle. Jeanie herself was the bonniest lassie in the whole town, but light-headed, and fonder of outgait and blether in the causey than was discreet of one of her uncertain parentage. She was, at the time when she met with her misfortune, in the service of Mrs Dalrymple, a colonel's widow, that came out of the army and settled among us on her jointure.

This Mrs Dalrymple, having been long used to the loose morals of camps and regiments, did not keep that strict hand over poor Jeanie, and her other serving lass, that she ought to have done, and so the poor guileless creature fell into the snare of some of the ne'er-do-weel gentlemen that used to play cards at night with Mrs Dalrymple. The truths of the story were never well known, nor who was the father, for the tragical issue barred all enquiry; but it came out that poor Jeanie was left to herself and, being instigated by the Enemy, after she had been delivered, did, while the midwife's back was turned, strangle the baby with a napkin. She was discovered in the very fact, with the bairn black in the face in the bed beside her.

The heinousness of the crime can by no possibility be lessened; but the beauty of the mother, her tender years, and her light-headedness, had won many favourers; and there was a great leaning in the hearts of all the town to compassionate her, especially when they thought of the ill example that had been set to her in the walk and conversation of her mother. It was not, however, within the power of the magistrates to overlook the accusation; so we were obligated to cause a precognition to be taken, and the search left no doubt of the wilfulness of the murder. Jeanie was in consequence removed to the tolbooth, where she lay till the lords were coming to Ayr, when she was sent thither to stand her trial before them; but, from the hour she did the deed, she never spoke.

Her trial was a short procedure, and she was cast to be hanged—and not only to be hanged, but ordered to be executed in our town, and her body given to the doctors to make anatomy. The execution of Jeanie was what all expected would happen; but when the news reached the town of the other parts of the sentence, the wail was as the sough of a pestilence, and fain would the council have got it dispensed with. But the Lord Advocate was just wud at the crime, both because there had been no previous concealment, so as to have been an extenuation for the shame of the birth, and because Jeanie would neither divulge the name of the father, nor make answer to all the interrogatories that were put to her—standing at the bar like a dumbie, and looking round her, and at the judges, like a demented creature, and beautiful as a Flanders' baby. It was thought by many, that her advocate might have made great use of her visible consternation, and pled that she was by herself; for in truth she had every appearance of being so. He was, however, a dure man, no doubt well enough versed in the particulars and punctualities of the law for an ordinary plea; but no of the right sort of knowledge and talent to take up the case of a forlorn lassie, misled by ill example and a winsome nature, and clothed in the allurement of loveliness, as the judge himself said to the jury.

On the night before the day of execution, she was brought over in a chaise from Ayr between two town-officers, and placed again in our hands, and still she never spoke.

Nothing could exceed the compassion that every one had for poor Jeanie, so she wasna committed to a common cell, but laid in the council-room, where the ladies of the town made up a comfortable bed for her, and some of them sat up all night and prayed for her; but her thoughts were gone, and she sat silent.

In the morning, by break of day, her wanton mother, that had been trolloping in Glasgow, came to the tolbooth door, and made a dreadful wally-waeing, and the ladies were obligated, for the sake of peace, to bid her be let in. But Jeanie noticed her not, still sitting with her eyes cast down, waiting the coming on of the hour of her doom. The wicked mother first tried to rouse her by weeping and distraction, and then she took to upbraiding; but Jeanie seemed to heed her not, save only once, and then she but looked at the misleart tinkler, and shook her head. I happened to come into the room at this time, and seeing all the charitable ladies weeping around, and the randy mother talking to the poor lassie as loudly and vehement as if she had been both deaf and sullen, I commanded the officers, with a voice of authority, to remove the mother, by which we had for a season peace, till the hour came.

There had not been an execution in the town in the memory of the oldest person then living; the last that suffered was one of the martyrs in the time of the persecution, so that we were not skilled in the business, and had besides no hangman, but were necessitated to borrow the Ayr one. Indeed, I being the youngest bailie, was in terror that the obligation might have fallen to me.

A scaffold was erected at the Tron, just under the tolbooth windows, by Thomas Gimblet, the master-of-work, who had a good penny of profit by the job, for he contracted with the town-council, and had the boards after the business was done to the bargain; but Thomas was then deacon of the wrights, and himself a member of our body.

At the hour appointed, Jeanie, dressed in white, was led out by the town-officers, and in the midst of the magistrates from among the ladies, with her hands tied behind her with a black riband. At the first sight of her at the tolbooth stairhead, a universal sob rose from all the multitude, and the sternest e'e couldna refrain from shedding a tear. We marched slowly down the stair, and on to the foot of the scaffold, where her younger brother, Willy, that was stable-boy at my lord's, was standing by himself, in an open ring made round him in the crowd; every one compassionating the dejected laddie, for he was a fine youth, and of an orderly spirit.

As his sister came towards the foot of the ladder, he ran towards her, and embraced her with a wail of sorrow that melted every heart, and made us all stop in the middle of our solemnity. Jeanie looked at him, (for her hands were tied,) and a silent tear was seen to drop from her cheek. But in the course of little more than a minute, all was quiet, and we proceeded to ascend the scaffold. Willy, who had by this time dried his eyes, went up with us, and when Mr Pittle had said the prayer, and sung the psalm, in which the whole multitude joined, as it were with the contrition of sorrow, the hangman stepped forward to put on the fatal cap, but Willy took it out of his hand, and placed it on his sister himself, and then kneeling down, with his back towards her, closing his eyes and shutting his ears with his hands, he saw not nor heard when she was launched into eternity.

When the awful act was over, and the stir was for the magistrates to return, and the body to be cut down, poor Willy rose, and without looking round, went down the steps of the scaffold; the multitude made a lane for him to pass, and he went on through them hiding his face, and gaed straight out of the town. As for the mother, we were obligated, in the course of the same year, to drum her out of the town, for stealing thirteen choppin bottles from William Gallon's, the vintner's, and selling them for whisky to Maggie Picken, that was tried at the same time for the reset.

Chapter 10

A Riot

Nothing very material after Jeanie Gaisling's affair, happened in the town till the time of my first provostry, when an event arose with an aspect of exceeding danger to the lives and properties of the whole town. I cannot indeed think of it at this day, though age has cooled me down in all concerns to a spirit of composure, without feeling the blood boil in my veins; so greatly, in the matter alluded to, was the king's dignity and the rightful government, by law and magistracy, insulted in my person.

From time out of mind, it had been an ancient and commendable custom in the burgh, to have, on the king's birth-day, a large bowl of punch made in the council-chamber, in order and to the end and effect of drinking his majesty's health at the cross; and for pleasance to the commonality, the magistrates were wont, on the same occasion, to allow a cart of coals for a bonfire. I do not now, at this distance of time, remember the cause how it came to pass, but come to pass it did, that the council resolved for time coming to refrain from giving the coals for the bonfire; and it so fell out that the first administration of this economy was carried into effect during my provostry, and the wyte of it was laid at my door by the trades' lads, and others, that took on them the lead in hobleshows at the fairs, and such like public doings. Now I come to the issue and particulars.

The birth-day, in progress of time, came round, and the morning was ushered in with the ringing of bells, and the windows of the houses adorned with green boughs and garlands. It was a fine bright day, and nothing could exceed the glee and joviality of all faces till the afternoon, when I went up to the council-chamber in the tolbooth, to meet the other magistrates and respectable characters of the town, in order to drink the king's health. In going thither, I was joined, just as I was stepping out of my shop, by Mr Stoup, the excise gauger, and Mr Firlot, the mealmonger, who had made a power of money a short time before, by a cargo of corn that he had brought from Belfast, the ports being then open, for which he was envied by some, and by the common sort was considered and reviled as a wicked hard-hearted forestaller. As for Mr Stoup, although he was a very creditable man, he had the repute of being overly austere in his vocation, for which he was not liked over and above the dislike that the commonality cherish against all of his calling; so that it was not possible that any magistrate, such as I endeavoured to be, adverse to ill-doers, and to vice and immorality of every kind, could have met at such a time and juncture, a greater misfortune than those two men, especially when it is considered, that the abolition of the bonfire was regarded as a heinous trespass on the liberties and privileges of the people. However, having left the shop, and being joined, as I have narrated, by Mr Stoup and Mr Firlot, we walked together at a sedate pace towards the tolbooth, before which, and at the cross, a great assemblage of people were convened; trades' lads, weavers with coats out at the elbow, the callans of the school; in short, the utmost gathering and congregation of the clanjamphry, who the moment they saw me coming, set up a great shout and howl, crying like desperation, "Provost, whar's the bonfire? Hae ye sent the coals, provost, hame to yersel, or selt them, provost, for meal to the forestaller?" with other such misleart phraseology that was most contemptuous, bearing every symptom of the rebellion and insurrection that they were then meditating. But I kept my temper, and went into the council-chamber, where others of the respectable inhabitants were met with the magistrates and town-council assembled.

"What's the matter, provost?" said several of them as I came in; "are ye ill; or what has fashed you?" But I only replied, that the mob without was very unruly for being deprived of their bonfire. Upon this, some of those present proposed to gratify them, by ordering a cart of coals, as usual; but I set my face against this, saying, that it would look like intimidation were we now to comply, and that all veneration for law and authority would be at an end by such weakness on the part of those entrusted with the exercise of power. There the debate, for a season, ended; and the punch being ready, the table was taken out of the council-chamber and carried to the cross, and placed there, and then the bowl and glasses—the magistrates following, and the rest of the company.

Seeing us surrounded by the town-officers with their halberts, the multitude made way, seemingly with their wonted civility, and, when his majesty's health was drank, they shouted with us, seemingly, too, as loyally as ever; but that was a traitorous device to throw us off our guard, as, in the upshot, was manifested; for no sooner had we filled the glasses again, than some of the most audacious of the rioters began to insult us, crying, "The bonfire! the bonfire!—No fire, no bowl!—Gentle and semple should share and share alike." In short, there was a moving backwards and forwards, and a confusion among the mob, with snatches of huzzas and laughter, that boded great mischief; and some of my friends near me said to me no to be alarmed, which only alarmed me the more, as I thought they surely had heard something. However, we drank our second glass without any actual molestation; but when we gave the three cheers, as the custom was, after the same, instead of being answered joyfully, the mob set up a frightful yell, and, rolling like the waves of the sea, came on us with such a shock, that the table, and punch-bowl, and glasses, were couped and broken. Bailie Weezle, who was standing on the opposite side, got his shins so ruffled by the falling of the table, that he was for many a day after confined to the house with two sore legs; and it was feared he would have been a lameter for life. The dinging down of the table was the signal of the rebellious ringleaders for open war. Immediately there was an outcry and a roaring, that was a terrification to hear; and I know not how it was, but before we kent where we were, I found myself, with many of those who had been drinking the king's health, once more in the council-chamber, where it was proposed that we should read the riot act from the windows; and this awful duty, by the nature of my office as provost, it behoved me to perform. Nor did I shrink from it; for by this time my corruption was raised, and I was determined not to let the royal authority be set at nought in my hands.

Accordingly, Mr Keelivine, the town clerk, having searched out among his law books for the riot act, one of the windows of the council-chamber was opened, and the bellman having, with a loud voice, proclaimed the "O yes!" three times, I stepped forward with the book in my hands. At the sight of me, the rioters, in the most audacious manner, set up a blasphemous laugh; but, instead of finding me daunted thereat, they were surprised at my fortitude; and, when I began to read, they listened in silence. But this was a concerted stratagem; for the moment that I had ended, a dead cat came whizzing through the air like a comet, and gave me such a clash in the face that I was knocked down to the floor, in the middle of the very council-chamber. What ensued is neither to be told nor described; some were for beating the fire-drum; others were for arming ourselves with what weapons were in the tolbooth; but I deemed it more congenial to the nature of the catastrophe, to send off an express to Ayr for the regiment of soldiers that was quartered there—the roar of the rioters without, being all the time like a raging flood.

Major Target, however, who had seen service in foreign wars, was among us, and he having tried in vain to get us to listen to him, went out of his own accord to the rioters, and was received by them with three cheers. He then spoke to them in an exhorting manner, and represented to them the imprudence of their behaviour; upon which they gave him three other cheers, and immediately dispersed and went home. The major was a vain body, and took great credit to himself, as I heard, for this; but, considering the temper of mind the mob was at one time in, it is quite evident that it was no so much the major's speech and exhortation that sent them off, as their dread and terror of the soldiers that I had sent for.

All that night the magistrates, with other gentlemen of the town, sat in the council-chamber, and sent out, from time to time, to see that every thing was quiet; and by this judicious proceeding, of which we drew up and transmitted a full account to the king and government in London, by whom the whole of our conduct was highly applauded, peace was maintained till the next day at noon, when a detachment, as it was called, of four companies came from the regiment in Ayr, and took upon them the preservation of order and regularity. I may here notice, that this was the first time any soldiers had been quartered in the town since the forty-five; and a woeful warning it was of the consequences that follow rebellion and treasonable practices; for, to the present day, we have always had a portion of every regiment, sent to Ayr, quartered upon us.

Chapter 11

Policy

Just about the end of my first provostry, I began to make a discovery. Whether it was that I was a little inordinately lifted up by reason of the dignity, and did not comport myself with a sufficient condescension and conciliation of manner to the rest of the town-council, it would be hard to say. I could, however, discern that a general ceremonious insincerity was performed by the members towards me, especially on the part of those who were in league and conjunct with the town-clerk, who comported himself, by reason of his knowledge of the law, as if he was in verity the true and effectual chief magistrate of the burgh; and the effect of this discovery, was a consideration and digesting within me how I should demean myself, so as to regain the vantage I had lost; taking little heed as to how the loss had come, whether from an ill-judged pride and pretending in myself, or from the natural spirit of envy, that darkens the good-will of all mankind towards those who get sudden promotion, as it was commonly thought I had obtained, in being so soon exalted to the provostry.

Before the Michaelmas I was, in consequence of this deliberation and counselling with my own mind, fully prepared to achieve a great stroke of policy for the future government of the town. I saw that it would not do for me for a time to stand overly eminent forward, and that it was a better thing, in the world, to have power and influence, than to show the possession of either. Accordingly, after casting about from one thing to another, I bethought with myself, that it would be a great advantage if the council could be worked with, so as to nominate and appoint My Lord the next provost after me. In the proposing of this, I could see there would be no difficulty; but the hazard was, that his lordship might only be made a tool of instrumentality to our shrewd and sly town-clerk, Mr Keelivine, while it was of great importance that I should keep the management of my lord in my own hands. In this strait, however, a thing came to pass, which strongly confirms me in the opinion, that good-luck has really a great deal to say with the prosperity of men. The earl, who had not for years been in the country, came down in the summer from London, and I, together with the other magistrates and council, received an invitation to dine with him at the castle. We all of course went, "with our best breeding," as the old proverb says, "helped by our brawest deeding;" but I soon saw that it was only a *pro forma* dinner, and that there was nothing of cordiality in all the civility with which we were treated, both by my lord and my lady. Nor, indeed, could I, on an afterthought, blame our noble entertainers for being so on their guard; for in truth some of the deacons, (I'll no say any of the bailies,) were so transported out of themselves with the glory of my lord's banquet, and the thought of dining at the castle, and at the first table too, that when the wine began to fiz in their noddles, they forgot themselves entirely, and made no more of the earl than if he had been one of themselves. Seeing to what issue the matter was tending, I set a guard upon myself; and while my lord, out of a parly-voo politess, was egging them on, one after another, to drink deeper and deeper of his old wines, to the manifest detriment of their own senses, I kept myself in a degree as sober as a judge, warily noting all things that came to pass.

The earl had really a commendable share of common sense for a lord, and the discretion of my conduct was not unnoticed by him; in so much, that after the major part of the council had become, as it may be said, out o' the body, cracking their jokes with one another, just as if all present had been carousing at the Cross-Keys, his lordship wised to me to come and sit beside him, where we had a very private and satisfactory conversation together; in the which conversation, I said, that it was a pity he would not allow himself to be nominated our provost. Nobody had ever minted to him a thought of the thing before; so it was no wonder that his lordship replied, with a look of surprise, saying, "That so far from refusing, he had never heard of any such proposal."

"That is very extraordinary, my lord," said I; "for surely it is for your interests, and would to a certainty be a great advantage to the town, were your lordship to take upon you the nominal office of provost; I say nominal, my lord, because being now used to the duties, and somewhat experienced therein, I could take all the necessary part of the trouble off your lordship's hands, and so render the provostry in your lordship's name a perfect nonentity." Whereupon, he was pleased to say, if I would do so, and he commended my talents and prudence, he would have no objection to be made the provost at the ensuing election. Something more explicit might have ensued at that time; but Bailie McLucre and Mr Sharpset, who was the dean of guild, had been for about the space of half an hour carrying on a vehement argument anent some concern of the guildry, in which, coming to high words, and both being beguiled and ripened into folly by the earl's wine, they came into such a manifest quarrel, that Mr Sharpset pulled off the bailie's best wig, and flung it with a damn into the fire: the which stramash caused my lord to end the sederunt; but none of the magistrates, save myself was in a condition to go with his lordship to My Lady in the drawing-room.

Chapter 12

The Spy

Soon after the foregoing transaction, a thing happened that, in a manner, I would fain conceal and suppress from the knowledge of future times, although it was but a sort of sprose to make the world laugh. Fortunately for my character, however, it did not fall out exactly in my hands, although it happened in the course of my provostry. The matter spoken of, was the affair of a Frenchman who was taken up as a spy; for the American war was then raging, and the French had taken the part of the Yankee rebels.

One day, in the month of August it was, I had gone on some private concernment of my own to Kilmarnock, and Mr Booble, who was then oldest Bailie, naturally officiated as chief magistrate in my stead.

There have been, as the world knows, a disposition on the part of the grand monarque of that time, to invade and conquer this country, the which made it a duty incumbent on all magistrates to keep a vigilant eye on the in-comings and out-goings of aliens and other suspectable persons. On the said day, and during my absence, a Frenchman, that could speak no manner of English, somehow was discovered in the Cross-Key inns. What he was, or where he came from, nobody at the time could tell, as I was informed; but there he was, having come into the house at the door, with a bundle in his hand, and a portmanty on his shoulder, like a traveller out of some vehicle of conveyance. Mrs Drammer, the landlady, did not like his looks; for he had toozy black whiskers, was lank and wan, and moreover deformed beyond human nature, as she said, with a parrot nose, and had no cravat, but only a bit black riband drawn through two buttonholes, fastening his ill-coloured sark neck, which gave him altogether something of an unwholesome, outlandish appearance.

Finding he was a foreigner, and understanding that strict injunctions were laid on the magistrates by the king and government anent the egressing of such persons, she thought, for the credit of her house, and the safety of the community at large, that it behoved her to send word to me, then provost, of this man's visibility among us; but as I was not at home, Mrs Pawkie, my wife, directed the messenger to Bailie Booble's. The bailie was, at all times, overly ready to claught at an alarm; and when he heard the news, he went straight to the council-room, and sending for the rest of the council, ordered the alien enemy, as he called the forlorn Frenchman, to be brought before him. By this time, the suspicion of a spy in the town had spread far and wide; and Mrs Pawkie told me, that there was a palid consternation in every countenance when the black and yellow man-for he had not the looks of the honest folks of this country—was brought up the street between two of the town-officers, to stand an examine before Bailie Booble.

Neither the bailie, nor those that were then sitting with him, could speak any French language, and "the alien enemy" was as little master of our tongue. I have often wondered how the bailie did not jealouse that he could be no spy, seeing how, in that respect, he wanted the main faculty. But he was under the enchantment of a panic, partly thinking also, perhaps, that he was to do a great exploit for the government in my absence.

However, the man was brought before him, and there was he, and them all, speaking loud out to one another as if they had been hard of hearing, when I, on my coming home from Kilmarnock, went to see what was going on in the council. Considering that the procedure had been in handsome time before my arrival, I thought it judicious to leave the whole business with those present, and to sit still as a spectator; and really it was very comical to observe how the bailie was driven to his wit's-end by the poor lean and yellow Frenchman, and in what a pucker of passion the pannel put himself at every new interlocutor, none of which he could understand. At last, the bailie getting no satisfaction—how could he?—he directed the man's portmanty and bundle to be opened; and in the bottom of the forementioned package, there, to be sure, was found many a mystical and suspicious paper, which no one could read; among others, there was a strange map, as it then seemed to all present.

"I' gude faith," cried the bailie, with a keckle of exultation, "here's proof enough now. This is a plain map o' the Frith o' Clyde, all the way to the tail of the bank o' Greenock. This muckle place is Arran; that round ane is the craig of Ailsa; the wee ane between is Plada. Gentlemen, gentlemen, this is a sore discovery; there will be hanging and quartering on this." So he ordered the man to be forthwith committed as a king's prisoner to the tolbooth; and turning to me, said:—"My lord provost, as ye have not been present throughout the whole of this troublesome affair, I'll e'en gie an account my sel to the lord advocate of what we have done." I thought, at the time, there was something fey and overly forward in this, but I assented; for I know not what it was, that seemed to me as if there was something neither right nor regular; indeed, to say the truth, I was no ill pleased that the bailie took on him what he did; so I allowed him to write himself to the lord advocate; and, as the sequel showed, it was a blessed prudence on my part that I did so, for no sooner did his lordship receive the bailie's terrifying letter, than a special king's messenger was sent to take the spy into Edinburgh Castle; and nothing could surpass the great importance that Bailie Booble made of himself, on the occasion, on getting the man into a coach, and two dragoons to guard him into Glasgow.

But oh! what a dejected man was the miserable Bailie Booble, and what a laugh rose from shop and chamber, when the tidings came out from Edinburgh that "the alien enemy" was but a French cook coming over from Dublin, with the intent to take up the trade of a confectioner in Glasgow, and that the map of the Clyde was nothing but a plan for the outset of a fashionable table—the bailie's island of Arran being the roast beef, and the craig of Ailsa the plum-pudding, and Plada a butter-boat. Nobody enjoyed the jocularity of the business more than mysel; but I trembled when I thought of the escape that my honour and character had with the lord advocate. I trow, Bailie Booble never set himself so forward from that day to this.

Chapter 13

The Meal-Mob

After the close of the American war, I had, for various reasons of a private nature, a wish to sequestrate myself for a time, from any very ostensible part in public affairs. Still, however, desiring to retain a mean of resuming my station, and of maintaining my influence in the council, I bespoke Mr Keg to act in my place as deputy for My Lord, who was regularly every year at this time chosen into the provostry.

This Mr Keg was a man who had made a competency by the Isle-of-Man trade, and had come in from the laighlands, where he had been apparently in the farming line, to live among us; but for many a day, on account of something that happened when he was concerned in the smuggling, he kept himself cannily aloof from all sort of town matters; deporting himself with a most creditable sobriety; in so much, that there was at one time a sough that Mr Pittle, the minister, our friend, had put him on the leet for an elder. That post, however, if it was offered to him, he certainly never accepted; but I jealouse that he took the rumour o't for a sign that his character had ripened into an estimation among us, for he thenceforth began to kithe more in public, and was just a patron to every manifestation of loyalty, putting more lights in his windows in the rejoicing nights of victory than any other body, Mr McCreesh, the candlemaker, and Collector Cocket, not excepted. Thus, in the fulness of time, he was taken into the council, and no man in the whole corporation could be said to be more zealous than he was. In respect, therefore, to him, I had nothing to fear, so far as the interests, and, over and above all, the loyalty of the corporation, were concerned; but something like a quailing came over my heart, when, after the breaking up of the council on the day of election, he seemed to shy away from me, who had been instrumental to his advancement. However, I trow he had soon reason to repent of that ingratitude, as I may well call it; for when the troubles of the meal mob came upon him, I showed him that I could keep my distance as well as my neighbours.

It was on the Friday, our market-day, that the hobleshow began, and in the afternoon, when the farmers who had brought in their victual for sale were loading their carts to take it home again, the price not having come up to their expectation. All the forenoon, as the wives that went to the meal-market, came back railing with toom pocks and basins, it might have been foretold that the farmers would have to abate their extortion, or that something would come o't before night. My new house and shop being forenent the market, I had noted this, and said to Mrs Pawkie, my wife, what I thought would be the upshot, especially when, towards the afternoon, I observed the commonality gathering in the market-place, and no sparing in their tongues to the farmers; so, upon her advice, I directed Thomas Snakers to put on the shutters.

Some of the farmers were loading their carts to go home, when the schools skailed, and all the weans came shouting to the market. Still nothing happened, till tinkler Jean, a randy that had been with the army at the siege of Gibraltar, and, for aught I ken, in the Americas, if no in the Indies likewise;—she came with her meal-basin in her hand, swearing, like a trooper, that if she didna get it filled with meal at fifteen-pence a peck, (the farmers demanded sixteen), she would have the fu' o't of their heart's blood; and the mob of thoughtless weans and idle fellows, with shouts and yells, encouraged Jean, and egged her on to a catastrophe. The corruption of the farmers was thus raised, and a young rash lad, the son of James Dyke o' the Mount, whom Jean was blackguarding at a dreadful rate, and upbraiding on account of some ploy he had had with the Dalmailing session anent a bairn, in an unguarded moment lifted his hand, and shook his neive in Jean's face, and even, as she said, struck her. He himself swore an affidavit that he gave her only a ding out of his way; but be this as it may, at him rushed Jean with open mouth, and broke her timber meal-basin on his head, as it had been an eggshell. Heaven only knows what next ensued; but in a jiffy the whole market-place was as white with scattered meal as if it had been covered with snow, and the farmers were seen flying helter skelter out at the townhead, pursued by the mob, in a hail and whirlwind of stones and glaur. Then the drums were heard beating to arms, and the soldiers were seen flying to their rendezvous. I stood composedly at the dining room window, and was very thankful that I wasna provost in such a hurricane, when I saw poor Mr Keg, as pale as a dishclout, running to and fro bareheaded, with the town-officers and their halberts at his heels, exhorting and crying till he was as hoarse as a crow, to the angry multitude, that was raging and tossing like a sea in the market-place. Then it was that he felt the consequence of his pridefulness towards me; for, observing me standing in serenity at the window, he came, and in a vehement manner cried to me for the love of heaven to come to his assistance, and pacify the people. It would not have been proper in me to have refused; so out I went in the very nick of time: for when I got to the door, there was the soldiers in battle array, coming marching with fife and drum up the gait with Major Blaze at their head, red and furious in the face, and bent on some bloody business. The first thing I did was to run to the major, just as he was facing the men for a "charge bagonets" on the people, crying to him to halt; for the riot act wasna yet read, and the murder of all that might be slain would lie at his door; at which to hear he stood aghast, and the men halted. Then I flew back to the provost, and I cried to him, "Read the riot act!" which some of the mob hearing, became terrified thereat, none knowing the penalties or consequences thereof, when backed by soldiers; and in a moment, as if they had seen the glimpse of a terrible spirit in the air, the whole multitude dropped the dirt and stones out of their hands, and, turning their backs, flew into doors and closes, and were skailed before we knew where we were. It is not to be told the laud and admiration that I got for my ability in this business; for the major was so well pleased to have been saved from a battle, that, at my suggestion, he wrote an account of the whole business to the commander-in-chief, assuring him that, but for me, and my great weight and authority in the town, nobody could tell what the issue might have been; so that the Lord Advocate, to whom the report was shown by the general, wrote me a letter of thanks in the name of the government; and I, although not provost, was thus seen and believed to be a person of the foremost note and consideration in the town.

But although the mob was dispersed, as I have related, the consequences did not end there; for, the week following, none of the farmers brought in their victual; and there was a great lamentation and moaning in the market-place when, on the Friday, not a single cart from the country was to be seen, but only Simon Laidlaw's, with his timber caps and luggies; and the talk was, that meal would be half-a-crown the peck. The grief, however, of the business wasna visible till the Saturday—the wonted day for the poor to seek their meat—when the swarm of beggars that came forth was a sight truly calamitous. Many a decent auld woman that had patiently eiked out the slender thread of a weary life with her wheel, in privacy, her scant and want known only to her Maker, was seen going from door to door with the salt tear in her e'e, and looking in the face of the pitiful, being as yet unacquainted with the language of beggary; but the worst sight of all was two bonny bairns, dressed in their best, of a genteel demeanour, going from house to house like the hungry babes in the wood: nobody kent who they were, nor whar they came from; but as I was seeing them served myself at our door, I spoke to them, and they told me that their mother was lying sick and ill at home. They were the orphans of a broken merchant from Glasgow, and, with their mother, had come out to our town the week before, without knowing where else to seek their meat.

Mrs Pawkie, who was a tender-hearted mother herself, took in the bairns on hearing this, and we made of them, and the same night, among our acquaintance, we got a small sum raised to assist their mother, who proved a very well-bred and respectable lady-like creature. When she got better, she was persuaded to take up a school, which she kept for some years, with credit to herself and benefit to the community, till she got a legacy left her by a brother that died in India, the which, being some thousands, caused her to remove into Edinburgh, for the better education of her own children; and its seldom that legacies are so well bestowed, for she never forgot Mrs Pawkie's kindness, and out of the fore-end of her wealth she sent her a very handsome present. Divers matters of elegance have come to us from her, year by year, since syne, and regularly on the anniversary day of that sore Saturday, as the Saturday following the meal mob was ever after called.

Chapter 14

The Second Provostry

I have had occasion to observe in the course of my experience, that there is not a greater mollifier of the temper and nature of man than a constant flowing in of success and prosperity. From the time that I had been dean of guild, I was sensible of a considerable increase of my worldly means and substance; and although Bailie McLucre played me a soople trick at the election, by the inordinate sale and roup of his potatoe-rig, the which tried me, as I do confess, and nettled me with disappointment; yet things, in other respects, went so well with me that, about the eighty-eight, I began to put forth my hand again into public affairs, endowed both with more vigour and activity than it was in the first period of my magisterial functions. Indeed, it may be here proper for me to narrate, that my retiring into the background during the last two or three years, was a thing, as I have said, done on mature deliberation; partly, in order that the weight of my talents might be rightly estimated; and partly, that men might, of their own reflections, come to a proper understanding concerning them. I did not secede from the council. Could I have done that with propriety, I would assuredly not have scrupled to make the sacrifice; but I knew well that, if I was to resign, it would not be easy afterwards to get myself again chosen in. In a word, I was persuaded that I had, at times, carried things a little too highly, and that I had the adversary of a rebellious feeling in the minds and hearts of the corporation against me. However, what I did, answered the end and purpose I had in view; folk began to wonder and think with themselves, what for Mr Pawkie had ceased to bestir himself in public affairs; and the magistrates and council having, on two or three occasions, done very unsatisfactory things, it was said by one, and echoed by another, till the whole town was persuaded of the fact, that, had I lent my shoulder to the wheel, things would not have been as they were. But the matter which did the most service to me at this time, was a rank piece of idolatry towards my lord, on the part of Bailie McLucre, who had again got himself most sickerly installed in the guildry. Sundry tacks came to an end in this year of eighty-eight; and among others, the Niggerbrae park, which, lying at a commodious distance from the town, might have been relet with a rise and advantage. But what did the dean of guild do? He, in some secret and clandestine manner, gave a hint to my lord's factor to make an offer for the park on a two nineteen years' lease, at the rent then going—the which was done in a my lord's name, his lordship being then provost. The Niggerbrae was accordingly let to him, at the same rent which the town received for it in the sixty-nine. Nothing could be more manifest than that there was some jookerie cookerie in this affair; but in what manner it was done, or how the dean of guild's benefit was to ensue, no one could tell, and few were able to conjecture; for my lord was sorely straitened for money, and had nothing to spare out of hand. However, towards the end of the year, a light broke in upon us.

Gabriel McLucre, the dean of guild's fifth son, a fine spirited laddie, somehow got suddenly a cadetcy to go to India; and there were uncharitably-minded persons, who said, that this was the payment for the Niggerbrae job to my lord. The outcry, in consequence, both against the dean of guild, and especially against the magistrates and council for consenting thereto, was so extraordinary, and I was so openly upbraided for being so long lukewarm, that I was, in a manner, forced again forward to take a prominent part; but I took good care to let it be well known, that, in resuming my public faculties, I was resolved to take my own way, and to introduce a new method and reformation into all our concerns. Accordingly, at the Michaelmas following, that is, in the eighty-nine, I was a second time chosen to the provostry, with an understanding, that I was to be upheld in the office and dignity for two years; and that sundry improvements, which I thought the town was susceptible of, both in the causey of the streets and the reparation of the kirk, should be set about under my direction; but the way in which I handled the same, and brought them to a satisfactory completeness and perfection, will supply abundant matter for two chapters.

Chapter 15

On the Improvement of the Streets

In ancient times, Gudetown had been fortified with ports and gates at the end of the streets; and in troublesome occasions, the country people, as the traditions relate, were in the practice of driving in their families and cattle for shelter. This gave occasion to that great width in our streets, and those of other royal burghs, which is so remarkable; the same being so built to give room and stance for the cattle. But in those days the streets were not paved at the sides, but only in the middle, or, as it was called, the crown of the causey; which was raised and backed upward, to let the rain-water run off into the gutters. In progress of time, however, as the land and kingdom gradually settled down into an orderly state, the farmers and country folk having no cause to drive in their herds and flocks, as in the primitive ages of a rampageous antiquity, the proprietors of houses in the town, at their own cost, began, one after another, to pave the spaces of ground between their steadings and the crown of the causey; the which spaces were called lones, and the lones being considered as private property, the corporation had only regard to the middle portion of the street—that which I have said was named the crown of the causey.

The effect of this separation of interests in a common good began to manifest itself, when the pavement of the crown of the causey, by neglect, became rough and dangerous to loaded carts and gentlemen's carriages passing through the town; in so much that, for some time prior to my second provostry, the carts and carriages made no hesitation of going over the lones, instead of keeping the highway in the middle of the street; at which many of the burgesses made loud and just complaints.

One dark night, the very first Sunday after my restoration to the provostry, there was like to have happened a very sore thing by an old woman, one Peggy Waife, who had been out with her gown-tail over her head for a choppin of strong ale. As she was coming home, with her ale in a greybeard in her hand, a chaise in full bir came upon her and knocked her down, and broke the greybeard and spilt the liquor. The cry was terrible; some thought poor Peggy was killed outright, and wives, with candles in their hands, started out at the doors and windows. Peggy, however, was more terrified than damaged; but the gentry that were in the chaise, being termagant English travellers, swore like dragoons that the streets should be indicted as a nuisance; and when they put up at the inns, two of them came to me, as provost, to remonstrate on the shameful condition of the pavement, and to lodge in my hands the sum of ten pounds for the behoof of Peggy; the which was greater riches than ever the poor creature thought to attain in this world. Seeing they were gentlemen of a right quality, I did what I could to pacify them, by joining in every thing they said in condemnation of the streets; telling them, at the same time, that the improvement of the causey was to be the very first object and care of my provostry. And I bade Mrs Pawkie bring in the wine decanters, and requested them to sit down with me and take a glass of wine and a sugar biscuit; the civility of which, on my part, soon brought them into a peaceable way of thinking, and they went away, highly commending my politess and hospitality, of which they spoke in the warmest terms, to their companion when they returned to the inns, as the waiter who attended them overheard, and told the landlord, who informed me and others of the same in the morning. So that on the Saturday following, when the town-council met, there was no difficulty in getting a minute entered at the sederunt, that the crown of the causey should be forthwith put in a state of reparation.

Having thus gotten the thing determined upon, I then proposed that we should have the work done by contract, and that notice should be given publicly of such being our intent. Some boggling was made to this proposal, it never having been the use and wont of the corporation, in time past, to do any thing by contract, but just to put whatever was required into the hands of one of the council, who got the work done in the best way he could; by which loose manner of administration great abuses were often allowed to pass unreproved. But I persisted in my resolution to have the causey renewed by contract; and all the inhabitants of the town gave me credit for introducing such a great reformation into the management of public affairs.

When it was made known that we would receive offers to contract, divers persons came forward; and I was a little at a loss, when I saw such competition, as to which ought to be preferred. At last, I bethought me, to send for the different competitors, and converse with them on the subject quietly; and I found in Thomas Shovel, the tacksman of Whinstone-quarry, a discreet and considerate man. His offer was, it is true, not so low as some of the others; but he had facilities to do the work quickly, that none of the rest could pretend to; so, upon a clear understanding of that, with the help of the dean of guild McLucre's advocacy, Thomas Shovel got the contract. At first, I could not divine what interest my old friend, the dean of guild, had to be so earnest in behalf of the offering contractor; in course of time, however, it spunkit out that he was a sleeping partner in the business, by which he made a power of profit. But saving two three carts of stones to big a dyke round the new steading which I had bought a short time before at the town-end, I had no benefit whatever. Indeed, I may take it upon me to say, that should not say it, few provosts, in so great a concern, could have acted more on a principle than I did in this; and if Thomas Shovel, of his free-will, did, at the instigation of the dean of guild, lay down the stones on my ground as aforesaid, the town was not wronged; for, no doubt, he paid me the compliment at some expense of his own profit.

Chapter 16

About the Repair of the Kirk

The repair of the kirk, the next job I took in hand, was not so easily managed as that of the causey; for it seems, in former times, the whole space of the area had been free to the parish in general, and that the lofts were constructions, raised at the special expense of the heritors for themselves. The fronts being for their families, and the back seats for their servants and tenants. In those times there were no such things as pews; but only forms, removeable, as I have heard say, at pleasure.

It, however, happened, in the course of nature, that certain forms came to be sabbathly frequented by the same persons; who, in this manner, acquired a sort of prescriptive right to them. And those persons or families, one after another, finding it would be an ease and convenience to them during divine worship, put up backs to their forms. But still, for many a year, there was no inclosure of pews; the first, indeed, that made a pew, as I have been told, was one Archibald Rafter, a wright, and the grandfather of Mr Rafter, the architect, who has had so much to do with the edification of the new town of Edinburgh. This Archibald's form happened to be near the door, on the left side of the pulpit; and in the winter, when the wind was in the north, it was a very cold seat, which induced him to inclose it round and round, with certain old doors and shutters, which he had acquired in taking down and rebuilding the left wing of the Whinnyhill house. The comfort in which this enabled him and his family to listen to the worship, had an immediate effect; and the example being of a taking nature, in the course of little more than twenty years from the time, the whole area of the kirk had been pewed in a very creditable manner.

Families thus getting, as it were, portions of the church, some, when removing from the town, gave them up to their neighbours on receiving a consideration for the expense they had been at in making the pews; so that, from less to more, the pews so formed became a lettable and a vendible property. It was, therefore, thought a hard thing, that in the reparation which the seats had come to require in my time, the heritors and corporation should be obligated to pay the cost and expense of what was so clearly the property of others; while it seemed an impossibility to get the whole tot of the proprietors of the pews to bear the expense of new-seating the kirk. We had in the council many a long and weighty sederunt on the subject, without coming to any practical conclusion. At last, I thought the best way, as the kirk was really become a disgrace to the town, would be, for the corporation to undertake the repair entirely, upon an understanding that we were to be paid eighteenpence a bottom-room, *per annum*, by the proprietors of the pews; and, on sounding the heritors, I found them all most willing to consent thereto, glad to be relieved from the awful expense of gutting and replenishing such a great concern as the kirk was. Accordingly, the council having agreed to this proposal, we had plans and estimates made, and notice given to the owners of pews of our intention. The whole proceedings gave the greatest satisfaction possible to the inhabitants in general , who lauded and approved of my discernment more and more.

By the estimate, it was found that the repairs would cost about a thousand pounds; and by the plan, that the seats, at eighteenpence a sitter, would yield better than a hundred pounds a-year; so that there was no scruple, on the part of the town-council, in borrowing the money wanted. This was the first public debt ever contracted by the corporation, and people were very fain to get their money lodged at five per cent. on such good security; in so much, that we had a great deal more offered than we required at that time and epoch.

Chapter 17

The Law Plea

The repair of the kirk was undertaken by contract with William Plane, the joiner, with whom I was in terms at the time anent the bigging of a land of houses on my new steading at the town-end. A most reasonable man in all things he was, and in no concern of my own had I a better satisfaction than in the house he built for me at the conjuncture when he had the town's work in the kirk; but there was at that period among us a certain person, of the name of Nabal Smeddum, a tobacconist by calling, who, up to this season, had been regarded but as a droll and comical body at a coothy crack. He was, in stature, of the lower order of mankind, but endowed with an inclination towards corpulency, by which he had acquired some show of a belly, and his face was round, and his cheeks both red and sleeky. He was, however, in his personalities, chiefly remarkable for two queer and twinkling little eyes, and for a habitual custom of licking his lips whenever he said any thing of pith or jocosity, or thought that he had done so, which was very often the case. In his apparel, as befitted his trade, he wore a suit of snuff-coloured cloth, and a brown round-eared wig, that curled close in to his neck.

Mr Smeddum, as I have related, was in some estimation for his comicality; but he was a dure hand at an argument, and would not see the plainest truth when it was not on his side of the debate. No occasion or cause, however, had come to pass by which this inherent cross-grainedness was stirred into action, till the affair of reseating the kirk—a measure, as I have mentioned, which gave the best satisfaction; but it happened that, on a Saturday night, as I was going soberly home from a meeting of the magistrates in the clerk's chamber, I by chance recollected that I stood in need of having my box replenished; and accordingly, in the most innocent and harmless manner that it was possible for a man to do, I stepped into this Mr Smeddum, the tobacconist's shop, and while he was compounding my mixture from the two canisters that stood on his counter, and I was in a manner doing nothing but looking at the number of counterfeit sixpences and shillings that were nailed thereon as an admonishment to his customers, he said to me, "So, provost, we're to hae a new lining to the kirk. I wonder, when ye were at it, that ye didna rather think of bigging another frae the fundament, for I'm thinking the walls are no o' a capacity of strength to outlast this seating."

Knowing, as I did, the tough temper of the body, I can attribute my entering into an argument with him on the subject to nothing but some inconsiderate infatuation; for when I said heedlessly, the walls are very good, he threw the brass snuff-spoon with an ecstasy into one of the canisters, and lifting his two hands into a posture of admiration, cried, as if he had seen an unco———

"Good! surely, provost, ye hae na had an inspection; they're crackit in divers places; they're shotten out wi' infirmity in others. In short, the whole kirk, frae the coping to the fundament, is a fabric smitten wi' a paralytic."

"It's very extraordinar, Mr Smeddum," was my reply, "that nobody has seen a' this but yoursel'."

"Na, if ye will deny the fact, provost," quo' he, "it's o' no service for me to say a word; but there has to a moral certainty been a slackness somewhere, or how has it happened that the wa's were na subjected to a right inspection before this job o' the seating?"

By this time, I had seen the great error into the which I had fallen, by entering on a confabulation with Mr Smeddum; so I said to him, "It' no a matter for you and me to dispute about, so I'll thank you to fill my box;" the which manner of putting an end to the debate he took very ill; and after I left the shop, he laid the marrow of our discourse open to Mr Threeper the writer, who by chance went in, like mysel', to get a supply of rappee for the Sabbath. That limb of the law discerning a sediment of litigation in the case, eggit on Mr Smeddum into a persuasion that the seating of the kirk was a thing which the magistrates had no legal authority to undertake. At this critical moment, my ancient adversary and seeming friend, the dean of guild, happened to pass the door, and the bickering snuff-man seeing him, cried to him to come in.

It was a very unfortunate occurrence; for Mr McLucre having a secret interest, as I have intimated, in the whinstone quarry, when he heard of taking down walls and bigging them up again, he listened with greedy ears to the dubieties of Mr Threeper, and loudly, and to the heart's content of Mr Smeddum, condemned the frailty and infirmity of the kirk, as a building in general.

It would be overly tedious to mention, however, all the outs and ins of the affair; but, from less to more, a faction was begotten, and grew to head, and stirring among the inhabitants of the town, not only with regard to the putting of new seats within the old walls, but likewise as to the power of the magistrates to lay out any part of the public funds in the reparation of the kirk; and the upshot was, a contribution among certain malecontents, to enable Mr Threeper to consult on all the points.

As in all similar cases, the parties applying for legal advice were heartened into a plea by the opinion they got, and the town-council was thrown into the greatest consternation by receiving notice that the malecontents were going to extremities.

Two things I saw it was obligational on me to urge forward; the one was to go on still with the reparations, and the other to contest the law-suit, although some were for waiting in the first case till the plea was settled, and in the second to make no defence, but to give up our intention anent the new-seating. But I thought that, as we had borrowed the money for the repairs, we should proceed; and I had a vista that the contribution raised by the Smeddumites, as they were called, would run out, being from their own pockets, whereas we fought with the public purse in our hand; and by dint of exhortation to that effect, I carried the majority to go into my plan, which in the end was most gratifying, for the kirk was in a manner made as good as new, and the contributional stock of the Smeddumites was entirely rookit by the lawyers, who would fain have them to form another, assuring them that, no doubt, the legal point was in their favour. But every body knows the uncertainty of a legal opinion; and although the case was given up, for lack of a fund to carry it on, there was a living ember of discontent left in its ashes, ready to kindle into a flame on the first puff of popular dissatisfaction.

Chapter 18

The Suppression of the Fairs

The spirit by which the Smeddumites were actuated in ecclesiastical affairs, was a type and taste of the great distemper with which all the world was, more or less, at the time inflamed, and which cast the ancient state and monarchy of France into the perdition of anarchy and confusion. I think, upon the whole, however, that our royal burgh was not afflicted to any very dangerous degree, though there was a sort of itch of it among a few of the sedentary orders, such as the weavers and shoemakers, who, by the nature of sitting long in one posture, are apt to become subject to the flatulence of theoretical opinions; but although this was my notion, yet knowing how much better the king and government were acquainted with the true condition of things than I could to a certainty be, I kept a steady eye on the proceedings of the ministers and parliament at London, taking them for an index and model for the management of the public concerns, which, by the grace of God, and the handling of my friends, I was raised up and set forward to undertake.

Seeing the great dread and anxiety that was above, as to the inordinate liberty of the multitude, and how necessary it was to bridle popularity, which was become rampant and ill to ride, kicking at all established order, and trying to throw both king and nobles from the saddle, I resolved to discountenance all tumultuous meetings, and to place every reasonable impediment in the way of multitudes assembling together: indeed, I had for many years been of opinion, that fairs were become a great political evil to the regular shopkeepers, by reason of the packmen, and other travelling merchants, coming with their wares and underselling us; so that both private interest and public principle incited me on to do all in my power to bring our fair-days into disrepute. It cannot be told what a world of thought and consideration this cost me before I lighted on the right method, nor, without a dive into the past times of antiquity, is it in the power of man to understand the difficulties of the matter.

Some of our fair-days were remnants of the papistical idolatry, and instituted of old by the Pope and Cardinals, in order to make an income from the vice and immorality that was usually rife at the same. These, in the main points, were only market-days of a blither kind than the common. The country folks came in dressed in their best, the schools got the play, and a long rank of sweety-wives and their stands, covered with the wonted dainties of the occasion, occupied the sunny side of the High Street; while the shady side was, in like manner, taken possession of by the packmen, who, in their booths, made a marvellous display of goods of an inferior quality, with laces and ribands of all colours, hanging down in front, and twirling like pinnets in the wind. There was likewise the allurement of some compendious show of wild beasts; in short, a swatch of every thing that the art of man has devised for such occasions, to wile away the bawbee.

Besides the fairs of this sort, that may be said to be of a pious origin, there were others of a more boisterous kind, that had come of the times of trouble, when the trades paraded with war-like weapons, and the banners of their respective crafts; and in every seventh year we had a resuscitation of King Crispianus in all his glory and regality, with the man in the coat-of-mail, of bell-metal, and the dukes, and lord mayor of London, at the which, the influx of lads and lasses from the country was just prodigious, and the rioting and rampaging at night, the brulies and the dancing, was worse than Vanity Fair in the Pilgrim's Progress.

To put down, and utterly to abolish, by stress of law, or authority, any ancient pleasure of the commonality, I had learned, by this time, was not wisdom, and that the fairs were only to be effectually suppressed by losing their temptations, and so to cease to call forth any expectation of merriment among the people. Accordingly, with respect to the fairs of pious origin, I, without expounding my secret motives, persuaded the council, that, having been at so great an expense in new-paving the streets, we ought not to permit the heavy caravans of wild beasts to occupy, as formerly, the front of the Tolbooth towards the Cross; but to order them, for the future, to keep at the Greenhead. This was, in a manner, expurgating them out of the town altogether; and the consequence was, that the people, who were wont to assemble in the High Street, came to be divided, part gathering at the Greenhead, round the shows, and part remaining among the stands and the booths; thus an appearance was given of the fairs being less attended than formerly, and gradually, year after year, the venerable race of sweety-wives, and chatty packmen, that were so detrimental to the shopkeepers, grew less and less numerous, until the fairs fell into insignificance.

At the parade fair, the remnant of the weapon-showing, I proceeded more roundly to work, and resolved to debar, by proclamation, all persons from appearing with arms; but the deacons of the trades spared me the trouble of issuing the same, for they dissuaded their crafts from parading. Nothing, however, so well helped me out as the volunteers, of which I will speak by and by; for when the war began, and they were formed, nobody could afterwards abide to look at the fantastical and disorderly marching of the trades, in their processions and paradings; so that, in this manner, all the glory of the fairs being shorn and expunged, they have fallen into disrepute, and have suffered a natural suppression.

Chapter 19

The Volunteers

The volunteers began in the year 1793, when the democrats in Paris threatened the downfall and utter subversion of kings, lords, and commons. As became us who were of the council, we drew up an address to his majesty, assuring him that our lives and fortunes were at his disposal. To the which dutiful address, we received, by return of post, a very gracious answer; and, at the same time, the lord-lieutenant gave me a bit hint, that it would be very pleasant to his majesty to hear that we had volunteers in our town, men of creditable connexions, and willing to defend their property.

When I got this note from his lordship, I went to Mr Pipe, the wine- merchant, and spoke to him concerning it, and we had some discreet conversation on the same; in the which it was agreed between us that, as I was now rather inclined to a corpulency of parts, and being likewise chief civil magistrate, it would not do to set myself at the head of a body of soldiers, but that the consequence might be made up to me in the clothing of the men; so I consented to put the business into his hands upon this understanding. Accordingly, he went the same night with me to Mr Dinton, that was in the general merchandizing line, a part-owner in vessels, a trafficker in corn, and now and then a canny discounter of bills, at a moderate rate, to folk in straits and difficulties. And we told him—the same being agreed between us, as the best way of fructifying the job to a profitable issue—that, as provost, I had got an intimation to raise a corps of volunteers, and that I thought no better hand could be got for a co-operation than him and Mr Pipe, who was pointed out to me as a gentleman weel qualified for the command.

Mr Dinton, who was a proud man, and an offset from one of the county families, I could see was not overly pleased at the preferment over him given to Mr Pipe, so that

I was in a manner constrained to loot a sort ajee, and to wile him into good-humour with all the ability in my power, by saying that it was natural enough of the king and government to think of Mr Pipe as one of the most proper men in the town, he paying, as he did, the largest sum of the king's dues at the excise, and being, as we all knew, in a great correspondence with foreign ports—and I winkit to Mr Pipe as I said this, and he could with a difficulty keep his countenance at hearing how I so beguiled Mr Dinton into a spirit of loyalty for the raising of the volunteers.

The ice being thus broken, next day we had a meeting, before the council met, to take the business into public consideration, and we thereat settled on certain creditable persons in the town, of a known principle, as the fittest to be officers under the command of Mr Pipe, as commandant, and Mr Dinton, as his colleague under him. We agreed among us, as the custom was in other places, that they should be elected major, captain, lieutenants, and ensigns, by the free votes of the whole corps, according to the degrees that we had determined for them. In the doing of this, and the bringing it to pass, my skill and management was greatly approved and extolled by all who had a peep behind the curtain.

The town-council being, as I have intimated, convened to hear the gracious answer to the address read, and to take into consideration the suggesting anent the volunteering, met in the clerk's chamber, where we agreed to call a meeting of the inhabitants of the town by proclamation, and by a notice in the church. This being determined, Mr Pipe and Mr Dinton got a paper drawn up, and privately, before the Sunday, a number of their genteeler friends, including those whom we had noted down to be elected officers, set their names as willing to be volunteers.

On the Sunday, Mr Pittle, at my instigation, preached a sermon, showing forth the necessity of arming ourselves in the defence of all that was dear to us. It was a discourse of great method and sound argument, but not altogether so quickened with pith and bir as might have been wished for; but it paved the way to the reading out of the summons for the inhabitants to meet the magistrates in the church on the Thursday following, for the purpose, as it was worded by the town-clerk, to take into consideration the best means of saving the king and kingdom in the then monstrous crisis of public affairs.

The discourse, with the summons, and a rumour and whispering that had in the mean time taken place, caused the desired effect; in so much, that, on the Thursday, there was a great congregation of the male portion of the people. At the which, old Mr Dravel—a genteel man he was, well read in matters of history, though somewhat over-portioned with a conceit of himself—got up on the table, in one of the table-seats forenent the poopit, and made a speech suitable to the occasion; in the which he set forth what manful things had been done of old by the Greeks and the Romans for their country, and, waxing warm with his subject, he cried out with a loud voice, towards the end of the discourse, giving at the same time a stamp with his foot, "Come, then, as men and as citizens; the cry is for your altars and your God."

"Gude save's, Mr Dravel, are ye gane by yoursel?" cried Willy Coggle from the front of the loft, a daft body that was aye far ben on all public occasions—"to think that our God's a Pagan image in need of sick feckless help as the like o' thine?" The which outcry of Willy raised a most extraordinary laugh at the fine paternoster, about the ashes of our ancestors, that Mr Dravel had been so vehemently rehearsing; and I was greatly afraid that the solemnity of the day would be turned into a ridicule. However, Mr Pipe, who was upon the whole a man no without both sense and capacity, rose and said, that our business was to strengthen the hands of government, by coming forward as volunteers; and therefore, without thinking it necessary, among the people of this blessed land, to urge any arguments in furtherance of that object, he would propose that a volunteer corps should be raised; and he begged leave of me, who, as provost, was in the chair, to read a few words that he had hastily thrown together on the subject, as the outlines of a pact of agreement among those who might be inclined to join with him. I should here, however, mention, that the said few words of a pact was the costive product overnight of no small endeavour between me and Mr Dinton as well as him.

When he had thus made his motion, Mr Dinton, as we had concerted, got up and seconded the same, pointing out the liberal spirit in which the agreement was drawn, as every person signing it was eligible to be an officer of any rank, and every man had a vote in the preferment of the officers. All which was mightily applauded; and upon this I rose, and said, "It was a pleasant thing for me to have to report to his majesty's government the loyalty of the inhabitants of our town, and the unanimity of the volunteering spirit among them—and to testify," said I, "to all the world, how much we are sensible of the blessings of the true liberty we enjoy, I would suggest that the matter of the volunteering be left entirely to Mr Pipe and Mr Dinton, with a few other respectable gentlemen, as a committee, to carry the same into effect;" and with that I looked, as it were, round the church, and then said, "There's Mr Oranger, a better couldna be joined with them." He was a most creditable man, and a grocer, that we had waled out for a captain; so I desired, having got a nod of assent from him, that Mr Oranger's name might be added to their's, as one of the committee. In like manner I did by all the rest whom we had previously chosen. Thus, in a manner, predisposing the public towards them for officers.

In the course of the week, by the endeavours of the committee, a sufficient number of names was got to the paper, and the election of the officers came on on the Tuesday following; at which, though there was a sort of a contest, and nothing could be a fairer election, yet the very persons that we had chosen were elected, though some of them had but a narrow chance. Mr Pipe was made the commandant, by a superiority of only two votes over Mr Dinton.

Chapter 20

The Clothing

It was an understood thing at first, that, saving in the matter of guns and other military implements, the volunteers were to be at all their own expenses; out of which, both tribulation and disappointment ensued; for when it came to be determined about the uniforms, Major Pipe found that he could by no possibility wise all the furnishing to me, every one being disposed to get his regimentals from his own merchant; and there was also a division anent the colour of the same, many of the doucer sort of the men being blate of appearing in scarlet and gold-lace, insisting with a great earnestness, almost to a sedition, on the uniform being blue. So that the whole advantage of a contract was frustrated, and I began to be sorry that I had not made a point of being, notwithstanding the alleged weight and impediment of my corpulence, the major-commandant myself. However, things, after some time, began to take a turn for the better; and the art of raising volunteers being better understood in the kingdom, Mr Pipe went into Edinburgh, and upon some conference with the lord advocate, got permission to augment his force by another company, and leave to draw two days' pay a-week for account of the men, and to defray the necessary expenses of the corps. The doing of this bred no little agitation in the same; and some of the forward and upsetting spirits of the younger privates, that had been smitten, though not in a disloyal sense, with the insubordinate spirit of the age, clamoured about the rights of the original bargain with them, insisting that the officers had no privilege to sell their independence, and a deal of trash of that sort, and finally withdrew from the corps, drawing, to the consternation of the officers, the pay that had been taken in their names; and which the officers could not refuse, although it was really wanted for the contingencies of the service, as Major Pipe himself told me.

When the corps had thus been rid of these turbulent spirits, the men grew more manageable and rational, assenting by little and little to all the proposals of the officers, until there was a true military dominion of discipline gained over them; and a joint contract was entered into between Major Pipe and me, for a regular supply of all necessaries, in order to insure a uniform appearance, which, it is well known, is essential to a right discipline. In the end, when the eyes of men in civil stations had got accustomed to military show and parade, it was determined to change the colour of the cloth from blue to red, the former having at first been preferred, and worn for some time; in the accomplishment of which change I had (and why should I disguise the honest fact?) my share of the advantage which the kingdom at large drew, in that period of anarchy and confusion, from the laudable establishment of a volunteer force.

Chapter 21

The Press Gang

During the same just and necessary war for all that was dear to us, in which the volunteers were raised, one of the severest trials happened to me that ever any magistrate was subjected to. I had, at the time, again subsided into an ordinary counsellor; but it so fell out that, by reason of Mr Shuttlethrift, who was then provost, having occasion and need to go into Glasgow upon some affairs of his own private concerns, he being interested in the Kilbeacon cotton-mill; and Mr Dalrye, the bailie, who should have acted for him, being likewise from home, anent a plea he had with a neighbour concerning the bounds of their rigs and gables; the whole authority and power of the magistrates devolved, by a courtesy on the part of their colleague, Bailie Hammerman, into my hands.

For some time before, there had been an ingathering among us of sailor lads from the neighbouring ports, who on their arrival, in order to shun the press-gangs, left their vessels and came to scog themselves with us. By this, a rumour or a suspicion rose that the men-of-war's men were suddenly to come at the dead hour of the night and sweep them all away. Heaven only knows whether this notice was bred in the fears and jealousies of the people, or was a humane inkling given, by some of the men-of-war's men, to put the poor sailor lads on their guard, was never known. But on a Saturday night, as I was on the eve of stepping into my bed, I shall never forget it—Mrs Pawkie was already in, and as sound as a door-nail—and I was just crooking my mouth to blow out the candle, when I heard a rap. As our bed-room window was over the door, I looked out. It was a dark night; but I could see by a glaik of light from a neighbour's window, that there was a man with a cocked hat at the door.

"What's your will?" said I to him, as I looked out at him in my nightcap. He made no other answer, but that he was one of his majesty's officers, and had business with the justice.

I did not like this Englification and voice of claim and authority; however, I drew on my stockings and breeks again, and taking my wife's flannel coaty about my shoulders—for I was then troubled with the rheumatiz—I went down, and, opening the door, let in the lieutenant.

"I come," said he, "to show you my warrant and commission, and to acquaint you that, having information of several able-bodied seamen being in the town, I mean to make a search for them."

I really did not well know what to say at the moment; but I begged him, for the love of peace and quietness, to defer his work till the next morning: but he said he must obey his orders; and he was sorry that it was his duty to be on so disagreeable a service, with many other things, that showed something like a sense of compassion that could not have been hoped for in the captain of a pressgang.

When he had said this, he then went away, saying, for he saw my tribulation, that it would be as well for me to be prepared in case of any riot. This was the worst news of all; but what could I do? I thereupon went again to Mrs Pawkie, and shaking her awake, told her what was going on, and a terrified woman she was. I then dressed myself with all possible expedition, and went to the town-clerk's, and we sent for the town-officers, and then adjourned to the council-chamber to wait the issue of what might betide.

In my absence, Mrs Pawkie rose out of her bed, and by some wonderful instinct collecting all the bairns, went with them to the minister's house, as to a place of refuge and sanctuary.

Shortly after we had been in the council-room, I opened the window and looked out, but all was still; the town was lying in the defencelessness of sleep, and nothing was heard but the clicking of the town-clock in the steeple over our heads. By and by, however, a sough and pattering of feet was heard approaching; and shortly after, in looking out, we saw the pressgang, headed by their officers, with cutlasses by their side, and great club-sticks in their hands. They said nothing; but the sound of their feet on the silent stones of the causey, was as the noise of a dreadful engine. They passed, and went on; and all that were with me in the council stood at the windows and listened. In the course of a minute or two after, two lassies, with a callan, that had been out, came flying and wailing, giving the alarm to the town. Then we heard the driving of the bludgeons on the doors, and the outcries of terrified women; and presently after we saw the poor chased sailors running in their shirts, with their clothes in their hands, as if they had been felons and blackguards caught in guilt, and flying from the hands of justice.

The town was awakened with the din as with the cry of fire; and lights came starting forward, as it were, to the windows. The women were out with lamentations and vows of vengeance. I was in a state of horror unspeakable. Then came some three or four of the pressgang with a struggling sailor in their clutches, with nothing but his trousers on—his shirt riven from his back in the fury. Syne came the rest of the gang and their officers, scattered as it were with a tempest of mud and stones, pursued and battered by a troop of desperate women and weans, whose fathers and brothers were in jeopardy. And these were followed by the wailing wife of the pressed man, with her five bairns, clamouring in their agony to heaven against the king and government for the outrage. I couldna listen to the fearful justice of their outcry, but sat down in a corner of the council-chamber with my fingers in my ears.

In a little while a shout of triumph rose from the mob, and we heard them returning, and I felt, as it were, relieved; but the sound of their voices became hoarse and terrible as they drew near, and, in a moment, I heard the jingle of twenty broken windows rattle in the street. My heart misgave me; and, indeed, it was my own windows. They left not one pane unbroken; and nothing kept them from demolishing the house to the ground-stone but the exhortations of Major Pipe, who, on hearing the uproar, was up and out, and did all in his power to arrest the fury of the tumult. It seems, the mob had taken it into their heads that I had signed what they called the press-warrants; and on driving the gang out of the town, and rescuing the man, they came to revenge themselves on me and mine; which is the cause that made me say it was a miraculous instinct that led Mrs Pawkie to take the family to Mr Pittle's; for, had they been in the house, it is not to be told what the consequences might have been.

Before morning the riot was ended, but the damage to my house was very great; and I was intending, as the public had done the deed, that the town should have paid for it. "But," said Mr Keelivine, the town-clerk," I think you may do better; and this calamity, if properly handled to the government, may make your fortune," I reflected on the hint; and accordingly, the next day, I went over to the regulating captain of the pressgang, and represented to him the great damage and detriment which I had suffered, requesting him to represent to government that it was all owing to the part I had taken in his behalf. To this, for a time, he made some scruple of objection; but at last he drew up, in my presence, a letter to the lords of the admiralty, telling what he had done, and how he and his men had been ill-used, and that the house of the chief-magistrate of the town had been in a manner destroyed by the rioters.

By the same post I wrote off myself to the lord advocate, and likewise to the secretary of state, in London; commending, very properly, the prudent and circumspect manner in which the officer had come to apprize me of his duty, and giving as faithful an account as I well could of the riot; concluding with a simple notification of what had been done to my house, and the outcry that might be raised in the town were any part of the town's funds to be used in the repairs.

Both the lord advocate and Mr Secretary of State wrote me back by retour of post, thanking me for my zeal in the public service; and I was informed that, as it might not be expedient to agitate in the town the payment of the damage which my house had received, the lords of the treasury would indemnify me for the same; and this was done in a manner which showed the blessings we enjoy under our most venerable constitution; for I was not only thereby enabled, by what I got, to repair the windows, but to build up a vacant steading; the same which I settled last year on my dochter, Marion, when she was married to Mr Geery, of the Gatherton Home.

Chapter 22

The Wig Dinner

The affair of the Press Gang gave great concern to all of the council; for it was thought that the loyalty of the burgh would be called in question, and doubted by the king's ministers, notwithstanding our many assurances to the contrary; the which sense and apprehension begat among us an inordinate anxiety to manifest our principles on all expedient occasions. In the doing of this, divers curious and comical things came to pass; but the most comical of all was what happened at the Michaelmas dinner following the riot.

The weather, for some days before, had been raw for that time of the year, and Michaelmas-day was, both for wind and wet and cold, past ordinar; in so much that we were obligated to have a large fire in the council-chamber, where we dined. Round this fire, after drinking his majesty's health and the other appropriate toasts, we were sitting as cozy as could be; and every one the longer he sat, and the oftener his glass visited the punch-bowl, waxed more and more royal, till everybody was in a most hilarious temperament, singing songs and joining chorus with the greatest cordiality.

It happened, among others of the company, there was a gash old carl, the laird of Bodletonbrae, who was a very capital hand at a joke; and he, chancing to notice that the whole of the magistrates and town council then present wore wigs, feigned to become out of all bounds with the demonstrations of his devotion to king and country; and others that were there, not wishing to appear any thing behind him in the same, vied in their sprose of patriotism, and bragging in a manful manner of what, in the hour of trial, they would be seen to do. Bodletonbrae was all the time laughing in his sleeve at the way he was working them on, till at last, after they had flung the glasses twice or thrice over their shoulders, he proposed we should throw our wigs in the fire next. Surely there was some glammer about us that caused us not to observe his devilry, for the laird had no wig on his head. Be that, however, as it may, the instigation took effect, and in the twinkling of an eye every scalp was bare, and the chimley roaring with the roasting of gude kens how many powdered wigs well fattened with pomatum. But scarcely was the deed done, till every one was admonished of his folly, by the laird laughing, like a being out of his senses, at the number of bald heads and shaven crowns that his device had brought to light, and by one and all of us experiencing the coldness of the air on the nakedness of our upper parts.

The first thing that we then did was to send the town-officers, who were waiting on as usual for the dribbles of the bottles and the leavings in the bowls, to bring our nightcaps, but I trow few were so lucky as me, for I had a spare wig at home, which Mrs Pawkie, my wife, a most considerate woman, sent to me; so that I was, in a manner, to all visibility, none the worse of the ploy; but the rest of the council were perfect oddities within their wigs, and the sorest thing of all was, that the exploit of burning the wigs had got wind; so that, when we left the council-room, there was a great congregation of funny weans and misleart trades' lads assembled before the tolbooth, shouting, and like as if they were out of the body with daffing, to see so many of the heads of the town in their nightcaps, and no, maybe, just so solid at the time as could have been wished. Nor did the matter rest here; for the generality of the sufferers being in a public way, were obligated to appear the next day in their shops, and at their callings, with their nightcaps—for few of them had two wigs like me—by which no small merriment ensued, and was continued for many a day. It would hardly, however, be supposed, that in such a matter any thing could have redounded to my advantage; but so it fell out, that by my wife's prudence in sending me my other wig, it was observed by the commonality, when we sallied forth to I had on my wig, and it was thought I had a very meritorious command of myself, and was the only man in the town fit for a magistrate; for in every thing I was seen to be most cautious and considerate. I could not, however, when I saw the turn the affair took to my advantage, but reflect on what small and visionary grounds the popularity of public men will sometimes rest.

Chapter 23

The Death of Mr McLucre

Shortly after the affair recorded in the foregoing chapter, an event came to pass in the burgh that had been for some time foreseen.

My old friend and adversary, Bailie McLucre, being now a man well stricken in years, was one night, in going home from a gavawlling with some of the neighbours at Mr Shuttlethrift's, the manufacturer's, (the bailie, canny man, never liket ony thing of the sort at his own cost and outlay,) having partaken largely of the bowl, for the manufacturer was of a blithe humour—the bailie, as I was saying, in going home, was overtaken by an apoplexy just at the threshold of his own door, and although it did not kill him outright, it shoved him, as it were, almost into the very grave; in so much that he never spoke an articulate word during the several weeks he was permitted to doze away his latter end; and accordingly he died, and was buried in a very creditable manner to the community, in consideration of the long space of time he had been a public man among us.

But what rendered the event of his death, in my opinion, the more remarkable, was, that I considered with him the last remnant of the old practice of managing the concerns of the town came to a period. For now that he is dead and gone, and also all those whom I found conjunct with him, when I came into power and office, I may venture to say, that things in yon former times were not guided so thoroughly by the hand of a disinterested integrity as in these latter years. On the contrary, it seemed to be the use and wont of men in public trusts, to think they were free to indemnify themselves in a left-handed way for the time and trouble they bestowed in the same. But the thing was not so far wrong in principle as in the hugger-muggering way in which it was done, and which gave to it a guilty colour, that, by the judicious stratagem of a right system, it would never have had. In sooth to say, through the whole course of my public life, I met with no greater difficulties and trials than in cleansing myself from the old habitudes of office. For I must in verity confess, that I myself partook, in a degree, at my beginning, of the caterpillar nature; and it was not until the light of happier days called forth the wings of my endowment, that I became conscious of being raised into public life for a better purpose than to prey upon the leaves and flourishes of the commonwealth. So that, if I have seemed to speak lightly of those doings that are now denominated corruptions, I hope it was discerned therein that I did so rather to intimate that such things were, than to consider them as in themselves commendable. Indeed, in their notations, I have endeavoured, in a manner, to be governed by the spirit of the times in which the transactions happened; for I have lived long enough to remark, that if we judge of past events by present motives, and do not try to enter into the spirit of the age when they took place, and to see them with the eyes with which they were really seen, we shall conceit many things to be of a bad and wicked character that were not thought so harshly of by those who witnessed them, nor even by those who, perhaps, suffered from them. While, therefore, I think it has been of a great advantage to the public to have survived that method of administration in which the like of Bailie McLucre was engendered, I would not have it understood that I think the men who held the public trusts in those days a whit less honest than the men of my own time. The spirit of their own age was upon them, as that of ours is upon us, and their ways of working the wherry entered more or less into all their trafficking, whether for the commonality, or for their own particular behoof and advantage.

I have been thus large and frank in my reflections anent the death of the bailie, because, poor man, he had outlived the times for which he was qualified; and, instead of the merriment and jocularity that his wily by-hand ways used to cause among his neighbours, the rising generation began to pick and dab at him, in such a manner, that, had he been much longer spared, it is to be feared he would not have been allowed to enjoy his earnings both with ease and honour. However, he got out of the world with some respect, and the matters of which I have now to speak, are exalted, both in method and principle, far above the personal considerations that took something from the public virtue of his day and generation.

Chapter 24

The Windy Yule

It was in the course of the Winter, after the decease of Bailie McLucre, that the great loss of lives took place, which every body agreed was one of the most calamitous things that had for many a year befallen the town.

Three or four vessels were coming with cargoes of grain from Ireland; another from the Baltic with Norawa deals; and a third from Bristol, where she had been on a charter for some Greenock merchants.

It happened that, for a time, there had been contrary winds, against which no vessel could enter the port, and the ships, whereof I have been speaking, were all lying together at anchor in the bay, waiting a change of weather. These five vessels were owned among ourselves, and their crews consisted of fathers and sons belonging to the place, so that, both by reason of interest and affection, a more than ordinary concern was felt for them; for the sea was so rough, that no boat could live in it to go near them, and we had our fears that the men on board would be very ill off. Nothing, however, occurred but this natural anxiety, till the Saturday, which was Yule. In the morning the weather was blasty and sleety, waxing more and more tempestuous till about mid-day, when the wind checked suddenly round from the nor-east to the sou-west, and blew a gale as if the prince of the powers of the air was doing his utmost to work mischief. The rain blattered, the windows clattered, the shop-shutters flapped, pigs from the lum-heads came rattling down like thunder-claps, and the skies were dismal both with cloud and carry. Yet, for all that, there was in the streets a stir and a busy visitation between neighbours, and every one went to their high windows, to look at the five poor barks that were warsling against the strong arm of the elements of the storm and the ocean.

Still the lift gloomed, and the wind roared, and it was as doleful a sight as ever was seen in any town afflicted with calamity, to see the sailors' wives, with their red cloaks about their heads, followed by their hirpling and disconsolate bairns, going one after another to the kirkyard, to look at the vessels where their helpless breadwinners were battling with the tempest. My heart was really sorrowful, and full of a sore anxiety to think of what might happen to the town, whereof so many were in peril, and to whom no human magistracy could extend the arm of protection. Seeing no abatement of the wrath of heaven, that howled and roared around us, I put on my big-coat, and taking my staff in my hand, having tied down my hat with a silk handkerchief, towards gloaming I walked likewise to the kirkyard, where I beheld such an assemblage of sorrow, as few men in situation have ever been put to the trial to witness.

In the lea of the kirk many hundreds of the town were gathered together; but there was no discourse among them. The major part were sailors' wives and weans, and at every new thud of the blast, a sob rose, and the mothers drew their bairns closer in about them, as if they saw the visible hand of a foe raised to smite them. Apart from the multitude, I observed three or four young lasses standing behind the Whinnyhill families' tomb, and I jealoused that they had joes in the ships; for they often looked to the bay, with long necks and sad faces, from behind the monument. A widow woman, one old Mary Weery, that was a lameter, and dependent on her son, who was on board the Louping Meg, (as the Lovely Peggy was nicknamed at the shore,) stood by herself, and every now and then wrung her hands, crying, with a woeful voice, "The Lord giveth and the Lord taketh away, blessed be the name of the Lord;"—but it was manifest to all that her faith was fainting within her. But of all the piteous objects there, on that doleful evening, none troubled my thoughts more than three motherless children, that belonged to the mate of one of the vessels in the jeopardy. He was an Englishman that had been settled some years in the town, where his family had neither kith nor kin; and his wife having died about a month before, the bairns, of whom the eldest was but nine or so, were friendless enough, though both my gudewife, and other well-disposed ladies, paid them all manner of attention till their father would come home. The three poor little things, knowing that he was in one of the ships, had been often out and anxious, and they were then sitting under the lea of a headstone, near their mother's grave, chittering and creeping closer and closer at every squall. Never was such an orphan-like sight seen.

When it began to be so dark that the vessels could no longer be discerned from the churchyard, many went down to the shore, and I took the three babies home with me, and Mrs Pawkie made tea for them, and they soon began to play with our own younger children, in blythe forgetfulness of the storm; every now and then, however, the eldest of them, when the shutters rattled and the lum-head roared, would pause in his innocent daffing, and cower in towards Mrs Pawkie, as if he was daunted and dismayed by something he knew not what.

Many a one that night walked the sounding shore in sorrow, and fires were lighted along it to a great extent; but the darkness and the noise of the raging deep, and the howling wind, never intermitted till about midnight: at which time a message was brought to me, that it might be needful to send a guard of soldiers to the beach, for that broken masts and tackle had come in, and that surely some of the barks had perished. I lost no time in obeying this suggestion, which was made to me by one of the owners of the Louping Meg; and to show that I sincerely sympathized with all those in affliction, I rose and dressed myself, and went down to the shore, where I directed several old boats to be drawn up by the fires, and blankets to be brought, and cordials prepared, for them that might be spared with life to reach the land; and I walked the beach with the mourners till the morning.

As the day dawned, the wind began to abate in its violence, and to wear away from the sou-west into the norit, but it was soon discovered that some of the vessels with the corn had perished; for the first thing seen, was a long fringe of tangle and grain along the line of the highwater mark, and every one strained with greedy and grieved eyes, as the daylight brightened, to discover which had suffered. But I can proceed no further with the dismal recital of that doleful morning. Let it suffice here to be known, that, through the haze, we at last saw three of the vessels lying on their beam-ends with their masts broken, and the waves riding like the furious horses of destruction over them. What had become of the other two was never known; but it was supposed that they had foundered at their anchors, and that all on board perished.

The day being now Sabbath, and the whole town idle, every body in a manner was down on the beach, to help and mourn as the bodies, one after another, were cast out by the waves. Alas! few were the better of my provident preparation, and it was a thing not to be described, to see, for more than a mile along the coast, the new-made widows and fatherless bairns, mourning and weeping over the corpses of those they loved. Seventeen bodies were, before ten o'clock, carried to the desolated dwelling of their families; and when old Thomas Pull, the betheral, went to ring the bell for public worship, such was the universal sorrow of the town, that Nanse Donsie, an idiot natural, ran up the street to stop him, crying, in the voice of a pardonable desperation, "Wha, in sic a time, can praise the Lord?"

Chapter 25

The Subscription

The calamity of the storm opened and disposed the hearts of the whole town to charity; and it was a pleasure to behold the manner in which the tide of sympathy flowed towards the sufferers. Nobody went to the church in the forenoon; but when I had returned home from the shore, several of the council met at my house to confer anent the desolation, and it was concerted among us, at my suggestion, that there should be a meeting of the inhabitants called by the magistrates, for the next day, in order to take the public compassion with the tear in the eye—which was accordingly done by Mr Pittle himself from the pulpit, with a few judicious words on the heavy dispensation. And the number of folk that came forward to subscribe was just wonderful. We got well on to a hundred pounds in the first two hours, besides many a bundle of old clothes. But one of the most remarkable things in the business was done by Mr Macandoe. He was, in his original, a lad of the place, who had gone into Glasgow, where he was in a topping line; and happening to be on a visit to his friends at the time, he came to the meeting and put down his name for twenty guineas, which he gave me in banknotes—a sum of such liberality as had never been given to the town from one individual man, since the mortification of fifty pounds that we got by the will of Major Bravery that died in Cheltenham, in England, after making his fortune in India. The sum total of the subscription, when we got my lord's five-and-twenty guineas, was better than two hundred pounds sterling—for even several of the country gentlemen were very generous contributors, and it is well known that they are not inordinately charitable, especially to town folks—but the distribution of it was no easy task, for it required a discrimination of character as well as of necessities. It was at first proposed to give it over to the session. I knew, however, that, in their hands, it would do no good; for Mr Pittle, the minister, was a vain sort of a body, and easy to be fleeched, and the bold and the bardy with him would be sure to come in for a better share than the meek and the modest, who might be in greater want. So I set myself to consider what was the best way of proceeding; and truly upon reflection, there are few events in my history that I look back upon with more satisfaction than the part I performed in this matter; for, before going into any division of the money, I proposed that we should allot it to three classes—those who were destitute; those who had some help, but large families; and those to whom a temporality would be sufficient—and that we should make a visitation to the houses of all the sufferers, in order to class them under their proper heads aright. By this method, and together with what I had done personally in the tempest, I got great praise and laud from all reflecting people; and it is not now to be told what a consolation was brought to many a sorrowful widow and orphan's heart, by the patience and temperance with which the fund of liberality was distributed; yet because a small sum was reserved to help some of the more helpless at another time, and the same was put out to interest in the town's books, there were not wanting evil-minded persons who went about whispering calumnious innuendos to my disadvantage; but I know, by this time, the nature of the world, and how impossible it is to reason with such a seven-headed and ten-horned beast as the multitude. So I said nothing; only I got the town-clerk's young man, who acted as clerk to the committee of the subscription, to make out a fair account of the distribution of the money, and to what intent the residue had been placed in the town-treasurer's hand; and this I sent unto a friend in Glasgow to get printed for me, the which he did; and when I got the copies, I directed one to every individual subscriber, and sent the town-drummer an end's errand with them, which was altogether a proceeding of a method and exactness so by common, that it not only quenched the envy of spite utterly out, but contributed more and more to give me weight and authority with the community, until I had the whole sway and mastery of the town.

Chapter 26

Of the Public Lamps

Death is a great reformer of corporate bodies, and we found, now and then, the benefit of his helping hand in our royal burgh. From the time of my being chosen into the council; and, indeed, for some years before, Mr Hirple had been a member, but, from some secret and unexpressed understanding among us, he was never made a bailie; for he was not liked; having none of that furthy and jocose spirit so becoming in a magistrate of that degree, and to which the gifts of gravity and formality make but an unsubstantial substitute. He was, on the contrary, a queer and quistical man, of a small stature of body, with an outshot breast, the which, I am inclined to think, was one of the main causes of our never promoting him into the ostensible magistracy; besides, his temper was exceedingly brittle; and in the debates anent the weightiest concerns of the public, he was apt to puff and fiz, and go off with a pluff of anger like a pioye; so that, for the space of more than five-and-twenty years, we would have been glad of his resignation; and, in the heat of argument, there was no lack of hints to that effect from more than one of his friends, especially from Bailie Picken, who was himself a sharp-tempered individual, and could as ill sit quiet under a contradiction as any man I ever was conjunct with. But just before the close of my second provostry, Providence was kind to Mr Hirple, and removed him gently away from the cares, and troubles, and the vain policy of this contending world, into, as I hope and trust, a far better place.

It may seem, hereafter, to the unlearned readers among posterity, particularly to such of them as may happen not to be versed in that state of things which we were obliged to endure, very strange that I should make this special mention of Mr Hirple at his latter end, seeing and observing the small store and account I have thus set upon his talents and personalities. But the verity of the reason is plainly this: we never discovered his worth and value till we had lost him, or rather, till we found the defect and gap that his death caused, and the affliction that came in through it upon us in the ill-advised selection of Mr Hickery to fill his vacant place.

The spunky nature of Mr Hirple was certainly very disagreeable often to most of the council, especially when there was any difference of opinion; but then it was only a sort of flash, and at the vote he always, like a reasonable man, sided with the majority, and never after attempted to rip up a decision when it was once so settled. Mr Hickery was just the even down reverse of this. He never, to be sure, ran himself into a passion, but then he continued to speak and argue so long in reply, never heeding the most rational things of his adversaries, that he was sure to put every other person in a rage; in addition to all which, he was likewise a sorrowful body in never being able to understand how a determination by vote ought to and did put an end to every questionable proceeding; so that he was, for a constancy, ever harping about the last subject discussed, as if it had not been decided, until a new difference of opinion arose, and necessitated him to change the burden and o'ercome of his wearysome speeches.

It may seem remarkable that we should have taken such a plague into the council, and be thought that we were well served for our folly; but we were unacquaint with the character of the man—for although a native of the town, he was in truth a stranger, having, at an early age, espoused his fortune, and gone to Philadelphia in America;

and no doubt his argol-bargolous disposition was an inheritance accumulated with his other conquest of wealth from the mannerless Yankees. Coming home and settling among us, with a power of money, (some said eleven thousand pounds,) a short time before Mr Hirple departed this life, we all thought, on that event happening, it would be a very proper compliment to take Mr Hickery into the council, and accordingly we were so misfortunate as to do so; but I trow we soon had reason to repent our indiscretion, and none more than myself, who had first proposed him.

Mr Hickery having been chosen to supply the void caused by the death of Mr Hirple, in the very first sederunt of the council after his election, he kithed in his true colours.

Among other things that I had contemplated for the ornament and edification of the burgh, was the placing up of lamps to light the streets, such as may be seen in all well regulated cities and towns of any degree. Having spoken of this patriotic project to several of my colleagues, who all highly approved of the same, I had no jealousy or suspicion that a design so clearly and luminously useful would meet with any other opposition than, may be, some doubt as to the fiscal abilities of our income. To be sure Mr Dribbles, who at that time kept the head inns, and was in the council, said, with a wink, that it might be found an inconvenience to sober folk that happened, on an occasion now and then, to be an hour later than usual among their friends, either at his house or any other, to be shown by the lamps to the profane populace as they were making the best of their way home; and Mr Dippings, the candlemaker, with less public spirit than might have been expected from one who made such a penny by the illuminations on news of victory, was of opinion that lamps would only encourage the commonality to keep late hours; and that the gentry were in no need of any thing of the sort, having their own handsome glass lanterns, with two candles in them, garnished and adorned with clippit paper; an equipage which he prophesied would soon wear out of fashion when lamps were once introduced, and the which prediction I have lived to see verified; for certainly, now-a-days, except when some elderly widow lady, or maiden gentlewoman, wanting the help and protection of man, happens to be out at her tea and supper, a tight and snod serving lassie, with a three-cornered glass lantern, is never seen on the causey. But, to return from this digression; saving and excepting the remarks of Mr Dribbles and Mr Dippings, and neither of them could be considered as made in a sincere frame of mind, I had no foretaste of any opposition. I was, therefore, but ill prepared for the worrying argument with which Mr Hickery seized upon the scheme, asserting and maintaining, among other apparatus-like reasoning, that in such a northern climate as that of Scotland, and where the twilight was of such long duration, it would be a profligate waste of the public money to employ it on any thing so little required as lamps were in our streets.

He had come home from America in the summer time, and I reminded him, that it certainly could never be the intention of the magistrates to light the lamps all the year round; but that in the winter there was a great need of them; for in our northern climate the days were then very short, as he would soon experience, and might probably recollect. But never, surely, was such an endless man created. For, upon this, he immediately rejoined, that the streets would be much more effectually lighted, than by all the lamps I proposed to put up, were the inhabitants ordered to sit with their window-shutters open. I really did not know what answer to make to such a proposal, but I saw it would never do to argue with him; so I held my tongue quietly, and as soon as possible, on a pretence of private business, left the meeting, not a little mortified to find such a contrary spirit had got in among us.

After that meeting of the council, I went cannily round to all the other members, and represented to them, one by one, how proper it was that the lamps should be set up, both for a credit to the town, and as a conformity to the fashion of the age in every other place. And I took occasion to descant, at some length, on the untractable nature of Mr Hickery, and how it would be proper before the next meeting to agree to say nothing when the matter was again brought on the carpet, but just to come to the vote at once. Accordingly this was done, but it made no difference to Mr Hickery; on the contrary, he said, in a vehement manner, that he was sure there must be some corrupt understanding among us, otherwise a matter of such importance could not have been decided by a silent vote; and at every session of the council, till some new matter of difference cast up, he continued cuckooing about the lamp-job, as he called it, till he had sickened every body out of all patience.

Chapter 27

The Plainstones

The first question that changed the bark of Mr Hickery, was my proposal for the side plainstones of the high street. In the new paving of the crown of the causey, some years before, the rise in the middle had been levelled to an equality with the side loans, and in disposing of the lamp-posts, it was thought advantageous to place them halfway from the houses and the syvers, between the loans and the crown of the causey, which had the effect at night, of making the people who were wont, in their travels and visitations, to keep the middle of the street, to diverge into the space and path between the lamp-posts and the houses. This, especially in wet weather, was attended with some disadvantages; for the pavement, close to the houses, was not well laid, and there being then no ronns to the houses, at every other place, particularly where the nepus-gables were towards the streets, the rain came gushing in a spout, like as if the windows of heaven were opened. And, in consequence, it began to be freely conversed, that there would be a great comfort in having the sides of the streets paved with flags, like the plainstones of Glasgow, and that an obligation should be laid on the landlords, to put up ronns to kepp the rain, and to conduct the water down in pipes by the sides of the houses;—all which furnished Mr Hickery with fresh topics for his fasherie about the lamps, and was, as he said, proof and demonstration of that most politic, corrupt, and short-sighted job, the consequences of which would reach, in the shape of some new tax, every ramification of society;—with divers other American argumentatives to the same effect. However, in process of time, by a judicious handling and the help of an advantageous free grassum, which we got for some of the town lands from Mr Shuttlethrift the manufacturer, who was desirous to build a villa-house, we got the flagstone part of the project accomplished, and the landlords gradually, of their own free-will, put up the ronns, by which the town has been greatly improved and convenienced.

But new occasions call for new laws; the side pavement, concentrating the people, required to be kept cleaner, and in better order, than when the whole width of the street was in use; so that the magistrates were constrained to make regulations concerning the same, and to enact fines and penalties against those who neglected to scrape and wash the plainstones forent their houses, and to denounce, in the strictest terms, the emptying of improper utensils on the same; and this, until the people had grown into the habitude of attending to the rules, gave rise to many pleas, and contentious appeals and bickerings, before the magistrates. Among others summoned before me for default, was one Mrs Fenton, commonly called the Tappit-hen, who kept a small change-house, not of the best repute, being frequented by young men, of a station of life that gave her heart and countenance to be bardy, even to the bailies. It happened that, by some inattention, she had, one frosty morning, neglected to soop her flags, and old Miss Peggy Dainty being early afoot, in passing her door committed a false step, by treading on a bit of a lemon's skin, and her heels flying up, down she fell on her back, at full length, with a great cloyt. Mrs Fenton, hearing the accident, came running to the door, and seeing the exposure that perjink Miss Peggy had made of herself, put her hands to her sides, and laughed for some time as if she was by herself. Miss Peggy, being sorely hurt in the hinder parts, summoned Mrs Fenton before me, where the whole affair, both as to what was seen and heard, was so described, with name and surname, that I could not keep my composure. It was, however, made manifest, that Mrs Fenton had offended the law, in so much, as her flags had not been swept that morning; and therefore, to appease the offended delicacy of Miss Peggy, who was a most respectable lady in single life, I fined the delinquent five shillings.

"Mr Pawkie," said the latheron, "I'll no pay't. Whar do ye expeck a widow woman like me can get five shillings for ony sic nonsense?"

"Ye must not speak in that manner, honest woman," was my reply; "but just pay the fine."

"In deed and truth, Mr Pawkie," quo she, "it's ill getting a breek off a highlandman. I'll pay no sic thing—five shillings—that's a story!"

I thought I would have been constrained to send her to prison, the woman grew so bold and contumacious, when Mr Hickery came in, and hearing what was going forward, was evidently working himself up to take the randy's part; but fortunately she had a suspicion that all the town-council and magistrates were in league against her, on account of the repute of her house, so that when he enquired of her where she lived, with a view, as I suspect, of interceding, she turned to him, and with a leer and a laugh, said, "Dear me, Mr Hickery, I'm sure ye hae nae need to speer that!"

The insinuation set up his birses; but she bamboozled him with her banter, and raised such a laugh against him, that he was fairly driven from the council room, and I was myself obliged to let her go, without exacting the fine.

Who would have thought that this affair was to prove to me the means of an easy riddance of Mr Hickery? But so it turned out; for whether or not there was any foundation for the traffickings with him which she pretended, he never could abide to hear the story alluded to, which, when I discerned, I took care, whenever he showed any sort of inclination to molest the council with his propugnacity, to joke him about his bonny sweetheart, "the Tappit hen," and he instantly sang dumb, and quietly slipped away; by which it may be seen how curiously events come to pass, since, out of the very first cause of his thwarting me in the lamps, I found, in process of time, a way of silencing him far better than any sort of truth or reason.

Chapter 28

The Second Crop of Volunteers

I have already related, at full length, many of the particulars anent the electing of the first set of volunteers; the which, by being germinated partly under the old system of public intromission, was done with more management and slight of art than the second. This, however, I will ever maintain, was not owing to any greater spirit of corruption; but only and solely to following the ancient dexterous ways, that had been, in a manner, engrained with the very nature of every thing pertaining to the representation of government as it existed, not merely in burgh towns, but wheresoever the crown and ministers found it expedient to have their lion's paw.

Matters were brought to a bearing differently, when, in the second edition of the late war, it was thought necessary to call on the people to resist the rampageous ambition of Bonaparte, then champing and trampling for the rich pastures of our national commonwealth. Accordingly, I kept myself aloof from all handling in the pecuniaries of the business; but I lent a friendly countenance to every feasible project that was likely to strengthen the confidence of the king in the loyalty and bravery of his people. For by this time I had learnt, that there was a wakerife common sense abroad among the opinions of men; and that the secret of the new way of ruling the world was to follow, not to control, the evident dictates of the popular voice; and I soon had reason to felicitate myself on this prudent and seasonable discovery. For it won me great reverence among the forward young men, who started up at the call of their country; and their demeanour towards me was as tokens and arles, from the rising generation, of being continued in respect and authority by them. Some of my colleagues, who are as well not named, by making themselves over busy, got but small thank for their pains. I was even preferred to the provost, as the medium of communicating the sentiments of the volunteering lads to the lord-lieutenant; and their cause did not suffer in my hands, for his lordship had long been in the habit of considering me as one of the discreetest men in the burgh; and although he returned very civil answers to all letters, he wrote to me in the cordial erudition of an old friend—a thing which the volunteers soon discerned, and respected me accordingly.

But the soldiering zeal being spontaneous among all ranks, and breaking forth into a blaze without any pre-ordered method, some of the magistrates were disconcerted, and wist not what to do. I'll no take it upon me to say that they were altogether guided by a desire to have a finger in the pie, either in the shape of the honours of command or the profits of contract. This, however, is certain, that they either felt or feigned a great alarm and consternation at seeing such a vast military power in civil hands, over which they had no natural control; and, as was said, independent of the crown and parliament. Another thing there could be no doubt of: in the frame of this fear they remonstrated with the government, and counselled the ministers to throw a wet blanket on the ardour of the volunteering, which, it is well known, was very readily done; for the ministers, on seeing such a pressing forward to join the banners of the kingdom, had a dread and regard to the old leaven of Jacobinism, and put a limitation on the number of the armed men that were to be allowed to rise in every place—a most ill-advised prudence, as was made manifest by what happened among us, of which I will now rehearse the particulars, and the part I had in it myself.

As soon as it was understood among the commonality that the French were determined to subdue and make a conquest of Britain, as they had done of all the rest of Europe, holding the noses of every continental king and potentate to the grindstone, there was a prodigious stir and motion in all the hearts and pulses of Scotland, and no where in a more vehement degree than in Gudetown. But, for some reason or an other which I could never dive into the bottom of, there was a slackness or backwardness on the part of government in sending instructions to the magistrates to step forward; in so much that the people grew terrified that they would be conquered, without having even an opportunity to defend, as their fathers did of old, the hallowed things of their native land; and, under the sense of this alarm, they knotted themselves together, and actually drew out proposals and resolutions of service of their own accord; by which means they kept the power of choosing their officers in their own hands, and so gave many of the big-wigs of the town a tacit intimation that they were not likely to have the command. While things were in this process, the government had come to its senses; and some steps and measures were taken to organize volunteer corps throughout the nation. Taking heart from them, other corps were proposed on the part of the gentry, in which they are themselves to have the command; and seeing that the numbers were to be limited, they had a wish and interest to keep back the real volunteer offers, to and to get their own accepted in their stead. A suspicion of this sort getting vent, an outcry of discontent thereat arose against them; and to the consternation of the magistrates, the young lads, who had at the first come so briskly forward, called a meeting of their body, and, requesting the magistrates to be present, demanded to know what steps had been taken with their offer of service; and, if transmitted to government, what answer had been received.

This was a new era in public affairs; and no little amazement and anger was expressed by some of the town-council, that any set of persons should dare to question and interfere with the magistrates. But I saw it would never do to take the bull by the horns in that manner at such a time; so I commenced with Bailie Sprose, my lord being at the time provost, and earnestly beseeched him to attend the meeting with me, and to give a mild answer to any questions that might be put; and this was the more necessary, as there was some good reason to believe, that, in point of fact, the offer of service had been kept back.

We accordingly went to the meeting, where Mr Sprose, at my suggestion, stated, that we had received no answer; and that we could not explain how the delay had arisen. This, however, did not pacify the volunteers; but they appointed certain of their own number, a committee, to attend to the business, and to communicate with the secretary of state direct; intimating, that the members of the committee were those whom they intended to elect for their officers. This was a decisive step, and took the business entirely out of the hands of the magistrates; so, after the meeting, both Mr Sprose and myself agreed, that no time should be lost in communicating to the lord lieutenant what had taken place.

Our letter, and the volunteers' letter, went by the same post; and on receiving ours, the lord-lieutenant had immediately some conference with the secretary of state, who, falling into the views of his lordship, in preferring the offers of the corps proposed by the gentry, sent the volunteers word in reply, that their services, on the terms they had proposed, which were of the least possible expense to government, could not be accepted.

It was hoped that this answer would have ended the matter; but there were certain propugnacious spirits in the volunteers' committee; and they urged and persuaded the others to come into resolutions, to the effect that, having made early offers of service, on terms less objectionable in every point than those of many offers subsequently made and accepted, unless their offer was accepted, they would consider themselves as having the authority of his majesty's government to believe and to represent, that there was, in truth, no reason to apprehend that the enemy meditated any invasion; and these resolutions they sent off to London forthwith, before the magistrates had time to hear or to remonstrate against the use of such novel language from our burgh to his majesty's ministers.

We, however, heard something; and I wrote my lord, to inform him that the volunteers had renewed their offer, (for so we understood their representation was) and he, from what he had heard before from the secretary of state, not expecting the effect it would have, answered me, that their offer could not be accepted. But to our astonishment, by the same post, the volunteers found themselves accepted, and the gentlemen they recommended for their officers gazetted; the which, as I tell frankly, was an admonition to me, that the peremptory will of authority was no longer sufficient for the rule of mankind; and, therefore, I squared my after conduct more by a deference to public opinion, than by any laid down maxims and principles of my own; the consequence of which was, that my influence still continued to grow and gather strength in the community, and I was enabled to accomplish many things that my predecessors would have thought it was almost beyond the compass of man to undertake.

Chapter 29

Captain Armour

In the course of these notadums, I have, here and there, touched on divers matters that did not actually pertain to my own magisterial life, further than as showing the temper and spirit in which different things were brought to a bearing; and, in the same way, I will now again step aside from the regular course of public affairs, to record an occurrence which, at the time, excited no small wonderment and sympathy, and in which it was confessed by many that I performed a very judicious part. The event here spoken of, was the quartering in the town, after the removal of that well-behaved regiment, the Argyle fencibles, the main part of another, the name and number of which I do not now recollect; but it was an English corps, and, like the other troops of that nation, was not then brought into the sobriety of discipline to which the whole British army has since been reduced, by the paternal perseverance of his Royal Highness the Duke of York; so that, after the douce and respectful Highlanders, we sorely felt the consequences of the outstropolous and galravitching Englishers, who thought it no disgrace to fill themselves as fou as pipers, and fight in the streets, and march to the church on the Lord's day with their band of music. However, after the first Sunday, upon a remonstrance on the immorality of such irreligious bravery, Colonel Cavendish, the commandant, silenced the musicians.

Among the officers, there was one Captain Armour, an extraordinar well demeaned, handsome man, who was very shy of accepting any civility from the town gentry, and kept himself aloof from all our ploys and entertainments, in such a manner, that the rest of the officers talked of him, marvelling at the cause, for it was not his wont in other places.

One Sabbath, during the remembering prayer, Mr Pittle put up a few words for criminals under sentence of death, there being two at the time in the Ayr jail, at the which petition I happened to look at Captain Armour, who, with the lave of the officers, were within the magistrates' loft, and I thought he had, at the moment, a likeness to poor Jeanie Gaisling, that was executed for the murder of her bastard bairn.

This notion at the time disturbed me very much, and one thought after another so came into my head, that I could pay no attention to Mr Pittle, who certainly was but a cauldrife preacher, and never more so than on that day. In short, I was haunted with the fancy, that Captain Armour was no other than the misfortunate lassie's poor brother, who had in so pathetical a manner attended her and the magistrates to the scaffold; and, what was very strange, I was not the only one in the kirk who thought the same thing; for the resemblance, while Mr Pittle was praying, had been observed by many; and it was the subject of discourse in my shop on the Monday following, when the whole history of that most sorrowful concern was again brought to mind. But, without dwelling at large on the particularities, I need only mention, that it began to be publicly jealoused that he was indeed the identical lad, which moved every body; for he was a very good and gallant officer, having risen by his own merits, and was likewise much beloved in the regiment. Nevertheless, though his sister's sin was no fault of his, and could not impair the worth of his well-earned character, yet some of the thoughtless young ensigns began to draw off from him, and he was visited, in a manner, with the disgrace of an excommunication.

Being, however, a sensible man, he bore it for a while patiently, may be hoping that the suspicion would wear away; but my lord, with all his retinue, coming from London to the castle for the summer, invited the officers one day to dine with him and the countess, when the fact was established by a very simple accident.

Captain Armour, in going up the stairs, among the crooked old passages of the castle, happened to notice that the colonel, who was in the van, turned to the wrong hand, and called to him to take the other way, which circumstance convinced all present that he was domestically familiar with the labyrinths of the building; and the consequence was, that, during dinner, not one of the officers spoke to him, some from embarrassment and others from pride.

The earl perceiving their demeanour, enquired of the colonel, when they had returned from the table to the drawing-room, as to the cause of such a visible alienation, and Colonel Cavendish, who was much of the gentleman, explaining it, expressing his grief that so unpleasant a discovery had been made to the prejudice of so worthy a man, my lord was observed to stand some time in a thoughtful posture, after which he went and spoke in a whisper to the countess, who advised him, as her ladyship in the sequel told me herself, to send for me, as a wary and prudent man. Accordingly a servant was secretly dispatched express to the town on that errand; my lord and my lady insisting on the officers staying to spend the evening with them, which was an unusual civility at the pro forma dinners at the castle.

When I arrived, the earl took me into his private library, and we had some serious conversation about the captain's sister; and, when I had related the circumstantialities of her end to him, he sent for the captain, and with great tenderness, and a manner most kind and gracious, told him what he had noticed in the conduct of the officers, offering his mediation to appease any difference, if it was a thing that could be done.

While my lord was speaking, the captain preserved a steady and unmoved countenance: no one could have imagined that he was listening to any thing but some grave generality of discourse; but when the earl offered to mediate, his breast swelled, and his face grew like his coat, and I saw his eyes fill with water as he turned round, to hide the grief that could not be stifled. The passion of shame, however, lasted but for a moment. In less time than I am in writing these heads, he was again himself, and with a modest fortitude that was exceedingly comely, he acknowledged who he was, adding, that he feared his blameless disgrace entailed effects which he could not hope to remove, and therefore it was his intention to resign his commission. The earl, however, requested that he would do nothing rashly, and that he should first allow him to try what could be done to convince his brother officers that it was unworthy of them to act towards him in the way they did. His lordship then led us to the drawing-room, on entering which, he said aloud to the countess, in a manner that could not be misunderstood, "In Captain Armour I have discovered an old acquaintance, who by his own merits, and under circumstances that would have sunk any man less conscious of his own purity and worth, has raised himself, from having once been my servant, to a rank that makes me happy to receive him as my guest."

I need not add, that this benevolence of his lordship was followed with a most bountiful alteration towards the captain from all present, in so much that, before the regiment was removed from the town, we had the satisfaction of seeing him at divers of the town-ploys, where he received every civility.

Chapter 30

The Trades Ball

At the conclusion of my second provostry, or rather, as I think, after it was over, an accident happened in the town that might have led to no little trouble and contention but for the way and manner that I managed the same. My friend and neighbour, Mr Kilsyth, an ettling man, who had been wonderful prosperous in the spirit line, having been taken on for a bailie, by virtue of some able handling on the part of Deacon Kenitweel, proposed and propounded, that there should be a ball and supper for the trades; and to testify his sense of the honour that he owed to all the crafts, especially the wrights, whereof Mr Kenitweel was then deacon, he promised to send in both wine, rum, and brandy, from his cellar, for the company. I did not much approve of the project, for divers reasons; the principal of which was, because my daughters were grown into young ladies, and I was, thank God, in a circumstance to entitle them to hold their heads something above the trades. However, I could not positively refuse my compliance, especially as Mrs Pawkie was requested by Bailie Kilsyth, and those who took an active part in furtherance of the ploy, to be the lady directress of the occasion. And, out of an honour and homage to myself, I was likewise entreated to preside at the head of the table, over the supper that was to ensue after the dancing.

In its own nature, there was surely nothing of an objectionable principle, in a "trades' ball;" but we had several young men of the gentle sort about the town, blythe and rattling lads, who were welcome both to high and low, and to whom the project seemed worthy of a ridicule. It would, as I said at the time, have been just as well to have made it really a trades' ball, without any adulteration of the gentry; but the hempies alluded to jouked themselves in upon us, and obligated the managers to invite them; and an ill return they made for this discretion and civility, as I have to relate.

On the night set for the occasion, the company met in the assembly-room, in the New-inns, where we had bespoke a light genteel supper, and had McLachlan, the fiddler, over from Ayr, for the purpose. Nothing could be better while the dancing lasted; the whole concern wore an appearance of the greatest genteelity. But when supper was announced, and the company adjourned to partake of it, judge of the universal consternation that was visible in every countenance, when, instead of the light tarts, and nice jellies and sillybobs that were expected, we beheld a long table, with a row down the middle of rounds of beef, large cold veal-pies on pewter plates like tea-trays, cold boiled turkeys, and beef and bacon hams, and, for ornament in the middle, a perfect stack of celery.

The instant I entered the supper-room, I saw there had been a plot: poor Bailie Kilsyth, who had all the night been in triumph and glory, was for a season speechless; and when at last he came to himself, he was like to have been the death of the landlord on the spot; while I could remark, with the tail of my eye, that secret looks of a queer satisfaction were exchanged among the beaux before mentioned. This observe, when I made it, led me to go up to the bailie as he was storming at the bribed and corrupt innkeeper, and to say to him, that if he would leave the matter to me, I would settle it to the content of all present; which he, slackening the grip he had taken of the landlord by the throat, instantly conceded. Whereupon, I went back to the head of the table, and said aloud, " that the cold collection had been provided by some secret friends, and although it was not just what the directors could have wished, yet it would be as well to bring to mind the old proverb, which instructs us no to be particular about the mouth of a gi'en horse. " But I added, "before partaking thereof, we'll hae in our bill frae the landlord, and settle it, "—and it was called accordingly. I could discern, that this was a turn that the conspirators did not look for. It, however, put the company a thought into spirits, and they made the best o't. But, while they were busy at the table, I took a canny opportunity of saying, under the rose to one of the gentlemen, "that 1 saw through the joke, and could relish it just as well as the plotters; but as the thing was so plainly felt as an insult by the generality of the company, the less that was said about it the better; and that if the whole bill, including the cost of Bailie Kilsyth's wine and spirits, was defrayed, I would make no enquiries, and the authors might never be known." This admonishment was not lost, for by-and-by, I saw the gentleman confabbing together; and the next morning, through the post, I received a twenty-pound note in a nameless letter, requesting the amount of it to be placed against the expense of the ball. I was overly well satisfied with this to say a great deal of what I thought, but I took a quiet step to the bank, where, expressing some doubt of the goodness of the note, I was informed it was perfectly good, and had been that very day issued from the bank to one of the gentlemen, whom, even at this day, it would not be prudent to expose to danger by naming.

Upon a consultation with the other gentlemen, who had the management of the ball, it was agreed, that we should say nothing of the gift of twenty pounds, but distribute it in the winter to needful families, which was done; for we feared that the authors of the derision would be found out, and that ill-blood might be bred in the town.

Chapter 31

The Bailie's Head

But although in the main I was considered by the events and transactions already rehearsed, a prudent and sagacious man, yet I was not free from the consequences of envy. To be sure, they were not manifested in any very intolerant spirit, and in so far they caused me rather molestation of mind than actual suffering; but still they kithed in evil, and thereby marred the full satisfactory fruition of my labours and devices. Among other of the outbreakings alluded to that not a little vexed me, was one that I will relate, and just in order here to show the animus of men's minds towards me.

We had in the town a clever lad, with a geni of a mechanical turn, who made punch-bowls of leather, and legs for cripples of the same commodity, that were lighter and easier to wear than either legs of cork or timber. His name was Geordie Sooplejoint, a modest, douce, and well-behaved young man—caring for little else but the perfecting of his art. I had heard of his talent, and was curious to converse with him; so I spoke to Bailie Pirlet, who had taken him by the hand, to bring him and his leather punch-bowl, and some of his curious legs and arms, to let me see them; the which the bailie did, and it happened that while they were with me, in came Mr Thomas McQueerie, a dry neighbour at a joke. After some generality of discourse concerning the inventions, whereon Bailie Pirlet, who was naturally a gabby prick-me-dainty body, enlarged at great length, with all his well dockit words, as if they were on chandler's pins, pointing out here the utility of the legs to persons maimed in the wars of their country, and showing forth there in what manner the punch-bowls were specimens of a new art that might in time supplant both China and Staffordshire ware, and deducing therefrom the benefits that would come out of it to the country at large, and especially to the landed interest, in so much as the increased demand which it would cause for leather, would raise the value of hides, and per consequence the price of black cattle—to all which Mr McQueerie listened with a shrewd and a thirsty ear; and when the bailie had made an end of his paternoster, he proposed that I should make a filling of Geordie's bowl, to try if it did not leak.

"Indeed, Mr Pawkie," quo' he, "it will be a great credit to our town to hae had the merit o' producing sic a clever lad, who, as the bailie has in a manner demonstrated, is ordained to bring about an augmentation o' trade by his punch-bowls, little short of what has been done wi' the steam-engines. Geordie will be to us what James Watt is to the ettling town of Greenook, so we can do no less than drink prosperity to his endeavours." I did not much like this bantering of Mr McQueerie, for I saw it made Geordie's face grow red, and it was not what he had deserved; so to repress it, and to encourage the poor lad, I said, "Come, come, neighbour, none of your wipes—what Geordie has done, is but arles of what he may do."

"That's no to be debated," replied Mr McQueerie, "for he has shown already that he can make very good legs and arms; and I'm sure I shouldna be surprised were he in time to make heads as good as a bailie's."

I never saw any mortal man look as that pernickity personage, the bailie, did at this joke, but I suppressed my own feelings; while the bailie, like a bantam cock in a passion, stotted out of his chair with the spunk of a birslet pea, demanding of Mr McQueerie an explanation of what he meant by the insinuation. It was with great difficulty that I got him pacified; but unfortunately the joke was oure good to be forgotten, and when it was afterwards spread abroad, as it happened to take its birth in my house, it was laid to my charge, and many a time was I obligated to tell all about it, and how it couldna be meant for me, but had been incurred by Bailie Pirlet's conceit of spinning out long perjink speeches.

Chapter 32

The Town Drummer

Nor did I get everything my own way, for I was often thwarted in matters of small account, and suffered from them greater disturbance and molestation than things of such little moment ought to have been allowed to produce within me; and I do not think that any thing happened in the whole course of my public life, which gave me more vexation than what I felt in the last week of my second provostry.

For many a year, one Robin Boss had been town drummer; he was a relic of some American-war fencibles, and was, to say the God's truth of him, a divor body, with no manner of conduct, saving a very earnest endeavour to fill himself fou as often as he could get the means; the consequence of which was, that his face was as plooky as a curran' bun, and his nose as red as a partan's tae.

One afternoon there was a need to send out a proclamation to abolish a practice that was growing into a custom, in some of the bye parts of the town, of keeping swine at large—ordering them to be confined in proper styes, and other suitable places. As on all occasions when the matter to be proclaimed was from the magistrates, Thomas, on this, was attended by the town-officers in their Sunday garbs, and with their halberts in their hands; but the abominable and irreverent creature was so drunk, that he wamblet to and fro over the drum, as if there had not been a bane in his body. He was seemingly as soople and as senseless as a bolster.—Still, as this was no new thing with him, it might have passed; for James Hound, the senior officer, was in the practice, when Robin was in that state, of reading the proclamations himself.—On this occasion, however, James happened to be absent on some hue and cry quest, and another of the officers (I forget which) was appointed to perform for him. Robin, accustomed to James, no sooner heard the other man begin to read, than he began to curse and swear at him as an incapable nincompoop—an impertinent term that he was much addicted to. The grammar school was at the time skailing, and the boys seeing the stramash, gathered round the officer, and yelling and shouting, encouraged Robin more and more into rebellion, till at last they worked up his corruption to such a pitch, that he took the drum from about his neck, and made it fly like a bombshell at the officer's head.

The officers behaved very well, for they dragged Robin by the lug and the horn to the tolbooth, and then came with their complaint to me. Seeing how the authorities had been set at nought, and the necessity there was of making an example, I forthwith ordered Robin to be cashiered from the service of the town; and as so important a concern as a proclamation ought not to be delayed, I likewise, upon the spot, ordered the officers to take a lad that had been also a drummer in a marching regiment, and go with him to make the proclamation.

Nothing could be done in a more earnest and zealous public spirit than this was done by me. But habit had begot in the town a partiality for the drunken ne'er-do-well, Robin; and this just act of mine was immediately condemned as a daring stretch of arbitrary power; and the consequence was, that when the council met next day, some sharp words flew from among us, as to my usurping an undue authority; and the thank I got for my pains was the mortification to see the worthless body restored to full power and dignity, with no other reward than an admonition to behave better for the future. Now, I leave it to the unbiassed judgment of posterity to determine if any public man could be more ungraciously treated by his colleagues than I was on this occasion. But, verily, the council had their reward.

Chapter 33

An Alarm

The divor, Robin Boss, being, as I have recorded, reinstated in office, soon began to play his old tricks. In the course of the week after the Michaelmas term at which my second provostry ended, he was so insupportably drunk that he fell head foremost into his drum, which cost the town five-and-twenty shillings for a new one—an accident that was not without some satisfaction to me; and I trow I was not sparing in my derisive commendations on the worth of such a public officer. Nevertheless, he was still kept on, some befriending him for compassion, and others as it were to spite me.

But Robin's good behaviour did not end with breaking the drum, and costing a new one.—In the course of the winter it was his custom to beat, "Go to bed, Tom," about ten o'clock at night, and the reveille at five in the morning.—In one of his drunken fits he made a mistake, and instead of going his rounds as usual at ten o'clock, he had fallen asleep in a change house, and waking about the midnight hour in the terror of some whisky dream, he seized his drum, and running into the streets, began to strike the fire-beat in the most awful manner.

It was a fine clear frosty moonlight, and the hollow sound of the drum resounded through the silent streets like thunder.—In a moment every body was a-foot, and the cry of "Whar is't? whar's the fire?" was heard echoing from all sides.—Robin, quite unconscious that he alone was the cause of the alarm, still went along beating the dreadful summons. I heard the noise and rose; but while I was drawing on my stockings, in the chair at the bed-head, and telling Mrs Pawkie to compose herself, for our houses were all insured, I suddenly recollected that Robin had the night before neglected to go his rounds at ten o'clock as usual, and the thought came into my head that the alarm might be one of his inebriated mistakes; so, instead of dressing myself any further, I went to the window, and looked out through the glass, without opening it, for, being in my night clothes, I was afraid of taking cold. The street was as throng as on a market day, and every face in the moonlight was pale with fear.—Men and lads were running with their coats, and carrying their breeches in their hands; wives and maidens were all asking questions at one another, and even lasses were fleeing to and fro, like water nymphs with urns, having stoups and pails in their hands.—There was swearing and tearing of men, hoarse with the rage of impatience, at the tolbooth, getting out the fire-engine from its stance under the stair; and loud and terrible afar off, and over all, came the peal of alarm from drunken Robin's drum.

I could scarcely keep my composity when I beheld and heard all this, for I was soon thoroughly persuaded of the fact. At last I saw Deacon Girdwood, the chief advocate and champion of Robin, passing down the causey like a demented man, with a red nightcap, and his big-coat on—for some had cried that the fire was in his yard.—"Deacon," cried I, opening the window, forgetting in the jocularity of the moment the risk I ran from being so naked, "whar away sae fast, deacon?"

The deacon stopped and said, "Is't out? is't out?"

"Gang your ways home," quo' I very coolly, "for I hae a notion that a' this hobleshow's but the fume of a gill in your friend Robin's head."

"It's no possible!" exclaimed the deacon.

"Possible here or possible there, Mr Girdwood," quo' I, "it's oure cauld for me to stand talking wi' you here; we'll learn the rights o't in the morning; so, good-night;" and with that I pulled down the window. But scarcely had I done so, when a shout of laughter came gathering up the street, and soon after poor drunken Robin was brought along by the cuff of the neck, between two of the town-officers, one of them carrying his drum. The next day he was put out of office for ever, and folk recollecting in what manner I had acted towards him before, the outcry about my arbitrary power was forgotten in the blame that was heaped upon those who had espoused Robin's cause against me.

Chapter 34

The County Gentry

For a long period of time, I had observed that there was a gradual mixing in of the country gentry among the town's folks. This was partly to be ascribed to a necessity rising out of the French Revolution, whereby men of substance thought it an expedient policy to relax in their ancient maxims of family pride and consequence; and partly to the great increase and growth of wealth which the influx of trade caused throughout the kingdom, whereby the merchants were enabled to vie and ostentate even with the better sort of lairds. The effect of this, however, was less protuberant in our town than in many others which I might well name, and the cause thereof lay mainly in our being more given to deal in the small way; not that we lacked of traders possessed both of purse and perseverance; but we did not exactly lie in the thoroughfare of those mighty masses of foreign commodities, the through going of which left, to use the words of the old proverb, "goud in goupins" with all who had the handling of the same. Nevertheless, we came in for our share of the condescensions of the country gentry; and although there was nothing like a melting down of them among us, either by marrying or giving in marriage, there was a communion that gave us some insight, no overly to their advantage, as to the extent and measure of their capacities and talents. In short, we discovered that they were vessels made of ordinary human clay; so that, instead of our reverence for them being augmented by a freer intercourse, we thought less and less of them, until, poor bodies, the bit prideful lairdies were just looked down upon by our gawsie big-bellied burgesses, not a few of whom had heritable bonds on their estates. But in this I am speaking of the change when it had come to a full head; for in verity it must be allowed that when the country gentry, with their families, began to intromit among us, we could not make enough of them. Indeed, we were deaved about the affability of old crabbit Bodle of Bodletonbrae, and his sister, Miss Jenny, when they favoured us with their company at the first inspection ball. I'll ne'er forgot that occasion; for being then in my second provostry, I had, in course of nature, been appointed a deputy lord-lieutenant, and the town-council entertaining the inspecting officers, and the officers of the volunteers, it fell as a duty incumbent on me to be the director of the ball afterwards, and to the which I sent an invitation to the laird and his sister, little hoping or expecting they would come. But the laird, likewise being a deputy lord-lieutenant, he accepted the invitation, and came with his sister in all the state of pedigree in their power. Such a prodigy of old-fashioned grandeur as Miss Jenny was!—but neither shop nor mantua maker of our day and generation had been the better o't. She was just, as some of the young lasses said, like Clarissa Harlowe, in the cuts and copperplates of Mrs Rickerton's set of the book, and an older and more curious set than Mrs Rickerton's was not in the whole town; indeed, for that matter, I believe it was the only one among us, and it had edified, as Mr Binder the bookseller used to say, at least three successive generations of young ladies, for he had himself given it twice new covers. We had, however, not then any circulating library. But for all her antiquity and lappets, it is not to be supposed what respect and deference Miss Jenny and her brother, the laird, received—nor the small praise that came to my share, for having had the spirit to invite them. The ball was spoken of as the genteelest in the memory of man, although to my certain knowledge, on account of the volunteers, some were there that never thought to mess or mell in the same chamber with Bodletonbrae and his sister, Miss Jenny.

Chapter 35

Tests of Success

Intending these notions for the instruction of posterity, it would not be altogether becoming of me to speak of the domestic effects which many of the things that I have herein jotted down had in my own family. I feel myself however, constrained in spirit to lift aside a small bit of the private curtain, just to show how Mrs Pawkie comported herself in the progressive vicissitudes of our prosperity, in the act and doing of which I do not wish to throw any slight on her feminine qualities; for, to speak of her as she deserves at my hand, she has been a most excellent wife, and a decent woman, and had aye a ruth and ready hand for the needful. Still, to say the truth, she is not without a few little weaknesses like her neighbours, and the ill-less vanity of being thought far ben with the great is among others of her harmless frailities.

Soon after the inspection ball before spoken of, she said to me that it would be a great benefit and advantage to our family if we could get Bodletonbrae and his sister, and some of the other country gentry, to dine with us. I was not very clear about how the benefit was to come to book, for the outlay I thought as likely o'ergang the profit; at the same time, not wishing to baulk Mrs Pawkie of a ploy on which I saw her mind was bent, I gave my consent to her and my daughters to send out the cards, and make the necessary preparations. But herein I should not take credit to myself for more of the virtue of humility than was my due; therefore I open the door of my secret heart so far ajee, as to let the reader discern that I was content to hear our invitations were all accepted.

Of the specialities and dainties of the banquet prepared, it is not fitting that I should treat in any more particular manner, than to say they were the best that could be had, and that our guests were all mightily well pleased. Indeed, my wife was out of the body with exultation when Mrs Auchans of that Ilk begged that she would let her have a copy of the directions she had followed in making a flummery, which the whole company declared was most excellent. This compliment was the more pleasant, as Lady Auchans was well known for her skill in savoury contrivances, and to have anything new to her of the sort was a triumph beyond our most sanguine expectations. In a word, from that day we found that we had taken, as it were, a step above the common in the town. There were, no doubt, some who envied our good fortune; but, upon the whole, the community at large were pleased to see the consideration in which their chief magistrate was held. It reflected down, as it were, upon themselves a glaik of the sunshine that shone upon us; and although it may be a light thing, as it is seemingly a vain one, to me to say, I am now pretty much of Mrs Pawkie's opinion, that our cultivation of an intercourse with the country gentry was, in the end, a benefit to our family, in so far as it obtained, both for my sons and daughters, a degree of countenance that otherwise could hardly have been expected from their connexions and fortune, even though I had been twice provost.

Chapter 36

Retribution

But a sad accident shortly after happened, which had the effect of making it as little pleasant to me to vex Mr Hickery with a joke about the Tappit-hen, as it was to him. Widow Fenton, as I have soberly hinted; for it is not a subject to be openly spoken of, had many ill-assorted and irregular characters among her customers; and a gang of play-actors coming to the town, and getting leave to perform in Mr Dribble's barn, batches of the young lads, both gentle and semple, when the play was over, used to adjourn to her house for pies and porter, the commodities in which she chiefly dealt. One night, when the deep tragedy of Mary Queen of Scots was the play, there was a great concourse of people at "The Theatre Royal," and the consequence was, that the Tappit-hen's house, both but and ben, was, at the conclusion, filled to overflowing.

The actress that played Queen Elizabeth, was a little-worth termagant woman, and, in addition to other laxities of conduct, was addicted to the immorality of taking more than did her good, and when in her cups, she would rant and ring fiercer than old Queen Elizabeth ever could do herself. Queen Mary's part was done by a bonny genty young lady, that was said to have run away from a boarding-school, and, by all accounts, she acted wonderful well. But she too was not altogether without a flaw, so that there was a division in the town between their admirers and visiters; some maintaining, as I was told, that Mrs Beaufort, if she would keep herself sober, was not only a finer woman, but more of a lady, and a better actress, than Miss Scarborough, while others considered her as a vulgar regimental virago.

The play of Mary Queen of Scots, causing a great congregation of the rival partizans of the two ladies to meet in the Tappit-hen's public, some contention took place about the merits of their respective favourites, and, from less to more, hands were raised, and blows given, and the trades'-lads, being as hot in their differences as the gentlemen, a dreadful riot ensued. Gillstoups, porter bottles, and penny pies flew like balls and bomb-shells in battle. Mrs Fenton, with her mutch off, and her hair loose, with wide and wild arms, like a witch in a whirlwind, was seen trying to sunder the challengers, and the champions. Finding, however, her endeavours unavailing, and fearing that murder would be committed, she ran like desperation into the streets, crying for help. I was just at the time stepping into my bed, when I heard the uproar, and, dressing myself again, I went out to the street; for the sound and din of the riot came raging through the silence of the midnight, like the tearing and swearing of the multitude at a house on fire, and I thought no less an accident could be the cause.

On going into the street, I met several persons running to the scene of action, and, among others, Mrs Beaufort, with a gallant of her own, and both of them no in their sober senses. It's no for me to say who he was; but assuredly, had the woman no been doited with drink, she never would have seen any likeness between him and me, for he was more than twenty years my junior. However, onward we all ran to Mrs Fenton's house, where the riot, like a raging caldron boiling o'er, had overflowed into the street.

The moment I reached the door, I ran forward with my stick raised, but not with any design of striking man, woman, or child, when a ramplor devil, the young laird of Swinton, who was one of the most outstrapolous rakes about the town, wrenched it out of my grip, and would have, I dare say, made no scruple of doing me some dreadful bodily harm, when suddenly I found myself pulled out of the crowd by a powerful-handed woman, who cried, "Come, my love; love, come:" and who was this but that scarlet strumpet, Mrs Beaufort, who having lost her gallant in the crowd, and being, as I think, blind fou, had taken me for him, insisting before all present that I was her dear friend, and that she would die for me—with other siclike fantastical and randy ranting, which no queen in a tragedy could by any possibility surpass. At first I was confounded and overtaken, and could not speak; and the worst of all was, that, in a moment, the mob seemed to forget their quarrel, and to turn in derision on me. What might have ensued it would not be easy to say; but just at this very critical juncture, and while the drunken latheron was casting herself into antic shapes of distress, and flourishing with her hands and arms to the heavens at my imputed cruelty, two of the town-officers came up, which gave me courage to act a decisive part; so I gave over to them Mrs Beaufort, with all her airs, and, going myself to the guardhouse, brought a file of soldiers, and so quelled the riot. But from that night I thought it prudent to eschew every allusion to Mrs Fenton, and tacitly to forgive even Swinton for the treatment I had received from him, by seeming as if I had not noticed him, although I had singled him out by name.

Mrs Pawkie, on hearing what I had suffered from Mrs Beaufort, was very zealous that I should punish her to the utmost rigour of the law, even to drumming her out of the town; but forbearance was my best policy, so I only persuaded my colleagues to order the players to decamp, and to give the Tappit-hen notice, that it would be expedient for the future sale of her pies and porter, at untimeous hours, and that she should flit her howff from our town. Indeed, what pleasure would it have been to me to have dealt unmercifully, either towards the one or the other, for surely the gentle way of keeping up a proper respect for magistrates, and others in authority, should ever be preferred; especially, as in cases like this, where there had been no premeditated wrong. And I say this with the greater sincerity; for in my secret conscience, when I think of the affair at this distance of time, I am pricked not a little in reflecting how I had previously crowed and triumphed over poor Mr Hickery, in the matter of his mortification at the time of Miss Peggy Dainty's false step.

Chapter 37

The Duel

Heretofore all my magisterial undertakings and concerns had thriven in a very satisfactory manner. I was, to be sure, now and then, as I have narrated, subjected to opposition, and squibs, and a jeer; and envious and spiteful persons were not wanting in the world to call in question my intents and motives, representing my best endeavours for the public good as but a right-handed method to secure my own interests. It would be a vain thing of me to deny, that, at the beginning of my career, I was misled by the wily examples of the past times, who thought that, in taking on them to serve the community, they had a privilege to see that they were full-handed for what benefit they might do the public; but as I gathered experience, and saw the rising of the sharp-sighted spirit that is now abroad among the affairs of men, I clearly discerned that it would be more for the advantage of me and mine to act with a conformity thereto, than to seek, by any similar wiles or devices, an immediate and sicker advantage. I may therefore say, without a boast, that the two or three years before my third provostry were as renowned and comfortable to myself, upon the whole, as any reasonable man could look for. We cannot, however, expect a full cup and measure of the sweets of life, without some adulteration of the sour and bitter; and it was my lot and fate to prove an experience of this truth, in a sudden and unaccountable falling off from all moral decorum in a person of my brother's only son, Richard, a lad that was a promise of great ability in his youth.

He was just between the tyning and the winning, as the saying is, when the playactors, before spoken off, came to the town, being then in his eighteenth year. Naturally of a light-hearted and funny disposition, and possessing a jocose turn for mimickry, he was a great favourite among his companions, and getting in with the players, it seems drew up with that little-worth, demure daffodel, Miss Scarborough, through the instrumentality of whose condisciples and the randy Mrs Beaufort, that riot at Widow Fenton's began, which ended in expurgating the town of the whole gang, bag and baggage. Some there were, I shall here mention, who said that the expulsion of the players was owing to what I had heard anent the intromission of my nephew; but, in verity, I had not the least spunk or spark of suspicion of what was going on between him and the miss, till one night, some time after, Richard and the young laird of Swinton, with others of their comrades, forgathered, and came to high words on the subject, the two being rivals, or rather, as was said, equally in esteem and favour with the lady.

Young Swinton was, to say the truth of him, a fine bold rattling lad, warm in the temper, and ready with the hand, and no man's foe so much as his own; for he was a spoiled bairn, through the partiality of old Lady Bodikins, his grandmother, who lived in the turreted house at the town-end, by whose indulgence he grew to be of a dressy and rakish inclination, and, like most youngsters of the kind, was vain of his shames, the which cost Mr Pittle's session no little trouble. But—not to dwell on his faults—my nephew and he quarrelled, and nothing less would serve them than to fight a duel, which they did with pistols next morning; and Richard received from the laird's first shot a bullet in the left arm, that disabled him in that member for life. He was left for dead on the green where they fought—Swinton and the two seconds making, as was supposed, their escape.

When Richard was found faint and bleeding by Tammy Tout, the town-herd, as he drove out the cows in the morning, the hobleshow is not to be described; and my brother came to me, and insisted that I should give him a warrant to apprehend all concerned. I was grieved for my brother, and very much distressed to think of what had happened to blithe Dicky, as I was wont to call my nephew when he was a laddie, and I would fain have gratified the spirit of revenge in myself but I brought to mind his roving and wanton pranks, and I counselled his father first to abide the upshot of the wound, representing to him, in the best manner I could, that it was but the quarrel of the young men, and that maybe his son was as muckle in fault as Swinton.

My brother was, however, of a hasty temper, and upbraided me with my slackness, on account, as he tauntingly insinuated, of the young laird being one of my best customers, which was a harsh and unrighteous doing; but it was not the severest trial which the accident occasioned to me; for the same night, at a late hour, a line was brought to me by a lassie, requesting I would come to a certain place—and when I went there, who was it from but Swinton and the two other young lads that had been the seconds at the duel.

"Bailie," said the laird on behalf of himself and friends, "though you are the uncle of poor Dick, we have resolved to throw ourselves into your hands, for we have not provided any money to enable us to flee the country; we only hope you will not deal overly harshly with us till his fate is ascertained."

I was greatly disconcerted, and wist not what to say; for knowing the rigour of our Scottish laws against duelling, I was wae to see three brave youths, not yet come to years of discretion, standing in the peril and jeopardy of an ignominious end, and that, too, for an injury done to my own kin; and then I thought of my nephew and of my brother, that, maybe, would soon be in sorrow for the loss of his only son. In short, I was tried almost beyond my humanity. The three poor lads, seeing me hesitate, were much moved, and one of them (Sandy Blackie) said,

"I told you how it would be; it was even-down madness to throw ourselves into the lion's mouth." To this Swinton replied, "Mr Pawkie, we have cast ourselves on your mercy as a gentleman."

What could I say to this, but that I hoped they would find me one; and without speaking any more at that time—for indeed I could not, my heart beat so fast—I bade them follow me, and taking them round by the back road to my garden yett, I let them in, and conveyed them into a warehouse where I kept my bales and boxes. Then slipping into the house, I took out of the pantry a basket of bread and a cold leg of mutton, which, when Mrs Pawkie and the servant lassies missed in the morning, they could not divine what had become of; and giving the same to them, with a bottle of wine-for they were very hungry, having tasted nothing all day—I went round to my brother's to see at the latest how Richard was. But such a stang as I got on entering the house, when I heard his mother wailing that he was dead, he having fainted away in getting the bullet extracted; and when I saw his father coming out of the room like a demented man, and heard again his upbraiding of me for having refused a warrant to apprehend the murderers—I was so stunned with the shock, and with the thought of the poor young lads in my mercy, that I could with difficulty support myself along the passage into a room where there was a chair, into which I fell rather than threw myself. I had not, however, been long seated, when a joyful cry announced that Richard was recovering, and presently he was in a manner free from pain; and the doctor assured me the wound was probably not mortal. I did not, however, linger long on hearing this; but hastening home, I took what money I had in my scrutoire, and going to the malefactors, said, "Lads, take thir twa three pounds, and quit the town as fast as ye can, for Richard is my nephew, and blood, ye ken, is thicker than water, and I may be tempted to give you up."

They started on their legs, and shaking me in a warm manner by both the hands, they hurried away without speaking, nor could I say more, as I opened the back yett to let them out, than bid them take tent of themselves.

Mrs Pawkie was in a great consternation at my late absence, and when I went home she thought I was ill, I was so pale and flurried, and she wanted to send for the doctor, but I told her that when I was calmed, I would be better; however, I got no sleep that night. In the morning I went to see Richard, whom I found in a composed and rational state: he confessed to his father that he was as muckle to blame as Swinton, and begged and entreated us, if he should die, not to take any steps against the fugitives: my brother, however, was loth to make rash promises, and it was not till his son was out of danger that I had any ease of mind for the part I had played. But when Richard was afterwards well enough to go about, and the duellers had come out of their hidings, they told him what I had done, by which the whole affair came to the public, and I got great fame thereby, none being more proud to speak of it than poor Dick himself, who, from that time, became the bosom friend of Swinton; in so much that, when he was out of his time as a writer, and had gone through his courses at Edinburgh, the laird made him his man of business, and, in a manner, gave him a nest egg.

Chapter 38

An Interlocutor

Upon a consideration of many things, it appears to me very strange, that almost the whole tot of our improvements became, in a manner, the parents of new plagues and troubles to the magistrates. It might reasonably have been thought that the lamps in the streets would have been a terror to evil-doers, and the plainstone side-pavements paths of pleasantness to them that do well; but, so far from this being the case, the very reverse was the consequence. The servant lasses went freely out (on their errands) at night, and at late hours, for their mistresses, without the protection of lanterns, by which they were enabled to gallant in a way that never could have before happened: for lanterns are kenspeckle commodities, and of course a check on every kind of gavaulling. Thus, out of the lamps sprung no little irregularity in the conduct of servants, and much bitterness of spirit on that account to mistresses, especially to those who were of a particular turn, and who did not choose that their maidens should spend their hours a-field, when they could be profitably employed at home.

Of the plagues that were from the plainstones, I have given an exemplary specimen in the plea between old perjink Miss Peggy Dainty, and the widow Fenton, that was commonly called the Tappit-hen. For the present, I shall therefore confine myself in this nota bena to an accident that happened to Mrs Girdwood, the deacon of the coopers' wife—a most managing, industrious, and indefatigable woman, that allowed no grass to grow in her path.

Mrs Girdwood had fee'd one Jeanie Tirlet, and soon after she came home, the mistress had her big summer washing at the public washing-house on the green—all the best of her sheets and napery—both what had been used in the course of the winter, and what was only washed to keep clear in the colour, were in the boyne. It was one of the greatest doings of the kind that the mistress had in the whole course of the year, and the value of things intrusted to Jeanie's care was not to be told, at least so said Mrs Girdwood herself.

Jeanie and Marion Sapples, the washerwoman, with a pickle tea and sugar tied in the corners of a napkin, and two measured glasses of whisky in an old doctor's bottle, had been sent with the foul clothes the night before to the washing-house, and by break of day they were up and at their work; nothing particular, as Marion said, was observed about Jeanie till after they had taken their breakfast, when, in spreading out the clothes on the green, some of the ne'er-do-weel young clerks of the town were seen gaffawing and haverelling with Jeanie, the consequence of which was, that all the rest of the day she was light-headed; indeed, as Mrs Girdwood told me herself, when Jeanie came in from the green for Marion's dinner, she couldna help remarking to her goodman, that there was something fey about the lassie, or, to use her own words, there was a storm in her tail, light where it might. But little did she think it was to bring the dule it did to her.

Jeanie having gotten the pig with the wonted allowance of broth and beef in it for Marion, returned to the green, and while Marion was eating the same, she disappeared. Once away, aye away; hilt or hair of Jeanie was not seen that night. Honest Marion Sapples worked like a Trojan to the gloaming, but the light latheron never came back; at last, seeing no other help for it, she got one of the other women at the washing-house to go to Mrs Girdwood and to let her know what had happened, and how the best part of the washing would, unless help was sent, be obliged to lie out all night.

The deacon's wife well knew the great stake she had on that occasion in the boyne, and was for a season demented with the thought; but at last summoning her three daughters, and borrowing our lass, and Mr Smeddum the tobacconist's niece, she went to the green, and got everything safely housed, yet still Jeanie Tirlet never made her appearance.

Mrs Girdwood and her daughters having returned home, in a most uneasy state of mind on the lassie's account, the deacon himself came over to me, to consult what he ought to do as the head of a family. But I advised him to wait till Jeanie cast up, which was the next morning. Where she had been, and who she was with, could never be delved out of her; but the deacon brought her to the clerk's chamber, before Bailie Kittlewit, who was that day acting magistrate, and he sentenced her to be dismissed from her servitude with no more than the wage she had actually earned. The lassie was conscious of the ill turn she had played, and would have submitted in modesty; but one of the writers' clerks, an impudent whippersnapper, that had more to say with her than I need to say, bade her protest and appeal against the interlocutor, which the daring gipsy, so egged on, actually did, and the appeal next court day came before me. Whereupon, I, knowing the outs and ins of the case, decerned that she should be fined five shillings to the poor of the parish, and ordained to go back to Mrs Girdwood's, and there stay out the term of her servitude, or failing by refusal so to do, to be sent to prison, and put to hard labour for the remainder of the term.

Every body present, on hearing the circumstances, thought this a most judicious and lenient sentence; but so thought not the other servant lasses of the town; for in the evening, as I was going home, thinking no harm, on passing the Cross-well, where a vast congregation of them were assembled with their stoups discoursing the news of the day, they opened on me like a pack of hounds at a tod, and I verily believed they would have mobbed me had I not made the best of my way home. My wife had been at the window when the hobleshow began, and was just like to die of diversion at seeing me so set upon by the tinklers; and when I entered the dining-room she said, "Really, Mr Pawkie, ye're a gallant man, to be soweel in the good graces of the ladies." But although I have often since had many a good laugh at the sport, I was not overly pleased with Mrs Pawkie at the time—particularly as the matter between the deacon's wife and Jeanie did not end with my interlocutor. For the latheron's friend in the court having discovered that I had not decerned she was to do any work to Mrs Girdwood, but only to stay out her term, advised her to do nothing when she went back but go to her bed, which she was bardy enough to do, until my poor friend, the deacon, in order to get a quiet riddance of her, was glad to pay her full fee, and board wages for the remainder of her time. This was the same Jeanie Tirlet that was transported for some misdemeanour, after making both Glasgow and Edinburgh owre het to hold her.

Chapter 39

The Newspaper

Shortly after the foregoing tribulation, of which I cannot take it upon me to say that I got so well rid as of many other vexations of a more grievous nature, there arose a thing in the town that caused to me much deep concern, and very serious reflection. I had been, from the beginning, a true government man, as all loyal subjects ought in duty to be; for I never indeed could well understand how it would advantage, either the king or his ministers, to injure and do detriment to the lieges; on the contrary, I always saw and thought that his majesty, and those of his cabinet, had as great an interest in the prosperity and well-doing of the people, as it was possible for a landlord to have in the thriving of his tenantry. Accordingly, giving on all occasions, and at all times and seasons, even when the policy of the kingdom was overcast with a cloud, the king and government, in church and state, credit for the best intentions, however humble their capacity in performance might seem in those straits and difficulties, which, from time to time, dumfoundered the wisest in power and authority, I was exceedingly troubled to hear that a newspaper was to be set up in the burgh, and that, too, by hands not altogether clean of the coom of jacobinical democracy.

The person that first brought me an account of this, and it was in a private confidential manner, was Mr Scudmyloof, the grammar schoolmaster, a man of method and lear, to whom the fathers of the project had applied for an occasional cast of his skill, in the way of Latin head-pieces, and essays of erudition concerning the free spirit among the ancient Greeks and Romans; but he, not liking the principle of the men concerned in the scheme, thought that it would be a public service to the community at large, if a stop could be put, by my help, to the opening of such an ettering sore and king's evil as a newspaper, in our heretofore and hitherto truly royal and loyal burgh; especially as it was given out that the calamity, for I can call it no less, was to be conducted on liberal principles, meaning, of course, in the most afflicting and vexatious manner towards his majesty's ministers.

"What ye say," said I to Mr Scudmyloof when he told me the news, "is very alarming, very much so indeed; but as there is no law yet actually and peremptorily prohibiting the sending forth of newspapers, I doubt it will not be in my power to interfere."

He was of the same opinion; and we both agreed it was a rank exuberance of liberty, that the commonality should be exposed to the risk of being inoculated with anarchy and confusion, from what he, in his learned manner, judiciously called the predilections of amateur pretension. The parties engaged in the project being Mr Absolom the writer—a man no overly reverential in his opinion of the law and lords when his clients lost their pleas, which, poor folk, was very often—and some three or four young and inexperienced lads, that were wont to read essays, and debate the kittle points of divinity and other hidden knowledge, in the Cross-Keys monthly, denying the existence of the soul of man, as Dr Sinney told me, till they were deprived of all rationality by foreign or British spirits. In short, I was perplexed when I heard of the design, not knowing what to do, or what might be expected from me by government in a case of such emergency as the setting up of it newspaper so declaredly adverse to every species of vested trust and power; for it was easy to forsee that those immediately on the scene would be the first opposed to the onset and brunt of the battle. Never can any public man have a more delicate task imposed upon him, than to steer clear of offence in such a predicament. After a full consideration of the business, Mr Scudmyloof declared that he would retire from the field, and stand aloof; and he rehearsed a fine passage in the Greek language on that head, pat to the occasion, but which I did not very thoroughly understand, being no deacon in the dead languages, as I told him at the time.

But when the dominie had left me, I considered with myself, and having long before then observed that our hopes, when realized, are always light in the grain, and our fears, when come to pass, less than they seemed as seen through the mists of time and distance, I resolved with myself to sit still with my eyes open, watching and saying nothing; and it was well that I deported myself so prudently; for when the first number of the paper made its appearance, it was as poor a job as ever was "open to all parties, and influenced by none;" and it required but two eyes to discern that there was no need of any strong power from the lord advocate to suppress or abolish the undertaking; for there was neither birr nor smeddum enough in it to molest the high or to pleasure the low; so being left to itself, and not ennobled by any prosecution, as the schemers expected, it became as foisonless as the "London Gazette" on ordinary occasions. Those behind the curtain, who thought to bounce out with a grand stot and strut before the world, finding that even I used it as a convenient vehicle to advertise my houses when need was, and which I did by the way of a canny seduction of policy, joking civilly with Mr Absolom anent his paper trumpet, as I called it, they were utterly vanquished by seeing themselves of so little account in the world, and forsook the thing altogether; by which means it was gradually transformed into a very solid and decent supporter of the government—Mr Absolom, for his pains, being invited to all our public dinners, of which he gave a full account, to the great satisfaction of all who were present, but more particularly to those who were not, especially the wives and ladies of the town, to whom it was a great pleasure to see the names of their kith and kin in print. And indeed, to do Mr Absolom justice, he was certainly at great pains to set off every thing to the best advantage, and usually put speeches to some of our names which showed that, in the way of grammaticals, he was even able to have mended some of the parliamentary clishmaclavers, of which the Londoners, with all their skill in the craft, are so seldom able to lick into any shape of common sense. Thus, by a judicious forbearance in the first instance, and a canny wising towards the undertaking in the second, did I, in the third, help to convert this dangerous political adversary into a very respectable instrument of governmental influence and efficacy.

Chapter 40

The School-house scheme

The spirit of opposition that kithed towards me in the affair of Robin Boss, the drummer, was but an instance and symptom of the new nature then growing up in public matters. I was not long done with my second provostry, when I had occasion to congratulate myself on having passed twice through the dignity with so much respect; for, at the Michaelmas term, we had chosen Mr Robert Plan into the vacancy caused by the death of that easy man, Mr Weezle, which happened a short time before. I know not what came over me, that Mr Plan was allowed to be chosen, for I never could abide him; being, as he was, a great stickler for small particularities, more zealous than discreet, and even more intent to carry his own point, than to consider the good that might flow from a more urbane spirit. Not that the man was devoid of ability—few, indeed, could set forth a more plausible tale; but he was continually meddling, keeking, and poking, and always taking up a suspicious opinion of every body's intents and motives but his own. He was, besides, of a retired and sedentary habit of body; and the vapour of his stomach, as he was sitting by himself, often mounted into his upper story, and begat, with his over zealous and meddling imagination, many unsound and fantastical notions. For all that, however, it must be acknowledged that Mr Plan was a sincere honest man, only he sometimes lacked the discernment of the right from the wrong; and the consequence was, that, when in error, he was even more obstinate than when in the right; for his jealousy of human nature made him interpret falsely the heat with which his own headstrong zeal, when in error, was ever very properly resisted.

In nothing, however, did his molesting temper cause so much disturbance, as when, in the year 1809, the bigging of the new school-house was under consideration. There was, about that time, a great sough throughout the country on the subject of education, and it was a fashion to call schools academies; and out of a delusion rising from the use of that term, to think it necessary to decry the good plain old places, wherein so many had learnt those things by which they helped to make the country and kingdom what it is, and to scheme for the ways and means to raise more edificial structures and receptacles. None was more infected with his distemperature than Mr Plan; and accordingly, when he came to the council-chamber, on the day that the matter of the new school-house was to be discussed, he brought with him a fine castle in the air, which he pressed hard upon us; representing, that if we laid out two or three thousand pounds more than we intended, and built a beautiful academy and got a rector thereto, with a liberal salary, and other suitable masters, opulent people at a distance—yea, gentlemen in the East and West Indies—would send their children to be educated among us, by which, great fame and profit would redound to the town.

Nothing could be more plausibly set forth; and certainly the project, as a notion, had many things to recommend it; but we had no funds adequate to undertake it; so, on the score of expense, knowing, as I did, the state of the public income, I thought it my duty to oppose it in toto; which fired Mr Plan to such a degree, that he immediately insinuated that I had some end of my own to serve in objecting to his scheme; and because the wall that it was proposed to big round the moderate building which we were contemplating, would inclose a portion of the backside of my new steading at the Westergate, he made no scruple of speaking, in a circumbendibus manner, as to the particular reasons that I might have for preferring it to his design, which he roused, in his way, as more worthy of the state of the arts and the taste of the age.

It was not easy to sit still under his imputations; especially as I could plainly see that some of the other members of the council leant towards his way of thinking. Nor will I deny that, in preferring the more moderate design, I had a contemplation of my own advantage in the matter of the dyke; for I do not think it any shame to a public man to serve his own interests by those of the community, when he can righteously do so.

It was a thing never questionable, that the school-house require the inclosure of a wall, and the outside of that wall was of a natural necessity constrained to be a wing of inclosure to the ground beyond. Therefore, I see not how a corrupt motive ought to have been imputed to me, merely because I had a piece of ground that marched with the spot whereon it was intended to construct the new building; which spot, I should remark, belonged to the town before I bought mine. However, Mr Plan so worked upon this material, that, what with one thing and what with another, he got the council persuaded to give up the moderate plan, and to consent to sell the ground where it had been proposed to build the new school, and to apply the proceeds towards the means of erecting a fine academy on the Green.

It was not easy to thole to be so thwarted, especially for such an extravagant problem, by one so new to our councils and deliberations. I never was more fashed in my life; for having hitherto, in all my plans for the improvement of the town, not only succeeded, but given satisfaction, I was vexed to see the council run away with such a speculative vagary. No doubt, the popular fantasy anent education and academies, had quite as muckle to do in the matter as Mr Plan's fozey rhetoric, but what availed that to me, at seeing a reasonable undertaking reviled and set aside, and grievous debts about to be laid on the community for a bubble as unsubstantial as that of the Ayr Bank. Besides, it was giving the upper hand in the council to Mr Plan, to which, as a new man, he had no right. I said but little, for I saw it would be of no use; I, however, took a canny opportunity of remarking to old Mr Dinledoup, the English teacher, that this castle-building scheme of an academy would cause great changes probably in the masters; and as, no doubt, it would oblige us to adopt the new methods of teaching, I would like to have a private inkling of what salary he would expect on being superannuated.

The worthy man was hale and hearty, not exceeding three score and seven, and had never dreamt of being superannuated. He was, besides, a prideful body, and, like all of his calling, thought not a little of himself. The surprise, therefore, with which he heard me was just wonderful. For a space of time he stood still and uttered nothing; then he took his snuff-box out of the flap pocket of his waistcoat, where he usually carried it, and, giving three distinct and very comical raps, drew his mouth into a purse. "Mr Pawkie," at last he said; "Mr Pawkie, there will be news in the world before I consent to be superannuated."

This was what I expected, and I replied, "Then, why do not you and Mr Scudmyloof, of the grammar school, represent to the magistrates that the present school-house may, with a small repair, serve for many years." And so I sowed an effectual seed of opposition to Mr Plan, in a quarter he never dreamt of; the two dominies, in the dread of undergoing some transmogrification, laid their heads together, and went round among the parents of the children, and decried the academy project, and the cess that the cost of it would bring upon the town; by which a public opinion was begotten and brought to a bearing, that the magistrates could not resist; so the old school-house was repaired, and Mr Plan's scheme, as well as the other, given up. In this, it is true, if I had not the satisfaction to get a dyke to the backside of my property, I had the pleasure to know that my interloping adversary was disappointed; the which was a sort of compensation.

Chapter 41

Benefits of Neutrality

The General Election of 1812 was a source of trouble and uneasiness to me; both because our district of burghs was to be contested, and because the contest was not between men of opposite principles, but of the same side. To neither of them had I any particular leaning; on the contrary, I would have preferred the old member, whom I had, on different occasions, found an accessible and tractable instrument, in the way of getting small favours with the government and India company, for friends that never failed to consider them as such things should be. But what could I do? Providence had placed me in the van of the battle, and I needs must fight; so thought every body, and so for a time I thought myself. Weighing, however, the matter one night soberly in my mind, and seeing that whichever of the two candidates was chosen, I, by my adherent loyalty to the cause for which they were both declared, the contest between them being a rivalry of purse and personality, would have as much to say with the one as with the other, came to the conclusion that it was my prudentest course not to intermeddle at all in the election. Accordingly, as soon as it was proper to make a declaration of my sentiments, I made this known, and it caused a great wonderment in the town; nobody could imagine it possible that I was sincere, many thinking there was something aneath it, which would kithe in time to the surprise of the public.

However, the peutering went on, and I took no part. The two candidates were as civil and as liberal, the one after the other, to Mrs Pawkie and my daughters, as any gentlemen of a parliamentary understanding could be. Indeed, I verily believe, that although I had been really chosen delegate, as it was at one time intended I should be, I could not have hoped for half the profit that came in from the dubiety which my declaration of neutrality caused; for as often as I assured the one candidate that I did not intend even to be present at the choosing of the delegate, some rich present was sure to be sent to my wife, of which the other no sooner heard than he was upsides with him. It was just a sport to think of me protesting my neutrality, and to see how little I was believed. For still the friends of the two candidates, like the figures of of the four quarters of the world round Britannia in a picture, came about my wife, and poured into her lap a most extraordinary paraphernalia from the horn of their abundance.

The common talk of the town was, that surely I was bereft of my wonted discretion, to traffic so openly with corruption; and that it could not be doubted I would have to face the House of Commons, and suffer the worst pains and penalties of bribery. But what did all this signify to me, who was conscious of the truth and integrity of my motives and talents? "They say!—what say they?—let them say!"—was what I said, as often as any of my canny friends came to me, saying, "For God's sake, Mr Pawkie, tak' tent"—"I hope, Mr Pawkie, ye ken the ground ye stand on"—or, "I wish that some folks were aware of what's said about them." In short, I was both angered and diverted by their clishmaclavers; and having some need to go into Glasgow just on the eve of the election, I thought I would, for diversion, give them something in truth to play with; so saying nothing to my shop lad the night before, nor even to Mrs Pawkie, (for the best of women are given to tattling), till we were in our beds, I went off early on the morning of the day appointed for choosing the delegate.

The consternation in the town at my evasion was wonderful. Nobody could fathom it; and the friends and supporters of the rival candidates looked, as I was told, at one another, in a state of suspicion that was just a curiosity to witness. Even when the delegate was chosen, every body thought that something would be found wanting, merely because I was not present. The new member himself, when his election was declared, did not feel quite easy; and more than once, when I saw him after my return from Glasgow, he said to me, in a particular manner—"But tell me now, bailie, what was the true reason of your visit to Glasgow?" And, in like manner, his opponent also hinted that he would petition against the return; but there were some facts which he could not well get at without my assistance—insinuating that I might find my account in helping him.

At last, the true policy of the part I had played began to be understood; and I got far more credit for the way in which I had turned both parties so well to my own advantage, than if I had been the means of deciding the election by my single vote.

Chapter 42

The New Member

But the new member was, in some points, not of so tractable a nature as many of his predecessors had been; and notwithstanding all the couthy jocosity and curry-favouring of his demeanour towards us before the election, he was no sooner returned, than he began, as it were, to snap his fingers in the very faces of those of the council to whom he was most indebted, which was a thing not of very easy endurance, considering how they had taxed their consciences in his behalf; and this treatment was the more bitterly felt, as the old member had been, during the whole of his time, as considerate and obliging as could reasonably be expected; doing any little job that needed his helping hand when it was in his power, and when it was not, replying to our letters in a most discreet and civil manner. To be sure, poor man, he had but little to say in the way of granting favours; for being latterly inclined to a whiggish principle, he was, in consequence, debarred from all manner of government patronage, and had little in his gift but soft words and fair promises. Indeed, I have often remarked, in the course of my time, that there is a surprising difference, in regard to the urbanities in use among those who have not yet come to authority, or who have been cast down from it, and those who are in the full possession of the rule and domination of office; but never was the thing plainer than in the conduct of the new member.

He was by nature and inclination one of the upsetting sort; a kind of man who, in all manner of business, have a leaven of contrariness, that makes them very hard to deal with; and he, being conjunct with his majesty's ministers at London, had imbibed and partook of that domineering spirit to which all men are ordained, to be given over whenever they are clothed in the garments of power. Many among us thought, by his colleaguing with the government, that we had got a great catch, and they were both blythe and vogie when he was chosen; none doubting but he would do much good servitude to the corporation, and the interests of the burgh. However he soon gave a rebuff, that laid us all on our backs in a state of the greatest mortification. But although it behoved me to sink down with the rest, I was but little hurt: on the contrary, I had a good laugh in my sleeve at the time; and afterwards, many a merry tumbler of toddy with my brethren, when they had recovered from their discomfiture. The story was this:—

About a fortnight after the election, Mr Scudmyloof, the schoolmaster, called one day on me, in my shop, and said, "That being of a nervous turn, the din of the school did not agree with him; and that he would, therefore, be greatly obliged to me if I would get him made a gauger." There had been something in the carriage of our new member, before he left the town, that was not satisfactory to me, forbye my part at the election, the which made me loth to be the first to ask for any grace, though the master was a most respectable and decent man; so I advised Mr Scudmyloof to apply to Provost Pickandab, who had been the delegate, as the person to whose instrumentality the member was most obliged; and to whose application, he of course would pay the greatest attention.

Whether Provost Pickandab had made any observe similar to mine, I never could rightly understand, though I had a notion to that effect: he, however, instead of writing himself, made the application for Mr Scudmyloof an affair of the council; recommending him as a worthy modest man, which he really was, and well qualified for the post. Off went this notable letter, and by return of post from London, we got our answer as we were all sitting in council; deliberating anent the rebuilding of the Cross-well, which had been for some time in a sore state of dilapidation; and surely never was any letter more to the point and less to the purpose of an applicant. It was very short and pithy, just acknowledging receipt of ours; and adding thereto, "circumstances do not allow me to pay any attention to such applications." We all with one accord, in sympathy and instinct, threw ourselves back in our chairs at the words, looking at Provost Pickandab, with the pragmatical epistle in his hand, sitting in his place at the head of the table, with the countenance of consternation.

When I came to myself I began to consider that there must have been something no right in the provost's own letter on the subject, to cause such an uncourteous rebuff; so after condemning, in very strong terms, the member's most ungenteel style, in order to procure for myself a patient hearing, I warily proposed that the provost's application should be read, a copy thereof being kept, and I had soon a positive confirmation of my suspicion. For the provost, being fresh in the dignity of his office, and naturally of a prideful turn, had addressed the parliament man as if he was under an obligation to him; and as if the council had a right to command him to get the gauger's post, or indeed any other, for whomsoever they might apply. So, seeing whence the original sin of the affair had sprung, I said nothing; but the same night I wrote a humiliated letter from myself to the member, telling him how sorry we all were for the indiscretion that had been used towards him, and how much it would pleasure me to heal the breach that had happened between him and the burgh, with other words of an oily and conciliating policy.

The indignant member, by the time my letter reached hand, had cooled in his passion, and, I fancy, was glad of an occasion to do away the consequence of the rupture; for with a most extraordinary alacrity he procured Mr Scudmyloof the post, writing me, when he had done so, in the civilest manner, and saying many condescending things concerning his regard for me; all which ministered to maintain and uphold my repute and consideration in the town, as superior to that of the provost.

Chapter 43

My Third Provostry

It was at the Michaelmas 1813 I was chosen provost for the third time, and at the special request of my lord the earl, who, being in ill health, had been advised by the faculty of doctors in London to try the medicinal virtues of the air and climate of Sicily, in the Mediterranean sea; and there was an understanding on the occasion, that I should hold the post of honour for two years, chiefly in order to bring to a conclusion different works that the town had then in hand.

At the two former times when I was raised to the dignity, and indeed at all times when I received any advancement, I had enjoyed an elation of heart, and was, as I may say, crouse and vogie; but experience had worked a change upon my nature, and when I was saluted on my election with the customary greetings and gratulations of those present, I felt a solemnity enter into the frame of my thoughts, and I became as it were a new man on the spot. When I returned home to my own house, I retired into my private chamber for a time, to consult with myself in what manner my deportment should be regulated; for I was conscious that heretofore I had been overly governed with a disposition to do things my own way, and although not in an avaricious temper, yet something, I must confess, with a sort of sinister respect for my own interests. It may be, that standing now clear and free of the world, I had less incitement to be so grippy, and so was thought of me, I very well know; but in sobriety and truth I conscientiously affirm, and herein record, that I had lived to partake of the purer spirit which the great mutations of the age had conjured into public affairs, and I saw that there was a necessity to carry into all dealings with the concerns of the community, the same probity which helps a man to prosperity in the sequestered traffic of private life.

This serious and religious communing wrought within me to a benign and pleasant issue, and when I went back in the afternoon to dine with the corporation in the council-room, and looked around me on the bailies, the councillors, and the deacons, I felt as if I was indeed elevated above them all, and that I had a task to perform, in which I could hope for but little sympathy from many; and the first thing I did was to measure, with a discreet hand, the festivity of the occasion.

At all former and precedent banquets, it had been the custom to give vent to muckle wanton and luxurious indulgence, and to galravitch, both at hack and manger, in a very expensive manner to the funds of the town. I therefore resolved to set my face against this for the future; and accordingly, when we had enjoyed a jocose temperance of loyalty and hilarity, with a decent measure of wine, I filled a glass, and requesting all present to do the same, without any preliminary reflections on the gavaulling of past times, I drank good afternoon to each severally, and then rose from the table, in a way that put an end to all the expectations of more drink.

But this conduct did not give satisfaction to some of the old hands, who had been for years in the habit and practice of looking forward to the provost's dinner as to a feast of fat things. Mr Peevie, one of the very sickerest of all the former sederunts, came to me next morning, in a remonstrating disposition, to enquire what had come over me, and to tell me that every body was much surprised, and many thought it not right of me to break in upon ancient and wonted customs in such a sudden and unconcerted manner.

This Mr Peevie was, in his person, a stumpy man, well advanced in years. He had been, in his origin, a bonnet-maker; but falling heir to a friend that left him a property, he retired from business about the fiftieth year of his age, doing nothing but walking about with an ivory-headed staff, in a suit of dark blue cloth with yellow buttons, wearing a large cocked hat, and a white three-tiered wig, which was well powdered every morning by Duncan Curl, the barber. The method of his discourse and conversation was very precise, and his words were all set forth in a style of consequence, that took with many for a season as the pith and marrow of solidity and sense. The body, however, was but a pompous trifle, and I had for many a day held his observes and admonishments in no very reverential estimation. So that, when I heard him address me in such a memorializing manner, I was inclined and tempted to set him off with a flea in his lug. However, I was enabled to bridle and rein in this prejudicial humour, and answer him in his own way.

"Mr Peevie," quo' I, "you know that few in the town hae the repute that ye hae for a gift of sagacity by common, and therefore I'll open my mind to you in this matter, with a frankness that would not be a judicious polity with folk of a lighter understanding."

This was before the counter in my shop. I then walked in behind it, and drew the chair that stands in the corner nearer to the fire, for Mr Peevie. When he was seated thereon, and, as was his wont in conversation, had placed both his hands on the top of his staff, and leant his chin on the same, I subjoined.

"Mr Peevie, I need not tell to a man of your experience, that folk in public stations cannot always venture to lay before the world the reasons of their conduct on particular occasions; and therefore, when men who have been long in the station that I have filled in this town, are seen to step aside from what has been in time past, it is to be hoped that grave and sensible persons like you, Mr Peevie, will no rashly condemn them unheard; nevertheless, my good friend, I am very happy that ye have spoken to me anent the stinted allowance of wine and punch at the dinner, because the like thing from any other would have made me jealouse that the complaint was altogether owing to a disappointed appetite, which is a corrupt thing, that I am sure would never affect a man of such a public spirit as you are well known to be."

Mr Peevie, at this, lifted his chin from off his hands, and dropping his arms down upon his knees, held his staff by the middle, as he replied, looking upward to me,

"What ye say, Provost Pawkie, has in it a solid commodity of judgment and sensibility; and ye may be sure that I was not without a cogitation of reflection, that there had been a discreet argument of economy at the bottom of the revolution which was brought to a criticism yesterday's afternoon. Weel aware am I, that men in authority cannot appease and quell the inordinate concupiscence of the multitude, and that in a' stations of life there are persons who would mumpileese the retinue of the king and government for their own behoof and eeteration, without any regard to the cause or effect of such manifest predilections. But ye do me no more than a judicature, in supposing that, in this matter, I am habituated wi' the best intentions. For I can assure you, Mr Pawkie, that no man in this community has a more literal respect for your character than I have, or is more disposed for a judicious example of continence in the way of public entertEenment than I have ever been; for, as you know, I am of a constipent principle towards every extravagant and costive outlay. Therefore, on my own account, I had a satisfaction at seeing the abridgement which you made of our former inebrieties; but there are other persons of a conjugal nature, who look upon such castrations as a deficiency of their rights, and the like of them will find fault with the best procedures."

"Very true, Mr Peevie," said I, "that's very true; but if his Majesty's government, in this war for all that is dear to us as men and Britons, wish us, who are in authority under them, to pare and save, in order that the means of bringing the war to a happy end may not be wasted, an example must be set, and that example, as a loyal subject and a magistrate, it's my intent so to give, in the hope and confidence of being backed by every person of a right way of thinking."

"It's no to be deputed, Provost Pawkie," replied my friend, somewhat puzzled by what I had said; "it's no to be deputed, that we live in a gigantic vortex, and that every man is bound to make an energetic dispensation for the good of his country; but I could not have thought that our means had come to sic an alteration and extremity, as that the reverent homage of the Michaelmas dinners could have been enacted, and declared absolute and abolished, by any interpolation less than the omnipotence of parliament."

"Not abolished, Mr Peevie," cried I, interrupting him; "that would indeed be a stretch of power. No, no; I hope we're both ordained to partake of many a Michaelmas dinner thegether yet; but with a meted measure of sobriety. For we neither live in the auld time nor the golden age, and it would not do now for the like of you and me, Mr Peevie, to be seen in the dusk of the evening, toddling home from the town-hall wi' goggling een and havering tongues, and one of the town-officers following at a distance in case of accidents; sic things ye ken, hae been, but nobody would plead for their continuance."

Mr Peevie did not relish this, for in truth it came near his own doors, it having been his annual practice for some years at the Michaelmas dinner to give a sixpence to James Hound, the officer, to see him safe home, and the very time before he had sat so long, that honest James was obligated to cleek and oxter him the whole way; and in the way home, the old man, cagie with what he had gotten, stood in the causey opposite to Mr McVest's door, then deacon of the taylors, and trying to snap his fingers, sang like a daft man,

> The sheets they were thin and the blankets were sma',
> And the taylor fell through the bed, thimble and a'.

So that he was disconcerted by my innuendo, and shortly after left the shop, I trow, with small inclination to propagate any sedition against me, for the abbreviation I had made of the Michaelmas galravitching.

Chapter 44

The Church Vacant

I had long been sensible that in getting Mr Pittle the kirk, I had acted with the levity and indiscretion of a young man; but at that time I understood not the nature of public trust, nor, indeed, did the community at large. Men in power then ruled more for their own ends than in these latter times; and use and wont sanctioned and sanctified many doings, from the days of our ancestors, that, but to imagine, will astonish and startle posterity. Accordingly, when Mr Pittle, after a lingering illness, was removed from us, which happened in the first year of my third provostry, I bethought me of the consequences which had ensued from his presentation, and resolved within myself to act a very different part in the filling up of the vacancy. With this intent, as soon as the breath was out of his body, I sent round for some of the most weighty and best considered of the councillors and elders, and told them that a great trust was, by the death of the minister, placed in our hands, and that, in these times, we ought to do what in us lay to get a shepherd that would gather back to the establishment the flock which had been scattered among the seceders, by the feckless crook and ill-guiding of their former pastor.

They all agreed with me in this, and named one eminent divine after another; but the majority of voices were in favour of Dr Whackdeil of Kirkbogle, a man of weight and example, both in and out the pulpit, so that it was resolved to give the call to him, which was done accordingly.

It however came out that the Kirkbogle stipend was better than ours, and the consequence was, that having given the call, it became necessary to make up the deficiency; for it was not reasonable to expect that the reverend doctor, with his small family of nine children, would remove to us at a loss. How to accomplish this was a work of some difficulty, for the town revenues were all eaten up with one thing and another; but upon an examination of the income, arising from what had been levied on the seats for the repair of the church, it was discovered that, by doing away a sinking fund, which had been set apart to redeem the debt incurred for the same, and by the town taking the debt on itself, we could make up a sufficiency to bring the doctor among us. And in so far as having an orthodox preacher, and a very excellent man for our minister, there was great cause to be satisfied with that arrangement.

But the payment of the interest on the public debt, with which the town was burdened, began soon after to press heavily on us, and we were obligated to take on more borrowed money, in order to keep our credit, and likewise to devise ways and means, in the shape of public improvements, to raise an income to make up what was required. This led me to suggest the building of the new bridge, the cost of which, by contract, there was no reason to complain of, and the toll thereon, while the war lasted, not only paid the interest of the borrowed money by which it was built, but left a good penny in the nook of the treasurer's box for other purposes.

Had the war continued, and the nation to prosper thereby as it did, nobody can doubt that a great source of wealth and income was opened to the town; but when peace came round, and our prosperity began to fall off, the traffic on the bridge grew less and less, insomuch that the toll, as I now understand, (for since my resignation, I meddle not with public concerns,) does not yield enough to pay the five per cent on the prime cost of the bridge, by which my successors suffer much molestation in raising the needful money to do the same. However, every body continues well satisfied with Dr Whackdeil, who was the original cause of this perplexity; and it is to be hoped that, in time, things will grow better, and the revenues come round again to indemnify the town for its present tribulation.

Chapter 45

The Stramash in the Council

As I have said, my third provostry was undertaken in a spirit of sincerity, different in some degree from that of the two former; but strange and singular as it may seem, I really think I got less credit for the purity of my intents, than I did even in the first. During the whole term from the election in the year 1813 to the Michaelmas following, I verily believe that no one proposal which I made to the council was construed in a right sense; this was partly owing to the repute I had acquired for canny management, but chiefly to the perverse views and misconceptions of that Yankee thorn-in-the-side, Mr Hickery, who never desisted from setting himself against every thing that sprang from me, and as often found some show of plausibility to maintain his argumentations. And yet, for all that, he was a man held in no esteem or respect in the town; for he had wearied every body out by his everlasting contradictions. Mr Plan was likewise a source of great tribulation to me; for he was ever and anon coming forward with some new device, either for ornament or profit, as he said, to the burgh; and no small portion of my time, that might have been more advantageously employed, was wasted in the thriftless consideration of his schemes: all which, with my advanced years, begat in me a sort of distaste to the bickerings of the council chamber; so I conferred and communed with myself, anent the possibility of ruling the town without having recourse to so unwieldy a vehicle as the wheels within wheels of the factions which the Yankee reformator, and that projectile Mr Plan, as he was called by Mr Peevie, had inserted among us.

I will no equivocate that there was, in this notion, an appearance of taking more on me than the laws allowed; but then my motives were so clean to my conscience, and I was so sure of satisfying the people by the methods I intended to pursue, that there could be no moral fault in the trifle of illegality, which, may be, I might have been led on to commit. However, I was fortunately spared from the experiment, by a sudden change in the council.—One day Mr Hickery and Mr Plan, who had been for years colleaguing together for their own ends, happened to differ in opinion, and the one suspecting that this difference was the fruit of some secret corruption, they taunted each other, and came to high words, and finally to an open quarrel, actually shaking their neeves across the table, and, I'll no venture to deny, maybe exchanging blows.

Such a convulsion in the sober councils of a burgh town was never heard of. It was a thing not to be endured, and so I saw at the time, and was resolved to turn it to the public advantage. Accordingly, when the two angry men had sat back in their seats, bleached in the face with passion, and panting and out of breath, I rose up in my chair at the head of the table, and with a judicial solemnity addressed the council, saying, that what we had witnessed was a disgrace not to be tolerated in a Christian land; that unless we obtained indemnity for the past, and security for the future, I would resign; but in doing so I would bring the cause thereof before the Fifteen at Edinburgh, yea, even to the House of Lords at London; so I gave the offending parties notice, as well as those who, from motives of personal friendship, might be disposed to overlook the insult that had been given to the constituted authority of the king, so imperfectly represented in my person, as it would seem, by the audacious conflict and misdemeanour which had just taken place.

This was striking while the iron was hot: every one looked at my sternness with surprise, and some begged me to be seated, and to consider the matter calmly.— "Gentlemen," quo' I, "dinna mistake me. I never was in more composure all my life.— It's indeed no on my own account that I feel on this occasion. The gross violation of all the decent decorum of magisterial authority, is not a thing that affects me in my own person; it's an outrage against the state; the prerogatives of the king's crown are endamaged; atonement must be made, or punishment must ensue. It's a thing that by no possibility can be overlooked: it's an offence committed in open court, and we cannot but take cognizance thereof."

I saw that what I said was operating to an effect, and that the two troublesome members were confounded. Mr Hickery rose to offer some apology; but, perceiving I had now got him in a girn, I interposed my authority, and would not permit him to proceed.

"Mr Hickery," said I, "it's of no use to address yourself to me. I am very sensible that ye are sorry for your fault; but that will not do. The law knows no such thing as repentance; and it is the law, not me nor our worthy friends here, that ye have offended. In short, Mr Hickery, the matter is such that, in one word, either you and Mr Plan must quit your seats at this table of your own free-will, or I must quit mine, and mine I will not give up without letting the public know the shame on your part that has compelled me."

He sat down and I sat down; and for some time the other councillors looked at one another in silence and wonder. Seeing, however, that my gentle hint was not likely to be taken, I said to the town-clerk, who was sitting at the bottom of the table,

"Sir, it's your duty to make a minute of everything that is done and said at the sederunts of the council; and as provost, I hereby require of you to record the particularities of this melancholy crisis."

Mr Keelevine made an endeavour to dissuade me; but I set him down with a stern voice, striking the table at the same time with all my birr, as I said, "Sir, you have no voice here. Do you refuse to perform what I order? At your peril I command the thing to be done."

Never had such austerity been seen in my conduct before. The whole council sat in astonishment; and Mr Keelevine prepared his pen, and took a sheet of paper to draw out a notation of the minute, when Mr Peevie rose, and after coughing three times, and looking first at me and syne at the two delinquents, said—"My Lord Provost, I was surprised, and beginning to be confounded, at the explosion which the two gentlemen have committed. No man can designate the extent of such an official malversation, demonstrated, as it has been here, in the presence of us all, who are the lawful custodiers of the kingly dignity in this his majesty's royal burgh. I will, therefore, not take it upon me either to apologise or to obliviate their offence; for, indeed, it is an offence that merits the most condign animadversion, and the consequences might be legible for ever, were a gentleman, so conspicable in the town as you are, to evacuate the magistracy on account of it. But it is my balsamic advice, that rather than promulgate this matter, the two malcontents should abdicate, and that a precept should be placarded at this sederunt as if they were not here, but had resigned and evaded their places, precursive to the meeting."

To this I answered, that no one could suspect me of wishing to push the matter further, provided the thing could be otherwise settled; and therefore, if Mr Plan and Mr Hickery would shake hands, and agree never to notice what had passed to each other, and the other members and magistrates would consent likewise to bury the business in oblivion, I would agree to the balsamic advice of Mr Peevie, and even waive my obligation to bind over the hostile parties to keep the king's peace, so that the whole affair might neither be known nor placed upon record.

Mr Hickery, I could discern, was rather surprised; but I found that I had thus got the thief in the wuddy, and he had no choice; so both he and Mr Plan rose from their seats in a very sheepish manner, and looking at us as if they had unpleasant ideas in their minds, they departed forth the council-chamber; and a minute was made by the town-clerk that they, having resigned their trust as councillors, two other gentlemen at the next meeting should be chosen into their stead.

Thus did I, in a manner most unexpected, get myself rid and clear of the two most obdurate oppositionists, and by taking care to choose discreet persons for their successors, I was enabled to wind the council round my finger, which was a far more expedient method of governing the community than what I had at one time meditated, even if I could have brought it to a bearing. But, in order to understand the full weight and importance of this, I must describe how the choice and election was made, because, in order to make my own power and influence the more sicker, it was necessary that I should not be seen in the business.

Chapter 46

The New Councillors

Mr Peevie was not a little proud of the part he had played in the storm of the council. and his words grew, if possible, longer-nebbit and more kittle than before, in so much that the same evening, when I called on him after dusk, by way of a device to get him to help the implementing of my intents with regard to the choice of two gentlemen to succeed those whom he called "the expurgated dislocators," it was with a great difficulty that I could expiscate his meaning. "Mr Peevie," said I, when we were cozily seated by ourselves in his little back parlour—the mistress having set out the gardevin and tumblers, and the lass brought in the hot water—"I do not think, Mr Peevie, that in all my experience, and I am now both an old man and an old magistrate, that I ever saw any thing better managed than the manner in which ye quelled the hobleshow this morning, and therefore we maun hae a little more of your balsamic advice, to make a' heal among us again; and now that I think o't, how has it happent that ye hae never been a bailie? I'm sure it's due both to your character and circumstance that ye should take upon you a portion of the burden of the town honours. Therefore, Mr Peevie, would it no be a very proper thing, in the choice of the new councillors, to take men of a friendly mind towards you, and of an easy and manageable habit of will. "

The old man was mightily taken with this insinuation, and acknowledged that it would give him pleasure to be a bailie next year. We then cannily proceeded, just as if one thing begat another, to discourse anent the different men that were likely to do as councillors, and fixed at last on Alexander Hodden the blanket merchant, and Patrick Fegs the grocer, both excellent characters of their kind. There was not, indeed, in the whole burgh at the time, a person of such a flexible easy nature as Mr Hodden; and his neighbour, Mr Fegs, was even better, for he was so good-tempered, and kindly, and complying, that the very callants at the grammar school had nicknamed him Barley-sugar Pate.

"No better than them can be,"said I to Mr Peevie; "they are likewise both well to do in the world, and should be brought into consequence; and the way o't canna be in better hands than your own. I would, therefore, recommend it to you to see them on the subject, and, if ye find them willing, lay your hairs in the water to bring the business to a bearing."

Accordingly, we settled to speak of it as a matter in part decided, that Mr Hodden and Mr Fegs were to be the two new councillors; and to make the thing sure, as soon as I went home I told it to Mrs Pawkie as a state secret, and laid my injunctions on her not to say a word about it, either to Mrs Hodden or to Mrs Fegs, the wives of our two elect; for I knew her disposition, and that, although to a certainty not a word of the fact would escape from her, yet she would be utterly unable to rest until she had made the substance of it known in some way or another; and, as I expected, so it came to pass. She went that very night to Mrs Rickerton, the mother of Mr Feg's wife, and, as I afterwards picked out of her, told the old lady that maybe, erelong, she would hear of some great honour that would come to her family, with other mystical intimations that pointed plainly to the dignities of the magistracy; the which, when she had returned home, so worked upon the imagination of Mrs Rickerton, that, before going to bed, she felt herself obliged to send for her daughter, to the end that she might be delivered and eased of what she had heard. In this way Mr Fegs got a foretaste of what had been concerted for his advantage; and Mr Peevie, in the mean time, through his helpmate, had, in like manner, not been idle; the effect of all which was, that next day, every where in the town, people spoke of Mr Hodden and Mr Fegs as being ordained to be the new councillors, in the stead of the two who had, as it was said, resigned in so unaccountable a manner, so that no candidates offered, and the election was concluded in the most candid and agreeable spirit possible; after which I had neither trouble nor adversary, but went on, in my own prudent way, with the works in hand—the completion of the new bridge, the reparation of the tolbooth steeple, and the bigging of the new schools on the piece of ground adjoining to my own at the Westergate; and in the doing of the latter job I had an opportunity of manifesting my public spirit; for when the scheme, as I have related, was some years before given up, on account of Mr Plan's castles in the air for educating tawny children from the East and West Indies, I inclosed my own ground, and built the house thereon now occupied by Collector Gather's widow, and the town, per consequence, was not called on for one penny of the cost, but saved so much of a wall as the length of mine extended—a part not less than a full third part of the whole. No doubt, all these great and useful public works were not done without money; but the town was then in great credit, and many persons were willing and ready to lend; for every thing was in a prosperous order, and we had a prospect of a vast increase of income, not only from the toll on the new bridge, but likewise from three very excellent shops which we repaired on the ground floor of the tolbooth. We had likewise feued out to advantage a considerable portion of the town moor; so that had things gone on in the way they were in my time, there can be no doubt that the burgh would have been in very flourishing circumstances, and instead of being drowned, as it now is, in debt, it might have been in the most topping way; and if the project that I had formed for bringing in a supply of water by pipes, had been carried into effect, it would have been a most advantageous undertaking for the community at large.

But my task is now drawing to an end; and I have only to relate what happened at the conclusion of the last act of my very serviceable and eventful life, the which I will proceed to do with as much brevity as is consistent with the nature of that free and faithful spirit in which the whole of these notandums have been indited.

Chapter 47

Resignation

Shortly after the Battle of Waterloo, I began to see that a change was coming in among us. There was less work for the people to do, no outgate in the army for roving and idle spirits, and those who had tacks of the town lands complained of slack markets; indeed, in my own double vocation of the cloth shop and wine cellar, I had a taste and experience of the general declension that would of a necessity ensue, when the great outlay of government and the discharge from public employ drew more and more to an issue. So I bethought me, that being now well stricken in years, and, though I say it that should not, likewise a man in good respect and circumstances, it would be a prudent thing to retire and secede entirely from all farther intromissions with public affairs.

Accordingly, towards the midsummer of the year 1816, I commenced in a far off way to give notice, that at Michaelmas I intended to abdicate my authority and power, to which intimations little heed was at first given; but gradually the seed took with the soil, and began to swell and shoot up, in so much that, by the middle of August, it was an understood thing that I was to retire from the council, and refrain entirely from the part I had so long played with credit in the burgh.

When people first began to believe that I was in earnest, I cannot but acknowledge I was remonstrated with by many, and that not a few were pleased to say my resignation would be a public loss; but these expressions, and the disposition of them, wore away before Michaelmas came; and I had some sense of the feeling which the fluctuating gratitude of the multitude often causes to rise in the breasts of those who have ettled their best to serve the ungrateful populace. However, I considered with myself that it would not do for me, after what I had done for the town and commonality, to go out of office like a knotless thread, and that, as a something was of right due to me, I would be committing an act of injustice to my family if I neglected the means of realizing the same. But it was a task of delicacy, and who could I prompt to tell the town-council to do what they ought to do? I could not myself speak of my own services—I could ask nothing. Truly it was a subject that cost me no small cogitation; for I could not confide it even to the wife of my bosom. However, I gained my end, and the means and method thereof may advantage other public characters, in a similar strait, to know and understand.

Seeing that nothing was moving onwards in men's minds to do the act of courtesy to me, so justly my due, on the Saturday before Michaelmas I invited Mr Mucklewheel, the hosier, (who had the year before been chosen into the council, in the place of old Mr Peevie, who had a paralytic, and never in consequence was made a bailie,) to take a glass of toddy with me, a way and method of peutering with the councillors, one by one, that I often found of a great efficacy in bringing their understandings into a docile state; and when we had discussed one cheerer with the usual clishmaclaver of the times, I began, as we were both birzing the sugar for the second, to speak with a circumbendibus about my resignation of the trusts I had so long held with profit to the community.

"Mr Mucklewheel," quo' I "ye're but a young man, and no versed yet, as ye will be, in the policy and diplomatics that are requisite in the management of the town, and therefore I need not say any thing to you about what I have got an inkling of, as to the intents of the new magistrates and council towards me. It's very true that I have been long a faithful servant to the public, but he's a weak man who looks to any reward from the people; and after the experience I have had, I would certainly prove myself to be one of the very weakest, if I thought it was likely, that either anent the piece of plate and the vote of thanks, any body would take a speciality of trouble."

To this Mr Mucklewheel answered, that he was glad to hear such a compliment was intended; "No man," said he, "more richly deserves a handsome token of public respect, and I will surely give the proposal all the countenance and support in my power possible to do."

"As to that," I replied, pouring in the rum and helping myself to the warm water, "I entertain no doubt, and I have every confidence that the proposal, when it is made, will be in a manner unanimously approved. But, Mr Mucklewheel, what's every body's business, is nobody's. I have heard of no one that's to bring the matter forward; it's all fair and smooth to speak of such things in holes and corners, but to face the public with them is another sort of thing. For few men can abide to see honours conferred on their neighbours, though between ourselves, Mr Mucklewheel, every man in a public trust should, for his own sake, further and promote the bestowing of public rewards on his predecessors; because looking forward to the time when he must himself become a predecessor, he should think how he would feel were he, like me, after a magistracy of near to fifty years, to sink into the humility of a private station, as if he had never been any thing in the world. In sooth, Mr Mucklewheel, I'll no deny that it's a satisfaction to me to think that maybe the piece of plate and the vote of thanks will be forthcoming; at the same time, unless they are both brought to a bearing in a proper manner, I would rather nothing was done at all."

"Ye may depend on't," said Mr Mucklewheel, that it will be done very properly, and in a manner to do credit both to you and the council. I'll speak to Bailie Shuttlethrift, the new provost, to propose the thing himself, and that I'll second it."

"Hooly, hooly, friend," quo' I, with a laugh of jocularity, no ill—pleased to see to what effect I had worked upon him; "that will never do; ye're but a greenhorn in public affairs. The provost maun ken nothing about it, or let on that he doesna ken, which is the same thing, for folk would say that he was ettling at something of the kind for himself, and was only eager for a precedent. It would, therefore, ne'er do to speak to him. But Mr Birky, who is to be elected into the council in my stead, would be a very proper person. For ye ken coming in as my successor, it would very naturally fall to him to speak modestly of himself. compared with me, and therefore I think he is the fittest person to make the proposal, and you, as the next youngest that has been taken in, might second the same." Mr Mucklewheel agreed with me, that certainly the thing would come with the best grace from my successor. "But I doubt," was my answer, "if he kens aught of the matter; ye might however enquire. In short, Mr Mucklewheel, ye see it requires a canny hand to manage public affairs, and a sound discretion to know who are the fittest to work in them. If the case were not my own, and if I was speaking for an other that had done for the town what I have done, the task would be easy. For I would just rise in my place, and say as a thing of course, and admitted on all hands, 'Gentlemen, it would be a very wrong thing of us, to let Mr Mucklewheel, (that is, supposing you were me,) who has so long been a fellow-labourer with us, to quit his place here without some mark of our own esteem for him as a man, and some testimony from the council to his merits as a magistrate. Every body knows that he has been for near to fifty years a distinguished character, and has thrice filled the very highest post in the burgh; that many great improvements have been made in his time, wherein his influence and wisdom was very evident; I would therefore propose, that a committee should be appointed to consider of the best means of expressing our sense of his services, in which I shall be very happy to assist, provided the provost will consent to act as chairman.'

"That's the way I would open the business; and were I the seconder, as you are to be to Mr Birky, I would say, 'The worthy councillor has but anticipated what every one was desirous to propose, and although a committee is a very fit way of doing the thing respectfully, there is yet a far better, and that is, for the council now sitting to come at once to a resolution on the subject, then a committee may be appointed to carry that resolution into effect.'

"Having said this, you might advert first to the vote of thanks, and then to the piece of plate, to remain with the gentleman's family as a monumental testimony of the opinion which was entertained by the community of his services and character."

Having in this judicious manner primed Mr Mucklewheel as to the procedure, I suddenly recollected that I had a letter to write to catch the post, and having told him so, "Maybe," quo' I, "ye would step the length of Mr Birky's and see how he is inclined, and by the time I am done writing, ye can be back; for after all that we have been saying, and the warm and friendly interest you have taken in this business, I really would not wish my friends to stir in it, unless it is to be done in a satisfactory manner."

Mr Mucklewheel accordingly went to Mr Birky, who had of course heard nothing of the subject, but they came back together, and he was very vogie with the notion of making a speech before the council, for he was an upsetting young man. In short, the matter was so set forward, that, on the Monday following, it was all over the town that I was to get a piece of plate at my resignation, and the whole affair proceeded so well to an issue, that the same was brought to a head to a wish. Thus had I the great satisfaction of going to my repose as a private citizen with a very handsome silver cup, bearing an inscription in the Latin tongue, of the time I had been in the council, guildry, and magistracy; and although, in the outset of my public life, some of my dealings may have been leavened with the leaven of antiquity, yet, upon the whole, it will not be found, I think, that, one thing weighed with another, I have been an unprofitable servant to the community. Magistrates and rulers must rule according to the maxims and affections of the world; at least, whenever I tried any other way, strange obstacles started up in the opinions of men against me, and my purest intents were often more criticised than some which were less disinterested; so much is it the natural humour of mankind to jealouse and doubt the integrity of all those who are in authority and power, especially when they see them deviating from the practices of their predecessors. Posterity, therefore, or I am far mistaken, will not be angered at my plain dealing with regard to the small motives of private advantage of which I have made mention, since it has been my endeavour to show and to acknowledge, that there is a reforming spirit abroad among men, and that really the world is gradually growing better—slowly I allow; but still it is growing better, and the main profit of the improvement will be reaped by those who are ordained to come after us.

The Entail, or The Lairds of Grippy

TO THE KING
SIRE,

with the profoundest sense of your Majesty's gracious condescension, the Author of this work has now the honour to lay it, by permission, at your Majesty's feet.

It belongs to a series of sketches, in which he has attempted to describe characters and manners peculiar to the most ancient, and most loyal, portion of all your Majesty's dominions;—it embraces a great part of the last century, the most prosperous period in the annals of Scotland, and singularly glorious to the administration of your Majesty's Illustrious Family;—it has been written since the era of your Majesty's joyous Visit to the venerable home of your Royal Ancestors;—and it is presented as a humble memorial of the feelings with which the Author, in common with all his countrymen, did homage to the King at Holyrood.

He has the happiness to be,
SIRE,
Your Majesty's
Most dutiful and most faithful
subject and servant

Edinburgh, 3d December 1822.

Chapter I

Claud Walkinshaw was the sole surviving male heir of the Walkinshaws of Kittlestonheugh. His grandfather, the last Laird of the line, deluded by the golden visions that allured so many of the Scottish gentry to embark their fortunes in the Darien Expedition, sent his only son, the father of Claud, in one of the ships fitted out at Cartsdyke, and with him an adventure in which he had staked more than the whole value of his estate. But, as it is not our intention to fatigue the reader with any very circumstantial account of the state of the Laird's family, we shall pass over, with all expedient brevity, the domestic history of Claud's childhood. He was scarcely a year old when his father sailed, and his mother died of a broken heart, on hearing that her husband, with many of his companions, had perished of disease and famine among the swamps of the Mosquito shore. The Kittlestonheugh estate was soon after sold, and the Laird, with Claud, retired into Glasgow, where he rented the upper part of a back house, in Aird's Close, in the Drygate. The only servant whom, in this altered state, he could afford to retain, or rather the only one that he could not get rid of, owing to her age and infirmities, was Maudge Dobbie, who, in her youth, was bairnswoman to his son. She had been upwards of forty years in the servitude of his house; and the situation she had filled to the father of Claud did not tend to diminish the kindliness with which she regarded the child, especially when, by the ruin of her master, there was none but herself to attend him.

The charms of Maudge had, even in her vernal years, been confined to her warm and affectionate feelings; and, at this period, she was twisted east and west, and hither and yont, and Time, in the shape of old age, hung so embracingly round her neck, that this weight had bent her into a hoop. Yet, thus deformed and aged, she was not without qualities that might have endeared her to a more generous boy. Her father had been schoolmaster in the village of Kittleston; and under his tuition, before she was sent, as the phrase then was, to seek her bread in the world, she had acquired a few of the elements of learning beyond those which, in that period, fell to the common lot of female domestics: and she was thus enabled, not only to teach the orphan reading and writing, but even to supply him with some knowledge of arithmetic, particularly addition and the multiplication table. She also possessed a rich stock of goblin lore and romantic stories, the recital of which had given the father of Claud the taste for adventure that induced him to embark in the ill-fated expedition. These, however, were not so congenial to the less sanguine temperament of the son, who early preferred the history of Whittington and his Cat to the achievements of Sir William Wallace; and 'Tak your auld cloak about you,' ever seemed to him a thousand times more sensible than Chevy Chace. As for that doleful ditty, the Flowers of the Forest, it was worse than the Babes in the Wood; and Gil Morrice more wearisome than Death and the Lady.

The solitary old Laird had not been long settled in his sequestered and humble town-retreat, when a change became visible both in his appearance and manners. He had been formerly bustling, vigorous, hearty, and social; but from the first account of the death of his son, and the ruin of his fortune, he grew thoughtful and sedentary, and shunned the approach of strangers, and retired from the visits of his friends. Sometimes he sat for whole days, without speaking, and without even noticing the kitten-like gambols of his grandson; at others he would fondle over the child, and caress him with more than a grandfather's affection; again, he would peevishly brush the boy away as he clasped his knees, and hurry out of the house with short and agitated steps. His respectable portliness disappeared; his clothes began to hang loosely upon him; his colour fled; his face withered; and his legs wasted into meagre shanks. Before the end of the first twelve months, he was either unwilling or unable to move unassisted from the old arm chair, in which he sat from morning to night, with his grey head drooping over his breast; and one evening, when Maudge went to assist him to undress, she found he had been for some time dead.

After the funeral, Maudge removed with the pennyless orphan to a garret room in the Saltmarket, where she endeavoured to earn for him and herself the humble aliment of meal and salt, by working stockings; her infirmities and figure having disqualified her from the more profitable industry of the spinning-wheel. In this condition she remained for some time, pinched with poverty, but still patient with her lot, and preserving, nevertheless, a neat and decent exterior.

It was only in the calm of the summer Sabbath evenings that she indulged in the luxury of a view of the country; and her usual walk on those occasions, with Claud in her hand, was along the brow of Whitehill, which she perhaps preferred, because it afforded her a distant view of the scenes of her happier days; and while she pointed out to Claud the hills and lands of his forefathers, she exhorted him to make it his constant endeavour to redeem them, if possible, from their new possessors, regularly concluding her admonition with some sketch or portrait of the hereditary grandeur of his ancestors.

One afternoon, while she was thus engaged, Provost Gorbals and his wife made their appearance.

The Provost was a man in flourishing circumstances, and he was then walking with his lady to choose a scite for a country-house which they had long talked of building. They were a stately corpulent couple, well befitting the magisterial consequence of the husband.

Mrs Gorbals was arrayed in a stiff and costly yellow brocade, magnificently embroidered with flowers, the least of which was peony; but the exuberance of her ruffle cuffs and flounces, the richness of her lace apron, with the vast head-dress of catgut and millinery, together with her blue satin mantle, trimmed with ermine, are items in the gorgeous paraphernalia of the Glasgow ladies of that time, to which the pencil of some abler limner can alone do justice.

The appearance of the Provost himself became his dignity, and corresponded with the affluent garniture of his lady: it was indeed such, that, even had he not worn the golden chains of his dignity, there would have been no difficulty in determining him to be some personage dressed with at least a little brief authority. Over the magisterial vestments of black velvet, he wore a new scarlet cloak, although the day had been one of the sultriest in July; and, with a lofty consequential air, and an ample display of the corporeal acquisition which he had made at his own and other well furnished tables, he moved along, swinging at every step his tall golden-headed cane with the solemnity of a mandarine.

Claud was filled with wonder and awe at the sight of such splendid examples of Glasgow pomp and prosperity, but Maudge speedily rebuked his juvenile admiration.

'They're no worth the looking at,' said she; 'had ye but seen the last Leddy Kittleston heugh, your ain muckle respekit grandmother, and her twa sisters, in their hench-hoops, with their fans in their han's—the three in a row would hae soopit the whole breadth o'the Trongate—ye would hae seen something. They were nane o' your new-made leddies, but come o' a pedigree. Foul would hae been the gait, and drooking the shower, that would hae gart them jook their heads intil the door o' ony sic thing as a Glasgow bailie—Na; Claudie, my lamb, thou maun lift thy een aboon the trash o' the town, and ay keep mind that the hills are standing yet that might hae been thy ain; and so may they yet be, an thou can but master the pride o' back and belly, and seek for something mair solid than the bravery o' sic a Solomon in all his glory as yon Provost Gorbals.—Heh, sirs, what a kyteful o' pride's yon'er! and yet I would be nane surprised the morn to hear that the Nechabudnezzar was a' gane to pigs and whistles, and driven out wi' the divors bill to the barren pastures of bankruptcy.'

Chapter II

After taking a stroll round the brow of the hill, Provost Gorbals and his lady approached the spot where Maudge and Claud were sitting. As they drew near, the old woman rose, for she recognised in Mrs Gorbals one of the former visitors at Kittlestonheugh. The figure of Maudge herself was so remarkable, that, seen once, it was seldom forgotten, and the worthy lady, almost at the same instant, said to the Provost,—

'Eh! Megsty, gudeman, if I dinna think yon's auld Kittlestonheugh's crookit bairnswoman. I won'er what's come o' the Laird, poor bodie, sin' he was rookit by the Darien. Eh! what an alteration it was to Mrs Walkinshaw, his gudedochter. She was a bonny bodie; but frae the time o' the sore news, she croynt awa, and her life gied out like the snuff o' a can'le. Hey, Magdalene Dobbie, come hither to me, I'm wanting to speak to thee.'

Maudge, at this shrill obstreperous summons, leading Claud by the hand, went forward to the lady, who immediately said,—

'Ist 'tou aye in Kittlestonheugh's service, and what's come o' him, sin' his lan' was roupit?'

Maudge replied respectfully, and with the tear in her eye, that the Laird was dead.

'Dead!' exclaimed Mrs Gorbals, 'that's very extraordinare. I doubt he was ill off at his latter end. Whar did he die, poor man?'

'We were obligated,' said Maudge, somewhat comforted by the compassionate accent of the lady, 'to come intil Glasgow, where he fell into a decay o' nature.' And she added, with a sigh that was almost a sob, ' 'Deed, it's vera true, he died in a sare straitened circumstance, and left this helpless laddie upon my hands.'

The Provost, who had in the meantime been still looking about in quest of a site for his intended mansion, on hearing this, turned round, and putting his hand in his pocket, said,—

'An' is this Kittlestonheugh's oe? I'm sure it's a vera pityful thing o' you, lucky, to tak compassion on the orphan; hae, my laddie, there's a saxpence.'

'Saxpence, gudeman!' exclaimed the Provost's lady, 'ye'll ne'er even your han' wi' a saxpence to the like of Kittlestonheugh, for sae we're bound in nature to call him, landless though his laird-ship now be; poor bairn, I'm wae for't. Ye ken his mother was sib to mine by the father's side, and blood's thicker than water ony day.'

Generosity is in some degree one of the necessary qualifications of a Glasgow magistrate, and Provost Gorbals being as well endowed with it as any of his successors have been since, was not displeased with the benevolent warmth of his wife, especially when he understood that Claud was of their own kin. On the contrary, he said affectionately,—

'Really it was vera thoughtless o' me, Liezy, my dear; but ye ken I have na an instinct to make me acquaint wi' the particulars of folk, before hearing about them. I'm sure no living soul can have a greater compassion than myself for gentle blood come to need-cessity.' Mrs Gorbals, however, instead of replying to this remark—indeed, what could she say, for experience had taught her that it was perfectly just—addressed herself again to Maudge.

'And whar dost t'ou live? and what hast t'ou to live upon?'

'I hae but the mercy of Providence,' was the humble answer of honest Maudge, 'and a garret-room in John Sinclair's lan'. I ettle as weel as I can for a morsel, by working stockings; but Claud's a rumbling laddie, and needs mair than I hae to gi'e him: a young appetite's a growing evil in the poor's aught.'

The Provost and his wife looked kindly at each other, and the latter added,—

'Gudeman, ye maun do something for them. It'll no fare the waur wi' our basket and our store.'

And Maudge was in consequence requested to bring Claud with her that evening to the Provost's house in the Bridgegate. 'I think,' added Mrs Gorbals, 'that our Hughoc's auld claes will just do for him; and Maudge, keep a good heart, we'll no let thee want. I won'er 'tou did na think of making an application to us afore.'

'No,' replied the old woman, 'I could ne'er do that—I would hae been in an unco strait before I would hae begget on my own account; and how could I think o' disgracing the family? Any help that the Lord may dispose your hearts to gi'e, I'll accept wi' great thankfulness, but an almous is what I hope he'll ne'er put it upon me to seek; and though Claud be for the present a weight and burden, yet, an he's sparet, he'll be able belyve to do something for himsel.'

Both the Provost and Mrs Gorbals commended her spirit; and, from this interview, the situation of Maudge was considerably improved by their constant kindness. Doubtless, had Mr Gorbals lived, he would have assisted Claud into business, but, dying suddenly, his circumstances were discovered to be less flourishing than the world had imagined, and his widow found herself constrained to abridge her wonted liberality.

Maudge, however, wrestled with poverty as well as she could, till Claud had attained his eleventh year, when she thought he was of a sufficient capacity to do something for himself. Accordingly, she intimated to Mrs Gorbals that she hoped it would be in her power to help her with the loan of a guinea to set him out in the world with a pack. This the lady readily promised, but advised her to make application first to his relation Miss Christiana Heritage.

'She's in a bein' circumstance,' said Mrs Gorbals, 'for her father, auld Windywa's, left her weel on to five hundred pounds, and her cousin, Lord Killycrankie, ane of the fifteen that ay staid in our house when he rode the Circuit, being heir of entail to her father, alloos her the use of the house, so that she's in a way to do muckle for the laddie, if her heart were so inclined.'

Maudge, agreeably to this suggestion, went next day to Windywalls; but we must reserve our account of the mansion and its mistress to enrich our next chapter, for Miss Christiana was, even in our day and generation, a personage of no small consequence in her own eyes: indeed, for that matter, she was no less in ours, if we may judge by the niche which she occupies in the gallery of our recollection, after the lapse of more than fifty years.

Chapter III

In the course of the same summer in which we commenced those grammar-school acquirements, that, in after life, have been so deservedly celebrated, our revered relative, the late old Lady Havers, carried us in her infirm dowagerian chariot to pay her annual visit to Miss Christiana Heritage. In the admiration with which we contemplated the venerable mansion and its ancient mistress, an indistinct vision rises in our fancy of a large irregular white-washed house, with a tall turnpike stair-case; over the low and dwarfish arched door of which a huge cable was carved in stone, and dropped in a knotted festoon at each side. The traditions of the neighbourhood ascribed this carving to the Pictish sculptors, who executed the principal ornaments of the High Kirk of Glasgow.

On entering under this feudal arch we ascended a spiral stair, and were shown into a large and lofty room, on three sides of which, each far in a deep recess, was a narrow window glazed with lozens of yellow glass, that seemed scarcely more transparent than horn. The walls were hung with tapestry, from which tremendous forms, in warlike attitudes and with grim aspects, frowned in apparitional obscurity.

But of all the circumstances of a visit, which we must ever consider as a glimpse into the presence-chamber of the olden time, none made so deep and so vivid an impression upon our young remembrance as the appearance and deportment of Miss Christiana herself. She had been apprised of Lady Havers coming, and was seated in state to receive her, on a large settee adorned with ancestral needle work. She rose as our venerable relation entered the room. Alas! we have lived to know that we shall never again behold the ceremonial of a reception half so solemnly performed.

Miss Christiana was dressed in a courtly suit of purple Genoese velvet; her petticoat, spread by her hoop, extended almost to arms-length at each side. The ruffle cuffs which hung at her elbows loaded with lead, were coeval with the Union, having been worn by her mother when she attended her husband to that assembly of the States of Scotland, which put an end to the independence and poverty of the kingdom. But who, at this distance of time, shall presume to estimate the altitude of the Babylonian tower of toupees and lappets which adorned Miss Christiana's brow?

It is probable, that the reception which she gave to poor Maudge and Claud was not quite so ceremonious as ours; for the substantial benison of the visit was but half-a-crown. Mrs Gorbals, on hearing this, exclaimed with a just indignation against the near-be-gawn Miss Christiana, and setting herself actively to work, soon collected, among her acquaintance, a small sum sufficient to enable Maudge to buy and furnish a pack for Claud. James Bridle the saddlemaker, who had worked for his father, gave him a present of a strap to sling it over his shoulder; and thus, with a judicious selection of godly and humorous tracts, curtain rings, sleeve buttons, together with a compendious assortment of needles and pins, thimbles, stay-laces and garters, with a bunch of ballads and excellent new songs, Claud Walkinshaw espoused his fortune.

His excursions at first were confined to the neighbouring villages, and as he was sly and gabby, he soon contrived to get in about the good-will of the farmers' wives, and in process of time, few pedlars in all the west country were better liked, though every one complained that he was the dearest and the gairest.

His success equalled the most sanguine expectations of Maudge, but Mrs Gorbals thought he might have recollected, somewhat better than he did, the kindness and care with which the affectionate old creature had struggled to support him in his helplessness. As often, however, as that warm-hearted lady inquired if he gave her any of his winnings, Maudge was obliged to say, 'I hope, poor lad, he has more sense than to think o' the like o' me. Is na he striving to make a conquest of the lands of his forefathers? Ye ken he's come o' gentle blood, and I am nae better than his servan'.'

But although Maudge spoke thus generously, still sometimes, when she had afterwards become bedrid, and was left to languish and linger out the remnant of age in her solitary garret, comforted only by the occasional visits and charitable attentions of Mrs Gorbals, the wish would now and then rise, that Claud, when he was prospering in the traffic of the Borders, would whiles' think of her forlorn condition. But it was the lambent play of affection, in which anxiety to see him again before she died was stronger than any other feeling, and as often as she felt it moving her to repine at his inattention, she would turn herself to the wall, and implore the Father of Mercies to prosper his honest endeavours, and that he might ne'er be troubled in his industry with any thought about such a burden as it had pleased Heaven to make her to the world.

After having been bedrid for about the space of two years, Maudge died. Claud, in the mean time, was thriving as well as the prigging wives and higgling girls in his beat between the Nith and the Tyne would permit.

Nor was there any pedlar better known at the fairs of the Border towns, or who displayed on those occasions such a rich assortment of goods. It was thought by some, that, in choosing that remote country for the scene of his itinerant trade, he was actuated by some sentiment of reverence for the former consequence of his family. But, as faithful historians, we are compelled to remind the reader, that he was too worldly wise to indulge himself with any thing so romantic; the absolute fact being, that, after trying many other parts of the country, he found the Borders the most profitable, and that the inhabitants were also the most hospitable customers,—no small item in the arithmetical philosophy of a pedlar.

Chapter IV

About twenty years after the death of Maudge, Claud returned to Glasgow with five hundred pounds above the world, and settled himself as a cloth-merchant, in a shop under the piazza of a house which occupied part of the ground where the Exchange now stands. The resolution which he had early formed to redeem the inheritance of his ancestors, and which his old affectionate benefactress had perhaps inspired, as well as cherished, was grown into a habit. His carefueness, his assiduity, his parsimony, his very honesty, had no other object nor motive; it was the actuating principle of his life. Some years after he had settled in Glasgow, his savings and gathering enabled him to purchase the farm of Grippy, a part of the patrimony of his family.

The feelings of the mariner returning home, when he again beholds the rising hills of his native land, and the joys and fears of the father's bosom, when, after a long absence, he approaches the abode of his children, are tame and calm, compared to the deep and greedy satisfaction with which the persevering pedlar received the earth and stone that gave him infeftment of that cold and sterile portion of his forefathers' estate. In the same moment he formed a resolution worthy of the sentiment he then felt,—a sentiment which, in a less sordid breast, might have almost partaken of the pride of virtue. He resolved to marry, and beget children, and entail the property, that none of his descendants might ever have it in their power to commit the imprudence which had brought his grandfather to a morsel, and thrown himself on the world. And the same night, after maturely considering the prospects of all the heiresses within the probable scope of his ambition, he resolved that his affections should be directed towards Miss Girzy Hypel, the only daughter of Malachi Hypel, the Laird of Plealands.

They were in some degree related, and he had been led to think of her from an incident which occurred on the day he made the purchase. Her father was, at the time, in Glasgow, attending the Circuit; for, as often as the judges visited the city, he had some dispute with a neighbour or a tenant that required their interposition. Having heard of what had taken place, he called on Claud to congratulate him on the recovery of so much of his family inheritance.

'I hear,' said the Laird, on entering the shop, and proffering his hand across the counter, 'that ye hae gotten a sappy bargain o' the Grippy. It's true some o' the lands are but cauld; howsever, cousin, ne'er fash your thumb, Glasgow's on the thrive, and ye hae as many een in your head, for an advantage, as ony body I ken. But now that ye hae gotten a house, wha's to be the leddy? I'm sure ye might do waur than cast a sheep's e'e in at our door; my dochter Girzy's o' your ain flesh and blood; I dinna see ony moral impossibility in her becoming, as the Psalmist says, "bone of thy bone."'

Claud replied in his wonted couthy manner:

'Nane o' your jokes, Laird,—me even mysel to your dochter? Na, na, Plealands, that canna be thought o' now a days. But, no to make a ridicule of sic a solemn concern, it's vera true that, had na my grandfather, when he was grown doited, sent out a' the Kittlestonheugh in a cargo o' playocks to the Darien, I might hae been in a state and condition to look at Miss Girzy; but, ye ken, I hae a lang clue to wind before I maun think o' playing the ba' wi' Fortune, in ettling so far aboun my reach.'

'Snuffs o' tobacco,' exclaimed the Laird,—'are nae ye sib to oursels? and, if ye dinna fail by your ain blateness, our Girzy's no surely past speaking to. Just lay your leg, my man, o'er a side o' horse flesh, and come your ways, some Saturday, to spier her price.'

It was upon this delicate hint that Grippy was induced to think of Miss Girzy Hypel; but finding that he was deemed a fit match for her, and might get her when he would, he deferred the visit until he had cast about among the other neighbouring lairds' families for a better, that is to say, a richer match. In this, whether he met with repulsive receptions, or found no satisfactory answers to his inquiries, is not quite certain; but, as we have said, in the same night on which he took legal possession of his purchase, he resolved to visit Plealands; and in order that the family might not be taken unawares, he sent a letter next day by the Ayr carrier to apprise the Laird of his intention, provided it was convenient to receive him for a night. To this letter, by the return of Johnny Drizen, the carrier, on the week following, he received such a cordial reply, that he was induced to send for Cornelius Luke, the tailor, a douce and respectable man, and one of the elders of the Tron Kirk.

'Come your ways, Cornie,' said the intending lover; 'I want to speak to you anent what's doing about the new kirk on the Green Know.'

'Doing, Mr Walkinshaw!—it's a doing that our bairns' bairns will ne'er hear the end o'—a rank and carnal innovation on the spirit o' the Kirk o' Scotland,' replied the elder—'It's to be after the fashion o' some prelatic Babel in Lon'on, and they hae christened it already by the papistical name o' St Andrew—a sore thing that, Mr Walkinshaw; but the Lord has set his face against it, and the builders thereof are smitten as wi' a confusion o' tongues, in the lack o' siller to fulfil their idolatrous intents—Blessed be His name for evermore! But was na Mr Kilfuddy, wha preached for Mr Anderson last Sabbath, most sweet and delectable on the vanities of this life, in his forenoon lecture? and did na ye think, when he spoke o' that seventh wonder o' the world, the temple of Diana, and enlarged wi' sic pith and marrow on the idolaters in Ephesus, that he was looking o'er his shouther at Lowrie Dinwiddie and Provost Aiton, who are no wrang't in being wytid wi' the sin o' this inordinate superstructure?—Mr Walkinshaw, am nae prophet, as ye will ken, but I can see that the day's no far aff, when ministers of the gospel in Glasgow will be seen chambering and wantoning to the sound o' the kist fu' o' whistles, wi' the seven-headed beast routing its choruses at every o'ercome o' the spring.'

Which prediction was in our own day and generation to a great degree fulfilled; at the time, however, it only served to move the pawkie cloth-merchant to say,

'Nae doubt, Cornie, the world's like the tod's whelp, aye the aulder the waur; but I trust we'll hear news in the land before the like o' that comes to pass. Howsever, in the words of truth and holiness, "sufficient for the day is the evil thereof," and let us hope, that a regenerating spirit may go forth to the ends o' the earth, and that all the sons of men will not be utterly cut up, root and branch.'

'No: be thankit,' said Cornelius, the tailor—'even of those that shall live in the latter days, a remnant will be saved.' 'That's a great comfort, Mr Luke, to us a',' replied Claud;—'but, talking o' remnants, I hae a bit blue o' superfine; it has been lang on hand, and the moths are beginning to meddle wi't—I won'er if ye could mak me a coat o't?'

The remnant was then produced on the counter, and Cornelius, after inspecting it carefully, declared, that, 'with the help of a steek or twa of darning, that would na be percep, it would do very well.' The cloth was accordingly delivered to him, with strict injunctions to have it ready by Friday, and with all the requisite et ceteras to complete a coat, he left the shop greatly edified, as he told his wife, by the godly salutations of Mr Walkinshaw's spirit; 'wherein,' as he said, 'there was a kithing of fruit meet for repentance; a foretaste o' things that pertain not to this life; a receiving o' the erls of righteousness and peace, which passeth all understanding, and endureth for evermore.'

'I'm blithe to hear't,' was the worthy woman's answer, 'for he's an even down Nabal—a perfect penure pig, that I ne'er could abide since he wauld na lend poor old Mrs Gorbals, the provost's widow, that, they say, set him up in the world, the sma' soom o' five pounds, to help her wi' the outfit o' her oe when he was gaun to Virginia, a clerk to Bailie Cross.'

Chapter V

When Claud was duly equipped by Cornelius Luke, in the best fashion of that period, for a bien cloth-merchant of the discreet age of forty-seven, a message was sent by his shop lad, Jock Gleg, to Rob Wallace, the horsecouper in the Gallowgate, to have his beast in readiness next morning by seven o'clock, the intending lover having, several days before, bespoke it for the occasion.

Accordingly, at seven o'clock on Saturday morning, Rob was with the horse himself, at the entry to Cochran's Land, in the Candleriggs, where Claud then lodged, and the wooer, in the sprucest cut of his tailor, with a long silver-headed whip in his hand, borrowed from his friend and customer, Bailie Murdoch, attended by Jock Gleg, carrying a stool, came to the close mouth.

'I'm thinking, Mr Walkinshaw,' said Rob, the horse-couper, 'that ye would na be the waur of a spur, an it were only on the ae heel.'

'We maun do our best without that commodity, Rob,' replied Claud, trying to crack his whip in a gallant style, but unfortunately cutting his own leg through the dark blue rig-and-fur gamashins; for he judiciously considered, that, for so short a journey, and that, too, on speculation, it was not worth his while to get a pair of boots.

Rob drew up the horse, and Jock having placed the stool, Claud put his right foot in the stirrup, at which Rob and some of the students of the college, who happened to be attracted to the spot, with diverse others then and there present, set up a loud shout of laughter, much to his molestation. But surely no man is expected to know by instinct the proper way of mounting a horse; and this was the first time that Claud had ever ascended the back of any quadruped.

When he had clambered into the saddle, Rob led the horse into the middle of the street, and the beast, of its own accord, walked soberly across the Trongate towards the Stock well. The conduct of the horse, for some time, was indeed most considerate, and, in consequence, although Claud hung heavily over his neck, and held him as fast as possible with his knees, he passed the bridge, and cleared the buildings beyond, without attracting, in any particular degree, the admiration of the public towards his rider. But, in an unguarded moment, the infatuated Claud rashly thought it necessary to employ the Bailie's whip, and the horse, so admonished, quickened his pace to a trot. 'Heavens, ca' they this riding?' exclaimed Claud, and almost bit his tongue through in the utterance. However, by the time they reached Cathcart, it was quite surprising to see how well he worked in the saddle; and, notwithstanding the continued jolting, how nobly he preserved his balance. But, on entering that village, all the dogs, in the most terrifying manner, came rushing out from the cottage doors, and pursued the trotting horse with such bark and bay, that the poor animal saw no other for't, but to trot from them faster and faster. The noise of the dogs, and of a passenger on horseback, drew forth the inhabitants, and at every door might be seen beldams with flannel caps, and mothers with babies in their arms, and clusters of children around them. It was the general opinion among all the spectators, on seeing the spruce new clothes of Claud, and his vaulting horsemanship, that he could be no less a personage than the Lord Provost of Glasgow.

Among them were a few country lads, who, perceiving how little the rider's seat of honour was accustomed to a saddle, had the wickedness to encourage and egg on the dogs to attack the horse still more furiously; but, notwithstanding their malice, Claud still kept his seat, until all the dogs but one devil of a terrier had retired from the pursuit: nothing could equal the spirit and pertinacity with which that implacable cur hung upon the rear, and snapped at the heels of the horse. Claud, who durst not venture to look behind, lest he should lose his balance, several times damned the dog with great sincerity, and tried to lash him away with Bailie Murdoch's silver-headed whip, but the terrier would not desist.

How long the attack might have continued, there is certainly no telling, as it was quickly determined by one of those lucky hits of fortune which are so desirable in life. The long lash of the Bailie's whip, in one of Claud's blind attempts, happily knotted itself round the neck of the dog. The horse, at the same moment, started forward into that pleasant speed at which the pilgrims of yore were wont to pass from London to the shrine of St Thomas a Becket at Canterbury, (which, for brevity, is in vulgar parlance called, in consequence, a canter;) and Claud dragged the terrier at his whip-string end, like an angler who has hooked a salmon that he cannot raise out of the water, until he met with Johnny Drizen, the Ayr carrier, coming on his weekly journey to Glasgow.

'Lordsake, Mr Walkinshaw!' exclaimed the carrier, as he drew his horse aside—'in the name of the Lord, whare are ye gaun,' and what's that ye're hauling ahint you?'

'For the love of Heaven, Johnny,' replied the distressed cloth-merchant, pale with apprehension, and perspiring at every pore,—'for the love of Heaven, stop this desperate beast!'

The tone of terror and accent of anguish in which this invocation was uttered, had such an effect on the humanity and feelings of the Ayr carrier, that he ran towards Claud with the ardour of a philanthropist, and seized the horse by the bridle rings. Claud, in the same moment, threw down the whip, with the strangled dog at the lash; and, making an endeavour to vault out of the saddle, fell into the mire, and materially damaged the lustre and beauty of his new coat. However, he soon regained his legs, but they so shook and trembled, that he could scarcely stand, as he bent forward with his feet widely asunder, being utterly unable for some time to endure in any other position the pain of that experience of St Sebastian's martyrdom which he had locally suffered.

His first words to the carrier were, 'Man, Johnny, this is the roughest brute that ever was created. Twa dyers wi' their beetles could na hae done me mair detriment. I dinna think I'll e'er be able to sit down again.'

This colloquy was, however, speedily put an end to, by the appearance of a covered cart, in which three ministers were returning from the synod to their respective parishes in Ayrshire; for at that time neither post-chaise nor stage-coach was numbered among the luxuries of Glasgow. One of them happened to be the identical Mr Kilfuddy of Braehill, who had lectured so learnedly about the Temple of Diana on the preceding Sunday in the Tron Church; and he being acquainted with Claud, said, as he looked out and bade the driver to stop,—

'Dear me, Mr Walkinshaw, but ye hae gotten an unco cowp. I hope nae banes are broken?'

'No,' replied Claud a little pawkily, 'no; thanks be and praise—the banes, I believe, are a' to the fore; but it's no to be expressed what I hae suffer't in the flesh.'

Some further conversation then ensued, and the result was most satisfactory, for Claud was invited to take a seat in the cart with the ministers, and induced to send his horse back to Rob Wallace by Johnny Drizen the carrier. Thus, without any material augmentation of his calamity, was he conveyed to the gate which led to Plealands. The Laird, who had all the morning been anxiously looking out for him, on seeing the cart approaching, left the house, and was standing ready at the yett to give him welcome.

Chapter VI

Plealands house stood on the bleak brow of a hill. It was not of great antiquity, having been raised by the father of Malachi; but it occupied the site of an ancient fortalice, the materials of which were employed in its construction; and as no great skill of the sculptor had been exerted to change the original form of the lintels and their ornaments, it had an air of antiquity much greater than properly belonged to its years.

About as much as the habitation had been altered from its primitive character, the master too had been modernized. But, in whatever degree he may have been supposed to have declined from the heroic bearing of his ancestors, he still inherited, in unabated vigour, the animosity of their spirit; and if the coercive influence of national improvement prevented him from being distinguished in the feud and foray, the books of sederunt, both of the Glasgow Circuit and of the Court of Session, bore ample testimony to his constancy before them in asserting supposed rights, and in vindicating supposed wrongs.

In his personal appearance, Malachi Hypel had but few pretensions to the air and grace of the gentlemen of that time. He was a coarse hard-favoured fresh-coloured carl, with a few white hairs thinly scattered over a round bald head. His eyes were small and grey, quick in the glance, and sharp in the expression. He spoke thickly and hurriedly, and although his words were all very cogently strung together, there was still an unaccountable obscurity in the precise meaning of what he said. In his usual style of dress he was rude and careless, and he commonly wore a large flat brimmed blue bonnet; but on the occasion when he came to the gate to receive Claud, he had on his Sunday suit and hat.

After the first salutations were over, he said to Claud, on seeing him walking lamely and uneasily, 'What's the matter, Grippy, that ye seem sae stiff and sair?'

'I met wi' a bit accident,' was Claud's reply: 'Rob Wallace, the horse-couper, gied me sic a deevil to ride as, I believe, never man before mounted. I would na wish my sworn enemy a greater ill than a day's journey on that beast's back, especially an he was as little used to riding as me.'

The latter clause of the sentence was muttered inwardly, for the Laird did not hear it; otherwise he would probably have indulged his humour a little at the expence of his guest, as he had a sort of taste for caustic jocularity, which the hirpling manner of Claud was, at the moment, well calculated to provoke.

On reaching the brow of the rising ground where the house stood, the leddy, as Mrs Hypel was emphatically called by the neighbouring cottars, with Miss Girzy, came out to be introduced to their relative.

Whether the leddy, a pale, pensive, delicate woman, had been informed by the Laird of the object of Claud's visit, we do not thoroughly know, but she received him with a polite and friendly respectfulness. Miss Girzy certainly was in total ignorance of the whole business, and was, therefore, not embarrassed with any virgin palpitations, nor blushing anxieties; on the contrary, she met him with the ease and freedom of an old acquaintance.

It might here be naturally expected that we should describe the charms of Miss Girzy's person, and the graces of her mind; but, in whatever degree she possessed either, she had been allowed to reach the discreet years of a Dumbarton youth in unsolicited maidenhood; indeed, with the aid of all the prospective interest of the inheritance around her, she did not make quite so tender an impression on the heart of her resolved lover as he himself could have wished. But why should we expatiate on such particulars? Let the manners and virtues of the family speak for themselves, while we proceed to relate what ensued.

Chapter VII

'Girzy,' said the Laird to his daughter, as they entered the dining-room, 'gae to thy bed and bring a cod for Mr Walkinshaw, for he'll no can thole to sit down on our hard chairs.'

Miss Girzy laughed as she retired to execute the order, while her mother continued, as she had done from the first introduction, to inspect Claud from head to foot, with a curious and something of a suspicious eye; there was even an occasional flush that gleamed through the habitual paleness of her thoughtful countenance, redder and warmer than the hectic glow of mere corporeal indisposition. Her attention, however, was soon drawn to the spacious round table, in the middle of the room, by one of the maids entering with a large pewter tureen, John Drappie, the man servant, having been that morning sent on some caption and horning business of the Laird's to Gabriel Beagle, the Kilmarnock lawyer. But, as the critics hold it indelicate to describe the details of any refectionary supply, however elegant, we must not presume to enumerate the series and succession of Scottish fare, which soon crowned the board, all served on pewter as bright as plate. Our readers must endeavour, by the aid of their own fancies, to form some idea of the various forms in which the head and harigals of the sheep, that had been put to death for the occasion, were served up, not forgetting the sonsy, savoury, sappy haggis, together with the gude fat hen, the float whey, which, in a large china punch-bowl, graced the centre of the table, and supplied the place of jellies, tarts, tartlets, and puddings.

By the time the table was burdened, Miss Girzy had returned with the pillow, which she herself placed in one of the armchairs, shaking and patting it into plumpness, as she said,—

'Come round here, Mr Walkinshaw,—I trow ye'll fin' this a saft easy seat,—well do I ken what it is to be saddle-sick mysel'. Lordsake, when I gaed in ahint my father to see the robber hang'd at Ayr, I was for mair than three days just as if I had sat doun on a heckle.'

When the cloth was removed, and the ladies had retired, the Laird opened his mind by stretching his arm across the table towards his guest, and, shaking him again heartily by the hand,—

'Weel, Grippy,' said he, 'but am blithe to see you here; and, if am no mistaen, Girzy will no be ill to woo.—Is na she a coothy and kind creature?—She'll make you a capital wife.—There's no another in the parish that kens better how to manage a house.— Man, it would do your heart gude to hear how she rants among the servan' lasses, lazy sluts, that would like nothing better than to live at heck and manger, and bring their master to a morsel; but I trow Girzy gars them keep a trig house and a birring wheel.'

'No doubt, Laird,' replied Claud, 'but it's a comfort to hae a frugal woman for a helpmate; but ye ken now-a-days it's no the fashion for bare legs to come thegither— The wife maun hae something to put in the pot as well as the man.—And, although Miss Girzy may na be a' thegither objectionable, yet it would still be a pleasant thing baith to hersel' and the man that gets her, an ye would just gi'e a bit inkling o' what she'll hae.'

'Is na she my only dochter? That's a proof and test that she'll get a',—naebody needs to be teld mair.'

'Vera true, Laird,' rejoined the suitor, 'but the leddy's life's in her lip, and if ony thing were happening to her, ye're a hale man, and wha kens what would be the upshot o' a second marriage?'

'That's looking far ben,' replied the Laird, and he presently added, more briskly, 'My wife, to be sure, is a frail woman, but she's no the gear that 'ill traike.'

In this delicate and considerate way, the overture to a purpose of marriage was opened; and, not to dwell on particulars, it is sufficient to say, that, in the course of little more than a month thereafter, Miss Girzy was translated into the Leddy of Grippy; and in due season presented her husband with a son and heir, who was baptized by the name of Charles.

When the birth was communicated to the Laird, he rode expressly to Grippy to congratulate his son-in-law on the occasion; and, when they were sitting together, in the afternoon, according to the fashion of the age, enjoying the contents of the gardevin entire, Claud warily began to sound him on a subject that lay very near his heart.

'Laird,' said he, 'ye ken the Walkinshaws of Kittlestonheugh are o' a vera ancient blood, and but for the doited prank o' my grandfather, in sending my father on that gouk's errand to the Darien, the hills are green and the land broad that should this day hae been mine; and, therefore, to put it out o' the power of posterity to play at any sic wastrie again, I mean to entail the property of the Grippy.'

'That's a very good conceit,' replied the Laird, 'and I hae mysel' had a notion of entailing the Plealands likewise.'

'So I hae heard you say,' rejoined Claud, 'and now that the bairn's born, and a laddie too, we may make ae work o't.'

'Wi' a' my heart,' replied the Laird, 'nothing can be more agreeable to me; but as I wish to preserve the name of my family, than whilk there's no a more respectit in Scotland, I'll only covenant that when Charlie succeeds me, that he'll take the name o' Hypel.'

'Ye surely, Laird, would ne'er be so unreasonable,' replied Grippy, a little somewhat hastily; 'ye can ne'er be sae unreasonable as to expect that the lad would gie up his father's name, the name o' Walkinshaw, and take only that of Hypel.'

' 'Deed would I,' said the Laird, 'for no haeing a son o' my own to come after me, it's surely very natural that I would like the Hypels to kittle again in my oe through my only dochter.'

'The Walkinshaws, I doubt,' replied Claud emphatically, 'will ne'er consent to sic an eclipse as that.'

'The lands of Plealands,' retorted the Laird, 'are worth something.'

'So it was thought, or I doubt the heir o't would nae hae been a Walkinshaw,' replied Claud, still more pertinaciously.

'Weel, weel,' said the Laird, 'dinna let us argol bargol about it; entail your own property as ye will, mine shall be on the second son; ye can ne'er object to that.'

'Second son, and the first scarce sax days auld! I tell you what it is, an ye'll no make the entail on the first, that is, on Charlie Walkinshaw, to be Walkinshaw, mind that, I'll no say what may happen in the way o' second sons.'

'The Plealands' my ain, and though I canna weel will it awa', and ne'er will sell't, yet get it wha will, he maun tak the name o' Hypel. The thing's sae settled, Grippy, and it's no for you and me to cast out about it.'

Claud made several attempts to revive the subject, and to persuade the Laird to change his mind, but he was inflexible. Still, however, being resolved, as far as in him lay, to anticipate the indiscretion of his heirs, he executed a deed of entail on Charles; and for a considerable time after the Laird was not a little confirmed in his determination not to execute any deed in favour of Charles, but to reserve his lands for the second son, by the very reason that might have led another sort of person to act differently, namely, that he understood there was no prospect of any such appearing.

Towards the end, however, of the third year after the birth of Charles, Claud communicated to the Laird, that, by some unaccountable dispensation, Mrs Walkinshaw was again in the way to be a mother, adding, 'Noo, Laird, ye'll hae your ain way o't;' and, accordingly, as soon as Walter, the second son, was born, and baptized, the lands of Plealands were entailed on him, on condition, as his grandfather intended, that he should assume the name of Hypel.

Chapter VIII

For several years after the birth of Walter, no event of any consequence happened in the affairs of Claud. He continued to persevere in the parsimonious system which had so far advanced his fortune. His wife was no less industrious on her part, for, in the meantime, she presented him with a daughter and another son, and had reared calves and grumphies innumerable, the profit of which, as she often said, was as good as the meal and malt o' the family. By their united care and endeavours, Grippy thus became one of the wealthiest men of that age in Glasgow; but although different desirable opportunities presented themselves for investing his money in other and more valuable land, he kept it ever ready to redeem any portion of his ancestral estate that might be offered for sale.

The satisfaction which he enjoyed from his accumulative prospects was not, however, without a mixture of that anxiety with which the cup of human prosperity, whether really full, or only foaming, is always embittered. The Laird, his father-in-law, in the deed of entail which he executed of the Plealands, had reserved to himself a power of revocation, in the event of his wife dying before him, in the first instance, and of Walter and George, the two younger sons of Grippy, either dying under age, or refusing to take the name of Hypel, in the second. This power, both under the circumstances, and in itself, was perfectly reasonable; and perhaps it was the more vexatious to the meditations of Claud, that it happened to be so. For he often said to his wife, as they sat of an evening by the fire-side in the dark, for the Leddy was no seamstress, and he had as little taste for literature, of course, they burned no candles when by themselves, and that was almost every night,—' I marvel, Girzy, what could gar your father put that most unsafe claw in his entail. I would na be surprised if out o' it were to come a mean of taking the property entirely frae us. For ye see, if your mither was dead, and, poor woman, she has lang been in a feckless way, there's no doubt but your father would marry again,—and married again, there can be as little doubt that he would hae childer,—so what then would become o 'ours—'

To this the worthy Leddy of Grippy would as feelingly reply,

'I'm thinking, gudeman, that ye need na tak the anxieties sae muckle to heart; for, although my mither has been, past the memory o' man, in a complaining condition, I ken nae odds o' her this many a year; her ail's like water to leather; it makes her life the tougher; and I would put mair confidence in the durability of her complaint than in my father's health; so we need na fash ourselves wi' controverting anent what may come o' the death o' either the t'ane or the t'ither.'

'But then,' replied Claud, 'ye forget the other claw about Watty and Geordie. Supposing, noo, that they were baith dead and gone, which, when we think o' the frush green kail-custock-like nature of bairns, is no an impossibility in the hands of their Maker. Will it no be the most hardest thing that ever was seen in the world for Charlie no to inherit the breadth o' the blade of a cabaudge o' a' his father's matrimonial conquest? But even should it please the Lord to spare Watty, is't no an afflicting thing, to see sic a braw property as the Plealands destined to a creature that I am sure his brother Geordie, if he lives to come to years o' discretion, will no fail to tak the law o' him for a haverel?'

'I won'er to hear you, gudeman,' exclaimed the Leddy, 'ay mislikening Watty at that gait. I'm sure he's as muckle your ain as ony o' the ither bairns; and he's a weel-tempered laddie, lilting like a linty at the door-cheek frae morning to night, when Charlie's rampaging about the farm, riving his claes on bush and brier a' the summer, tormenting the birds and mawkins out o' their vera life.'

'Singing, Girzy, I'm really distressed to hear you,' replied the father; 'to ca' yon singing; it's nothing but lal, lal, lal, lal, wi' a bow and a bend, backwards and forwards, as if the creature had na the gumpshion o' the cuckoo, the whilk has a note mair in its sang, although it has but twa.'

'It's an innocent sang for a' that; and I wish his brothers may ne'er do waur than sing the like o't. But ye just hae a spite at the bairn, gudeman, 'cause my father has made him the heir to the Plealands. That's the gospel truth o' your being so fain to gar folk trow that my Watty's daft.'

'Ye're daft, gudewife—are na we speaking here in a rational manner anent the concerns o' our family? It would be a sair heart to me to think that Watty, or any o' my bairns, were na like the lave o' the warld; but ye ken there are degrees o' capacity, Girzy, and Watty's, poor callan, we maun alloo, between oursels, has been meted by a sma' measure.'

'Weel, if ever I heard the like o' that—if the Lord has dealt the brains o' our family in mutchkins and chapins, it's my opinion, that Watty got his in the biggest stoup; for he's farther on in every sort of education than Charlie, and can say his questions without missing a word, as far as "What is forbidden in the tenth commandment?" And I ne'er hae been able to get his brother beyond "What is effectual calling?" Though, I'll no deny, he's better at the Mother's Carritches; but that a' comes o' the questions and answers being so vera short.'

'That's the vera thing, Girzy, that disturbs me,' replied the father, 'for the callan can get ony thing by heart, but, after all, he's just like a book, for every thing he learns is dead within him, and he's ne'er a prin's worth the wiser o't. But it's some satisfaction to me, that, since your father would be so unreasonably obstinate as to make away the Plealands past Charlie, he'll be punished in the gouk he's chosen for heir.'

'Gude guide us; is na that gouk your ain bairn?' exclaimed the indignant mother. 'Surely the man's fey about his entails and his properties, to speak o' the illess laddie, as if it were no better than a stirk or a stot.—Ye'll no hae the power to wrang my wean, while the breath o' life's in my bodie; so, I redde ye, tak tent to what ye try.'

'Girzy, t'ou has a head, and so has a nail.'

'Gudeman, ye hae a tongue, and so has a bell.'

'Weel, weel, but what I was saying a' concerns the benefit and advantage o' our family,' said Claud,' and ye ken as it is our duty to live for one another, and to draw a' thegither, it behoves us twa, as parents, to see that ilk is properly yocket, sin' it would surely be a great misfortune, if, after a' our frugality and gathering, the cart were cowpit in the dirt at last by ony neglek on our part.'

'That's ay what ye say,' replied the Leddy,—'a's for the family, and nothing for the dividual bairns—noo that's what I can never understand, for is na our family, Charlie, Watty, Geordie, and Meg?'

'My family,' said Claud emphatically, 'was the Walkinshaws of Kittlestonheugh, and let me tell you, Girzy Hypel, if it had na been on their account, there would ne'er hae been a Charlie nor a Watty either between you and me to plea about.'

'I'm no denying your parentage—I ne'er said a light word about it, but I canna comprehend how it is, that ye would mak step-bairns o' your ain blithesome childer on account o' a wheen auld dead patriarchs that hae been rotten, for ought I ken to the contrary, since before Abraham begat Isaac.'

'Haud thy tongue, woman, haud thy tongue. It's a thrashing o' the water, and a raising o' bells, to speak to ane o' thy capacity on things so far aboon thy understanding. Gae but the house, and see gin the supper's ready.'

In this manner, the conversations between Grippy and his Leddy were usually conducted to their natural issue, a quarrel, which ended in a rupture that was only healed by a peremptory command, which sent her on some household mission, during the performance of which the bickering was forgotten.

Chapter IX

In the meantime, as much friendliness and intercourse was maintained between the families of Grippy and Plealands as could reasonably be expected from the characters and dispositions of the respective inmates.

Shortly, however, after the conversation related in the preceding Chapter had taken place, it happened that, as Malachi was returning on horseback from Glasgow, where he had lost a law-suit, long prosecuted with the most relentless pertinacity against one of his tenants, he was overtaken on the Mairns Moor by one of those sudden squalls and showers, which the genius of the place so often raises, no doubt purposely, to conceal from the weary traveller the dreariness of the view around, and being wetted into the skin, the cold which he caught in consequence, and the irritation of his mind, brought on a fever, that terminated fatally on the fifth day.

His funeral was conducted according to the fashion of the age; but the day appointed was raw, windy, and sleety; not, however, so much so as to prevent the friends of the deceased from flocking in from every quarter. The assemblage that arrived far transcended all that can be imagined, in these economical days, of the attendance requisite on any such occasion. The gentry were shown into the dining-room, and into every room that could be fitted up with planks and deals for their reception. The barn received the tenantry, and a vast multitude—the whole clanjamphry from all the neighbouring parishes—assembled on the green in front of the house.

The Laird in his lifetime maintained a rough and free hospitality; and, as his kindred and acquaintance expected, there was neither scant nor want at his burial. The profusion of the services of seedcake and wine to the in-door guests was in the liberalest spirit of the time; and tobacco-pipes, shortbread, and brandy, unadulterated by any immersion of the gauger's rod, were distributed, with unmeasured abundance, to those in the barn and on the green.

Mr Kilfuddy, the parish minister, said grace to the gentry in the dining-room; and the elders, in like manner, performed a similar part in the other rooms. We are not sure if we may venture to assert, that grace was said to the company out of doors. Mr Taws, the dominie of Bodleton, has indeed repeatedly declared, that he did himself ask a blessing; but he has never produced any other evidence that was satisfactory to us. Indeed, what with the drinking, the blast, and the sleet, it was not reasonable to expect much attention would be paid to any prayer; and therefore we shall not insist very particularly on this point.

The Braehill church-yard was at a considerable distance from Plealands house, and hearses not being then in fashion in that part of the country, one of the Laird's own carts was drawn out, and the coffin placed on it for conveyance, while the services were going round the company. How it happened, whether owing to the neglect of Thomas Cabinet, the wright, who acted the part of undertaker, and who had, with all his men, more to attend to than he could well manage, in supplying the multitude with refreshments; or whether John Drappie, the old servant that was to drive the cart, had, like many others, got a service overmuch, we need not pause to inquire:—it, however, so happened, that, by some unaccountable and never explained circumstance, the whole body of the assembled guests arranged themselves in funereal array as well and as steadily as the generality of them could, and proceeded towards the church-yard—those in the van believing that the cart with the coffin was behind, and their followers in the rear committing a similar mistake, by supposing that it was before them in front. Thus both parties, in ignorance of the simple fact, that the coffin and cart were still standing at the house door, proceeded, with as much gravity and decorum as possible, to the church-yard gate, where they halted. As the gentlemen in front fell back to the right and left, to open an avenue for the body to be brought up, the omission was discovered, and also that there was no other way of performing the interment but by returning, as expeditiously as possible, to the house for the body.

By this time the weather, which had been all the morning cold and blustering, was become quite tempestuous. The wind raved in the trees and hedges—the sleet was almost thickened into a blinding snow, insomuch, that, when the company reached the house, the greater number of them were so chilled that they stood in need of another service, and another was of course handed round on the green; of which the greater number liberally and freely partaking, were soon rendered as little able to wrestle against the wind as when they originally set out. However, when the procession was formed a second time, Thomas Cabinet taking care to send the cart with the coffin on before, the whole moved again towards the church-yard, it is said, with a degree of less decorum than in their former procession. Nay, there is no disguising the fact, that more than two or three of the company, finding themselves, perhaps, unable to struggle against the blast, either lay down of their own voluntary accord on the road, or were blown over by the wind.

When the procession had a second time reached the churchyard, and Thomas Cabinet, perspiring at every pore, was wiping his bald head with his coat sleeve, his men got the coffin removed from the cart, and placed on the spokes, and the relatives, according to the irrespective degrees of propinquity, arranged themselves to carry it. The bearers, however, either by means of the headstones and the graves over which their path lay, or by some other cause, walked so unevenly, that those on the one side pushed against their corresponding kindred on the other, in such a manner, that the coffin was borne rollingly along for some time, but without any accident, till the relations on the right side gave a tremendous lurch, in which they drew the spokes out of the hands of the mourners on the left, and the whole pageant fell with a dreadful surge to the ground.

This accident, however, was soon rectified; the neighbours, who were not bearers, assisted the fallen to rise, and Thomas Cabinet, with his men, carried the coffin to its place of rest, and having laid it on the two planks which were stretched across the grave, assembled the nearest kin around, and gave the cords into their hands, that they might lower the Laird into his last bed. The betherel and his assistant then drew out the planks, and the sudden jirk of the coffin, when they were removed, gave such a tug to those who had hold of the cords, that it pulled them down, head foremost, into the grave after it. Fortunately, however, none were buried but the body; for, by dint of the best assistance available on the spot, the living were raised, and thereby enabled to return to their respective homes, all as jocose and as happy as possible.

Chapter X

On examining the Laird's papers after the funeral, Mr Keelevin, the father of the celebrated town-clerk of Gudetoun, the lawyer present on the occasion, discovered, in reading over the deed which had been executed by the deceased, in favour of Walter, the second son of Claud, that it was, in some essential points, imperfect as a deed of entail, though in other respects valid as a testamentary conveyance. The opinion of counsel, as in all similar cases, was in consequence forthwith taken; and the suspicions of Mr Keelevin being confirmed, Walter was admitted as heir to the estate, but found under no legal obligation to assume his grandfather's name,—the very obligation which the old gentleman had been most solicitous to impose upon him.

How it happened that the clause respecting so important a point should have been so inaccurately framed, remains for those gentlemen of the law, who commit such inadvertencies, to explain. The discovery had the effect of inducing Claud to apply to our old master, the late Gilbert Omit, writer, to examine the entail of the Grippy, which he had himself drawn up; and it too was found defective, and easily to be set aside. Really, when one considers how much some lawyers profit by their own mistakes, one might almost be tempted to do them the injustice to suspect that they now and then have an eye to futurity, and carve out work for themselves. There have, however, been discoveries of legal errors, which have occasioned more distress than this one; for, instead of giving the old man any uneasiness, he expressed the most perfect satisfaction on being informed, in answer to a plain question on the subject, that it was still in his power to disinherit his first-born. Well do we recollect the scene, being seated at the time on the opposite side of Mr Omit's desk, copying a codicil which Miss Christiana Heritage, then in her ninety-second year, was adding to her will, for the purpose of devising, as heir-looms, the bedstead and blankets in which Prince Charles Edward slept, when he passed the night in her house, after having levied that contribution on the loyal and godly city of Glasgow, for which the magistrates and council were afterwards so laudably indemnified by Parliament. We were not then quite so well versed in the secrets of human nature as experience has since so mournfully taught us, and the words of Claud at the time sounded strangely and harshly in our ear, especially when he inquired, with a sharp, and as it were a greedy voice, whether it was practicable to get Walter to conjoin with him in a deed that would unite his inheritance of Plealands to the Grippy, and thereby make a property as broad and good as the ancestral estate of Kittlestonheugh?

'Ye ken, Mr Omit,' said he, 'how I was defrauded, as a bodie may say, of my patrimony, by my grandfather; and now, since it has pleased Providence to put it in my power, by joining the heritage of Plealands and Grippy, to renew my ancestry, I would fain mak a settlement with Watty to that effek.'

Mr Omit, with all that calm and methodical manner which a long experience of those devices of the heart, to which lawyers in good practice, if at all men of observation, generally attain, replied,—

'Nothing can be done in that way while Walter is under age. But certainly, when the lad comes to majority, if he be then so inclined, there is no legal impediment in the way of such an arrangement; the matter, however, would require to be well considered, for it would be an unco like thing to hear of a man cutting off his firstborn for no fault, but only because he could constitute a larger inheritance by giving a preference to his second.'

Whatever impression this admonitory remark made on the mind of Claud at the moment, nothing further took place at that time; but he thoughtfully gathered his papers together, and, tying them up with a string, walked away from the office, and returned to Grippy, where he was not a little surprised to see Mr Allan Dreghorn's wooden coach at the door; the first four-wheeled gentleman's carriage started in Glasgow, and which, according to the praise-worthy history of Bailie Cleland, was made by Mr Dreghorn's own workmen, he being a timber merchant, carpenter, and joiner. It was borrowed for the day by Mr and Mrs Kilfuddy, who were then in Glasgow, and who, in consequence of their parochial connection with the Plealands family, had deemed it right and proper to pay the Leddy of Grippy a visit of sympathy and condolence, on account of the loss she had sustained in her father.

Chapter XI

The Reverend Mr Kilfuddy was a little, short, erect, sharp-looking, brisk tempered personage, with a red nose, a white powdered wig, and a large cocked hat. His lady was an ample, demure, and solemn matron, who, in all her gestures, showed the most perfect consciousness of enjoying the supreme dignity of a minister's wife in a country parish.

According to the Scottish etiquette of that period, she was dressed for the occasion in mourning; but the day being bleak and cold, she had assumed her winter mantle of green satin, lined with grey rabbit skin, and her hands ceremoniously protruded through the loop holes, formed for that purpose, reposed in full consequentiality within the embraces of each other, in a large black satin muff of her own making, adorned with a bunch of flowers in needlework, which she had embroidered some thirty years before, as the last and most perfect specimen of all her accomplishments. But, although they were not so like the blooming progeny of Flora, as a Linwood might, perhaps, have liked, they possessed a very competent degree of resemblance to the flowers they were intended to represent, insomuch that there was really no great risk of mistaking the roses for lilies. And here we cannot refrain from ingeniously suspecting that the limner who designed those celebrated emblematic pictures of the months which adorned the drawing-room of the Craiglands, and on which the far-famed Miss Mysie Cuningham set so great a value, must have had the image of Mrs Kilfuddy in his mind's eye, when he delineated the matronly representative of November.

The minister, after inquiring with a proper degree of sympathetic pathos into the state of the mourner's health, piously observed, 'That nothing is so uncertain as the things of time. This dispensation,' said he, 'which has been vouchsafed, Mrs Walkinshaw, to you and yours, is an earnest of what we have all to look for in this world. But we should not be overly cast down by the like o't, but lippen to eternity; for the sorrows of perishable human nature are erls given to us of joys hereafter. I trust, therefore, and hope, that you will soon recover this sore shock, and in the cares of your young family, find a pleasant pastime for the loss of your worthy father, whom, I am blithe to hear, has died in better circumstances than could be expected, considering the trouble he has had wi' his lawing; leaving, as they say, the estate clear of debt, and a heavy soom of lying siller.'

'My father, Mr Kilfuddy,' replied the lady, 'was, as you well know, a most worthy character, and I'll no say has na left a nest egg—the Lord be thankit, and we maun compose oursels to thole wi' what He has been pleased, in his gracious ordinances to send upon us for the advantage of our poor sinful souls. But the burial has cost the gudeman a power o' money; for my father being the head o' a family, we hae been obligated to put a' the servants, baith here, at the Grippy, and at the Plealands, in full deep mourning; and to hing the front o' the laft in the kirk, as ye'll see next Sabbath, wi' very handsome black cloth, the whilk cost twenty-pence the ell, first cost out o' the gudeman's ain shop; but, considering wha my father was, we could do no less in a' decency.'

'And I see,' interfered the minister's wife, 'that ye hae gotten a bombazeen o' the first quality; nae doubt ye had it likewise frae Mr Walkinshaw's own shop, which is a great thing, Mrs Walkinshaw, for you to get.'

'Na, Mem,' replied the mourner, 'ye dinna know what a misfortune I hae met wi'. I was, as ye ken, at the Plealands when my father took his departal to a better world, and sent for my mournings frae Glasgow, and frae the gudeman, as ye would naturally expek, and I had Mally Trimmings in the house ready to mak them when the box would come. But it happened to be a day o' deluge, so that my whole commodity, on Baldy Slowgaun's cart, was drookit through and through, and baith the crape and bombazeen were rendered as soople as pudding skins. It was, indeed, a sight past expression, and obligated me to send an express to Kilmarnock for the things I hae on, the outlay of whilk was a clean total loss, besides being at the dear rate. But, Mr Kilfuddy, every thing in this howling wilderness is ordered for the best; and, if the gudeman has been needcessited to pay for twa sets o' mournings, yet, when he gets what he'll get frae my father's gear, he ought to be very well content that it's nae waur.'

'What ye say, Mrs Walkinshaw,' replied the minister, 'is very judicious; for it was spoken at the funeral, that your father, Plealands, could nae hae left muckle less than three thousand pounds of lying money.'

'No, Mr Kilfuddy, it's no just so muckle; but I'll no say it's ony waur than twa thousand.'

'A braw soom, a braw soom,' said the spiritual comforter:—but what farther of the customary spirituality of this occasion might have ensued is matter of speculative opinion; for, at this juncture, Watty, the heir to the deceased, came rumbling into the room, crying,

'Mither, mither, Meg Draiks winna gie me a bit of auld daddy's burial bread, though ye brought o'er three farls wi' the sweeties on't, and twa whangs as big as peats o' the fine sugar seed-cake.'

The composity of the minister and his wife were greatly tried, as Mrs Kilfuddy herself often afterwards said, by this 'outstrapolous intrusion;' but quiet was soon restored by Mrs Walkinshaw ordering in the bread and wine, of which Walter was allowed to partake. The visitors then looked significantly at each other; and Mrs

Kilfuddy, replacing her hands in her satin muff, which, during the refectionary treat from the funeral relics, had been laid on her knees, rose and said,—

'Noo, I hope, Mrs Walkinshaw, when ye come to see the leddy, your mither, at the Plealands, that ye'll no neglek to gie us a ca' at the Manse, and ye'll be sure to bring the young Laird wi' you, for he's a fine spirity bairn—every bodie maun alloo that.'

'He's as he came frae the hand o' his Maker,' replied Mrs Walkinshaw, looking piously towards the minister; 'and it's a great consolation to me to think he's so weel provided for by my father.'

'Then it's true,' said Mr Kilfuddy, 'that he gets a' the Plealands property?'

''Deed is't, sir, and a braw patrimony I trow it will be by the time he arrives at the years o' discretion.'

'That's a lang look,' rejoined the minister a little slyly, for Walter's defect of capacity was more obvious than his mother imagined; but she did not perceive the point of Mr Kilfuddy's sarcasm, her attention at the moment being drawn to the entrance of her husband, evidently troubled in thought, and still holding the papers in his hand as he took them away from Mr Omit's desk.

Chapter XII

Experience had taught Mrs Walkinshaw, as it does most married ladies, that when a husband is in one of his moody fits, the best way of reconciling him to the cause of his vexation is to let him alone, or, as the phrase is, to let him come again to himself. Accordingly, instead of teasing him at the moment with any inquiries about the source of his molestation, she drew Mrs Kilfuddy aside, and retired into another room, leaving him in the hands of the worthy divine, who, sidling up to him, said,—

'I'm weel content to observe the resigned spirit of Mrs Walkinshaw under this heavy dispensation,—and it would be a great thing to us a' if we would lay the chastisement rightly to heart. For wi' a' his faults, and no mere man is faultless, Plealands was na without a seasoning o' good qualities, though, poor man, he had his ain tribulation in a set of thrawn-natured tenants. But he has won away, as we a' hope, to that pleasant place where the wicked cease from troubling, and the weary rest in peace. Nae doubt, Mr Walkinshaw, it maun hae been some sma' disappointment to you, to find that your second son is made the heir, but it's no an affliction past remedy, so ye should na let it fash you oure muckle.'

'No, bethankit,' replied Claud, 'it's no past remede, as Gibby Omit tells me; but I'm a thought troubled anent the means, for my auld son Charlie's a fine callan, and I would grudge to shove him out o' the line o' inheritance. It's an unco pity, Mr Kilfuddy, that it had na pleased the Lord to mak Watty like him.'

The minister, who did not very clearly understand this, said, 'A'thing considered, Mr Walkinshaw, ye'll just hae to let the law tak its course, and though ye canna hae the lairdship in ae lump, as ye aiblins expekit, it's nevertheless in your ain family.'

'I'm no contesting that,' rejoined Claud, 'but I would fain hae the twa mailings in ae aught, for if that could be brought about, I would na doubt of making an excambio o' the Plealands for the Divethill and Kittleston, the twa farms that wi' the Gippy made up the heritage o' my forefathers; for Mr Auchincloss, the present propreeator, is frae the shire o' Ayr, and I hae had an inklin that he wouldna be ill pleased to mak a swap, if there was ony possibility in law to alloo't.'

'I canna say,' replied the Reverend Mr Kilfuddy, 'that I hae ony great knowledge o' the laws o' man; I should, however, think it's no impossible; but still, Mr Walkinshaw, ye would hae to mak a reservation for behoof of your son Walter, as heir to his grandfather. It would be putting adders in the creel wi' the eggs if ye did na.'

'That's the very fasherie o' the business, Mr Kilfuddy, for it would be na satisfaction to me to leave a divided inheritance; and the warst o't is, that Watty, haverel though it's like to be, is no sae ill as to be cognos't; and what maks the case the mair kittle, even though he were sae, his younger brother Geordie, by course o' law and nature, would still come in for the Plealands afore Charlie. In short, I see nothing for't, Mr Kilfuddy, but to join the Grippy in ae settlement wi' the Plealands, and I would do sae outright, only I dinna like on poor Charlie's account.—Do ye think there is ony sin in a man setting aside his first-born? Ye ken Jacob was all oot to get the blessing and the birthright o' his elder brother Esau.'

Mr Kilfuddy, notwithstanding a spice of worldly-mindedness in his constitution, was, nevertheless, an honest and pious Presbyterian pastor; and the quickness of his temper at the moment stirred him to rebuke the cold-hearted speculations of this sordid father.

'Mr Walkinshaw,' said he severely, 'I can see no point o' comparison between the case o' your twa sons and that o' Jacob and Esau; and what's mair, the very jealousing that there may be sin in what ye wish to do, is a clear demonstration that it is vera sinful; for, O man! it's a bad intent indeed that we canna excuse to oursels. But to set you right in ae point, and that ye may hae nae apology drawn from scriptural acts, for the unnatural inclination to disinherit your first-born, out o' the prideful phantasy of leaving a large estate, I should tell you that there was a mystery of our holy religion hidden in Jacob's mess o' porridge, and it's a profane thing to meddle with that which appertaineth to the Lord, for what He does, and what He permits, is past the understanding o' man, and woe awaits on all those that would bring ought to pass contrary to the manifest course of his ordained method. For example, he taketh the breath of life away at his pleasure, but has he not commanded that no man shall commit murder?—Mr Walkinshaw, Mr Walkinshaw, ye maun strive against this sin of the flesh, ye maun warsle wi' the devil, and hit him weel on the hip till ye gar him loosen the grip that he has ta'en to draw you on to sic an awful sin. Heh, man! an ye're deluded on to do this thing! What a bonny sight it will be to see your latter end, when Belzebub, wi' his horns, will be sitting upon your bosom, boring through the very joints and marrow o' your poor soul wi' the red-het gimblets o' a guilty conscience.'

Claud shuddered at the picture, and taking the reproving minister by the hand, said, 'We canna help the wicked thoughts that sometimes rise, we dinna ken whar frae within us.'

'Ye dinna ken whar frae?—I'll tell you whar frae—frae hell; sic thoughts are the cormorants that sit on the apple trees in the devil's kailyard, and the souls o' the damned are the carcases they mak their meat o'.'

'For Heaven's sake, Mr Kilfuddy,' exclaimed Claud, trembling in every limb; 'be patient, and no speak that gait, ye gar my hair stand on end.'

'Hair! O man, it would be weel for you, if your precious soul would stand on end, and no only on end, but humlet to the dust, and that ye would retire into a corner, and scrape the leprosy of sic festering sins wi' a potsherd o' the gospel, till ye had cleansed yourself for a repentance unto life.'

These ghostly animadversions may, perhaps, sound harsh to the polite ears of latter days, but denunciation was, at that time, an instrument of reasoning much more effectual than persuasion, and the spiritual guides of the people, in warning them of the danger of evil courses, made no scruple, on any occasion, to strengthen their admonitions with the liveliest imagery that religion and enthusiasm supplied. Yet, with all the powerful aid of such eloquence, their efforts were often unavailing, and the energy of Mr Kilfuddy, in this instance, had, perhaps, no other effect than to make Claud for a time hesitate, although, before they parted, he expressed great contrition for having, as he said, yielded to the temptation of thinking that he was at liberty to settle his estate on whom he pleased.

Chapter XIII

At the death of the Laird of Plealands, the Grippy family, as we have already stated, consisted of three sons and a daughter. Charles, the eldest, was, as his father intimated to Mr Kilfuddy, a fine, generous, open-hearted, blithe-faced boy.

Towards him Claud cherished as much affection as the sterile sensibilities of his own bosom could entertain for any object; but Mrs Walkinshaw, from some of those unaccountable antipathies with which nature occasionally perplexes philosophy, almost hated her first-born, and poured the full flow of her uncouth kindness on Walter, who, from the earliest dawnings of observation, gave the most indubitable and conclusive indications of being endowed with as little delicacy and sense as herself. The third son, George, was, at this period, too young to evince any peculiar character; but, in after life, under the appearance of a dull and inapt spirit, his indefatigable, calculating, and persevering disposition demonstrated how much he had inherited of the heart and mind of his father. The daughter was baptized Margaret, which her mother elegantly abbreviated into Meg; and, as the course of our narrative requires that we should lose sight of her for some time, we may here give a brief epitome of her character. To beauty she had no particular pretensions, nor were her accomplishments of the most refined degree; indeed, her chief merit consisted in an innate predilection for thrift and household management; and what few elements of education which she had acquired were chiefly derived from Jenny Hirple, a lameter woman, who went round among the houses of the heritors of the parish with a stilt, the sound of which, and of her feet on the floors, plainly pronounced the words one pound ten. Jenny gave lessons in reading, knitting, and needlework, and something that resembled writing; and under her tuition, Miss Meg continued till she had reached the blooming period of sixteen, when her father's heart was so far opened, that, in consideration of the fortune he found he could then bestow with her hand, he was induced to send her for three months to Edinburgh; there, and in that time, to learn manners, 'and be perfited,' as her mother said, 'wi' a boarding-school education.' But, to return to Charles, the first-born, to whose history it is requisite our attention should at present be directed, nothing could seem more auspicious than the spring of his youth, notwithstanding the lurking inclination of his father to set him aside in the order of succession. This was principally owing to his grandmother, who had, during the life of the Laird, her husband, languished, almost from her wedding-day, in a state of uninterested resignation of spirit, so quiet, and yet so melancholy, that it partook far more of the nature of dejection than contentment. Immediately after his death, her health and her spirits began to acquire new energy; and before he was six months in the earth, she strangely appeared as a cheerful old lady, who delighted in society, and could herself administer to its pleasures.

In the summer following she removed into Glasgow, and Charles, being then about ten years old, was sent to reside with her for the advantages of attending the schools. Considering the illiterate education of his father, and the rough-spun humours and character of his mother, this was singularly fortunate; for the old lady had, in her youth, been deemed destined for a more refined sphere than the householdry of the Laird of Plealands.

Her father was by profession an advocate in Edinburgh, and had sat in the last assembly of the States of Scotland. Having, however, to the last, opposed the Union with all the vehemence in his power, he was rejected by the Government party of the day; and in consequence, although his talents and acquirements were considered of a superior order, he was allowed to hang on about the Parliament-house, with the empty celebrity of abilities, that, with more prudence, might have secured both riches and honours.

The leisure which he was thus obliged to possess was devoted to the cultivation of his daughter's mind, and the affection of no father was ever more tender, till about the period when she attained her twentieth year. Her charms were then in full blossom, and she was seen only to be followed and admired. But, in proportion as every manly heart was delighted with the graces and intelligence of the unfortunate girl, the solicitude of her father to see her married grew more and more earnest, till it actually became his exclusive and predominant passion, and worked upon him to such a degree, that it could no longer be regarded but as tinctured with some insane malady; insomuch, that his continual questions respecting the addresses of the gentlemen, and who or whether any of them sincerely spoke of love, embittered her life, and deprived her of all the innocent delight which the feminine heart, in the gaiety and triumph of youth, naturally enjoys from the homage of the men.

At this juncture Malachi Hypel was in Edinburgh, drinking the rounds of an advocate's studies; for he had no intention to practise, and with students of that kind the bottle then supplied the place of reviews and magazines. He was a sturdy, rough, hard-riding and free-living fellow, entitled by his fortune and connections almost to the best society; but qualified by his manners and inclinations to relish the lowest more joyously. Unluckily he was among the loudest and the warmest admirers of the ill-fated girl, and one night after supper, flushed with claret and brandy, he openly, before her father, made her a tender of his hand. The old man grasped it with an avaricious satisfaction, and though the heart of the poor girl was ready to burst at the idea of becoming the wife of one so coarse and rugged, she was nevertheless induced, in the space of little more than a month after, to submit to her fate.

The conduct of her father was at that time quite inexplicable, but when he soon afterwards died, unable to witness the misery to which he had consigned his beloved child, the secret came out. His circumstances were in the most ruinous condition; his little patrimony was entirely consumed, and he acknowledged on his death-bed, while he implored with anguish the pardon of his daughter, that the thought of leaving her in poverty had so overset his reason, that he could think of nothing but of securing her against the horrors of want. A disclosure so painful should have softened the harsh nature of her husband towards her, but it had quite a contrary effect. He considered himself as having been in some degree overreached, and although he had certainly not married her with any view to fortune, he yet reviled her as a party to her father's sordid machination. This confirmed the sadness with which she had yielded to become his bride, and darkened the whole course of her wedded life with one continued and unvaried shade of melancholy.

The death of her husband was in consequence felt as a deliverance from thraldom. The event happened late in the day, but still in time enough to allow the original brightness of her mind to shine out in the evening with a serene and pleasing lustre, sufficient to show what, in happier circumstances, she might have been. The beams fell on Charles with the cherishing influence of the summer twilight on the young plant, and if the tears of memory were sometimes mingled with her instructions, they were like the gracious dews that improve the delicacy of the flower, and add freshness to its fragrance.

Beneath her care, his natural sensibility was exalted and refined, and if it could not be said that he was endowed with genius, he soon appeared to feel, with all the tenderness and intelligence of a poet. In this respect his ingenuous affections served to recall the long vanished happiness of her juvenile hopes, and yielding to the sentiments which such reflections were calculated to inspire, she devoted, perhaps, too many of her exhortations in teaching him to value Love as the first of earthly blessings and of human enjoyments.

'Love,' she often said to the wondering boy, who scarcely understood the term, 'is like its emblem fire; it comes down from Heaven, and when once kindled in two faithful bosoms, grows brighter and stronger as it mingles its flames, ever rising and pointing towards the holy fountain-head from whence it came.'—These romantic lessons were ill calculated to fit him to perform that wary part in the world which could alone have enabled him to master the malice of his fortune, and to overcome the consequences of that disinheritance which his father had never for a moment ceased to meditate, but only waited for an appropriate opportunity to carry into effect.

Chapter XIV

Charles, in due time, was sent to College, and while attending the classes, formed an intimate friendship with a youth of his own age, of the name of Colin Fatherlans, the only son of Fatherlans of that Ilk. He was at this time about eighteen, and being invited by his companion to spend a few weeks at Fatherlans house in Ayrshire, he had soon occasion to feel the influence of his grandmother's lectures on affection and fidelity.

Colin had an only sister, and Charles, from the first moment that he saw her, felt the fascinations of her extraordinary beauty, and the charms of a mind, still more lovely in its intelligence than the bloom and graces of her form. Isabella Fatherlans was tall and elegant, but withal so gentle, that she seemed, as it were, ever in need of protection; and the feeling which this diffidence of nature universally inspired, converted the homage of her admirers into a sentiment of tenderness, which, in the impassioned bosom of Charles Walkinshaw, was speedily warmed into love.

For several successive years, he had the gratification of spending some weeks in the company of Isabella; and the free intercourse permitted between them soon led to the disclosure of a mutual passion. No doubt at that time clouded the sunshine that shone along the hopes and promises in the vista of their future years. Every thing, on the contrary, was propitious. His lineage and prospects rendered him acceptable to her parents, and she was viewed by his father as a match almost beyond expectation desirable. Time alone seemed to be the only adversary to their affection; but with him Fortune was in league, and the course of true love never long runs smooth.

The father of Isabella was one of those unfortunate lairds who embarked in the Mississippian project of the Ayr Bank, the inevitable fate of which, at the very moment when the hopes of the lovers were as gay as the apple boughs with blossoms in the first fine mornings of spring, came like a nipping frost, and blighted their happiness for ever. Fatherlans was ruined, and his ruin was a sufficient reason, with the inflexible Claud, to command Charles to renounce all thoughts of that fond connection which he had himself considered as the most enviable which his son could hope to obtain. But the altered fortunes of Isabella only served to endear her more and more to her lover; and the interdict of his father was felt as a profane interference with that hallowed enthusiasm of mingled love and sorrow with which his breast was at the moment filled.

'It is impossible,' said he; 'and even were it in my power to submit to the sacrifice you require, honour, and every sentiment that makes life worthy, would forbid me. No, sir; I feel that Isabella and I are one; Heaven has made us so, and no human interposition can separate minds which God and Nature have so truly united. The very reason that you urge against the continuance of my attachment, is the strongest argument to make me cherish it with greater devotion than ever. You tell me she is poor, and must be pennyless. Is not that, sir, telling me that she has claims upon my compassion as well as on my love? You say her father must be driven to the door. Gracious Heaven! and in such a time shall I shun Isabella? A common stranger, one that I had ever before known, would, in such adversity and distress, be entitled to any asylum I could offer; but Isabella—in the storm that has unroofed her father's house—shall she not claim that shelter which, by so many vows, I have sworn to extend over her through life?'

'Weel, weel, Charlie,' replied the old man, 'rant awa, and tak thy tocherless bargain to thee, and see what thou'll mak o't. But mind my words—when Poverty comes in at the door, Love jumps out at the window.'

'It is true,' said the lover, a little more calmly, 'that we cannot hope to live in such circumstances as I had so often reason to expect; but still, you will not refuse to take me into partnership, which, in the better days of her father, you so often promised?'

'We'll hae twa words about that,' replied the father; 'it's ae thing to take in a partner young, clever, and sharp, and another to take a needful man with the prospect o' a family. But, Charlie, I'll no draw back in my word to you, if ye'll just put off for a year or twa this calf love connection. May be by and by ye'll think better o' my counsel; at ony rate, something for a sair foot may be gathered in the mean time; and neither you nor Bell Fatherlans are sae auld but ye can afford to bide a while.'

This was said in the old man's most reflective and sedate manner, and after some farther conversation, Charles did consent to postpone for that time his marriage, on condition of being immediately admitted into partnership, with an understanding, that he should be free to marry at the end of twelve months, if he still continued so inclined. Both parties in this arrangement calculated without their host. The father thought that the necessary change in the exterior circumstances of Isabella would, in the course of the year, have a tendency to abate the ardour of her lover, and the son gave too much credit to his own self-denial, supposing, that, although the ruin of Fatherlans was declared, yet, as in similar cases, twelve months would probably elapse before the sequestration and sale of his estate would finally reduce the condition of his family. From the moment, however, that the affairs of the banking company were found irretrievable, Mr Fatherlans zealously bestirred himself to place his daughter above the hazards of want, even while he entertained the hope that it might not be necessary. He carried her with him to Glasgow, and, before calling at Claud's shop, secured for her an asylum in the house of Miss Mally Trimmings, a celebrated mantua maker of that time. When he afterwards waited on the inexorable pedlar, and communicated the circumstance, the latter, with unfeigned pleasure, commended the prudence of the measure, for he anticipated that the pride of his son would recoil at the idea of connecting himself with Isabella in her altered state. What the lover himself felt on hearing the news, we shall no attempt to describe, nor shall we so far intrude beyond the veil which should ever be drawn over the anxieties and the sorrows of young affection, under darkened prospects, as to relate what passed between the lovers when they next met. The resolution however, with which they both separated, was worthy of the purity of their mutual affections, and they agreed to pass the probationary year in a cheerful submission to their lot.

Chapter XV

When Charles parted from Isabella, he returned thoughtfully towards Grippy, which was situated on the south side of the Clyde, at the foot of the Cathkin hills. His road, after passing the bridge, lay across the fields as far as Rutherglen, where it diverged towards the higher ground, commanding at every winding a rich and variegated prospect.

The year was waning into autumn, and the sun setting in all that effulgence of glory, with which, in a serene evening, he commonly at that season terminates his daily course behind the distant mountains of Dumbartonshire and Argyle. A thin mist, partaking more of the lacy character of a haze than the texture of a vapour spreading from the river, softened the nearer features of the view while the distant were glowing in the golden blaze of the western skies, and the outlines of the city on the left appeared gilded with a brighter light, every window sparkling as if illuminated from within. The colour of the trees and hedges was beginning to change and here and there a tuft of yellow leaves, and occasionally the berries of the mountain ash, like clusters of fiery embers, with sheaves of corn, and reapers in a few of the neighbouring fields, showed that the summer was entirely past, and the harvest time begun.

The calm diffused over the face of the landscape—the numerous images of maturity and repose every where around—were calculated to soothe the spirit, to inspire gentle thoughts, and to awaken pleasing recollections; and there was something in the feelings with which the lovers had separated, if not altogether in unison with the graciousness of the hour, still so much in harmony with the general benignity of nature, that Charles felt his resolution and self-denial elevated with a sentiment of devotion, mingled with the fond enthusiasm of his passion. 'It is but a short time—a few months—and we shall be happy,' he exclaimed to himself; 'and our happiness will be the dearer that we shall have earned it by this sacrifice to prudence and to duty.'

But Charles and Isabella had estimated their fortitude too highly. They were both inexperienced in what the world really is; and her tender and sensitive spirit was soon found incapable of withstanding the trials and the humiliation to which she found herself subjected.

It was part of her business to carry home the dresses made up for Miss Mally's customers; and although the Glasgow ladies of that time were perhaps not more difficult to please with the style or fashion of their gowns and millinery than those of our own day, yet some of them were less actuated by a compassionate consideration for the altered fortunes of Isabella than all our fair contemporaries would undoubtedly have been. The unfortunate girl was, in consequence, often obliged to suffer taunts and animadversions, which, though levelled against the taste or inattention of her mistress, entered not the less painfully into her young and delicate bosom. Still, however, she struggled against the harsh circumstances to which she was exposed; but her sensibilities were stronger than her courage, and her beauty betrayed what she felt, and soon began to fade.

Charles was in the practice of accompanying her in the evenings when she commonly performed her disagreeable errands, and relieved her of the burden of her band-box, joyfully counting how much of the probationary year was already past, and cheering her with the assurance that her misfortunes had only endeared her to him the more. It happened, however, that, one Saturday, being late of reaching the place of rendezvous—the foot of the staircase which led to Miss Mally's dwelling—Isabella had gone away before he arrived, with a new dress to Mrs Jarvie, the wife of the far-famed Bailie Nicol, the same Matty who lighted the worthy magistrate to the Tolbooth, on that memorable night when he, the son of the deacon, found his kinsman Rob Roy there.

Matty at this time was a full-blown lady; the simple, modest, bare-footed lassie, having developed into a crimson, gorgeous, high-heeled madam,—well aware of the augmented width and weight of the bailie's purse, and jealous a little too much of her own consequence, perhaps, by recollecting the condition from which she had been exalted. The dress made up for her was a costly negligee; it not only contained several yards of the richest brocade more than any other Miss Mally Trimmings had ever made, but was adorned with cuffs and flounces in a style of such affluent magnificence, that we question if any grander has since been seen in Glasgow. Nor was it ordered for any common occasion, but to grace a formal dinner party, which Provost Anderson and his lady intended to give the magistrates and their wives at the conclusion of his eighth provostry. It was therefore not extraordinary that Mrs Jarvie should take particular interest in this dress; but the moment she began to try it on, poor Isabella discovered that it would not fit, and stood trembling from head to heel, while the bailie's wife, in great glee and good humour with the splendour of the dress, was loud in her praises of the cut of the ruffle-cuffs and the folds of the flounces. Having contemplated the flow of the negligee on both sides, and taken two or three stately steps across the room, to see how it would sweep behind, Mrs Jarvie took the wings of the body in her hands, and, drawing them together, found they would not nearly meet.

Isabella, with a beating heart and a diffident hand, approached to smooth the silk, that it might expand; but all would not do. Mrs Jarvie stood a monument of consternation, as silent as Lot's wife, when she looked back, and thought of the charming dresses she had left behind.

'O Chrystal!' were the first words to which the cidevant Matty could give utterance. 'O Chrystal! My God, is nae this moving? Your mistress, doited devil, as I maun ca' her, ought to be skelpit wi' nettles for this calamity. The goun's ruin't—my gude silk to be clippit in this nearbegaun way—past a' redemption. Gang out o' the gait, ye cutty, and no finger and meddle wi' me. This usage is enough to provoke the elect; as 'am a living soul, and that's a muckle word for me to say, I'll hae the old craighling scoot afore the Lords. The first cost was mair than five and twenty guineas. If there's law and justice atween God and man, she shall pay for't, or I'll hae my satisfaction on her flesh. Hither, maiden, and help me off wi' it. Siena beauty as it was. Tak it wi' you; tak it to you; out o' the house and my presence. How durst ye dare to bring sic a disgrace to me? But, let me look at it. Is't no possible to put in a gushet or a gore, and to make an eke?'

'I'll take it home and try,' said Isabella, timidly folding up the gown, which she had removed from Mrs Jarvie.

'Try,' said the bailie's wife, relapsing; 'a pretty like story, that sic a gown should stand in the jeopardy o' a try; but how could Miss Mally presume to send a silly thing like t'ee on this occasion? Lay down the gown this precious moment, and gae hame, and order her to come to me direkily: it's no to seek what I hae to say.'

The trembling and terrified girl let the unfortunate negligee fall, and hastily, in tears, quitted the room, and, flying from the house, met, in the street, her lover, who, having learnt where she was, had followed her to the house. A rapid and agitated disclosure of her feelings and situation followed. Charles, on the spot, resolved, at all hazards, rather to make her his wife at once, and to face the worst that might in consequence happen from his father's displeasure, than allow her to remain exposed to such contumelious treatment. Accordingly, it was agreed that they should be married, and on the Monday following, the ceremony was performed, when he conducted her to a lodging which he had provided in the interval.

Chapter XVI

On the morning after his marriage, Charles was anxious, doubtful, and diffident. His original intention was to go at once to his father, to state what he had done, and to persuade him, if possible, to overlook a step, that, from its suddenness, might be deemed rash, but, from the source and motives from which it proceeded, could, he thought, be regarded only as praiseworthy. Still, though this was his own opinion, he, nevertheless, had some idea that the old gentleman would not view it exactly in the same light; and the feeling which this doubt awakened made him hesitate at first, and finally to seek a mediator.

He had long remarked, that 'the lady,' his grandmother, sustained a part of great dignity towards his father; and he concluded, from the effect it appeared to produce, that her superiority was fully acknowledged. Under this delusion, after some consideration of the bearings and peculiarities of his case, he determined to try her interference, and, for that purpose, instead of going to Grippy, as he had originally intended, when he left Isabella, he proceeded to the house of the old lady, where he found her at home and alone.

The moment he entered her sitting-room, she perceived that his mind was laden with something which pressed heavily on his feelings; and she said,

'What has vext you, Charlie? has your father been severe upon you for ony misdemeanour, or hae ye done any thing that ye're afeared to tell?'

In the expression of these sentiments, she had touched the sensitive cord, that, at the moment, was fastened to his heart.

'I'm sure,' was his reply, 'that I hae done no ill, and dinna ken why I should be frightened in thinking on what every bodie that can feel and reflect will approve.'

'What is't?' said the lady, thoughtfully: 'What is't? If it's ought good, let me partake the solace wi' you; and if it's bad, speak it out, that a remedy may be, as soon as possible, applied.'

'Bell Fatherlans,' was his answer; but he could only articulate her name.

'Poor lassie,' said the venerable gentlewoman, 'her lot's hard, and I'm wae both for your sake and hers, Charlie, that your father's so dure as to stand against your marriage in the way he does. But he was aye a bargainer; alack! the world is made up o' bargainers; and a heart wi' a right affection is no an article o' meikle repute in the common market o' man and woman. Poor genty Bell! I wish it had been in my power to hae sweetened her lot; for I doubt and fear she's oure thin-skinned to thole long the needles and prins o' Miss Mally Trimmings' short temper; and, what's far waur, the tawpy taunts of her pridefu' customers.'

'She could suffer them no longer, nor would I let her,' replied the bridegroom, encouraged by these expressions to disclose the whole extent of his imprudence.

Mrs Hypel did not immediately return any answer, but sat for a few moments thoughtful, we might, indeed, say sorrowful—she then said,

'Ye should na, Charlie, speak to me. I canna help you, my dear, though I hae the will. Gang to your father and tell him a', and if he winna do what ye wish, then my poor bairn bravely trust to Providence, that gars' the heart beat as it should beat, in spite o' a' the devices o' man.'

'I fear,' replied Charles, with simplicity, 'that I hae done that already, for Bell and me were married yesterday. I could na suffer to see her snooled and cast down any longer by every fat-pursed wife that would triumph and glory in a new gown.'

'Married, Charlie!' said the old lady with an accent of surprise, mingled with sorrow; 'Married! weel, that's a step that canna be untrodden, and your tribulation is proof enough to me that you are awakened to the consequence. But what's to be done?'

'Nothing, Mem, but only to speak a kind word for us to my father,' was the still simple answer of the simple young husband.

'I'll speak for you, Charlie, I can do that, and I'll be happy and proud to gie you a' the countenance in my power; but your father, Charlie—the gude forgie me because he is your father—I'm darkened and dubious when I think o' him.'

'I hae a notion,' replied Charles, 'that we need be no cess on him: we're content to live in a sma' way; only I would like my wife to be countenanced as becomes her ain family, and mair especially because she is mine, so that, if my father will be pleased to tak her, and regard her as his gude-dochter, I'll ask nothing for the present, but do my part, as an honest and honourable man, to the very uttermost o' my ability.'

The kind and venerable old woman was profoundly moved by the earnest and frank spirit in which this was said; and she assured him, that so wise and so discreet a resolution could not fail to make his father look with a compassionate eye on his generous imprudence. 'So gae your ways home to Bell,' said she, 'and counsel and comfort her; the day's raw, but I'll even now away to the Grippy to intercede for you, and by the gloaming be you here wi' your bonny bride, and I trust, as I wish, to hae glad tidings for you baith.'

Charles, with great ardour and energy, expressed the sense which he felt of the old lady's kindness and partiality, but still he doubted the successful result of the mission she had undertaken. Nevertheless, her words inspired hope, and hope was the charm that spread over the prospects of Isabella and of himself, the light, the verdure, and the colours which enriched and filled the distant and future scenes of their expectations with fairer and brighter promises than they were ever destined to enjoy.

Chapter XVII

Claud was sitting at the window when he discovered his mother-in-law coming slowly towards the house, and he said to his wife,—

'In the name o' gude, Girzy, what can hae brought your mother frae the town on sic a day as this?'

'I hope,' replied the Leddy of Grippy, 'that nothing's the matter wi' Charlie, for he promised to be out on Sabbath to his dinner, and never came.'

In saying these words, she went hastily to the door to meet her mother, the appearance of whose countenance at the moment was not calculated to allay her maternal fears. Indeed, the old lady scarcely spoke to her daughter, but walking straight into the dining-room where Grippy himself was sitting, took a seat on a chair, and then threw off her cloak on the back of it, before she uttered a word.

'What's wrang, grannie?' said Claud, rising from his seat at the window, and coming towards her.—'What's wrang, ye seem fashed?'

'In truth, Mr Walkinshaw, I hae cause,' was the reply—'poor Charlie!'—

'What's happen'd to him?' exclaimed his mother.

'Has he met wi' ony misfortunate accident?' inquired the father.

'I hope it's no a misfortune,' said the old lady, somewhat recovering her self-possession. 'At the same time, it's what I jealouse, Grippy, ye'll no be vera content to hear.'

'What is't?' cried the father sharply, a little tantalized.

'Has he broken his leg?' said the mother.

'Haud that clavering tongue o' thine, Girzy,' exclaimed the Laird peevishly; 'wilt t' ou ne'er devaul' wi' sca'ding thy lips in other folks' kail?'

'He had amaist met wi' far waur than a broken leg,' interposed the grandmother. 'His heart was amaist broken.'

'It maun be unco brittle,' said Claud, with a hem. 'But what's the need o' this summering and wintering anent it?—Tell us what has happened?'

'Ye're a parent, Mr Walkinshaw,' replied the old lady seriously, 'and I think ye hae a fatherly regard for Charlie; but I'll be plain wi' you. I doubt ye hae na a right consideration for the gentle nature of the poor lad; and it's that which gars me doubt and fear that what I hae to say will no be agreeable.'

Claud said nothing in answer to this, but sat down in a chair on the right side of his mother-in-law, his wife having in the meantime taken a seat on the other side.—The old lady continued,—

'At the same time, Mr Walkinshaw, ye're a reasonable man, and what I'm come about is a matter that maun just be endured. In short, it's nothing less than to say, that, considering Fatherlans' misfortunes, ye ought to hae alloo't Charlie and Isabella to hae been married, for it's a sad situation she was placed in—a meek and gentle creature like her was na fit to bide the flyte and flights o' the Glasgow leddies.'

She paused, in the expectation that Claud would make some answer, but he still remained silent.—Mrs Walkinshaw, however, spoke,—

' 'Deed mither, that's just what I said—for ye ken it's an awfu' thing to thwart a true affection. Tro this't, gudeman; and ye should think what would hae been your ain tender feelings had my father stoppit our wedding after a' was settled.'

'There was some difference between the twa cases,' said the Dowager of Plealands dryly to her daughter;—'neither you nor Mr Walkinshaw were so young as Charlie and Miss Fatherlans—that was something—and may be there was a difference, too, in the character of the parties. Hows'ever, Mr Walkinshaw, marriages are made in heaven; and it's no in the power and faculty of man to controvert the coming to pass o' what is ordained to be. Charlie Walkinshaw and Bell Fatherlans were a couple marrowed by their Maker, and it's no right to stand in the way of their happiness.'

'I'm sure,' said Claud, now breaking silence, 'it can ne'er be said that I'm ony bar till't. I would only fain try a year's probation in case it's but calf love.'

Mrs Hypel shook her head as she said,—'It's vera prudent o' you, but ye canna put auld heads on young shouthers. In a word, Mr Walkinshaw, it's no reasonable to expek that young folk, so encouraged in their mutual affection as they were, can thole so lang as ye would wish. The days o' sic courtships as Jacob's and Rachel's are lang past.'

'I but bade them bide a year,' replied Claud.—

'A year's an unco time to love; but to make a lang tale short, what might hae been foreseen has come to pass, the fond young things hae gotten themselves married.'

'No possible!' exclaimed Claud, starting from his chair, which he instantly resumed.—

'Weel,' said Mrs Walkinshaw,—'if e'er I heard the like o' that!—Our Charlie a married man! the head o' a family!'—

The old lady took no notice of these and other interjections of the same meaning, which her daughter continued to vent, but looking askance and steadily at Claud, who seemed for a minute deeply and moodily agitated, she said,—

'Ye say nothing, Mr Walkinshaw.'

'What can I say?' was his answer.—'I had a better hope for Charlie,—I thought the year would hae cooled him,—and am sure Miss Betty Bodle would hae been a better bargain.'

'Miss Betty Bodle!' exclaimed the grandmother, 'she's a perfect tawpy.'

'Weel, weel,' said Grippy, ' it mak's no odds noo what she is,—Charlie has ravelled the skein o' his own fortune, and maun wind it as he can.'

'That will no be ill to do, Mr Walkinshaw, wi' your helping hand.—He's your first born, and a better-hearted lad never lived.'

'Nae doubt I maun help him,—there can be nae doubt o' that; but he canna expek, and the world can ne'er expek, that I'll do for him what I might hae done had he no been so rash and disobedient.'

'Very true, Mr Walkinshaw,' said the gratified old lady, happy to find that the reconciliation was so easily effected; and proud to be the messenger of such glad tidings to the young couple, she soon after returned to Glasgow. But scarcely had she left the house, when Claud appeared strangely disturbed,—at one moment he ran hastily towards his scrutoire, and opened it, and greedily seized the title-deeds of his property,—the next he closed it thoughtfully, and retreating to his seat, sat down in silence.

'What's the matter wi' you, gudeman? ye were na sae fashed when my mother was here,' said his wife.

'I'll do nothing rashly—I'll do nothing rashly,' was the mysterious reply.

'Eh, mither, mither,' cried Walter, bolting into the room,—'what would you think, our Charlie's grown a wife's gudeman like my father.'

'Out o' my sight, ye ranting cuif,' exclaimed Claud, in a rapture of rage, which so intimidated Walter that he fled in terror.

'It's dreadfu' to be sae tempted,—and a' the gude to gang to sic a haverel,' added Claud, in a low troubled accent, as he turned away and walked towards the window.

'Nae doubt,' said his wife, 'it's an awfu' thing to hear o' sic disobedience as Charlie in his rashness has been guilty o'.'

'It is, it is,' replied her husband, 'and many a ane for far less hae disinherited their sons,—cut them off wi' a shilling.'

'That's true,' rejoined the Leddy of Grippy. 'Did na Kilmarkeckle gie his only daughter but the legacy o' his curse, for running away wi' the Englisher captain, and leave a' to his niece Betty Bodle?'

'And a' she hae might hae been in our family but for this misfortune.—When I think o' the loss, and how pleased her father was when I proposed Charlie for her—It's

enough to gar me tak' some desperate step to punish the contumacious reprobate.—
He'll break my heart.'

'Dear keep me, gudeman, but ye're mair fashed than I could hae thought it was in
the power o' nature for you to be,'—said Mrs Walkinshaw, surprised at his agitation.

'The scoundrel! the scoundrel!' said Claud, walking quickly across the room—'To
cause sic a loss!—To tak' nae advice!—to run sic a ram-race!—I ought, I will gar him
fin' the weight o' my displeasure. Betty Bodle's tocher would hae been better than the
Grippy—But he shall suffer for't—I see na why a father may na tak' his own course
as weel as a son—I'll no be set at nought in this gait. I'll gang in to Mr Keelevin the
morn.'

'Dinna be oure headstrong, my dear, but compose yoursel',' —said the lady, perplexed,
and in some degree alarmed at the mention of the lawyer's name.—

'Compose thysel, Girzy, and no meddle wi' me,' was the answer, in a less confident
tone than the declaration he had just made, adding,

'I never thought he would hae used me in this way. I'm sure I was ay indulgent to
him.'

'Overly sae,' interrupted Mrs Walkinshaw, 'and often I told you that he would gie
you a het heart for't, and noo ye see my words hae come to pass.'

Claud scowled at her with a look of the fiercest aversion, for at that moment the
better feelings of his nature yearned towards Charles, and almost overcame the sordid
avidity with which he had resolved to cut him off from his birthright, and to entail
the estate of Grippy with the Plealands on Walter,—an intention which, as we have
before mentioned, he early formed, and had never abandoned, being merely deterred
from carrying it into effect by a sense of shame, mingled with affection, and as light
reverence for natural justice; all which, however, were loosened from their hold in his
conscience, by the warranty which the imprudence of the marriage seemed to give
him in the eyes of the world, for doing what he had so long desired to do. Instead,
however, of making her any reply, he walked out into the open air, and continued for
about half an hour to traverse the green in front of the house, sometimes with quick
short steps, at others with a slow and heavy pace. Gradually, however, his motion
became more regular, and ultimately ended in a sedate and firm tread, which indicated
that his mind was made up on the question, which he had been debating with himself.

Chapter XVIII

That abysm of legal dubieties, the office of Mr Keelevin, the writer, consisted of two
obscure apartments on the ground floor of McGregor's Land, in McWhinnie's Close,
in the Gallowgate. The outer room was appropriated to the clerks, and the inner for
the darker mysteries of consultation. To this place Claud repaired on the day following
the interesting communication, of which we have recorded the first impressions in the
foregoing chapter. He had ordered breakfast to be ready an hour earlier than usual; and
as soon as he had finished it, he went to his scrutoire, and taking out his title-deeds,
put them in his pocket, and without saying any thing to his wife of what he intended
to do, lifted his hat and stick from their accustomed place of repose, in the corner of
the dining-room, and proceeded, as we have said, to consult Mr Keelevin.

It is not the universal opinion of mankind, that the profession of the law is favourable to the preservation of simplicity of character or of benevolence of disposition; but this, no doubt, arises from the malice of disappointed clients, who, to shield themselves from the consequences of their own unfair courses, pretend that the wrongs and injustice of which they are either found guilty, or are frustrated in the attempt to effect, is owing to the faults and roguery of their own or their adversaries' lawyers. But why need we advocate any revision of the sentence pronounced upon the limbs of the law? for, grasping, as they do, the whole concerns and interests of the rest of the community, we think they are sufficiently armed with claws and talons to defend themselves. All, in fact, that we meant by this apologetic insinuation, was to prepare the reader for the introduction of Mr Keelevin, on whom the corrosive sublimate of a long and thorough professional insight of all kinds of equivocation and chicanery had, in no degree, deteriorated from the purity of his own unsuspicious and benevolent nature. Indeed, at the very time that Claud called, he was rebuking his young men on account of the cruelty of a contrivance they had made to catch a thief that was in the nocturnal practice of opening the window of their office, to take away what small change they were so negligent as to leave on or in their desks; and they were not only defending themselves, but remonstrating with him for having rendered their contrivance abortive. For, after they had ingeniously constructed a trap within the window, namely, a footless table, over which the thief must necessarily pass to reach their desks, he had secretly placed a pillow under it, in order that, when it fell down, the robber might not hurt himself in the fall.

'Gude morning, gude morning, Mr Keelevin; how're ye the day?' said Claud, as he entered.

'Gaily, gaily, Grippy; how're ye yoursel, and how's a' at hame? Come awa ben to my room,' was the writer's answer, turning round and opening the door; for experience had taught him, that visits from acquaintances at that hour were not out of mere civility.

Claud stepped in, and seated himself in an old armed chair which stood on the inner side of the table where Mr Keelevin himself usually wrote; and the lawyer followed him, after saying to the clerks, 'I redde ye, lads, tak tent to what I hae been telling you, and no encourage yourselves to the practice of evil that good may come o't. To devise snares and stratagems is most abominable—all that ye should or ought to do, is to take such precautions that the thief may not enter; but to wile him into the trap, by leaving the window unfastened, was nothing less than to be the cause of his sin. So I admonish you no to do the like o't again.'

In saying this he came in, and, shutting the door, took his own seat at the opposite side of the table, addressing himself to Claud, 'And so ye hae gotten your auld son married? I hope it's to your satisfaction.'

'An he has brewed good yill, Mr Keelevin, he'll drink the better,' was the reply; 'but I hae come to consult you anent a bit alteration that I would fain make in my testament.'

'That's no a matter of great difficulty, Laird; for, sin' we found out that the deed of entail that was made after your old son was born can never stand, a' ye have is free to be destined as ye will, both heritable and moveable.'

'And a lucky discovery that was;—many a troubled thought I hae had in my own breast about it; and now I'm come to confer wi' you, Mr Keelevin, for I would na trust the hair o' a dog to the judgment o' that tavert bodie, Gibby Omit, that gart me pay nine pounds seven shillings and saxpence too for the parchment; for it ne'er could be called an instrument, as it had na the pith o' a windlestrae to bind the property; and over and aboon that, the bodie has lang had his back to the wa', wi' the 'poplexy; so that I maun put my trust in this affair into your hands, in the hope and confidence that ye're able to mak something mair sicker.'

'We'll do our endeavour, Mr Walkinshaw; hae ye made ony sort o' scantling o' what you would wish done?'

'No, but I hae brought the teetles o' the property in my pouch, and ye'll just conform to them. As for the bit saving of lying money, we'll no fash wi' it for the present; I'm only looking to get a solid and right entail o' the heritable.'

'Nothing can be easier. Come as ye're o' an ancient family, no doubt your intent is to settle the Grippy on the male line; and, failing your sons and their heirs, then on the heirs of the body of your daughter.'

'Just sae, just sae. I'll make no change on my original disposition; only, as I would fain hae what cam by the gudewife made part and portion o' the family heritage, and as her father's settlement on Watty canna be broken without a great risk, I would like to begin the entail o' the Grippy wi' him.'

'I see nothing to prevent that; ye could gie Charlie, the auld son, his liferent in't, and as Watty, no to speak disrespectful of his capacity, may ne'er marry, it might be so managed.'

'Oh, but that's no what I mean, and what for may na Watty marry? Is na he o' capacity to execute a deed, and surely that should qualify him to take a wife?'

'But heavens preserve me, Mr Walkinshaw, are ye sensible of the ill ye would do to that fine lad, his auld brother, that's now a married man, and in the way to get heirs? Sic a settlement as ye speak o' would be cutting him off a' thegither: it would be most iniquitous!'

'An it should be sae, the property is my own conquesting, Mr Keelevin, and surely I may mak a kirk and a mill o't an I like.'

'Nobody, it's true, Mr Walkinshaw, has ony right to meddle wi' how ye dispone of your own, but I was thinking ye may be did na reflect that sic an entail as ye speak o' would be rank injustice to poor Charlie, that I hae ay thought a most excellent lad.'

'Excellent here, or excellent there, it was na my fault that he drew up wi' a tocherless tawpy, when he might hae had Miss Betty Bodle.'

'I am very sorry to hear he has displeased you; but the Fatherlans family, into whilk he has married, has ay been in great repute and estimation.'

'Aye, afore the Ayr Bank; but the silly bodie the father was clean broken by that venture.'

'That should be the greater reason, Mr Walkinshaw, wi' you to let your estate go in the natural way to Charlie.'

'A' that may be very true, Mr Keelevin; I did na come here, however, to confer with you anent the like of that, but only of the law. I want you to draw the settlement, as I was saying; first, ye'll entail it on Walter and his heirs-male, syne on Geordie and his heirs-male, and failing them, ye may gang back, to please yoursel, to the heirs-male o' Charlie, and failing them, to Meg's heirs-general.'

'Mr Walkinshaw,' said the honest writer, after a pause of about a minute, 'there's no Christianity in this.'

'But there may be law, I hope.'

'I think, Mr Walkinshaw, my good and worthy friend, that you should reflect well on this matter, for it is a thing by ordinare to do.'

'But ye ken, Mr Keelevin, when Watty dies, the Grippy and the Plealands will be a' ae heritage, and will na that be a braw thing for my family?'

'But what for would ye cut off poor Charlie from his rightful inheritance?'

'Me cut him off frae his inheritance! When my grandfather brake on account o' the Darien, then it was that he lost his inheritance. He'll get frae me a' that I inherited frae our forbears, and may be mair; only, I'll no alloo he has ony heritable right on me, but what stands with my pleasure to gie him as an almous.'

'But consider, he's your own firstborn?'—'Weel, then, what o' that?'

'And it stands with nature surely, Mr Walkinshaw, that he should hae a bairn's part o' your gear.'

'Stands wi' nature, Mr Keelevin? A coat o' feathers or a pair o' hairy breeks is a' the bairn's part o' gear that I ever heard o' in nature, as the fowls o' the air and the beasts o' the field can very plainly testify.—No, no, Mr Keelevin, we're no now in a state o' nature but a state o' law, and it would be an unco thing if we did na make the best o't. In short, ye'll just get the settlements drawn up as soon as a possibility will alloo, for it does na do to lose time wi' sic things, as ye ken, and I'll come in wi' Watty neest market day and get them implemented.'

'Watty's no requisite,' said Mr Keelevin, somewhat thoughtfully; 'it can be done without him. I really wish ye would think better o't before we spoil any paper.'

'I'm no fear't about the paper, in your hands, Mr Keelevin,—ye'll do every thing right wi' sincerity,—and mind, an it should be afterwards found out that there are ony flaws in the new deed, as there were in the auld, which the doited creature Gibby Omit made out, I'll gar you pay for't yoursel; so tak tent, for your own sake, and see that baith Watty's deed and mine are right and proper in every point of law.'

'Watty's! what do you mean by Watty's?'

'Have na I been telling you that it's my wis that the Plealands and the Grippy should be made one heritage, and is na Watty concos mancos enough to be conjunct wi' me in the like o' that? Ye ken the flaw in his grandfather's settlement, and that, though the land has come clear and clean to him, yet it's no sae tethered but he may wise it awa as it likes him to do, for he's noo past one-and-twenty. Therefore, what I want is, that ye will mak a paper for him, by the whilk he's to 'gree that the Plealands gang the same gait, by entail, as the Grippy.'

'As in duty bound, Mr Walkinshaw, I maun do your will in this business,' said Mr Keelevin; 'but really I ken na when I hae been more troubled about the specialities of any settlement. It's no right o' you to exercise your authority oure Watty; the lad's truly no in a state to be called on to implement ony such agreement as what ye propose. He should na be meddled wi', but just left to wear out his time in the world, as little observed as possible.'

'I canna say, Mr Keelevin, that I like to hear you misliken the lad sae, for did na ye yourself, with an ettling of pains that no other body could hae gane through but yoursel, prove, to the satisfaction of the fifteen at Edinburgh, that he was a young man of a very creditable intellect, when Plealands' will was contested by his cousin?'

'Waes me, Mr Walkinshaw, that ye should cast up to me the sincerity with which I did but my duty to a client. However, as ye're bent on this business, I'll say na mair in objection, but do my best to make a clear and tight entail, according to your instructions—trusting that I shall be accounted hereafter as having been but the innocent agent; and yet I beg you again, before it's oure late, to reflect on the consequence to that fine lad Charlie, who is now the head of a house, and in the way of having a family—It's an awfu' thing ye're doing to him.'

'Weel, weel, Mr Keelevin, as I was saying, dinna ye fash your thumb, but mak out the papers in a sicker manner,—and may be though ye think sae ill o' me, it winna be the waur for Charlie after a's come and gane.'

'It's in the Lord's power certainly,' replied the worthy lawyer piously, 'to make it all up to him.'

'And maybe it's in my power too, for when this is done, I'll hae to take another cast o' your slight o' hand in the way of a bit will for the moveables and lying siller, but I would just like this to be weel done first.'

'Man, Laird, I'm blythe to hear that,—but ye ken that ye told me last year when you were clearing the wadset that was left on the Grippy, that ye had na meikle mair left—But I'm blithe to hear ye're in a condition to act the part of a true father to a' your bairns, though I maun say that I canna approve, as a man and a frien', of this crotchet of entailing your estate on a haverel, to the prejudice of a braw and gallant lad like Charlie. Hows' ever, sin' it is sae, we'll say nae mair about it. The papers will be ready for you by Wednesday come eight days, and I'll tak care to see they are to your wish.'

'Na, an ye dinna do that, the cost shall be on your own risk, for the deil a plack or bawbee will I pay for them, till I hae a satisfaction that they are as they ought to be. Howsever, gude day, Mr Keelevin, and we'll be wi' you on Wednesday by ten o'clock.'

In saying this, Claud, who had in the mean time risen from his seat, left the office without turning his head towards the desk, where the clerks, as he walked through the outer room, were sitting, winking at one another, as he plodded past them, carrying his staff in his left hand behind him, a habit which he had acquired with his ellwand when he travelled the Borders as a pedlar.

Chapter XIX

On the Saturday evening after the instructions had been given to prepare the new deed of entail, Grippy was thoughtful and silent, and his wife observing how much he was troubled in mind, said,

'I'm thinking, gudeman, though ye hae no reason to be pleased with this match Charlie has made for himsel, ye ken, as it canna be helpit noo, we maun just put up wi't.'

To this observation, which was about one of the most sensible that ever the Leddy o' Grippy made in her life, Claud replied, with an ill articulated grumph, that partook more of the sound and nature of a groan than a growl, and she continued,—

'But, poor laddie, bare legs need happing; I would fain hope ye'll no be oure dure;— ye'll hae to try an there be any moully pennies in the neuk o' your coffer that can be spar'd and no miss't.'

'I hae thought o' that, Girzy, my dawty,' said he somewhat more cordially than he was in the practice of doing to his wife; 'and we'll gang o'er the morn and speer for Charlie. I wish he had na been so headstrong; but it's a' his ain fault: howsever, it would na be canny to gang toom-handed, and I hae got a bit bill for five score pounds that I'm mindit to gie him.'

'Five score pounds, gudeman! that's the whole tot o' a hundred. Na, gudeman, I would hae thought the half o't an unco almous frae you. I hope it's no a fedam afore death. Gude preserve us! ye're really ta'en wi' a fit o' the liberalities; but Charlie, or am mista'en, will hae need o't a', for yon Flanders baby is no for a poor man's wife. But for a' that, I'm blithe to think ye're gaun to be sae kind, though I need na wonder at it, for Charlie was ay your darling chevalier, I'm sure nobody can tell what for, and ye ay lookit down on poor good-natured Watty.'

'Haud that senseless tongue o' thine, Girzy; Watty's just like the mither o't, a haverel; and if it were na more for ae thing than anither, the deil a penny would the silly gouk get frae me, aboon an aliment to keep him frae beggary. But what's ordain't will come to pass, and it's no my fault that the sumph Watty was na Charlie. But it's o' nae use to contest about the matter; ye'll be ready betimes the morn's morning to gang in wi' me to the town to see the young folks.'

Nothing more then passed, but Claud, somewhat to the surprise of his lady, proposed to make family worship that evening. 'It's time now, gudewife,' said, he, 'when we're in a way to be made ancestors, that we should be thinking o' what's to come o' our sinful souls hereafter. Cry ben the servants, and I'll read a chapter to them and you, by way o' a change, for I kenna what's about me, but this rash action o' that thoughtless laddie fashes me, and yet it would na be right o' me to do any other way than what I'm doing.'

The big ha' Bible was accordingly removed by Mrs Walkinshaw from the shelf where it commonly lay undisturbed from the one sacramental occasion to the other, and the dust being blown off, as on the Saturday night prior to the action sermon, she carried it to the kitchen to be more thoroughly wiped, and soon after returned with it followed by the servants. Claud, in the meantime, having drawn his elbow-chair close to the table, and placed his spectacles on his nose, was sitting when the mistress laid the volume before him ready to begin. As some little stir was produced by the servants taking their places, he accidentally turned up the cover, and looked at the page in which he had inserted the dates of his own marriage and the births of his children. Mrs Walkinshaw observing him looking at the record, said,

'Atweel, Charlie need na been in sic a haste, he's no auld enough yet to be the head o' a family. How auld were ye, gude-man, when we were marriet? But he's no blest wi' the forethought o' you.'

'Will that tongue o' thine, Girzy, ne'er be quiet? In the presence o' thy Maker, wheest, and pay attention, while I read a chapter of His holy word.'

The accent in which this was uttered imposed at once silence and awe, and when he added, 'Let us worship God, by reading a portion of the Scriptures of truth,' the servants often afterwards said, 'he spoke like a dreadfu' divine.'

Not being, as we have intimated, much in the practice of domestic worship, Claud had avoided singing a Psalm, nor was he so well acquainted with the Bible, as to be able to fix on any particular chapter or appropriate passage from recollection. In this respect he was, indeed, much inferior to the generality of the Glasgow merchants of that age, for, although they were considerably changed from the austerity by which their fathers had incurred the vengeance of Charles the Second's government, they were still regular in the performance of their religious domestic duties. Some excuse, however, might be made for Claud, on account of his having spent so many years on the English Borders, a region in no age or period greatly renowned for piety, though plentifully endowed, from a very ancient date, with ecclesiastical mansions for the benefit of the outlaws of the two nations. Not, however, to insist on this topic, instead of reverently waling a portion with judicious care, he opened the book with a degree of superstitious trepidation, and the first passage which caught his eye was the thirty-second verse of the twenty-seventh chapter of Genesis. He paused for a moment; and the servants and the family having also opened their Bibles, looked towards him in expectation that he would name the chapter he intended to read. But he closed the volume over upon his hand, which he had inadvertently placed on the text, and lay back on his chair, unconscious of what he had done, leaving his hand still within the book.

'We're a' ready,' said Mrs Walkinshaw; 'whare's the place?'

Roused by her observation from the reverie into which he had momentarily sunk, without reflecting on what he did, he hastily opened the Bible, by raising his hand, which threw open the leaves, and again he saw and read,—

'And Isaac his father said unto him, Who art thou? and he said, I am thy son,—thy first-born, Esau; And Isaac trembled very exceedingly.'

'What's the matter wi' you, gudeman?' said the Leddy; 'are ye no weel?' as he again threw himself back in his chair, leaving the book open before him. He, however, made no reply, but only drew his hand over his face, and slightly rubbed his forehead.

'Im thinking, gudeman,' added the Leddy, 'as ye're no used wi' making exercise, it may be as weel for us at the beginning to read a chapter intil oursels.'

'I'll chapse that place,' said Walter, who was sitting opposite to his father, putting, at the same time, unobserved into the book a bit of stick which he happened to be slily gnawing.

Claud heard what his wife suggested, but for about a minute made no answer: shutting the Bible, without noticing the mark which Walter had placed in it, he said,—

'I'm thinking ye're no far wrang, gudewife. Sirs, ye may gae but the house, and ilk read a chapter wi' sobriety, and we'll begin the worship the morn's night, whilk is the Lord's.'

The servants accordingly retired; and Walter reached across the table to lay hold of the big Bible, in order to read his chapter where he had inserted the stick; but his father angrily struck him sharply over the fingers, saying,—

'Hast t'ou neither grace nor gumshion, that t'ou daurs to tak awa the word o' God frae before my very face? Look to thy ain book, and mind what it tells thee, an t'ou has the capacity of an understanding to understand it.'

Walter, rebuked by the chastisement, withdrew from the table; and, taking a seat sulkily by the fireside, began to turn over the leaves of his pocket Bible, and from time to time he read mutteringly a verse here and there by the light of the grate. Mrs Walkinshaw, with Miss Meg, having but one book between them, drew their chairs close to the table; and the mother, laying her hand on her daughter's shoulders, overlooked the chapter which the latter had selected.

Although Claud had by this time recovered from the agitation into which he had been thrown, by the admonition he had as it were received from the divine oracle, he yet felt a profound emotion of awe as he again stretched his hand towards the sacred volume, which, when he had again opened, and again beheld the self-same words, he trembled very exceedingly, in so much that he made the table shake violently.

'In the name of God, what's that!' cried his wife, terrified by the unusual motion, and raising her eyes from the book, with a strong expression of the fear which she then felt.

Claud was so startled, that he looked wildly behind him for a moment, with a ghastly and superstitious glare. Naturally possessing, however, a firm and steady mind, his alarm scarcely lasted a moment; but the pious business of the evening was so much disturbed, and had been to himself so particularly striking, that he suddenly quitted the table, and left the room.

Chapter XX

The Sabbath morning was calm and clear, and the whole face of Nature fresh and bright. Every thing was animated with glee; and the very flowers, as they looked up in the sunshine, shone like glad faces. Even the Leddy o' Grippy partook of the gladdening spirit which glittered and frolicked around her; and as she walked a few paces in front of her husband down the footpath from the house to the highway leading to Glasgow, she remarked, as their dog ran gamboling before them, that

'Auld Colley, wi' his daffing, looks as he had a notion o' the braw wissing o' joy Charlie is to get. The brute, gudeman, ay took up wi' him, which was a wonderfu' thing to me; for he did nothing but weary its life wi' garring it loup for an everlasting after sticks and chucky stanes. Hows'ever, I fancy dogs are like men—leavened, as Mr Kilfuddy says, wi' the leaven of an ungrateful heart—for Colley is as doddy and crabbit to Watty as if he was its adversary, although, as ye ken, he gathers and keeps a' the banes for't.'

'Wilt t'ou ne'er devaul' wi' thy havering tongue? I'm sure the dumb brute, in favouring Charlie, showed mair sense than his mother, poor fellow.'

'Aye, aye, gudeman, so ye say; but every body knows your most unnatural partiality.'

'Thy tongue, woman,' exclaimed her husband, 'gangs like the clatter-bane o' a goose's——'

'Eh, Megsty me!' cried the Leddy; 'wha's yon at the yett tirling at the pin?'

Claud, roused by her interjection, looked forward, and beheld, with some experience of astonishment, that it was Mr Keelevin, the writer.

'We'll hae to turn and gang back with him,' said Mrs Walkinshaw, when she observed who it was.

'I'll be damn'd if I do ony sic thing,' growled the old man, with a fierceness of emphasis that betrayed apprehension and alarm, while it at the same time denoted a rivetted determination to persevere in the resolution he had taken; and, mending his pace briskly, he reached the gate before the worthy lawyer had given himself admittance.

'Gude day, Mr Keelevin!—What's brought you so soon afield this morning?'

'I hae just ta'en a bit canter oure to see you, and to speak anent yon thing.'

'Hae ye got the papers made out?'

'Surely—it can never be your serious intent—I would fain hope—nay, really Mr Walkinshaw, ye maunna think o't.'

'Hoot, toot, toot; I thought ye had mair sense, Mr Keelevin. But I'm sorry we canna gae back wi' you, for we're just sae far in the road to see Charlie and his lady landless.

' 'Deed are we,' added Mrs Walkinshaw; 'and ye'll no guess what the gudeman has in his pouch to gie them for hansel to their matrimony: the whole tot of a hundred pound, Mr Keelevin—what think you o' that?'

The lawyer looked first at the Leddy, and then at the Laird, and said, 'Mr Walkinshaw, I hae done you wrong in my thought.'

'Say nae mair about it, but hae the papers ready by Wednesday, as I directed,' replied Claud.

'I hope and trust, Mr Keelevin,' said Mrs Walkinshaw, 'that he's no about his will and testament: I redde ye, an he be, see that I'm no neglekit; and dinna let him do an injustice to the lave for the behoof of Charlie, wha is, as I say, his darling chevalier.'

Mr Keelevin was as much perplexed as ever any member of the profession was in his life; but he answered cheerfully,

'Ye need na be fear't, Mrs Walkinshaw, I'll no wrang either you or any one of the family;' and he added, looking towards her husband, 'if I can help it.'

'Na, thanks be an' praise, as I understand the law, that's no in your power; for I'm secured wi' a jointure on the Grippy by my marriage articles; and my father, in his testament, ordained me to hae a hundred a year out of the harming o' his lying money; the whilk, as I have myself counted, brings in to the gudeman, frae the wadset that he has on the Kilmarkeckle estate, full mair than a hundred and twenty-seven pounds; so I would wis both you and him to ken, that I'm no in your reverence; and likewise, too, Mr Keelevin, that I'll no faik a farthing o' my right.'

Mr Keelevin was still more perplexed at the information contained in this speech; for he knew nothing of the mortgage, or, as the Leddy called it, the wadset which Claud had on his neighbour Kilmarkeckle's property, Mr Omit having been employed by him in that business. Indeed, it was a regular part of Grippy's pawkie policy, not to let his affairs be too well known, even to his most confidential legal adviser; but, in common transactions, to employ any one who could be safely trusted in matters of ordinary professional routine. Thus the fallacious impression which Claud had in some degree made on the day in which he instructed the honest lawyer respecting the entail was, in a great measure, confirmed; so that Mr Keelevin, instead of pressing the remonstrance which he had come on purpose from Glasgow that morning to urge, marvelled exceedingly within himself at the untold wealth of his client.

In the meantime, Grippy and his Leddy continued walking towards the city, but the lawyer remounted his horse, pondering on what he had heard, and almost persuaded that Claud, whom he knew to be so close and wary in worldly matters, was acting a very prudent part. He conceived that he must surely be much richer than the world supposed; and that, seeing the natural defects of his second son, Walter, how little he was superior to an idiot, and judging he could make no good use of ready money, but might, on the contrary, become the prey of knavery, he had, perhaps, determined, very wisely, to secure to him his future fortune by the entail proposed, meaning to indemnify Charles from his lying money. The only doubt that he could not clear off entirely to his satisfaction, was the circumstance of George, the youngest son, being preferred in the limitations of the entail to his eldest brother. But even this admitted of something like a reasonable explanation; for, by the will of the grandfather, in the event of Walter dying without male issue, George was entitled to succeed to the Plealands, as heir of entail; the effect of all which, in the benevolent mind of honest Mr Keelevin, contributed not a little to rebuild the good opinion of his client, which had suffered such a shock from the harshness of his instructions, as to induce him to pay the visit which led to the rencounter described; and in consequence he walked his horse beside the Laird and Leddy, as they continued to pick their steps along the shady side of the road.—Mrs Walkinshaw, with her petticoats lifted half leg high, still kept the van, and her husband followed stooping forward in his gait, with his staff in his left hand behind him—the characteristic and usual position in which, as we have already mentioned, he was wont to carry his ellwand when a pedlar.

Chapter XXI

The young couple were a good deal surprised at the unexpected visit of their father and mother; for although they had been led to hope, from the success of the old lady's mission, that their pardon would be conceded, they had still, by hearing nothing farther on the subject, passed the interval in so much anxiety, that it had materially impaired their happiness. Charles, who was well aware of the natural obduracy of his father's disposition, had almost entirely given up all expectation of ever being restored to his favour; and the despondency of the apprehensions connected with this feeling underwent but little alleviation when he observed the clouded aspect, the averted eye, and the momentary glances, with which his wife was regarded, and the troubled looks from time to time thrown towards himself. Nevertheless, the visit, which was at first so embarrassing to all parties, began to assume a more cordial character; and the generosity of Charles' nature, which led him to give a benevolent interpretation to the actions and motives of every man, soon mastered his anxieties; and he found himself, after the ice was broken, enabled to take a part in the raillery of his mother, who, in high glee and good humour, joked with her blooming and blushing daughter-in-law, with all the dexterity and delicacy of which she was so admirable a mistress.

'Eh!' said she, 'but this was a galloping wedding o' yours, Charlie. It was an unco like thing, Bell—na, ye need na look down, for ye maunna expek me to ca' you by your lang-nebbit baptismal name, now that ye're my gudedochter—for ceremony's a cauld rife commodity amang near frien's. surely, Bell, it would hae been mair wiselike had ye been cried in the kirk three distink Sabbaths, as me and your gude-father was, instead o' gallanting awa under the scog and cloud o' night, as if ye had been fain and fey. Howsever, it's done noo; and the gudeman means to be vastly genteel. I'm sure the post should get a hag when we hear o' him coming wi' hundreds o' pounds in his pouch, to gi'e awa for deil-be-licket but a gratus gift o' gude will, in hansel to your matrimonial. But Charlie, your gudeman, Bell, was ay his pett, and so am nane surprised at his unnatural partiality, only I ken they'll hae clear e'en and bent brows that 'ill see him gi'eing ony sic almous to Watty.'

When the parental visitors had sat about an hour, during the great part of which the Leddy o' Grippy continued in this strain of clishmaclaver, the Laird said to her it was time to take the road homeward. Charles pressed them to stay dinner. This, however, was decidedly refused by his father, but not in quite so gruff a manner as he commonly gave his refusals, for he added, giving Charles the bank-bill, as he moved across the room, towards the door,—

'Hae, there's something to help to keep the banes green, but be careful, Charlie, for I doubt ye'll hae need, noo that ye're the head o' a family, to look at baith sides o' the bawbee before ye part wi't.'

'It's for a whole hundred pound,' exclaimed Lady Grippy in an exulting whisper to her daughter-in-law—while the old man, after parting with the paper, turned briskly round to his son, as if to interrupt his thankfulness, and said,—'Charlie, ye maun come wi' Watty and me on Wednesday; I hae a bit alteration to make in my papers; and, as we need na cry sic things at the Cross, I'm mindit to hae you and him for the witnesses.'

Charles readily promised attendance; and the old people then made their congees and departed.

In the walk homeward Claud was still more taciturn than in the morning; he was even sullen, and occasionally peevish; but his wife was in full pipe and glee; and, as soon as they were beyond hearing, she said,—

'Every body maun alloo that she's a well far't lassie yon; and, if she's as good as she's bonny, Charlie's no to mean wi' his match. But, dear me, gudeman, ye were unco scrimpit in your talk to her—I think ye might hae been a thought mair complaisant and jocose, considering it was a marriage occasion; and I wonder what came o'er mysel that I forgot to bid them come to the Grippy and tak their dinner the morn, for ye ken we hae a side o' mutton in the house; for, since ye hae made a conciliation free gratus wi' them, we need na be standing on stapping-stanes; no that I think the less of the het heart that Charlie has gi'en to us baith; but it was his forton, and we maun put up wi't. Howsever, gudeman, ye'll alloo me to make an observe to you anent the hundred pound. I think it would hae been more prudent to hae gi'en them but the half o't, or ony smaller sum, for Charlie's no a very gude guide;—siller wi' him gangs like snaw aff a dyke; and as for his lily-white handit madam, a' the jingling o' her spinnit will ne'er make up for the winsome tinkle o' Betty Bodle's tocher purse. But I hae been thinking, gudeman, noo that Charlie's by hand and awa, as the ballad o' Woo't and Married and a'sings, could na ye persuade our Watty to mak up to Betty, and sae get her gear saved to us yet?'

This suggestion was the only wise thing, in the opinion of Claud, that ever he had heard his wife utter; it was, indeed, in harmonious accordance with the tenor of his own reflections, not only at the moment, but from the hour in which he was first informed of the marriage. For he knew, from the character of Miss Betty Bodle's father, that the entail of the Grippy, in favour of Walter, would be deemed by him a satisfactory equivalent for any intellectual defect. The disinheritance of Charles was thus, in some degree, palliated to his conscience as an act of family policy rather than of resentment; in truth, resentment had perhaps very little to say in the feeling by which it was dictated;—for, as all he did and thought of in life was with a view to the restoration of the Walkinshaws of Kittlestonheugh, we might be justified, for the honour of human nature, to believe, that he actually contemplated the sacrifice which he was making of his first-born to the Moloch of ancestral pride, with reluctance, nay, even with sorrow.

In the meantime, as he returned towards Grippy with his wife, thus discoursing on the subject of Miss Betty Bodle and Walter, Charles and Isabella were mutually felicitating themselves on the earnest which they had so unexpectedly received of what they deemed a thorough reconciliation.

There had, however, been something so heartless in the behaviour of the old man during the visit, that, notwithstanding the hopes which his gift encouraged, it left a chill and comfortless sensation in the bosom of the young lady, and her spirit felt it as the foretaste of misfortune. Averse, however, to occasion any diminution of the joy which the visit of his parents had afforded to her husband, she endeavoured to suppress the bodement, and to partake of the gladdening anticipations in which he indulged. The effort to please others never fails to reward ourselves. In the afternoon, when the old dowager called, she was delighted to find them both satisfied with the prospect, which had so suddenly opened, and so far too beyond her most sanguine expectations, that she also shared in their pleasure, and with her grandson inferred, from the liberal earnest he had received, that, in the papers and deeds he was invited to witness, his father intended to make some provision to enable him to support the rank in society to which Isabella had been born, and in which his own taste prompted him to move. The evening, in consequence, was spent by them with all the happiness which the children of men so often enjoy with the freest confidence, while the snares of adversity are planted around them, and the demons of sorrow and evil are hovering unseen, awaiting the signal from destiny to descend on their blind and unsuspicious victims.

Chapter XXII

Grippy passed the interval between the visit and the day appointed for the execution of the deeds of entail with as much comfort of mind as Heaven commonly bestows on a man conscious of an unjust intention, and unable to excuse it to himself. Charles, who, in the meantime, naturally felt some anxiety to learn the precise nature of the intended settlement, was early afoot on the morning of Wednesday, and walked from the lodgings where he resided with his wife in Glasgow to meet his father and brother, on their way to the town. Being rather before the time appointed, he went forward to the house, on the green plot in front of which the old man was standing, with his hands behind, and his head thoughtfully bent downwards.

The approach of his son roused Claud from his reverie; and he went briskly forward to meet him, shaking him heartily by the hand, and inquiring, with more kindness than the occasion required, for the health of his young wife. Such unusual cordiality tended to confirm the delusion which the gift of the bank bill on Sunday had inspired; but the paroxysm of affection produced by the effort to disguise the sense which the old man suffered of the irreparable wrong he was so doggedly resolved to commit, soon went off; and, in the midst of his congratulations, conscience smote him with such confusion, that he was obliged to turn away, to conceal the embarrassment which betrayed the insincerity of the warmth he had so well assumed. Poor Charles, however, was prevented from observing the change in his manner and countenance, by Walter appearing at the door in his Sunday clothes, followed by his mother, with his best hat in her hand, which she was smoothing at the same time with the tail of her apron.

'I redde ye, my bairn,' said she to Walter, as she gave him the hat, 'to take care o' thysel, for ye ken they're an unco crew ay in the Trongate on Wednesday; and mind what I hae been telling you, no to put your hand to pen and ink unless Mr Keelevin tells you it's to be for your advantage; for Charlie's your father's ain chevalier, and nae farther gane than the last Lord's day, he gied him, as I telt you, a whole hundred pound for hansel to his tocherless matrimony.'

Charles, at this speech, reddened and walked back from the house, without speaking to his mother; but he had not advanced many steps towards the gate, when she cried,—

'Hey, Charlie! are ye sae muckle ta'en up wi' your bonny bride, that your mother's already forgotten?'

He felt the reproof, and immediately turned and went back to make some apology, but she prevented him by saying,—

'See that this is no a Jacob and Esau business, Charlie, and that ye dinna wrang poor Watty; for he's an easy good-natured lad, and will just do what either you or his father bids him.'

Charles laughed, and replied,—

'I think, mother, your exhortation should rather be to Watty than me; for ye ken Jacob was the youngest, and beguiled his auld brother of the birth-right.'

The old man heard the remark, and felt it rush through his very soul with the anguish of a barbed and feathered arrow; and he exclaimed, with an accent of remorse as sharp and bitter as the voice of anger,—

'Hae done wi' your clavers, and come awa. Do ye think Mr Keelevin has nothing mair to do than to wait for us, while ye're talking profanity, and taigling at this gait? Come awa, Watty, ye gumshionless cuif, as ever father was plagued wi'; and Charlie, my lad, let us gang thegither, the haverel will follow; for if it has na the colley-dog's sense, it has something like its instinct.'

And so saying, he stepped on hastily towards the gate, swinging his staff in his right hand, and walking faster and more erectly than he was wont.

The two sons, seeing the pace at which their father was going forward, parted from their mother and followed him, Charles laughing and jeering at the beau which Walter had made of himself.

During the journey the old man kept aloof from them, turning occasionally round to rebuke their mirth, for there was something in the freedom and gaiety of Charles's laugh that reproached his spirit, and the folly of Walter was never so disagreeable to him before.

When they reached the office of Mr Keelevin, they found him with the parchments ready on the desk; but before reading them over, he requested the Laird to step in with him into his inner-chamber.

'Noo, Mr Walkinshaw,' said he, when he had shut the door, 'I hope ye have well reflected on this step, for when it is done, there's nae power in the law o' Scotland to undo it. I would, therefore, fain hope ye're no doing this out of any motive or feeling of resentment for the thoughtless marriage, it may be, of your auld son.'

Claud assured him, that he was not in the slightest degree influenced by any such sentiment; adding, 'But, Mr Keelevin, though I employ you to do my business, I dinna think ye ought to catechise me. Ye're, as I would say, but the pen in this matter, and the right or the wrong o't's a' my ain.

I would, therefore, counsel you, noo that the papers are ready, that they should be implemented, and for that purpose, I hae brought my twa sons to be the witnesses themselves to the act and deed.'

Mr Keelevin held up his hands, and, starting back, gave a deep sigh as he said,—'It's no possible that Charlie can be consenting to his own disinheritance, or he's as daft as his brother.'

'Consenting here, or consenting there, Mr Keelevin,' replied the father, 'ye'll just bring in the papers and read them o'er to me; ye need na fash to ca' ben the lads, for that might breed strife atween them.'

'Na! as sure's death, Mr Walkinshaw,' exclaimed the honest writer, with a warmth and simplicity rather obsolete among his professional brethren now-a-days, however much they may have been distinguished for those qualities in the innocent golden age; 'Na! as sure's death, Mr Walkinshaw, this is mair than I hae the conscience to do; the lads are parties to the transaction, by their reversionary interest, and it is but right and proper they should know what they are about.'

'Mr Keelevin,' cried the Laird, peevishly, 'ye're surely growing doited. It would be an unco like thing if witnesses to our wills and testaments had a right to ken what we bequeathe. Please God, neither Charlie nor Watty sall be ony the wiser o' this day's purpose, as lang as the breath's in my body.'

'Weel, Mr Walkinshaw,' replied the lawyer, 'ye'll tak your own way o't, I see that; but, as ye led me to believe, I hope an' trust it's in your power to make up to Charles the consequences of this very extraordinary entail; and I hope ye'll lose no time till ye hae done sae.'

'Mr Keelevin, ye'll read the papers,' was the brief and abrupt answer which Claud made to this admonition; and the papers were accordingly brought in and read.

During the reading, Claud was frequently afflicted by the discordant cheerfulness of Charles's voice in the outer room, joking with the clerks, at the expence of his fortunate brother; but the task of aforesaids and hereafters being finished, he called them in, with a sharp and peevish accent, and signed the deeds in their presence. Charles took the pen from his father, and also at once signed as witness, while Mr Keelevin looked the living image of amazement; but, when the pen was presented to Watty, he refused to take it.

'What am I to get by this?' said the natural, mindful of his mother's advice. 'I would like to ken that. Nobody writes papers without payment.'

'T'ou's a born idiot,' said the father; 'wilt t'ou no do as t'ou's bidden?'

'I'll do ony other thing ye like, but I'll no sign that drum-head paper, without an advantage: ye would na get Mr Keelevin to do the like o't without payment; and what for should ye get me? Have na I come in a' the gait frae the Grippy to do this; and am I no to get a black bawbee for my pains?'

The Laird masked the vexation with which this idiot speech of his destined heir troubled his self-possession, while Charles sat down in one of the chairs, convulsed with laughter. Claud was not, however, to be deterred from his purpose by the absurdity of his son: on the contrary, he was afraid to make the extent of the fool's folly too evident, lest it might afterwards be rendered instrumental to set aside the entail. He called in one of the clerks from the outer-chamber, and requested him to attest his signature. Walter loudly complained of being so treated; and said, that he expected a guinea, at the very least, for the trouble he had been put to; for so he interpreted the advantage to which his mother had alluded.

'Weel, weel,' said his father, 'ha'd thy tongue, and t'ou sail get a guinea; but first sign this other paper,' presenting to him the second deed; by which, as possessor of the Plealands' estate, he entailed it in the same manner, and to the same line of succession, as he had himself destined the Grippy.

The assurance of the guinea was effectual; Walter signed the deed, which was witnessed by Charles and the clerk; and the disinheritance was thus made complete.

Chapter XXIII

On leaving the office of Mr Keelevin, Charles invited his father and brother to go home with him; but the old man abruptly turned away. Walter, however, appeared inclined to accept the invitation, and was moving off with Charles, when their father looked back, and chidingly commanded him to come along.

At any other time, this little incident would have been unnoticed by Charles, who, believing the old man had made some liberal provision for him or for his wife, was struck with the harsh contrast of such behaviour to the paternal affection by which he thought him actuated; and he paused, in consequence, thoughtfully looking after him as he walked towards the Cross, followed by Walter.

Grippy had not proceeded above twenty or thirty paces when he stopped, and turning round, called to his son, who immediately obeyed the summons.

'Charlie,' said he, 'I hope t'ou'll let nae daffing nor ploys about this marriage o' thine tak up thy attention frae the shop; for business maun be minded; and I'm thinking t'ou had as weel be making up a bit balance-sheet, that I may see how the counts stand between us.'

This touched an irksome recollection, and recalled to mind the observation which his father had made on the occasion of Fatherlans' ruin, with respect to the hazards of taking into partnership a man with the prospect of a family.

'I hope,' was his reply, 'that it is not your intention, sir, to close accounts with me?'

'No, Charlie, no,' was his answer.—'I'll may be mak things better for thee—t'ou'll no be out o' the need o't. But atween hands mak up the balance-sheet, and come doun on Saturday wi' thy wife to Grippy, and we'll hae some discourse anent it.'

With these words, the old man and Walter again went on towards the Cross, leaving Charles standing perplexed, and unable to divine the source and motives of his father's behaviour. It seemed altogether so unaccountable, that for a moment he thought of going back to Mr Keelevin to ask him concerning the settlements; but a sense of propriety restrained him, and he thought it alike indelicate and dishonourable, to pry into an affair which was so evidently concealed from him. But this restraint, and these considerations, did not in any degree tend to allay the anxiety which the mysteriousness of his father's conduct had so keenly excited; so that, when he returned home to Isabella, he appeared absent and thoughtful, which she attributed to some disappointment in his expectations,—an idea the more natural to her, as she had, from the visit on Sunday, been haunted with an apprehension that there was something unsound in the reconciliation.

Upon being questioned as to the cause of his altered spirits, Charles could give no feasible reason for the change. He described what had passed, he mentioned what his father had said, and he communicated the invitation, in all which there was nothing that the mind could lay hold of, nor ought to justify his strange and indescribable apprehension, if that feeling might be called an apprehension, to which his imagination could attach no danger, nor conjure up any thing to be feared. On the contrary, so far from having reason to suspect that evil was meditated against him, he had received a positive assurance that his circumstances would probably receive an immediate improvement; but for all that, there had been, in the reserve of the old man's manner, and in the vagueness of his promises, a something which sounded hollowly to his hope, and deprived him of confidence in the anticipations he had cherished.

While Isabella and he were sitting together conversing on the subject, the old Lady Plealands came in, anxious to hear what had been done, having previously been informed of the intended settlements, but not of their nature and objects. In her character, as we have already intimated, there was a considerable vein, if not of romantic sentiment, unquestionably of morbid sensibility. She disliked her son-in-law from the first moment in which she saw him; and this dislike had made her so averse to his company, that, although their connection was now nearly of four-and-twenty years standing, she had still but a very imperfect notion of his character. She regarded him as one of the most sordid of men, without being aware that avarice with him was but an agent in the pursuit of that ancestral phantom which he worshipped as the chief, almost the only good in life; and, therefore, could neither imagine any possible ground for supposing, that, after being reconciled, he could intend his first-born any injury, nor sympathize with the anxieties which her young friends freely confessed both felt, while she could not but deplore the unsatisfactory state of their immediate situation.

In the meantime, Walter and his father were walking homeward. The old man held no communion with his son; but now and then he rebuked him for hallooing at birds in the hedges, or chasing butterflies, a sport so unbecoming his years.

In their way they had occasion to pass the end of the path which led to Kilmarkeckle, where Miss Bodle, the heiress, resided with her father.

'Watty,' said Grippy to his son, 'gae thy ways hame by thysel, and tell thy mither that am gaun up to the Kilmarkeckle to hae some discourse wi' Mr Bodle, so that she need na weary if I dinna come hame to my dinner.'

'Ye had better come hame,' said Watty, 'for there's a sheep's head in the pat, wi' a cuff o' the neck like ony Glasgow bailie's.—Ye'll no get the like o't at Kilmarkeckle, where the kail's sae thin that every pile o' barley runs roun' the dish, bobbing and bidding gude day to its neighbour.'

Claud had turned into the footpath from the main road, but there was something in this speech which did more than provoke his displeasure; and he said aloud, and with an accent of profound dread,—'I hope the Lord can forgi'e me for what I hae done to this fool!'

Walter was not so void of sense as to be incapable of comprehending the substance of this contrite exclamation; and instantly recollecting his mother's admonition, and having some idea, imperfect as it was, of the peril of parchments with seals on them, he began, with obstreperous sobs and wails, to weep and cry, because, as he said, 'My father and our Charlie had fastened on me the black bargain o' a law plea to wrang me o' auld daddy's mailing.'

Grippy was petrified; it seemed to him that his son was that day smitten in anger to him by the hand of Heaven, with a more disgusting idiocy than he had ever before exhibited, and, instigated by the aversion of the moment, he rushed towards him, and struck him so furiously with his stick, that he sent him yelling homeward as fast as he could run. The injustice and the rashness of the action were felt at once, and, overpowered for a few seconds by shame, remorse, and grief, the old man sat down on a low dry-stone wall that bounded the road on one side, and clasping his hands fervently together, confessed with bitter tears that he doubted he had committed a great sin. It was, however, but a transitory contrition, for, hearing some one approaching, he rose abruptly, and lifting his stick, which he had dropped in his agitation, walked up the footpath towards Kilmarkeckle; but he had not advanced many paces when a hand was laid on his shoulder. He looked round, and it was Walter, with his hat folded together in his hand.

'Father,' said the fool, 'I hae catched a muckle bum-bee; will ye help to haud it till I take out the honey blob?'

'I'll go hame, Watty—I'll go hame,' was the only answer he made, in an accent of extreme sorrow, 'I'll go hame; I daur do nae mair this day,' and he returned back with Walter to the main road, where, having again recovered his self-possession, he said, 'I'm dafter than thee to gang on in this fool gait; go, as I bade thee, hame and tell thy mother no to look for me to dinner, for I'll aiblins bide wi' Kilmarkeckle.' In saying which, he turned briskly round, and, without ever looking behind, walked with an alert step, swinging his staff courageously, and never halted till he reached Kilmarkeckle-house, where he was met at the door by Mr Bodle himself, who, seeing him approaching up the avenue, came out to meet him.

Chapter XXIV

Bodle of Kilmarkeckle, like all the lairds of that time, was come of an ancient family, in some degree related to the universal stock of Adam, but how much more ancient, no historian has yet undertaken to show. Like his contemporaries of the same station, he was, of course, proud of his lineage; but he valued himself more on his own accomplishments than even on the superior purity of his blood. We are, however, in doubt, whether he ought to be described as an artist or a philosopher, for he had equal claims to the honour of being both, and certainly without question, in the art of delineating hieroglyphical resemblances of birds and beasts on the walls of his parlour with snuff, he had evinced, if not talent or genius, at least considerable industry. In the course of more than twenty years, he had not only covered the walls with many a curious and grotesque form, but invented,—and therein lay the principle of his philosophy—a particular classification, as original and descriptive as that of Linnaeus.

At an early age he had acquired the habit of taking snuff, and in process of time became, as all regular snuff-takers are, acute in discriminating the shades and inflections of flavour in the kind to which he was addicted. This was at once the cause and the principle of his science. For the nature of each of the birds and beasts which he modelled resembled, as he averred, some peculiarity in the tobacco of which the snuff that they severally represented had been made; and really, to do him justice, it was quite wonderful to hear with what ingenuity he could explain the discriminative qualities in which the resemblance of attributes and character consisted. But it must be confessed, that he sometimes fell into that bad custom remarkable among philosophers, of talking a great deal too much to every body, and on every occasion, of his favourite study. Saving this, however, the Laird of Kilmarkeckle was in other respects a harmless easy-tempered man, of a nature so kind and indulgent, that he allowed all about him to grow to rankness. The number of cats of every size and age which frisked in his parlour, or basked at the sunny side of the house, exceeded all reasonable credibility, and yet it was a common saying among the neighbours, that Kilmarkeckle's mice kittled twice as often as his cats.

In nothing was his easy and indulgent nature more shown than in his daughter, Miss Betty, who having, at an early age, lost her mother, he had permitted to run unbridled among the servants, till the habits which she had acquired in consequence rendered every subsequent attempt to reduce her into the requisite subjection of the sex totally unavailing.

She had turned her twentieth year, and was not without beauty, but of such a sturdy and athletic kind, that, with her open ruddy countenance, laughing eyes, white well-set teeth, and free and joyous step and air, justly entitled her to the nickname of Fun, bestowed by Charles Walkinshaw.

She was fond of dogs and horses, and was a better shot than the Duke of Douglas's gamekeeper. Bold, boisterous, and frank, she made no scruple of employing her whip when rudely treated, either by master or man; for she frequently laid herself open to freedoms from both, and she neither felt nor pretended to any of her sex's gentleness nor delicacy. Still she was not without a conciliatory portion of feminine virtues, and perhaps, had she been fated to become the wife of a sportsman or a soldier, she might possibly have appeared on the turf or in the tent to considerable advantage.

Such a woman, it may be supposed, could not but look with the most thorough contempt on Walter Walkinshaw; and yet, from the accidental circumstance of being often his playmate in childhood, and making him, in the frolic of their juvenile amusements, her butt and toy, she had contracted something like an habitual affection for the creature; in so much, that, when her father, after Claud's visit, proposed Walter for her husband, she made no serious objection to the match; on the contrary, she laughed, and amused herself with the idea of making him fetch and carry as whimsically as of old, and do her hests and biddings as implicitly as when they were children. Every thing thus seemed auspicious to a speedy and happy union of the properties of Kilmarkeckle and Grippy,—indeed, so far beyond the most sanguine expectations of Claud, that, when he saw the philosophical Laird coming next morning, with a canister of snuff in his hand, to tell him the result of the communication to Miss Betty, his mind was prepared to hear a most decided, and even a menacing refusal, for having ventured to make the proposal.

'Come away, Kilmarkeckle,' said he, meeting him at the door: 'come in by—what's the best o' your news this morning? I hope nothing's wrang at hame, to gar you look sae as ye were fasht?'

'Troth,' replied Kilmarkeckle, 'I hae got a thing this morning that's very vexatious. Last year, at Beltane, ye should ken, I coft frae Donald McSneeshen, the tobacconist aboon the Cross of Glasgow, a canister of a kind that I ca'd the Linty. It was sae brisk in the smeddum, so pleasant to the smell, garring ye trow in the sniffling that ye were sitting on a bonny green knowe in hay time, by the side of a blooming whin-bush, hearkening to the blythe wee birdies singing sangs, as it were, to pleasure the summer's sun; and what would ye think, Mr Walkinshaw, here is another canister of a sort that I'll defy ony ordinary nose to tell the difference, and yet, for the life o' me, I canna gie't in conscience anither name than the Hippopotamus.'

'But hae ye spoken to your dochter?' said Grippy, interrupting him, and apprehensive of a dissertation.

'O aye, atweel I hae done that.'

'And what did Miss Betty say?'

'Na, an ye had but seen and heard her, ye would just hae dee't, Mr Walkinshaw. I'm sure I wonder wha the lassie taks her light-hearted merriment frae, for her mother was a sober and sedate sensible woman; I never heard her jocose but ance, in a' the time we were thegither, and that was when I expounded to her how Maccaba is like a nightingale, the whilk, as I hae seen and read in print, is a feathert fowl that has a great notion o' roses.'

'I was fear't for that,' rejoined Claud, suspecting that Miss Betty had ridiculed the proposal.

'But to gae back to the Linty and the Hippopotamus,' resumed Kilmarkeckle. 'The snuff that I hae here in this canister—tak a pree o't, Mr Walkinshaw—it was sent me in a present frae Mr Glassford, made out of the primest hogget in his last cargo—what think ye o't? Noo, I would just speer gin ye could tell wherein it may be likened to a hippopotamus, the which is a creature living in the rivers of Afrikaw, and has twa ivory teeth, bigger, as I am creditably informed, than the blade o' a scythe.'

Claud, believing that his proposal had been rejected, and not desirous of reverting to the subject, encouraged the philosopher to talk, by saying, that he could not possibly imagine how snuff could be said to resemble any such creature.

'That's a' that ye ken?' said Kilmarkeckle, chuckling with pleasure, and inhaling a pinch with the most cordial satisfaction. 'This snuff is just as like a hippopotamus as the other sort that was sae like it, was like a linty; and nothing could be plainer; for, even now when I hae't in my nostril, I think I see the creature wallowing and wantoning in some wide river in a lown sunny day, wi' its muckle glad e'en, wamling wi' delight in its black head, as it lies lapping in the clear callour water, wi' its red tongue, twirling and twining round its ivory teeth, and every now and then giving another lick.'

'But I dinna see any likeness in that to snuff, Mr Bodle,' said Claud.

'That's most extraordinary, Mr Walkinshaw; for surely there is a likeness somewhere in every thing that brings another thing to mind; and although as yet I'll no point out to you the vera particularity in a hippopotamus by which this snuff gars me think o' the beast, ye must, nevertheless, allow past a' dispute, that there is a particularity.'

Claud replied with ironical gravity, that he thought the snuff much more like a meadow, for it had the smell and flavour of new hay.

'Ye're no far frae the mark, Grippy; and now I'll tell you wherein the likeness lies. The hay, ye ken, is cut down by scythes in meadows; meadows lie by water sides: the teeth of the hippopotamus is as big as scythes; and he slumbers and sleeps in the rivers of Afrikaw; so the snuff, smelling like hay, brings a' thae things to mind; and therefore it is like a hippopotamus.'

After enjoying a hearty laugh at this triumph of his reasoning, the philosopher alighted from his hobby, and proceeded to tell Claud that he had spoken to his daughter, and that she had made no objection to the match.

'Heavens preserve us, Mr Bodle!' exclaimed Grippy; 'wha were ye havering sae about a brute beast, and had sic blithsome news to tell me?'

They then conversed somewhat circumstantially regarding the requisite settlements, Kilmarkeckle agreeing entirely with every thing that the sordid and cunning bargainer proposed, until the whole business was arranged, except the small particular of ascertaining how the appointed bridegroom stood affected. This however, his father undertook to manage, and also that Walter should go in the evening to Kilmarkeckle, and in person make a tender of his heart and hand to the blooming, boisterous, and bouncing Miss Betty.

Chapter XXV

'Watty,' said the Laird o' Grippy to his hopeful heir, calling him into the room, after Kilmarkeckle had retired,—

'Watty, come ben and sit down; I want to hae some solid converse wi' thee. Dist t'ou hearken to what I'm saying?—Kilmarkeckle has just been wi' me—Hear'st t'ou me?—deevil an I saw the like o' thee—what's t'ou looking at? As I was saying Kilmarkeckle has been here, and he was thinking that you and his dochter'—

'Weel,' interrupted Watty, 'if ever I saw the like o' that. There was a Jenny Langlegs bumming at the corner o' the window, when down came a spider wabster as big as a puddock, and claught it in his arms; and he's off and awa wi' her intil his nest;—I ne'er saw the like o't.'

'It's most extraordinar, Watty Walkinshaw,' exclaimed his father peevishly, 'that I canna get a mouthful o' common sense out o' thee, although I was just telling thee o' the greatest advantage that t'ou's ever likely to meet wi' in this world. How would ye like Miss Betty Bodle for a wife?'

'O father!'

'I'm saying, would na she make a capital Leddy o' the Plealands?'

Walter made no reply, but laughed, and chuckingly rubbed his hands, and then delightedly patted the sides of his thighs with them.

'I'm sure ye canna fin' ony fau't wi' her; there's no a brawer nor a better tocher'd lass in the three shires.—What think'st t'ou?'

Walter suddenly suspended his ecstasy; and grasping his knees firmly, he bent forward, and, looking his father seriously in the face, said,—

'But will she no thump me? Ye mind how she made my back baith black and blue.—I'm frightit.'

'Haud thy tongue wi' sic nonsense; that happened when ye were but bairns. I'm sure there's no a blither, bonnier quean in a' the kintra side.'

'I'll no deny that she has red cheeks, and e'en like blobs o' honey dew in a kail-blade; but father—Lord, father! she has a neive like a beer mell.'

'But for a' that, a sightly lad like you might put up wi' her, Watty. I'm sure ye'll gang far, baith east and west, before ye'll meet wi' her marrow; and ye should reflek on her tocher, the whilk is a wull-ease that's no to be found at ilka dykeside.'

'Aye, so they say; her uncle 'frauded his ain only dochter, and left her a stocking fu' o' guineas for a legacy.—But will she let me go halffer?'

'Ye need na misdoubt that; na, an ye fleech her weel, I would na be surprised if she would gi'e you the whole tot; and I'm sure ye ne'er hae seen ony woman that ye can like better.'

'Aye, but I hae though,' replied Watty confidently.

'Wha is't?' exclaimed his father, surprised and terrified.

'My mother.'

The old man, sordid as he was, and driving thus earnestly his greedy purpose, was forced to laugh at the solemn simplicity of this answer; but he added, resuming his perseverance,—

'True! I did na think o' thy mother, Watty—but an t'ou was ance marriet to Betty Bodle, t'ou would soon like her far better than thy mother.'

'The fifth command says, "Honour thy father and thy mother, that thy days may be long in the land;" and there's no ae word about liking a wife in a' the rest.'

'Weel, weel, but what I hae to say is, that me and Kilmarkeckle hae made a paction for thee to marry his dochter, and t'ou maun just gang o'er the night and court Miss Betty.'

'But I dinna ken the way o't, father; I ne'er did sic a thing a' my days; odd, I'm unco blate to try't.'

'Gude forgi'e me,' said Claud to himself, 'but the creature grows sillier and sillier every day—I tell thee, Watty Walkinshaw, to pluck up the spirit o' manhood, and gang o'er this night to Kilmarkeckle, and speak to Miss Betty by yoursel about the wedding.

'Atweel, I can do that, and help her to buy her parapharnauls,—We will hae a prime apple-pye that night, wi' raisins in't.'

The old man was petrified.—It seemed to him that it was utterly impossible the marriage could ever take place, and he sat for some time stricken, as it were, with a palsy of the mind. But these intervals of feeling and emotion were not of long duration; his inflexible character, and the ardour with which his whole spirit was devoted to the attainment of one object, soon settled an silenced all doubt, contrition, and hesitation; and considering, so far as Walter was concerned, the business decided, he summoned his wife to communicate to her the news.—'Girzy Hypel,' said he as she entered the room, holding by the neck a chicken, which she was assisting the maids in the kitchen to pluck for dinner, and the feathers of which were sticking thickly on the blue worsted apron which she had put on to protect her old red quilted silk petticoat.

'Girzy Hypel, be nane surprised to hear of a purpose of marriage soon between Watty and Betty Bodle.'

'No possible!' exclaimed the Leddy, sitting down, with vehemence in her astonishment, and flinging, at the same time the chicken across her lap, with a certain degree of instinctive or habitual dexterity.

'What for is't no possible?' said the Laird, angrily through his teeth, apprehensive that she was going to raise some foolish objection.

'Na, gudeman, an that's to be a come-to-pass—let nobody talk o' miracles to me. For although it's a thing just to the nines o' my wishes, I hae ay jealoused that Betty Bodle would na tak him, for she's o' a rampant nature, and he's a sober weel-disposed lad. My word, Watty, t'ou has thy ain luck—first thy grandfather's property o' the Plealands, and syne'—She was going to add, 'sic a bonny braw-tochered lass as Betty Bodle'—but her observation struck jarringly on the most discordant string in her husband's bosom and he interrupted her, sharply, saying,—

'Every thing that's ordained will come to pass; and a' that I hae for the present to observe to you, Girzy, is to tak tent that the lad gangs over wiselike, at the gloaming, to Kilmarkeckle, in order to see Miss Betty anent the wedding.'

'I'm sure,' retorted the Leddy, 'I hae no need to green for weddings in my family, for, instead o' any pleasance to me, the deil-be-licket's my part and portion o' the pastime but girns and gowls. Gudeman, ye should learn to keep your temper, and be of a composed spirit, and talk wi' me in a sedate manner, when our bairns are changing their life. Watty, my lad, mind what your mother says—"Marriage is a creel, where ye maun catch," as the auld byword runs, "an adder or an eel." But, as I was rehearsing, I could na hae thought that Betty Bodle would hae fa'en just at ance into your grip; for I had a notion that she was oure souple in the tail to be easily catched. But it's the Lord's will, Watty; and I hope ye'll enjoy a' manner o' happiness wi' her, and be a confort to ane anither, like your father and me,—bringing up your bairns in the fear o' God, as we hae done you, setting them, in your walk and conversation, a patren of sobriety and honesty, till they come to years of discretion, when, if it's ordained for them, nae doubt they'll look, as ye hae done, for a settlement in the world, and ye maun part wi' them, as we are obligated, by course of nature, to part with you.'

At the conclusion of which pathetic address, the old lady lifted her apron to wipe the gathered drops from her eyes, when Watty exclaimed,—

'Eh! mother, ane o' the hen's feathers is playing at whirley wi' the breath o' your nostril!'

Thus ended the annunciation of the conjugal felicity of which Grippy was the architect.

After dinner, Walter, dressed and set off to the best advantage by the assistance of his mother, walked, accompanied by his father, to Kilmarkeckle; and we should do him injustice if we did not state, that, whatever might be his intellectual deficiencies, undoubtedly in personal appearance, saving, perhaps, some little lack of mental light in his countenance, he was cast in a mould to find favour in any lady's eye. Perhaps he did not carry himself quite as firmly as if he had been broke in by a serjeant of dragoons, and in his air and gait we shall not undertake to affirm that there was nothing lax nor slovenly but still, upon the whole, he was, as his mother said, looking after him as he left the house, 'a braw bargain of manhood, him wha would.'

Chapter XXVI

After Kilmarkeckle had welcomed Grippy and Walter, he began to talk of the hippopotamus, by showing them the outlines of a figure which he intended to fill up with the snuff on the wall. Claud, however, cut him short, by proposing, in a whisper, that Miss Betty should be called in, and that she and Walter should be left together, while they took a walk to discuss the merits of the hippopotamus. This was done quickly, and, accordingly, the young lady made her appearance, entering the room with a blushing giggle, perusing her Titan of a suitor from head to heel with the beam of her eye.

'We'll leave you to yoursels,' said her father jocularly, 'and, Watty, be brisk wi' her, lad; she can thole a touzle, I'se warrant.'

This exhortation had, however, no immediate effect, for Walter, from the moment she made her appearance, looked awkward and shamefaced, swinging his hat between his legs, with his eyes fixed on the brazen head of the tongs, which were placed upright astradle in front of the grate; but every now and then he peeped at her from the corner of his eye with a queer and luscious glance, which, while it amused, deterred her for some time from addressing him. Diffidence, however, had nothing to do with the character of Miss Betty Bodle, and a feeling of conscious superiority soon overcame the slight embarrassment which arose from the novelty of her situation.

Observing the perplexity of her lover, she suddenly started from her seat, and advancing briskly towards him, touched him on the shoulder, saying,—

'Watty,—I say, Watty, what's your will wi' me?'

'Nothing,' was the reply, while he looked up knowingly in her face.

'What are ye fear't for? I ken what ye're come about,'said she, 'my father has telt me.'

At these encouraging words, he leaped from his chair with an alacrity unusual to his character, and attempted to take her in his arms; but she nimbly escaped from his clasp, giving him, at the same time, a smart slap on the cheek.

'That's no fair, Betty Bodle,' cried the lover, rubbing his cheek, and looking somewhat offended and afraid.

'Then what gart you meddle wi' me?' replied the bouncing girl, with a laughing bravery that soon reinvigorated his love.

'I'm sure I was na gaun to do you ony harm,' was the reply;—'no, as sure's death, Betty, I would rather cut my finger than do you ony scaith, for I like you so weel—I canna tell you how weel; but, if ye'll tak me, I'll mak you the Leddy o' the Plealands in a jiffy, and my mother says that my father will gie me a hundred pound to buy you parapharnauls and new plenishing.'

The young lady was probably conciliated by the manner in which this was said; for she approached towards him, and while still affecting to laugh, it was manifest even to Walter himself that she was not displeased by the alacrity with which he had come to the point. Emboldened by her freedom, he took her by the hand, looking, however, away from her, as if he was not aware of what he had done; and in this situation they stood for the space of two or three minutes without speaking. Miss Betty was the first to break silence:—

'Weel, Watty,' said she, 'what are ye going to say to me?'

'Na,' replied he, becoming almost gallant; 'it's your turn to speak noo. I hae spoken my mind, Betty Bodle—Eh! this is a bonny hand; and what a sonsy arm ye hae—I could amaist bite your cheek, Betty Bodle—I could.'

'Gude preserve me, Watty! ye're like a wud dog.'

'An I were sae, I would worry you,' was his animated answer, while he turned round, and devoured her with kisses; a liberty which she instantaneously resented, by vigorously pushing him from her, and driving him down into her father's easy chair; his arm in the fall rubbing off half a score of the old gentleman's snuffy representatives.

But, notwithstanding this masculine effort of maiden modesty, Miss Betty really rejoiced in the ardent intrepidity of her lover, and said, merrily,

'I redde you, Watty, keep your distance; man and wife's man and wife; but I'm only Betty Bodle, and ye're but Watty Walkinshaw.'

'Od, Betty,' replied Watty, not more than half-pleased, as he rubbed his right elbow, which was hurt in the fall, 'ye're desperate strong, woman; and what were ye the waur o' a bit slaik o' a kiss?' Howsever, my bonny dawty, we'll no cast out for a' that; for if ye'll just marry me, and I'm sure ye'll no get any body that can like you half so weel, I'll do any thing ye bid me, as sure's death I will—there's my hand, Betty Bodle, I will; and I'll buy you the bravest satin gown in a' Glasgow, wi' far bigger flowers on't than on any ane in a' Mrs Bailie Nicol Jarvie's aught. And we'll live in the Plealands-house, and do nothing frae dawn to dark but shoo ane another on a swing between the twa trees on the green; and I'll be as kind to you, Betty Bodle, as I can be, and buy you likewise a side-saddle, and a poney to ride on; and when the winter comes, sowing the land wi' hailstones to grow frost and snaw, we'll sit cosily at the chumley-lug, and I'll read you a chapter o' the Bible, or aiblins Patie and Roger,—as sure's death I will, Betty Bodle.'

It would seem, indeed, that there is something exalting and inspiring in the tender passion; for the earnest and emphatic manner in which this was said gave a degree of energy to the countenance of Watty, that made him appear in the eyes of his sweetheart, to whom moral vigour was not an object of primary admiration, really a clever and effectual fellow.

'I'll be free wi' you, Watty,' was her answer; 'I dinna objek to tak you, but,' and she hesitated.—

'But what?' said Watty, still exalted above his wont.

'Ye maunna hurry the wedding oure soon.'

'Ye'll get your ain time, Betty Bodle, I'll promise you that,' was his soft answer; 'but when a bargain's struck, the sooner payment's made the better; for, as the copy-line at the school says, "Delays are dangerous."—So, if ye like, Betty, we can be bookit on Saturday, and cried, for the first time, on Sabbath, and syne, a second time next Lord's day, and the third time on the Sunday after, and marriet on the Tuesday following."

'I dinna think, Watty,' said she, laying her hand on his shoulder, 'that we need sic a fasherie o' crying.'

'Then, if ye dinna like it, Betty Bodle, I'm sure neither do I, so we can be cried a' out on ae day, and married on Monday, like my brother and Bell Fatherlans.'

What more might have passed, as the lovers had now come to a perfect understanding with each other, it is needless to conjecture, as the return of the old gentlemen interrupted their conversation; so that, not to consume the precious time of our readers with any unnecessary disquisition, we shall only say, that some objection being stated by Grippy to the first Monday as a day too early for the requisite settlements to be prepared, it was agreed that the booking should take place, as Walter had proposed, on the approaching Saturday, and that the banns should be published, once, on the first Sunday, and twice on the next, and that the wedding should be held on the Tuesday following.

Chapter XXVII

When Charles and Isabella were informed that his brother and Betty Bodle were to be bookit on Saturday, that is, their names recorded, for the publication of the banns, in the books of the kirk-session,—something like a gleam of light seemed to be thrown on the obscurity which invested the motives of the old man's conduct. They were perfectly aware of Walter's true character, and concluded, as all the world did at the time, that the match was entirely of his father's contrivance; and they expected, when Walter's marriage settlement came to be divulged, that they would then learn what provision had been made for themselves. In the meantime, Charles made out the balance-sheet, as he had been desired, and carried it in his pocket when he went on Saturday with his wife to dine at Grippy.

The weather that day was mild for the season, but a thin grey vapour filled the whole air, and saddened every feature of the landscape. The birds sat mute and ourie, and the Clyde, increased by recent upland rains, grumbled with the hoarseness of his wintry voice. The solemnity of external nature awakened a sympathetic melancholy in the minds of the young couple, as they walked towards their father's, and Charles once or twice said that he felt a degree of depression which he had never experienced before.

'I wish, Isabella,' said he, 'that this business of ours were well settled, for I begin, on your account, to grow anxious. I am not superstitious; but I kenna what's in't—every now and then a thought comes over me that I am no to be a long liver—I feel, as it were, that I have na a firm grip of the world—a sma' shock, I doubt, would easily shake me off.'

'I must own,' replied his wife with softness, 'that we have both some reason to regret our rashness. I ought not to have been so weak as to feel the little hardships of my condition so acutely; but, since it is done, we must do our best to bear up against the anxiety that I really think you indulge too much. My advice is, that we should give up speaking about your father's intents, and strive, as well as we can, to make your income, whatever it is, serve us.'

'That's kindly said, my dear Bell, but you know that my father's no a man that can be persuaded to feel as we feel, and I would not be surprised were he to break up his partnership with me, and what should we then do?'

In this sort of anxious and domestic conversation, they approached towards Grippy-house, where they were met on the green in front by Margaret and George, who had not seen them since their marriage.

Miss Meg, as she was commonly called, being at the time on a visit in Argyleshire with a family to whom their mother was related, the Campbells of Glengrowlmaghallochan, and George was also absent on a shooting excursion with some of his acquaintance at the Plealands, the mansion-house of which happened to be then untenanted. Their reception by their brother and sister, especially by Miss Meg, was kind and sisterly, for although in many points she resembled her mother, she yet possessed much more warmth of heart.

The gratulations and welcomings being over, she gave a description of the preparations which had already commenced for Walter's wedding.

'Na, what would ye think,' said she, laughing, 'my father gied him ten pounds to gang intil Glasgow the day to buy a present for the bride, and ye'll hardly guess what he has sent her,—a cradle,—a mahogany cradle, shod wi' roynes, that it may na waken the baby when its rocking.'

'But that would na tak all the ten pounds?' said Charles, diverted by the circumstance; 'what has he done wi' the rest?'

'He could na see any other thing to please him, so he tied it in the corner of his napkin, but as he was coming home flourishing it round his head, it happened to strike the crookit tree at the water side, and the whole tot o' the siller, eight guineas, three half-crowns, and eighteenpence, played whir to the very middle o' the Clyde. He has na got the grief o' the loss greetten out yet.'

Before there was time for any observation to be made on this misfortune, the bridegroom came out to the door, seemingly in high glee, crying, 'See what I hae gotten,' showing another note for ten pounds, which his father had given to pacify him, before Kilmarkeckle and the bride arrived; they being also expected to dinner.

It happened that Isabella, dressed in her gayest apparel for this occasion, had brought in her hand, wrapt in paper, a pair of red Morocco shoes, which, at that period, were much worn among lairds' daughters; for the roads, being deep and sloughy, she had, according to the fashion of the age, walked in others of a coarser kind; and Walter's eye accidentally lighting on the shoes, he went up, without preface, to his sister-in-law, and, taking the parcel gently out of her hand, opened it, and contemplating the shoes, holding one in each hand at arm's length, said, 'Bell Fatherlans, what will ye tak to sell thir bonny red cheeket shoon?—I would fain buy them for Betty Bodle.'

Several minutes elapsed before it was possible to return any answer; but when composure was in some degree regained, Mrs Charles Walkinshaw said,—

'Ye surely would never buy old shoes for your bride? I have worn them often. It would be an ill omen to give her a second-hand present, Mr Walter; besides, I don't think they would fit.'

This little incident had the effect of tuning the spirits of Charles and his wife into some degree of unison with the main business of the day; and the whole party entered the house bantering and laughing with Walter. But scarcely had they been seated, when their father said,—

'Charlie, has t'ou brought the balance-sheet, as I bade thee?'

This at once silenced both his mirth and Isabella's, and the old man expressed his satisfaction on receiving it, and also that the profits were not less than he expected.

Having read it over carefully, he then folded it slowly up, and put it into his pocket, and, rising from his seat, walked three or four times across the room, followed by the eyes of his beating-hearted son and daughter-in-law—at last he halted.

'Weel, Charlie,' said he, 'I'll no be waur than my word to thee—t'ou sail hae a' the profit made between us since we came thegither in the shop; that will help to get so me bits o' plenishing for a house—and I'll mak, for time coming, an eke to thy share. But, Charlie and Bell, ca' canny; bairns will rise among you, and ye maun bear in mind that I hae baith Geordie and Meg to provide for yet.'

This was said in a fatherly manner, and the intelligence was in so many respects agreeable, that it afforded the anxious young couple great pleasure.

Walter was not, however, satisfied at hearing no allusion to him, and he said,—'And are ye no gaun to do any thing for me, father?'

These words, like the cut of a scourge, tingled to the very soul of the old man, and he looked with a fierce and devouring eye at the idiot;—but said nothing. Walter was not, however, to be daunted; setting up a cry, something between a wail and a howl, he brought his mother flying from the kitchen, where she was busy assisting the maids in preparing dinner—to inquire what had befallen the bridegroom.

'My father's making a step-bairn o' me, mother, and has gi'en Charlie a' the outcome frae the till, and says he's gaun to hain but for Geordie and Meg.'

'Surely, gudeman,' said the Leddy o' Grippy, addressing her husband, who for a moment stood confounded at this obstreperous accusation—'Surely ye'll hae mair naturality than no to gi'e Watty a bairn's part o' gear? Has na he a right to share and share alike wi' the rest, over and aboon what he got by my father? If there's law, justice, or gospel in the land, ye'll be obligated to let him hae his right, an I should sell my coat to pay the cost.'

The old man made no answer; and his children sat in wonder, for they inferred from his silence that he actually did intend to make a step-bairn of Watty.

'Weel;' said the Leddy emphatically, 'but I jealoused something o' this;—I kent there could be nae good at the bottom o' that huggermuggering wi' Keelevin. Hows'ever, I'll see til't, Watty, and I'll gar him tell what he has put intil that abomination o' a paper that ye were deluded to sign.'

Claud, at these words, started from his seat, with the dark face, and pale quivering lips of guilt and vengeance; and, giving a stamp with his foot that shook the whole house, cried,—

'If ye daur to mak or meddle wi' what I hae done.'—

He paused for about the space of half a minute, and then he added, in his wonted calm and sober voice,—'Watty, t'ou has been provided more—I hae done mair for thee than I can weel excuse to mysel—and I charge baith thee and thy mother never, on pain of my curse and everlasting ill-will, to speak ony sic things again.'

'What hae ye done? canna ye tell us, and gie a bodie a satisfaction?' exclaimed the Leddy.

But the wrath again mustered and lowered in his visage, and he said, in a voice so deep and dreadful, so hollow and so troubled, from the very innermost caverns of his spirit, that it made all present tremble,—

'Silence, woman, silence.'

'Eh! there's Betty Bodle and her father,' exclaimed Watty, casting his eyes, at that moment, towards the window, and rushing from his seat, with an extravagant flutter, to meet them, thus happily terminating a scene which threatened to banish the anticipated festivity and revels of the day.

Chapter XXVIII

Leddy Grippy having been, as she herself observed, 'cheated baith o' bridal and in fare by Charlie's moonlight marriage,'was resolved to have all made up to her, and every jovial and auspicious rite performed at Walter's wedding.—Accordingly, the interval between the booking and the day appointed for the ceremony was with her all bustle and business. Nor were the preparations at Kilmarkeckle to send forth the bride in proper trim, in any degree less active or liberal. Among other things, it had been agreed that each of the two families should kill a cow for the occasion, but an accident rendered this unnecessary at Grippy.

At this time, Kilmarkeckle and Grippy kept two bulls who cherished the most deadly hatred of each other, in so much, that their respective herds had the greatest trouble to prevent them from constantly fighting. And on the Thursday preceding the wedding-day, Leddy Grippy, in the multitude of her cares and concerns, having occasion to send a message to Glasgow, and, unable to spare any of the other servants, called the cow-boy from the field, and dispatched him on the errand. Bausy, as their bull was called, taking advantage of his keeper's absence, went muttering and growling for some time round the inclosure, till at last discovering a gap in the hedge, he leapt through, and, flourishing his tail, and grumbling as hoarse as an earthquake, he ran, breathing wrath and defiance, straight on towards a field beyond where Gurl, Kilmarkeckle's bull, was pasturing in the most conjugal manner with his sultanas.

Gurl knew the voice of his foe, and, raising his head from the grass, bellowed a hoarse and sonorous answer to the challenger, and, in the same moment, scampered to the hedge, on the outside of which Bausy was roaring his threats of vengeance and slaughter. The two adversaries glared for a moment at each other, and then galloped along the sides of the hedge in quest of an opening through which they might rush to satisfy their rage.

In the meantime, Kilmarkeckle's herd-boy had flown to the house for assistance, and Miss Betty, heading all the servants, and armed with a flail, came, at double quick time, to the scene of action. But, before she could bring up her forces, Bausy burst headlong through the hedge, like a hurricane. Gurl, however, received him with such a thundering batter on the ribs, that he fell reeling from the shock. A repetition of the blow laid him on the ground, gasping and struggling with rage, agony, and death, so that, before the bride and her allies were able to drive Gurl from his fallen antagonist, he had gored and fractured him in almost every bone with the force and strength of the beam of a steam-engine. Thus was Leddy Grippy prevented from killing the cow which she had allotted for the wedding-feast, the carcase of Bausy being so unexpectedly substituted.

But, saving this accident, nothing went amiss in the preparations for the wedding either at Grippy or Kilmarkeckle. All the neighbours were invited, and the most joyous anticipations universally prevailed; even Claud himself seemed to be softened from the habitual austerity which had for years gradually encrusted his character, and he partook of the hilarity of his family, and joked with the Leddy in a manner so facetious, that her spirits mounted, and, as she said herself, 'were flichtering in the very air.'

The bridegroom alone, of all those who took any interest in the proceedings, appeared thoughtful and moody; but it was impossible that any lover could be more devoted to his mistress: from morning to night he hovered round the skirts of her father's mansion, and as often as he got a peep of her, he laughed, and then hastily retired, wistfully looking behind, as if he hoped that she would follow. Sometimes this manoeuvre proved successful, and Miss Betty permitted him to encircle her waist with his arm, as they ranged the fields in amatory communion together.

This, although perfectly agreeable to their happy situation, was not at all times satisfactory to his mother; and she frequently chided Watty for neglecting the dinner hour, and 'curdooing,' as she said, 'under cloud o' night.' However, at last every preparatory rite but the feet-washing was performed; and that it also might be accomplished according to the most mirthful observance of the ceremony at that period, Charles and George brought out from Glasgow, on the evening prior to the wedding-day, a score of their acquaintance to assist in the operation on the bridegroom; while Miss Meg, and all the maiden friends of the bride, assembled at Kilmarkeckle to officiate there. But when the hour arrived, Watty was absent. During the mixing of a large bowl of punch, at which Charles presided, he had slily escaped, and not answering to their summons, they were for some time surprised, till it was suggested that possibly he might have gone to the bride, whither they agreed to follow him.

Meanwhile the young ladies had commenced their operations with Miss Betty. The tub, the hot water, and the ring, were all in readiness; her stockings were pulled off, and loud laughter and merry scuffling, and many a freak of girlish gambol was played, as they rubbed her legs, and winded their fingers through the water to find the ring of Fortune, till a loud exulting neigh of gladness at the window at once silenced their mirth.

The bride raised her eyes; her maidens turning round from the tub, looked towards the window, where they beheld Watty standing, his white teeth and large delighted eyes glittering in the light of the room. It is impossible to describe the consternation of the ladies at this profane intrusion on their peculiar mysteries. The bride was the first that recovered her self-possession: leaping from her seat, and over-setting the tub in her fury, she bounded to the door, and, seizing Watty by the cuff of the neck, shook him as a tygress would a buffalo.

'The deevil ride a hunting on you, Watty Walkinshaw, I'll gar you glower in at windows,' was her endearing salutation, seconded by the whole vigour of her hand in a smack on the face, so impressive, that it made him yell till the very echoes yelled again. 'Gang hame wi' you, ye roaring bull o' Bashen, or I'll take a rung to your back,' then followed; and the terrified bridegroom instantly fled coweringly, as if she actually was pursuing him with a staff.

'I trow,' said she, addressing herself to the young ladies who had come to the door after her, I'll learn him better manners, before he's long in my aught.'

'I would be none surprised were he to draw back,' said Miss Jenny Shortridge, a soft and diffident girl, who, instead of joining in the irresistible laughter of her companions, had continued silent, and seemed almost petrified.

'Poo!' exclaimed the bride; 'he draw back! Watty Walkinshaw prove false to me! He dare na, woman, for his very life; but, come, let us gang in and finish the fun.'

But the fun had suffered a material abatement by the breach which had thus been made in it. Miss Meg Walkinshaw, however, had the good luck to find the ring, a certain token that she would be the next married.

In the meantime, the chastised bridegroom, in running homeward, was met by his brothers and their companions, to whose merriment he contributed quite as much as he had subtracted from that of the ladies, by the sincerity with which he related what had happened,—declaring, that he would rather stand in the kirk than tak Betty Bodle; which determination Charles, in the heedlessness and mirth of the moment, so fortified and encouraged, that, before they had returned back to the punch-bowl, Walter was swearing that neither father nor mother would force him to marry such a dragoon. The old man seemed more disturbed than might have been expected from his knowledge of the pliancy of Walter's disposition at hearing him in this humour, while the Leddy said, with all the solemnity suitable to her sense of the indignity which her favourite had suffered,—

'Biting and scarting may be Scotch folks wooing; but, if that's the gait Betty Bodle means to use you, Watty, my dear, I would see her, and a' the Kilmarkeckles that ever were cleck it, doon the water, or strung in a wooddie, before I would hae ony thing to say to ane come o' their seed or breed. To lift her hands to her bridegroom!—The like o't was never heard tell o' in a Christian land—Na, gudeman, nane o' your winks and glooms to me,—I will speak out. She's a perfect drum-major,—the randy cutty— deevil-dome good o' her—it's no to seek what I'll gie her the morn.'

'Dinna grow angry, mother,' interposed Walter, thawing, in some degree, from the sternness of his resentment. 'It was na a very sair knock after a'.'

'T'ou's a fool and a sumph to say any thing about it, Watty,' said Grippy himself; 'many a brawer lad has met wi' far waur; and, if t'ou had na been egget on by Charlie to mak a complaint, it would just hae passed like a pat for true love.'

'Eh na, father, it was na a pat, but a scud like the clap o' a fir deal,' said the bridegroom.

'Weel, weel, Watty,' exclaimed Charlie, 'you must just put up wi't, ye're no a penny the waur o't.' By this sort of conversation Walter was in the end pacified, and reconciled to his destiny.

Chapter XXIX

Never did Nature show herself better pleased on any festival than on Walter's wedding-day. The sun shone out as if his very rays were as much made up of gladness as of light. The dew-drops twinkled as if instinct with pleasure. The birds lilted—the waters and the windows sparkled; cocks crowed as if they were themselves bridegrooms, and the sounds of laughing girls, and cackling hens, made the riant banks of the Clyde joyful for many a mile.

It was originally intended that the minister should breakfast at Kilmarkeckle, to perform the ceremony there; but this, though in accordance with newer and genteeler fashions, was overruled by the young friends of the bride and bridegroom insisting that the wedding should be celebrated with a ranting dance and supper worthy of the olden, and, as they told Leddy Grippy, better times. Hence the liberality of the preparations, as intimated in the preceding chapter.

In furtherance of this plan, the minister, and all his family, were invited, and it was arranged, that the ceremony should not take place till the evening, when the whole friends of the parties, with the bride and bridegroom at their head, should walk in procession after the ceremony from the manse to Grippy, where the barn, by the fair hands of Miss Meg and her companions, was garnished and garlanded for the ball and banquet. Accordingly, as the marriage hour drew near, and as it had been previously concerted by 'the best men' on both sides, a numerous assemblage of the guests took place, both at Grippy and Kilmarkeckle—and, at the time appointed, the two parties, respectively carrying with them the bride and bridegroom, headed by a piper playing 'Hey let us a' to the bridal,' proceeded to the manse, where they were met by their worthy parish pastor at the door.

The Reverend Doctor Denholm was one of those old estimable stock characters of the best days of the presbytery, who, to great learning and sincere piety, evinced an inexhaustible fund of couthy jocularity. He was far advanced in life, an aged man, but withal hale and hearty, and as fond of an innocent ploy, such as a wedding or a christening, as the blithest spirit in its teens of any lad or lass in the parish. But he was not quite prepared to receive so numerous a company; nor, indeed, could any room in the manse have accommodated half the party. He, therefore, proposed to perform the ceremony under the great tree, which sheltered the house from the south-west wind in winter, and afforded shade and shelter to all the birds of summer that ventured to trust themselves beneath its hospitable boughs.

To this, however, Walter, the bridegroom, seemed disposed to make some objection, alleging that it might be a very good place for field-preaching, or for a tent on sacramental occasions, 'but it was an unco like thing to think of marrying folk under the canopy of the heavens; adding, that he did na think it was canny to be married under a tree.'

The Doctor soon, however, obviated this objection, by assuring him that Adam and Eve had been married under a tree.

'Gude keep us a' frae sic a wedding as they had,' replied Watty; 'where the deil was best-man? Howsever, Doctor, sin it's no an apple-tree, I'll mak a conformity.' At which the pipes again struck up, and, led by the worthy Doctor bare-headed, the whole assemblage proceeded to the spot.

'Noo, Doctor,' said the bridegroom, as all present were composing themselves to listen to the religious part of the ceremony—'Noo, Doctor, dinna scrimp the prayer, but tie a sicker knot; I hae nae broo o' the carnality o' five minute marriages, like the Glasgowers, and ye can weel afford to gie us half an hour, 'cause ye're weel payt for the wind o' your mouth: the hat and gloves I sent you cost me four-and-twenty shillings, clean countit out to my brother Charlie, that would na in his niggerality faik me a saxpence on a' the liveries I bought frae him.'

This address occasioned a little delay, but order being again restored, the Reverend Doctor, folding his hands together, and lowering his eyelids, and assuming his pulpit voice, began the prayer.

It was a calm and beautiful evening, the sun at the time appeared to be resting on the flaky amber that adorned his western throne, to look back on the world, as if pleased to see the corn and the fruits gathered, with which he had assisted to fill the wide lap of the matronly earth. We happened at the time to be walking alone towards Blantyre, enjoying the universal air of contentment with which all things at the golden sunsets of autumn invites the anxious spirit of man to serenity and repose.

As we approached the little gate that opened to the footpath across the glebe by which the road to the village was abridged to visitors on foot, our attention was first drawn towards the wedding party, by the kindly, pleasing, deep-toned voice of the venerable pastor, whose solemn murmurs rose softly into the balmy air, diffusing all around an odour of holiness that sweetened the very sense of life.

We paused, and uncovering, walked gently and quietly towards the spot, which we reached just as the worthy Doctor had bestowed the benediction. The bride looked blushing and expectant, but Walter, instead of saluting her in the customary manner, held her by the hand at arm's length, and said to the Doctor, 'Be served.'

'Ye should kiss her, bridegroom,' said the minister.

'I ken that,' replied Watty, 'but no till my betters be served. Help yoursel, Doctor.'

Upon which the Doctor, wiping his mouth with the back of his hand, enjoyed himself as he was requested.

'It's the last buss,' added Walter, 'it's the last buss, Betty Bodle, ye'll e'er gie to mortal man while am your gudeman.'

'I did na think,' said the Reverend Doctor aside to us, 'that the creature had sic a knowledge o' the vows.'

The pipes at this crisis being again filled, the guests, hand in hand, following the bridegroom and bride, then marched to the ornamented barn at Grippy, to which we were invited to follow; but what then ensued deserves a new Chapter.

Chapter XXX

Having accepted the invitation to come with the minister's family to the wedding, we stopped and took tea at the manse with the Reverend Doctor and Mrs Denholm,— the young ladies and their brother having joined the procession. For all our days we have been naturally of a most sedate turn of mind; and although then but in our twenty-third year, we preferred the temperate good humour of the Doctor's conversation, and the householdry topics of his wife, to the boisterous blair of the bagpipes. As soon, however, as tea was over, with Mrs Denholm dressed in her best, and the pastor in his newest suit, we proceeded towards Grippy.

By this time the sun was set, but the speckless topaz of the western skies diffused a golden twilight, that tinged every object with a pleasing mellow softness. Like the wedding-ring of a bashful bride, the new moon just showed her silver rim, and the evening star was kindling her lamp, as we approached the foot of the avenue which led to the house, the windows of which sparkled with festivity; while from the barn the merry yelps of two delighted fiddles, and the good-humoured grumbling of a well pleased bass, mingling with laughter and squeaks, and the thudding of bounding feet, made every pulse in our young blood circle as briskly as the dancers in their reeling.

When we reached the door, the moment that the venerable minister made his appearance, the music stopped, and the dancing was suspended, by which we were enabled to survey the assembly for a few minutes, in its most composed and ceremonious form. At the upper end of the barn stood two arm chairs, one of which, appropriated to the bridegroom, was empty; in the other sat the bride, panting from the vigorous efforts she had made in the reel that was interrupted by our entrance. The bridegroom himself was standing near a table close to the musicians, stirring a large punch-bowl, and filling from time to time the glasses. His father sat in a corner by himself, with his hands leaning on his staff, and his lips firmly drawn together, contemplating the scene before him with a sharp but thoughtful eye. Old Kilmarkeckle, with an ivory snuff-box, mounted with gold, in his hand, was sitting with Mr Keelevin on the left hand of Claud, evidently explaining some remarkable property in the flavour of the snuff, to which the honest lawyer was paying the utmost attention, looking at the philosophical Laird, however, every now and then, with a countenance at once expressive of admiration, curiosity, and laughter. Leddy Grippy sat on the left of the bride, apparelled in a crimson satin gown, made for the occasion, with a stupendous fabric of gauze and catgut, adorned with vast convolutions of broad red ribbons for a head-dress, and a costly French shawl, primly pinned open, to show her embroidered stomacher. At her side sat the meek and beautiful Isabella, like a primrose within the shadow of a peony; and on Isabella's left the aged Lady Plealands, neatly dressed in white silk, with a close cap of black lace, black silk mittens, and a rich black apron. But we must not attempt thus to describe all the guests, who, to the number of nearly a hundred, young and old, were seated in various groups around the sides of the barn; for our attention was drawn to Milrookit, the Laird of Dirdumwhamle, a hearty widower for the second time, about forty five—he might be older—who, cozily in a corner, was engaged in serious courtship with Miss Meg.

When the formalities of respect, with which Doctor Denholm was so properly received, had been duly performed, the bridegroom bade the fiddlers again play up, and, going towards the minister, said, 'Do ye smell ony thing gude, Sir?'

'No doubt, bridegroom,' replied the Doctor, 'I canna be insensible to the pleasant savour of the supper.'

'Come here, then,' rejoined Watty, 'and I'll show you a sight would do a hungry body good—weel I wat my mother has na spared her skill and spice.'—In saying which, he lifted aside a carpet that had been drawn across the barn like a curtain behind the seats at the upper end of the ball-room, and showed him the supper table, on which about a dozen men and maid-servants were in the act of piling joints and pyes that would have done credit to the Michaelmas dinner of the Glasgow magistrates—'Is na that a gallant banquet?' said Watty—'Look at yon braw pastry pye wi' the King's crown on't.'

The Reverend Pastor declared that it was a very edificial structure, and he had no doubt it was as good as it looked—'Would ye like to pree't, Doctor? I'll just nip off ane o' the pearlies on the crown to let you taste how good it is. It'll never be missed.'

The bride, who overheard part of this dialogue, started up at these words, and as Walter was in the act of stretching forth his hand to plunder the crown, she pulled him by the coat-tail, and drew him into the chair appropriated for him, sitting down, at the same time, in her own on his left, saying, in an angry whisper,—'Are ye fou' already, Watty Walkinshaw? If ye mudge out o' that seat again this night, I'll mak you as sick o' pyes and puddings as ever a dog was o' het kail.'

Nothing more particular happened before supper; and every thing went off at the banquet as mirthfully as on any similar occasion. The dancing was then resumed, and during the bustle and whirl of the reels, the bride and bridegroom were conducted quietly to the house to be bedded.

When they were undressed, but before the stocking was thrown, we got a hint from Charles to look at the bridal chamber, and accordingly ran with him to the house, and bolting into the room, beheld the happy pair sitting up in bed, with white napkins drawn over their heads like two shrouds, and each holding one of their hands, so as to conceal entirely their modest and downcast faces. But, before we had time to say a word, the minister, followed by the two pipers, and the best-men and bride's-maids, bringing posset and cake, came in,—and while the distribution, with the customary benedictions, was going forward, dancing was recommenced in the bedroom.

How it happened, or what was the cause, we know not; but the dancing continued so long, and was kept up with so much glee, that somehow, by the crowded state of the apartment, the young pair in bed were altogether forgotten, till the bridegroom, tired with sitting so long like a mummy, lost all patience, and, in a voice of rage and thunder, ordered every man and mother's son instantly to quit the room,—a command which he as vehemently repeated with a menace of immediate punishment,—putting, at the same time, one of his legs out of bed, and clenching his fist, in the act of rising. The bride cowered in giggling beneath the coverlet, and all the other ladies, followed by the men and the pipers, fled pell-mell, and hurly-burly, glad to make their escape.

Chapter XXXI

When Claud first proposed the marriage to Kilmarkeckle, it was intended that the young couple should reside at Plealands; but an opportunity had occurred, in the meantime, for Mr Keelevin to intimate to Mr Auchincloss, the gentleman who possessed the two farms, which, with the Grippy, constituted the ancient estate of Kittlestonheugh, that Mr Walkinshaw would be glad to make an excambio with him, and not only give Plealands, but even a considerable inducement in money. This proposal, particularly the latter part of it, was agreeable to Mr Auchincloss, who, at the time, stood in want of ready money to establish one of his sons in the Virginia trade; and, in consequence, the negotiation was soon speedily brought to a satisfactory termination.

But, in this affair, Grippy did not think fit to confer with any of his sons. He was averse to speak to Charles on the subject, possibly from some feeling connected with the deed of entail; and, it is unnecessary to say, that, although Walter was really principal in the business, he had no regard for what his opinion might be. The consequence of which was, that the bridegroom was not a little amazed to find, next day, on proposing to ride the Brous, to his own house at Plealands, and to hold the Infare there, that it was intended to be assigned to Mr Auchincloss, and that, as soon as his family were removed thither, the house of Divethill, one of the exchanged farms, would be set in order for him in its stead.

The moment that this explanation was given to Walter, he remembered the parchments which he had signed, and the agitation of his father on the way home, and he made no scruple of loudly and bitterly declaring, with many a lusty sob, that he was cheated out of his inheritance by his father and Charles. The old man was confounded at this view which the Natural plausibly enough took of the arrangement; but yet, anxious to conceal from his first-born the injustice with which he had used him in the entail, he at first attempted to silence Walter by threats, and then to cajole him with promises, but without effect; at last, so high did the conflict rise between them, that Leddy Grippy and Walter's wife came into the room to inquire what had happened.

'O Betty Bodle!' exclaimed Walter, the moment he saw them; 'what are we to do? My father has beguiled me o' the Plealands, and I hae neither house nor ha' to tak you to. He has gart me wise it awa to Charlie, and we'll hae nathing as lang as Kilmarkeckle lives, but scant and want and beggary. It's no my fau't, Betty Bodle, that ye'll hae to work for your daily bread, the sin o't a' is my father's. But I'll help you a' I can, Betty, and if ye turn a washerwoman on the Green of Glasgow, I'll carry your boynes, and water your claes, and watch them, that ye may sleep when ye're weary't, Betty Bodle,—for though he's a false father, I'll be a true gudeman.'

Betty Bodle sat down in a chair, with her back to the window, and Walter, going to her, hung over her with an air of kindness, which his simplicity rendered at once affecting and tender; while Leddy Grippy, petrified by what she heard, also sat down, and, leaning herself back in her seat, with a look of amazement, held her arms streaked down by her side, with all her fingers stretched and spread to the utmost. Claud, himself, was for a moment overawed, and had almost lost his wonted self-possession, at the just accusation of being a false father; but, exerting all his firmness and fortitude, he said calmly,—

'I canna bear this at thy hand, Watty. I hae secured for thee far mair than the Plealands; and is the satisfaction that I thought to hae had this day, noo when I hae made a conquest of the lands o' my forefathers, to be turned into sadness and bitterness o' heart?'

'What hae ye secur'd?' exclaimed Leddy Grippy. 'Is na it ordaint that Charlie, by his birthright, will get your lands? How is't then that ye hae wrang't Watty of his ain? the braw property that my worthy father left him both by will and testament. An he had been to the fore, ye durst na, gudeman, hae played at sic jookery pookery; for he had a skill o' law, and kent the kittle points in a manner that ye can never fathom; weel wat I, that your ellwand would hae been a jimp measure to the sauvendie o' his books and Latin taliations. But, gudeman, ye's no get a' your ain way. I'll put on my cloak, and, Betty Bodle, put on yours, and Watty, my ill-used bairn, get your hat. We'll oure for Kilmarkeckle, and gang a' to Mr Keelevin together to make an interlocutor about this most dreadful extortioning.'

The old man absolutely shuddered; his face became yellow, and his lips white with anger and vexation at this speech.

'Girzy Hypel,' said he, with a troubled and broken voice, 'were t'ou a woman o' understanding, or had t'at haverel get o' thine the gumshion o' a sucking turkey, I could speak, and confound your injustice, were I no restrained by a sense of my own shame.'

'But what's a' this stoor about?' said the young wife, addressing herself to her father-in-law. 'Surely ye'll no objek to mak me the wiser?'

'No, my dear,' replied Claud, 'I hope I can speak and be understood by thee. I hae gotten Mr Auchincloss to mak an excambio of the Divethill for the Plealands, by the whilk the whole of the Kittlestonheugh patrimony will be redeemed to the family; and I intend and wis you and Watty to live at the Divethill, our neighbours here, and your father's neighbours; that, my bairn, is the whole straemash.'

'But,' said she, 'when ye're dead, will we still hae the Divethill?'

'No doubt o' that, my dawty,' said the old man delighted; 'and even far mair.'

'Then, Watty Walkinshaw, ye gaumeril,'said she, addressing her husband, 'what would ye be at?—Your father's a most just man, and will do you and a' his weans justice.'

'But, for a' that,' said Leddy Grippy to her husband, somewhat bamboozled by the view which her daughter-in-law seemed to take of the subject,—

'When will we hear o' you giving hundreds o' pounds to Watty, as ye did to Charlie, for a matrimonial hansel?'

'I'm sure,'replied the Laird, 'were the like o' that to quiet thy unruly member, Girzy, and be any satisfaction to thee, that I hae done my full duty to Walter, a five score pound should na be wanting to stap up the gap.'

'I'll tell you what it is, father,' interrupted Walter, 'if ye'll gie the whole soom o' a hundre pound, I care na gin ye mak drammock o' the Plealands.'

'A bargain be't,' said Claud, happy to be relieved from their importunity; but he added, with particular emphasis, to Watty's wife,—

'Dinna ye tak ony care about what's passed; the Divethill's a good excambio for the Plealands, and it sail be bound as stiffly as law and statute can tether to you and your heirs by Walter.'

Thus so far Grippy continued to sail before the wind, and, perhaps, in the steady pursuit of his object, he met with as few serious obstacles as most adventurers. What sacrifice of internal feeling he may have made, may be known hereafter. In the mean time, the secrets and mysteries of his bosom were never divulged; but all his thoughts and anxieties as carefully hidden from the world as if the disclosure of them would have brought shame on himself. Events, however, press; and we must proceed with the current of our history.

Chapter XXXII

Although Claud had accomplished the great object of all his strivings, and although, from the Divethill, where the little castle of his forefathers once stood, he could contemplate the whole extent of the Kittlestonheugh estate, restored, as he said, to the Walkinshaws, and by his exertions, there was still a craving void in his bosom that yearned to be satisfied. He felt as if the circumstance of Watty having a legal interest in the property, arising from the excambio for the Plealands, made the conquest less certainly his own than it might have been, and this lessened the enjoyment of the self-gratulation with which he contemplated the really proud eminence to which he had attained.

But keener feelings and harsher recollections were also mingled with that regret; and a sentiment of sorrow, in strong affinity with remorse, embittered his meditations, when he thought of the precipitancy with which he had executed the irrevocable entail, to the exclusion of Charles; to whom, prior to that unjust transaction, he had been more attached than to any other human being. It is true, that, when he adopted that novel resolution, he had, at the same time, appeased his conscience with intentions to indemnify his unfortunate first-born; but in this, he was not aware of the mysteries of the heart, nor that there was a latent spring in his breast, as vigorous and elastic in its energy, as the source of that indefatigable perseverance by which he had accomplished so much.

The constant animadversions of his wife, respecting his partiality for Charles and undisguised contempt for Watty, had the effect of first awakening the powers of that dormant engine. They galled the sense of his own injustice, and kept the memory of it so continually before him, that, in the mere wish not to give her cause to vex him for his partiality, he estranged himself from Charles in such a manner, that it was soon obvious and severely felt. Conscious that he had done him wrong,—aware that the wrong would probably soon be discovered,—and conscious, too, that this behaviour was calculated to beget suspicion, he began to dislike to see Charles, and alternately to feel in every necessary interview, as if he was no longer treated by him with the same respect as formerly. Still, however, there was so much of the leaven of original virtue in the composition of his paternal affection, and in the general frame of his character, that this disagreeable feeling never took the decided nature of enmity. He did not hate because he had injured,—he was only apprehensive of being upbraided for having betrayed hopes which he well knew his particular affection must have necessarily inspired.

Perhaps, had he not, immediately after Walter's marriage, been occupied with the legal arrangement consequent to an accepted proposal from Milrookit of Dirdumwhamle, to make Miss Meg his third wife, this apprehension might have hardened into animosity, and been exasperated to aversion; but the cares and affairs of that business came, as it were, in aid of the father in his nature, and while they seemingly served to excuse his gradually abridged intercourse with Charles and Isabella, they prevented such an incurable induration of his heart from taking place towards them, as the feelings at work within him had an undoubted tendency to produce. We shall not, therefore, dwell on the innumerable little incidents arising out of his estrangement, by which the happiness of that ill-fated pair was deprived of so much of its best essence,—contentment,—and their lives, with the endearing promise of a family, embittered by anxieties of which it would be as difficult to describe the importance, as to give each of them an appropriate name.

In the meantime, the marriage of Miss Meg was consummated, and we have every disposition to detail the rites and the revels, but they were all managed in a spirit so much more moderate than Walter's wedding, that the feast would seem made up but of the cold bake-meats of the former banquet. Indeed, Mr Milrookit, the bridegroom, being, as Leddy Grippy called him, a waster of wives, having had two before, and who knows how many more he may have contemplated to have, it would not have been reasonable to expect that he should allow such a free-handed junketting as took place on that occasion. Besides this, the dowry with Grippy's daughter was not quite so liberal as he had expected; for when the old man was stipulating for her jointure, he gave him a gentle hint not to expect too much.

'Two hundred pounds a-year, Mr Milrookit,' said Grippy, 'is a bare enough sufficiency for my dochter; but I'll no be overly extortionate, sin it's no in my power, even noo, to gie you meikle in hand, and I would na lead you to expek any great deal hereafter, for ye ken it has cost me a world o' pains and ettling to gather the needful to redeem the Kittlestonheugh, the whilk maun ay gang in the male line; but failing my three sons and their heirs, the entail gangs to the heirs general o' Meg, so that ye hae a' to look in that airt; that, ye maun alloo, is worth something. Howsever, I dinna objek to the two hundred pounds; but I would like an ye could throw a bit fifty tilt, just as a cast o'the hand to mak lucky measure.'

'I would na begrudge that, Grippy,' replied the gausey widower of Dirdumwhamle; 'but ye ken I hae a sma' family: the first Mrs Milrookit brought me sax sons, and the second had four, wi' five dochters. It's true that the bairns o' the last clecking are to be provided for by their mother's uncle, the auld General wi' the gout at Lon'on; but my first family are dependent on myself, for, like your Charlie, I made a calf-love marriage, and my father was na sae kind as ye hae been to him, for he put a' past me that he could, and had he no deet amang hands in one o' his scrieds wi' the Lairds o' Kilpatrick, I'm sure I canna think what would hae come o' me and my first wife. So you see, Grippy'—

'I wis, Dirdumwhamle,' interrupted the old man, 'that ye would either ca' me by name or Kittlestonheugh, for the Grippy's but a pendicle o' the family property; and though, by reason o'the castle being ta'en down when my grandfather took a wadset on'frae the public, we are obligated to live here in this house that was on the land when I made a conquest o't again, yet a' gangs noo by the ancient name o' Kittlestonheugh, and a dochter of the Walkinshaws o' the same is a match for the best laird in the shire though she had na ither tocher than her snood and cockernony.'

'Weel, Kittlestonheugh,' replied Dirdumwhamle, 'I'll e'e mak it better than the twa hunder and fifty—I'll make it whole three hunder, if ye'll get a paction o' consent and conneevance wi' your auld son Charles, to pay to Miss Meg, or to the offspring o'my marriage wi'her, a yearly soom during his liferent in the property, you yoursel' undertaking in your lifetime to be as good. I'm sure that's baith fair and a very great liberality on my side.'

Claud received this proposal with a convulsive gurgle of the heart's blood. It seemed to him, that, on every occasion, the wrong which he had done Charles was to be brought in the most offensive form before him, and he sat for the space of two or three minutes without making any reply; at last he said,—

'Mr Milrookit, I ne'er rue't anything in my life but the consequence of twa three het words that ance passed between me and my gudefather Plealands, anent our properties; and I hae lived to repent my obduracy. For this cause I'll say nae mair about an augmentation of the proposed jointure, but just get my dochter to put up wi' the two hundred pounds, hoping that hereafter, an ye can mak it better, she'll be none the waur of her father's confidence in you on this occasion.'

Thus was Miss Meg disposed of, and thus did the act of injustice which was done to one child operate, through the mazy feelings of the father's conscious spirit, to deter him, even in the midst of such sordid bargaining, not only from venturing to insist on his own terms, but even from entertaining a proposal which had for its object a much more liberal provision for his daughter than he had any reason, under all the circumstances, to expect.

Chapter XXXIII

Soon after the marriage of Miss Meg, George, the third son, and youngest of the family, was placed in the counting-house of one of the most eminent West Indian merchants at that period in Glasgow. This incident was in no other respect important in the history of the Lairds of Grippy, than as serving to open a career to George, that would lead him into a higher class of acquaintance than his elder brothers: for it was about this time that the general merchants of the royal city began to arrogate to themselves that aristocratic superiority over the shopkeepers, which they have since established into an oligarchy, as proud and sacred, in what respects the reciprocities of society, as the famous Seignories of Venice and of Genoa.

In the character, however, of George, there was nothing ostensibly haughty, or rather his pride had not shown itself in any strong colour, when he first entered on hismercantile career. Like his father, he was firm and persevering; but he wanted something of the old man's shrewdness; and there was more of avarice in his hopes of wealth than in the sordidness of his father, for they were not elevated by any such ambitious sentiment as that which prompted Claud to strive with such constancy for the recovery of his paternal inheritance. In fact, the young merchant, notwithstanding the superiority of his education and other advantages, we may safely venture to assert, was a more vulgar character than the old pedlar. But his peculiarities did not manifest themselves till long after the period of which we are now speaking.

In the meantime, every thing proceeded with the family much in the same manner as with most others. Claud and his wife had daily altercations about their household affairs. Charles and Isabella narrowed themselves into a small sphere, of which his grandmother, the venerable Lady Plealands, now above fourscore, was their principal associate, and their mutual affection was strengthened by the birth of a son. Walter and Betty Bodle resided at the Divethill; and they, too, had the prospect of adding, as a Malthusian would say, to the mass of suffering mankind. The philosophical Kilmarkeckle continued his abstruse researches as successfully as ever into the affinities between snuff and the natures of beasts and birds, while the Laird of Dirdumwhamle and his Lady struggled on in the yoke together, as well as a father and stepmother, amidst fifteen children, the progeny of two prior marriages, could reasonably be expected to do, where neither party was particularly gifted with delicacy or forbearance. In a word, they all moved along with the rest of the world during the first twelve months, after the execution of the deed of entail, without experiencing any other particular change in their relative situations than those to which we have alluded.

But the epoch was now drawing near, when Mrs Walter Walkinshaw was required to prepare herself for becoming a mother, and her husband was no less interested than herself in the event. He did nothing for several months, from morning to night, but inquire how she felt herself, and contrive, in his affectionate simplicity, a thousand insufferable annoyances to one of her disposition, for the purpose of affording her ease and pleasure; all of which were either answered by a laugh, or a slap, as the humour of the moment dictated. Sometimes, when she, regardless of her maternal state, would, in walking to Grippy or Kilmarkeckle, take short cuts across the fields, and over ditches, and through hedges, he would anxiously follow her at a distance, and when he saw her in any difficulty to pass, he would run kindly to her assistance. More than once, at her jocular suggestion, he has lain down in the dry ditches to allow her to step across on his back. Never had wife a more loving or obedient husband. She was allowed in every thing, not only to please herself, but to make him do whatever she pleased; and yet, with all her whims and caprice, she proved so true and so worthy a wife, that he grew every day more and more uxorious.

Nor was his mother less satisfied with Betty Bodle. They enjoyed together the most intimate communion of minds on all topics of household economy; but it was somewhat surprising, that, notwithstanding the care and pains which the old leddy took to instruct her daughter-in-law in all the mysteries of the churn and cheesset, Mrs Walter's butter was seldom fit for market, and the huxters of the royal city never gave her near so good a price for her cheese as Leddy Grippy regularly received for hers, although, in the process of the making, they both followed the same recipes.

The conjugal felicities of Walter afforded, however, but little pleasure to his father. The obstreperous humours of his daughter-in-law jarred with his sedate dispositions, and in her fun and freaks she so loudly showed her thorough knowledge of her husband's defective intellects, that it for ever reminded him of the probable indignation with which the world would one day hear of the injustice he had done to Charles. The effect of this gradually led him to shun the society of his own family, and having neither from nature nor habit any inclination for general company, he became solitary and morose. He only visited Glasgow once a week, on Wednesday, and generally sat about an hour in the shop, in his old elbow chair, in the corner; and, saving a few questions relative to the business, he abstained from conversing with his son. It would seem, however, that, under this sullen taciturnity, the love which he had once cherished for Charles still tugged at his heart; for, happening to come into the shop, on the morning after Isabella had made him a grandfather, by the birth of a boy, on being informed of that happy event, he shook his son warmly by the hand, and said, in a serious and impressive manner,—

'An it please God, Charlie, to gie thee ony mair childer, I redde thee, wi' the counsel o' a father, to mak na odds among them, but remember they are a' alike thine, and that t'ou canna prefer ane aboon anither without sin;'—and he followed this admonition with a gifty of twenty pounds to buy the infant a christening frock.

But from that day he never spoke to Charles of his family; on the contrary, he became dark and more obdurate in his manner to every one around him. His only enjoyment seemed to be a sort of doating delight in contemplating, from a rude bench which he had constructed on a rising ground behind the house of Grippy, the surrounding fields of his forefathers. There he would sit for hours together alone, bending forward with his chin resting on the ivory head of his staff, which he held between his knees by both hands, and with a quick and eager glance survey the scene for a moment, and then drop his eyelids, and look only on the ground.

Whatever might be the general tenor of his reflections as he sat on that spot, they were evidently not always pleasant; for one afternoon, as he was sitting there, his wife, who came upon him, suddenly and unperceived, to tell him a messenger was sent to Glasgow from Divethill for the midwife, she was surprised to find him agitated and almost in tears.

'Dear me, gudeman,'said she, 'what's come o'er you, that ye're sitting here hanging your gruntel like a sow playing on a trump? Hae na ye heard that Betty Bodle's time's come? I'm gaun ower to the crying, and if ye like ye may walk that length wi' me. I hope, poor thing, she'll hae an easy time o't, and that we'll hae blithes-meat before the sun gangs doun.'

'Gang the gait thysel, Girzy Hypel,' said Claud, raising his head, 'and no fash me with thy clishmaclavers.'

'Heh, gudeman! but ye hae been eating sourrocks instead o' lang-kail. But e'ens ye like, Meg dorts, as Patie and Roger says, I can gang mysel'; and with that, whisking pettishly round, she walked away.

Claud being thus disturbed in his meditations, looked after her as she moved along the footpath down the slope, and for the space of a minute or two, appeared inclined to follow her, but relapsing into some new train of thought, before she had reached the bottom, he had again resumed his common attitude, and replaced his chin on the ivory head of his staff.

Chapter XXXIV

There are times in life when every man feels as if his sympathies were extinct. This arises from various causes; sometimes from vicissitudes of fortune; sometimes from the sense of ingratitude, which, like the canker in the rose, destroys the germ of all kindness and charity; often from disappointments in affairs of the heart, which leave it incapable of ever again loving; but the most common cause is the consciousness of having committed wrong, when the feelings recoil inward, and, by some curious mystery in the nature of our selfishness, instead of prompting atonement, irritate us to repeat and to persevere in our injustice.

Into one of these temporary trances Claud had fallen when his wife left him; and he continued sitting, with his eyes rivetted on the ground, insensible to all the actual state of life, contemplating the circumstances and condition of his children, as if he had no interest in their fate, nor could be affected by any thing in their fortunes.

In this fit of apathy and abstraction, he was roused by the sound of some one approaching; and on looking up, and turning his eyes towards the path which led from the house to the bench where he was then sitting, he saw Walter coming.

There was something unwonted in the appearance and gestures of Walter, which soon interested the old man. At one moment he rushed forward several steps, with a strange wildness of air. He would then stop and wring his hands, gaze upward, as if he wondered at some extraordinary phenomenon in the sky; but seeing nothing, he dropped his hands, and, at his ordinary pace, came slowly up the hill.

When he arrived within a few paces of the bench, he halted, and looked, with such an open and innocent sadness, that even the heart of his father, which so shortly before was as inert to humanity as case-hardened iron, throbbed with pity, and was melted to a degree of softness and compassion, almost entirely new to its sensibilities.

'What's the matter wi' thee, Watty? 'said he, with unusual kindliness. The poor natural, however, made no reply,—but continued to gaze at him with the same inexpressible simplicity of grief.

'Hast t'ou lost ony thing, Watty?'—'I dinna ken,' was the answer, followed by a burst of tears.

'Surely something dreadfu' has befallen the lad,' said Claud to himself, alarmed at the astonishment of sorrow with which his faculties seemed to be bound up.

'Can t'ou no tell me what has happened, Watty?'

In about the space of half a minute, Walter moved his eyes slowly round, as if he saw and followed something which filled him with awe and dread.

He then suddenly checked himself, and said, 'It's naething; she's no there.'

'Sit down beside me, Watty,'exclaimed his father, alarmed; 'sit down beside me, and compose thysel.'

Walter did as he was bidden, and stretching out his feet, hung forward in such a posture of extreme listlessness and helpless despondency, that all power of action appeared to be withdrawn.

Claud rose, and believing he was only under the influence of some of those silly passions to which he was occasionally subject, moved to go away, when he looked up, and said,—

'Father, Betty Bodle's dead!—My Betty Bodle's dead!'

'Dead!' said Claud, thunderstruck.

'Aye, father, she's dead! My Betty Bodle's dead!'

'Dost t'ou ken what t'ou's saying?' But Walter, without attending to the question, repeated, with an accent of tenderness still more simple and touching,—

'My Betty Bodle's dead! She's awa up aboon the skies yon'er, and left me a wee wee baby'; in saying which, he again burst into tears, and rising hastily from the bench, ran wildly back towards the Divethill-house, whither he was followed by the old man, where the disastrous intelligence was confirmed, that she had died in giving birth to a daughter.

Deep and secret as Claud kept his feelings from the eyes of the world, this was a misfortune which he was ill prepared to withstand. For although in the first shock he betrayed no emotion, it was soon evident that it had shattered some of the firmest intents and purposes of his mind. That he regretted the premature death of a beautiful young woman in such interesting circumstances, was natural to him as a man; but he felt the event more as a personal disappointment, and thought it was accompanied with something so like retribution, that he inwardly trembled as if he had been chastised by some visible arm of Providence. For he could not disguise to himself that a female heir was a contingency he had not contemplated; that, by the catastrophe which had happened to the mother, the excambio of the Plealands for the Divethill would be rendered of no avail; and that, unless Walter married again, and had a son, the re-united Kittlestonheugh property must again be disjoined, as the Divethill would necessarily become the inheritance of the daughter.

The vexation of this was, however, alleviated, when he reflected on the pliancy of Walter's character, and he comforted himself with the idea, that, as soon as a reasonable sacrifice of time had been made to decorum, he would be able to induce the natural to marry again. Shall we venture to say, it also occurred in the cogitations of his sordid ambition, that, as the infant was prematurely born, and was feeble and infirm, he entertained some hope it might die, and not interfere with the entailed destination of the general estate? But if, in hazarding this harsh supposition, we do him any injustice, it is certain that he began to think there was something in the current of human affairs over which he could acquire no control, and that, although, in pursuing so steadily the single purpose of recovering his family inheritance, his endeavours had, till this period, proved eminently successful, he yet saw, with dismay, that, from the moment other interests came to be blended with those which he considered so peculiarly his own, other causes also came into operation, and turned, in spite of all his hedging and prudence, the whole issue of his labours awry. He perceived that human power was set at nought by the natural course of things, and nothing produced a more painful conviction of the wrong he had committed against his first-born, than the frustration of his wishes by the misfortune which had befallen Walter. His reflections were also embittered from another source; by his parsimony he foresaw that, in the course of a few years, he would have been able, from his own funds, to have redeemed the Divethill without having had recourse to the excambio; and that the whole of the Kittlestonheugh might thus have been his own conquest, and, as such, without violating any of the usages of society, he might have commenced the entail with Charles. In a word, the death of Walter's wife and the birth of the daughter disturbed all his schemes, and rent from roof to foundation the castles which he had been so long and so arduously building. But it is necessary that we should return to poor Walter, on whom the loss of his beloved Betty Bodle acted with the incitement of a new impulse, and produced a change of character that rendered him a far less tractable instrument than his father expected to find.

Chapter XXXV

The sorrow of Walter, after he had returned home, assumed the appearance of a calm and settled melancholy. He sat beside the corpse with his hands folded and his head drooping. He made no answer to any question; but as often as he heard the infant's cry, he looked towards the bed, and said, with an accent of indescribable sadness, 'My Betty Bodle!'

When the coffin arrived, his mother wished him to leave the room, apprehensive, from the profound grief in which he was plunged, that he might break out into some extravagance of passion, but he refused; and, when it was brought in, he assisted with singular tranquillity in the ceremonial of the coffining. But when the lid was lifted and placed over the body, and the carpenter was preparing to fasten it down for ever, he shuddered for a moment from head to foot; and, raising it with his left hand, he took a last look of the face, removing the veil with his right, and touching the sunken cheek as if he had hoped still to feel some ember of life; but it was cold and stiff.

'She's clay noo,' said he.—'There's nane o' my Betty Bodle here.'

And he turned away with a careless air, as if he had no farther interest in the scene. From that moment his artless affections took another direction; he immediately quitted the death-room, and, going to the nursery where the infant lay asleep in the nurse's lap, he contemplated it for some time, and then, with a cheerful and happy look and tone, said,—'It's a wee Betty Bodle; and it's my Betty Bodle noo.' And all his time and thoughts were thenceforth devoted to this darling object, in so much that, when the hour of the funeral was near, and he was requested to dress himself to perform the husband's customary part in the solemnity, he refused, not only to quit the child, but to have any thing to do with the burial.

'I canna understand,' said he, 'what for a' this fykerie's about a lump o' yird? Sho'el't intil a hole, and no fash me.'

'It's your wife, my lad,' replied his mother; 'ye'll surely never refuse to carry her head in a gudemanlike manner to the kirk-yard.'

'Na, na, mother, Betty Bodle's my wife, yon clod in the black kist is but her auld boddice; and when she flang't off, she put on this bonny wee new cleiding o' clay,' said he, pointing to the baby.

The Leddy, after some farther remonstrance, was disconcerted by the pertinacity with which he continued to adhere to his resolution, and went to beg her husband to interfere.

'Ye'll hae to gang ben, gudeman,' said she, 'and speak to Watty.—I wis the poor thing hasna gane by itsel wi' a broken heart. He threeps that the body is no his wife's, and ca's it a hateral o' clay and stones, and says we may fling't, Gude guide us, ayont the midden for him.—We'll just be affrontit if he'll no carry the head.'

Claud, who had dressed himself in the morning for the funeral, was sitting in the elbow chair, on the right side of the chimney-place, with his cheek resting on his hand, and his eyelids dropped, but not entirely shut, and on being thus addressed, he instantly rose, and went to the nursery.

'What's t'ou doing there like a hussy-fellow?' said he. 'Rise and get on thy mournings, and behave wise-like, and leave the bairn to the women.'

'It's my bairn,' replied Watty, 'and ye hae naething, father, to do wi't.—Will I no tak care o' my ain baby—my bonny wee Betty Bodle?'

'Do as I bid thee, or I'll maybe gar thee fin' the weight o' my staff,' cried the old man sharply, expecting immediate obedience to his commands, such as he always found, however positively Walter, on other occasions, at first refused; but in this instance he was disappointed; for the widower looked him steadily in the face, and said,—

'I'm a father noo; it would be an awfu' thing for a decent greyheaded man like you, father, to strike the head o' a motherless family.'

Claud was so strangely affected by the look and accent with which this was expressed, that he stood for some time at a loss what to say, but soon recovering his self-possession, he replied, in a mild and persuasive manner,—

'The frien's expek, Watty, that ye'll attend the burial, and carry the head, as the use and wont is in every weel-doing family.'

'It's a thriftless custom, father, and what care I for burial-bread and services o' wine? They cost siller, father, and I'll no wrang Betty Bodle for ony sic outlay on her auld yirden garment. Ye may gang, for fashion's cause, wi' your weepers and your mourning strings, and lay the black kist i' the kirk-yard hole, but I'll no mudge the ba' o' my muckle tae in ony sic road.'

'T'ou's past remede, I fear,' replied his father thoughtfully; 'but, Watty, I hope in this t'ou'll oblige thy mother and me, and put on thy new black claes;—t'ou kens they're in a braw fasson,—and come ben and receive the guests in a douce and sober manner.'

'The minister, I'm thinking, will soon be here, and t'ou should be in the way when he comes.'

'No,' said Watty, 'no, do as ye like, and come wha may, it's a' ane to me: I'm positeeve.'

The old man, losing all self-command at this extraordinary opposition, exclaimed,—

'There's a judgment in this; and, if there's power in the law o' Scotland, I'll gar thee rue sic dourness. Get up, I say, and put on thy mournings, or I'll hae thee cognost, and sent to bedlam.'

'I'm sure I look for nae mair at your hands, father,' replied Walter simply; 'for my mither has often telt me, when ye hae been sitting sour and sulky in the nook, that ye would na begrudge crowns and pounds to mak me compos mentis for the benefit of Charlie.'

Every pulse in the veins of Claud stood still at this stroke, and he staggered, overwhelmed with shame, remorse, and indignation, into a seat.

'Eh!' said the Leddy, returning into the room at this juncture, 'what's come o'er you, gudeman? Pity me, will he no do your bidding?'

'Girzy Hypel,' was the hoarse and emphatic reply, 'Girzy Hypel, t'ou's the curse o' my life; the folly in thee has altered to idiotical depravity in him, and the wrong I did against my ain nature in marrying thee, I maun noo, in my auld age, reap the fruits o' in sorrow, and shame, and sin.'

'Here's composity for a burial!' exclaimed the Leddy. 'What's the matter, Watty Walkinshaw?'

'My father's in a passion.'

Claud started from his seat, and, with fury in his eyes, and his hands clenched, rushed across the room towards the spot where Walter was sitting, watching the infant in the nurse's lap. In the same moment, the affectionate natural also sprang forward, and placed himself in an attitude to protect the child. The fierce old man was confounded, and turning round hastily, quitted the room, wringing his hands, unable any longer to master the conflicting feelings which warred so wildly in his bosom.

'This is a pretty like house o' mourning,' said the Leddy; 'a father and a son fighting, and a dead body waiting to be ta'en to the kirk-yard. O Watty Walkinshaw! Watty Walkinshaw! many a sore heart ye hae gi'en your parents,—will ye ne'er divaul till ye hae brought our grey hairs wi' sorrow to the grave? There's your poor father flown demented, and a' the comfort in his cup and mine gane like water spilt on the ground. Many a happy day we hae had, till this condumacity o' thine grew to sic a head. But tak your ain way o't. Do as ye like. Let strangers carry your wife to the kirk-yard, and see what ye'll mak o't.'

But notwithstanding all these, and many more equally persuasive and commanding arguments, Walter was not to be moved, and the funeral, in consequence, was obliged to be performed without him. Yet still, though thus tortured in his feelings, the stern old man inflexibly adhered to his purpose. The entail which he had executed was still with him held irrevocable; and, indeed, it had been so framed, that, unless he rendered himself insolvent, it could not be set aside.

Chapter XXXVI

For some time after the funeral of Mrs Walter Walkinshaw, the affairs of the Grippy family ran in a straight and even current. The estrangement of the old man from his first-born suffered no describable increase, but Charles felt that it was increasing. The old Leddy, in the meanwhile, had a world of cares upon her hands in breaking up the establishment which had been formed for Walter at the house on the Divethill, and in removing him back with the infant and the nurse to Grippy. And scarcely had she accomplished these, when a letter from her daughter, Mrs Milrookit, informed her that the preparations for an addition to the 'sma family' of Dirdumwhamle were complete, and that she hoped her mother could be present on the occasion, which was expected to come to pass in the course of a few weeks from the date.

Nothing was more congenial to the mind and habits of the Leddy, than a business of this sort, or, indeed, any epochal domestic event, such as, in her own phraseology, was entitled to the epithet of a handling. But when she mentioned the subject to her husband, he objected, saying,—

'It's no possible, Girzy, for ye ken Mr and Mrs Givan are to be here next week with their dochter, Miss Peggy, and I would fain hae them to see an ony thing could be brought to a head between her and our Geordie. He's noo o' a time o' life when I would like he were settled in the world, and amang a' our frien's there's no a family I would be mair content to see him connected wi' than the Givans, who are come o' the best blood, and are, moreover, o' great wealth and property.'

'Weel, if e'er there was the like o' you, gudeman,' replied the Leddy, delighted with the news; 'an ye were to set your mind on a purpose o' marriage between a goose and a grumphie, I dinna think but ye would make it a' come to pass. For wha would hae thought o' this plot on the Givans, who, to be sure, are a most creditable family, and Miss Peggy, their dochter, is a vera genty creature, although it's my notion she's no o' a capacity to do meikle in the way o' throughgality. Howsever, she's a bonny playock, and noo that the stipend ye alloo't to Watty is at an end, by reason of that heavy loss which we all met wi'in his wife, ye'll can weel afford to help Geordie to keep her out in a station o' life; for times, gudeman, are no noo as when you and me cam thegither. Then a bein house, and a snod but and ben, was a' that was lookit for; but sin genteelity came into fashion, lads and lasses hae grown leddies and gentlemen, and a Glasgow wife saullying to the kirk wi' her muff and her mantle, looks as puckered wi' pride as my lord's leddy.'

Claud, who knew well that his helpmate was able to continue her desultory consultations as long as she could keep herself awake, here endeavoured to turn the spate of her clatter into a new channel, by observing, that hitherto they had not enjoyed any great degree of comfort in the marriages of their family.

'Watty's,' said he, 'ye see, has in a manner been waur than nane; for a' we hae gotten by't is that weakly lassie bairn; and the sumph himsel is sae ta'en up wi't, that he's a perfect obdooracy to every wis o' mine, that he would tak another wife to raise a male-heir to the family.'

'I'm sure,' replied the Leddy, 'it's just a sport to hear you, gudeman, and your male-heirs. What for can ye no be content wi' Charlie's son?'

The countenance of Grippy was instantaneously clouded, but in a moment the gloom passed, and he said,—

'Girzy Hypel, t'ou kens naething about it. Will na Watty's dochter inherit the Divethill by right o' her father, for the Plealands, and so rive the heart again out o' the Kittlestonheugh, and mak a' my ettling fruitless? Noo, what I wis is, that Geordie should tak a wife to himsel as soon as a possibility will alloo, and if he has a son, by course o' nature, it might be wised in time to marry Watty's dochter, and so keep the property frae ganging out o' the family.'

'Noo, gudeman, thole wi' me, and no be angry,' replied the Leddy; 'for I canna but say it's a thing past ordinar, that ye never seem to refleck, that Charlie's laddie might just as weel be wised to marry Watty's dochter, as ony son that Geordie's like to get; and over and moreover, the wean's in the world already, gudeman, but a' Geordie's are as trouts in the water; so I redde you to consider weel what ye're doing, and gut nae fish till ye catch them.'

During this speech, Claud's face was again overcast; the harsh and agonizing discord of his bosom rudely jangled through all the depths of his conscience, and reminded him how futile his wishes and devices might be rendered either by the failure of issue, or the birth of daughters. Every thing seemed arranged by Providence, to keep the afflicting sense of the wrong he had done his first-born constantly galled. But it had not before occurred to him, that even a marriage between the son of Charles and Walter's daughter could not remedy the fault he had committed. The heirs-male of George had a preference in the entail; and such a marriage would, in no degree, tend to prevent the Kittlestonheugh from being again disjoined. In one sentence, the ambitious old man was miserable; but rather than yet consent to retrace any step he had taken, he persevered in his original course, as if the fire in his heart could be subdued by adding fresh piles of the same fuel. The match which he had formed for George was accordingly brought to what he deemed a favourable issue; for George, possessing but little innate delicacy, and only eager to become rich, had no scruple in proposing himself, at his father's suggestion, to Miss Peggy Givan; and the young lady being entirely under the control of her mother, who regarded a union with her relations, the Grippy family, as one of the most desirable, peaceably acquiesced in the arrangement.

Prior, however, to the marriage taking place, Mr Givan, a shrewd and worldly man, conceiving, that, as George was a younger son, his elder brother married, and Walter's daughter standing between him and the succession to the estate,—he stipulated that the bridegroom should be settled as a principal in business. A short delay in consequence occurred between the arrangement and the solemnization; but the difficulty was overcome, by the old man advancing nearly the whole of his ready money as a proportion of the capital which was required by the house that received George into partnership. Perhaps he might have been spared this sacrifice, for as such he felt it, could he have brought himself to divulge to Mr Givan the nature of the entail which he had executed; but the shame of that transaction had by this time sunk so deep, that he often wished and tried to consider the deed as having no existence.

Meanwhile, Mrs Milrookit had become the mother of a son; the only occurrence which, for some time, had given Claud any unalloyed satisfaction. But it also was soon converted into a new source of vexation and of punishment; for Leddy Grippy, ever dotingly fond of Walter, determined, from the first hour in which she heard of the birth of Walkinshaw Milrookit, as the child was called, to match him with her favourite's Betty; and the mere possibility of such an event taking place filled her husband with anxiety and fear; the expressions of which, and the peevish and bitter accents that he used in checking her loquacity on the subject, only served to make her wonderment at his prejudices the more and more tormenting.

END OF VOLUME FIRST

VOLUME II

Chapter I

In the meantime, Charles and Isabella had enjoyed a large share of domestic felicity, rendered the more endearingly exquisite by their parental anxiety, for it had pleased Heaven at once to bless and burden their narrow circumstances with two beautiful children, James and Mary. Their income arising from the share which the old man had assigned of the business had, during the first two or three years subsequent to their marriage, proved sufficient for the supply of their restricted wants; but their expences began gradually to increase, and about the end of the third year Charles found that they had incurred several small debts above their means of payment.

These, in the course of the fourth, rose to such a sum, that, being naturally of an apprehensive mind, he grew uneasy at the amount, and came to the resolution to borrow two hundred pounds to discharge them. This, he imagined, there could be no difficulty in procuring; for, believing that he was the heir of entail to the main part of the estate which his father had so entirely redeemed, he conceived that he might raise the money on his reversionary prospects, and, with this view, he called one morning on Mr Keelevin to request his agency in the business.

'I'm grieved, man,' said the honest lawyer, 'to hear that ye're in such straits; but had na ye better speak to your father? It might bring on you his displeasure if he heard ye were borrowing money to be paid at his death. It's a thing nae frien', far less a father, would like done by himsel.'

'In truth,' replied Charles, 'I am quite sensible of that; but what can I do? for my father, ever since my brother Watty's marriage, has been so cold and reserved about his affairs to me, that every thing like confidence seems as if it were perished from between us.'

Mr Keelevin, during this speech, raised his left arm on the elbow from the table at which he was sitting, and rested his chin on his hand. There was nothing in the habitual calm of his countenance which indicated what was passing in his heart, but his eyes once or twice glimmered with a vivid expression of pity.

'Mr Walkinshaw,' said he, 'if you dinna like to apply to your father yoursel, could na some friend mediate for you? Let me speak to him.'

'It's friendly of you, Mr Keelevin, to offer to do that; but really, to speak plainly, I would far rather borrow the money from a stranger, than lay myself open to any remarks. Indeed, for myself, I don't much care; but ye ken my father's narrow ideas about household charges; and may be he might take it on him to make remarks to my wife that I would na like to hear o'.'

'But, Mr Charles, you know that money canna be borrow't without security.'

'I am aware of that; and it's on that account I want your assistance. I should think that my chance of surviving my father is worth something.'

'But the whole estate is strictly entailed, Mr Charles,' replied the lawyer, with compassionate regard.

'The income, however, is all clear, Mr Keelevin.'

'I dinna misdoubt that, Mr Charles, but the entail—Do you ken how it runs?'

'No; but I imagine much in the usual manner.'

'No, Mr Charles,' said the honest writer, raising his head, and letting his hand fall on the table, with a mournful emphasis; 'No, Mr Charles, it does na run in the usual manner; and I hope ye'll no put ony reliance on't. It was na right o' your father to let you live in ignorance so long. Maybe it has been this to-look that has led you into the debts ye want to pay.'

The manner in which this was said affected the unfortunate firstborn more than the meaning; but he replied,—

'No doubt, Mr Keelevin, I may have been less scrupulous in my expences than I would have been, had I not counted on the chance of my birth-right.'

'Mr Charles, I'm sorry for you; but I would na do a frien's part by you, were I to keep you ony langer in the dark. Your father, Mr Charles, is an honest man; but there's a bee in his bonnet, as we a' ken, anent his pedigree. I need na tell you how he has warslet to get back the inheritance o' his forefathers; but I am wae to say, that in a pursuit so meritorious, he has committed ae great fault. Really, Mr Charles, I have na hardly the heart to tell you.'

'What is it?' said Charles, with emotion and apprehension.

'He has made a deed,' said Mr Keelevin, 'whereby he has cut you off frae the succession, in order that Walter, your brother, might be in a condition to make an exchange of the Plealands for the twa mailings that were wanting to make up wi' the Grippy property, a restoration of the auld estate of Kittlestonheugh; and I doubt it's o' a nature in consequence, that, even were he willing, canna be easily altered.'

To this heart-withering communication Charles made no answer. He stood for several minutes astonished; and then giving Mr Keelevin a wild look, shuddered and quitted the office.

Instead of returning home, he rushed with rapid and unequal steps down the Gallowgate, and, turning to the left hand in reaching the end of the street, never halted till he had gained the dark firs which overhang the cathedral and skirt the Molindinar Burn, which at the time was swelled with rains, and pouring its troubled torrent almost as violently as the tide of feelings that struggled in his bosom. Unconscious of what he did, and borne along by the whirlwind of his own thoughts, he darted down the steep, and for a moment hung on the rocks at the bottom as if he meditated some frantic leap. Recoiling and trembling with the recollections of his family, he then threw himself on the ground, and for some time shut his eyes as if he wished to believe that he was agitated only by a dream.

The scene and the day were in unison with the tempest which shook his frame and shivered his mind. The sky was darkly overcast. The clouds were rolling in black and lowering masses, through which an occasional gleam of sunshine flickered for a moment on the towers and pinnacles of the cathedral, and glimmered in its rapid transit on the monuments and graves in the church-yard. A gloomy shadow succeeded; and then a white and ghastly light hovered along the ruins of the bishop's castle, and darted with a strong and steady ray on a gibbet which stood on the rising ground beyond. The gusty wind howled like a death dog among the firs, which waved their dark boughs like hearse plumes over him, and the voice of the raging waters encouraged his despair.

He felt as if he had been betrayed into a situation which compelled him to surrender all the honourable intents of his life, and that he must spend the comfortless remainder of his days in a conflict with poverty, a prey to all its temptations, expedients, and crimes. At one moment, he clenched his grasp, and gnashed his teeth, and smote his forehead, abandoning himself to the wild and headlong energies and instincts of a rage that was almost revenge; at another, the image of Isabella, so gentle and so defenceless, rose in a burst of tenderness and sorrow, and subdued him with inexpressible grief. But the thought of his children in the heedless days of their innocence, condemned to beggary by a fraud against nature, again scattered these subsiding feelings like the blast that brushes the waves of the ocean into spindrift.

This vehemence of feeling could not last long without producing some visible effect. When the storm had in some degree spent itself, he left the wild and solitary spot where he had given himself so entirely up to his passion, and returned towards his home; but his limbs trembled, his knees faltered, and a cold shivering vibrated through his whole frame. An intense pain was kindled in his forehead; every object reeled and shuddered to him as he passed; and, before he reached the house, he was so unwell that he immediately retired to bed. In the course of the afternoon he became delirious, and a rapid and raging fever terrified his ill-fated wife.

Chapter II

Mr Keelevin, when Charles had left him, sat for some time with his cheek resting on his hand, reflecting on what had passed; and in the afternoon, he ordered his horse, and rode over to Grippy, where he found the Laird sitting sullenly by himself in the easy chair by the fire-side, with a white night-cap on his head, and grey worsted stockings drawn over his knees.

'I'm wae, Mr Walkinshaw,' said the honest lawyer, as he entered the room, 'to see you in sic an ailing condition; what's the matter wi' you, and how lang hae ye been sae indisposed?'

Claud had not observed his entrance; for, supposing the noise in opening the door had been made by the Leddy in her manifold household cares, or by some one of the servants, he never moved his head, but kept his eyes ruminatingly fixed on a peeling of soot that was ominously fluttering on one of the ribs of the grate, betokening, according to the most credible oracles of Scottish superstition, the arrival of a stranger, or the occurrence of some remarkable event. But, on hearing the voice of his legal friend, he turned briskly round.

'Sit ye doun, Mr Keelevin, sit ye doun forenent me. What's brought you here the day? Man, this is sore weather for ane at your time o' life to come so far afield,' was the salutation with which he received him.

'Aye,' replied Mr Keelevin, 'baith you and me, Grippy, are beginning to be the waur o' the wear; but I didna expek to find you in sic a condition as this. I hope it's no the gout or the rheumatism.'

Claud, who had the natural horror of death as strong as most country gentlemen of a certain age, if not of all ages, did not much relish either the observation or the inquiries. He, however, said, with affected indifference,—

'No! be thankit, it's neither the t'ane nor the t'ither, but just a waff o' cauld that I got twa nights ago;—a bit towt that's no worth the talking o'.'

'I'm extraordinar glad to hear't; for, seeing you in sic a frail and feckless state, I was fear't that ye were na in a way to converse on any concern o' business. No that I hae muckle to say, but ye ken a' sma' things are a great fasherie to a weakly person, and I wouldna discompose you, Mr Walkinshaw, unless you just felt yoursel in your right ordinar, for, at your time o' life, ony disturbance....'

'My time o' life?' interrupted the old man tartly. 'Surely I'm no sae auld that ye need to be speaking o' my time o' life? But what's your will, Mr Keelevin, wi' me?'

Whether all this sympathetic condolence, on the part of the lawyer, was said in sincerity, or with any ulterior view, we need not pause to discuss, for the abrupt question of the invalid brought it at once to a conclusion.

'In truth, Laird,' replied Mr Keelevin, 'I canna say that I hae ony thing o' a particular speciality to trouble you anent, for I came hither more in the way o' friendship than o' business,—having had this morning a visit frae your son Charles, a fine weel-doing young man as can be.'

'He's weel enough,' said the old man gruffly, and the lawyer continued,—

'Deed, Mr Walkinshaw, he's mair than weel enough. He's by common, and it was with great concern I heard that you and him are no on sic a footing of cordiality as I had thought ye were.'

'Has he been making a complaint o' me?' said Claud looking sharply, and with a grim and knotted brow as if he was, at the same time, apprehensive and indignant.

'He has mair sense and discretion,' replied Mr Keelevin; 'but he was speaking to me on a piece of business, and I was surprised he did na rather confer wi' you; till, in course of conversation, it fell out, as it were unawares, that he did na like to speak to you anent it; the which dislike, I jealouse, could only proceed o' some lack o' confidence between you, mair than should ever be between a father and a weel-behaved son like Mr Charles.'

'And what was't?' said Grippy drily.

'I doubt that his income is scant to his want, Mr Walkinshaw.'

'He's an extravagant fool; and ne'er had a hand to thraw a key in a lock;—when I began the world I had na'——

'Surely,' interrupted Mr Keelevin, 'ye could ne'er think the son o' a man in your circumstances should hain and hamper as ye were necessitated to do in your younger years. But no to mak a hearing or an argument concerning the same—Mr Charles requires a sma' sum to get him free o' a wee bit difficulty, for, ye ken, there are some folk, Mr Walkinshaw, that a flea-bite molests like the lash o' a whip.'

The old man made no answer to this; but sat for some time silent, drawing down his brows and twirling his thumbs. Mr Keelevin waited in patience till he should digest the reply he so evidently meditated.

'I hae ay thought Charlie honest, at least,' said Grippy; 'but I maun say that this fashes me, for if he's in sic straits, there's no telling what liberties he may be led to tak wi' my property in the shop.'

Mr Keelevin, who, in the first part of this reply, had bent eagerly forward, was so thunderstruck by the conclusion, that he threw himself back in his chair with his arms extended; but in a moment recovering from his consternation, he said, with fervour,—

'Mr Walkinshaw, I mind weel the reproof ye gave me when I remonstrated wi' you against the injustice ye were doing the poor lad in the entail, but there's no consideration on this earth will let me alloo you to gang on in a course of error and prejudice. Your son is an honest young man. I wish I could say his father kent his worth, or was worthy o' him—and I'll no see him wrangeously driven to the door, without taking his part, and letting the world ken wha's to blame. I'll no say ye hae defrauded him o' his birthright, for the property was your ain—but if ye drive him forth the shop, and cast him wi' his sma family on the scrimp mercy of mankind, I would be wanting to human nature in general, if I did na say it was most abominable, and that you yoursel, wi' a' your trumpery o' Walkinshaws and Kittlestonheughs, ought to be scourged by the hands o' the hangman. So do as ye like, Mr Walkinshaw, ride to the deevil at the full gallop for ought I care, but ye's no get out o' this world without hearing the hue and cry, that every Christian soul canna but raise after you.'

Claud was completely cowed both by the anger and menace of the honest lawyer, but still more by the upbraidings of his own startled conscience—and he said, in a humiliated tone, that almost provoked contempt,—

'Ye're owre hasty, Mr Keelevin. I did na mint a word about driving him forth the shop. Did he tell you how muckle his defect was?'

'Twa miserable hundred pounds,' replied Mr Keelevin, somewhat subsiding into his wonted equanimity.

'Twa hundred pound o' debt!' exclaimed Claud.

'Aye,' said Mr Keelevin, 'and I marvel it's no mair, when I consider the stinting and the sterile father o' him.'

'If I had the siller, Mr Keelevin,' replied Claud, 'to convince baith you and him that I'm no the niggar ye tak me for, I would gi'e you't wi' hearty gude will; but the advance I made to get Geordie into his partnership has for the present rookit me o' a' I had at command.'

'No possible!' exclaimed Mr Keelevin, subdued from his indignation; adding, 'and heavens preserve us, Mr Walkinshaw, an ony thing were happening on a sudden to carry you aff, ye hae made na provision for Charlie nor your dochter.'

There was something in this observation which made the old man shrink up into himself, and vibrate from head to heel. In the course, however, of less than a minute, he regained his self-possession, and said,—

' 'Deed your observe, Mr Keelevin, is very just, and I ought to do something to provide for what may come to pass. I maun try and get Watty to concur wi' me in some bit settlement that may lighten the disappointment to Charlie and Meg, should it please the Lord to tak me to himsel without a reasonable warning. Can sic a paper be made out?'

'O, yes,' replied the worthy lawyer, delighted with so successful an issue to his voluntary mission; 'ye hae twa ways o' doing the business; either by getting Watty to agree to an aliment, or by making a bond of provision to Charles and Mrs Milrookit.'

Claud said he would prefer the former mode; observing, with respect to the latter, that he thought it would be a cheating o' the law to take the other course.

'As for cheating the law,' said the lawyer, 'ye need gie yoursel no uneasiness about it, provided ye do honestly by your ain bairns, and the rest o' the community.'

And it was in consequence agreed, that, in the course of a day or two, Claud should take Walter to Glasgow, to execute a deed, by which, in the event of surviving his father, he would undertake to pay a certain annuity for the behoof of Charles's family, and that of his sister, Mrs Milrookit.

Chapter III

In furtherance of the arrangement agreed upon, as we have described in the foregoing chapter, as soon as Mr Keelevin had retired, Claud summoned Walter into the parlour. It happened, that the Leddy, during the period of the lawyer's visit, had been so engaged in another part of the house, that she was not aware of the conference, till, by chance, she saw him riding down the avenue. We need not, therefore, say that she experienced some degree of alarm, at the idea of a lawyer having been with her husband, unknown to her; and particularly, when, so immediately after his departure, her darling was requested to attend his father.

The mother and son entered the room together. Walter came from the nursery, where he had been dandling his child, and his appearance was not of the most prepossessing kind. From the death of his wife, in whose time, under her dictation, he was brushed up into something of a gentlemanly exterior, he had become gradually more and more slovenly. He only shaved on Saturday night, and buttoned his breeches knees on Sunday morning. Nor was the dress of Leddy Grippy at all out of keeping with that of her hopeful favourite. Her, time-out-of-mind, red quilted silk petticoat was broken into many holes;—her thrice dyed double tabinet gown, of bottle-green, with large ruffle cuffs, was in need of another dip; for, in her various culinary inspections, it had received many stains, and the superstructure of lawn and catgut, ornamented with ribbons, dyed blea in ink, surmounting her ill-toiletted toupee, had every appearance of having been smoked into yellow, beyond all power of blanching in the bleacher's art.

'And so, gudeman,' said she, on entering the room, 'ye hae had that auld sneck-drawer, Keelevin, wi' you? I won'er what you and him can hae to say in sic a clandestine manner, that the door maun be ay steekit when ye're thegither at your confabbles. Surely there's nae honesty that a man can hae, whilk his wife ought na to come in for a share of.'

'Sit down, Girzy Hypel, and haud thy tongue,' was the peevish command which this speech provoked.

'What for will I haud my tongue? a fool posture that would be, and no very commodious at this time; for ye see my fingers are coomy.'

'Woman, t'ou's past bearing!' exclaimed her disconcerted husband.

'An it's nae shame to me, gudeman; for every body kens I'm a grannie.'

The Laird smote his right thigh, and shook his left hand, with vexation; presently, however, he said,—

'Weel, weel; but sit ye down, and Watty, tak t'ou a chair beside her; for I want to consult you anent a paper that I'm mindit to hae drawn out for a satisfaction to you a'; for nane can tell when their time may come.'

'Ye ne'er made a mair sensible observe, gudeman, in a' your days,' replied the Leddy, sitting down; 'and it's vera right to make your will and testament; for ye ken what a straemash happened in the Glengowlmahallaghan family, by reason o' the Laird holographing his codicil; whilk, to be sure, was a dreadfu' omission, as my cousin, his wife, fand in her widowhood; for a' the moveables thereby gaed wi' the heritage to his auld son by the first wife—even the vera silver pourie that I gied her mysel wi' my own hands, in a gift at her marriage—a' gaed to the heir.'

'T'ou kens,' said Claud, interrupting her oration, 'that I hae provided thee wi' the liferent o' a house o' fifteen pounds a-year, furniture, and a jointure of a hundred and twenty over and aboon the outcoming o' thy father's gathering. So t'ou canna expek, Girzy, that I would wrang our bairns wi' ony mair overlay on thy account.'

'Ye're grown richer, gudeman, than when we came thegither,' replied the Leddy; 'and ne'er a man made siller without his wife's leave. So it would be a most hard thing, after a' my toiling and moiling, to make me nae better o't than the stricts o' the law in my marriage articles and my father's will; whilk was a gratus amous, that made me nane behauden to you.—No, an ye mean to do justice, gudeman, I'll get my thirds o' the conquest ye hae gotten sin the time o' our marriage; and I'll be content wi' nae less.'

'Weel, weel, Girzy, we'll no cast out about a settlement for thee.'

'It would be a fearful thing to hear tell o' an we did,' replied the Leddy: 'Living as we hae lived, a comfort to ane anither for thirty years, and bringin up sic a braw family, wi' so meikle credit. No, gudeman, I hae mair confidence in you than to misdoot your love and kindness, noo that ye're drawing so near your latter end as to be seriously thinking o' making a will. But, for a' that, I would like to ken what I'm to hae.'

'Very right, Girzy; very right,' said Claud; 'but, before we can come to a clear understanding, me and Watty maun conform in a bit paper by oursels, just that there may be nae debate hereafter about his right to the excambio we made for the Plealands.'

'I'll no put hand to ony drumhead paper again,' said Watty, 'for fear it wrang my wee Betty Bodle.'

Although this was said in a vacant heedless manner, it yet disturbed the mind of his father exceedingly, for the strange obstinacy with which the natural had persisted in his refusal to attend the funeral of his wife, had shown that there was something deeper and more intractable in his character than any one had previously imagined. But opposition had only the effect of making Claud more pertinacious, while it induced him to change his mode of operation. Perceiving, or at least being afraid that he might again call his obduracy into action, he accordingly shifted his ground, and, instead of his wonted method of treating Walter with commands and menaces, he dexterously availed himself of the Leddy's auxiliary assistance.

'Far be it, Watty, frae me, thy father,' said he, 'to think or wis wrang to thee or thine; but t'ou kens that in family settlements, where there's a patch't property like ours, we maun hae conjunk proceedings. Noo, as I'm fain to do something satisfactory to thy mother, t'ou'll surely never objek to join me in the needfu' instruments to gie effek to my intentions.'

'I'll do every thing to serve my mother,' replied Walter, 'but I'll no sign ony papers.'

'Surely, Watty Walkinshaw,' exclaimed the old Leddy, surprised at this repetition of his refusal, 'ye would na see me in want, and driven to a needcessity to gang frae door to door, wi' a meal-pock round my neck, and an oaken rung in my hand?'

'I would rather gie you my twa dollars, and the auld French half-a-crown, that I got long syne, on my birth-day, frae grannie,' said Watty.

'Then what for will ye no let your father make a rightfu' settlement?' cried his mother.

'I'm sure I dinna hinder him. He may mak fifty settlements for me; I'll ne'er fin' fau't wi' him.'

'Then,' said the Leddy, 'ye canna objek to his reasonable request.'

'I objek to no reasonable request; I only say, mother, that I'll no sign ony paper whatsomever, wheresomever, howsomever, nor ever and ever—so ye need na try to fleetch me.'

'Ye're ah outstrapolous ne'er-do-weel,' cried the Leddy, in a rage, knocking her neives smartly together, 'to speak to thy mother in that way; t'ou sail sign the paper, an te life be in thy body.'

'I'll no wrang my ain bairn for father nor mother; I'll gang to Jock Harrigals, the flesher, and pay him to hag aff my right hand, afore I put pen to law-paper again.'

'This is a' I get for my love and affection,' exclaimed the Leddy, bursting into tears; while her husband, scarcely less agitated by the firmness with which his purpose was resisted, sat in a state of gloomy abstraction, seemingly unconscious of the altercation. 'But,' added Mrs Walkinshaw,

'I'm no in thy reverence, t'ou unnatural Absalom, to rebel sae against thy parents. I hae may be a hoggar, and I ken whan I die wha s'all get the gouden guts o't—Wilt t'ou sign the paper?'

'I'll burn aff my right hand in the lowing fire, that I may ne'er be able to write the scrape o' a pen;' and with these emphatic words, said in a soft and simple manner, he rose from his seat, and was actually proceeding towards the fire-place, when a loud knocking at the door disturbed, and put an end to the conversation. It was a messenger sent from old Lady Plealands, to inform her daughter of Charles' malady, and to say that the doctor, who had been called in, was greatly alarmed at the rapid progress of the disease.

Chapter IV

Leddy Grippy was one of those worthy gentlewomen, who, without the slightest interest or feeling in any object or purpose with which they happen to be engaged, conceive themselves bound to perform all the customary indications of the profoundest sympathy and the deepest sensibility. Accordingly, no sooner did she receive the message of her son's melancholy condition, than she proceeded forthwith to prepare herself for going immediately to Glasgow.

'I canna expek, gudeman,'said she, 'that wi' your host ye'll come wi' me to Glasgow on this very sorrowful occasion; therefore I hope ye'll tak gude care o' yoursel, and see that the servan' lasses get your water-gruel, wi' a tamarind in't, at night, if it should please Charlie's Maker, by reason o 'the dangerous distemper, no to alloo me to come hame.'

The intelligence, however, had so troubled the old man, that he scarcely heard her observation. The indisposition of his son seemed to be somehow connected with the visit of Mr Keelevin, which it certainly was; and while his wife busily prepared for her visit, his mind wandered in devious conjectures, without being able to reach any thing calculated either to satisfy his wonder or to appease his apprehension.

'It's very right, Girzy, my dear,' said he, 'that ye sou'd gang in and see Charlie, poor lad; I'm extraordinar sorry to hear o' this income, and ye'll be sure to tak care he wants for nothing. Hear'st t'ou; look into the auld pocketbook in the scrutoire neuk; t'ou'l aiblins fin' there a five-pound note,—tak it wi' thee—there's no sic an extravagant commodity in ony man's house as a delirious fever.'

'Ah!' replied the Leddy, looking at her darling and ungrateful Walter, 'ye see what it is to hae a kind father; but ill ye deserve ony attention either frae father or mother, for your condumacity is ordained to break our hearts.'

'Mother,' said Walter, 'dinna be in sic a hurry—I hae something that 'ill do Charlie good.' In saying which, he rose and went to the nursery, whence he immediately returned with a pill box.

'There, mother! tak that wi' you; it's a box o' excellent medicaments, either for the cough, or the cauld, or shortness o' breath; to say naething amang frien's o' a constipation. Gie Charlie twa at bed-time and ane in the morning, and ye'll see an effek sufficient to cure every impediment in man or woman.'

Leddy Grippy, with the utmost contempt for the pills, snatched the box out of his hand, and flung it behind the fire. She then seated herself in the chair opposite her husband, and while she at the same time tied her cloak and placed on her bonnet, she said,—

'I'll alloo at last, gudeman, that I hae been a' my days in an error, for I could na hae believed that Watty was sic an idiot o' a naturalist, had I no lived to see this day. But the will o' Providence be done on earth as it is in heaven, and let us pray that he may be forgiven the sair heart he has gi'en to us his aged parents, as we forgive our debtors. I won'er, howsever, that my mother did na send word o' the nature o' this delirietness o' Charlie, for to be surely it's a very sudden come-to-pass, but the things o' time are no to be lippent to, and life fleeth away like a weaver's shuttle, and no man knoweth wheresoever it findeth rest for the sole of its foot. But, before I go, ye'll no neglek to tell Jenny in the morning to tak the three spyniels o' yarn to Josey Thrums, the weaver, for my Dornick towelling; and ye'll be sure to put Tarn Modiwart in mind that he's no to harl the plough out o'er the green brae till I get my big washing out o' hand. As for t'ee, Watty, stay till this calamity's past, and I'll let ee ken what it is to treat baith father and mother wi' sae little reverence. Really, gudeman, I begin to hae a notion, that he's, as auld Elspeth Freet, the midwife, ance said to me, a ta'en awa, and I would be nane surprised, that whoever lives to see him dee will find in the bed a benweed or a windlestrae, instead o'a Christian corpse. But sufficient for the day is the evil there of; and this sore news o' our auld son should mak us walk humbly, and no repine at the mercies set before us in this our sinfu' estate.'

The worthy Leddy might have continued her edifying exhortation for some time longer, but her husband grew impatient, and harshly interrupted her eloquence, by reminding her that the day was far advanced, and that the road to Glasgow was both deep and dreigh.

'I would counsel you, Girzy Hypel,' said he, 'no to put off your time wi' sic havers here, but gang intil the town, and send us out word in the morning, if ye dinna come hame, how Charlie may happen to be; for I canna but say that thir news are no just what I could hae wiss'd to hear at this time. As for what we hae been saying to Watty, we baith ken he's a kind-hearted chiel, and he'll think better or the morn o' what we were speaking about—will na ye, Watty?'

'I'll think as muckle's ye like,' said the faithful natural; 'but I'll sign nae papers; that's a fact afore divines. What for do ye ay fash me wi' your deeds and your instruments? I'm sure baith Charlie and Geordie could write better than me, and ye ne'er troublet them. But I jealouse the cause—an my grandfather had na left me his lawful heir to the Plealands, I might hae sat at the chumley lug whistling on my thumb. We a' hae frien's anew when we hae ony thing, and so I see in a' this flyting and fleetching; but ye'll flyte and ye'll fleetch till puddocks grow chucky-stanes before ye'll get me to wrang my ain bairn, my bonny wee Betty Bodle, that has na ane that cares for her, but only my leafu' lane.'

The Leddy would have renewed her remonstratory animadversions on his obstinacy, but the Laird again reminded her of the length of the journey in such an evening before her, and after a few half advices and half reproaches, she left the house.

Indisposed as Claud had previously felt himself, or seemed to be, she had not been long away, when he rose from his easy chair, and walked slowly across the room, with his hands behind, swinging his body heavily as he paced the floor. Walter, who still remained on his seat, appeared for some time not to notice his father's gestures; but the old man unconsciously began to quicken his steps, and at last walked so rapidly that his son's attention was roused.

'Father,' said he, 'hae ye been taking epicacco, for that was just the way that I was telt to gang, when I was last no weel?'

'No, no,' exclaimed the wretched old man; 'but I hae drank the bitterest dose o' life. There's nae vomit for a sick soul—nae purge for a foul conscience.'

These were, however, confessions that escaped from him unawares, like the sparks that are elicited in violent percussions,—for he soon drew himself firmly and bravely up, as if he prepared himself to defy the worst that was in store for him; but this resolution also as quickly passed away, and he returned to his easy chair, and sat down, as if he had been abandoned of all hope, and had resigned himself into a dull and sleepy lethargy.

For about half an hour he continued in this slumbering and inaccessible state, at the end of which he called one of the servants, and bade him be ready to go to Glasgow by break of day, and bring Mr Keelevin before breakfast. 'Something maun be done,' said he as the servant, accompanied by Walter, left the room; 'the curse of God has fallen upon me, my hands are tied, a dreadfu' chain is fastened about me; I hae cheated mysel, and there's nae bail—no, not in the Heavens—for the man that has wilfully raffled away his own soul in the guilty game o' pride.'

Chapter V

Meanwhile, the disease which had laid Charles prostrate was proceeding with a terrific and devastating fury. Before his mother reached the house, he had lost all sense of himself and situation, and his mind was a chaos of the wildest and most extravagant phantasies. Occasionally, however, he would sink into a momentary calm, when a feeble gleam of reason would appear amidst his ravings, like the transient glimmer of a passing light from the shore on the black waves of the stormy ocean, when the cry has arisen at midnight of a vessel on the rocks, and her crew in jeopardy. But these breathing pauses of the fever's rage were, perhaps, more dreadful than its violence, for they were accompanied with a return of the moral anguish which had brought on his malady; and as often as his eye caught the meek, but desponding countenance of Isabella, as she sat by his bed-side, he would make a convulsive effort to raise himself, and instantly relapse into the tempestuous raptures of the delirium. In this state he passed the night.

Towards morning symptoms of a change began to show themselves,—the turbulence of his thoughts subsided,—his breathing became more regular; and both Isabella and his mother were persuaded that he was considerably better. Under this impression, the old lady, at day-break, dispatched a messenger to inform his father of the favourable change, who, in the interval, had passed a night, in a state, not more calm, and far less enviable, than that of his distracted son.

Whatever was the motive which induced Claud, on the preceding evening, to determine on sending for Mr Keelevin, it would appear that it did not long maintain its influence; for, before going to bed, he countermanded the order. Indeed, his whole behaviour that night indicated a strange and unwonted degree of indecision. It was evident that he meditated some intention, which he hesitated to carry into effect; and the conflict banished sleep from his pillow. When the messenger from Glasgow arrived, he was already dressed, and, as none of the servants were stirring, he opened the door himself. The news certainly gave him pleasure, but they also produced some change in the secret workings of his mind, of no auspicious augury to the fulfilment of the parental intention which he had probably formed; but which he was as probably reluctant to realize, as it could not be carried into effect without material detriment to that one single dominant object to which his whole life, efforts, and errors, had been devoted. At least from the moment he received the agreeable intelligence that Charles was better, his agitation ceased, and he resumed his seat in the elbow chair, by the parlour fire-side, as composedly as if nothing had occurred, in any degree, to trouble the apparently even tenor of his daily unsocial and solitary reflections. In this situation he fell asleep, from which he was roused by another messenger with still more interesting intelligence to him, than even the convalescence, as it was supposed, of his favourite son.

Mrs George Walkinshaw had, for some time, given a large promise, in her appearance, of adding to the heirs of Kittlestonheugh; but, by her residence in Glasgow, and holding little intercourse with the Grippy family, owing to her own situation, and to her dislike of the members, especially after Walter had been brought back with his child; the Laird and Leddy were less acquainted with her maternal progress than might have been expected, particularly when the anxiety of the old man, with respect to male issue, is considered. Such things, however, are of common occurrence in all families; and it so happened, that, during the course of this interesting night, Mrs George had been delivered; and that her husband, as in duty bound, in the morning, dispatched a maid-servant to inform his father and mother of the joyous event.

The messenger, Jenny Purdie, had several years before been in the servitude of the Laird's house, from which she translated herself to that of George. Being something forward, at the same time sly and adroit, and having heard how much her old master had been disappointed that Walter's daughter was not a son, she made no scruple of employing a little address in communicating her news. Accordingly, when the Laird, disturbed in his slumber by her entrance, roused himself, and turned round to see who it was that had come into the room, she presented herself, as she had walked from the royal city muffled up in a dingy red cloak, her dark blue and white striped petticoat, sorely scanty, and her glowing purple legs, and well spread shoeless feet, bearing liberal proof of the speed with which she had spattered and splashed along the road.

'I wis you meikle joy, Laird! I hae brought you blithe smeat,' was her salutation.

'What is't, Jenny?' said the old man.

'I'll let you guess that, unless ye promise to gi'e me half-a-crown,' was her reply.

'T'ou canna think I would ware less on sic errand as t'ou's come on. Is't a laddie?'

'It's far better, Laird,' said Jenny triumphantly.

'Is't twins?' exclaimed the Laird, sympathizing with her exultation.

'A half-crown, a half-crown, Laird,' was, however, all the satisfaction he received. 'Down wi' the dust.'

'An t'ou's sae on thy peremptors, I fancy I maun comply. There, take it, and welcome,' said he, pulling the money from under the flap of his waistcoat pocket; while Jenny, stretching her arm, as she hoisted it from under the cloak, eagerly bent forward and took the silver out of his hand, instantaneously affecting the greatest gravity of face.

'Laird,' said she, 'ye mauna be angry wi' me, but I did na like just to dumbfoun'er you a' at ance wi' the news; my mistress, it's very true, has been brought to bed, but it's no as ye expekit.'

'Then it's but a dochter?' replied the Laird discontentedly.

'No, Sir, it's no a dochter.—It's twa dochters, Sir!' exclaimed Jenny, scarcely able to repress her risibility, while she endeavoured to assume an accent of condolence.

Claud sank back in his chair, and, drooping his head, gave a deep sigh.

'But,' rejoined the adroit Jenny, 'it's a gude earnest of a braw family, so keep up your heart, Laird, aiblins the neist birds may be a' cocks; there ne'er was a goose without a gander.'

'Gae bot the house, and fash na me wi' thy clishmaclavers. I say gae bot the house,' cried the Laird, in a tone so deep and strong, that Jenny's disposition to gossip was most effectually daunted, and she immediately retired.

For some time after she had left the room, Claud continued sitting in the same posture with which he had uttered the command, leaning slightly forward, and holding the arms of the easy-chair graspingly by both his hands, as if in the act of raising himself. Gradually, however, he relaxed his hold, and subsided slowly and heavily into the position in which he usually fell asleep. Shutting his eyes, he remained in that state for a considerable time, exhibiting no external indication of the rush of mortified feelings, which, like a subterranean stream of some acrid mineral, struggled through all the abysses of his bosom.

This last stroke—the birth of twin daughters—seemed to perfect the signs and omens of that displeasure with which he had for some time thought the disinheritance of his first-born was regarded; and there was undoubtedly something sublime in the fortitude with which he endured the gna wings of remorse.—It may be impossible to consider the course of his sordid ambition without indignation; but the strength of character which enabled him to contend at once with his paternal partiality, and stand firm in his injustice before what he awfully deemed the frowns and the menaces of Heaven, forms a spectacle of moral bravery that cannot be contemplated without emotions of wonder mingled with dread.

Chapter VI

The fallacious symptoms in the progress of Charles's malady, which had deceived his wife and mother, assumed, on the third day, the most alarming appearance. Mr Keelevin, who, from the interview, had taken an uncommon interest in his situation, did not, however, hear of his illness till the doctors, from the firmest persuasion that he could not survive, had expressed some doubts of his recovery; but, from that time, the inquiries of the honest lawyer were frequent; and, not withstanding what had passed on the former occasion, he resolved to make another attempt on the sympathies of the father. For this purpose, on the morning of the fifth day, which happened to be Sunday, he called at Charles's house, to inquire how he was, previous to the visit which he intended to pay to Grippy. But the servant who attended the door was in tears, and told him that her master was in the last struggles of life.

Any other general acquaintance would, on receiving such intelligence, however deeply he might have felt affected, have retired; but the ardent mind and simplicity of Mr Keelevin prompted him to act differently; and without replying to the girl, he softly slipped his feet from his shoes, and stepping gently to the sick chamber, entered it unobserved; so much were those around the death-bed occupied with the scene before them.

Isabella was sitting at the bed-head, holding her dying husband by both the hands, and bending over him almost as insensible as himself. His mother was sitting near the foot of the bed, with a phial in one hand, and a towel, resting on her knee, in the other, looking over her left shoulder towards her son, with an eager countenance, in which curiosity, and alarm, and pity, were, in rapid succession, strangely and vacantly expressed. At the foot of the bed, the curtains of which were drawn aside, the two little children stood wondering in solemn innocence at the mournful mystery which Nature was performing with their father. Mr Keelevin was more moved by their helpless astonishment than even by the sight of the last and lessening heavings and pantings of his dying friend; and, melted to tears, he withdrew, and wept behind the door.

In the course of three or four minutes, a rustle in the chamber roused him; and on looking round, he saw Isabella standing on the floor, and her mother-in-law, who had dropped the phial, sitting, with a look of horror, holding up her hand, which quivered with agitation. He stepped forward, and giving a momentary glance at the bed, saw that all was over; but, before he could turn round to address himself to the ladies, the children uttered a shrill piercing shriek of terror; and running to their mother, hid their little faces in her dress, and clasped her fearfully in their arms.

For some minutes he was overcome. The young, the beautiful, the defenceless widow, was the first that recovered her self-possession. A flood of tears relieved her heart; and bending down, and folding her arms round her orphans, she knelt, and said, with an upward look of supplication, 'God will protect you.'

Mr Keelevin was still unable to trust himself to say a word; but he approached, and gently assisting her to rise, led her, with the children, into the parlour, where old Lady Plealands was sitting alone, with a large psalm-book in her hand. Her spectacles lying on a table in the middle of the room, showed that she had been unable to read.

He then returned to bring Leddy Grippy also away from the body, but met her in the passage. We dare not venture to repeat what she said to him, for she was a mother; but the result was, a request from her that he would undertake to communicate the intelligence to her husband, and to beg him either to come to her in the course of the day, or send her some money: 'For,' said she, 'this is a bare house, Mr Keelevin; and Heaven only knows what's to become o' the wee orphans.'

The kind-hearted lawyer needed, however, no argument to spur him on to do all that he could in such a time, and in such circumstances, to lighten the distress and misery of a family whose necessities he so well knew. On quitting the house, he proceeded immediately towards Grippy, ruminating on the scene he had witnessed, and on the sorrows which he foresaw the desolate widow and her children were destined to suffer.

The weather, for some days before, had been unsettled and boisterous; but it was that morning uncommonly fine for the advanced state of the season. Every thing was calm and in repose, as if Nature herself had hallowed the Sabbath. Mr Keelevin walked thoughtfully along, the grief of his reflections being gradually subdued by the benevolence of his intentions; but he was a man well stricken in years, and the agitation he had undergone made the way appear to him so long, that he felt himself tired, insomuch, that when he came to the bottom of the lane which led to Kilmarkeckle, he sat down to rest himself on the old dike, where Claud himself had sat, on his return from the town, after executing the fatal entail. Absorbed in the reflections to which the event of the morning naturally gave rise, he leaned for some time pensively forward, supporting his head on his hand, insensible to every object around, till he was roused by the cooing of a pigeon in the field behind him. The softness and the affectionate sound of its tones comforted his spirits as he thought of his client's harsh temper, and he raised his eyes and looked on the beautiful tranquillity of the landscape before him, with a sensation of freshness and pleasure, that restored him to confidence in the charity of his intentions. The waters of the river were glancing to the cloudless morning sun,—a clear bright cheerfulness dwelt on the foreheads of the distant hills,—the verdure of the nearer fields seemed to be gladdened by the presence of spring,—and a band of little schoolboys, in their Sunday clothes, playing with a large dog on the opposite bank of the river, was in unison with the general benevolence that smiled and breathed around, but was liveliest in his own heart.

Chapter VII

The benevolent lawyer found the old man in his accustomed seat by the fireside. Walter was in the room with him, dressed for church, and dandling his child. At first Mr Keelevin felt a little embarrassment, not being exactly aware in what manner the news he had to communicate might be received; but seeing how Walter was engaged, he took occasion to commend his parental affection.

'That's acting like a father, Mr Walter,' said he; 'for a kind parent innocently pleasuring his bairn is a sight that the very angels are proud to look on. Mak muckle o' the poor wee thing, for nobody can tell how long she may be spared to you. I dare say, Mr Walkinshaw,' he added, addressing himself to Claud, 'ye hae mony a time been happy in the same manner wi' your own children?'

'I had something else to tak up my mind,' replied the old man gruffly, not altogether pleased to see the lawyer, and apprehensive of some new animadversions.

'Nae doubt, your's has been an eydent and industrious life,' said Mr Keelevin, 'and hitherto it has na been without a large scare o' comfort. Ye canna, however, expek a greater constancy in fortune and the favour o' Providence than falls to the common lot of man; and ye maun lay your account to meet wi' troubles and sorrows as weel as your neighbours.'

This was intended by the speaker as a prelude to the tidings he had brought, and was said in a mild and sympathetic manner; but the heart of Claud, galled and skinless by the corrosion of his own thoughts, felt it as a reproach, and he interrupted him sharply.

'What ken ye, Mr Keelevin, either o' my trumps or my troubles?' And he subjoined, in his austerest and most emphatic manner, 'The inner man alone knows, whether, in the gifts o' fortune, he has gotten gude, or but only gowd. Mr Keelevin, I hae lived long eneugh to mak an observe on prosperity,—the whilk is, that the doited and heedless world is very ready to mistak the smothering growth of the ivy, on a doddered stem, for the green boughs o' a sound and flourishing tree.'

To which Walter added singingly, as he swung his child by the arms,—

'Near planted by a river,
Which in his season yields his fruit,
And his leaf fadeth never.'

'But no to enter upon any controversy, Mr Walkinshaw,' said Mr Keelevin,—'ye'll no hae heard the day how your son Charles is?'

'No,' replied Claud, with a peculiarly impressive accent; 'but, at the latest last night, the gudewife sent word he was very ill.'

'I'm greatly concerned about him,' resumed the lawyer, scarcely aware of the address with which, in his simplicity, he was moving on towards the fatal communication; 'I am greatly concerned about him, but mair for his young children—they'll be very helpless orphans, Mr Walkinshaw.'

'I ken that,' was the stern answer, uttered with such a dark and troubled look, that it quite daunted Mr Keelevin at the moment from proceeding.

'Ye ken that!' cried Walter, pausing, and setting down the child on the floor, and seating himself beside it; 'how do ye ken that, father?'

The old man eyed him for a moment with a fierce and strong aversion, and, turning to Mr Keelevin, shook his head, but said nothing.

'What's done, is done, and canna be helped,' resumed the lawyer; 'but reparation may yet, by some sma cost and cooking, be made; and I hope Mr Walkinshaw, considering what has happened, ye'll do your duty.'

'I'll sign nae papers,' interposed Walter; 'I'll do nothing to wrang my wee Betty Bodle,'—and he fondly kissed the child.

Mr Keelevin looked compassionately at the natural, and then, turning to his father, said,—

'I hae been this morning to see Mr Charles.'

'Weel, and how is he?' exclaimed the father eagerly.

The lawyer, for about the term of a minute, made no reply, but looked at him steadily in the face, and then added solemnly,

'He's no more!'

At first the news seemed to produce scarcely any effect; the iron countenance of the old man underwent no immediate change—he only remained immoveable in the position in which he had received the shock; but presently Mr Keelevin saw that he did not fetch his breath, and that his lips began to contract asunder, and to expose his yellow teeth with the grin almost of a skull.

'Heavens preserve us, Mr Walkinshaw!' cried Mr Keelevin, rising to his assistance; but, in the same moment, the old man uttered a groan so deep and dreadful, so strange and superhuman, that Walter snatched up his child, and rushed in terror out of the room. After this earthquake-struggle, he in some degree recovered himself, and the lawyer returned to his chair, where he remained some time silent.

'I had a fear o't, but I was na prepar't, Mr Keelevin, for this,' said the miserable father; 'and noo I'll kick against the pricks nae langer. Wonderful God! I bend my aged grey head at thy footstool. O lay not thy hand heavier upon me than I am able to bear. Mr Keelevin, ye ance said the entail cou'd be broken if I were to die insolvent—mak me sae in the name of the God I have dared so long to fight against. An Charlie's dead—murdered by my devices! Weel do I mind, when he was a playing bairn, that I first kent the blessing of what it is to hae something to be kind to;—aften and aften did his glad and bright young face thaw the frost that had bound up my heart, but ay something new o' the world's pride and trash cam in between, and hardent it mair and mair.—But a's done noo, Mr Keelevin—the fight's done and the battle won, and the avenging God of righteousness and judgment is victorious.'

Mr Keelevin sat in silent astonishment at this violence of sorrow. He had no previous conception of that vast abyss of sensibility which lay hidden and unknown within the impenetrable granite of the old man's pride and avarice; and he was amazed and overawed when he beheld it burst forth, as when the fountains of the great deep were broken up, and the deluge swept away the earliest and the oldest iniquities of man.

The immediate effect, when he began to recover from his wonder, was a sentiment of profound reverence.

'Mr Walkinshaw,' said he, 'I have long done you great injustice;' and he was proceeding to say something more as an apology, but Claud interrupted him.

'You hae ne'er done me any manner of wrong, Mr Keelevin; but I hae sinned greatly and lang against my ain nature, and it's time I sou'd repent. In a few sorrowful days I maun follow the lamb I hae sacrificed on the altars o' pride; speed a' ye dow to mak the little way I hae to gang to the grave easy to one that travels wi' a broken heart. I gie you nae further instructions—your skill and honest conscience will tell you what is needful to be done; and when the paper's made out, come to me. For the present leave me, and in your way hame bid Dr Denholm come hither in the afternoon.'

'I think, Mr Walkinshaw,' replied Mr Keelevin, falling into his professional manner on receiving these orders, 'that it would be as weel for me to come back the morn, when ye're more composed, to get the particulars of what ye wish done.'

'O man!' exclaimed the hoary penitent, 'ye ken little o' me. Frae the very dawn o' life I hae done nothing but big and build an idolatrous image; and when it was finished, ye saw how I laid my first-born on its burning and brazen altar. But ye never saw what I saw—the face of an angry God looking constantly from behind a cloud that darkened a' the world like the shadow of death to me; and ye canna feel what I feel now, when His dreadful right hand has smashed my idol into dust. I hae nae langer part interest nor portion in the concerns of this life; but only to sign ony paper that ye can devise, to restore their rights to the twa babies that my idolatry has made fatherless.'

'I hope, in mercy, Mr Walkinshaw, that ye'll be comforted,' said the worthy lawyer, deeply affected by his vehemence.

'I hope so too, but I see na whar at present it's to come frae,' replied Claud, bursting into tears, and weeping bitterly. 'But,' he added, 'I would fain, Mr Keelevin, be left to mysel—alack! alack! I hae been owre lang left to mysel. Howsever, gang away the day, and remember Dr Denholm as ye pass;—but I'll ne'er hae peace o' mind till the paper's made and signed; so, as a Christian, I beg you to make haste, for it will be a Samaritan's act of charity.'

Mr Keelevin perceived that it was of no use at that time to offer any farther consolation, and he accordingly withdrew.

Chapter VIII

During the remainder of the day, after Mr Keelevin had left him, Claud continued to sit alone, and took no heed of any thing that occurred around him.—Dinner was placed on the table at the usual hour; but he did not join Walter.

'I won'er , father,' said the natural, as he was hewing at the joint, 'that ye're no for ony dinner the day; for ye ken if a' the folk in the world were to die but only ae man, it would behove that man to hae his dinner.'

To this sage observation the grey-haired penitent made no reply; and Walter finished his meal without attempting to draw him again into conversation.

In the afternoon Claud left his elbow chair, and walked slowly and heavily up the path which led to the bench he had constructed on the rising ground, where he was so often in the practice of contemplating the lands of his forefathers; and on gaining the brow of the hill, he halted, and once more surveyed the scene.

For a moment it would seem that a glow of satisfaction passed over his heart; but it was only a hectical flush, instantly succeeded by the nausea of moral disgust; and he turned abruptly round, and seated himself with his back towards the view which had afforded him so much pleasure. In this situation he continued some time, resting his forehead on his ivory-headed staff, and with his eyes fixed on the ground.

In the meantime, Mr Keelevin having called on the Reverend Dr Denholm, according to Claud's wish, to request he would visit him in the afternoon, the venerable minister was on his way to Grippy. On reaching the house, he was informed by one of the maid-servants, that her master had walked to his summer-seat on the hill, whither he immediately proceeded, and found the old man still rapt in his moody and mournful meditations.

Claud had looked up, as he heard him approach, and pointing to the bench, beckoned him to be seated. For some time they sat together without speaking; the minister appearing to wait in expectation that the penitent would address him first; but observing him still disposed to continue silent, he at last said,—

'Mr Keelevin told me, Mr Walkinshaw, that ye wished to see me under this dispensation with which the hand o' a righteous Providence has visited your family.'

'I'm greatly obliged to Mr Keelevin,' replied Claud, thoughtfully; 'he's a frien'ly and a very honest man. It would hae been happy wi' me the day, Dr Denholm, had I put mair confidence in him; but I doobt, I doobt, I hae been a' my life a sore hypocrite.'

'I was ay o' that notion,' said the Reverend Doctor, not quite sure whether the contrition so humbly expressed was sincere or affected, but the meek look of resignation with which the desolate old man replied to the cutting sarcasm, moved the very heart of the chastiser with strong emotions of sympathy and grief; and he added, in his kindliest manner,—

'But I hope, Mr Walkinshaw, I may say to you, "Brother, be of good cheer;" for if this stroke, by which your first-born is cut off from the inheritance of the years that were in the promise of his winsome youth, is ta'en and borne as the admonition of the vanity of setting your heart on the things of carnal life, it will prove to you a great blessing for evermore.'

There was something in the words in which this was couched, that, still more painfully than the taunt, affected the disconsolate penitent, and he burst into tears, taking hold of the minister's right hand graspingly with his left, saying, 'Spare me, doctor! O spare me, an it be possible—for the worm that never dieth hath coiled itsel within my bosom, and the fire that's never quenched is kindled around me—What an it be forever?'

'Ye shouldna, Mr Walkinshaw,' replied the clergyman, awed by the energy and solemnity of his manner—'Ye should na entertain such desperate thoughts, but hope for better things; for it's a blithe thing for your precious soul to be at last sensible o' your own unworthiness.'

'Aye, doctor, but, alack for me! I was ay sensible o' that. I hae sinned wi' my e'en open, and I thought to mak up for't by a strict observance o' church ordinances.'

' 'Deed, Mr Walkinshaw, there are few shorter roads to the pit than through the kirk-door; and many a Christian has been brought nigh to the death, thinking himsel cheered and guided by the sound o' gospel preaching, when, a' the time, his ear was turned to the sough o' perdition.'

'What shall I do to be saved?' said the old man, reverentially and timidly.

'Ye can do naething yoursel, Mr Walkinshaw,' replied the minister; and he proceeded, with the fearlessness of a champion and the energy of an apostle, to make manifest to his understanding the corruption of the human heart, and its utter unworthiness in the pure eyes of Him that alone can wash away the Ethiopian hue of original sin, and eradicate the Leopard spots of personal guilt.

While he spoke the bosom of Claud was convulsed—he breathed deeply and fearfully—his eyes glared—and the manner in which he held his hands, trembling and slightly raised, showed that his whole inward being was transfixed as it were, with a horrible sense of some tremendous apocalypse.

'I fear, I fear, Doctor Denholm,' he exclaimed, 'that I can hae no hope.'

The venerable pastor was struck with the despair of the expression, and, after a short pause, said, 'Dinna let yoursel despond; tak comfort in the mercy of God; surely your life has na been blacken't wi' ony great crime?'

'It has been one continued crime,' cried the penitent—'frae the first hour that my remembrance can look back to, down to the vera last minute, there has been no break nor interruption in the constancy of my iniquity. I sold my soul to the Evil One in my childhood, that I might recover the inheritance of my forebears. O the pride of that mystery! and a' the time there was a voice within me that would na be pacified wi' the vain promises I made to become another man, as soon as ever my conquest was complete.'

'I see but in that,' said the pious Doctor, in a kind and consoling manner, 'I see but in a' that, Mr Walkinshaw, an inordinate love of the world; and noo that ye're awakened to a sense of your danger, the Comforter will soon come. Ye hae ay been reputed an honest man, and no deficient in your moral duties, as a husband, a parent, a master, and a friend.'

Claud clasped his hands fervently together, exclaiming, 'O God! thou hast ever seen my hypocrisy!—Dr Denholm,' and he took him firmly by the hand;—'when I was but a bairn, I kent na what it was to hae the innocence o'a young heart. I used to hide the sma' presents of siller I got frae my frien's, even when Maudge Dobbie, the auld kind creature that brought me up, could na earn a sufficiency for our scrimpit meals; I did na gang near her when I kent she was in poor tith and bedrid, for fear my heart would relent, and gar me gie her something out o' the gathering I was making for the redemption o' this vile yird that is mair grateful than me, for it repays with its fruits the care o' the tiller. I stiffled the very sense o' loving kindness within me; and in furtherance of my wicked avarice, I married a woman—Heaven may forgie the aversion I had to her; but my own nature never can.'

Dr Denholm held up his hands, and contemplated in silence the humbled and prostrate spirit that was thus proceeding with the frightful confession of its own baseness and depravity.

'But,' cried the penitent, 'I canna hope that ye're able to thole the sight that I would lay open in the inner sepulchre of my guilty conscience—for in a' my reprobation I had ever the right before me, when I deliberately preferred the wrang. The angel of the Lord ceased not, by night nor by day, to warsle for me; but I clung to Baal, and spurned and kicked whenever the messenger of brightness and grace tried to tak me away.'

The old man paused, and then looking towards the minister, who still continued silent, regarding him with compassionate amazement, said,—

371

'Doctor, what can I expek?'

'O! Mr Walkinshaw, but ye hae been a doure sinner,' was the simple and emphatic reply; 'and I hope that this sense o' the evil of your way is an admonition to a repentance that may lead you into the right road at last.

Be ye, therefore, thankful for the warning ye hae now gotten of the power and the displeasure of God.'

'Many a warning,' said Claud, 'in tokens sairer than the plagues o' Egypt, which but grieved the flesh, hae I had in the spirit; but still my heart was harden't till the destroying angel slew my first-born.'

'Still I say, be thankful, Mr Walkinshaw! ye hae received a singular manifestation of the goodness of God. Your son, we're to hope, is removed into a better world. He's exposed no more to the temptations of this life—a' care wi' him is past—a' sorrow is taken from him. It's no misfortune to die, but a great risk to be born; and nae Christian should sorrow, like unto those who are without hope, when Death, frae ahint the black yett, puts forth his ancient hand, and pulls in a brother or a sister by the skirts of the garment of flesh. The like o' that, Mr Walkinshaw, is naething; but when, by the removal of a friend, we are taught to see the error of our way, it's a great thing for us—it's a blithe thing; and, therefore, I say unto you again, brother, be of good cheer, for in this temporal death of your son, may be the Lord has been pleased to bring about your own salvation.'

'And what may be the token whereby I may venture to take comfort frae the hope?'

'There's nae surer sign gi'en to man than that token—when ye see this life but as a pilgrimage, then ye may set forward in your way rejoicing—when ye behold nothing in your goods and gear but trash and splendid dirt, then may ye be sure that ye hae gotten better than silver or gold—when ye see in your herds and flocks but fodder for a carnal creature like the beasts that perish, then shall ye eat of the heavenly manna—when ye thirst to do good, then shall the rock be smitten, and the waters of life, flowing forth, will follow you wheresoever you travel in the wilderness of this world.'

The venerable pastor suddenly paused, for at that moment Claud laid aside his hat, and, falling on his knees, clasped his hands together, and looking towards the skies, his long grey hair flowing over his back, he said with awful solemnity, 'Father, thy will be done!—in the devastation of my earthly heart, I accept the erls of thy service.'

He then rose with a serene countenance, as if his rigid features had undergone some benignant transformation. At that moment a distant strain of wild and holy music, rising from a hundred voices, drew their attention towards a shaggy bank of natural birch and hazel, where, on the sloping ground in front, they saw a number of Cameronians from Glasgow, and the neighbouring villages, assembled to commemorate in worship the persecutions which their forefathers had suffered there for righteousness sake.

After listening till the psalm was finished, Claud and Dr Denholm returned towards the house, where they found Leddy Grippy had arrived. The old man, in order to avoid any unnecessary conversation, proposed that the servants should be called in, and that the Doctor should pray—which he did accordingly, and at the conclusion retired.

Chapter IX

On Monday Claud rose early, and, without waiting for breakfast, or heeding the remonstrances of his wife on the risk he ran in going afield fasting, walked to Glasgow, and went directly to the house of his mother-in-law, the aged Lady Plealands, now considerably above four-score. The natural delicacy of her constitution had received so great a shock from the death of Charles, that she was unable that morning to leave her room. Having, however, brought home with her the two orphans, until after the funeral, their grandfather found them playing in the parlour, and perhaps he was better pleased to meet with them than had she been there herself.

Although they knew him perfectly, yet the cold and distant intercourse which arose from his estrangement towards their father, had prevented them from being on those terms of familiarity which commonly subsist between children and their grandfathers; and when they saw him enter the room, they immediately left their toys on the floor, and, retiring to a corner, stood looking at him timidly, with their hands behind.

The old man, without seeming to notice their innocent reverence, walked to a chair near the window, and sat down. His demeanour was as calm, and his features as sedate, as usual, but his eyes glittered with a slight sprinkling of tears, and twice or thrice he pressed his elbows into his sides, as if to restrain some inordinate agitation of the heart. In the course of a few minutes he became quite master of himself, and, looking for a short time compassionately at the children, he invited them to come to him. Mary, the girl, who was the youngest, obeyed at once the summons; but James, the boy, still kept back.

'What for wilt t'ou no come to me?' said Claud.

'I'll come, if ye'll no hurt me,' replied the child.

'Hurt thee! what for, poor thing, should I hurt thee?' inquired his grandfather, somewhat disturbed by the proposed condition.

'I dinna ken,' said the boy, still retreating,—'but I am feart, for ye hurt papa for naething, and mamma used to greet for't.'

Claud shuddered, and in the spasmodic effort which he made to suppress his emotion, he unconsciously squeezed the little hand of the girl so hardly, as he held her between his knees, that she shrieked with the pain, and flew towards her brother, who, equally terrified, ran to shelter himself behind a chair.

For some time the old man was so much affected, that he felt himself incapable of speaking to them. But he said to himself,—

'It is fit that I should endure this. I sowed tares, and mauna expek wheat.'

The children, not finding themselves angrily pursued, began to recover courage, and again to look at him.

'I did na mean to hurt thee, Mary,' said he, after a short interval. 'Come, and we'll mak it up;'—and, turning to the boy, he added, 'I'm very wae that e'er I did ony wrang to your father, my bonny laddie, but I'll do sae nae mair.'

'That's cause ye canna help it,' replied James boldly, 'for he's dead—he's in a soun' soun' sleep—nobody but an angel wi' the last trumpet at his vera lug is able to waken him—and Mary and me, and mamma—we're a' gaun to lie down and die too, for there's nobody now in the world that cares for us.'

'I care for you, my lambie, and I'll be kind to you; I'll be as kind as your father.'

It would appear that these words had been spoken affectionately, for the little girl, forgetful of her hurt, returned, and placed herself between his knees; but her brother still stood aloof.

'But will ye be kind to mamma?' said the boy, with an eager and suspicious look.

'That I will,' was the answer. 'She'll ne'er again hae to blame me—nor hae reason to be sorrowful on my account.'

'But were nae ye ance papa's papa?' rejoined the child, still more suspiciously.

The old man felt the full force of all that was meant by these simple expressions, and he drew his hand hastily over his eyes to wipe away the rising tears.

'And will ye never trust me?' said he sorrowfully to the child, who, melted by the tone in which it was uttered, advanced two or three steps towards him.

'Ay, if ye'll say as sure's death that ye'll no hurt me.'

'Then I do say as sure's death,' exclaimed Claud fervently, and held out his hand, which the child, running forward, caught in his, and was in the same moment folded to his grandfather's bosom.

Lady Plealands had, in the meantime, been told who was her visitor, and being anxious, for many reasons, to see him at this crisis, opened the door. Feeble, pale, and delicate, the venerable gentlewoman was startled at seeing a sight she so little expected, and stood several minutes with the door in her hand before she entered.

'Come in,' said Claud to her—'come in—I hae something to say to you anent thir bairns—Something maun be done for them and their mother; and I would fain tak counsel wi' you concerning 't. Bell Fatherlans is o' oure frush a heart to thole wi' the dinging and fyke o' our house, or I would tak them a' hame to Grippy; but ye maun devise some method wi' her to mak their loss as light in worldly circumstances as my means will alloo; and whatsoever you and her 'gree upon Mr Keelevin will see executed baith by deed and paction.'

'Is't possible that ye're sincere, Mr Walkinshaw?' replied the old lady.

Claud made no answer, but, disconsolately, shook his head.

'This is a mercy past hope, if ye're really sincere.'

'I am sincere,' said the stern old man, severely; 'and I speak wi' humiliation and contrition. I hae borne the rebuke of thir babies, and their suspicion has spoken sermons of reproaches to my cowed spirit and broken heart.'

'What have ye done?' inquired the Lady, surprised at his vehemence—'what have ye done to make you speak in such a way, Mr Walkinshaw?'

'In an evil hour I was beguiled by the Moloch o' pride and ambition to disinherit their father, and settle a' my property on Watty, because he had the Plealands. But, from that hour, I hae never kent what comfort is, or amaist what it is to hope for heavenly mercy. But I hae lived to see my sin, and I yearn to mak atonement. When that's done, I trust that I may be permitted to lay down my head, and close my een in peace.'

Mrs Hypel did not well know what answer to make, the disclosure seemed to her so extraordinary, that she looked at Claud as if she distrusted what she heard, or was disposed to question the soundness of his mind.

'I see,' he added, 'that, like the orphans, ye dinna believe me; but, like them, Mrs Hypel, ye'll may be in time be wrought to hae compassion on a humbled and contrite heart. A', therefore, that I can say for the present is, consult wi' Bell, and confer wi' Mr Keelevin; he has full power frae me to do whatsoever he may think just and right; and what ye do, do quickly, for a heavy hand is on my shouther; and there's one before me in the shape o' my braw Charlie, that waves his hand, and beckons me to follow him.'

The profound despondency with which this was uttered overwhelmed the feelings of the old Lady; even the children were affected, and, disengaging themselves from his arms, retired together, and looked at him with wonder and awe.

'Will ye go and see their mother? '—said the lady, as he rose, and was moving towards the door. He halted, and for a few seconds appeared to reflect; but suddenly looking round, he replied, with a deep and troubled voice,—

'No. I hae been enabled to do mair than I ever thought it was in my power to do; but I canna yet,—no, not this day,—I canna yet venture there.—I will, however, by and by. It's a penance I maun dree, and I will go through it a'.'

And with these words he quitted the house, leaving the old gentlewoman and the children equally amazed, and incapable of comprehending the depth and mystery of a grief which, mournful as the immediate cause certainly was, undoubtedly partook in some degree of religious despair.

Chapter X

Between the interview described in the preceding chapter and the funeral, nothing remarkable appeared in the conduct of Claud. On the contrary, those habits of reserve and taciturnity into which he had fallen, from the date of the entail, were apparently renewed, and, to the common observation of the general eye, he moved and acted as if he had undergone no inward change.

The domestics, however, began to notice, that, instead of the sharp and contemptuous manner which he usually employed in addressing himself to Walter, his voice was modulated with an accent of compassion,—and that, on the third day after the death of Charles, he, for the first time, caressed and fondled the affectionate natural's darling, Betty Bodle.

It might have been thought that this simple little incident would have afforded pleasure to her father, who happened to be out of the room, when the old man took her up in his arms; but so far from this being the case, the moment that Walter returned he ran towards him, and snatched the child away.

'What for do'st t'ou tak the bairn frae me sae frightedly, Watty?' said Claud in a mild tone of remonstrance, entirely different from any thing he had ever before addressed to him.

Walter, however, made no reply, but retiring to a distant part of the room, carefully inspected the child, and frequently inquired where she was hurt, although she was laughing and tickled with his nursery-like proceedings.

'What gars t'ee think, Watty,' rejoined his father, 'that I would hurt the wean?"

'Cause I hae heard you wish that the Lord would tak the brat to himsel.'

'An I did, Watty, it was nae ill wis.'

'So I ken, or else the minister lies,' replied Walter; 'but I would na like, for a' that, to hae her sent till him; and noo, as they say ye're ta'en up wi' Charlie's bairns, I jealouse ye hae some end o' your ain for rooketty-cooing wi' my wee Betty Bodle. I canna understand this new kythed kindness,—so, gin ye like, father, we'll just be fair gude e'en and fair gude day, as we were wont.'

This sank deeper into the wounded heart of his father than even the distrust of the orphans; but the old man made no answer. Walter, however, observed him muttering something to himself, as he leant his head back, with his eyes shut, against the shoulder of the easy chair in which he was sitting; and rising softly with the child in his arms, walked cautiously behind the chair, and bent forward to listen. But the words were spoken so inwardly and thickly, that nothing could be overheard. While in this position, the little girl playfully stretched out her hand and seized her grandfather by the ear.

Startled from his prayer or his reverie, Claud, yielding to the first impulse of the moment, turned angrily round at being so disturbed, and, under the influence of his old contemptuous regard for Watty, struck him a severe blow on the face,—but almost in the same instant, ashamed of his rashness, he shudderingly exclaimed, throbbing with remorse and vexation,—

'Forgi'e me, Watty, for I know not what I do;' and he added, in a wild ejaculation, 'Lord! Lord! O lighter, lighter lay the hand o' thy anger upon me. The reed is broken—O, if it may stand wi' thy pleasure, let it not thus be trampled in the mire! But why should I supplicate for any favour?—Lord of justice and of judgment, let thy will be done!'

Walter was scarcely more confounded by the blow than by these impassioned exclamations; and hastily quitting the room, ran, with the child in his arms, to his mother, who happened at the time, as was her wont, to be in the kitchen on household cares intent, crying, 'Mother! mother! my father's gane by himsel; he's aff at the head; he's daft; and ta'en to the praising o' the Lord at this time o' day.'

But, excepting this trivial incident, nothing, as we have already stated, occurred between the interview with Lady Plealands and the funeral to indicate, in any degree, the fierce combustion of distracted thoughts which was raging within the unfathomable caverns of the penitent's bosom—all without, save but for this little effusion, was calm and stable. His external appearance was as we have sometimes seen Mount Etna in the sullenness of a wintry day, when the chaos and fires of its abyss uttered no sound, and an occasional gasp of vapour was heavily breathed along the grey and gloomy sky. Everything was still and seemingly stedfast. The woods were silent in all their leaves; the convents wore an awful aspect of unsocial solemnity; and the ruins and remains of former ages appeared as if permitted to moulder in unmolested decay. The very sea, as it rolled in a noiseless swell towards the black promontories of lava, suggested strange imageries of universal death, as if it had been the pall of the former world heavily moved by the wind. But that dark and ominous tranquillity boded neither permanence nor safety—the traveller and the inhabitant alike felt it as a syncope in nature, and dreaded an eruption or a hurricane.

Such was the serenity in which Claud passed the time till Saturday, the day appointed for the funeral. On the preceding evening his wife went into Glasgow to direct the preparations, and about noon he followed her, and took his seat, to receive the guests, at the door of the principal room arranged for the company, with James, the orphan, at his knee. Nothing uncommon passed for some time; he went regularly through the ceremonial of assistant chief mourner, and in silence welcomed, by the customary shake of the hand, each of the friends of the deceased as they came in. When Dr Denholm arrived, it was observed that his limbs trembled, and that he held him a little longer by the hand than any other; but he too was allowed to pass on to his seat. After the venerable minister, Mr Keelevin made his appearance. His clothes were of an old-fashioned cut, such as even still may occasionally be seen at west country funerals among those who keep a special suit of black for the purpose of attending the burials of their friends; and the sort of quick eager look of curiosity which he glanced round the room, as he lifted his small cocked hat from off his white, well-powdered, ionic curled tie-wig, which he held firm with his left forefinger, provoked a smile, in despite of the solemnity of the occasion.

Claud grasped him impatiently by the hand, and drew him into a seat beside himself. 'Hae ye made out the instrument?' said he.

'It's no just finished,' replied Mr Keelevin; 'but I was mindit to ca' on you the morn, though it's Sabbath, to let you see, for approbation, what I have thought might be sufficient.'

'Ye ought to hae had it done by this time,' said Claud, somewhat chidingly.

' 'Deed should I,' was the answer, 'but ye ken the Lords are coming to the town next week, and I hae had to prepare for the defence of several unfortunate creatures.'

'It's a judgment time indeed,' said Claud; and, after a pause of several minutes, he added, 'I would fain no be disturbed on the Lord's day, so ye need na come to Grippy, and on Monday morning I'll be wi' you betimes; I hope a' may be finished that day, for, till I hae made atonement, I can expek no peace o' mind.'

Nothing farther was allowed at that time to pass between them, for the betherils employed to carry round the services of bread and wine came in with their trays, and Deacon Gardner, of the Wrights, who had charge of the funeral, having nodded to the Reverend Dr John Hamilton, the minister of the Inner High Church, in the district of which the house was situated, the worthy divine rose, and put an end to all farther private whispering, by commencing the prayer.

When the regular in-door rites and ceremonies were performing, and the body had, in the meantime, been removed into the street, and placed on the shoulders of those who were to carry it to the grave, Claud took his grandson by the hand, and followed at the head, with a firmly knotted countenance, but with faultering steps.

In the procession to the church-yard no particular expression of feeling took place; but when the first shovelful of earth rattled hollowly on the coffin, the little boy, who still held his grandfather by the finger, gave a shriek, and ran to stop the grave-digger from covering it up. But the old man softly and composedly drew him back, telling him it was the will of God, and that the same thing must be done to every body in the world.

'And to me too?' said the child, inquiringly and fearfully.

'To a' that live,' replied his grandfather; and the earth being, by this time, half filled in, he took off his hat, and looking at the grave for a moment, gave a profound sigh, and again covering his head, led the child home.

Chapter XI

Immediately after the funeral Claud returned home to Grippy, where he continued during the remainder of the day secluded in his bed-chamber.

Next morning, being Sunday, he was up and dressed earlier than usual; and after partaking slightly of breakfast, he walked into Glasgow, and went straight to the house of his daughter-in-law.

The widow was still in her own room, and not in any state or condition to be seen; but the children were dressed for church, and when the bells began to ring, he led them out, each holding him by the hand, innocently proud of their new black clothes.

In all the way up the High Street, and down the pathway from the church-yard gate to the door of the cathedral, he never raised his eyes; and during the sermon he continued in the same apparent state of stupor. In retiring from the church, the little boy drew him gently aside from the path to show his sister the spot where their father was laid; and the old man, absorbed in his own reflections, was unconsciously on the point of stepping on the grave, when James checked him,—

'It's papa—dinna tramp on him.'

Aghast and recoiling, as if he had trodden upon an adder, he looked wildly around, and breathed quickly and with great difficulty, but said nothing. In an instant his countenance underwent a remarkable change—his eyes became glittering and glassy, and his lips white. His whole frame shook, and appeared under the influence of some mortal agitation. His presence of mind did not, however, desert him, and he led the children hastily home. On reaching the door, he gave them in to the servant that opened it without speaking, and went immediately to Grippy, where, the moment he had seated himself in his elbow chair, he ordered one of the servants to go for Mr Keelevin.

'What ails you, father?' said Walter, who was in the room at the time; 'ye speak unco drumly—hae ye bitten your tongue?' But scarcely had he uttered these words, when the astonished creature gave a wild and fearful shout, and, clasping his hands above his head, cried, 'Help! help! something's riving my father in pieces!'

The cry brought in the servants, who, scarcely less terrified, found the old man smitten with a universal paralysis, his mouth and eyes dreadfully distorted, and his arms powerless.

In the alarm and consternation of the moment, he was almost immediately deserted; every one ran in quest of medical aid. Walter alone remained with him, and continued gazing in his face with a strange horror, which idiocy rendered terrific.

Before any of the servants returned, the violence of the shock seemed to subside, and he appeared to be sensible of his situation. The moment that the first entered the room he made an effort to speak, and the name of Keelevin was two or three times so distinctly articulated, that even Walter understood what he meant, and immediately ran wildly to Glasgow for the lawyer. Another messenger was dispatched for the Leddy, who had, during the forenoon, gone to her daughter-in-law, with the intention of spending the day.

In the meantime a Doctor was procured, but he seemed to consider the situation of the patient hopeless; he, however, as in all similar cases, applied the usual stimulants to restore energy, but without any decisive effect.

The weather, which had all day been lowering and hazy, about this time became drizzly, and the wind rose, insomuch that Leddy Grippy, who came flying to the summons, before reaching home was drenched to the skin, and was for some time, both from her agitation and fatigue, incapable of taking any part in the bustle around her husband.

Walter, who had made the utmost speed for Mr Keelevin, returned soon after his mother; and, on appearing before his father, the old man eagerly spoke to him; but his voice was so thick, that few of his words were intelligible. It was, however, evident that he inquired for the lawyer; for he threw his eyes constantly towards the door, and several times again was able to articulate his name.

At last, Mr Keelevin arrived on horseback, and came into the room, dressed in his trotcosey; the hood of which, over his cocked hat, was drawn so closely on his face, that but the tip of his sharp aquiline nose was visible.

But, forgetful or regardless of his appearance, he stalked with long strides at once to the chair where Claud was sitting; and taking from under the skirt of the trotcosey a bond of provision for the widow and children of Charles, and for Mrs Milrookit, he knelt down, and began to read it aloud.

'Sir,' said the Doctor, who was standing at the other side of the patient, 'Mr Walkinshaw is in no condition to understand you.'

Still, however, Mr Keelevin read on; and when he had finished, he called for pen and ink.

'It is impossible that he can write,' said the Doctor.

'Ye hae no business to mak ony sic observation,' exclaimed the benevolent lawyer. 'Ye shou'd say nothing till we try. In the name of justice and mercy, is there nobody in this house that will fetch me pen and ink?'

It was evident to all present that Claud perfectly understood what his friend said; and his eyes betokened eagerness and satisfaction; but the expression with which his features accompanied the assent in his look was horrible and appalling. At this juncture Leddy Grippy came rushing, half dressed, into the room, her dishevelled grey hair flying loosely over her shoulders, exclaiming,—'What's wrang noo?—what new judgment has befallen us?—Whatna fearfu' image is that like a corpse out o' a tomb, that's making a' this rippet for the cheatrie instruments o' pen and ink, when a dying man is at his last gasp?'

'Mrs Walkinshaw, for Heaven's sake be quiet;—your gudeman,' replied Mr Keelevin, opening the hood of his trotcosey, and throwing it back; taking off, at the same time, his cocked hat—'Your gudeman kens very weel what I hae read to him. It's a provision for Mrs Charles and her orphans.'

'But is there no likewise a provision in't for me?' cried the Leddy.

'O, Mrs Walkinshaw, we'll speak o' that hereafter; but let us get this executed affhand,' replied Mr Keelevin. 'Ye see your gudeman kens what we're saying, and looks wistfully to get it done. I say, in the name of God, get me pen and ink.'

'Ye's get neither pen nor ink here, Mr Keelevin, till my rights are cognost in a record o' sederunt and session.'

'Hush!' exclaimed the Doctor—all was silent, and every eye turned on the patient, whose countenance was again hideously convulsed;—a troubled groan struggled and heaved for a moment in his breast, and was followed by short quivering through his whole frame.

'It is all over!' said the Doctor. At these words the Leddy rushed towards the elbow chair, and, with frantic cries and gestures, flew on the body, and acted an extravagance of sorrow ten times more outrageous than grief. Mr Keelevin stood motionless, holding the paper in his hand; and, after contemplating the spectacle before him for about two or three minutes, shook his head disconsolately, and replacing his cocked hat, drew the hood of the trotcosey again over his face, and left the house.

Chapter XII

As soon as the nature of the settlement which Claud had made of his property was known, Lady Plealands removed Mrs Charles and the children to her own house, and earnestly entreated her daughter the Leddy, who continued to reside at Grippy, managing the household cares there as usual, to exert her influence with Walter to make some provision for his unfortunate relations. Even George, who, engrossed by his business and his own family, cared almost as little as any man for the concerns of others, felt so ashamed of his father's conduct, that, on the Sunday after the funeral, he went to pay a visit of condolence to his mother, and to join his exhortations to hers, in the hope that something might be done. But Walter was inexorable.

'If my father,' said he, 'did sic a wicked thing to Charlie as ye a' say, what for would ye hae me to do as ill and as wrang to my bairn? Is na wee Betty Bodle my first-born, and, by course o' nature and law, she has a right to a' I hae; what for then would ye hae me to mak away wi' ony thing that pertains to her? I'll no be guilty o' ony sic sin.'

'But you know, Walter,' replied George, 'that our father did intend to make some provision both for Mrs Charles her family and our sister, and it's really a disgrace to us all if nothing be done for them. It was but a chance that the bond of provision was na signed.'

'Ye may say sae, Geordie, in your cracks at the Yarn Club, o'er the punch-bowl, but I think it was the will o' Providence; for, had it been ordain't that Bell Fatherlans and her weans were to get a part o' father's gear, they would hae gotten't. But ye saw the Lord took him to Abraham's bosom before the bond was signed, which was a clear proof and testimony to me, that it does na stand wi' the pleasure o' Heaven that she should get ony thing. She'll get nothing frae me.'

'But,' again interposed George, 'if you will do nothing in consideration of our father's intention, you ought in charity to think of her distress.'

'Charity begins at hame, Geordie, and wha kens but I may be brought to want if I dinna tak care?'

'I'm sure,' replied the merchant, sharply, 'that many a one has who less deserved it.'

'How do ye ken what I deserve?' cried the natural, offended. 'It's speaking ill o' the understanding o' Providence, to say I dinna deserve what it has gi'en me. I'm thinking, Geordie, Providence kens my deserts muckle better than you.'

Leddy Grippy, who, during this conversation, was sitting at the table, in all the pomp of her new widow's weeds, with the big Bible before her, in which she was trying to read that edifying chapter, the tenth of Nehemiah, here interposed.

'Wheesht, wheesht, Watty, and dinna blaspheme,' said she; 'and no be overly condumacious. Ye ken your father was a good man, and nothing but the dart o' death prevented him frae making a handsome provision for a' his family, forbye you; and no doubt, when ye hae gotten the better o' the sore stroke o' the sudden removal of the golden candlestick o' his life from among us, ye'll do every thing in a rational and just manner.'

''Deed I'll do nae sic things, mother,' was the reply; 'I'm mindit to haud the grip I hae gotten.'

'But ye're a Christian, Watty,' resumed the Leddy, still preserving her well put on mourning equanimity, 'and it behoves you to reflek, that a' in your power is gi'en to you but as a steward.'

'Ye need na tell me that; but wha's steward am I? Is na the matter a trust for my bairn? I'm wee Betty Bodle's steward, and no man shall upbraid me wi' being unfaithfu',' replied Walter.

'Aye, aye, Watty, that's very true in a sense,' said she, 'but whosoever giveth to the poor lendeth to the Lord.'

'That's what I canna comprehend; for the Lord has no need to borrow; he can make a world o' gold for the poor folk, if he likes, and if he keeps them in poor tith, he has his ain reasons for't.'

'Ah, weel I wat!' exclaimed the Leddy pathetically; 'noo I fin' to my cost, that my cousin, Ringan Gilhaize, the Mauchlin maltster, had the rights o't when he plea't my father's will, on account of thy concos montis; and, but for auld pawky Keelevin, he would hae gotten the property that's sae ill waur't on thee.'

All this, however, made no impression; but George, in walking back to Glasgow, several times thought of what had fallen from his mother respecting the attempt which had been made to set aside her father's settlement, on the score of Walter's idiocy; and once or twice it occurred to him that the thing was still not impracticable, and that, being next heir of entail, and nearest male relative, it might be of advantage to his own family to get the management of the estate. Thus, by a conversation intended to benefit the disinherited heirs, the seed was sown of new plans and proceedings, worthy of the father's son. From that period, George took no farther interest in the affairs of his sister-in-law, but his visits became unusually frequent to Grippy, and he was generally always attended by some friend, whom he led into conversation with his brother, calculated to call forth the least equivocal disclosures of the state of Walter's mind.

But whatever were his motives for these visits, and this kind of conduct, he kept them close within his own breast. No one suspected him of any sinister design, but many applauded his filial attentions to his mother; for so his visits were construed, and they were deemed the more meritorious on account of the state of his own family, his wife, after the birth of her twin daughters, having fallen into ill health. Indeed, he was in general contemplated with sentiments of compassion and respect. Every body had heard of his anxiety, on the death of his father, to procure some provision for his deceased brother's family, and sympathised with the regret which he expressed at finding Walter so niggardly and intractable; for not a word was breathed of his incapacity. The increased thoughtfulness and reserve of his manner which began, we may say, from the conversation quoted, was in consequence attributed to the effect of his comfortless domestic situation, and the public sympathy was considerably augmented, when, in the course of the same year in which his father died, he happened to lose one of his daughters.

There were, however, among his friends, as there are always about most men, certain shrewd and invidious characters, and some among them did not give him credit for so much sensibility as their mutual acquaintance in common parlance ascribed to him.

On the contrary, they openly condemned his indelicacy, in so often exposing the fooleries of his brother; and those who had detected the well hidden sordid meanness of his disposition, wondered that he had so quietly acquiesced in Walter's succession. But they had either forgotten, or had never heard of, the circumstance to which his mother alluded with respect to her relation, the Mauchlin maltster's attempt to invalidate her father's will, and, of course, were not aware of the address requisite to prove the incapacity of a man whose situation had been already investigated, and who, by a solemn adjudication, was declared in the full possession of all his faculties.

Their wonderment was not, however, allowed to continue long, for an event, which took place within a little more than three months after the death of his daughter, ended all debates and controversies on the subject.

Chapter XIII

Death, it is said, rarely enters a house without making himself familiar to the inmates. Walter's daughter, a premature child, had from her birth been always infirm and delicate. In the course of the spring after her grandfather's death, she evidently grew worse, and towards the end of summer it was the opinion of all who saw her that she could not live long. The tenderness and solicitude of her father knew no bounds. She was, indeed, the sole object that interested him in life; he doated over her with the most single and entire affection; and when she died, he would not believe, nor allow himself to think, she had expired, but sat by the bedside, preserving silence, and preventing her from being touched, lest it should awaken her from a slumber which he fondly imagined was to establish her recovery. No inducement could be contrived to draw him from his vigilant watch, nor by any persuasion could permission be obtained to dress her corpse.

George, in the meanwhile, called several times at the house, and took occasion, in going there one day, to ask the Reverend Doctor Denholm to accompany him, under the pretext that perhaps he might prevail with Walter to allow the body to be removed, as it was beginning to grow offensive. But, when they reached the house, Walter was missing—he had suddenly and unobserved quitted the room where the corpse lay, and his mother, availing herself of his absence, was busily preparing for the interment.

They waited some time in expectation of his return, believing he had only walked into the fields, in consequence of the air of the chamber having become intolerable; but, after conversing upwards of an hour on general topics, some anxiety began to be expressed for his appearance, and his mother grew so alarmed, that servants were dispatched in all directions in quest of him. They had not, however, proceeded far, when he was met on the Glasgow road, coming with his niece Mary in his arms, followed by Lady Plealands' maid-servant, loudly remonstrating with him for carrying off the child, and every now and then making an attempt to snatch it from his arms.

'What hae ye been about?' cried his mother, as she saw him approaching towards the house. He, however, made no answer; but, carrying the child into the nursery, he immediately stripped it naked, and dressed her in the clothes of his own daughter, caressing and pleasing her with a thousand fond assurances—calling her his third Betty Bodle, and betraying all the artless delight and satisfaction with which a child regards a new toy.

Dr Denholm happening to be among those who wondered that his brother had permitted him to succeed his father unmolested, and on seeing this indisputable proof of idiocy according to the notions of society, said,—

'I canna refrain, Mr George, from telling you, that I think it's no right to alloo such a fine property as your father left, to be exposed to wastrie and ruination in the possession of such a haverel. It's neither doing justice to the world nor to your ain family; and I redde you look about you—for wha kens what he may do next?'

Such an admonition, the involuntary incitement of the moment, was not lost. George had, in fact, been long fishing for something of the kind, but nothing had occurred to provoke so explicit an opinion of Walter's obvious incapacity. He, however, replied cautiously,—

'Some allowance, Doctor, must be made for the consternation of his sorrow; and ye should know that it's a kittle point of law to determine when a man has or has not his sufficient senses.'

''Deed, Dr Denholm,' added Leddy Grippy, who happened to be present,—'what ye say is very true; for I can ne'er abide to think that Watty's as he ought to be, since he refus't to make good his honest father's kind intents to the rest o' the family. Here am I toiling and moiling frae morning to night for his advantage; and would ye believe me, Doctor, when I tell you, that he'll no alloo a black bawbee for any needful outlay? and I'm obligated to tak frae my ain jointure money to pay the cost o' everything the house stands in need of.'

'Not possible!' said George, with every indication of the sincerest astonishment.

'Whether it's possible, or whether it's probable, I ken best mysel,' replied the Leddy;—'and this I ken likewise, that what I say is the even-down truth; and nae farther gain than Monday was eight days, I paid Deacon Paul, the Glasgow mason, thirteen shillings, a groat, and a bawbee, for the count o' his sklater that pointed the skews o' the house at Martinmas; and though I would supplicate, an it were on my knees, like Queen Esther, the doure Ahasuerus, that he is, has no mercy. Indeed, I'll be nane surprised gin he leaves me to pay a' the charge o' his bairn's burial, which will be a black shame if he does.'

'This must not be endured,' said George, gravely; 'and I am surprised, mother, ye never spoke of such treatment before. I cannot sit patient and hear that ye're used in such a cruel and unnatural manner.'

'It would be a blot on your character, Mr George,' rejoined the minister, 'if ye did. Your brother has been from his youth upward an evident idiot; and ever since the death of his wife, ony little wit he had has been daily growing less.'

'What ye say, Doctor,' resumed the Leddy, 'is no to be controverted; for, poor lad, he certainly fell intil a sore melancholic at that time; and it's my conceit he has ne'er rightly got the better o't; for he was—hegh, sirs!—he was till that time the kindest o' a' my bairns; but, frae the day and hour that his wife took her departel in childbed, he has been a changed creature. Ye'll mind how outstrapolous and constipated he was at her burial; and it's wi' a heavy heart that I maun say't, when his kind father, soon after, wanted to mak a will and testament to keep us a' right and comfortable, he was just like to burn the house aboon our heads wi' his condumacity.'

'I am well aware of the truth of much that you have said; but it's a painful thing for a man to think of taking steps against the capacity of his brother,' replied George. 'For, in the event of not succeeding, he must suffer great obloquy in the opinion of the world; and you know that, with respect to Walter, the attempt was once made already.'

'And every body said,' cried the Leddy, 'that, but for the devices of auld draughty Keelevin, he would hae been proven as mad as a March hare; and nae doubt, as he kens how he jookit the law afore, he might be o' an instrumentality were the thing to gang to a revisidendo. No that I would like to see my bairn put into bedlam; at the same time, Dr Denholm, I would na be doing a Christian and a parent's part to the lave o' my family, an I were to mak a mitigation against it.'

'I do not think,' replied George, looking inquiringly at the Reverend Doctor—'that when a man is proved incapable of conducting his affairs, it is necessary to confine him.'

'O, no; not at all, Mr George,' was the unsuspicious minister's answer. 'It would mak no odds to your brother; it would only oblige you to take the management of the estate.'

'That,' replied George, 'would be far from convenient, for the business of the counting-house requires my whole attention. Ye can have no notion, Dr Denholm, how much this rebellion in America has increased the anxieties of merchants. At the same time, I would be greatly wanting in duty and respect towards my mother, were I to allow her to remain any longer in such an unhappy state, to say nothing of the manifest injustice of obliging her to lay out her own proper jointure in repairs and other expences of the house.'

Little more passed at that time on the subject; but, in the course of walking back to Glasgow, George was fortified in his intentions by the conversation of the Doctor— or, what is, perhaps, more correct, he appeared so doubtful and scrupulous, that the guileless pastor thought it necessary to argue with him against allowing his delicacy to carry him too far.

Chapter XIV

After the minister and George had left the house, the cares, we should say the enjoyments, of the Leddy were considerably increased, when she had leisure to reflect on the singular transaction by which Walter had supplied himself with another child. What with the requisite preparations for the funeral of his daughter next day, and 'this new income,' as she called the adopted orphan, 'that, in itself, was a handling little short o' a birth,' she had not, from the death of her husband, found herself half so earnestly occupied as on this sorrowful occasion. The house rung with her admonitions to the servants, and her short quick steps, in consequence of walking with old shoes down the heel, clattered as cleverly as her tongue. But all this bustle and prodigality of anxieties suffered a sudden suspension, by the arrival of Mrs Charles Walkinshaw, in quest of her child. The little girl, however, was by this time so delighted with the fondling and caresses of her uncle, that she was averse to return home with her mother.

'I won'er,' said Leddy Grippy, 'how ane in your straitened circumstance, Bell Fatherlans, canna be thankfu' for sic a gratus amous as this. Watty's a kind-hearted creature, and ye may be sure that neither scaith nor scant will be alloo't to come near the wean while it stays in this house. For my part, I think his kidnapping her has been nothing less than an instigation o' Providence, since he would na be constrained, by any reason or understanding, to settle an aliment on you.'

'I cannot, however, part with my child to him. You know there are many little peculiarities about Mr Walter that do not exactly fit him for taking charge of children.'

'But, since he's willing to bear the cost and charge o' her,' said the Leddy, 'ye should mak no objek, but conform; for ye ken, I'll hae the direction o' her edication; and am sure ye would na wis to see her any better brought up than was our Meg, Mrs Milrookit, who could once play seven tunes and a march on the spinet, and sewed a satin piece, at Embrough, of Adam and Eve eating the forbidden fruit under the tree of life;—the like of which had na before been seen in a' this kintra side. In short, Bell, my dear, it's my advice to you to let the lassie bide wi' us; for, unless Watty is put out o' the way, it may prove a great thing baith for her and you; for he's a most conomical creature; and the siller he'll save belyve will be just a portion.'

'What do you mean,' replied the young widow, eagerly, 'about putting him out of the way?'

'Ah! Bell Fatherlans,' exclaimed the Leddy, in her most pathetic manner;—'little ken ye yet what it is to hae a family. This has, indeed, been a house o' mourning the day, even though we had na a body in it waiting for interment. The minister has been here wi' Geordie, and it's his solid opinion—we a'ken what a man o' lair and judgment Dr Denholm is;—he thinks that Watty's no o' a faculty to maintain the salvation of the family property; and when your gudebrother heard how I hae been used, he said, that neither law nor justice should oblige him to let his mother live any longer in this house o' bondage and land o' Egypt; so that, when we get the wean put aneath the ground, there aiblins will be some terrogation as to the naturality of Watty's capacity, which, ye may be sure, is a most sore heart to me, his mother, to hear tell o'. But if it's the Lord's will, I maun submit; for really, in some things, Watty's no to be thol't; yet, for a' that, Bell, my dear, I would let him tak his own way wi' your bairn, till we see what's to be the upshot. For, and though I maun say it, who is his parent, that it canna be weel denied, that he's a thought daft by course o' nature; he may, nevertheless, be decreet it douce enough by course o' law. Therefore, it's neither for you nor me to mak or meddle in the matter; but gather the haws afore the snaws, betide whatever may betide.'

We cannot venture to say that Mrs Charles Walkinshaw was exactly what we should call surprised at this information. She knew enough of the characters of her mother-in-law and of George, to hear even more extraordinary communications from the former unmoved. We need scarcely add, however, that the Leddy's argument was not calculated with her to produce the effect intended; on the contrary, she said,—

'What you tell me only serves to convince me of the impropriety I should be guilty of in leaving my child with Walter.'

But their conversation was interrupted at this juncture by the entrance of Walter, leading Mary.

'I'm come,' said he, 'Bell Fatherlans, to tell you that ye're to gang away hame, and bring Jamie here to stay wi' us. The house is big enough to haud us a', and it'll be a grand ploy to my mother—for ye ken she has such a heart for a thrangerie butt and ben, that, rather than want wark, she'll mak a baby o' the beetle, and dance til't, cracking her thumbs, and singing,

> Dance to your deddie, my bonny leddie;
> Jink through the reelie; jook round and wheelie;
> Bob in the setting, my bonny lamb;
> And ye's get a slide o' a dishie nicie—
> Red cheekit apples and a mutton ham.

So just gang hame at ance, Bell, and bring your laddie, and we'll a' live thegither, and rookettycoo wi' ane anither like doos in a doocot.'

But although Leddy Grippy certainly did like a bustle with all her heart and spirit, she had still that infirmity which ever belongs to human nature gifted with similar propensities,—namely, a throbbing apprehension at the idea of it, such as mankind in general suffer in the prospect of enjoying pleasure; and the expression of this feeling with her took commonly the form and language of repugnance and reluctance, yea sometimes it even amounted to refusal.

'What say ye?' cried she to Walter, under a strong impression of it at the moment,—'are ye utterly bereav't o' your senses, to speak o' bringing the lade o' another family on my hands?'

'I'm sure,' was his answer, 'if ye dinna like to tak the pleasure o't, ye're free to set up your jointure house, and live the life o' dowager duchess, for me, mother. But Bell Fatherlans and her bairns are to come here,—for this is my house, ye ken—settled on me and mine, past a' power o' law, by my father—and what's my ain I'll mak my ain.'

'Wha would hae thought o' sic outcoming o' kindness as this!' replied the Leddy. 'I fancy, Bell, ye'll hae to come and resident wi' us?'

'An she does na,' said Walter, 'I'll gang away where never one kent me, and tak her wee Mary on my back in a basket, like Jenny Nettles—that's what I will; so put the matter to your knee and straight it.'

'I'll mak a bargain, Mr Walter,' replied Mrs Charles,—'I'll leave Mary to-night, and come, after the burial to-morrow, with James, and stay a few days.'

'Ye'll stay a' your days,' exclaimed Walter; 'and as ye're a leddy o' mair genteelity than my mother, ye shall hae the full rule and power o' the house, and mak jam and jelly;—a' the cast o' her grace and skill gangs nae farther than butter and cheese.'

His mother was confounded, and unable for some time to utter a word.

At last, putting her hands firmly into her sides, she said,—'My word, but thou's no blate. But it's no worth my while to gang intil a passion for a born idiot. Your reign, my lad, 's no ordain to be lang, if there's either law or gospel among the fifteen at Embro. To misliken his mother! to misuse me as I were nae better than an auld bachle, and, in a manner, to turn me out the house!'

'O don't disturb yourself,' interposed Mrs Charles; 'they were but words of course. You know his humour, and need not be surprised at what he says.'

The indignant mother was not, however, soon appeased,—her wrath for some time burnt fiercely, and it required no little dexterity on the part of her daughter-in-law to allay the altercation which ensued; but in the end her endeavours proved successful, and the result was an arrangement, that the child should be left for a day or two, to ascertain whether Walter's attachment was dictated by caprice or a transfer of his affections. And in order to preserve quiet, and to prevent any extravagance that might be injurious to the little girl, it was also arranged that her mother and brother should likewise spend a few weeks at Grippy.

Chapter XV

The news of the arrangement, when communicated to Doctor Denholm and George, at the funeral next day, produced on them very opposite effects. The minister, who was naturally of a warm and benevolent disposition, persuaded himself that the proposal of Walter, to receive his sister-in-law and her family, was dictated by a sense of duty and of religion, and regretted that he had so hastily expressed himself so strongly respecting his incapacity. Indeed, every one who heard the story put upon it nearly the same sort of construction, and applauded the uncouth kindness of the natural as brotherly and Christian.

George, however, saw it, perhaps, more correctly; but he was exceedingly disturbed by the favourable impression which it made on the minds of his acquaintance, and hesitated to indulge his desire to obtain the management of the estate. But still he continued his visits to Grippy, and took every opportunity of drawing the attention of his friends to the imbecility of his brother. Nothing, however, occurred to further his wishes till the term of Martinmas after the incident mentioned in the foregoing chapter; when, on receiving his rents, he presented his sister-in-law with a ten pound note, at the same time counting out, to the calculation of a halfpenny, the balance he owed his mother of her jointure, but absolutely refusing to repay her any of the money she had, in the mean time, disbursed for different little household concerns and repairs, saying, that all she had laid out was nothing in comparison to what she was due for bed and board. This was the unkindest cut of all; for she justly and truly estimated her services to him as of far more value. However, she said nothing; but next day, on the pretext of going to see her mother, who was now very infirm, and unable to quit her chamber, she went to Glasgow and called on George, to whom she made a loud and long complaint of the insults she had received, and of the total unfitness and unworthiness of his brother to continue uncontrolled in the possession of the estate.

George sympathized with her sorrows and her sufferings like a dutiful son, and comforted her with the assurance that he would lose no time in taking some steps for her relief, and the preservation of the property. And, as she consented to remain that day to dinner, it was thought, considering the disposition Walter had shown to squander his gifts on his sister-in-law, without any consideration for the rest of the family, it might be as well to consult Mr Keelevin on the occasion. A message was, accordingly, dispatched to the honest lawyer, begging him to call after dinner; in short, every demonstration was made by George to convince his mother how much better her worth was appreciated by him than by his brother;—and she was not only consoled, but delighted with the sincerity of his attentions.

In due time Mr Keelevin made his appearance; and the Leddy began a strong representation of all the indignities which she had endured, but her son softly and mildly interposed, saying,—

'It is of no use, my dear mother, to trouble Mr Keelevin with these things; he knows the infirmities of Walter as well as we do. No doubt,' he added, turning to the lawyer, 'you have heard of the very extraordinary manner in which my brother took Mrs Charles and her family to Grippy.'

'I really,' replied the honest-hearted man, 'had no idea that he possessed so muckle feeling and common sense, but I was very happy to hear't. For, his own wean being no more, I'm sure he can do nothing better than make up to the disinherited orphans some portion of that which, but for your father's sudden death, would hae been provided for them.'

George knew not what reply to make to this; but his mother, who, like the rest of her sex, had an answer for all subjects and occasions ever ready, said,—

'It's weel to ca't sense and feeling, but if I were obligated to speak the truth, I would baptize it wi' another name. It's no to be rehearsed by the tongue o' man, Mr Keelevin, what I hae borne at the hands of the haverel idiot, since the death of him that's awa— your auld friend, Mr Keelevin;—he was a man of a capacity, and had he been spared a comfort to me, as he was, and aye sae couthy wi' his kindness, I would na kent what it is to be a helpless widow. But surely there maun be some way o' remedde for us a' in thir straits? It's no possible that Walter can be alloo't to riot and ravage in sic a most rabiator-like manner; for I need na tell you, that he's gane beyond all counsel and admonition. Noo, do ye think, Mr Keelevin, by your knowledge and skill in law, that we can get him cognost, and the rents and rule o' the property ta'en out of his hands? for, if he gangs on at the gait he's going, I'll be herri't, and he'll no leave himself ae bawbee to rub on anither.'

'What has he done?' inquired the lawyer, a little thoughtfully.

'Done! what has he no done? He gied Bell Fatherlands a ten pound note, and was as dour as a smith's vice in the grip, when I wantit him to refund me a pour o' ready money that I was obligated to lay out for the house.'

George, who had watched the lawyer's countenance in the meantime, said,—'I doubt, mother, few will agree in thinking of that in the way you do. My sister-in-law stands in need of his kindness, but your jointure is more than you require; for, after all your terrible outlays,' and he smiled to Mr Keelevin as he said the words, 'you have already saved money.'

'But what's that to him?' exclaimed the Leddy. 'Is nae a just debt a just debt—was na he bound to pay what I paid for him—and is't no like a daft man and an idiot, to say he'll no do't? I'm sure, Mr Keelevin, I need na tell you that Watty was ne'er truly concos montes. How ye got him made sound in his intellectuals when the law plea was about my father's will, ye ken best yoursel; but the straemash that was there anent is a thing to be remembered.'

Mr Keelevin gave a profound sigh, adding, in a sort of apologistic manner,—

'But Walter has maybe undergone some change since that time?'

'Yes,' said George, 'the grief and consternation into which he was thrown by the sudden death of his wife had undoubtedly a great effect on his mind.'

'He was clean dementit at that time,' cried the Leddy; 'he would neither buff nor stye for father nor mother, friend nor foe; a' the King's forces would na hae gart him carry his wife's head in a wise-like manner to the kirk-yard. I'm sure, Mr Keelevin, for ye were at the burial, ye may mind that her father, Kilmarkeckle, had to do't, and lost his Canary snuff by a twirl o' the wind, when he was taking a pinch, as they said, after lowering her head intil the grave; which was thought, at the time, a most unparent-like action for any man to be about at his only dochter's burial.'

Mr Keelevin replied, 'I will honestly confess to you, that I do think there has of late been signs of a want about Mr Walter. But in his kindness to his poor brother's widow and family, there's great proof and evidence, both of a sound mind, reason, and a right heart. Ye'll just, Mrs Walkinshaw, hae to fight on wi' him as well as ye can, for in the conscience o' me I would, knowing what I know of the family, be wae and sorry to disturb such a consolatory manifestation of brotherly love.'

'That's just my opinion,' said George, 'and I would fain persuade my mother to put up with the slights and ill usage to which she is so distressingly subjected—at the same time, I cannot say, but I have my fears, that her situation is likely to be made worse rather than better, for Walter appears disposed, not only to treat her in a very mean and unworthy manner, but to give the whole dominion of the house to Mrs Charles.'

'Na,' exclaimed the Leddy, kindling at this dexterous awakening of her wrongs. 'He did far waur, he a'maist turnt me out o' the house by the shouthers.'

'Did he lay hands on you, his mother?' inquired Mr Keelevin with his professional accent and earnestness. But George prevented her from replying, by saying that his mother naturally felt much molested in receiving so harsh a return for the particular partiality with which she had always treated his brother—and was proceeding in his wily and insidious manner to fan the flame he seemed so anxious to smother. Mr Keelevin, however, of a sudden, appeared to detect his drift, and gave him such a rebuking look, that he became confused and embarrassed, during which the honest lawyer rose and wished them good afternoon—saying to George, who accompanied him to the door,—

'The deil needs baith a syde cloak and a wary step to hide his cloven foot—I'll say nae mair, Mr George; but dinna mak your poor brother's bairns waur than they are—and your mother should na be egget on in her anger, when she happens, poor body, to tak the dods now and then—for the most sensible of women hae their turns o' tantrums, and need baith rein and bridle.'

Chapter XVI

'I hope and trust', said Leddy Grippy, as George returned from conducting the lawyer to the door, 'that ye'll hae mair compassion for your mother than to be sway't by the crooked counsels o' yon quirkie bodie. I could see vera weel that he has a because o' his ain for keeping his thumb on Watty's unnaturality. But Geordie, he's no surely the only lawyer in the town? I wat there are scores baith able and willing to tak the business by the hand; and if there shou'd be nane o' a sufficient capacity in Glasgow, just tak a step in til Enbro', where, I hae often heard my honest father say, there are legions o' a capacity to contest wi' Belzebub himsel.'

'I am very anxious, mother, to do every thing to promote your happiness,' was the reply; 'but the world will be apt to accuse me of being actuated by some sinister and selfish motive. It would be most disgraceful to me were I to fail.'

'It will be a black burning shame to alloo a daft man any longer to rule and govern us like a tyrant wi' a rod o' iron, pooking and rooking me, his mother, o' my ain lawful jointure and honest hainings, forbye skailing and scattering his inheritance in a manner, as if ten pound notes were tree-leaves at Hallowe'en.'

'I am quite sensible of the truth and justice of all you say; but you know the uncertainty of the law,' said George, 'and the consequences would be fatal to me were we not to succeed.'

'And what will be the consequences if he were taking it in his head to marry again? He would mak nae scruple of sending me off frae Grippy at an hour's warning.'

This touched the keenest nerve of her son's anxieties; and he was immediately alarmed by a long visionary vista of unborn sons, rising between him and the succession to the estate;—but he only appeared to sympathise with his mother.

'It's not possible,' said he, 'even were he to marry again, that he could be so harsh. You have lived ever since your marriage with my father at Grippy. It's your home, and endeared to you by many pleasing recollections. It would be extreme cruelty now, in your declining years, to force you to live in the close air, and up the dirty turnpike stairs o' Glasgow.'

'It would soon be the death o' me,' exclaimed the Leddy, with a sigh, wiping one of her eyes with the corner of her apron. 'In short, Geordie, if ye dinna step out and get him put past the power o' marrying, I'll regard you as little better than art and part in his idiocety. But it's time I were taking the road, for they'll a' be marvelling what keeps me. There's, however, ae thing I would advise you, and that is, to take gude care and no mint what we hae been speaking o' to living creature, for nobody can tell what detriment the born idiot might do to us baith, were he to get an inkling before a's ready to put the strait waiscoat o' the law on him; so I redde you set about it in a wary and wily manner, that he may hae nae cause to jealouse your intent.'

There was, however, no great occasion for the latter part of this speech, George being perfectly aware of all the difficulties and delicacies of the case; but he said,—

'Did he ever attempt actually to strike you?'

'O, no,' replied his mother; 'to do the fool thing justice, it's kindly enough in its manner; only it will neither be governed nor guided by me as it used to be; which is a sore trial.'

'Because,' rejoined George, 'had he ever dared to do so, there would then have been less trouble or scruple in instituting proceedings against him.'

'Na; an it's ony way to commode the business, we might soon provoke him to lift his hand; but it's a powerful creature, and I'm fear't. However, Geordie, ye might lay yoursel out for a bit slaik o' its paw; so just come o'er the morn's morning and try; for it'll no do to stand shilly-shallying, if we hope to mak a right legality o't'.'

Cowardice is the best auxiliary to the police, and George had discretion enough not to risk the danger of rousing the sleeping lion of his brother's Herculean sinews. But, in other respects, he took his mother's advice; and, avoiding the guilt of causing an offence, in order that he might be able to prosecute the offender, he applied to

Gabriel Pitwinnoch, the writer, from whose character he expected to encounter fewer scruples and less scrutiny than with Mr Keelevin.

In the meantime, the Leddy, who had returned home to Grippy, preserved the most entire reserve upon the subject to all the inmates of the family, and acted her part so well, that even a much more suspicious observer than her daughter-in-law would never have suspected her of double dealing. Indeed, any change that could be perceived in her manner was calculated to lull every suspicion,—for she appeared more than usually considerate and attentive towards Walter, and even condescended to wheedle and coax him on different occasions, when it would have been more consonant to her wonted behaviour had she employed commands and reproaches.

In the course of a week after the interview with Mr Keelevin, George went to Edinburgh, and he was accompanied in his journey by the wary Gabriel Pitwinnoch. What passed between them on the road, and who they saw, and what advice they received in the intellectual city, we need not be particular in relating; but the result was, that, about a week after their return, Gabriel came to Grippy, accompanied by a stranger, of whose consequence and rank it would appear the Leddy had some previous knowledge, as she deported herself towards him with a degree of ceremonious deference very unusual to her habits. The stranger, indeed, was no less a personage than Mr Threeper the advocate, a gentleman of long standing and great practice in the Parliament House, and much celebrated for his shrewd perception of technical flaws, and clever discrimination of those nicer points of the law that are so often at variance with justice.

It happened, that, when this learned doctor of the Caledonian Padua arrived with his worthy associate, Mrs Charles Walkinshaw was in the fields; but, the moment her son James saw him, he was so struck with his appearance, that he ran to tell her. Walter also followed him, under the influence of the same feeling, and said,—

'Come in, Bell Fatherlans, and see what a warld's won'er Pitwinnoch the writer has brought to our house. My mother says it's a haud the cat, and that it gangs about the town o' Embro, walking afore the Lords, in a black gown, wi' a wig ont's head. I marvel what the creature's come here for. It has a silver snuffbox, that it's ay pat patting; and ye would think, to hear it speak, that King Solomon, wi' a' his hundreds o' wives and concubines, was but a fool to him.'

Mrs Charles was alarmed at hearing of such a visitor; for the journey of George and Pitwinnoch to Edinburgh immediately occurred to her, and a feeling of compassion, mingled with gratitude for the kindness which Walter had lately shown to herself and her children, suggested that she ought to put him on his guard.

'Walter,' said she, 'I would not advise you to go near the house while the two lawyers are there,—for who knows what they may do to you? But go as fast as ye can to Glasgow, and tell Mr Keelevin what has happened; and say that I have some reason to fear it's a visit that bodes you no good, and therefore ye'll stand in need of his advice and assistance.'

The natural, who had an instinctive horror of the law, made no reply, but, with a strong expression of terror in his countenance, immediately left her, and went straight to Glasgow.

Chapter XVII

During the journey of George and Pitwinnoch to Edinburgh, a Brief of Chancery had been quietly obtained, directing the Sheriff of the county to summon a jury, to examine into the alleged fatuity of Walter; and the visit of the latter with Mr Threeper, the advocate, to Grippy, was to meet George, for the purpose of determining with respect to the evidence that it might be requisite to adduce before the inquest. All this was conducted, as it was intended to appear, in a spirit of the greatest delicacy towards the unfortunate *fatuus*, consistent with the administration of public justice.

'I can assure you,' said our friend Gabriel to Mr Threeper, as they walked towards the house—the advocate perusing the ground as he poked his way along with his cane, and occasionally taking snuff; 'I can assure you, that nothing but the most imperious necessity could have induced Mr George Walkinshaw to institute these proceedings; for he is a gentleman of the utmost respectability; and to my knowledge has been long and often urged in vain to get his brother cognost; but, until the idiot's conduct became so intolerable, that his mother could no longer endure it, he was quite inexorable.'

'Is Mr George in affluent circumstances?' said the advocate, dryly.

'He is but a young man; the house, however, in which he is a partner is one of the most flourishing in Glasgow,' was the answer.

'He has, perhaps, a large family?'

'O dear no; only one daughter; and his wife,' said Gabriel, 'is, I understand, not likely to have any more.'

'She may, however, have sons, Pitwinnoch,' rejoined the advocate, wittily—at the same time taking snuff. 'But you say it is the mother that has chiefly incited Mr Walkinshaw to this action.'

'So he told me,' replied the writer.

'Her evidence will be most important; for it is not natural that a mother would urge a process of such a nature, without very strong grounds indeed, unless she has some immediate or distinct prospective interest in the result. Have you any idea that such is the case?'

'I should think not,' said Gabriel.

'Do you imagine that such allowance as the Court might grant for the custody of the *fatuus* would have any influence with her?' inquired Mr Threeper, without raising his eyes from the road.

'I have always understood,' was the reply, 'that she is in the possession, not only of a handsome jointure, but of a considerable provision, specially disponed to her by the will of old Plealands, her father.'

'Ah! was she the daughter of old Plealands?' said the advocate. 'It was in a cause of his that I was first retained. He had the spirit of litigation in a very zealous degree.'

In this manner the two redressers of wrongs chattingly proceeded towards Grippy, by appointment, to meet George; and they arrived, as we have related in the foregoing chapter, a few minutes before he made his appearance.

In the meantime, Watty hastened with rapid steps, goaded by a mysterious apprehension of some impending danger, to the counting-house of Mr Keelevin, whom he found at his desk.

'Weel, Mr Walter,' said the honest writer, looking up from a deed he was perusing, somewhat surprised at seeing him—'What's the best o' your news the day, and what's brought you frae Grippy?'

'Mr Keelevin,' replied Walter, going towards him on tiptoe, and whispering audibly in his ear, 'I'll tell you something, Mr Keelevin:—twa gleds o' the law hae lighted yonder; and ye ken, by your ain ways, that the likes o' them dinna flee afield for naething.'

'No possible!' exclaimed Mr Keelevin; and the recollection of his interview with George and the Leddy flashing upon him at the moment, he at once divined the object of their visit; and added, 'It's most abominable;—but ken ye what they're seeking, Mr Walter?'

'No,' said he. 'But Bell Fatherlans bade me come and tell you; for she thought I might need your counsel.'

'She has acted a true friend's part; and I'm glad ye're come,' replied the lawyer; 'and for her and her bairns' sake, I hope we'll be able to defeat their plots and devices. But I would advise you, Mr Walter, to keep out o' harm's way, and no gang in the gate o' the gleds, as ye ca' them.'

'Hae ye ony ark or amrie, Mr Keelevin, where a body might den himsel till they're out o' the gate and away?' cried Walter timidly, and looking anxiously round the room.

'Ye should na speak sic havers, Mr Walter, but conduct yourself mair like a man,' said his legal friend grievedly. 'Indeed, Mr Walter, as I hae some notion that they're come to tak down your words—may be to spy your conduct, and mak nae gude report thereon to their superiors—tak my advice, and speak as little as possible.'

'I'll no say ae word—I'll be a dumbie—I'll sit as quiet as ony ane o' the images afore Bailie Glassford's house at the head o' the Stockwell. King William himsel, on his bell-metal horse at the Cross, is a popular preacher, Mr Keelevin, compared to what I'll be.'

The simplicity and sincerity with which this was said moved the kindhearted lawyer at once to smile and sigh.

'There will, I hope, Mr Walter,' said he, 'be no occasion to put any restraint like that upon yoursel; only it's my advice to you as a friend, to enter into no conversation with any one you do not well know, and to dress in your best clothes, and shave yoursel,—and in a' things demean and deport yoursel, like the laird o' Kittlestonheugh, and the representative of an ancient and respected family.'

'O, I can easily do that,' replied the natural; 'and I'll tak my father's ivory-headed cane, with the golden virl, and the silver e'e for a tassel, frae ahint the scrutoire, where it has ay stood since his death, and walk up and down the front of the house like a Glasgow magistrate.'

'For the love o' Heaven, Mr Walter,' exclaimed the lawyer, 'do nae sic mad like action! The like o' that is a' they want.'

'In whatna other way, then,' said Walter helplessly, 'can I behave like a gentleman, or a laird o' yird and stane, wi' the retinue o' an ancient pedigree like my father's Walkinshaws o' Kittlestonheugh?'

' 'Deed,' said Mr Keelevin compassionately, 'I'm wae to say't— but I doot, I doot, it's past the compass o' my power to advise you.'

'I'm sure,' exclaimed Walter despairingly, 'that the maker was ill aff for a turn when he took to the creating o' lawyers. The deils are but prentice work compared to them.

I dinna ken what to do, Mr Keelevin—I wish that I was dead, but I'm no like to dee, as Jenny says in her wally-wae about her father's cow and auld Robin Gray.'

'Mr Walter,' said his friend, after a pause of several minutes, 'go you to Mrs Hypel, your grandmother, for the present, and I'll out to Grippy, and sift the meaning o' this visitation. When I have gathered what it means, we'll hae the better notion in what way we ought to fight with the foe.'

'I'll smash them like a fore hammer,' exclaimed Walter proudly. 'I'll stand ahint a dike, and gie them a belter wi' stanes, till I hae na left the souls in their bodies—that's what I will,—if ye approve o't, Mr Keelevin.'

'Weel, weel, Mr Walter,' was the chagrined and grieved reply, 'we'll see to that when I return; but it's a terrible thing to think o' proving a man non compos mentis for the only sensible action he ever did in all his life.

Nevertheless, I will not let myself despond; and I have only for the present to exhort you to get yoursel in an order and fitness to appear as ye ought to be;—for really, Mr Walter, ye alloo yoursel to gang sae like a divor, that I dinna wonder ye hae been ta'en notice o'. So I counsel you to mak yoursel trig, and no to play ony antics.'

Walter assured him, that his advice would in every respect be followed; and, leaving the office, he went straight to the residence of his grandmother, while Mr Keelevin, actuated at once by his humanity and professional duty, ordered his horse, and reached Grippy just as the advocate, Mr Pitwinnoch, and George, were on the point of coming away, after waiting in vain for the return of Walter, whom Mr Threeper was desirous of conversing with personally.

Chapter XVIII

The triumvirate and Leddy Grippy were disconcerted at the appearance of Mr Keelevin—for, at that moment, the result of Mr Threeper's inquiries among the servants had put them all in the most agreeable and unanimous opinion with respect to the undoubted certainty of poor Watty's fatuity.—'We have just to walk over the course,' the advocate was saying; when George, happening to glance his eye towards the window, beheld the benevolent lawyer coming up the avenue.

'Good Heavens!' said he, 'what can that old pest, Keelevin, want here?'

'Keelevin!' exclaimed the Leddy,—'that's a miracle to me. I think, gentlemen,' she added, 'ye had as weel gang away by the back door—for ye would na like, may be, to be fashed wi' his confabbles. He's no a man, or I'm far mista'en, that kens muckle about the prejinketties o' the law, though he got the poor daft creature harl't through the difficulties o' the plea wi' my cousin Gilhaise, the Mauchlin maltster. I'm very sure, Mr Threeper, he's no an acquaintance ye would like to cultivate, for he has na the talons o' an advocate versed in the devices o' the courts, but is a quirkie bodie, capable o' making law no law at a', according to the best o' my discernment, which, to be sure, in matters o' locutories and decreets, is but that o' a hamely household woman, so I would advise you to eschew his company at this present time.'

Mr Threeper, however, saw farther into the lady's bosom than she suspected; and as it is never contrary, either to the interest of advocate or agent, to avoid having causes contested, especially when there is, as was in this case, substance enough to support a long and zealous litigation, that gentleman said,—

'Then Mr Keelevin is the agent who was employed in the former action?'

'Just sae,' resumed the Leddy, 'and ye ken he could na, wi' ony regard to himsel, be art and part on this occasion.'

'Ah, but, madam,' replied the advocate, earnestly, 'he may be agent for the *fatuus*. It is, therefore, highly proper we should set out with a right understanding respecting that point; for, if the allegations are to be controverted, it is impossible to foresee what obstacles may be raised, although, in my opinion, from the evidence I have heard, there is no doubt that the fatuity of your son is a fact which cannot fail to be in the end substantiated. Don't you think, Mr Pitwinnoch, that we had as well see Mr Keelevin?'

'Certainly,' said Gabriel. 'And, indeed, considering that, by the brief to the Sheriff, the Laird is a party, perhaps, even though Mr Keelevin should not have been employed, it would be but fair, and look well towards the world, were he instructed to take up this case on behalf of the *fatuus*. What say you, Mr Walkinshaw?'

George did not well know what to say, but he replied, that, for many reasons, he was desirous the whole affair should be managed as privately as possible. 'If, however, the forms of the procedure required that an agent should act for Walter, I have no objection; at the same time, I do not think Mr Keelevin the fittest person.'

'Heavens and earth!' exclaimed the Leddy, 'here's a respondenting and a hearing, and the Lord Ordinary and a' the fifteen Lords frae Embro' come to herry us out o' house and hall. Gentlemen, an ye'll tak my advice, who, in my worthy father's time, had some inkling o' what the cost o' law pleas are, ye'll hae naething to do wi' either Keelevin, Gardevine, or ony other Vines in the shape o' pro forma agents: but settle the business wi' the Sheriff in a douce and discreet manner.'

Mr Threeper, looking towards Mr Pitwinnoch and George, rapped his ivory snuff-box, rimmed and garnished with gold, and smiling, took a pinch as Mr Keelevin was shown into the room.

'Mr George,' said Mr Keelevin sedately, after being seated; 'I am not come here to ask needless questions, but as Man of Business for your brother, it will be necessary to serve me with the proper notices as to what you intend.'

Mr Threeper again had recourse to his box, and Gabriel looked inquiringly at his client—who could with difficulty conceal his confusion, while the old lady, who had much more presence of mind, said,—'May I be sae bold, Mr Keelevin, as to speer wha sent you here, at this time?'

'I came at Mr Walter's own particular and personal request,' was the reply; and he turned at the same time towards the advocate, and added, 'That does not look very like fatuity.'

'He never could hae done that o' his own free will. I should na wonder if the interloper, Bell Fatherlans, sent him—but I'll soon get to the bottom o't,' exclaimed the Leddy, and she immediately left the room in quest of Mrs Charles, to inquire. During her absence, Mr Keelevin resumed,—'It is not to be contested, Mr Threeper,' for he knew the person of the advocate, 'that the Laird is a man o' singularities and oddities—we a' hae our foibles; but he got a gude education, and his schoolmaster bore testimony on a former occasion to his capacity; and if it can be shown that he does not manage his estate so advantageously as he might do, surely that can never be objected against him, when we every day see so many o' the wisest o' our lairds, and lords, and country gentry, falling to pigs and whistles, frae even doun inattention or prodigality. I think it will be no easy thing to prove Mr Walter incapable o' managing his own affairs, with his mother's assistance.'

'Ah! Mr Keelevin, with his mother's assistance!' exclaimed the acute Mr Threeper. 'It's time that he were out of leading-strings, and able to take care of himself, without his mother's assistance—if he's ever likely to do so.'

At this crisis, the Leddy returned into the room flushed with anger. 'It's just as I jealoused,' cried she; 'it's a' the wark o' my gude-dochter—it was her that sent him; black was the day she e'er came to stay here; many a sore heart in the watches o' the night hae I had sin syne, for my poor weak misled lad; for if he were left to the freedom o' his own will, he would na stand on stepping stanes, but, without scrupulosity, would send me, his mother, to crack sand, or mak my leaving where I could, after wastering a' my jointure.'

This speech made a strong impression on the minds of all the lawyers present. Mr Keelevin treasured it up, and said nothing. Our friend Gabriel glanced the tail of his eye at the advocate, who, without affecting to have noticed the interested motive which the Leddy had betrayed, said to Mr Keelevin,—

'The case, Sir, cannot but go before a jury; for, although the *fatuus* be of a capacity to repeat any injunction which he may have received, and which is not inconsistent with a high degree of fatuity—it does not therefore follow that he is able to originate such motions or volitions of the mind as are requisite to constitute what may be denominated a legal modicum of understanding, the possession of which in Mr Walter Walkinshaw is the object of the proposed inquiry to determine.'

'Very well, gentlemen, since such is the case,' replied Mr Keelevin, rising, 'as I have undertaken the cause, it is unnecessary for us to hold any further conversation on the subject. I shall be prepared to protect my client.'

With these words he left the room, in some hope that possibly they might induce George still to stay proceedings. But the cupidity of George's own breast, the views and arguments of his counsel, and the animosity of his mother, all co-operated to weaken their effect; so that, in the course of as short a time as the forms of the judicature permitted, a jury was impannelled before the Sheriff, according to the tenor of the special brief of Chancery which had been procured for the purpose, and evidence as to the state of poor Watty's understanding and capacity regularly examined;—some account of which we shall proceed to lay before our readers, premising, that Mr Threeper opened the business in a speech replete with eloquence and ingenuity, and all that metaphysical refinement for which the Scottish bar was then, as at present, so justly celebrated. Nothing, indeed, could be more subtile, nor less applicable to the coarse and daily tear and wear of human concerns, than his definition of what constituted 'the minimum of understanding, or of reason, or of mental faculty in general, which the law, in its wisdom, required to be enjoyed by every individual claiming to exercise the functions that belong to man, as a subject, a citizen, a husband, a father, a master, a servant,—in one word, to enable him to execute those different essential duties, which every gentleman of the jury so well knew, and so laudably, so respectably, and so meritoriously performed.'—

But we regret that our limits do not allow us to enter upon the subject; and the more so, as it could not fail to prove highly interesting to our fair readers, in whose opinion the eloquence of the Parliament House of Edinburgh, no doubt, possesses many charming touches of sentiment, and amiable pathetic graces.

Chapter XIX

The first witness examined was Jenny Purdie, servant to Mr George Walkinshaw. She had previously been several years in the service of his father, and is the same who, as our readers will perhaps recollect, contrived so femininely to seduce half-a-crown from the pocket of the old man, when she brought him the news of the birth of his son's twin daughters.

'What is your opinion of Mr Walter Walkinshaw?' inquired Mr Threeper.

''Deed, Sir,' said Jenny, 'I hae but a sma' opinion o' him—he's a daft man, and has been sae a' his days.'

'But what do you mean by a daft man?'

'I thought every body kent what a daft man is,' replied Jenny; 'he's just silly, and tavert, and heedless, and o' an inclination to swattle in the dirt like a grumphie.'

'Well, but do you mean to say,' interrupted the advocate, 'that, to your knowledge, he has been daft all his days?'

'I never kent him ony better.'

'But you have not known him all his days—therefore, how can you say he has been daft all his days?—He might have been wise enough when you did not know him.'

'I dinna think it,' said Jenny;—'I dinna think it was ever in him to be wise—he's no o' a nature to be wise.'

'What do you mean by a nature?—Explain yourself.'

'I canna explain mysel ony better,' was the answer; 'only I ken that a cat's no a dog, nor o' a nature to be,—and so the Laird could ne'er be a man o' sense.'

'Very ingenious, indeed,' said Mr Threeper; 'and I am sure the gentlemen of the jury must be satisfied that it is not possible to give a clearer—a more distinctive impression of the deficiency of Mr Walkinshaw's capacity, than has been given by this simple and innocent country girl.—

But, Jenny, can you tell us of any instance of his daftness?'

'I can tell you o' naething but the sic like about him.'

'Cannot you remember any thing he said or did on any particular day?'

'O aye, at weel I wat can do that—on the vera day when I gaed hame, frae my service at the Grippy to Mr George's, the sheep were sheared, and Mr Watty said they were made sae naked, it was a shame to see them, and took one o' his mother's flannen polonies, to mak a hap to Mall Loup-the-Dike, the auld ewe, for decency.'

Jenny was then cross-questioned by Mr Queerie, the able and intelligent advocate employed for the defence by Mr Keelevin; but her evidence was none shaken, nor did it appear that her master had in any way influenced her. Before she left the box, the Sheriff said jocularly,—

'I'm sure, from your account, Jenny, that Mr Walkinshaw's no a man ye would like to marry?'

'There's no saying,' replied Jenny,—'the Kittlestonheugh's a braw estate; and mony a better born than me has been blithe to put up wi' houses and lan's, though wit and worth were baith wanting.'

The first witness thus came off with considerable eclat, and indeed gained the love and affections, it is said, of one of the jurors, an old bien carle, a bonnet-laird, to whom she was, in the course of a short time after, married.

The next witness was Mr Mordecai Saxheere, preses and founder of that renowned focus of sosherie the Yarn Club, which held its periodical libations of the vintage of the colonies in the buxom Widow Sheid's tavern, in Sourmilk John's Land, a stately pile that still lifts its lofty head in the Trongate. He was an elderly, trim, smooth, Quaker-faced gentleman, dressed in drab, with spacious buckram-lined skirts, that came round on his knees, giving to the general outline of his figure the appearance of a cone supported on legs in white worsted hose. He wore a highly powdered horse-hair wig, with a long queue; buckles at the knees and in his shoes, presenting, in the collective attributes of his dress and appearance, a respect-bespeaking epitome of competency, good-eating, honesty, and self-conceit. He was one of several gentlemen whom the long-forecasting George had carried with him to Grippy on those occasions when he was desirous to provide witnesses, to be available when the era should arrive that had now come to pass.

'Well, Mr Saxheere,' said the Edinburgh advocate, 'what have you to say with respect to the state of Mr Walter Walkinshaw?'

'Sir,' replied the preses of the Yarn Club, giving that sort of congratulatory smack with which he was in the practice of swallowing and sending round the dram that crowned the substantials, and was herald to what were called the liquidities of the club,—'Sir,' said Mordecai Saxheere, 'I have been in no terms of intromission with Mr Walkinshaw of Grippy, cept and except in the way of visitation; and on those occasions I always found him of a demeanour more sportive to others than congenial.'

'You are a merchant, I believe, Mr Saxheere,' said Mr Threeper; 'you have your shop in the High Street, near the Cross. On the market day you keep a bottle of whisky and a glass on the counter, from which, as I understand, you are in the practice of giving your customers a dram—first preeing or smelling the liquor yourself, and then handing it to them.—Now, I would ask you, if Mr Walkinshaw were to come to your shop on the market day, would you deal with him?—would you, on your oath, smell the glass, and then hand it across the counter, to be by him drunk off?'

The advocate intended this as a display of his intimate knowledge of the local habits and usages of Glasgow, though himself but an Edinburgh man,—in order to amaze the natives by his cleverness.

'Sir,' replied Mr Saxheere, again repeating his habitual congratulatory smack, 'much would rely on the purpose for which he came to custom. If he offered me yarn for sale, there could be no opponency on my side to give him the fair price of the day; but, if he wanted to buy, I might undergo some constipation of thought before compliance.'

'The doubtful credit of any wiser person might produce the same astringency,' said the advocate, slyly.

'No doubt it would,' replied the preses of the Yarn Club; 'but the predicament of the Laird of Grippy would na be under that denominator, but because I would have a suspicion of him in the way of judgment and sensibility.'

'Then he is not a man that you would think it safe to trade with as a customer?' said the Sheriff, desirous of putting an end to his prosing.

'Just so, Sir,' replied Mordecai; 'for, though it might be safe in the way of advantage, I could not think myself, in the way of character, free from an imputation, were I to intromit with him.'

It was not deemed expedient to cross question this witness; and another was called, a celebrated Professor of Mathematics in the University, the founder and preses of a club, called the 'Anderson Summer Saturday's.' The scientific attainments and abstract genius of this distinguished person were undisputed; but his simplicity of character and absence of mind were no less remarkable. The object that George probably had in view in taking him, as an occasional visitor, to see his brother, was, perhaps, to qualify the Professor to bear testimony to the arithmetical incapacity of Walter; and certainly the Professor had always found him sufficiently incapable to have warranted him to give the most decisive evidence on that head; but a circumstance had occurred at the last visit, which came out in the course of the investigation, by which it would appear the opinion of the learned mathematician was greatly shaken.

'I am informed, Professor, that you are acquainted with Mr Walter Walkinshaw. Will you have the goodness to tell the Court what is your opinion of that gentleman?' said the advocate.

'My opinion is, that he is a very extraordinary man; for he put a question to me when I last saw him, which I have not yet been able to answer.'

The advocate thought the Professor said this in irony,—and inquired, with a simper,—

'And, pray, what might that question be?'

'I was trying if he could calculate the aliquot parts of a pound; and he said to me, could I tell him the reason that there were but four and twenty bawbees in a shilling?'

'You may retire,' said the advocate, disconcerted; and the Professor immediately withdrew; for still the counsel in behalf of Walter declined to cross question.

'The next witness that I shall produce,' resumed Mr Threeper, is one whom I call with extreme reluctance. Every man must sympathise with the feelings of a mother on such an occasion as this,—and will easily comprehend, that, in the questions which my duty obliges me to put to Mrs Walkinshaw, I am, as it were, obliged, out of that sacred respect which is due to her maternal sensibility, to address myself in more general terms than I should otherwise do.'

The Leddy was then called,—and the advocate, with a solemn voice and pauses of lengthened sadness and commiseration, said,—

'Madam, the Court and the jury do not expect you to enter into any particular description of the state of your unfortunate son. They only desire to know if you think he is capable of conducting his affairs like other men.'

'Him capable!' exclaimed the Leddy. 'He's no o' a capacity to be advised.'

She would have proceeded farther,—but Mr Threeper interposed, saying, 'Madam, we shall not distress you farther; the Court and the jury must be satisfied.'

Not so was Mr Keelevin, who nodded to Mr Queerie, the counsel for Walter; and he immediately rose.

'I wish,' said he, 'just to put one question to the witness. How long is it since your son has been so incapable of acting for himself?'

'I canna gie you day nor date,' replied the Leddy; 'but he has been in a state of condumacity ever since his dochter diet.'

'Indeed!' said Mr Queerie; 'then he was not always incapable?'

'O no,' cried the Leddy; 'he was a most tractable creature, and the kindliest son,' she added, with a sigh; 'but since that time he's been neither to bind nor to haud, threatening to send me, his mother, a garsing—garing me lay out my own lawful jointure on the house, and using me in the most horridable manner—wastring his income in the most thoughtless way.'

Mr Threeper began to whisper to our friend Gabriel, and occasionally to look, with an afflicted glance, towards the Leddy.

Mr Queerie resumed,—

'Your situation, I perceive, has been for some time very unhappy—but, I suppose, were Mr Walkinshaw to make you a reasonable compensation for the trouble you take in managing his house, you would have no objections still to continue with him.'

'O! to be surely,' said the Leddy;—'only it would need to be something worth while; and my gude-dochter and her family would require to be obligated to gang hame.'

'Certainly, what you say, Madam, is very reasonable,' rejoined Mr Queerie;—'and I have no doubt that the Court perceives that a great part of your distress, from the idiotry of your son, arises from his having brought in the lady alluded to and her family.'

'It has come a' frae that,' replied the witness, unconscious of the force of what she was saying;—'for, 'cepting his unnaturality to me about them, his idiocety is very harmless.'

'Perhaps not worse than formerly?'

A look from George at this crisis put her on her guard; and she instantly replied, as if eager to redeem the effects of what she had just said,—

''Deed, Sir, it's no right to let him continue in the rule and power o' the property; for nobody can tell what he may commit.

At this juncture, Mr Queerie, perceiving her wariness, sat down; and the Reverend Dr Denholm being called by Mr Threeper, stated, in answer to the usual question,—

'I acknowledge, that I do not think Mr Walkinshaw entirely of a sound mind; but he has glaiks and gleams o' sense about him, that mak me very dootful if I could judicially swear, that he canna deport himsel wi' sufficient sagacity.'

'But,' said the advocate, 'did not you yourself advise Mr George Walkinshaw to institute these proceedings.'

'I'll no disown that,' replied the Doctor; 'but Mr Walter has since then done such a humane and a Christian duty to his brother's widow, and her two defenceless and portionless bairns, that I canna in my conscience, think now so lightly of him as I once did.'

Here the jury consulted together; and, after a short conference the foreman inquired if Mr Walkinshaw was in Court. On being answered in the negative, the Sheriff suggested an adjournment till next day, that he might be brought forward.

Chapter XX

When the Leddy returned from the Court to Grippy, Walter, who had in the meantime been somehow informed of the nature of the proceedings instituted against him, said to his mother,—

'Weel, mother, so ye hae been trying to mak me daft? but I'm just as wise as ever.'

'Thou's ordaint to bring disgrace on us a',' was her answer, dictated under a feeling of vague apprehension, arising from the uncertainty which seemed to lower upon the issue of the process by the evidence of Dr Denholm.

'I'm sure I hae nae hand in't,' said Walter; 'an ye had na meddlet wi' me, I would ne'er hae spoken to Keelevin, to vex you. But I suppose, mother, that you and that wily headcadab Geordie hae made naething o' your fause witnessing.'

'Haud thy fool tongue, and insult na me,' exclaimed the Leddy in a rage at the simpleton's insinuation, which was uttered without the slightest sentiment of reproach. 'But,' she added, 'ye'll see what it is to stand wi' a het face afore the Court the morn.'

'I'll no gang,' replied Walter; 'I hae nae broo o' Courts and law-pleas.'

'But ye shall gang, if the life be in your body.'

'I'll do nothing but what Mr Keelevin bids me.'

'Mr Keelevin,' exclaimed the Leddy, 'ought to be drum't out o' the town for bringing sic trebalation intil my family.—What business had he, wi' his controversies, to gumle law and justice in the manner he has done the day?' And while she was thus speaking, George and Mr Pitwinnoch made their appearance.

'Hegh man, Geordie!' said Watty,—'I'm thinking, instead o' making me daft, ye hae demented my mother, poor bodie; for she's come hame wi' a flyte proceeding out of her mouth like a two-edged sword.'

'If you were not worse than ye are,' said his brother, 'you would have compassion on your mother's feelings.'

'I'm sure,' said Watty, 'I hae every compassion for her; but there was nae need o' her to wis to mak me daft. It's a foul bird that files its ain nest; and really, to speak my mind, I think, Geordie, that you and her were na wise, but far left to yoursels, to put your heads intil the hangman's halter o' a law-plea anent my intellectuals.'

Gabriel Pitwinnoch, who began to distrust the effect of the evidence, was troubled not a little at this observation; for he thought, if Walter spoke as well to the point before the Court, the cause must be abandoned. As for George, he was scarcely in a state to think of any thing, so much was he confounded and vexed by the impression of Dr Denholm's evidence, the tenor of which was so decidedly at variance with all he had flattered himself it would be. He, however, said,—

'Ye're to be examined to-morrow, and what will you say for yourself?'

'I hae mair modesty,' replied Walter, 'than to be my ain trumpeter—I'll say naething but what Mr Keelevin bids me.'

Gabriel smiled encouragingly to George at this, who continued,—

'You had better tak care what ye say.'

'Na,' cried Watty, 'an that's the gait o't, I'll keep a calm sough—least said's soonest mendit—I'll haud my tongue.'

'But you must answer every question.'

'Is't in the Shorter or the Larger Catechism?' said Walter. 'I can say till the third petition o' the t'ane, and frae end to end o' the t'ither.'

'That's quite enough,' replied Gabriel, 'and more than will be required of you.'

But the satisfaction which such an agreeable exposure of the innocency of the simpleton was calculated to afford to all present, was disturbed at this juncture by the entrance of Mr Keelevin.

'I'm glad, gentlemen,' said he, the moment he came in, 'that I have found you here. I think you must all be convinced that the investigation should na gang farther. I'm sure Mr Walter will be willing to grant a reasonable consideration to his mother for her care and trouble in the house, and even to assign a moitie o' his income to you, Mr George. Be counselled by me:—let us settle the matter in that manner quietly.'

Pitwinnoch winked to his client,—and Watty said,—

'What for should I gie my mother ony more? Has na she bed, board, and washing, house-room and chattels, a' clear aboon her jointure? and I'm sure Geordie has nae lawful claim on me for ony aliment.—Oh, Mr Keelevin, it would be a terrible wastrie o' me to do the like o' that. They might weel mak me daft if I did sae.'

'But it will be far decenter and better for a' parties to enter into some agreement of that sort. Don't you think so, Mrs Walkinshaw, rather than to go on with this harsh business of proving your son an idiot?'

'I'm no an idiot, Mr Keelevin,' exclaimed Walter—'though it seems to me that there's a thraw in the judgment o' the family, or my mother and brother would ne'er hae raised this straemash about my capacity to take care o' the property. Did na I keep the cows frae the corn a' the last Ruglen fair-day, when Jock, the herd, got leave to gang in to try his luck and fortune at the roley-poleys?'

Honest Mr Keelevin wrung his hands at this.

'I'm sure, Sir,' said George, in his sleekiest manner, 'that you must yourself, Mr Keelevin, be quite sensible that the inquiry ought to proceed to a verdict.'

'I'm sensible o' nae sic things, Mr George,' was the indignant answer. 'Your brother is in as full possession of all his faculties as when your father executed the cursed entail, or when he was married to Kilmarkeckle's dochter.'

' 'Deed, Mr Keelevin,' replied Walter, 'ye're mista'en there; for I hae had twa teeth tuggit out for the toothache since syne; and I hae grown deaf in the left lug.'

'Did na I tell you,' said the worthy man, angrily, 'that ye were na to open your mouth?'

'Really, Mr Keelevin, I won'er to hear you,' replied the natural, with great sincerity; 'the mouth's the only trance-door that I ken to the belly.'

'Weel, weel,' again exclaimed his friend; 'mak a kirk and a mill o't; but be ruled by me, and let us draw up a reasonable agreement.'

'I'm thinking, Mr Keelevin, that ye dinna ken that I hae made a paction with mysel to sign nae law-papers, for fear it be to the injury of Betty Bodle.'

'Betty Bodle!' said Gabriel Pitwinnoch, eagerly; 'she has been long dead.'

'Ah!' said Walter, 'that's a' ye ken about it. She's baith living and life like.'

Mr Keelevin was startled and alarmed at this; but abstained from saying any thing. Gabriel also said nothing; but looked significantly to his client, who interposed, and put an end to the conversation.

'Having gone so far,' said he, 'I could, with no respect for my own character, allow the proceedings to be now arrested. It is, therefore, unnecessary either to consider your suggestion, or to hold any further debate here on the subject.'

Mr Keelevin made no reply to this; but said, as he had something to communicate in private to his client, he would carry him to Glasgow for that night. To so reasonable and so professional a proposal no objection was made. Walter himself also at once acquiesced, on the express condition, that he was not to be obliged to sign any law-papers.

Chapter XXI

Next day, when the Court again assembled, Walter was there, seated beside his agent, and dressed in his best. Every eye was directed towards him; and the simple expression of wonder, mingled with anxiety, which the scene around him occasioned, gave an air of so much intelligence to his features, which were regular, and, indeed, handsome, that he excited almost universal sympathy; even Mr Threeper was perplexed, when he saw him, at the proper time, rise from beside his friend, and, approaching the bottom of the table, make as low and profound bow, first to the Sheriff and then to the jury.

'You are Mr Walkinshaw, I believe?' said Mr Threeper.

'I believe I am,' replied Walter, timidly.

'What are you, Mr Walkinshaw?'

'A man, Sir.—My mother and brother want to mak me a daft ane.'

'How do you suspect them of any such intention?'

'Because ye see I'm here—I would na hae been here but for that.'

The countenance of honest Keelevin began to brighten, while that of George was clouded and overcast.

'Then you do not think you are a daft man?' said the advocate.

'Nobody thinks himsel daft. I dare say ye think ye're just as wise as me.'

A roar of laughter shook the Court, and Threeper blushed and was disconcerted; but he soon resumed, tartly,—

'Upon my word, Mr Walkinshaw, you have a good opinion of yourself. I should like to know for what reason?'

'That's a droll question to speer at a man,' replied Walter. 'A poll parrot thinks weel o' itsel, which is but a feathered creature, and short o' the capacity of a man by twa hands.'

Mr Keelevin trembled and grew pale; and the advocate, recovering full possession of his assurance, proceeded,—

'And so ye think, Mr Walkinshaw, that the two hands make all the difference between a man and a parrot?'

'No, no, Sir,' replied Walter, 'I dinna think that,—for ye ken the beast has feathers.'

'And why have not men feathers?'

'That's no a right question, Sir, to put to the like o' me, a weak human creature;—ye should ask their Maker,' said Walter gravely.

The advocate was again repulsed; Pitwinnoch sat doubting the intelligence of his ears, and George shivering from head to foot: a buzz of satisfaction pervaded the whole Court.

'Well, but not to meddle with such mysteries,' said Mr Threeper, assuming a jocular tone, 'I suppose you think yourself a very clever fellow?'

'At some things,' replied Walter modestly; 'but I dinna like to make a roos o' mysel.'

'And pray now, Mr Walkinshaw, may I ask what do you think you do best?'

'Man! and ye could see how I can sup curds and cream—there's no ane in a' the house can ding me.'

The sincerity and exultation with which this was expressed convulsed the Court, and threw the advocate completely on his beam-ends. However, he soon righted, and proceeded,—

'I don't doubt your ability in that way, Mr Walkinshaw; and I dare say you can play a capital knife and fork.'

'I'm better at the spoon,' replied Walter laughing.

'Well, I must confess you are a devilish clever fellow.'

'Mair sae, I'm thinking, than ye thought, Sir.—But noo, since,' continued Walter, 'ye hae speer't so many questions at me, will ye answer one yoursel?'

'O, I can have no possible objection to do that, Mr Walkinshaw.'

'Then,' said Walter, 'how muckle are ye to get frae my brother for this job?'

Again the Court was convulsed, and the questioner again disconcerted.

'I suspect, brother Threeper,' said the Sheriff, 'that you are in the wrong box.'

'I suspect so too,' replied the advocate laughing; but, addressing himself again to Walter, he said,—

'You have been married, Mr Walkinshaw?'

'Aye, auld Doctor Denholm married me to Betty Bodle.'

'And pray where is she?'

'Her mortal remains, as the headstone says, lie in the kirk-yard.'

The countenance of Mr Keelevin became pale and anxious—George and Pitwinnoch exchanged smiles of gratulation.

'You had a daughter?' said the advocate, looking knowingly to the jury, who sat listening with greedy ears.

'I had,' said Walter, and glanced anxiously towards his trembling agent.

'And what became of your daughter?'

No answer was immediately given—Walter hung his head, and seemed troubled; he sighed deeply, and again turned his eye inquiringly to Mr Keelevin. Almost every one present sympathised with his emotion, and ascribed it to parental sorrow.

'I say,' resumed the advocate, 'what became of your daughter?'

'I canna answer that question.'

The simple accent in which this was uttered interested all in his favour still more and more.

'Is she dead?' said the pertinacious Mr Threeper.

'Folk said sae; and what every body says maun be true.'

'Then you don't, of your own knowledge, know the fact?'

'Before I can answer that, I would like to ken what a fact is?'

The counsel shifted his ground, without noticing the question; and said,—

'But I understand, Mr Walkinshaw, you have still a child that you call your Betty Bodle?'

'And what business hae ye wi' that?' said the natural, offended. 'I never saw sic a stock o' impudence as ye hae in my life.'

'I did not mean to offend you, Mr Walkinshaw; I was only anxious, for the ends of justice, to know if you consider the child you call Betty Bodle as your daughter?'

'I'm sure,' replied Walter, 'that the ends o' justice would be meikle better served an ye would hae done wi' your speering.'

'It is, I must confess, strange that I cannot get a direct answer from you, Mr Walkinshaw. Surely, as a parent, you should know your child!' exclaimed the advocate, peevishly.

'An I was a mother ye might say sae.'

Mr Threeper began to feel, that, hitherto, he had made no impression; and forming an opinion of Walter's shrewdness far beyond what he was led to expect, he stooped, and conferred a short time with Mr Pitwinnoch. On resuming his wonted posture, he said,—

'I do not wish, Mr Walkinshaw, to harass your feelings; but I am not satisfied with the answer you have given respecting your child; and I beg you will be a little more explicit. Is the little girl that lives with you your daughter?'

'I dinna like to gie you any satisfaction on that head; for Mr Keelevin said, ye would bother me if I did.'

'Ah!' exclaimed the triumphant advocate, 'have I caught you at last?'

A murmur of disappointment ran through all the Court; and Walter looked around coweringly and afraid.

'So, Mr Keelevin has primed you, has he? He has instructed you what to say?'

'No,' said the poor natural; 'he instructed me to say nothing.'

'Then, why did he tell you that I would bother you?'

'I dinna ken, speer at himsel; there he sits.'

'No, Sir! I ask you,' said the advocate, grandly.

'I'm wearied, Mr Keelevin,' said Walter, helplessly, as he looked towards his disconsolate agent. 'May I no come away?'

The honest lawyer gave a deep sigh; to which all the spectators sympathisingly responded.

'Mr Walkinshaw,' said the Sheriff, 'don't be alarmed—we are all friendly disposed towards you; but it is necessary, for the satisfaction of the jury, that you should tell us what you think respecting the child that lives with you.'

Walter smiled and said, 'I hae nae objection to converse wi' a weel-bred gentleman like you; but that barking terrier in the wig, I can thole him no longer.'

'Well, then,' resumed the judge, 'is the little girl your daughter?'

'' Deed is she—my ain dochter.'

'How can that be, when, as you acknowledged, every body said your dochter was dead?'

'But I kent better mysel—my bairn and dochter, ye see, Sir, was lang a weakly baby, ay bleating like a lambie that has lost its mother; and she dwin't and dwinlet, and moant and grew sleepy sleepy, and then she clos'd her wee bonny een, and lay still; and I sat beside her three days and three nights, watching her a' the time, never lifting my een frae her face, that was as sweet to look on as a gowan in a lown May morning.

But I ken na how it came to pass—I thought, as I look't at her, that she was change't, and there began to come a kirkyard smell frae the bed, that was just as if the hand o' Nature was wising me to gae away; and then I saw, wi' the eye o' my heart, that my brother's wee Mary was grown my wee Betty Bodle, and so I gaed and brought her hame in my arms, and she is noo my dochter. But my mother has gaen on like a randy at me ever sin syne, and wants me to put away my ain bairn, which I will never, never do—No, Sir, I'll stand by her, and guard her, though fifty mothers, and fifty times fifty brother Geordies, were to flyte at me frae morning to night.'

One of the jury here interposed, and asked several questions relative to the management of the estate; by the answers to which it appeared, not only that Walter had never taken any charge whatever, but that he was totally ignorant of business, and even of the most ordinary money transactions.

The jury then turned round and laid their heads together; the legal gentlemen spoke across the table, and Walter was evidently alarmed at the bustle.—In the course of two or three minutes, the foreman returned a verdict of Fatuity.

The poor Laird shuddered, and, looking at the Sheriff, said, in an accent of simplicity that melted every heart, 'Am I found guilty?—O surely, Sir, ye'll no hang me, for I cou'dna help it?'

Chapter XXII

The scene in the parlour of Grippy, after the inquiry, was of the most solemn and lugubrious description.—The Leddy sat in the great chair, at the fire-side, in all the pomp of woe, wiping her eyes, and, ever and anon, giving vent to the deepest soughs of sorrow. Mrs Charles, with her son leaning on her knee, occupied another chair, pensive and anxious. George and Mr Pitwinnoch sat at the table, taking an inventory of the papers in the scrutoire, and Walter was playfully tickling his adopted daughter on the green before the window, when Mrs Milrookit, with her husband, the Laird of Dirdumwhamle, came to sympathise and condole with their friends, and to ascertain what would be the pecuniary consequences of the decision to them.

'Come awa, my dear,' said the Leddy to her daughter, as she entered the room;— 'Come away and tak a seat beside me. Your poor brother, Watty, has been weighed in the balance o' the Sheriff, and found wanting; and his vessels o' gold and silver, as I may say in the words o' Scripture, are carried away into captivity; for I understand that George gets no proper right to them, as I expeckit, but is obligated to keep them in custody, in case Watty should hereafter come to years o' discretion. Hegh Meg! but this is a sair day for us a'—and for nane mair sae than your afflicted gude-sister there and her twa bairns. She'll be under a needcessity to gang back and live again wi' my mother, now in her ninety-third year, and by course o' nature drawing near to her latter end.'

'And what's to become of you?' replied Mrs Milrookit.

'O I'll hae to bide here, to tak care o' every thing; and an aliment will be alloot to me for keeping poor Watty. Hegh Sirs! Wha would hae thought it, that sic a fine lad as he ance was, and preferred by his honest father as the best able to keep the property right, would thus hae been, by decreet o' court, proven a born idiot?'

'But,' interrupted Mrs Milrookit, glancing compassionately towards her sister-in-law, 'I think, since so little change is to be made, that ye might just as weel let Bell and her bairns bide wi' you—for my grandmother's income is little enough for her ain wants, now that she's in a manner bedrid.'

'It's easy for you, Meg, to speak,' replied her mother;—'but if ye had an experiment o' the heavy handfu' they hae been to me, ye would hae mair compassion for your mother. It's surely a dispensation sair enough, to hae the grief and heart-breaking sight before my eyes of a demented lad, that was so long a comfort to me in my widowhood. But it's the Lord's will, and I maun bend the knee o' resignation.'

'Is't your intent, Mr George,' said the Laird o' Dirdumwhamle, 'to mak any division o' what lying money there may hae been saved since your father's death?'

'I suspect there will not be enough to defray the costs of the process,' replied George; 'and if any balance should remain, the house really stands so much in need of repair, that I am persuaded there will not be a farthing left.'

' 'Deed,' said the Leddy, 'what he says, Mr Milrookit, is oure true; the house is in a frail condition, for it was like pu'ing the teeth out o' the head o' Watty to get him to do what was needful.'

'I think,' replied the Laird o' Dirdumwhamle, 'that since ye hae so soon come to the property, Mr George, and no likelihood o' any molestation in the possession, that ye might let us a' share and share alike o' the gethering, and be at the outlay o' the repairs frae the rental.'

'To this suggestion Mr George, however, replied, 'It will be time enough to consider that, when the law expences are paid.'

'They'll be a heavy soom, Mr Milrookit,' said the Leddy; 'weel do I ken frae my father's pleas what it is to pay law expences. The like o' Mr Pitwinnoch there, and Mr Keelevin, are men o' moderation and commonality in their charges—but yon awfu' folk wi' the cloaks o' darkness and the wigs o' wisdom frae Edinbro'—they are costly commodities.—But now that we're a' met here, I think it would be just as weel an we waur to settle at ance what I'm to hae, as the judicious curator o' Watty—for, by course o' law and nature, the aliment will begin frae this day.'

'Yes,' replied George, 'I think it will be just as well; and I'm glad, mother, that you have mentioned it. What is your opinion, Mr Milrookit, as to the amount that she should have?'

'All things considered,' replied the Laird of Dirdumwhamle, prospectively contemplating some chance of a reversionary interest to his wife in the Leddy's savings, 'I think you ought not to make it less than a hundred pounds a-year.'

'A hundred pounds a-year!' exclaimed the Leddy, 'that'll no buy saut to his kail. I hope and expek no less than the whole half o' the rents; and they were last year weel on to four hunder.'

'I think,' said George to Mr Pitwinnoch, 'I would not be justified to the Court were I to give any thing like that; but if you think I may, I can have no objection to comply with my mother's expectations.'

'O, Mr Walkinshaw,' replied Gabriel, 'you are no at a' aware o' your responsibility,—you can do no such things. Your brother has been found a *fatuus*, and, of course, entitled but to the plainest maintenance. I think that you will hardly be permitted to allow his mother more than fifty pounds; if, indeed, so much.'

'Fifty pounds! fifty placks,' cried the indignant Leddy. I'll let baith you and the Sheriff ken I'm no to be frauded o' my rights in that gait. I'll no faik a farthing o' a hundred and fifty.'

'In that case, I fear,' said Gabriel, 'Mr George will be obliged to seek another custodier for the *fatuus*, as assuredly, Mem, he'll ne'er be sanctioned to allow you any thing like that.'

'If ye think sae,' interposed Mrs Milrookit, compassionating the forlorn estate of her sister-in-law,—'I dare say Mrs Charles will be content to take him at a very moderate rate.'

'Megsty me!' exclaimed the Leddy. 'Hae I been buying a pig in a pock like that? Is't a possibility that he can be ta'en out o' my hands, and no reasonable allowance made to me at a'? Surely, Mr Pitwinnoch, surely, Geordie, this can never stand either by the laws of God or man.'

'I can assure you, Mrs Walkinshaw,' replied the lawyer, 'that fifty pounds a-year is as much as I could venture to advise Mr George to give; and seeing it is sae, you had as well agree to it at once.'

'I'll never agree to ony such thing.' I'll gang intil Embro mysel, and hae justice done me frae the Fifteen. I'll this very night consult Mr Keelevin, who is a most just man, and o' a right partiality.'

'I hope, mother,' said George, 'that you and I will not cast out about this; and to end all debates, if ye like, we'll leave the aliment to be settled by Mr Pitwinnoch and Mr Keelevin.'

'Nothing can be fairer,' observed the Laird of Dirdumwhamle, in the hope Mr Keelevin might be so wrought on as to insist, that at least a hundred should be allowed; and after some further altercation, the Leddy grudgingly assented to this proposal.

'But,' said Mrs Milrookit, 'considering now the altered state of Watty's circumstances, I dinna discern how it is possible for my mother to uphold this house and the farm?'

The Leddy looked a little aghast at this fearful intimation, while George replied,—

'I have reflected on that, Margaret, and I am quite of your opinion; and, indeed, it is my intention, after the requisite repairs are done to the house, to flit my family; for I am in hopes the change of air will be advantageous to my wife's health.'

The Leddy was thunderstruck, and unable to speak; but her eyes were eloquent with indignation.

'Perhaps, after all, it would be as well for our mother,' continued George, 'to take up house at once in Glasgow; and as I mean to settle an annuity of fifty pounds on Mrs Charles, they could not do better than all live together.'

All present but his mother applauded the liberality of George. To the young widow the intelligence of such a settlement was as fresh air to the captive; but before she could express her thankfulness, Leddy Grippy started up, and gave a tremendous stamp with her foot. She then resumed her seat, and appeared all at once calm and smiling; but it was a calm betokening no tranquillity, and a smile expressive of as little pleasure. In the course of a few seconds the hurricane burst forth, and alternately, with sobs and supplications, menaces, and knocking of nieves, and drumming with her feet, the hapless Leddy Grippy divulged and expatiated on the plots and devices of George. But all was of no avail—her destiny was sealed; and long before Messrs Keelevin and Pitwinnoch adjusted the amount of the allowance, which, after a great struggle on the part of the former, was settled at seventy five pounds, she found herself under the painful necessity of taking a flat up a turnpike stair in Glasgow, for herself and the *fatuus*.

Chapter XXIII

For some time after the decision of Walter's fatuity, nothing important occurred in the history of the Grippy family. George pacified his own conscience, and gained the approbation of the world, by fulfilling the promise of settling fifty pounds per annum on his sister-in-law. The house was enlarged and adorned, and the whole estate, under the ancient name of Kittlestonheugh, began to partake of that general spirit of improvement which was then gradually diffusing itself over the face of the west country.

In the meantime, Mrs Charles Walkinshaw, who had returned with her children to reside with their grandmother, found her situation comparatively comfortable; but an acute anxiety for the consequences that would ensue by the daily expected death of that gentlewoman, continued to thrill through her bosom, and chequer the sickly gleam of the uncertain sunshine that glimmered in her path. At last the old lady died, and she was reduced, as she had long foreseen, with her children, to the parsimonious annuity. As it was impossible for her to live in Glasgow, and educate her children, on so small a stipend, there, she retired to one of the neighbouring villages, where, in the family of the Reverend Mr Eadie, the minister, she found that kind of quiet intelligent society which her feelings and her misfortunes required.

Mrs Eadie was a Highland lady, and, according to the living chronicles of the region of clans and traditions, she was of scarcely less than illustrious birth. But for the last attempt to restore the royal line of the Stuarts, she would, in all probability, have moved in a sphere more spacious and suitable to the splendour of her pedigree than the humble and narrow orbit of a country clergyman's wife. Nor in her appearance did it seem that Nature and Fortune were agreed about her destiny; for the former had adorned her youth with the beauty, the virtues, and the dignity, which command admiration in the palace,—endowments but little consonant to the lowly duties of the rural manse.

At the epoch of which we are now speaking she was supposed to have passed her fiftieth year; but something in her air and manner gave her the appearance of being older—a slight shade of melancholy, the pale cast of thought, lent sweetness to the benign composure of her countenance; and she was seldom seen without inspiring interest, and awakening sentiments of profound and reverential respect. She had lost her only daughter about a year before; and a son, her remaining child, a boy about ten years of age, was supposed to have inherited the malady which carried off his sister. The anxiety which Mrs Eadie, in consequence, felt as a mother, partly occasioned that mild sadness of complexion to which we have alluded; but there was still a deeper and more affecting cause.

Before the ruin of her father's fortune, by the part he took in the Rebellion, she was betrothed to a youth who united many of the best Lowland virtues with the gallantry and enthusiasm peculiar to the Highlanders of that period. It was believed that he had fallen in the fatal field of Culloden; and, after a long period of virgin widowhood, on his account, she was induced, by the amiable manners and gentle virtues of Mr Eadie, to consent to change her life. He was then tutor in the family of a relation, with whom, on her father's forfeiture and death, she had found an asylum,—and when he was presented to the parish of Camrachle, they were married.

The first seven years, from the date of their union, were spent in that temperate state of enjoyment which is the nearest to perfect happiness; during the course of which their two children were born. In that time no symptom of the latent poison of the daughter's constitution appeared; but all around them, and in their prospects, was calm, and green, and mild, and prosperous.

In the course of the summer of the eighth year, in consequence of an often repeated invitation, they went, at the meeting of the General Assembly, to which Mr Eadie was returned a member, to spend a short time with a relation in Edinburgh, and among the strangers with whom they happened to meet at the houses of their friends were several from France, children and relations of some of those who had been out in the Forty-five.

A young gentleman belonging to these expatriated visitors, one evening interested Mrs Eadie, to so great a degree, that she requested to be particularly introduced to him, and, in the course of conversation, she learnt that he was the son of her former lover, and that his father was still alive, and married to a French woman, his mother. The shock which this discovery produced was so violent that she was obliged to leave the room, and falling afterwards into bad health, her singular beauty began to fade with premature decay.

Her husband, to whom she disclosed her grief, endeavoured to soften it by all the means and blandishments in his power; but it continued so long inveterate, that he, yielded himself to the common weakness of our nature, and growing peevish at her sorrow, chided her melancholy till their domestic felicity was mournfully impaired.

Such was the state in which Mrs Charles Walkinshaw found Mrs Eadie at their first acquaintance; and the disappointments and shadows which had fallen on the hopes of her own youth, soon led to an intimate and sympathetic friendship between them, the influence of which contributed at once to alleviate their reciprocal griefs, and to have the effect of reviving, in some degree, the withered affections of the minister. The gradual and irremediable progress of the consumption which preyed on his son, soon, however, claimed from that gentle and excellent man efforts of higher fortitude than he had before exerted, and from that inward exercise, and the sympathy which he felt for his wife's maternal solicitude, Mrs Walkinshaw had the satisfaction, in the course of a year, to see their mutual confidence and cordiality restored.

But in the same period the boy died; and though the long foreseen event deeply affected his parents, it proved a fortunate occurrence to the widow.

For the minister, to withdraw his reflections from the contemplation of his childless state, undertook the education of James, and Mrs Eadie, partly from the same motives, but chiefly to enjoy the society of her friend, proposed to unite with her in the education of Mary. 'We cannot tell,' said she to Mrs Walkinshaw, 'what her lot may be; but let us do our best to prepare her for the world, and leave her fortunes, as they ever must be, in the hands of Providence. The penury and obscurity of her present condition ought to be no objection to bestowing on her all the accomplishments we have it in our power to give. How little likely was it, in my father's time, that I should have been in this comparative poverty, and yet, but for those acquirements, which were studied for brighter prospects, how dark and sad would often have been my residence in this sequestered village?'

Chapter XXIV

In the meantime, the fortunes of George, whom we now regard as the third Laird of Grippy, continued to flourish. The estate rose in value, and his mercantile circumstances improved; but still the infirmities of his wife's health remained the same, and the want of a male heir was a craving void in his bosom, that no prosperity could supply.

The reflections, connected with this subject, were rendered the more afflicting, by the consideration, that, in the event of dying without a son, the estate would pass from his daughter to James, the son of his brother Charles—and the only consolation that he had to balance this was a hope that, perhaps, in time he might be able to bring to pass a marriage between them.

Accordingly, after a suspension of intercourse for several years, actuated by a perspective design of this kind, he, one afternoon, made his appearance in his own carriage, with his lady and daughter, at the door of Mrs Charles' humble dwelling, in the village of Camrachle.

'I am afraid,' said he, after they were all seated in her little parlour, the window of which was curtained without with honeysuckle and jessamine—and the grate filled with flowers;—'I am afraid, my dear sister, unless we occasionally renew our intercourse, that the intimacy will be lost between our families, which it ought to be the interest of friends to preserve. Mrs Walkinshaw and I have, therefore, come to request that you and the children will spend a few days with us at Kittlestonheugh, and if you do not object, we shall invite our mother and Walter to join you—you would be surprised to hear how much the poor fellow still dotes on the recollection of your Mary, as Betty Bodle, and bewails, because the law, as he says, has found him guilty of being daft, that he should not be allowed to see her.'

This visit and invitation were so unexpected, that even Mrs Charles, who was of the most gentle and confiding nature, could not avoid suspecting they were dictated by some unexplained purpose; but adversity had long taught her that she was only as a reed in the world, and must stoop as the wind blew. She, therefore, readily agreed to spend a few days at the mansion-house, and the children who were present, eagerly expressing a desire to see their uncle Walter, of whose indulgence and good nature they retained the liveliest recollection, it was arranged that, on the Monday following, the carriage should be sent for her and them, and that the Leddy and Walter should also be at Kittlestonheugh to meet them.

In the evening after this occurrence, Mrs Charles went to the manse, and communicated to the minister and Mrs Eadie what had happened.

They knew her story, and were partly acquainted with the history of the strange and infatuated Entail. Like her, they believed that her family had been entirely cut off from the succession, and, like her too, they respected the liberality of George, in granting her the annuity, small as it was. His character, indeed, stood fair and honourable with the world; he was a partner in one of the most eminent concerns in the royal city; his birth and the family estate placed him in the first class of her sons and daughters, that stately class who, though entirely devoted to the pursuit of lucre, still held their heads high as ancestral gentry. But after a suspension of intercourse for so long a period, so sudden a renewal of intimacy, and with a degree of cordiality never before evinced, naturally excited their wonder, and awakened their conjectures. Mrs Eadie, superior and high-minded herself, ascribed it to the best intentions. ' Your brother-in-law,' said she, 'is feeling the generous influence of prosperity, and is sensible that it must redound to his personal advantage with the world to continue towards you, on an enlarged scale, that friendship which you have already experienced.'

But the minister, who, from his humbler birth, and the necessity which it imposed on him to contemplate the movements of society from below, together with that acquired insight of the hidden workings of the heart, occasionally laid open in the confessional moments of contrition, when his assistance was required at the death-beds of his parishioners, appeared to entertain a different opinion.

'I hope his kindness proceeds,' said he, 'from so good a source; but I should have been better satisfied had it run in a constant stream, and not, after such an entire occultation, burst forth so suddenly. It is either the result of considerations with respect to things already past, recently impressed upon him, in some new manner, or springs from some sinister purpose that he has in view; and, therefore, Mrs Walkinshaw, though it may seem harsh in me to suggest so ill a return for such a demonstration of brotherly regard, I would advise you, on account of your children, to observe to what it tends.'

In the meantime, George, with his lady and daughter, had proceeded to his mother's residence in Virginia Street, to invite her and Walter to join Mrs Charles and the children.

His intercourse with her, after her domiciliation in the town had been established, was restored to the freest footing; for although, in the first instance, and in the most vehement manner, she declared, 'He had cheated her, and deprived Walter of his lawful senses; and that she ne'er would open her lips to him again,' he had, nevertheless, contrived to make his peace, by sending her presents, and paying her the most marked deference and respect; lamenting that the hard conditions of his situation as a trustee did not allow him to be in other respects more liberal. But still the embers of suspicion were not extinguished; and when, on this occasion, he told her where he had been, and the immediate object of his visit, she could not refrain from observing, that it was a very wonderful thing.

'Dear keep me, Geordie!' said she, 'what's in the wind noo, that ye hae been galloping awa in your new carriage to invite Bell Fatherlans and her weans to Grippy?'

George, eager to prevent her observations, interrupted her, saying,—'I am surprised, mother, that you still continue to call the place Grippy. You know it is properly Kittlestonheugh.'

'To be sure,' replied the Leddy, 'since my time and your worthy father's time, it has undergone a great transmogrification; what wi' your dining-rooms, and what wi' your drawing-rooms, and your new back jams and your wings.'

'Why, mother, I have but as yet built only one of the wings,' said he.

'And enough too,' exclaimed the Leddy. 'Geordie, tak my word for't, it 'ill a' flee fast enough away wi' ae wing. Howsever, I'll no objek to the visitation, for I hae had a sort o' wis to see my grand-childer, which is very natural I shou'd hae. Nae doot, by this time they are grown braw bairns; and their mother was ay a genty bodie, though, in a sense, mair for ornament than use.'

Walter, who, during this conversation, was sitting in his father's easy chair, that had, among other chattels, been removed from Grippy,—swinging backward and forwards, and occasionally throwing glances towards the visitors, said,—

'And is my Betty Bodle to be there?'

'O, yes,' replied George, glad to escape from his mother's remarks; 'and you'll be quite delighted to see her. She is uncommonly tall for her age.'

'I dinna like that,' said Walter; 'she should na hae grown ony bigger,—for I dinna like big folk.'

'And why not?'

"Cause ye ken, Geordie, the law's made only for them; and if you and me had ay been twa wee brotherly laddies, playing on the gowany brae, as we used to do, ye would ne'er hae thought o' bringing yon duty's claw frae Enbro' to prove me guilty o' daftness.'

'I'm sure, Watty,' said George, under the twinge which he suffered from the observation, 'that I could not do otherwise. It was required from me equally by what was due to the world and to my mother.'

'It may be sae,' replied Walter; 'but, as I'm daft, ye ken I dinna understand it;' and he again resumed his oscillations.

After some further conversation on the subject of the proposed visit, in which George arranged that he should call on Monday for his mother and Walter in the carriage, and take them out to the country with him, he took his leave.

Chapter XXV

On the same evening on which George and his family visited Mrs Charles at Camrachle, and while she was sitting in the manse parlour, Mrs Eadie received a letter by the post. It was from her cousin Frazer, who, as heir-male of Frazer of Glengael, her father's house, would, but for the forfeiture, have been his successor, and it was written to inform her, that, among other forfeited properties, the Glengael estate was to be soon publicly sold, and that he was making interest, according to the custom of the time, and the bearing in the minds of the Scottish gentry in general towards the unfortunate adherents of the Stuarts, to obtain a private preference at the sale; also begging that she would come to Edinburgh and assist him in the business, some of their mutual friends and relations having thought that, perhaps, she might herself think of concerting the means to make the purchase.

At one time, undoubtedly, the hereditary affections of Mrs Eadie would have prompted her to have made the attempt; but the loss of her children extinguished all the desire she had ever cherished on the subject, and left her only the wish that her kinsman might succeed. Nevertheless, she was too deeply under the influence of the clannish sentiments peculiar to the Highlanders, not to feel that a compliance with

Frazer's request was a duty. Accordingly, as soon as she read the letter, she handed it to her husband, at the same time saying,—

'I am glad that this has happened when we are about to lose for a time the society of Mrs Walkinshaw. We shall set out for Edinburgh on Monday, the day she leaves this, and perhaps we may be able to return about the time she expects to be back. For I feel,' she added, turning towards her, 'that your company has become an essential ingredient to our happiness.'

Mr Eadie was so much surprised at the decision with which his wife spoke, and the firmness with which she proposed going to Edinburgh, without reference to what he might be inclined to do, that, instead of reading the letter, he looked at her anxiously for a moment, perhaps recollecting the unpleasant incident of their former visit to the metropolis, and said, 'What has occurred?'

'Glengael is to be sold,' she replied, 'and my cousin, Frazer, is using all the influence he can to prevent any one from bidding against him. Kindness towards me deters some of our mutual friends from giving him their assistance; and he wishes my presence in Edinburgh to remove their scruples, and otherwise to help him.'

'You can do that as well by letter as in person,' said the minister, opening the letter; 'for, indeed, this year we cannot so well afford the expences of such a journey.'

'The honour of my father's house is concerned in this business,' replied the lady, calmly but proudly; 'and there is no immediate duty to interfere with what I owe to my family as the daughter of Glengael.'

Mrs Walkinshaw had, from her first interview, admired the august presence and lofty sentiments of Mrs Eadie; but nothing had before occurred to afford her even a glimpse of her dormant pride and sleeping energies, the sinews of a spirit capable of heroic and masculine effort; and she felt for a moment awed by the incidental disclosure of a power and resolution, that she had never once imagined to exist beneath the calm and equable sensibility which constituted the general tenor of her friend's character.

When the minister had read the letter, he again expressed his opinion that it was unnecessary to go to Edinburgh; but Mrs Eadie, without entering into any observation on his argument, said,—

'On second thoughts, it may not be necessary for you to go—but I must. I am summoned by my kinsman; and it is not for me to question the propriety of what he asks, but only to obey. It is the cause of my father's house.'

The minister smiled at her determination, and said, 'I suppose there is nothing else for me but also to obey. I do not, however, recollect who this Frazer is—Was he out with your father in the Forty-five?'

'No; but his father was,' replied Mrs Eadie, 'and was likewise executed at Carlisle. He, himself, was bred to the bar, and is an advocate in Edinburgh.' And, turning suddenly round to Mrs Walkinshaw, she added solemnly, 'There is something in this—There is some mysterious link between the fortunes of your family and mine. It has brought your brother-in-law here to-day, as if a new era were begun to you, and also this letter of auspicious omen to the blood of Glengael.'

Mr Eadie laughingly remarked, 'That he had not for a long time heard from her such a burst of Highland lore.'

But Mrs Walkinshaw was so affected by the solemnity with which it had been expressed, that she inadvertently said, 'I hope in Heaven it may be so.'

'I am persuaded it is,' rejoined Mrs Eadie, still serious; and emphatically taking her by the hand, she said, 'The minister dislikes what he calls my Highland freats, and believes they have their source in some dark remnants of pagan superstition; on that account, I abstain from speaking of many things that I see, the signs and forecoming shadows of events—nevertheless, my faith in them is none shaken, for the spirit has more faculties than the five senses, by which, among other things, the heart is taught to love or hate, it knows not wherefore—Mark, therefore, my words, and bear them in remembrance—for this day the fortunes of Glengael are mingled with those of your house.—The lights of both have been long set; but the time is coming, when they shall again shine in their brightness.'

'I should be incredulous no more,' replied the minister, 'if you could persuade her brother-in-law, Mr George Walkinshaw, to help Frazer with a loan towards the sum required for the purchase of Glengael.'

Perceiving, however, that he was treading too closely on a tender point, he turned the conversation, and nothing more particular occurred that evening. The interval between and Monday was occupied by the two families in little preparations for their respective journeys; Mr Eadie, notwithstanding the pecuniary inconvenience, having agreed to accompany his wife.

In the meantime, George, for some reason best known to himself, it would appear, had resolved to make the visit of so many connections a festival; for, on the day after he had been at Camrachle, he wrote to his brother-in-law, the Laird of Dirdumwhamle, to join the party with Mrs Milrookit, and to bring their son with them,—a circumstance which, when he mentioned it to his mother, only served to make her suspect that more was meant than met either the eye or ear in such extraordinary kindness; and the consequence was, that she secretly resolved to take the advice of Mr Keelevin, as to how she ought to conduct herself; for, from the time of his warsle, as she called it, with Pitwinnoch for the aliment, he had regained her good opinion. She had also another motive for being desirous of conferring with him, no less than a laudable wish to have her will made, especially as the worthy lawyer, now far declined into the vale of years, had been for some time in ill health, and unable to give regular attendance to his clients at the office: 'symptoms,' as the Leddy said when she heard it 'that he felt the cauld hand o' Death muddling about the root o' life, and a warning to a' that wanted to profit by his skill, no to slumber and sleep like the foolish virgins, that alloo't their cruises to burn out, and were wakened to desperation, when the shout got up that the bridegroom and the musickers were coming.'

But the worthy lawyer, when she called, was in no condition to attend any longer to worldly concerns,—a circumstance which she greatly deplored, as she mentioned it to her son George, who, however, was far from sympathising with her anxiety; on the contrary, the news, perhaps, afforded him particular satisfaction. For he was desirous that the world should continue to believe his elder brother had been entirely disinherited, and Mr Keelevin was the only person that he thought likely to set the heirs in that respect right.

Chapter XXVI

On the day appointed, the different members of the Grippy family assembled at Kittlestonheugh. Mrs Charles and her two children were the last that arrived; and during the drive from Camrachle, both James and Mary repeated many little instances of Walter's kindness, so lasting are the impressions of affection received in the artless and heedless hours of childhood; and they again anticipated, from the recollection of his good nature, a long summer day with him of frolic and mirth.

But they were now several years older, and they had undergone that unconscious change, by which, though the stores of memory are unaltered, the moral being becomes another creature, and can no longer feel towards the same object as it once felt. On alighting from the carriage, they bounded with light steps and jocund hearts in quest of their uncle; but, when they saw him sitting by himself in the garden, they paused, and were disappointed.

They recognised in him the same person whom they formerly knew, but they had heard he was daft; and they beheld him stooping forward, with his hands sillily hanging between his knees; and he appeared melancholy and helpless.

'Uncle Watty,' said James, compassionately, 'what for are ye sitting there alone?'

Watty looked up, and gazing at him vacantly for a few seconds, said,

''Cause naebody will sit wi' me, for I'm a daft man.' He then drooped his head, and sank into the same listless posture in which they had found him.

'Do ye no ken me?' said Mary.

He again raised his eyes, and alternately looked at them both, eagerly and suspiciously. Mary appeared to have outgrown his recollection, for he turned from her; but, after some time, he began to discover James; and a smile of curious wonder gradually illuminated his countenance, and developed itself into a broad grin of delight, as he said,—

'What a heap o' meat, Jamie Walkinshaw, ye maun hae eaten to mak you sic a muckle laddie;' and he drew the boy towards him to caress him as he had formerly done; but the child, escaping from his hands, retired several paces backward, and eyed him with pity, mingled with disgust.

Walter appeared struck with his look and movement; and again folding his hands, dropped them between his knees, and hung his head, saying to himself,—'But I'm daft; naebody cares for me noo; I'm a cumberer o' the ground, and a' my Betty Bodles are ta'en away.'

The accent in which this was expressed touched the natural tenderness of the little girl; and she went up to him, and said,—'Uncle, I'm your wee Betty Bodle; what for will ye no speak to me?'

His attention was again roused, and he took her by the hand, and, gently stroking her head, said, 'Ye're a bonny flower, a lily-like leddy, and leil in the heart and kindly in the e'e; but ye're no my Betty Bodle.' Suddenly, however, something in the cast of her countenance reminded him so strongly of her more childish appearance, that he caught her in his arms, and attempted to dandle her; but the action was so violent that it frightened the child, and she screamed, and struggling out of his hands, ran away. James followed her; and their attention being soon drawn to other objects, poor Walter was left neglected by all during the remainder of the forenoon.

At dinner he was brought in and placed at the table, with one of the children on each side; but he paid them no attention.

'What's come o'er thee, Watty?' said his mother. 'I thought ye would hae been out o' the body wi' your Betty Bodle; but ye ne'er let on ye see her.'

' 'Cause she's like a' the rest,' said he sorrowfully. 'She canna abide me; for ye ken I'm daft—It's surely an awfu' leprosy this daftness, that it gars every body flee me; but I canna help it—It's no my fau't, but the Maker's that made me, and the laws that found me guilty. But, Geordie,' he added, turning to his brother, 'What's the use o' letting me live in this world, doing nothing, and gude for naething?'

Mrs Charles felt her heart melt within her at the despondency with which this was said, and endeavoured to console him; he, however, took no notice of her attentions, but sat seemingly absorbed in melancholy, and heedless to the endeavours which even the compassionate children made to induce him to eat.

'No,' said he; I'll no eat ony mair—it's even down wastrie for sic a useless set-by thing as the like o' me to consume the fruits o' the earth. The cost o' my keep would be a braw thing to Bell Fatherlans, so I hope, Geordie, ye'll mak it o'er to her; for when I gae hame I'll lie doun and die.'

'Haud thy tongue, and no fright folk wi' sic blethers,' exclaimed his mother; 'but eat your dinner, and gang out to the green and play wi' the weans.'

'An I were na a daft creature, naebody would bid me play wi' weans—and the weans ken that I am sae, and mak a fool o' me for't—I dinna like to be every body's fool. I'm sure the law, when it found me guilty, might hae alloot me a mair merciful punishment. Meg Wilcat, that stealt Provost Murdoch's cocket-hat, and was whippit for't at the Cross, was pitied wi' many a watery e'e; but every body dauds and dings the daft Laird o' Grippy.'

'Na! as I'm to be trusted,' exclaimed the Leddy, 'if I dinna think, Geordie, that the creature's coming to its senses again; ' and she added laughing, 'and what will come o' your braw policy, and your planting and plenishing? for ye'll hae to gie't back, and count in the Court to the last bawbee for a' the rental besides.' George was never more at a loss than for an answer to parry this thrust; but, fortunately for him, Walter rose and left the room, and, as he had taken no dinner, his mother followed to remonstrate with him against the folly of his conduct. Her exhortations and her menaces were, however, equally ineffectual; the poor natural was not to be moved; he felt his own despised and humiliated state; and the expectation which he had formed of the pleasure he was to enjoy, in again being permitted to caress and fondle his Betty Bodle, was so bitterly disappointed, that it cut him to the heart. No persuasion, no promise, could entice him to return to the dining-room; but a settled and rivetted resolution to go back to Glasgow obliged his mother to desist, and allow him to take his own way. He accordingly quitted the house, and immediately on arriving at home went to bed. Overpowered by the calls of hunger, he was next day allured to take some food; and from day to day after, for several years, he was in the same manner tempted to eat; but all power of volition, from the period of the visit, appeared to have become extinct within him. His features suffered a melancholy change, and he never spoke—nor did he seem to recognize any one; but gradually, as it were, the whole of his mind and intellect ebbed away, leaving scarcely the merest instincts of life. But the woeful form which Nature assumes in the death-bed of fatuity admonishes us to draw the curtain over the last scene of poor Watty.

Chapter XXVII

In the foregoing Chapter we were led, by our regard for the simple affections and harmless character of the second Laird, to overstep a period of several years. We must now, in consequence, return, and resume the narrative from the time that Walter retired from the company; but, without entering too minutely into the other occurrences of the day, we may be allowed to observe, in the sage words of the Leddy, that the party enjoyed themselves with as much insipidity as is commonly found at the formal feasts of near relations.

Mrs Charles Walkinshaw, put on her guard by the conjectures of the minister of Camrachle, soon perceived an evident partiality on the part of her brother-in-law towards her son, and that he took particular pains to make the boy attentive to Robina, as his daughter was called. Indeed, the design of George was so obvious, and the whole proceedings of the day so peculiarly marked, that even the Leddy could not but observe them.

'I'm thinking,' said she, 'that the seeds of a matrimony are sown among us this day, for Geordie's a far-before looking soothsayer, and a Chaldee excellence like his father; and a bodie does na need an e'e in the neck to discern that he's just wising and wiling for a purpose of marriage hereafter between Jamie and Beenie. Gudespeed the wark! for really we hae had but little luck among us since the spirit o' disinheritance got the upper hand; and it would be a great comfort if a' sores could be salved and healed in the fulness of time, when the weans can be married according to law.'

'I do assure you, mother,' replied her dutiful son, 'that nothing would give me greater pleasure; and I hope, that, by the frequent renewal of these little cordial and friendly meetings, we may help forward so desirable an event.'

'But,' replied the old Leddy piously, 'marriages are made in Heaven; and, unless there has been a booking among the angels above, a' that can be done by man below, even to the crying, for the third and last time, in the kirk, will be only a thrashing the water and a raising of bells. Howsever, the prayers of the righteous availeth much; and we should a' endeavour, by our walk and conversation, to compass a work so meet for repentance until it's brought to a come-to-pass. So I hope, Bell Fatherlans, that ye'll up and be doing in this good work, watching and praying, like those who stand on the tower of Siloam looking towards Lebanon.'

'I think,' said Mrs Charles smiling, 'that you are looking far forward. The children are still but mere weans, and many a day must pass over their green heads before such a project ought even to be thought of.'

'It's weel kent, Bell,' replied her mother-in-law, 'that ye were ne'er a queen of Sheba, either for wisdom or forethought; but I hae heard my friend that's awa—your worthy father, Geordie—often say, that as the twig is bent the tree's inclined, which is a fine sentiment, and should teach us to set about our undertakings with a knowledge of better things than of silver and gold, in order that we may be enabled to work the work o' Providence.'

But just as the Leddy was thus expatiating away in high solemnity, a dreadful cry arose among the pre-ordained lovers.

The children had quarrelled; and, notwithstanding all the admonitions which they had received to be kind to one another, Miss Robina had given James a slap on the face, which he repaid with such instantaneous energy, that, during the remainder of the visit, they were never properly reconciled.

Other causes were also in operation destined to frustrate the long-forecasting prudence of her father. Mr and Mrs Eadie, on their arrival at Edinburgh, took up their abode with her relation Mr Frazer, the intending purchaser of Glengael; and they had not been many days in his house, till they came to the determination to adopt Ellen, his eldest daughter, who was then about the age of James. Accordingly, after having promoted the object of their journey, when they returned to the manse of Camrachle, they were allowed to take Ellen with them; and the intimacy which arose among the children in the progress of time ripened into love between her and James. For although his uncle, in the prosecution of his own purpose, often invited the boy to spend several days together with his cousin at Kittlestonheugh, and did every thing in his power during those visits to inspire the children with a mutual affection, their distaste for each other seemed only to increase.

Robina was sly and demure, observant, quiet, and spiteful. Ellen, on the contrary, was full of buoyancy and glee, playful and generous, qualities which assimilated much more with the dispositions of James than those of his cousin, so that, long before her beauty had awakened passion, she was to him a more interesting and delightful companion.

The amusements, also, at Camrachle, were more propitious to the growth of affection than those at Kittlestonheugh, where every thing was methodized into system, and where, if the expression may be allowed, the genius of design and purpose controlled and repressed nature. The lawn was preserved in a state of neatness too trim for the gambols of childhood; and the walks were too winding for the straightforward impulses of its freedom and joy. At Camrachle the fields were open, and their expanse unbounded. The sun, James often thought, shone brighter there than at Kittlestonheugh; the birds sung sweeter in the wild broom than in his uncle's shrubbery, and the moonlight glittered like gladness in the burns; but on the wide water of the Clyde it was always dull and silent.

There are few situations more congenial to the diffusion of tenderness and sensibility—the elements of affection—than the sunny hills and clear waters of a rural neighbourhood, and few of all the beautiful scenes of Scotland excel the environs of Camrachle. The village stands on the slope of a gentle swelling ground, and consists of a single row of scattered thatched cottages, behind which a considerable stream carries its tributary waters to the Cart. On the east end stands the little church, in the centre of a small cemetery, and close to it the modest mansion of the minister. The house which Mrs Walkinshaw occupied was a slated cottage near the manse. It was erected by a native of the village, who had made a moderate competency as a tradesman in Glasgow; and, both in point of external appearance and internal accommodation, it was much superior to any other of the same magnitude in the parish. A few ash trees rose among the gardens, and several of them were tufted with the nests of magpies, the birds belonging to which had been so long in the practice of resorting there, that they were familiar to all the children of the village.

But the chief beauty in the situation of Camrachle is a picturesque and extensive bank, shaggy with hazel, along the foot of which runs the stream already mentioned. The green and gowany brow of this romantic terrace commands a wide and splendid view of all the champaign district of Renfrewshire. And it was often observed, by the oldest inhabitants, that whenever any of the natives of the clachan had been long absent, the first spot they visited on their return was the crown of this bank, where they had spent the sunny days of their childhood. Here the young Walkinshaws and Ellen Frazer also instinctively resorted, and their regard for each other was not only ever after endeared by the remembrance of their early pastimes there, but associated with delightful recollections of glorious summer sunshine, the fresh green mornings of spring, and the golden evenings of autumn.

Chapter XXVIII

As James approached his fourteenth year, his uncle, still with a view to a union with Robina, proposed, that, when Mr Eadie thought his education sufficient for the mercantile profession, he should be sent to his countinghouse. But the early habits and the tenor of the lessons he had received were not calculated to insure success to James as a merchant. He was robust, handsome, and adventurous, fond of active pursuits, and had imbibed, from the Highland spirit of Mrs Eadie, a tinge of romance and enthusiasm. The bias of his character, the visions of his reveries, and the cast of his figure and physiognomy, were decidedly military. But the field of heroic enterprise was then vacant,—the American war was over, and all Europe slumbered in repose, unconscious of the hurricane that was then gathering; and thus, without any consideration of his own inclinations and instincts, James, like many of those who afterwards distinguished themselves in the great conflict, acceded to the proposal.

He had not, however, been above three or four years settled in Glasgow when his natural distaste for sedentary and regular business began to make him dislike the place; and his repugnance was heightened almost to disgust by the discovery of his uncle's sordid views with respect to him; nor, on the part of his cousin, was the design better relished; for, independent of an early and ungracious antipathy, she had placed her affections on another object; and more than once complained to the old Leddy of her father's tyranny in so openly urging on a union that would render her miserable, especially, as she said, when her cousin's attachment to Ellen Frazer was so unequivocal. But Leddy Grippy had set her mind on the match as strongly as her son; and, in consequence, neither felt nor showed any sympathy for Robina.

'Never fash your head,' she said to her one day, when the young lady was soliciting her mediation,—'Never fash your head, Beenie, my dear, about Jamie's calf-love for yon daffodil; but be an obedient child, and walk in the paths of pleasantness that ye're ordain't to, both by me and your father; for we hae had oure lang a divided family; and it's full time we were brought to a cordial understanding with one another.'

'But,' replied the disconsolate damsel, 'even though he had no previous attachment, I'll ne'er consent to marry him, for really I can never fancy him.'

'And what for can ye no fancy him? cried the Leddy—'I would like to ken that? But, to be plain wi' you, Beenie, it's a shame to hear a weel educated miss like you, brought up wi' a Christian principle, speaking about fancying young men. Sic a thing was never alloo't nor heard tell o' in my day and generation. But that comes o' your ganging to see Douglas tragedy, at that kirk o' Satan in Dunlop Street; where, as I am most creditably informed, the play-actors' court ane another afore a' the folk.'

'I am sure you have yourself experienced,' replied Robina, 'what it is to entertain a true affection, and to know that our wishes and inclinations are not under our own control.—How would you have liked had your father forced you to marry a man against your will?'

'Lassie, lassie!' exclaimed the Leddy, 'if ye live to be a grandmother like me, ye'll ken the right sense o' a lawful and tender affection. But there's no sincerity noo like the auld sincerity, when me and your honest grandfather, that was in mine, and is noo in Abraham's bosom, came thegither—we had no foistring and parley-vooing, like your novelle turtle-doves—but discoursed in a sober and wise-like manner anent the cost and charge o' a family; and the upshot was a visibility of solid cordiality and kindness, very different, Beenie, my dear, frae the puff-paste love o' your Clarissy Harlots.'

'Ah! but your affection was mutual from the beginning—you were not perhaps devoted to another?'

'Gude guide us, Beenie Walkinshaw! are ye devoted to another?—Damon and Phillis, pastorauling at hide and seek wi' their sheep, was the height o' discretion, compared wi' sic curdooing. My lass, I'll let no grass grow beneath my feet, till I hae gi'en your father notice o' this loup-the-window, and hey cockalorum-like love.'

'Impossible!' exclaimed the young lady; 'you will never surely be so rash as to betray me?'

'Wha is't wi'? But I need na speer; for I'll be none surprised to hear that it's a play-actor, or a soldier officer, or some other clandestine poetical.'

Miss possessed more shrewdness than her grandmother gave her credit for, and perceiving the turn and tendency of their conversation, she exerted all her address to remove the impression which she had thus produced, by affecting to laugh, saying,—

'What has made you suppose that I have formed any improper attachment? I was only anxious that you should speak to my father, and try to persuade him that I can never be happy with my cousin.'

'How can I persuade him o' ony sic havers? or how can ye hope that I would if it was in my power—when ye know what a comfort it will be to us a', to see such a prudent purpose o' marriage brought to perfection?—Na, na, Beenie, ye're an instrument in the hands o' Providence to bring aboot a great blessing to your family; and I would be as daft as your uncle Watty, when he gaed out to shoot the flees, were I to set mysel an adversary to such a righteous ordinance—so you maun just mak up your mind to conform. My word, but ye're weel aff to be married in your teens—I was past thirty before man speer't my price.'

'But,' said Robina, 'you forget that James himself has not yet consented—I am sure he is devoted to Ellen Frazer—and that he will never consent.'

'Weel, I declare if e'er I heard the like of sic upsetting.—I won'er what business either you or him hae to consenting or none consenting.—Is't no the pleasure o' your parentage that ye're to be married, and will ye dare to commit the sin of disobedient children? Beenie Walkinshaw, had I said sic a word to my father, who was a man o' past-ordinar sense, weel do I ken what I would hae gotten—I only just ance in a' my life, in a mistak, gied him a contradiction, and he declared that, had I been a son as I was but a dochter, he would hae grippit me by the cuff o' the neck and the back o' the breeks,' and shuttled me through the window. But the end o' the world is drawing near, and corruption's working daily to a head; a' modesty and maidenhood has departed frae womankind, and the sons of men are workers of iniquity—priests o' Baal, and transgressors every one—a', therefore, my leddy, that I hae to say to you is a word o' wisdom, and they ca't conform—Beenie, conform—and obey the fifth commandment.'

Robina was, however, in no degree changed by her grandmother's exhortations and animadversions; on the contrary, she was determined to take her own way, which is a rule that we would recommend to all young ladies, as productive of the happiest consequences in cases of the tender passion. But scarcely had she left the house, till Leddy Grippy, reflecting on what had passed, was not quite at ease in her mind, with respect to the sentimental insinuation of being devoted to another. For, although, in the subsequent conversation, the dexterity and address of the young lady considerably weakened the impression which it had at first made, still enough remained to make her suspect it really contained more than was intended to have been conveyed. But, to avoid unnecessary disturbance, she resolved to give her son a hint to observe the motions of his daughter, while, at the same time, she also determined to ascertain how far there was any ground to suppose that from the attachment of James to Ellen Frazer, there was reason to apprehend that he might likewise be as much averse to the projected marriage as Robina. And with this view she sent for him that evening—but what past will furnish matter for another Chapter.

Chapter XXIX

The Leddy was seated at her tea-table when young Walkinshaw arrived, and, as on all occasions when she had any intention in her head, she wore an aspect pregnant with importance. She was now an old woman, and had so long survived the sorrows of her widowhood, that even the weeds were thrown aside, and she had resumed her former dresses, unchanged from the fashion in which they were originally made. Her appearance, in consequence, was at once aged and ancient.

'Come your ways, Jamie,' said she, 'and draw in a chair and sit down; but, afore doing sae, tell the lass to bring ben the treck-pot,'—which he accordingly did; and as soon as the treck-pot, alias teapot, was on the board, she opened her trenches.

'Jamie,' she began, 'your uncle George has a great notion of you, and has done muckle for your mother, giving her, o' his own freewill, a handsome 'nuity; by the which she has brought you, and Mary your sister, up wi' great credit and confort. I would therefore fain hope, that, in the way o' gratitude, there will be no slackness on your part.'

James assured her that he had a very strong sense of his uncle's kindness; and that, to the best of his ability, he would exert himself to afford him every satisfaction; but that Glasgow was not a place which he much liked, and that he would rather go abroad, and push his fortune elsewhere, than continue confined to the counting-house.

'There's baith sense and sadness, Jamie, in what ye say,' replied the Leddy; 'but I won'er what ye would do abroad, when there's sic a bein beild biggit for you at home. Ye ken, by course o' nature, that your uncle's ordaint to die, and that he has only his ae dochter Beenie, your cousin, to inherit the braw conquest o' your worthy grandfather—the whilk, but for some mistak o' law, and the sudden o'ercome o' death amang us, would hae been yours by right o' birth. So that it's in a manner pointed out to you by the forefinger o' Providence to marry Beenie.'

James was less surprised at this suggestion than the old lady expected, and said, with a degree of coolness that she was not prepared for,—

'I dare say what you speak of would not be disagreeable to my uncle, for several times he has himself intimated as much, but it is an event that can never take place.'

'And what for no? I'm sure Beenie's fortune will be a better bargain than a landless lad like you can hope for at ony other hand.'

'True, but I'll never marry for money.'

'And what will ye marry for, then?' exclaimed the Leddy. 'Tak my word o' experience for't, my man,—a warm downseat's o' far mair consequence in matrimony than the silly low o' love; and think what a bonny business your father and mother made o' their gentle-shepherding. But, Jamie, what's the reason ye'll no tak Beenie?—there maun surely be some because for sic unnaturality?'

'Why,' said he laughing, 'I think it's time enough for me yet to be dreaming o' marrying.'

'That's no a satisfaction to my question; but there's ae thing I would fain gie you warning o', and that's, if ye'll no marry Beenie, I dinna think ye can hae ony farther to look, in the way o' patronage, frae your uncle.'

'Then,' said James indignantly, 'if his kindness is only given on such a condition as that, I ought not to receive it an hour longer.'

'Here's a tap o' tow!' exclaimed the Leddy. 'Aff and awa wi' you to your mother at Camrachle, and gallant about the braes and dyke-sides wi' that lang windlestrae-legget tawpie, Nell Frizel—She's the because o' your rebellion. 'Deed ye may think shame o't, Jamie; for it's a' enough to bring disgrace on a' manner o' affection to hear what I hae heard about you and her.'

'What have you heard?' cried he, burning with wrath and indignation.

'The callan's gaun aff at the head, to look at me as if his e'en were pistols—How dare ye, Sir?—But it's no worth my while to lose my temper wi' a creature that doesna ken the homage and honour due to his aged grandmother. Howsever, I'll be as plain as I'm pleasant wi' you my man; and if there's no an end soon put to your pastoraulity wi' yon Highland heron, and a sedate and dutiful compliancy vouchsafed to your benefactor, uncle George, there will be news in the land or lang.'

'You really place the motives of my uncle's conduct towards me in a strange light, and you forget that Robina is perhaps as strongly averse to the connection as I am.'

'So she would fain try to gar me true,' replied the Leddy; 'the whilk is a most mystical thing; but, poor lassie, I needna be surprised at it, when she jealouses that your affections are set on a loup-the-dyke Jenny Cameron like Nell Frizel. Howsever, Jamie, no to make a confabble about the matter, there can be no doubt if ye'll sing "We'll gang nae mair to yon toun," wi' your back to the manse o' Camrachle, that

Beenie, who is a most sweet-tempered and obedient fine lassie, will soon be wrought into a spirit of conformity wi' her father's will and my wishes.'

'I cannot but say,' replied Walkinshaw, 'that you consider affection as very pliant. Nor do I know why you take such liberties with Miss Frazer; who, in every respect, is infinitely superior to Robina.'

'Her superior!' cried the Leddy; 'but love's blin' as well as fey, or ye would as soon think o' likening a yird lead to a patrick or a turtle-dove, as Nell Frizel to Beenie Walkinshaw. Eh man! Jamie, but ye hae a poor taste; and I may say, as the auld sang sings, "Will ye compare a docken till a tansie?" I would na touch her wi' the tangs.'

'But you know,' said Walkinshaw, laughing at the excess of her contempt, 'that there is no accounting for tastes.'

'The craw thinks it's ain bird the whitest,' replied the Leddy; 'but, for a' that, it's as black as the back o' the bress; and, therefore, I would advise you to believe me, that Nell Frizel is just as ill-far't a creature as e'er came out the Maker's hand. I hae lived threescore and fifteen years in the world, and surely, in the course o' nature, should ken by this time what beauty is, and ought to be.'

How far the Leddy might have proceeded with her argument is impossible to say; for it was suddenly interrupted by her grandson bursting into an immoderate fit of laughter, which had the effect of instantly checking her eloquence, and turning the course of her ideas and animadversions into another channel. In the course, however, of a few minutes, she returned to the charge, but with no better success; and Walkinshaw left her, half resolved to come to some explanation on the subject with his uncle. It happened, however, that this discussion, which we have just related, took place on a Saturday night; and the weather next day being bright and beautiful, instead of going to his uncle's at Kittlestonheugh, as he commonly did on Sunday, from the time he had been placed in the counting-house, he rose early, and walked to Camrachle, where he arrived to breakfast, and afterwards accompanied his mother and sister to church.

The conversation with the old Leddy was still ringing in his ears, and her strictures on the beauty and person of Ellen Frazer seemed so irresistibly ridiculous, when he beheld her tall and elegant figure advancing to the minister's pew, that he could with difficulty preserve the decorum requisite to the sanctity of the place. Indeed, the effect was so strong, that Ellen herself noticed it; insomuch, that, when they met after sermon in the churchyard, she could not refrain from asking what had tickled him. Simple as the question was, and easy as the explanation might have been, he found himself, at the moment, embarrassed, and at a loss to answer her. Perhaps, had they been by themselves, this would not have happened; but Mrs Eadie, and his mother and sister, were present. In the evening, however, when he accompanied Mary and her to a walk, along the brow of the hazel bank, which overlooked the village, he took an opportunity of telling her what had passed, and of expressing his determination to ascertain how far his uncle was seriously bent on wishing him to marry Robina; protesting, at the same time, that it was a union which could never be—intermingled with a thousand little tender demonstrations, infinitely more delightful to the ears of Ellen than it is possible to make them to our readers. Indeed, Nature plainly shows, that the conversations of lovers are not fit for the public, by the care which she takes to tell the gentle parties, that they must speak in whispers, and choose retired spots and shady bowers, and other sequestered poetical places, for their conferences.

Chapter XXX

The conversations between the Leddy and her grandchildren were not of a kind to keep with her. On Monday morning she sent for her son, and, without explaining to him what had passed, cunningly began to express her doubts if ever a match would take place between James and Robina; recommending that the design should be given up, and an attempt made to conciliate a union between his daughter and her cousin Dirdumwhamle's son, by which, as she observed, the gear would still be kept in the family.

George, however, had many reasons against the match, not only with respect to the entail, but in consideration of Dirdumwhamle having six sons by his first marriage, and four by his second, all of whom stood between his nephew and the succession to his estate. It is, therefore, almost unnecessary to say, that he had a stronger repugnance to his mother's suggestion than if she had proposed a stranger rather than their relation.

'But,' said he, 'what reason have you to doubt that James and Robina are not likely to gratify our hopes and wishes? He is a very well-behaved lad; and though his heart does not appear to lie much to the business of the counting-house, still he is so desirous, apparently, to give satisfaction, that I have no doubt in time he will acquire steadiness and mercantile habits.'

'It would na be easy to say,' replied the Leddy, 'a' the whys and wherefores that I hae for my suspicion. But, ye ken, if the twa hae na a right true love and kindness for ane anither, it will be a doure job to make them happy in the way o' matrimonial felicity; and, to be plain wi' you, Geordie, I would be nane surprised if something had kittled between Jamie and a Highland lassie, ane Nell Frizel, that bides wi' the new-light minister o'Camrachle.'

The Laird had incidentally heard of Ellen, and once or twice, when he happened to visit his sister-in-law, he had seen her, and was struck with her beauty. But it had never occurred to him that there was any attachment between her and his nephew. The moment, however, that the Leddy mentioned her name, he acknowledged to himself its probability.

'But do you really think,' said he anxiously, 'that there is any thing of the sort between her and him?'

'Frae a' that I can hear, learn, and understand,' replied the Leddy, 'though it may na be probable-like, yet I fear it's oure true; for when he gangs to see his mother, and it's ay wi' him as wi' the saints,—"O mother dear Jerusalem, when shall I come to thee?"—I am most creditably informed that the twa do nothing but sauly forth hand in hand to walk in the green vallies, singing, "Low down in the broom," and "Pu'ing lilies both fresh and gay,"—which is as sure a symptom o' something very like love, as the hen's cackle is o' a new-laid egg.'

'Nevertheless,' said the Laird, 'I should have no great apprehensions, especially when he comes to understand how much it is his interest to prefer Robina.'

'That's a' true, Geordie; but I hae a misdoot that a's no right and sound wi' her mair than wi' him; and when we reflek how the mim maidens now-a-days hae delivered themselves up to the Little-gude in the shape and glamour o' novelles and Thomson's Seasons, we need be nane surprised to fin' Miss as headstrong in her obdooracy as the lovely young Lavinia that your sister Meg learnt to 'cite at the boarding-school.'

'It is not likely, however,' said the Laird, 'that she has yet fixed her affections on any one; and a very little attention on the part of James would soon overcome any prejudice that she may happen to have formed against him,—for now, when you bring the matter to mind, I do recollect that I have more than once observed a degree of petulance and repugnance on her part.'

'Then I mak no doot,' exclaimed the old lady, 'that she is in a begoted state to another, and it wou'd be wise to watch her. But, first and foremost, you should sift Jamie's tender passion—that's the novelle name for calf-love; and if it's within the compass o 'a possibility, get the swine driven through'!, or it may work us a' muckle dule, as his father's moonlight marriage did to your ain, worthy man!—That was indeed a sair warning to us a', and is the because to this day o' a' the penance o' vexation and tribulation that me and you, Geordie, are sae obligated to dree.'

The admonition was not lost; on the contrary, George, who was a decisive man of business, at once resolved to ascertain whether there were indeed any reasonable grounds for his mother's suspicions. For this purpose, on returning to the counting-house, he requested Walkinshaw to come in the evening to Kittlestonheugh, as he had something particular to say. The look and tone with which the communication was made convinced James that he could not be mistaken with respect to the topic intended, which, he conjectured, was connected with the conversation he had himself held with the Leddy on the preceding Saturday evening; and it was the more agreeable to him, as he was anxious to be relieved from the doubts which began to trouble him regarding the views and motives of his uncle's partiality. For, after parting from Ellen, he had, in the course of his walk back to Glasgow, worked himself up into a determination to quit the place, if any hope of the suggested marriage with Robina was the tenure by which he held her father's favour. His mind, in consequence, as he went to Kittlestonheugh in the evening, was occupied with many plans and schemes—the vague and aimless projects which fill the imagination of youth, when borne forward either by hopes or apprehensions. Indeed, the event contemplated, though it was still contingent on the spirit with which his uncle might receive his refusal, he yet, with the common precipitancy of youth, anticipated as settled, and his reflections were accordingly framed and modified by that conclusion. To leave Glasgow was determined; but where to go, and what to do, were points not so easily arranged; and ever and anon the image of Ellen Frazer rose in all the radiance of her beauty, like the angel to Balaam, and stood between him and his purpose.

The doubts, the fears, and the fondness, which alternately predominated in his bosom, received a secret and sympathetic energy from the appearance and state of external nature. The weather was cloudy but not lowering—a strong tempest seemed, however, to be raging at a distance; and several times he paused and looked back at the enormous masses of dark and troubled vapour, which were drifting along the whole sweep of the northern horizon, from Ben Lomond to the Ochils, as if some awful burning was laying waste the world beyond them; while a long and splendid stream of hazy sunshine, from behind the Cowal mountains, brightened the rugged summits of Dumbuck, and, spreading its golden fires over Dumbarton moor, gilded the brow of Dumgoin, and lighted up the magnificent vista which opens between them of the dark and distant Grampians.

The appearance of the city was also in harmony with the general sublimity of the evening. Her smoky canopy was lowered almost to a covering—a mist from the river hovered along her skirts and scattered buildings, but here and there some lofty edifice stood proudly eminent, and the pinnacles of the steeples glittering like spear-points through the cloud, suggested to the fancy strange and solemn images of heavenly guardians, stationed to oppose the adversaries of man.

A scene so wild, so calm, and yet so troubled and darkened, would, at any time, have heightened the enthusiasm of young Walkinshaw, but the state of his feelings made him more than ordinarily susceptible to the eloquence of its various lights and shadows. The uncertainty which wavered in the prospects of his future life, found a mystical reflex in the swift and stormy wrack of the carry, that some unfelt wind was silently urging along the distant horizon. The still and stationary objects around—the protected city and the everlasting hills, seemed to bear an assurance, that, however obscured the complexion of his fortunes might at that moment be, there was still something within himself that ought not to suffer any change, from the evanescent circumstances of another's frown or favour. This confidence in himself, felt perhaps for the first time that evening, gave a degree of vigour and decision to the determination which he had formed; and by the time he had reached the porch of his uncle's mansion, his step was firm, his emotions regulated, and a full and manly self-possession had succeeded to the fluctuating feelings, with which he left Glasgow, in so much that even his countenance seemed to have received some new impress, and to have lost the softness of youth, and taken more decidedly the cast and characteristics of manhood.

Chapter XXXI

Walkinshaw found his uncle alone, who, after some slight inquiries, relative to unimportant matters of business, said to him,—

'I have been desirous to see you, because I am anxious to make some family arrangements, to which, though I do not anticipate any objection on your part, as they will be highly advantageous to your interests, it is still proper that we should clearly understand each other respecting. It is unnecessary to inform you, that, by the disinheritance of your father, I came to the family estate, which, in the common course of nature, might have been yours—and you are quite aware, that, from the time it became necessary to cognosce your uncle, I have uniformly done more for your mother's family than could be claimed or was expected of me.'

'I am sensible of all that, Sir,' replied Walkinshaw, 'and I hope there is nothing which you can reasonably expect me to do, that I shall not feel pleasure in performing.'

His uncle was not quite satisfied with this; the firmness with which it was uttered, and the self-reservation which it implied—were not propitious to his wishes, but he resumed,—

'In the course of a short time, you will naturally be looking to me for some establishment in business, and certainly if you conduct yourself as you have hitherto done, it is but right that I should do something for you—much, however, will depend, as to the extent of what I may do, on the disposition with which you fall in with my views. Now, what I wish particularly to say to you is, that having but one child, and my circumstances enabling me to retire from the active management of the house, it is in my power to resign a considerable share in your favour—and this it is my wish to do in the course of two or three years; if—' and he paused, looking his nephew steadily in the face.

'I trust,' said Walkinshaw, 'it can be coupled with no condition that will prevent me from availing myself of your great liberality.'

His uncle was still more damped by this than by the former observation, and he replied peevishly,—

'I think, young man, considering your destitute circumstances, you might be a little more grateful for my friendship. It is but a cold return to suppose I would subject you to any condition that you would not gladly agree to.'

This, though hastily conceived, was not so sharply expressed as to have occasioned any particular sensation; but the train of Walkinshaw's reflections, with his suspicion of the object for which he was that evening invited to the country, made him feel it acutely, and his blood mounted at the allusion to his poverty. Still without petulance, but in an emphatic manner, he replied,—

'I have considered your friendship always as disinterested, and as such I have felt and cherished the sense of gratitude which it naturally inspired; but I frankly confess, that, had I any reason to believe it was less so than I hope it is, I doubt I should be unable to feel exactly as I have hitherto, felt.'

'And in the name of goodness!' exclaimed his uncle, at once surprised and apprehensive; 'what reason have you to suppose that I was not actuated by my regard for you as my nephew?'

'I have never had any, nor have I said so,' replied Walkinshaw; 'but you seem to suspect that I may not be so agreeable to some purpose you intend as the obligations you have laid me under, perhaps, entitle you to expect.'

'The purpose I intend,' said the uncle, 'is the strongest proof that I can give you of my affection. It is nothing less than founded on a hope that you will so demean yourself, as to give me the pleasure, in due time, of calling you by a dearer name than nephew.'

Notwithstanding all the preparations which Walkinshaw had made to hear the proposal with firmness, it overcame him like a thunder-clap—and he sat some time looking quickly from side to side, and unable to answer.

'You do not speak,' said his uncle, and he added, softly and inquisitively, 'Is there any cause to make you averse to Robina?—I trust I may say to you, as a young man of discretion and good sense, that there is no green and foolish affection which ought for a moment to weigh with you against the advantages of a marriage with your cousin—Were there nothing else held out to you, the very circumstance of regaining so easily the patrimony, which your father had so inconsiderately forfeited, should of itself be sufficient. But, besides that, on the day you are married to Robina, it is my fixed intent to resign the greatest part of my concern in the house to you, thereby placing you at once in opulence.'

While he was thus earnestly speaking, Walkinshaw recovered his self-possession; and being averse to give a disagreeable answer, he said, that he could not but duly estimate, to the fullest extent, all the advantages which the connection would insure; but, said he, 'Have you spoken to Robina herself?'

'No,' replied his uncle, with a smile of satisfaction, anticipating from the question something like a disposition to acquiesce in his views. 'No; I leave that to you—that's your part. You now know my wishes; and I trust and hope you are sensible that few proposals could be made to you so likely to promote your best interests.'

Walkinshaw saw the difficulties of his situation. He could no longer equivocate with them. It was impossible, he felt, to say that he would speak on the subject to Robina, without being guilty of duplicity towards his uncle. Besides this, he conceived it would sully the honour and purity of his affection for Ellen Frazer to allow himself to seek any declaration of refusal from Robina, however certain of receiving it. His uncle saw his perplexity, and said,—

'This proposal seems to have very much disconcerted you—but I will be plain; for, in a matter on which my heart is so much set, it is prudent to be candid. I do not merely suspect, but have some reason to believe, that you have formed a schoolboy attachment to Mrs Eadie's young friend. Now, without any other remark on the subject, I will only say, that, though Miss Frazer is a very fine girl, and of a most respectable family, there is nothing in the circumstances of her situation compared with those of your cousin, that would make any man of sense hesitate between them.'

So thought Walkinshaw; for, in his opinion, the man of sense would at once prefer Ellen.

'However,' continued his uncle,—'I will not at present press this matter farther. I have opened my mind to you, and I make no doubt, that you will soon see the wisdom and propriety of acceding to my wishes.'

Walkinshaw thought he would be acting unworthy of himself if he allowed his uncle to entertain any hope of his compliance; and, accordingly, he said, with some degree of agitation, but not so much as materially to affect the force with which he expressed himself,—

'I will not deny that your information with respect to Miss Frazer is correct; and the state of our sentiments renders it impossible that I should for a moment suffer you to expect I can ever look on Robina but as my cousin.'

'Well, well, James,' interrupted his uncle,—'I knew all that; and I calculated on hearing as much, and even more; but take time to reflect on what I have proposed; and I shall be perfectly content to see the result in your actions. So, let us go to your aunt's room, and take tea with her and Robina.'

'Impossible!—never!' exclaimed Walkinshaw, rising;—'I cannot allow you for a moment longer to continue in so fallacious an expectation. My mind is made up; my decision was formed before I came here; and no earthly consideration will induce me to forego an affection that has grown with my growth, and strengthened with my strength.'

His uncle laughed, and rubbed his hands, exceedingly amused at this rhapsody, and said, with the most provoking coolness,—

'I shall not increase your flame by stirring the fire—you are still but a youth—and it is very natural that you should have a love fit—all, therefore, that I mean to say at present is, take time—consider—reflect on the fortune you may obtain, and contrast it with the penury and dependence to which your father and mother exposed themselves by the rash indulgence of an inconsiderate attachment.'

'Sir,' exclaimed Walkinshaw, fervently, 'I was prepared for the proposal you have made, and my determination with respect to it was formed and settled before I came here.'

'Indeed!' said his uncle coldly; 'and pray what is it?'

'To quit Glasgow; to forego all the pecuniary advantages that I may derive from my connection with you—if '—and he made a full stop and looked his uncle severely in the face,—'if,' he resumed, 'your kindness was dictated with a view to this proposal.'

A short silence ensued, in which Walkinshaw still kept his eye brightly and keenly fixed on his uncle's face; but the Laird was too much a man of the world not to be able to endure this scrutiny.

'You are a strange fellow,' he at last said, with a smile, that he intended should be conciliatory; 'but as I was prepared for a few heroics I can forgive you.'

'Forgive!' cried the hot and indignant youth; 'what have I done to deserve such an insult? I thought your kindness merited my gratitude. I felt towards you as a man should feel towards a great benefactor; but now it would almost seem that you have in all your kindness but pursued some sinister purpose. Why am I selected to be your instrument? Why are my feelings and affections to be sacrificed on your sordid altars?'

He found his passion betraying him into irrational extravagance, and, torn by the conflict within him, he covered his face with his hands, and burst into tears.

'This is absolute folly, James,' said his uncle soberly.

'It is not folly,' was again his impassioned answer. 'My words may be foolish, but my feelings are at this moment wise. I cannot for ten times all your fortune, told a hundred times, endure to think I may be induced to barter my heart. It may be that I am ungrateful; if so, as I can never feel otherwise upon the subject than I do, send me away, as unworthy longer to share your favour; but worthy I shall nevertheless be of something still better.'

'Young man, you will be more reasonable to-morrow,' said his uncle contemptuously, and immediately left the room. Walkinshaw at the same moment also took his hat, and, rushing towards the door, quitted the house; but in turning suddenly round the corner, he ran against Robina, who, having some idea of the object of his visit, had been listening at the window to their conversation.

Chapter XXXII

The agitation in which Walkinshaw was at the moment when he encountered Robina, prevented him from being surprised at meeting her, and also from suspecting the cause which had taken her to that particular place so late in the evening. The young lady was more cool and collected, as we believe young ladies always are on such occasions, and she was the first who spoke.

'Where are you running so fast?' said she. 'I thought you would have staid tea. Will you not go back with me? My mother expects you.'

'Your father does not,' replied Walkinshaw tersely; 'and I wish it had been my fortune never to have set my foot within his door.'

'Dear me!' exclaimed Miss Robina, as artfully as if she had known nothing, nor overheard every word which had passed. 'What has happened? I hope nothing has occurred to occasion any quarrel between you. Do think, James, how prejudicial it must be to your interests to quarrel with my father.'

'Curse that eternal word interests!' was the unceremonious answer. 'Your father seems to think that human beings have nothing but interests; that the heart keeps a ledger, and values every thing in pounds sterling. Our best affections, our dearest feelings, are with him only as tare, that should pass for nothing in the weight of moral obligations.'

'But stop,' said Robina, 'don't be in such a hurry; tell me what all this means—what has affections and dear feelings to do with your countinghouse affairs?—I thought you and he never spoke of any thing but rum puncheons and sugar cargoes.'

'He is incapable of knowing the value of any thing less tangible and vendible!' exclaimed her cousin—'but I have done with both him and you.'

'Me!' cried Miss Robina, with an accent of the most innocent admiration, that any sly and shrewd miss of eighteen could possibly assume.—'Me! what have I to do with your hopes and your affections, and your tangible and vendible commodities?'

'I beg your pardon, I meant no offence to you, Robina—I am overborne by my feelings,' said Walkinshaw; 'and if you knew what has passed, you would sympathise with me.'

'But as I do not,' replied the young lady coolly, 'you must allow me to say that your behaviour appears to me very extravagant—surely nothing has passed between you and my father that I may not know?'

This was said in a manner that instantly recalled Walkinshaw to his senses. The deep and cunning character of his cousin he had often before remarked—with, we may say plainly, aversion—and he detected at once in the hollow and sonorous affectation of sympathy with which her voice was tuned, particularly in the latter clause of the sentence, the insincerity and hypocrisy of her conduct.—He did not, however, suspect that she had been playing the eaves-dropper; and, therefore, still tempered with moderation his expression of the sentiments she was so ingeniously leading him on to declare.

'No,' said he calmly, 'nothing has passed between your father and me that you may not know, but it will come more properly from him, for it concerns you, and in a manner that I can never take interest or part in.'

'Concerns me! concerns me!' exclaimed the actress; 'it is impossible that any thing of mine could occasion a misunderstanding between you.'

'But it has,' said Walkinshaw; 'and to deal with you, Robina, as you ought to be dealt with, for affecting to be so ignorant of your father's long evident wishes and intents—he has actually declared that he is most anxious we should be married.'

'I can see no harm in that,' said she, adding drily, 'provided it is not to one another.'

'But it is to one another,' said Walkinshaw, unguardedly, and in the simplicity of earnestness, which Miss perceiving, instantly with the adroitness of her sex turned to account—saying with well feigned diffidence,—

'I do not see why that should be so distressing to you.'

'No!' replied he. 'But the thing can never be, and it is of no use for us to talk of it—so good night.'

'Stay,' cried Robina,—'what you have told me deserves consideration.—Surely I have given you no reason to suppose that in a matter so important, I may not find it my interest to comply with my father's wishes.'

'Heavens!' exclaimed Walkinshaw, raising his clenched hands in a transport to the skies.

'Why are you so vehement?' said Robina.

'Because,' replied he solemnly, 'interest seems the everlasting consideration of our family—interest disinherited my father—interest made my uncle Walter consign my mother to poverty—interest proved the poor repentant wretch insane—interest claims the extinction of all I hold most precious in life,—and interest would make me baser than the most sordid of all our sordid race.'

'Then I am to understand you dislike me so much, that you have refused to accede to my father's wishes, for our mutual happiness?'

'For our mutual misery, I have refused to accede,' was the abrupt reply—'and if you had not some motive for appearing to feel otherwise—which motive I neither can penetrate nor desire to know, you would be as resolute in your objection to the bargain as I am—match I cannot call it, for it proceeds in a total oblivion of all that can endear or ennoble such a permanent connection.'

Miss was conscious of the truth of this observation, and with all her innate address, it threw her off her guard, and she said,—

'Why do you suppose that I am so insensible? My father may intend what he pleases, but my consent must be obtained before he can complete his intentions.' She had, however, scarcely said so much, when she perceived she was losing the 'vantage-ground that she had so dexterously occupied, and she turned briskly round and added, 'But, James, why should we fall out about this?—there is time enough before us to consider the subject dispassionately—my father cannot mean that the marriage should take place immediately.'

'Robina, you are your father's daughter, and the heiress of his nature as well as of his estate—no such marriage ever can or shall take place; nor do you wish it should—but I am going too far—it is enough that I declare my affections irrevocably engaged, and that I will never listen to a second proposition on that subject, which has to-night driven me wild. I have quitted your father—I intend it for ever—I will never return to his office.

All that I built on my connection with him is now thrown down—perhaps with it my happiness is also lost—but no matter, I cannot be a dealer in such bargaining as I have heard to-night. I am thankful to Providence that gave me a heart to feel better, and friends who taught me to think more nobly. However, I waste my breath and spirits idly; my resolution is fixed, and when I say Good night, I mean Farewell.'

With these words he hurried away, and, after walking a short time on the lawn, Robina returned into the house; and going up to her mother's apartment, where her father was sitting, she appeared as unconcerned and unconscious of the two preceding conversations, as if she had neither been a listener to the one, nor an actress in the other.

On entering the room, she perceived that her father had been mentioning to her mother something of what had passed between himself and her cousin; but it was her interest, on account of the direction which her affections had taken, to appear ignorant of many things, and studiously to avoid any topic with her father that might lead him to suspect her bent; for she had often observed, that few individuals could be proposed to him as a match for her, that he entertained so strong a prejudice against; although really, in point of appearance, relationship, and behaviour, it could hardly be said that the object of her preference was much inferior to her romantic cousin.

The sources and motives of that prejudice she was, however, regardless of discovering. She considered it in fact as an unreasonable and unaccountable antipathy, and was only anxious for the removal of any cause that might impede the consummation she devoutly wished. Glad, therefore, to be so fully mistress of Walkinshaw's sentiments as she had that night made herself, she thought, by a judicious management of her knowledge, she might overcome her father's prejudice;—and the address and dexterity with which she tried this we shall attempt to describe in the following Chapter.

Chapter XXXIII

'I thought,' said she, after seating herself at the tea-table, 'that my cousin would have stopped to-night; but I understand he has gone away.'

'Perhaps,' replied her father, 'had you requested him, he might have staid.'

'I don't think he would for me,' was her answer.—'He does not appear particularly satisfied when I attempt to interfere with any of his proceedings.'

'Then you do sometimes attempt to interfere?' said her father, somewhat surprised at the observation, and not suspecting that she had heard one word of what had passed, every syllable of which was carefully stored in the treasury of her bosom.

The young lady perceived that she was proceeding a little too quickly, and drew in her horns.

'All,' said she, 'that I meant to remark was, that he is not very tractable, which I regret;' and she contrived to give a sigh.

'Why should you regret it so particularly?' inquired her father, a little struck at the peculiar accent with which she had expressed herself.

'I cannot tell,' was her adroit reply; and then she added, in a brisker tone,—'But I wonder what business I have to trouble myself about him?'

For some time her father made no return to this; but, pushing back his chair from the tea-table till he had reached the chimney-corner, he leant his elbow on the mantle-piece, and appeared for several minutes in a state of profound abstraction. In the meantime, Mrs Walkinshaw had continued the conversation with her daughter, observing to her that she did, indeed, think her cousin must be a very headstrong lad; for he had spoken that night to her father in such a manner as had not only astonished but distressed him. 'However,' said she,—'he is still a mere boy; and, I doubt not, will, before long is past, think better of what his uncle has been telling him.'

'I am extremely sorry,' replied Robina, with the very voice of the most artless sympathy, though, perhaps, a little more accentuated than simplicity would have employed—'I am very sorry, indeed, that any difference has arisen between him and my father. I am sure I have always heard him spoken of as an amiable and very deserving young man. I trust it is of no particular consequence.'

'It is of the utmost consequence,' interposed her father; 'and it is of more to you than to any other besides.'

'To me, Sir! how is that possible?—What have I to do with him, or he with me? I am sure, except in being more deficient in his civilities than those of most of my acquaintance, I have had no occasion to remark any thing particular in his behaviour or conduct towards me.'

'I know it—I know it,' exclaimed her father; 'and therein lies the source of all my anxiety.'

'I fear that I do not rightly understand you,' said the cunning girl.

'Nor do I almost wish that you ever should; but, nevertheless, my heart is so intent on the business, that I think, were you to second my endeavours, the scheme might be accomplished.'

'The scheme—What scheme?' replied the most unaffected Robina.

'In a word, child,' said her father, 'How would you like James as a husband?'

'How can I tell?' was her simple answer. 'He has never given me any reason to think on the subject.'

'You cannot, however, but long have seen that it was with me a favourite object?'

'I confess it;—and, perhaps, I have myself,' she said, with a second sigh—'thought more of it than I ought to have done; but I have never had any encouragement from him.'

'How unhappy am I,' thought her father to himself—'The poor thing is as much disposed to the match as my heart could hope for.—Surely, surely, by a little address and perseverance, the romantic boy may be brought to reason and to reflect;' and he then said to her—'My dear Robina, you have been the subject of my conversation with James this evening; but I am grieved to say, that his sentiments, at present, are neither favourable to your wishes nor to mine.—He seems enchanted by Mrs Eadie's relation, and talked so much nonsense on the subject that we almost quarrelled.'

'I shall never accept of a divided heart,' said the young lady despondingly; 'and I entreat, my dear father, that you will never take another step in the business; for, as long as I can recollect, he has viewed me with eyes of aversion—and in all that time he has been the playmate, and the lover, perhaps, of Ellen Frazer.—Again I implore you to abandon every idea of promoting a union between him and me: It can never take place on his part but from the most sordid considerations of interest; nor on mine without feeling that I have been but as a bale bargained for.'

Her father listened with attention to what she said—it appeared reasonable—it was spirited; but there was something, nevertheless, in it which did not quite satisfy his mind, though the sense was clear and complete.

'Of course,' he replied guardedly; 'I should never require you to bestow your hand where you had not already given your affections; but it does not follow, that because the headstrong boy is at this time taken up with Miss Frazer, that he is always to remain of the same mind. On the contrary, Robina, were you to exert a little address, I am sure you would soon draw him from that unfortunate attachment.'

'What woman,' said she, with an air of supreme dignity, 'would submit to pilfer the betrothed affections of any man? No—Sir, I cannot do that—nor ought I; and pardon me when I use the expression, nor will I. Had my cousin made himself more agreeable to me, I do not say that such would have been my sentiments; but having seen nothing in his behaviour that can lead me to hope from him any thing but the same constancy in his dislike which I have ever experienced, I should think myself base, indeed, were I to allow you to expect that I may alter my opinion.'

Nothing farther passed at that time; for to leave the impression which she intended to produce as strong as possible, she immediately rose and left the room. Her father soon after also quitted his seat, and after taking two or three turns across the floor, went to his own apartment.

'I am the most unfortunate of men,' said he to himself, 'and my poor Robina is no less frustrated in her affections. I cannot, however, believe that the boy is so entirely destitute of prudence as not to think of what I have told him. I must give him time. Old heads do not grow on young shoulders. But it never occurred to me that Robina was attached to him; on the contrary, I have always thought that the distaste was stronger on her part than on his. But it is of no use to vex myself on the subject. Let me rest satisfied to-night with having ascertained that at least on Robina's part there is no objection to the match. My endeavours hereafter must be directed to detach James from the girl Frazer. It will, however, be no easy task, for he is ardent and enthusiastic, and she has undoubtedly many of those graces which readiest find favour in a young man's eye.'

He then hastily rose, and hurriedly paced the room.

'Why am I cursed,' he exclaimed, 'with this joyless and barren fate? Were Robina a son, all my anxieties would be hushed; but with her my interest in the estate of my ancestors terminates. Her mother, however, may yet'—and he paused. 'It is very weak,' he added, in a moment after, 'to indulge in these reflections. I have a plain task before me, and instead of speculating on hopes and chances, I ought to set earnestly about it, and leave no stone unturned till I have performed it thoroughly.'

With this he composed his mind for the remainder of the evening, and when he again joined Robina and her mother, the conversation by all parties was studiously directed to indifferent topics.

Chapter XXXIV

There are few things more ludicrous, and at the same time more interesting, than the state of a young man in love, unless, perhaps, it be that of an old man in the same unfortunate situation. The warmth of the admiration, the blindness of the passion, and the fond sincerity of the enthusiasm, which gives grace and sentiment to the instinct, all awaken sympathy, and even inspire a degree of compassionate regard; but the extravagance of feeling beyond what any neutral person can sympathise with, the ostrich-like simplicity of the expedients resorted to in assignations, and that self-approved sagacity and prudence in concealing what every body with half an eye can see, afford the most harmless and diverting spectacles of human absurdity. However, as we are desirous of conciliating the reverence of the young and fair, perhaps it may be as well to say nothing more on this head, but allow them to enjoy, in undisturbed faith, the amiable anticipation of that state of beatitude which Heaven, and all married personages, know is but a very very transient enchantment.

But we cannot, with any regard to the fidelity of circumstantial history, omit to relate what passed in young Walkinshaw's bosom, after he parted from his cousin.—To render it in some degree picturesque, we might describe his appearance; but when we spoke of him as a handsome manly youth for his inches and his eild, we said perhaps as much as we could well say upon that head, unless we were to paint the colour and fashion of his clothes,—a task in which we have no particular relish;—and, therefore, we may just briefly mention, that they were in the style of the sprucest clerks of Glasgow; and every body knows, that if the bucks of the Trongate would only button their coats, they might pass for gentlemen of as good blood and breeding as the best in Bond Street. But, even though Walkinshaw had been in the practice of buttoning his, he was that night in no condition to think of it. His whole bosom was as a flaming furnace—raging as fiercely as those of the Muirkirk Iron Works that served to illuminate his path.

He felt as if he had been held in a state of degradation; and had been regarded as so destitute of all the honourable qualities of a young man, that he would not scruple to barter himself in the most sordid manner. His spirit then mounting on the exulting wings of youthful hope, bore him aloft into the cloudy and meteoric region of romance, and visions of fortune and glory almost too splendid for the aching sight of his fancy, presented themselves in a thousand smiling forms, beckoning him away from the smoky confines and foetid airs of Glasgow, and pointing to some of the brightest and beaming bubbles that allure fantastic youth. But, in the midst of these glittering visions of triumphant adventure, 'a change came o'er the spirit of his dream,' and he beheld Ellen Frazer in the simple and tasteful attire in which she appeared so beautiful at Camrachle church. In the back ground of the sunny scene was a pretty poetical cottage, with a lamb tethered by the foot on the green, surrounded by a flock of snowy geese, enjoying their noontide siesta, and on the ground troops of cocks and hens, with several gabbling bandy-legged ducks; at the sight of which another change soon came o'er the spirit of his dream; and the elegant mansion that his uncle had made of the old house of Grippy, with all its lawns and plantations, and stately gate and porter's lodge, together with an elegant carriage in the avenue, presented a most alluring picture.—But it, too, soon vanished; and in the next change, he beheld Robina converted into his wife, carping at all his little pranks and humours, and studious only of her own enjoyments, without having any consideration for those that might be his. Then all was instantly darkened; and after a terrible burst of whirlwinds, and thunder and lightning, the cloud again opened, and he saw in its phantasmagorial mirror—a calm and summer sunset, with his beautiful Ellen Frazer in the shape of a venerable matron, partaking of the temperate pleasures of an aged man, seated on a rustic seat, under a tree, on the brow of Camrachlebank, enjoying the beauties of the view, and talking of their children's children; and in the visage of that aged man, he discovered a most respectable resemblance of himself.—So fine a close of a life, untroubled by any mischance, malady, or injustice, could not fail to produce the most satisfactory result. Accordingly, he decidedly resolved, that it should be his; and that, as he had previously determined, the connection with his uncle should thenceforth be cut for ever.

By the time that imagination rather than reason had worked him into this decision, he arrived at Glasgow; and being resolved to carry his intention into immediate effect, instead of going to the house where he was boarded, at his uncle's expence, he went to the Leddy's, partly with the intention of remaining there, but chiefly to remonstrate with her for having spoken of his attachment to Ellen Frazer; having concluded, naturally enough, that it was from her his uncle had received the information.

On entering the parlour he found the old lady seated alone, in her elbow chair, at the fireside. A single slender candle stood at her elbow, on a small claw-foot table; and she was winding the yarn from a pirn, with a hand-reel, carefully counting the turns. Hearing the door open, she looked round, and seeing who it was, said,—

'Is that thee, Jamie Walkinshaw?—six and thirty—where came ye frae—seven and thirty—at this time o' night?—eight and thirty—sit ye down—nine and thirty—snuff the candle—forty.'

'I'll wait till ye're done,' said he, 'as I wish to tell you something—for I have been out at Kittlestonheugh, where I had some words with my uncle.'

'No possible!—nine and forty,'—replied the Leddy;—'what hast been about?—fifty.'——

'He seems to regard me as if I had neither a will nor feelings, neither a head nor a heart.'

'I hope ye hae baith—five and fifty—but hae ye been condumacious?—seven and—plague tak the laddie, I'm out in my count, and I'll hae to begin the cutt again; so I may set by the reel. What were you saying, Jamie, anent an outcast wi' your uncle?'

'He has used me exceedingly ill—ripping up the obligations he has laid me under, and taunting me with my poverty.'

'And is't no true that ye're obligated to him, and that, but for the uncly duty he has fulfilled towards you, ye would this night hae been a bare lad?—gude kens an ye would na hae been as scant o' deeding as a salmon in the river.'

'It may be so, but when it is considered that he got the family estate by a quirk of law, he could scarcely have done less than he did for my unfortunate father's family. But I could have forgiven all that, had he not, in a way insulting to my feelings, intimated that he expected I would break with Ellen Frazer, and offer myself to Robina.'

'And sure am I, Jamie,' replied the Leddy, 'that it will be lang before you can do better.'

'My mind, however, is made up,' said he; 'and to-morrow morning I shall go to Camrachle, and tell my mother that I have resolved to leave Glasgow.—I will never again set my foot in the counting-house.'

'Got ye ony drink, Jamie, in the gait hame, that ye're in sic a wud humour for dancing "Auld Sir Simon the King," on the road to Camrachle?—Man, an I had as brisk a bee in the bonnet, I would set aff at ance, cracking my fingers at the moon and seven stars as I gaed louping alang.—But, to speak the words of soberness, I'm glad ye hae discretion enough to tak a night's rest first.'

'Do not think so lightly of my determination—It is fixed—and, from the moment I quitted Kittlestonheugh, I resolved to be no longer under any obligation to my uncle—He considers me as a mere passive instrument for his own ends.'

'Hegh, Sirs! man, but ye hae a great share o' sagacity,' exclaimed the Leddy; 'and because your uncle is fain that ye should marry his only dochter, and would, if ye did sae, leave you for dowry and tocher a braw estate and a bank o' siller, ye think he has pookit you by the nose.'

'No—not for that; but because he thinks so meanly of me, as to expect that, for mercenary considerations, I would bargain away both my feelings and my principles.'

'Sure am I he would ne'er mint ony sic matter,' replied the Leddy; 'and if he wantit you to break wi' yon galloping nymph o' the Highland heather, and draw up wi' that sweet primroser creature, your cousin Beenie, wha is a lassie o' sense and composity, and might be a match to majesty, it was a' for your honour and exaltation.'

'Don't distress me any farther with the subject,' said he. 'Will you have the goodness to let me stay here to-night? for, as I told you, there shall never now be any addition made to the obligations which have sunk me so low.'

' 'Deed my lad, an ye gang on in that deleerit manner, I'll no only gie you a bed, but send baith for a doctor and a gradawa, that your head may be shaved, and a' proper remedies—outwardly and inwardly—gotten to bring you back to a right way o' thinking.—But to end a' debates, ye'll just pack up your ends and your awls and gang hame to Mrs Spruil's, for the tow's to spin and the woo's to card that 'ill be the sheets and blankets o' your bed in this house the night—tak my word for't.'

'In that case, I will at once go to Camrachle. The night is fine, and the moon's up.'

'Awa wi' you, and show how weel ye hae come to years o' discretion, by singing as ye gang,—

'Scotsman ho! Scotsman lo!
Where shall this poor Scotsman go?
Send him east, send him west,
Send him to the craw's next.'

Notwithstanding the stern mood that Walkinshaw was in, this latter sally of his grandmother's eccentric humour compelled him to laugh, and he said gaily, 'But I shall be none the worse of a little supper before I set out. I hope you will not refuse me that?'

The old Lady, supposing that she had effectually brought him, as she said, round to himself, cheerfully acquiesced; but she was not a little disappointed, when, after some light and ludicrous conversation on general topics, he still so persisted either to remain in the house or to proceed to his mother's, that she found herself obliged to order a bed to be prepared for him—at the same time she continued to express her confidence, that he would be in a more docile humour next morning. 'I hope,' said she, 'nevertheless, that the spirit of obedience will soople that stiff neck o' thine, in the slumbers and watches of the night, or I ne'er would be consenting to countenance such outstrapulous rebellion.'

END OF VOLUME SECOND

VOLUME III

Chapter I

Walkinshaw passed a night of 'restless ecstasy.' Sometimes he reflected on the proposition with all the coolness that the Laird himself could have desired; but still and anon the centripetal movement of the thoughts and feelings which generated this prudence was suddenly arrested before they had gravitated into any thing like resolution, and then he was thrown as wild and as wide from the object of his uncle's solicitude as ever.

In the calmer, perhaps it may therefore be said, in the wiser course of his reflections, Robina appeared to him a shrewd and sensible girl, with a competent share of personal beauty, and many other excellent household qualities, to make her a commendable wife. With her he would at once enter on the enjoyment of opulence, and with it independence; and, moreover, and above all, have it in his power to restore his mother and sister to that state in society, to which, by birth and original expectations, they considered themselves as having some claim. This was a pleasing and a proud thought; and not to indulge it at the expence of a little sacrifice of personal feeling, seemed to him selfish and unmanly. But then he would remember with what high-toned bravery of determination he had boasted to his uncle of his pure and unalterable affections; how contemptuously he had spoken of pecuniary inducements, and in what terms, too, he had told Robina herself, that she had nothing to hope from him. It was, therefore, impossible that he could present himself to either with any expression of regret for what had passed, without appearing, in the eyes of both, as equally weak and unworthy. But the very thought of finding that he could think of entertaining the proposition at all, was more acute and mortifying than even this; and he despised himself when he considered how Ellen Frazer would look upon him, if she knew he had been so base as, for a moment, to calculate the sordid advantages of preferring his cousin.

But what was to be done? To return to the counting-house, after his resolute declaration; to embark again in that indoor and tame drudgery which he ever hated, and which was rendered as vile as slavery, by the disclosures which had taken place, could not be. He would be baser than were he to sell himself to his uncle's purposes, could he yield to such a suggestion.

To leave Glasgow was his only alternative; but how? and where to go? and where to obtain the means? were stinging questions that he could not answer; and then what was he to gain? To marry Robina was to sacrifice Ellen Frazer; to quit the country entailed the same consequence. Besides all that, in so doing, he would add to the sorrows and the disappointments of his gentle-hearted and affectionate mother, who had built renewed hopes on his success under the auspices of his uncle, and who looked eagerly forward to the time when he should be so established in business as to bring his sister before the world in circumstances befitting his father's child; for the hereditary pride of family was mingled with his sensibility; and even the beautiful and sprightly Ellen Frazer herself, perhaps, owed something of her superiority over Robina to the Highland pedigrees and heroic traditions which Mrs Eadie delighted to relate of her ancestors.

While tossing on these troubled and conflicting tides of the mind, he happened to recollect, that a merchant, a school-fellow of his father, and who, when he occasionally met him, always inquired, with more than common interest, for his mother and sister, had at that time a vessel bound for New York, where he intended to establish a store, and was in want of a clerk; and it occurred to him, that, perhaps, through that means, he might accomplish his wishes. This notion was as oil to his agitation, and hope restored soon brought sleep and soothing dreams to his pillow; but his slumbers were not of long duration, for before sunrise he awoke; and, in order to avoid the garrulous remonstrances of the Leddy, he rose and went to Camrachle for the purpose, as he persuaded himself, to consult his mother; but, for all that we have been able to understand, it was in reality only to communicate his determination. But these sort of self-delusions are very common to youths under age.

The morning air, as he issued from Glasgow, was cold and raw. Heavy blobs of water, the uncongenial distillations of the midnight fogs, hung so dully on the hoary hedges, that even Poesy would be guilty of downright extravagance, were she, on any occasion, to call such gross uncrystalline knobs of physic glass by any epithet implying dew. The road was not miry, but gluey, and reluctant, and wearisome to the tread. The smoke from the farmhouses rolled listlessly down the thatch, and lazily spread itself into a dingy azure haze, that lingered and lowered among the stacks of the farmyards. The cows, instead of proceeding, with their ordinary sedate common sense, to the pastures, stood on the loans, looking east and west, and lowing to one another—no doubt concerning the state of the weather. The birds chirped peevishly, as they hopped from bough to bough. The ducks walked in silence to their accustomed pools. The hens, creatures at all times of a sober temperament, condoled in actual sadness together under sheds and bushes; and chanticleer himself wore a paler crest than usual, and was so low in spirits, that he only once had heart enough to wind his bugle-horn. Nature was sullen—and the herd-boy drew his blanket-mantle closer round him, and snarlingly struck the calf as he grudgingly drove the herd a-field. On the ground, at the door of the toll-bar house, lay a gill-stoup on its side, and near it, on a plate, an empty glass and a bit of bread, which showed that some earlier traveller had, in despite of the Statute, but in consideration of the damp and unwholesome morning, obtained a dram from the gudewife's ain bottle.

In consequence of these sympathetic circumstances, before Walkinshaw reached Camrachle, his heart was almost as heavy as his limbs were tired.

His mother, when she saw him pass the parlour window, as he approached the door, was surprised at his appearance, and suffered something like a shock of fear when she perceived the dulness of his eye and the dejection of his features.

'What has brought you here?' was her first exclamation; 'and what has happened?'

But, instead of replying, he walked in, and seated himself at the fireside, complaining of his cold and uncomfortable walk, and the heaviness of the road. His sister was preparing breakfast, and happening not to be in the room, his mother repeated her anxious inquiries with an accent of more earnest solicitude.

'I fear,' said Walkinshaw, 'that I am only come to distress you;' and he then briefly recapitulated what had passed between himself and his uncle respecting Robina. But a sentiment of tenderness for his mother's anxieties, blended with a wish to save her from the disagreeable sensation with which he knew his determination to quit Glasgow would affect her, made him suppress the communication that he had come expressly to make.

Mrs Walkinshaw had been too long accustomed to the occasional anticipations in which her brother-in-law had indulged on the subject, to be surprised at what had taken place on his part; and both from her own observations, and from the repugnance her son expressed, she had no doubt that his attachment to Ellen Frazer was the chief obstacle to the marriage. The considerations and reflections to which this conclusion naturally gave rise, held her for some time silent. The moment, however, that Walkinshaw, encouraged by the seeming slightness of her regret at his declamations against the match, proceeded to a fuller disclosure of his sentiments, and to intimate his resolution to go abroad, her maternal fears were startled, and she was plunged into the profoundest sorrow. But still during breakfast she said nothing—misfortune and disappointment had indeed so long subdued her gentle spirit into the most patient resignation, that, while her soul quivered in all its tenderest feelings, she seldom even sighed, but, with a pale cheek and a meek supplication, expressed only by a heavenward look of her mild and melancholy eyes, she seemed to say, 'Alas! am I still doomed to suffer?' That look was ever irresistible with her children: in their very childhood it brought them, with all their artless and innocent caresses, to her bosom; and, on this occasion, it so penetrated the very core of Walkinshaw's heart, that he took her by the hand and burst into tears.

Chapter II

We are no casuists, and therefore cannot undertake to determine whether Jenny did right or wrong in marrying Auld Robin Gray for the sake of her poor father and mother; especially as it has been ever held by the most approved moralists, that there are principles to be abided by, even at the expence of great and incontrovertible duties. But of this we are quite certain, that there are few trials to which the generous heart can be subjected more severe than a contest between its duties and its affections—between the claims which others have upon the conduct of the man for their advantage, and the desires that he has himself to seek his own gratification. In this predicament stood young Walkinshaw; and at the moment when he took his mother by the hand, the claims of filial duty were undoubtedly preferred to the wishes of love.

'I am,' said he, 'at your disposal, mother—do with me as you think fit.—When I resented the mean opinion that my uncle seemed to hold of me, I forgot you—I thought only of myself. My first duties, I now feel, are due to the world, and the highest of them to my family.—But I wish that I had never known Ellen Frazer.'

'In that wish, my dear boy, you teach me what I ought myself to do.—No, James, I can never desire nor expect that my children will sacrifice themselves for me—for I regard it as no less than immolation when the heart revolts at the tasks which the hand performs. But my life has long been one continued sorrow; and it is natural that I should shrink at the approach of another and a darker cloud. I will not, however, ask you to remain with your uncle, nor even oppose your resolution to go abroad. But be not precipitate—consider the grief, the anxieties, and the humiliations, that both your father and I have endured, and think, were you united to Ellen Frazer, supposing her father and friends would consent to so unequal a match, what would be her fate were you , cut early off, as your father was?—It is the thought of that—of what I myself, with you and for you, have borne, which weighs so grievously at this moment on my spirits.'

'Do you wish me to return to Glasgow?' said Walkinshaw with an anxious and agitated voice.

'Not unless you feel yourself that you can do so without humiliation—for bitter, James, as my cup has been, and ill able as I am to wrestle with the blast, I will never counsel child of mine to do that which may lessen him in his own opinion. Heaven knows that there are mortifications ready enough in the world to humble us—we do not need to make any for ourselves—no, unless you can meet your uncle with a frank face and a free heart, do not return.'

'I am sure, then, that I never can,' replied Walkinshaw. 'I feel as if he had insulted my nature, by venturing to express what he seems to think of me; and a man can forgive almost any injury but a mean opinion of him.'

'But if you do not go to him, perhaps you will not find it difficult to obtain a situation in another counting-house?'

'If I am not to return to his, I would rather at once leave the place—I never liked it, and I shall now like it less than ever. In a word, my intention is to go, if possible, to America.'

'Go where you will, my blessing and tears is all, my dear boy, that I can give you.'

'Then you approve of my wish to go to America?'

'I do not object to it, James—It is a difficult thing for a mother to say that she approves of her son exposing himself to any hazard.'

'What would you have said, could I have obtained a commission in the army and a war raging?'

'Just what I say now—nor should I have felt more sorrow in seeing you go to a campaign than I shall feel when you leave me to encounter the yet to you untried perils of the world. Indeed, I may say, I should almost feel less, for, in the army, with all its hazard, there is a certain degree of assurance, that a young man, if he lives, will be fashioned into an honourable character.'

'I wish that there was a war,' said Walkinshaw with such sincere simplicity, that even his mother could scarcely refrain from smiling.

The conversation was, at this juncture, interrupted by the entrance of Mrs Eadie, who immediately perceived that something particular had occurred to disturb the tranquillity of her friend, and, for a moment, she looked at Walkinshaw with an austere and majestic eye. His mother observed the severity of her aspect, and thought it as well at once to mention what had happened.

Mrs Eadie listened to the recital of his uncle's proposal, and his resolution to go abroad, with a degree of juridical serenity, that lent almost as much solemnity to her appearance as it derived dignity from her august form; and, when Mrs Walkinshaw concluded, she said,—

'We have foreseen all this—and I am only surprised that now, when it has come to pass, it should affect you so much. I dreamt, last night, Mrs Walkinshaw, that you were dead, and laid out in your winding-sheet. I thought I was sitting beside the corpse, and that, though I was sorrowful, I was, nevertheless, strangely pleased. In that moment, my cousin, Glengael, came into the room, and he had a large ancient book, with brazen clasps on it, under his arm. That book he gave to Ellen Frazer, whom I then saw was also in the room, and she undid the brazen clasps, and opening it, showed her father a particular passage, which he read aloud, and, when he paused, I saw you rise, and, throwing aside the winding-sheet, you appeared richly dressed, with a chearful countenance, and on your hands were wedding-gloves. It was to tell you this auspicious dream that I came here this morning, and I have no doubt it betokens some happy change in your fortunes, to come by the agency of Glengael. Therefore, give yourself no uneasiness about this difference between James and his uncle; for, you may rest assured, it will terminate in some great good to your family; but there will be a death first, that's certain.'

Although Walkinshaw was familiar with the occasional gleams of the sybiline pretensions of Mrs Eadie, and always treated them with reverence, he could not resist from smiling at the earnestness with which she delivered her prediction, saying, 'But I do not see in what way the dream has anything to do with my case.'

'You do not see,' replied the Lady sternly, 'nor do I see; but it does not, therefore, follow, that there is no sympathy between them. The wheels of the world work in darkness, James, and it requires the sight of the seer to discern what is coming round, though the auguries of their index are visible to all eyes. But,' and she turned to Mrs Walkinshaw, 'it strikes me, that, in the present state of your circumstances, I might write to my cousin. The possession of Glengael gives him weight with Government, and, perhaps, his influence might be of use to your son.'

This afforded a ray of hope to Walkinshaw, of which he had never entertained the slightest notion, and it also, in some degree, lightened the spirits of his mother. They both expressed their sense of her kindness; and James said gaily, that he had no doubt the omens of her dream would soon be verified; but she replied solemnly,—

'No! though Glengael may be able, by his interest, to serve you, the agency of death can alone fulfil the vision; but, for the present, let us say no more on that head. I will write to-day to Mr Frazer, and inquire in what way he can best assist all our wishes.'

In the meantime, the Leddy had been informed by her maid of Walkinshaw's early departure for Camrachle; and, in consequence, as soon as she had breakfasted, a messenger was dispatched to the counting-house, to request that the Laird might be sent to her when he came to town; but this was unnecessary, for he had scarcely passed a more tranquil night than his nephew; and, before her messenger came back, he was in the parlour with Robina, whom he had brought with him in the carriage to spend the day with one of her friends. Why the young lady should have chosen so unpleasant a day for her visit, particularly as it was a volunteer, and had been, as she said, only concerted with herself after the conversation of the preceding evening, we must allow the sagacity of the reader to discover; but she appeared flurried, and put out of countenance, when her grandmother told her, that she expected Dirdumwhamle and Mrs Milrookit to dinner, and 'I think,' said she, 'Beenie, that ye ought to bide wi' me to meet them, for I expect Walky,' so she styled Walkinshaw, their son; 'and if ye're no to get the ae cousin, I dinna see but ye might set your cap for the other.'

'I trust and hope,' exclaimed the Laird, 'that she has more sense. Walkinshaw Milrookit has nothing.'

'And what has Jamie Walkinshaw?' said the Leddy. ' 'Deed, Geordie, though I canna but say ye're baith pawkie and auld farrant, it's no to be controversed that ye hae gotten your father's bee in the bonnet, anent ancestors and forbears, and nae gude can come out o' ony sic havers. Beenie, my Leddy, ne'er fash your head wi' your father's dodrums; but, an ye can hook Walky's heart wi' the tail o' your ee, ye's no want my helping hand at the fishing.'

'Mother,' said George vehemently, 'I am astonished that you can talk so lightly to the girl. I have my own reasons for being most decidedly averse to any such union. And though I do feel that James has used me ill, and that his headstrong conduct deserves my severest displeasure, I not only think it a duty to bring about a marriage between Robina and him, but will endeavour to act in it as such. Perhaps, had she been entirely free, I might have felt less interest in the business; but knowing, as I now do, that his coldness alone has prevented her from cherishing towards him a just and proper affection, I should be wanting in my obligations as a father, were I not to labour, by all expedient means, to promote the happiness of my child.'

During this speech the young lady appeared both out of countenance and inwardly amused, while her grandmother, placing her hands to her sides, looked at her with a queer and inquisitive eye, and said,—

'It's no possible, Beenie Walkinshaw, that thou's sic a masquerading cutty as to hae beguilt baith thy father and me? But, if ever I had an ee in my head, and could see wi' that ee, it's as true as the deil's in Dublin city, that I hae had a discernment o' thy heart-hatred to Jamie Walkinshaw. But let your father rin to the woody as he will— they're no to be born that' ill live to see that I hae a judgment and an understanding o' what's what. Howsever, Geordie, what's to be done wi' that ne'er-do-well water-wag-tail that's flown awa to its mother? Poor woman, she canna afford to gie't drammock. Something maun be done, and wi' your wis for a fresh decking of the pedigrees o' the Walkinshaws o' Kittlestonheugh, that I hae been sae lang deaved and driven doited wi', "for the space of forty years," I may say, in the words of the Psalmist, "the race hae grieved me." Ye canna do better than just tak a hurl in your chaise to Camrachle, and bring him in by the lug and horn, and nail him to the desk wi' a pin to his nose.'

There was worse advice, the Laird thought, than this; and, after some farther remarks to the same effect, he really did set off for Camrachle with the express intention of doing every thing in his power to heal the breach, and to conciliate again the affection and gratitude of his nephew.

Chapter III

As soon as the carriage had left the door, the Leddy resumed the conversation with her grand-daughter.

'Noo, Beenie Walkinshaw,' said she, 'I maun put you to the straights o' a question. Ye'll no tell me, lassie, that ye hae na flung stoor in your father's een, after the converse that we had thegither by oursels the other day; therefore and accordingly, I requeesht to know, what's at the bottom o' this black art and glamour that ye hae been guilty o'?—whatna scamp or hempy is't that the cutty has been gallanting wi', that she's trying to cast the glaiks in a' our een for?—Wha is't?—I insist to know—for ye'll ne'er gar me believe that there's no a because for your jookery pawkrie.'

'You said,' replied Miss, half blushing, half laughing, 'that you would lend a helping hand to me with Walkinshaw Milrookit.'

'Eh! Megsty me! I'm sparrow-blasted!' exclaimed the Leddy, throwing herself back in the chair, and lifting both her hands and eyes in wonderment.—'But thou, Beenie Walkinshaw, is a soople fairy; and so a' the time that thy father, as blin' as the silly blind bodie that his wife gart believe her gallant's horse was a milch cow sent frae her minny,—was wising and wyling to bring about a matrimony, or, as I should ca't, a matter-o'-money conjugality wi' your cousin Jamie, hae ye been linking by the dyke-sides, out o' sight, wi' Walky Milrookit? Weel, that beats print! Whatna novelle gied you that lesson, lassie? Hey Sirs! auld as I am, but I would like to read it. Howsever, Beenie, as the ae oe's as sib to me as the ither, I'll be as gude as my word; and when Dirdumwhamle and your aunty, wi' your joe, are here the day, we'll just lay our heads thegither for a purpose o' marriage, and let your father play the Scotch measure or shantruse, wi' the bellows and the shank o' the besom, to some warlock wallop o' his auld papistical and paternostering ancestors, that hae been—Gude preserve us!—for ought I ken to the contrary, suppin' brimstone broth wi' the deil lang afore the time o' Adam and Eve. Methuselah himself, I verily believe, could be naething less than half a cousin to the nine hundred and ninety-ninth Walkinshaw o' Kittlestonheugh. Howsever, Beenie, thou's a—thou's a—I'll no say what—ye little dooble cutty, to keep me in the dark, when I could hae gi'en you and Walky sae muckle convenience for courting. But, for a' that, I'll no be devoid o' grace, but act the part of a kind and affectionate grandmother, as it is well known I hae ay been to a' my bairns' childer; only I never thought to hae had a finger in the pye o' a Clarissy Harlot wedding.'

'But,' said Robina, 'what if my father should succeed in persuading James still to fall in with his wishes? My situation will be dreadful.'

''Deed, an that come to a possibility, I ken na what's to be done,' replied the Leddy; 'for ye know it will behove me to tak my ain son, your father's part; and as I was saying, Jamie Walkinshaw being as dear to me as Walky Milrookit, I can do no less than help you to him, which need be a matter of no diffeequalty, 'cause ye hae gart your father trow that ye're out o' the body for Jamie; so, as I said before, ye maun just conform.'

Miss looked aghast for a moment, and exclaimed, clasping her hands, at finding the total contempt with which her grandmother seemed to consider her affections,—

'Heaven protect me! I am ruined and undone!'

'Na, if that's the gait o't, Beenie, I hae nothing to say, but to help to tak up the loupen-steek in your stocking wi' as much brevity as is consistent wi' perspicuity, as the minister o' Port Glasgow says.'

'What do you mean? to what do you allude?' cried the young lady terrified.

'Beenie Walkinshaw, I'll be calm; I'll no lose my composity. But it's no to seek what I could say, ye Jerusalem concubine, to bring sic a crying sin into my family. O woman, woman! but ye're a silly nymph, and the black stool o' repentance is oure gude for you!'

Robina was so shocked and thunderstruck at the old lady's imputations and kindling animadversions, that she actually gasped with horror.

'But,' continued her grandmother,—'since it canna be helped noo, I maun just tell your father, as well as I can, and get the minister when we're a' thegither in the afternoon, and declare an irregular marriage, which is a calamity that never happened on my side of the house.'

Unable any longer to control her agitation, Robina started from her seat, exclaiming, 'Hear me, in mercy! spare such horrible—'

'Spare!' interrupted the Leddy, with the sharpest tone of her indignation,—'An' ye were my dochter as ye're but my grand-dochter, I would spare you, ye Israelitish handmaid, and randy o' Babylon. But pride ne'er leaves its master without a fa'—your father's weel serv't—he would tak nane o' my advice in your education; but instead o' sending you to a Christian school, got down frae Manchester, in England, a governess for miss, my leddy, wi' gumflowers on her head, and paint on her cheeks, and speaking in sic high English, that the Babel babble o' Mull and Moydart was a perfection o' sense when compar't wi't.'

'Good heavens! how have you fallen into this strange mistake?' said Robina, so much recovered, that she could scarcely refrain from laughing.

'Beenie, Beenie! ye may ca't a mistake; but I say it's a shame and a sin. O sic a blot to come on the 'scutcheon of my old age; and wha will tell your poor weakly mother, that, since the hour o' your luckless decking, has ne'er had a day to do weel. Lang, lang has she been sitting on the brink o' the grave, and this sore stroke will surely coup her in.'

'How was it possible,' at last exclaimed Robina, in full self-possession, 'that you could put such an indelicate construction on any thing that I have said?'

The Leddy had by this time melted into a flood of tears, and was searching for her handkerchief to wipe her eyes; but, surprised at the firmness with which she was addressed, she looked up as she leant forward, with one hand still in her pocket, and the other grasping the arm of the elbow chair in which she was seated.

'Yes,' continued Robina, 'you have committed a great error; and though I am mortified to think you could for a moment entertain so unworthy an opinion of me, I can hardly keep from laughing at the mistake.'

But although the Leddy was undoubtedly highly pleased to learn that she had distressed herself without reason, still, for the sake of her own dignity, which she thought somehow compromised by what she had said, she seemed as if she could have wished there had been a little truth in the imputation; for she said,—

'I'm blithe to hear you say sae, Beenie; but it was a very natural delusion on my part, for ye ken in thir novelle and play-actoring times nobody can tell what might happen. Howsever, I'm glad it's no waur; but ye maun alloo that it was a very suspectionable situation for you to be discovered colleaguing wi' Walky Milrookit in sic a clandestine manner; and, therefore, I see that na better can be made o't, but to bring a purpose o' marriage to pass between you, as I was saying, without fashing your father about it till it's by hand; when, after he has got his ramping and stamping over, he'll come to himsel, and mak us a' jocose.'

The conversation was continued with the same sort of consistency as far as the old lady was concerned, till Mrs Milrookit and Dirdumwhamle, with their son, arrived.

Young Milrookit, as we have already intimated, was, in point of personal figure, not much inferior to James; and though he certainly was attached to his cousin, Robina, with unfeigned affection, he had still so much of the leaven of his father in him, that her prospective chance of succeeding to the estate of Kittlestonheugh had undoubtedly some influence in heightening the glow of his passion.

A marriage with her was as early and as ardently the chief object of his father's ambition, as the union with his cousin Walkinshaw had been with her's; and the hope of seeing it consummated made the old gentleman, instead of settling him in any town business, resolve to make him a farmer, that he might one day be qualified to undertake the management of the Kittlestonheugh estate. It is, therefore, unnecessary to mention, that, when Robina and her lover had retired, on being told by their grandmother they might 'divert themselves in another room,' Dirdumwhamle engaged, with the most sympathetic alacrity, in the scheme, as he called it, to make the two affectionate young things happy. But what passed will be better told in a new Chapter.

Chapter IV

'Indeed, Leddy,'said the Laird of Dirdumwhamle, when she told him of the detection, as she called it, of Robina's notion of his son—'Blood ye ken's thicker than water; and I have na been without a thought mysel that there was something by the common o' cousinship atween them. But hearing, as we often a' have done, of the great instancy that my gude-brother was in for a match tweesh her and James, I could na think of making mysel an interloper. But if it's ordaint that she prefers Walky, I'm sure I can see nae harm in you and me giving the twa young things a bit canny shove onward in the road to a blithesome bridal.'

'I am thinking,' rejoined his wife, 'that, perhaps, it might be as prudent and more friendly to wait the upshot o' her father's endeavours wi' James,—for even although he should be worked into a compliancy, still there will be no marriage, and then Robina can avow her partiality for Walky.'

'Meg,' replied the Leddy, 'ye speak as one of the foolish women—ye ken naething about it; your brother Geordie's just his father's ain gett, and winna be put off frae his intents by a' the powers of law and government—let him ance get Jamie to conform, and he'll soon thraw Beenie into an obedience, and what will then become o' your Walky?—Na, na, Dirdumwhamle, heed her not, she lacketh understanding—it's you and me, Laird, that maun work the wherry in this breeze—y'ere a man o' experience in the ways o' matrimony, having been, as we all know, thrice married,—and I am an aged woman, that has na travelled the world for sax-and-seventy years without hearing the toast o' "Love and opportunity." Now, have na we the love ready-made to our hands in the fond affection of Beenie and Walky?—and surely neither o' us is in such a beggary o' capacity, that we're no able to conceit a time and place for an opportunity. Had it been, as I had at ae time this very day, a kind of a because to jealouse, I'll no say what—it was my purpose to hae sent for a minister or a magistrate, and got an un-regular marriage declared outright—though it would hae gi'en us a' het hearts and red faces for liveries. Noo, Laird, ye're a man o' sagacity and judgment, dinna ye think, though we hae na just sic an exploit to break our hearts wi' shame and tribulation, that we might ettle at something o' the same sort?—and there can be no sin in't, Meg; for is't no commanded in Scripture to increase and multiply? and what we are wising to bring about is a purpose o' marriage, which is the natural way o' plenishing the earth, and raising an increase o' the children of men.'

Much and devoutly as the Laird of Dirdumwhamle wished for such a consummation, he was not quite prepared for proceedings of so sudden and hasty a character. And being a personage of some worldly prudence, eagerly as he longed for the match, he was averse to expose himself to any strictures for the part he might take in promoting it. Accordingly, instead of acquiescing at once in his mother-in-law's suggestion, he said jocularly,

'Hooly, hooly, Leddy; it may come vera weel off Walky and Robina's hands to make a private marriage for themselves, poor young things, but it never will do for the like o' you and me to mess or mell in the matter, by ony open countenancing o' a ceremony. It's vera true that I see nae objection to the match, and would think I did nae ill in the way o' a quiet conneevance to help them on in their courtship, but things are no ripe for an aff-hand ploy.'

'I'm glad to hear you say sae,' interposed Mrs Milrookit; 'for really my mother seems fey about this connection; and nae gude can come o' ony thing sae rashly devised. My brother would, in my opinion, have great cause to complain, were the gudeman to be art or part in ony such conspiracy.'

The Leddy never liked to have her judgment called in question; (indeed, what ladies do?) and still less by a person so much her inferior in point of understanding (so she herself thought,) as her daughter.

'My word, Meg,' was her reply, 'but t'ou has a stock o' impudence, to haud up thy snout in that gait to the she that bore thee.—Am I one of these that hae, by reason of more strength, amaist attain't to the age of fourscore, without learning the right frae the wrang o' a' moral conduct, as that delightful man, Dr Pringle o' Garnock, said in his sermon on the Fast Day, when he preached in the Wynd Kirk, that t'ou has the spirit o' sedition, to tell me that I hae lost my solid judgment, when I'm labouring in the vineyard o' thy family?—Dirdumwhamle, your wife there, she's my dochter, and sorry am I to say't, but it's well known, and I dinna misdoot ye hae found it to your cost, that she is a most unreasonable, narrow, contracted woman, and wi' a' her 'conomical throughgality—her direction-books to mak grozette wine for deil-be-lickit, and her Katy Fisher's cookery, whereby she would gar us trow she can mak fat kail o' chucky stanes and an auld horse shoe—we a' ken, and ye ken, Laird, warst o' a', that she flings away the pease, and mak's her hotch-potch wi' the shawps, or, as the auld bye-word says, tyne's bottles gathering straes. So what need the like o' you and me sit in council, and the Shanedrims of the people, wi' ane o' the stupidest bawkie birds that e'er the Maker o't took the trouble to put the breath o' life in? Fey, did ye say?—that's a word o' discretion to fling at the head o' your aged parent. Howsever, it's no worth my condescendence to lose my temper wi' the like o' her. But, Meg Walkinshaw, or Mrs Milrookit, though ye be there afore your gudeman, the next time ye diminish my understanding, I'll may be let ye ken what it is to blaspheme your mother, so tak heed lest ye fall.

And now to wind up the thread o' what we were discoursing anent—It's my opinion, Dirdumwhamle, we should put no molestation in the way o' that purpose o' marriage. So, if ye dinna like to tell your son to gang for a minister, I'll do it myself; and the sooner it's by hand and awa, as the sang sings, the sooner we'll a' be in a situation to covenant and gree again wi' Beenie's father.'

The Laird was delighted to see the haste and heartiness with which the Leddy was resolved to consummate the match; but he said,—

'Do as ye like, Leddy—do as ye like; but I'll no coom my fingers wi' meddling in ony sic project. The wark be a' your ain.'

'Surely neither you nor that unreverent and misleart tumphy your wife, our Meg, would refuse to be present at the occasion?'

''Deed, Leddy, I'm unco sweert; I'll no deny that,' replied Dirdumwhamle.

'If it is to take place this day, and in this house, gudeman, I'm sure it will be ill put on blateness, both on your part and mine, no to be present,' said Mrs Milrookit.

'Noo, that's a word o' sense, Meg,' cried her mother, exultingly; 'that's something like the sagacity o' a Christian parent. Surely it would be a most Pagan-like thing, for the father and mother o' the bridegroom to be in the house, to ken o' what was going on, and fidging fain, as ye baith are, for the comfort it's to bring to us a', to sit in another room wi'a cloud on your brows, and your hands in a mournful posture. Awa, awa, Dirdumwhamle, wi' the like o' that; I hae nae brow o' sic worldly hypocrisy. But we hae nae time to lose, for your gude-brother will soon be back frae Camrachle, and I would fain hae a' o'er before he comes. Hey, Sirs! but it will be a sport if we can get him to be present at the wedding-dinner, and he ken naething about it. So I'll just send the lass at ance for Dr De'il fear; for it's a great thing, ye ken, to get a bridal blessed wi' the breath o' a sound orthodox; and I'll gae ben and tell Beenie and Walky, that they maun mak some sort o' a preparation.'

'But, when they are married, what's to become o' them?—where are they to bide?— and what hae they to live upon?'—said Mrs Milrookit, anxiously.

'Dinna ye fash your head, Meg,' said her mother, about ony sic trivialities. They can stay wi' me till after the reconciliation, when, nae doot, her father will alloo a genteel aliment; so we need na vex oursels about taking thought for to-morrow; sufficient for the day is the evil thereof. But ye hae bonny gooses and a' manner o' poultry at the Dirdumwhamle. So, as we'll need something to keep the banes green, ye may just send us a tasting; na, for that matter, we'll no cast outwi' the like o 'a sooking grumphie; or, if ye were chancing to kill a sheep, a side o' mutton's worth house-room; and butter and eggs, I'm no a novice, as the Renfrew Doctor said, butter and eggs may dine a provice, wi' the help o' bread for kitchen.'

In concluding this speech, the Leddy, who had, in the mean time, risen, gave a joyous geek with her head, and swept triumphantly out of the room.

Chapter V

In the meantime, Kittlestonheugh, as, according to the Scottish fashion, we should denominate Squire Walkinshaw, had proceeded to Camrachle, where he arrived at his sister-in-law's door just as Mrs Eadie was taking her leave, with the intention of writing to her relation Mr Frazer in behalf of James. As the carriage drove up, Mrs Charles, on seeing it approach, begged her to stop; but, upon second thoughts, it was considered better that she should not remain, and also that she should defer her letter to Glengael until after the interview. She was accordingly at the door when the Laird alighted, who, being but slightly acquainted with her, only bowed, and was passing on without speaking into the house, when she arrested him by one of her keen and supreme looks, of which few could withstand the searching brightness.

'Mr Walkinshaw,' said she, after eyeing him inquisitively for two or three seconds, 'before you go to Mrs Charles, I would speak with you.'

It would not be easy to explain the reason which induced Mrs Eadie so suddenly to determine on interfering, especially after what had just passed; but still, as she did so, we are bound, without investigating her motives too curiously, to relate the sequel.

Mr Walkinshaw bowed, thereby intimating his acquiescence; and she walked on towards the manse with slow steps and a majestic altitude, followed by the visitor in silence. But she had not advanced above four or five paces, when she turned round, and touching him emphatically on the arm, said,—

'Let us not disturb the minister, but go into the churchyard; we can converse there—the dead are fit witnesses to what I have to say.'

Notwithstanding all his worldliness, there was something so striking in her august air, the impressive melancholy of her countenance, and the solemn Siddonian grandeur of her voice, that Kittlestonheugh was awed, and could only at the moment again intimate his acquiescence by a profound bow. She then proceeded with her wonted dignity towards the churchyard, and entering the stile which opened into it, she walked on to the south side of the church. The sun by this time had exhaled away the morning mists, and was shining brightly on the venerable edifice, and on the humble tombs and frail memorials erected nigh.

'Here,' said she, stopping when they had reached the small turfless space which the feet of the rustic Sabbath pilgrims had trodden bare in front of the southern door,—'Here let us stop—the sun shines warmly here, and the church will shelter us from the cold north-east wind. Mr Walkinshaw, I am glad that we have met, before you entered yon unhappy house. The inmates are not in circumstances to contend with adversity: your sister loves her children too well not to wish that her son may obtain the great advantages which your proposal to him holds out; and he has too kind and generous a heart, not to go far, and willingly to sacrifice much on her account. You have it therefore in your power to make a family, which has hitherto known little else but misfortune, miserable or happy.'

'It cannot, I hope, Madam,' was his reply, 'be thought of me, that I should not desire greatly to make them happy.—Since you are acquainted with what has taken place, you will do me the justice to admit, that I could do nothing more expressive of the regard I entertain for my nephew, and of the esteem in which I hold his mother, than by offering him my only child in marriage, and with such a dowry, too, as no one in his situation could almost presume to expect.'

Mrs Eadie did not make any immediate answer, but again fixed her bright and penetrating eye for a few seconds so intensely on his countenance, that he turned aside from its irresistible ray.

'What you say, Sir, sounds well; but if, in seeking to confer that benefit, you mar for ever the happiness you wish to make, and know before that such must be the consequence, some other reason than either regard for your nephew, or esteem for his mother, must be the actuating spring that urges you to persevere.'

Firm of purpose, and fortified in resolution, as Kittlestonheugh was, something both in the tone and the substance of this speech made him thrill from head to foot.

'What other motive than my affection can I have?' said he.

'Interest,' replied Mrs Eadie, with a look that withered him to the heart,—'Interest; nothing else ever made a man force those to be unhappy whom he professed to love.'

'I am sorry, Madam, that you think so ill of me,' was his reply, expressed coldly and haughtily.

'I did not wish you to come here, that we should enter into any debate; but only to entreat that you will not press your wish for the marriage too urgently; because, out of the love and reverence which your nephew has for his mother, I fear he may be worked on to comply.'

'Fear! Madam—I cannot understand your meaning.'

The glance that Mrs Eadie darted at these words convinced him it was in vain to equivocate with her.

'Mr Walkinshaw,' said she, after another long pause, and a keen and suspicious scrutiny of his face—'It has always been reported, that some of my mother's family possessed the gift of a discerning spirit. This morning, when I saw you alight from your carriage I felt as if the mantle of my ancestors had fallen upon me. It is a hallowed and oracular inheritance; and, under its mysterious inspirations, I dare not disguise what I feel.—You have come to-day——'

'Really, Madam,' interrupted the merchant testily, 'I come for some better purpose than to listen to Highland stories about the second-sight. I must wish you good morning.'

In saying this, he turned round, and was moving to go away, when the lady, throwing back her shawl, magnificently raised her hand, and took hold of him by the arm—

'Stop, Mr Walkinshaw, this is a place of truth—There is no deceit in death and the grave—Life and the living may impose upon us; but here, where we stand, among the sincere—the dead—I tell you, and your heart, Sir, knows that what I tell you is true, there is no affection—no love for your nephew—nor respect for his mother, in the undivulged motives of that seeming kindness with which you are, shall I say plainly, seeking their ruin?'

The impassioned gestures and the suppressed energy with which this was said, gave an awful and mysterious effect to expressions that were in themselves simple, in so much that the astonished man of the world regarded her, for some time, with a mingled sentiment of wonder and awe. At last he said, with a sneer,—

'Upon my word, Mrs Eadie, the minister himself could hardly preach with more eloquence. It is a long time since I have been so lectured; and I should like to know by what authority I am so brought to book?'

The sarcastic tone in which this was said provoked the pride and Highland blood of the lady, who, stepping back, and raising her right arm with a towering grandeur, shook it over him as she said,—

'I have no more to say;—the fate of the blood of Glengael is twined and twisted with the destiny of Mrs Charles Walkinshaw's family; but at your dying hour you will remember what I have said, and, trembling, think of this place—of these tombs, these doors that lead into the judgment-chamber of Heaven, and of yon sun, that is the eye of the Almighty's chief sentinel over man.'

She then dropped her hand, and, walking slowly past him, went straight towards the manse, the door of which she had almost reached before he recovered himself from the amazement and apprehension with which he followed her with his eye. His feelings, however, he soon so far mastered in outward appearance, that he even assumed an air of ineffable contempt; but, nevertheless, an impression had been so stamped by her mystery and menace, that, in returning towards the dwelling of Mrs Charles, he gradually fell into a moody state of thoughtfulness and abstraction.

Chapter VI

Mrs Charles Walkinshaw had been a good deal surprised by the abrupt manner in which Mrs Eadie had intercepted her brother-in-law. Her son, not a little pleased of an opportunity to avoid his uncle, no sooner saw them pass the window than he made his escape from the house. Observing that they did not go to the manse, but turned off towards the churchyard, he hastened to take refuge with his old preceptor, the minister, possibly to see Ellen Frazer. The relation, however, of what passed in the manse does not fall within the scope of our narrative, particularly as it will be easily comprehended and understood by its effects. We have, therefore, only at present to mention, that Mrs Charles, in the meantime, sat in wonder and expectation, observing to her daughter, a mild and unobtrusive girl, who seldom spoke many sentences at a time, that she thought of late Mrs Eadie seemed unusually attentive to her Highland superstitions. 'She has been, I think, not so well of late,—her nerves are evidently in a high state of excitement. It is much to be regretted that she is so indisposed at this time, when we stand so much in need of her advice.'

Mary replied that she had noticed with sorrow a very great change indeed in their friend,—and she added,—

'Ellen says that she often walks out at night to the churchyard, and sits moaning over the graves of her children. It is strange after they have been so long dead, that her grief should have so unexpectedly broken out afresh. The minister, I am sure, is very uneasy—for I have noticed that he looks paler than he used to do, and with a degree of sadness that is really very affecting.'

While they were thus speaking Mr Walkinshaw came in, and the first words he said, before taking a seat, were,—

'Is the minister's wife in her right mind? She seems to me a little touched. I could with difficulty preserve my gravity at her fantastical nonsense.'

Mrs Charles, out of respect for her friend, did not choose to make any reply to this observation, so that her brother-in-law found himself obliged to revert to the business which had brought him to Camrachle.

'I thought James was here,' said he; 'what has become of him?'

'He has just stepped out.—I suspect he was not exactly prepared to meet you.'

'He is hot and hasty,' rejoined the uncle; 'we had rather an unpleasant conversation last night. I hope, since he has had time to reflect on what I said, he sees things differently.'

'I am grieved,' replied Mrs Charles with a sigh, 'that any thing should have arisen to mar the prospects that your kindness had opened to him.

But young men will be headstrong; their feelings often run away with their judgment.'

'But,' said Kittlestonheugh, 'I can forgive him. I never looked for any conduct in him different from that of others of his own age. Folly is the superfluous blossoms of youth: They drop off as the fruit forms. I hope he is not resolute in adhering to his declaration about leaving Glasgow.'

'He seems at present quite resolved,' replied his mother, with a deep and slow sigh, which told how heavily that determination lay upon her heart.

'Perhaps, then,' said his uncle, 'it may just be as well to leave him to himself for a few days; and I had better say nothing more to him on the subject.'

'I think,' replied Mrs Charles, timidly, as if afraid that she might offend,—'it is needless at present to speak to him about Robina: he must have time to reflect.'—She would have added, 'on the great advantages of the match to him;' but knowing, as she did, the decided sentiments of her son, she paused in the unfinished sentence, and felt vexed with herself for having said so much.

'But,' inquired her brother-in-law, in some degree solaced by the manner in which she had expressed herself—'But, surely, the boy will not be so ridiculous as to absent himself from the counting-house?'

'He speaks of going abroad,' was the soft and diffident answer.

'Impossible! he has not the means.'

She then told him what he had been considering with respect to his father's old acquaintance, who had the vessel going to America.

'In that case,' said his uncle, with an off-hand freedom that seemed much like generosity,—'I must undertake the expence of his outfit. He will be none the worse of seeing a little of the world; and he will return to us in the course of a year or two a wiser and a better man.'

'Your kindness, Sir, is truly extraordinary, and I shall be most happy if he can be persuaded to avail himself of it; but his mind lies towards the army, and, if he could get a cadetcy to India, I am sure he would prefer it above all things.'

'A cadetcy to India!' exclaimed the astonished uncle.—'By what chance or interest could he hope for such an appointment?'

'Mrs Eadie's cousin, who bought back her father's estate, she says, has some Parliamentary interest, and she intends to write him to beg his good offices for James.'

Kittlestonheugh was thunderstruck:—this was a turn in the affair that he had never once imagined within the scope and range of possibility. 'Do you think,' said he, 'that he had any view to this in his ungrateful insolence to me last night? If I thought so, every desire I had to serve him should be henceforth suppressed and extinguished.'

At this crisis the door was opened, and Mr Eadie, the minister, came in, by which occurrence the conversation was interrupted, and the vehemence of Mr Walkinshaw was allowed to subside during the interchange of the common reciprocities of the morning.

'I am much grieved, Mr Walkinshaw,' said the worthy clergyman, after a short pause, 'to hear of this unfortunate difference with your nephew. I hope the young man will soon come to a more considerate way of thinking.'

Mr Walkinshaw thought Mr Eadie a most sensible man, and could not but express his confidence, that, when the boy came to see how much all his best friends condemned his conduct, and were so solicitous for his compliance, he would repent his precipitation. 'We must, however,' said he, 'give him time. His mother tells me that he has resolved to go to America. I shall do all in my power to assist his views in that direction, not doubting in the end to reap the happiest effects.'

'But before taking any step in that scheme,' said the minister, 'he has resolved to wait the issue of a letter which I have left my wife writing to her relation—for he would prefer a military life to any other.'

'From all that I can understand,' replied the uncle, 'Mr Frazer, your friend, will not be slack in using his interests to get him to India; for he cannot but be aware of the pennyless condition of my nephew, and must be glad to get him out of his daughter's way.'

There was something in this that grated the heart of the mother, and jarred on the feelings of the minister.

'No,' said the latter; 'on the contrary, the affection which Glengael bears to his daughter would act with him as a motive to lessen any obstacles that might oppose her happiness. Were Mrs Eadie to say—but, for many reasons, she will not yet—that she believes her young friend is attached to Ellen, I am sure Mr Frazer would exert himself, in every possible way, to advance his fortune.'

'In that he would but do as I am doing,' replied the merchant with a smile of self-gratulation; and he added briskly, addressing himself to his sister-in-law, 'Will James accept favours from a stranger, with a view to promote a union with that stranger's daughter, and yet scorn the kindness of his uncle?'

The distressed mother had an answer ready; but long dependence on her cool and wary brother-in-law, together with her natural gentleness, made her bury it in her heart. The minister, however, who owed him no similar obligations, and was of a more courageous nature, did more than supply what she would have said.

'The cases, Mr Walkinshaw, are not similar. The affection between your nephew and Ellen is mutual; but your favour is to get him to agree to a union at which his heart revolts.'

'Revolts! you use strong language unnecessarily,' was the indignant retort.

'I beg your pardon, Mr Walkinshaw,' said the worthy Presbyter, disturbed at the thought of being so unceremonious; 'I am much interested in your nephew—I feel greatly for his present unhappy situation. I need not remind you that he has been to me, and with me, as my own son; and therefore you ought not to be surprised that I should take his part, particularly as, in so doing, I but defend the generous principles of a very noble youth.'

'Well, well,' exclaimed the Laird peevishly, 'I need not at present trouble myself any farther—I am as willing as ever to befriend him as I ought; but, from the humour he is in, it would serve no good purpose for me at present to interfere. I shall therefore return to Glasgow; and, when Mrs Eadie receives her answer, his mother will have the goodness to let me know.'

With these words he hastily bade his sister-in-law good morning, and hurried into his carriage.

'His conduct is very extraordinary,' said the minister as he drove off. 'There is something more than the mere regard and anxiety of an uncle in all this, especially when he knows that the proposed match is so obnoxious to his daughter. I cannot understand it; but come, Mrs Walkinshaw, let us go over to the manse—James is to dine with me to-day, and we shall be the better of all being together; for Mrs Eadie seems much out of spirits, and her health of late has not been good. Go, Mary, get your bonnet too, and come with us.'

So ended the pursuit to Camrachle; and we shall now beg the courteous reader to return with us to Glasgow, where we left the Leddy in high spirits, in the act of sending for the Reverend Dr De'il fear to marry her grandchildren.

Chapter VII

Long before Kittlestonheugh returned to Glasgow, the indissoluble knot was tied between his daughter and her cousin, Walkinshaw Milrookit. The Laird of Dirdumwhamle was secretly enjoying this happy consummation of a scheme which he considered as securing to his son the probable reversion of an affluent fortune, and a flourishing estate. Occasional flakes of fear floated, however, in the sunshine of his bosom, and fell cold for a moment on his heart. His wife was less satisfied. She knew the ardour with which her brother had pursued another object; she respected the consideration that was due to him as a parent in the disposal of his daughter; and she justly dreaded his indignation and reproaches. She was, therefore, anxious that Mr Milrookit should return with her to the country before he came back from Camrachle. But her mother, the Leddy, was in high glee, and triumphant, at having so cleverly, as she thought, accomplished a most meritorious stratagem, she would not for a moment listen to the idea of their going away before dinner.

'Na; ye'll just bide where ye are,' said she. 'It will be an unco like thing no to partake o' the marriage feast, though ye hae come without a wedding garment, after I hae been at the cost and outlay o' a jigot o' mutton, a fine young poney cock, and a florentine pye; dainties that the like o' hae na been in my house since Geordie, wi' his quirks o' law, wheedled me to connive wi' him to deprive uncle Watty o' his seven lawful senses, forbye the property. But I trow I hae now gotten the blin side o' him at last: he'll no daur to say a word to me about a huggery muggery matrimonial, take my word for't; for he kens the black craw I hae to pluck wi' him anent the prank he played me in the deevelry o' the concos mentos, whilk ought in course o' justice to have entitled me to a full half of the income o' the lands; and a blithe thing, Dirdumwhamle, that would hae been to you and your wife, could we hae wrought it into a come-to-pass; for sure am I, that, in my experience and throughgality, I would na hae tied my talent in a napkin, nor hid it in a stroopless tea-pot, in the corner o' the press, but laid it out to usury wi' Robin Carrick. Howsever, maybe, for a' that, Meg, when I'm dead and gone, ye'll find, in the bonny pocket-book ye sewed lang syne at the boarding-school for your father, a testimony o' the advantage it was to hae had a mother. But, Sirs, a wedding-day is no a time for molloncholious moralizing; so I'll mak a skip and a passover o' a matter and things pertaining to sic Death and the Leddy's confabbles as legacies, and kittle up your notions wi' a wee bit spree and sprose o' jocosity, afore the old man comes; for so, in course o' nature, it behoves us to ca' the bride's father, as he's now, by the benison o' Dr De'il fear, on the lawfu' toll-road to become, in due season, an ancestor. Nae doubt, he would hae liked better had it been to one of his ain Walkinshaws o' Kittlestonheugh; but when folk canna get the gouden goun, they should be thankful when they get the sleeve.'

While the Leddy was thus holding forth to the Laird and his wife, the carriage with George stopped at the door. Dirdumwhamle, notwithstanding all his inward pleasure, changed colour. Mrs Milrookit fled to another room, to which the happy pair had retired after the ceremony, that they might not be visible to any accidental visitors; and even the Leddy was for a time smitten with consternation. She, however, was the first who recovered her self-possession; and, before Mr Walkinshaw was announced, she was seated in her accustomed elbow chair with a volume of Mathew Henry's Commentary on her lap, and her spectacles on her nose, as if she had been piously reading. Dirdumwhamle sat opposite to her, and was apparently in a profound sleep, from which he was not roused until some time after the entrance of his brother-in-law.

'So, Geordie,' said the Leddy, taking off her spectacles, and shutting the book, as her son entered; 'what's come o' Jamie?—hae ye no brought the Douglas-tragedy-like mountebank, back wi' you?'

'Let him go to the devil,' was the answer.

'That's an ill wis, Geordie.—And so ye hae been a gouk's errant? But how are they a' at Camrachle?' replied the Leddy; 'and, to be sober, what's the callan gaun to do? And what did he say for himsel, the kick-at-the-benweed foal that he is? If his mother had laid on the taws better, he would nae hae been sae skeigh. But, sit down, Geordie, and tell me a' about it.—First and foremost, howsever, gie that sleepy bodie, Dirdumwhamle, a shoogle' out o' his dreams. What's set the man a snoring like the bars o' Ayr, at this time o' day, I won'er?'

But Dirdumwhamle did not require to be so shaken; for, at this juncture, he began to yawn and stretch his arms till, suddenly seeing his brother-in-law, he started wide awake.

'I am really sorry to say, mother,' resumed Kittlestonheugh, 'that my jaunt to Camrachle has been of no avail. The minister's wife, who, by the way, is certainly not in her right mind, has already written to her relation, Glengael, to beg his interest to procure a cadetship to India for James; and, until she receives an answer, I will let the fellow tak his own way.'

'Vera right, Geordie, vera right; ye could na act a more prudential and Solomon-like part,' replied his mother. 'But, since he will to Cupar, let him gang, and a' sorrow till him; and just compose your mind to approve o' Beenie's marriage wi' Walky, who is a lad of a methodical nature, and no a hurly-burly ramstam, like yon flea-luggit thing, Jamie.'

Dirdumwhamle would fain have said amen, but it stuck in his throat.

Nor had he any inducement to make any effort farther, by the decisive manner in which his brother-in-law declared, that he would almost as soon carry his daughter's head to the churchyard as see that match.

'Weel, weel; but I dare say, Geordie, ye need na mair waste your bir about it,' exclaimed the Leddy; 'for, frae something I hae heard the lad himsel say, this very day, it's no a marriage that ever noo is likely to happen in this warld;' and she winked significantly to the bridegroom's father.—'But, Geordie,' she continued, 'there is a because that I would like to understand. How is't that ye're sae doure against Walky Milrookit? I'm sure he's a very personable lad—come o' a gude family—sib to us a'; and, failing you and yours, heir o' entail to the Kittlestonheugh. Howsever, not of a shyou wi' the like o' that, as I see ye're kindling, I would, just by way o' diversion, be blithe to learn how it would gang wi' you, if Beenie, after a' this straemash, was to loup the window under cloud o' night wi' some gaberlunzie o' a crookit and blin' soldier-officer, or, wha kens, maybe a drunken drammatical divor frae the play-house, wi' ill-colour't darnt silk stockings; his coat out at the elbows, and his hat on ajee? How would you like that, Geordie?—Sic misfortunes are no uncos noo-a-days.'

Her son, notwithstanding the chagrin he suffered, was obliged to smile, saying, 'I have really a better opinion, both of Beenie's taste and her sense, than to suppose any such adventure possible.'

'So hae I,' replied the Leddy. 'But ye ken, if her character were to get sic a claut by a fox paw, ye would be obliged to tak her hame, and mak a genteel settlement befitting your only dochter.'

'I think,' said George, 'in such a case as you suppose, a genteel settlement would be a little more than could in reason be expected.'

'So think I, Geordie—I am sure I would ne'er counsel you into ony conformity; but, though we hae nae dread nor fear o' soldier-officers or drammaticals, it's o' the nature o' a possibility that she will draw up wi' some young lad o' very creditable connections and conduct; but wha, for some thraw o' your ain, ye would na let her marry.—What would ye do then, Geordie? Ye would hae to settle, or ye would be a most horridable parent.'

'My father, for so doing, disinherited Charles,' said George gravely, and the words froze the very spirit of Dirdumwhamle.

'That's vera true, Geordie,' resumed the Leddy; 'a bitter business it was to us a', and was the because o' your worthy father's sore latter end. But ye ken the property's entail't; and, when it pleases the Maker to take you to Himsel, by consequence Beenie will get the estate.'

'That's not so certain,' replied George, jocularly looking at Dirdumwhamle;—'my wife has of late been more infirm than usual, and were I to marry again, and had male heirs—'

'Hoot, wi' your male heirs, and your snuffies; I hate the vera name o' sic things—they hae been the pests o' my life.—It would hae been a better world without them,' exclaimed the Leddy, and then she added—'But we need na cast out about sic unborn babes o' Chevy Chase. Beenie's a decent lassie, and will, nae doubt, make a prudent conjugality; so a' I hae for the present is to say that I expek ye'll tak your dinner wi' us. Indeed, considering what has happened, it would na be pleasant to you to be seen on the plane-stanes the day,—for I'm really sorry to see, Geordie, that ye're no just in your right jocularity. Howsever, as we're to hae a bit ploy, I request and I hope ye'll bide wi' us, and help to carve the bubbly-jock, whilk is a beast, as I hae heard your father often say, that requir't the skill o' a doctor, the strength o' a butcher, and the practical hand o' a Glasgow Magistrate to diject.'

Nothing more particular passed before dinner, the hour of which was drawing near; but a wedding-feast is, at any time, worthy of a chapter.

Chapter VIII

The conversation which the Leddy, to do her justice, had, considering her peculiar humour and character, so adroitly managed with the bride's father, did not tend to produce the happiest feelings among the conscious wedding-guests.

Both the Laird of Dirdumwhamle and his wife were uneasy, and out of countenance, and the happy pair were as miserable as ever a couple of clandestine lovers, in the full possession of all their wishes, could possibly be. But their reverend grandmother, neither daunted nor dismayed, was in the full enjoyment of a triumph, and, eager in the anticipation of accomplishing, by her dexterous address, the felicitous work which, in her own opinion, she had so well begun. Accordingly, dinner was served, with an air of glee and pride, so marked, that Kittlestonheugh was struck with it, but said nothing; and, during the whole of the dijection of the dinner, as his mother persisted in calling the carving, he felt himself frequently on the point of inquiring what had put her into such uncommon good humour. But she did not deem the time yet come for a disclosure, and went on in the most jocund spirits possible, praising the dishes, and cajoling her guests to partake.

'It's extraordinar to me, Beenie,' said she to the bride, 'to lo and behold you sitting as mim as a May puddock, when you see us a' here met for a blithesome occasion—and, Walky, what's come o'er thee, that thou's no a bit mair brisk than the statute o' marble-stane, that I ance saw in that sink o' deceitfulness, the Parliament House o' Embrough? As for our Meg, thy mother, she was ay one of your Moll-on-the-coals, a sigher o' sadness, and I'm none surprised to see her in the hypocondoricals; but for Dirdumwhamle, your respectit father, a man o' property, family, and connections—the three cardinal points o' gentileety—to be as one in doleful dumps, is sic a doolie doomster, that uncle Geordie, there whar he sits, like a sow playing on a trump, is a perfect beautiful Absalom in a sense o' comparison. Howsever, no to let us just fa' knickitty-knock, frae side to side, till our harns are splattered at the bottom o' the well o' despair—I'll gie you a toast, a thing which, but at an occasion, I ne'er think o' minting, and this toast ye maun a' mak a lippy—Geordie, my son and bairn, ye ken as weel as I ken, what a happy matrimonial your sister has had wi' Dirdumwhamle—and, Dirdumwhamle, I need na say to you, ye hae found her a winsome helpmate; and, surely Meg, Mr Milrookit has been to you a most cordial husband. Noo, what I would propose for a propine, Geordie, is, Health and happiness to Mr and Mrs Milrookit, and may they long enjoy many happy returns o' this day.'

The toast was drank with great glee; but, without entering into any particular exposition of the respective feelings of the party, we shall just simply notice, as we proceed, that the Leddy gave a significant nod and a wink both to the bride and bridegroom, while the bride's father was seized with a most immoderate fit of laughing, at, what he supposed, the ludicrous eccentricity of his mother.

'Noo, Geordie, my man,' continued the Leddy, 'seeing ye're in sic a state o' mirth and jocundity, and knowing, as we a' know, that life is but a weaver's shuttle, and Time a wabster, that works for Death, Eternity, and Co. great whole merchants; but for a' that, I am creditably informed they'll be obligated, some day, to mak a sequester—Howsever, that's nane o' our concern just now,—but, Geordie, as I was saying, I would fain tell you o' an exploit.'

'I am sure,' said he laughing, 'you never appeared to me so capable to tell it well,—what is it?'

The Leddy did not immediately reply, but looking significantly round the table, she made a short pause, and then said,—

'Do you know that ever since Adam and Eve ate the forbidden fruit, the life o' man has been growing shorter and shorter? To me—noo sax-and seventy year auld—the monthly moon's but as a glaik on the wall—the spring but as a butterflee that taks the wings o' the morning—and a' the summer only as the tinkling o' a cymbal—as for hairst and winter, they're the shadows o' death; the whilk is an admonishment, that I should not be overly gair anent the world, but mak mysel and others happy, by taking the santified use o' what I hae—so, Geordie and Sirs, ye'll fill another glass.'

Another glass was filled, and the Leddy resumed, all her guests, save her son, sitting with the solemn aspects of expectation. The countenance of Kittlestonheugh alone was bright with admiration at the extraordinary spirits and garrulity of his mother.

'Noo, Geordie,'she resumed, 'as life is but a vapour, a puff out o' the stroop o' the tea-kettle o' Time—let us a' consent to mak one another happy—and there being nae likelihood that ever Jamie Walkinshaw will colleague wi' Beenie, your dochter; I would fain hope ye'll gie her and Walky there baith your benison and an aliment to mak them happy.'

George pushed back his chair, and looked as fiercely and as proudly as any angry and indignant gentleman could well do; but he said nothing.

'Na,'said the Leddy, 'if that's the gait o't, ye shall hae't as ye will hae't,—It's no in your power to mak them unhappy.'

'Mother, what do you mean?' was his exclamation.

'Just that I hae a because for what I mean; but, unless ye compose yoursel, I'll no tell you the night—and, in truth, for that matter, if ye dinna behave wi' mair reverence to your aged parent, and no bring my grey hairs wi' sorrow to the grave, I'll no tell you at a'.'

'This is inexplicable,' cried her son. 'In the name of goodness, to what do you allude?—of what do you complain?'

'Muckle, muckle hae I to complain o',' was the pathetic reply. 'If your worthy father had been to the fore, ye would na daur't to hae spoken wi' sic unreverence to me. But what hae I to expek in this world noo?—when the Laird lights the Leddy, so does a' the kitchen boys; and your behaviour, Geordie, is an unco warrandice to every one to lift the hoof against me in my auld days.'

'Good Heavens!' cried he, 'what have I done?'

'What hae ye no done?' exclaimed his mother.—'Was na my heart set on a match atween Beenie and Walky there—my ain grandchilder, and weel worthy o' ane anither; and hae na ye sworn, for ought I ken, a triple vow that ye would ne'er gie your consent?'

'And if I have done so—she is my daughter, and I have my own reasons for doing what I have done,' was his very dignified reply.

'Reasons here, or reasons there,' said his mother, 'I hae gude reason to know that it's no in your power to prevent it.—Noo, Beenie, and noo, Walky, down on your knees baith o' you, and mak a novelle confession that ye were married the day; and beg your father's pardon, who has been so jocose at your wedding feast, that for shame he canna refuse to conciliate, and mak a handsome aliment down on the nail.'

The youthful pair did as they were desired—George looked at them for about a minute, and was unable to speak. He then threw a wild and resentful glance round the table, and started from his seat.

'Never mind him,' said the Leddy, with the most perfect equanimity; 'rise, my bairns, and tak your chairs—he'll soon come to himsel.'

'He'll never come to himself—he is distracted—he is ruined—his life is blasted, and his fortune destroyed,' were the first words that burst from the astonished father;

and he subjoined impatiently, 'This cannot be true—it is impossible!—Do you trifle with me, mother?—Robina, can you have done this?'

' 'Deed, Geordie, I doubt it's o'er true,' replied his mother; 'and it cannot be helped noo.'

'But it may be punished!' was his furious exclamation.—'I will never speak to one of you again! To defraud me of my dearest purpose—to deceive my hopes—O you have made me miserable!'

'Ye'll be muckle the better o' your glass o' wine, Geordie—tak it, and compose yoursel like a decent and sedate fore-thinking man, as ye hae been ay reputed.'

He seized the glass, and dashed it into a thousand shivers on the table.

All by this time had risen but the Leddy—she alone kept her seat and her coolness.

'The man's gaen by himsel,' said she with the most matronly tranquillity.— 'He has scartit and dintit my gude mahogany table past a' the power o' beeswax and elbow grease to smooth. But, Sirs, sit down—I expekit far waur than a' this—I did na hope for ony thing like sic composity and discretion. Really, Geordie, it's heart salve to my sorrows to see that ye're a man o' a Christian meekness and resignation.'

The look with which he answered this was, however, so dark, so troubled, and so lowering, that it struck terror and alarm even into his mother's bosom, and instantly silenced her vain and vexatious attempt to ridicule the tempest of his feelings.—She threw herself back in her chair, at once overawed and alarmed; and he suddenly turned round and left the house.

Chapter IX

The shock which the delicate frame of Mrs Walkinshaw of Kittlestonheugh received on hearing of her daughter's precipitate marriage, and the distress which it seemed to give her husband, acted as a stimulus to the malady which had so long undermined her health, and the same night she was suddenly seized with alarming symptoms. Next day the disease evidently made such rapid progress, that even the Doctors ventured to express their apprehensions of a speedy and fatal issue.

In the meantime, the Leddy was doing all in her power to keep up the spirits of the young couple, by the reiterated declaration, that, as soon as her son 'had come to himsel,' as she said, 'he would come down with a most genteel settlement;' but day after day passed, and there was no indication of any relenting on his part; and Robina, as we still must continue to call her, was not only depressed with the thought of her rashness, but grieved for the effect it had produced on her mother.

None of the party, however, suffered more than the Laird of Dirdumwhamle. He heard of the acceleration with which the indisposition of Mrs Walkinshaw was proceeding to a crisis, and, knowing the sentiments of his brother-in-law with respect to male heirs, he could not disguise to himself the hazard that he ran of seeing his son cut out from the succession to the Kittlestonheugh estate; and the pang of this thought was sharpened and barbed by the reflection, that he had himself contributed and administered to an event which, but for the marriage, would probably have been procrastinated for years, during which it was impossible to say what might have happened.

At Camrachle, the news of the marriage diffused unmingled satisfaction.

Mrs Charles Walkinshaw saw in it the happy escape of her son from a connection that might have embittered his life; and cherished the hope that her brother-in-law would still continue his friendship and kindness.

Walkinshaw himself was still more delighted with the event than his mother. He laughed at the dexterity with which his grandmother had brought it about; and, exulting in the feeling of liberty which it gave to himself, he exclaimed, 'We shall now see whether, indeed, my uncle was actuated towards me by the affection he professed, or by some motive of which the springs are not yet discovered.'

The minister, who was present at this sally, said little; but he agreed with his young friend, that the event would soon put his uncle's affections to the test. 'I cannot explain to myself,' was his only observation, 'why we should all so unaccountably distrust the professions of your uncle, and suppose, with so little reason, in truth against the evidence of facts, that he is not actuated by the purest and kindest motives.'

'That very suspicion,' said Mrs Eadie mysteriously, 'is to me a sufficient proof that he is not so sincere in his professions as he gets the credit of being. But I know not how it is, that, in this marriage, and in the sudden illness of his wife, I perceive the tokens of great good to our friends.'

'In the marriage,' replied the minister, 'I certainly do see something which gives me reason to rejoice; but I confess that the illness of Mrs Walkinshaw does not appear to me to bode any good. On the contrary, I have no doubt, were she dying, that her husband will not be long without a young wife.'

'Did not I tell you,' said Mrs Eadie, turning to Mrs Charles, 'that there would be a death before the good to come by Glengael, to you or yours, would be gathered? Mrs Walkinshaw of Kittlestonheugh is doomed to die soon; when this event comes to pass, let us watch the issues and births of Time.'

'You grow more and more mystical every day,' said her husband pensively. 'I am sorry to observe how much you indulge yourself in superstitious anticipations; you ought to struggle against them.'

'I cannot,' replied the majestic Leddy, with solemnity—'The mortal dwelling of my spirit is shattered, and lights and glimpses of hereafter are breaking in upon me. It has been ever so with all my mother's race. The gift is an ancient inheritance of our blood; but it comes not to us till earthly things begin to lose their hold on our affections. The sense of it is to me an assurance that the bark of life has borne me to the river's mouth. I shall now soon pass that headland, beyond which lies the open sea:—from the islands therein no one ever returns.'

Mr Eadie sighed; and all present regarded her with compassion, for her benign countenance was strangely pale; her brilliant eyes shone with a supernatural lustre; and there was a wild and incommunicable air in her look, mysteriously in unison with the oracular enthusiasm of her melancholy.

At this juncture a letter was handed in. It was the answer from Glengael to Mrs Eadie's application respecting Walkinshaw; and it had the effect of changing the painful tenor of the conversation.

The contents were in the highest degree satisfactory. Mr Frazer not only promised his influence, declaring that he considered himself as the agent of the family interests, but said, that he had no doubt of procuring at once the cadetcy, stating, at the same time, that the progress and complexion of the French Revolution rendered it probable that Government would find it expedient to augment the army; in which case, a commission for young Walkinshaw would be readily obtained; and he concluded with expressions of his sorrow at hearing his kinswoman had of late been so unwell, urging her to visit him at Glengael Castle, to which the family was on the point of removing for the summer, and where her native air might, perhaps, essentially contribute to her recovery.

'Yes,' said she, after having read the letter aloud, and congratulated Walkinshaw on the prospect which had opened.—'Yes; I will visit Glengael. The spirits of my fathers hover in the silence of those mountains, and dwell in the loneliness of the heath. A voice within has long told me, that my home is there, and I have been an exile since I left it.'

'My dear Gertrude,' said Mr Eadie,—'you distress me exceedingly this morning. To hear you say so pains me to the heart. It seems to imply that you have not been happy with me.'

'I was happy with you,' was her impressive answer. 'I was happy; but then I thought the hopes of my youth had perished.—The woeful discovery that rose like a ghost upon me withered my spirit; and the death of my children has since extinguished the love of life. Still, while the corporeal tenement remained in some degree entire, I felt not as I now feel; but the door is thrown open for my departure. I feel the airs of the world of spirits blowing in upon me; and as I look round to see if I have set my house in order, all the past of life appears in a thousand pictures; and the most vivid in the series are the sunny landscapes of my early years.'

Mr Eadie saw that it was in vain to reason with his wife in such a mood; and the Walkinshaws sympathised with the tenderness that dictated his forbearance, while James turned the conversation, by proposing to his sister and Ellen, that they should walk into Glasgow next day, to pay their respects to the young couple.

Doubtless there was a little waggery at the bottom of this proposition; but there was also something of a graver feeling.—He was desirous to ascertain what effect the marriage of Robina had produced on his uncle with respect to himself, and also to communicate, through the medium of his grandmother, the favourable result of the application to Glengael, in the hope, that, if there was any sincerity in the professions of partiality with which he had been flattered, that his uncle would assist him in his outfit either for India or the army. Accordingly, the walk was arranged as he proposed; but the roads in the morning were so deep and sloughy, that the ladies did not accompany him; a disappointment which, however acute it might be to him, was hailed as a God-send by the Leddy, whose troubles and vexations of spirit had, from the wedding-day, continued to increase, and still no hope of alleviation appeared.

Chapter X

'Really,' said the Leddy, after Walkinshaw had told her the news, and that only the wetness of the road had prevented his sister and Ellen from coming with him to town,—'Really, Jamie, to tell you the gude's truth, though I would hae been blithe to see Mary, and that weel-bred lassie, your joe Nell Frizel—I'm very thankful they hae na come—for, unless I soon get some relief, I'll be herrit out o' house and hall wi' Beenie and Walky,—twa thoughtless wantons,—set them up wi' a clandestine marriage, in their teens! it's enough to put marriages out of fashion.'

'I thought,' replied Walkinshaw, playing with her humours, 'that the marriage was all your own doing.'

'My doing, Jamie Walkinshaw! wha daurs to say the like o' that? I'm as clear o't as the child unborn—to be sure they were married here, but that was no fault o' mine—my twa grand children, it could ne'er be expected that I would let them be married on the crown-o'-the-causey—But, wasna baith his mother and father present, and is that no gospel evidence, that I was but an innocent onlooker?—No, no, Jamie, whomsoever ye hear giving me the wyte o' ony sic Gretna Green job, I reddeye put your foot on the spark, and no let it singe my character.—I'm abundantly and overmuch punished already, for the harmless jocosity, in the cost and cumbering o' their keeping.'

'Well, but unless you had sanctioned their marriage, and approved o't beforehand, they would never have thought of taking up their residence with you.'

'Ye're no far wrang there, Jamie; I'll no deny that I gied my approbation, and I would hae done as muckle for your happiness, had ye been o' a right conforming spirit and married Beenie, by the whilk a' this hobbleshaw would hae been spare't; but there's a awful difference between approving o' a match, and providing a living and house-room, bed, board, and washing, for two married persons—and so, although it may be said in a sense, that I had a finger in the pye, yet every body who kens me, kens vera weel that I would ne'er hae meddled wi' ony sic gunpowder plot, had there been the least likelihood that it would bring upon me sic a heavy handful. In short, nobody, Jamie, has been more imposed upon than I hae been—I'm the only sufferer. De'il-be-lickit has it cost Dirdumwhamle, but an auld Muscovy duck, that he got sent him frae ane o' your uncle's Jamaica skippers two year ago, and it was then past laying—we smoor't it wi' ingons the day afore yesterday, but ye might as soon hae tried to mak a dinner o' a hesp o' seven heere yarn, for it was as teugh as the grannie of the cock that craw't to Peter.'

'But surely,' said Walkinshaw, affecting to condole with her, 'surely my uncle, when he has had time to cool, will come forward with something handsome,'

'Surely—Na, an he dinna do that, what's to become o' me?—Oh! Jamie, your uncle's no a man like your worthy grandfather,—he was a saint o' a Christian disposition—when your father married against both his will and mine, he did na gar the house dirl wi' his stamp to the quaking foundation; but on the Lord's day thereafter, took me by the arm—O! he was o' a kindly nature—and we gaed o'er thegither, and wis'd your father and mother joy, wi' a hunder pound in our hand—that was acting the parent's part!'

'But, notwithstanding all that kindness, you know he disinherited my father,' replied Walkinshaw seriously, 'and I am still suffering the consequences.'

'The best o' men, Jamie,' said the Leddy, sympathisingly, 'are no perfect, and your grandfather, I'll ne'er maintain, was na a no mere man—so anent the disinheritance, there was ay something I could na weel understand; for, although I had got an inkling o' the law frae my father, who was a deacon at a plea—as a' the Lords in Embro' could testificate, still there was a because in that act of sederunt and session, the whilk, in my opinion, required an interlocutor frae the Lord Ordinary to expiscate and expone, and, no doubt, had your grandfather been spare't, there would hae been a rectification.— But, wae's me, the Lord took him to himsel; in the very hour when Mr Keelevin, the lawyer, was doun on his knees reading a scantling o' a new last will and settlement.— Eh! Jamie, that was a moving sight,—before I could get a pen, to put in your dying grandfather's hand, to sign the paper, he took his departal to a better world, where, we are taught to hope, there are neither lawyers nor laws.'

'But if my uncle will not make a settlement on Robina, what will you do?' said Walkinshaw, laughing.

'Haud your tongue, and dinna terrify folk wi' ony sic impossility!' exclaimed the Leddy—'Poor man, he has something else to think o' at present. Is na your aunty brought nigh unto the gates o' death? Would ye expek him to be thinking o' marriage settlements and wedding banquets, when death's so busy in his dwelling? Ye're an unfeeling creature, Jamie—But the army's the best place for sic graceless getts, Whan do ye begin to spend your half-crown out o' saxpence a-day? And is Nell Frizel to carry your knapsack? Weel, I ay thought she was a cannonading character, and I'll be none surprised o' her fighting the French or the Yanky Doodles belyve, wi' a stone in the foot of a stocking, for I am most creditably informed, that that's the conduct o' the soldier's wives in the field o' battle.'

It was never very easy to follow the Leddy, when she was on what the sailors call one of her jawing tacks; and Walkinshaw, who always enjoyed her company most when she was in that humour, felt little disposed to interrupt her. In order, however, to set her off in a new direction, he said,—'But, when I get my appointment, I hope you'll give me something to buy a sword, which is the true bride o' a soldier.'

'And a poor tocher he gets wi' her,' said the Leddy;—'wounds and bruises, and putrefying sores, to make up a pack for beggary. No doubt, howsever, but I maun break the back o' a guinea for you.'

'Nay, I expect you'll give your old friend, Robin Carrick, a forenoon's call. I'll not be satisfied if you don't.'

'Well, if e'er I heard sic a stand-and-deliver-like speech since ever I was born,'— exclaimed his grandmother. 'Did I think, when I used to send the impudent smytcher, wi' my haining o' twa three pounds to the bank, that he was contriving to commit sic a highway robbery on me at last?'

'But,' said Walkinshaw, 'I have always heard you say, that there should be no stepbairns in families. Now, as you are so kind to Robina and Walky, it can never be held fair if you tie up your purse to me.'

'Thou's a wheedling creature, Jamie,' replied the Leddy, 'and nae doubt I maun do my duty, as every body knows I hae ay done, to a' my family; but I'll soon hae little to do't wi', if the twa new married eating moths are ordain't to devour a' my substance. But there's ae thing I'll do for thee, the whilk may be far better than making noughts in Robin Carrick's books. I'll gang out to the Kittlestonheugh, and speir for thy aunty; and though thy uncle, like a bull of Bashan, said he would not speak to me, I'll gar him fin' the weight o' a mother's tongue, and maybe, through my persuadgeon, he may be wrought to pay for thy sword and pistols, and other sinews o' war. For, to speak the truth, I'm wearying to mak a clean breast wi' him, and to tell him o' his unnaturality to his own dochter; and what's far waur, the sin, sorrow, and iniquity, of allooing me, his aged parent, to be rookit o' plack and bawbee by twa glaikit jocklandys that dinna care what they burn, e'en though it were themselves.'

But, before the Leddy got this laudable intention carried into effect, her daughter-in-law, to the infinite consternation of Dirdumwhamle, died; and, for some time after that event, no opportunity presented itself, either for her to be delivered of her grudge, or for any mutual friend to pave the way to a reconciliation. Young Mrs Milrookit saw her mother, and received her last blessing; but it was by stealth, and unknown to her father. So that, altogether, it would not have been easy, about the period of the funeral, to have named in all the royal city a more constipated family, as the Leddy assured all her acquaintance, the Walkinshaws and Milrookits, were baith in root and branch, herself being the wizent and forlorn trunk o' the tree.

Chapter XI

On the day immediately after the funeral of her sister-in-law, Mrs Charles Walkinshaw was surprised by a visit from the widower.

'I am come,' said he, 'partly to relieve my mind from the weight that oppresses it, arising from an occurrence to which I need not more particularly allude, and partly to vindicate myself from the harsh insinuations of James. He will find that I have not been so sordid in my views as he so unaccountably and so unreasonably supposed, and that I am still disposed to act towards him in the same liberal spirit I have ever done. What is the result of the application to Mrs Eadie's friend? And is there any way by which I can be rendered useful in the business?'

This was said in an off-hand man-of-the-world way. It was perfectly explicit. It left no room for hesitation; but still it was not said in such a manner as to bring with it the comfort it might have done to the meek and sensitive bosom of the anxious mother.

'I know not in what terms to thank you,' was her answer, diffidently and doubtingly expressed. 'Your assistance certainly would be most essential to James, for, now that he has received a commission in the King's army, I shall be reduced to much difficulty.'

'In the King's army! I thought he was going to India?' exclaimed her brother-in-law, evidently surprised.

'So it was originally intended; but,' said the mother, ' Mr Frazer thought, in the present state of Europe, that it would be of more advantage for him to take his chance in the regular army; and has in consequence obtained a commission in a regiment that is to be immediately increased. He has, indeed, proved a most valuable friend; for, as the recruiting is to be in the Highlands, he has invited James to Glengael, and is to afford him his countenance to recruit among his dependants, assuring Mrs Eadie that, from the attachment of the adherents of the family, he has no doubt that, in the course of the summer, James may be able to entitle himself to a Company, and then'——

This is very extraordinary friendship, thought the Glasgow merchant to himself. These Highlanders have curious ideas about friendship and kindred; but, nevertheless, when things are reduced to their money price, they are just like other people. 'But,' said he aloud, 'what do you mean is to take place when James has obtained a Company?'

'I suppose,' replied the gentle widow timidly, she knew not wherefore, 'that he will then not object to the marriage of James and Ellen.'

'I think,' said her brother-in-law, 'he ought to have gone to India. Were he still disposed to go there, my purse shall be open to him.'

'He could not hope for such rapid promotion as he may obtain through the means of Glengael,' replied Mrs Charles somewhat firmly; so steadily, indeed, that it disconcerted the Laird; still he preserved his external equanimity, and said,—

'Nevertheless, I am willing to assist his views in whichever way they lie. What has become of him?'

Mrs Charles then told him that, in consequence of the very encouraging letter from Mr Frazer, Walkinshaw had gone to mention to his father's old friend, who had the vessel fitting out for New York, the change that had taken place in his destination, and to solicit a loan to help his outfit.

Her brother-in-law bit his lips at this information. He had obtained no little reputation among his friends for the friendship which he had shown to his unfortunate brother's family; and all those who knew his wish to accomplish a match between James and his daughter, sympathised in sincerity with his disappointment. But something, it would not be easy to say what, troubled him when he heard this, and he said,—

'I think James carries his resentment too far. I had certainly done him no ill, and he might have applied to me before going to a stranger.'

'Favours,' replied the widow, 'owe all their grace and gratitude to the way in which they are conferred. James has peculiar notions, and perhaps he has felt more from the manner in which you spoke to him than from the matter you said.'

'Let us not revert to that subject—it recals mortifying reflections, and the event cannot be undone. But do you then think Mr Frazer will consent to allow his daughter to marry James? She is an uncommonly fine girl, and, considering the family connections, surely might do better.'

This was said in an easy disengaged style, but it was more assumed than sincere; indeed, there was something in it implying an estimate of considerations, independent of affections, which struck so disagreeably on the feelings, that his delicate auditor did not very well know what to say; but she added,—

'James intends, as soon as we are able to make the necessary arrangements, to set out for Glengael Castle, which, being in a neighbourhood where there are many old officers, he will be able to procure some information with respect to the best mode of proceeding with his recruiting; and Mr Frazer has kindly said that it will be for his advantage to start from the castle.'

'I suppose Miss Frazer will accompany him?' replied the widower drily.

'No,' said his sister-in-law, 'she does not go till she accompanies Mrs Eadie, who intends to pass the summer at Glengael.'

'I am glad of that; her presence might interfere with his duty.'

'Whom do you mean?' inquired Mrs Charles, surprised at the remark; 'whose presence?' and she subjoined smilingly, 'You are thinking of Ellen; and you will hardly guess that we are all of opinion here that both she and Mrs Eadie might be of great use to him on the spot. Mrs Eadie is so persuaded of it, that the very circumstance of their marriage being dependent on his raising a sufficient number of men to entitle him to a company, would, she says, were it known, make the sons of her father's clansmen flock around him.'

'It is to be deplored, that a woman, who still retains so many claims, both on her own account, and the high respectability of her birth, should have fallen into such a decay of mind,' said the merchant, at a loss for a more appropriate comment on his sister-in-law's intimation.—'But,' continued he, 'do not let James apply to any other person. I am ready and willing to advance all he may require; and, since it is determined that he ought immediately to avail himself of Mr Frazer's invitation, let him lose no time in setting off for Glengael. This, I trust,' said he in a gayer humour, which but ill suited with his deep mourning, 'will assure both him and Miss Frazer, that I am not so much their enemy as perhaps they have been led to imagine.'

Soon after this promise the widower took his leave; but, although his whole behaviour during the visit was unexpectedly kind and considerate, and although it was impossible to withhold the epithet of liberality—nay more, even of generosity—from his offer, still it did not carry that gladness to the widow's heart which the words and the assurance were calculated to convey. On the contrary, Mrs Charles sat for some time ruminating on what had passed; and when, in the course of about an hour after, Ellen Frazer, who had been walking on the brow of the hazel bank with Mary, came into the parlour, she looked at her for some time without speaking.

The walk had lent to the complexion of Ellen a lively rosy glow. The conversation which she had held with her companion related to her lover's hopes of renown, and it had excited emotions that at once sparkled in her eyes and fluctuated on her cheek. Her lips were vivid and smiling; her look was full of intelligence and naivete—simple at once and elegant—gay, buoyant, and almost as sly as artless, and a wreath, if the expression may be allowed, of those nameless graces in which the charms of beauty are mingled with the allurements of air and manners, garlanded her tall and blooming form.

She seemed to the mother of her lover a creature so adorned with loveliness and nobility, that it was impossible to imagine she was not destined for some higher sphere than the humble fortunes of Walkinshaw. But in that moment the mother herself forgot the auspices of her own youth, and how seldom it is that even beauty, the most palpable of all human excellence, obtains its proper place, or the homage of the manly heart that Nature meant it should enjoy.

Chapter XII

Mr Walkinshaw had not left Camrachle many minutes when his nephew appeared. James had in fact returned from Glasgow, while his uncle was in the house, but, seeing the carriage at the door, he purposely kept out of the way till it drove off.

His excursion had not been successful. He found his father's old acquaintance sufficiently cordial in the way of inquiries, and even disposed to sympathise with him, when informed of his determination to go abroad; but when the army was mentioned the merchant's heart froze; and after a short pause, and the expression of some frigiverous observations with respect to the licentiousness of the military life, it was suggested that his uncle was the proper quarter to apply to. In this crisis, their conversation was interrupted by the entrance of a third party, when Walkinshaw retired.

During his walk back to Camrachle, his heart was alternately sick and saucy, depressed and proud.

He could not conceive how he had been so deluded, as to suppose that he had any right to expect friendship from the gentleman he had applied to. He felt that in so doing he acted with the greenness of a boy, and he was mortified at his own softness. Had there been any reciprocity of obligations between his father and the gentleman, the case would have been different. 'Had they been for forty or fifty years,' thought he, 'in the mutual interchange of mercantile dependance, then perhaps I might have had some claim, and, no doubt, it would have been answered, but I was a fool to mistake civilities for friendship.' Perhaps, however, had the case been even as strong as he put it, he might still have found himself quite as much deceived.

'As to making any appeal to my uncle, that was none of his business,' said he to himself. 'I did not ask the fellow for advice, I solicited but a small favour. There is no such heart-scalding insolence as in refusing a solicitation, to refer the suppliant to others, and with prudential admonitions too—curse him who would beg, were it not to avoid doing worse.'

This brave humour lasted for the length of more than a mile's walk, during which the young soldier marched briskly along, whistling courageous tunes, and flourishing his stick with all the cuts of the broadsword, lopping the boughs of the hedges, as if they had been the limbs of Frenchmen, and switching away the heads of the thistles and benweeds in his path, as if they had been Parisian carmagnols, against whom, at that period, the loyalty of the British bosom was beginning to grow fretful and testy.

But the greater part of the next mile was less animated—occasionally, cowardly thoughts glimmered palely through the glorious turbulence of youthful heroism, and once or twice he paused and looked back towards Glasgow, wondering if there was any other in all that great city, who might be disposed to lend him the hundred pounds he had begged for his outfit.

'There is not one,' said he, and he sighed, but in a moment after he exclaimed, 'and who the devil cares? It does not do for soldiers to think much; let them do their duty at the moment; that's all they have to think of; I will go on in the track I have chosen, and trust to fortune for a windfall;' again 'In the Garb of Old Gaul' was gallantly whistled, and again the hedges and thistles felt the weight of his stick.

But as he approached Camrachle, his mood shifted into the minor key, and when the hazel-bank and the ash-trees, with the nests of the magpies in them, appeared in sight, the sonorous bravery of the Highland march, became gradually modulated into a low and querulous version of 'Lochaber no more,' and when he discovered the carriage at his mother's door, his valour so subsided into boyish bashfulness, that he shrunk away, as we have already mentioned, and did not venture to go home, till he saw that his uncle had left the house.

On his entrance, however, he received a slight sensation of pleasure, at seeing both his mother and sister with more comfort in their looks than he had expected, and he was, in consequence, able to tell them, with comparative indifference, the failure of his mission. His mother then related what had passed with his uncle.

The news perplexed Walkinshaw; they contradicted the opinion he had so warmly felt and expressed of his uncle; they made him feel he had acted rashly and ungratefully—but still such strange kindness occasioned a degree of dubiety, which lessened the self-reproaches of his contrition.

'However,' said he, with a light and joyous heart, 'I shall not again trouble either myself or him, as I have done; but in this instance, at least, he has acted disinterestedly, and I shall cheerfully avail myself of his offer, because it is generous—I accept it also as encouragement—after my disappointment, it is a happy omen; I will take it as a brave fellow does his bounty-money—a pledge from Fortune of some famous "all hail hereafter."'

What his sentiments would have been, had he known the tenor of his uncle's mind at that moment,—could he even but have suspected that the motive which dictated such seeming generosity, so like an honourable continuance of his former partiality, was prompted by a wish to remove him as soon as possible from the company of Ellen Frazer, in order to supplant him in her affections, we need not attempt to imagine how he would have felt. It is happy for mankind, that they know so little of the ill said of them behind their backs, by one another, and of the evil that is often meditated in satire and in malice, and still oftener undertaken from motives of interest and envy. Walkinshaw rejoicing in the good fortune that had so soon restored the alacrity of his spirits—so soon wiped away the corrosive damp of disappointment from its brightness—did not remain long with his mother and sister, but hastened to communicate the inspiring tidings to Ellen Frazer.

She was standing on the green in front of the manse, when she saw him coming bounding towards her, waving his hat in triumph and exultation, and she put on a grave face, and looked so rebukingly, that he halted abruptly, and said—'What's the matter?'

'It's very ridiculous to see any body behaving so absurdly,' was her cool and solemn answer.

'But I have glorious news to tell you; my uncle has come forward in the handsomest manner, and all's clear for action.'

This was said in an animated manner, and intended to upset her gravity, which, from his knowledge of her disposition, he suspected, was a sinless hypocrisy, put on only to teaze him. But she was either serious or more resolute in her purpose than he expected; for she replied with the most chastising coolness,—'I thought you were never to have any thing to say again to your uncle?'

Walkinshaw felt this pierce deeper than it was intended to do, and he reddened exceedingly, as he said, awkwardly.

'True! but I have done him injustice; and had he not been one of the best dispositioned men, he would never have continued his kindness to me as he has done; for I treated him harshly.'

'It says but little for you, that, after enjoying his good-will so long, you should have thrown his favours at him, and so soon after be obliged to confess you have done him wrong.'

Walkinshaw hung his head, still more and more confused. There was too much truth in the remark not to be felt as a just reproach; and, moreover, he thought it somewhat hard, as his folly had been on her account, that she should so taunt him. But Ellen, perceiving she had carried the joke a little too far, threw off her disguise, and, with one of her most captivating looks and smiles, said,—'Now, that I have tamed you into rational sobriety, let's hear what you have got to say. Men should never be spoken to when they are huzzaing. Remember the lesson when you are with your regiment.'

What further followed befits not our desultory pen to rehearse; but, during this recital of what had taken place at Glasgow, and the other incidents of the day, the lovers unconsciously strayed into the minister's garden, where a most touching and beautiful dialogue ensued, of which having lost our notes, we regret, on account of our fair readers, and all his Majesty's subalterns, who have not yet joined, that we cannot furnish a transcript.—The result, however, was, that, when Ellen returned into the manse, after parting from Walkinshaw, her beautiful eyes looked red and watery, and two huge tears tumbled out of them, when she told her aunt that he intended to set off for Glengael in the course of two or three days.

Chapter XIII

Next day Walkinshaw found himself constrained, by many motives, to go into Glasgow, in order to thank his uncle for the liberality of his offer, and, in accepting it, to ask pardon for the rudeness of his behaviour.

His reception in the counting-house was all he could have wished; it was even more cordial than the occasion required, and the cheque given, as the realization of the promise, considerably exceeded the necessary amount. Emboldened by so much kindness, Walkinshaw, who felt for his cousins, and really sympathised with the Leddy under the burden of expence which she had brought upon herself, ventured to intercede in their behalf, and he was gratified with his uncle's answer.

'I am pleased, James,' said he, ' that you take so great an interest in them; but, make your mind easy, for, although I have been shamefully used, and cannot but long resent it, still, as a man, I ought not to indulge my anger too far. I, therefore, give you liberty to go and tell them, that, although I do not mean to hold any intercourse with Robina and her husband, I have, nevertheless, ordered my man of business to prepare a deed of settlement on her, such as I ought to make on my daughter.'

Walkinshaw believed , when he heard this, that he possessed no faculty whatever to penetrate the depths of character, so bright and shining did all the virtues of his uncle at that moment appear;—virtues of which, a month before, he did not conceive he possessed as inglespark. It may, therefore, be easily imagined, that he hastened with light steps and long strides towards his grandmother's house, to communicate the generous tidings. But, on reaching the door, he met the old lady, wrapped up, as it seemed, for a journey, with her maid, coming out, carrying a small trunk under her arm. On seeing him, she made a movement to return; but, suddenly recollecting herself, she said,—'Jamie, I hae nae time, for I'm gaun to catch the Greenock flying coach at the Black Bull, and ye can come wi' me.'

'But, what has become o' Robina?' cried he, surprised at this intelligence and sudden movement.

His grandmother took hold of him by the arm, and giving it an indescribable squeeze of exultation, said,—'I'll tell you, it's just a sport. They would need long spoons that sup parridge wi' the de'il, or the like o' me, ye maun ken. I was just like to be devour't into beggary by them. Ae frien' after another calling, glasses o' wine ne'er devauling; the corks playing clunk in the kitchen frae morning to night, as if they had been in a change-house on a fair-day. I could stand it no longer. So yesterday, when that nabal, Dirdumwhamle, sent us a pair o' his hunger't hens, I told baith Beenie and Walky, that they were obligated to go and thank their parents, and to pay them a marriage visit for a day or twa, although we're a' in black for your aunty, her mother; and so this morning I got them off, Lord be praised; and I am noo on my way to pay a visit to Miss Jenny Purdie, my cousin, at Greenock.'

'Goodness! and is this to throw poor Beenie and Walky adrift?' exclaimed Walkinshaw.

'Charity, Jamie, my bairn, begins at hame, and they hae a nearer claim on Dirdumwhamle, who is Walky's lawful father, than on me; so e'en let them live upon him till I invite them back again.'

Walkinshaw, though really shocked, he could not tell why, was yet so tickled by the Leddy's adroitness, that he laughed most immoderately, and was unable for some time in consequence to communicate the message, of which he was the joyous bearer; but when he told her, she exclaimed,—

'Na, if that's the turn things hae ta'en, I'll defer my visit to Miss Jenny for the present; so we'll return back. For surely, baith Beenie and Walky will no be destitute of a' consideration when they come to their kingdom, for the dreadfu' cost and outlay that I hae been at the last five weeks. But, if they're guilty o' sic niggerality, I'll mak out a count—bed, board, and washing, at five and twenty shillings a-week, Mrs Scrimpit, the minister's widow of Toomgarnels, tells me, would be a charge o' great moderation;— and if they pay't, as pay't they shall, or I'll hae them for an affront to the Clerk's Chambers; ye's get the whole half o't, Jamie, to buy yoursel a braw Andrew Ferrara. But I marvel, wi' an exceeding great joy, at this cast o' grace that's come on your uncle. For, frae the hour he saw the light, he was o' a most voracious nature for himsel; and while the fit lasts, I hope ye'll get him to do something for you.'

Walkinshaw then told her not only what his uncle had done, but with the ardour in which the free heart of youth delights to speak of favours, he recapitulated all the kind and friendly things that had been said to him.

'Jamie, Jamie, I ken your uncle Geordie better than you,—for I hae been his mother. It's no for a courtesy o' causey clash that he's birling his mouldy pennies in sic firlots;— tak my word for't.'

'There is no possible advantage can arise to him from his kindness to me.'

'That's to say, my bairn, that ye hae na a discerning spirit to see't; but if ye had the second sight o' experience as I hae, ye would fin' a whaup in the nest, or I am no a Christian sister, bapteesed Girzel.'

By this time they had returned to the house, and the maid having unlocked the door, and carried in the trunk, Walkinshaw followed his grandmother into the parlour, with the view of enjoying what she herself called, the observes of her phlosification; but the moment she had taken her seat, instead of resuming the wonted strain of her jocular garrulity, she began to sigh deeply, and weep bitterly, a thing which he never saw her do before, but in a way that seldom failed to amuse him; on this occasion, however, her emotion was unaffected, and it moved him to pity her. 'What's the matter with you?' said he, kindly;—she did not, however, make any answer for some time, but at last she said,—

'Thou's gaun awa to face thy faes,—as the sang sings, "far far frae me and Logan braes,"—and I am an aged person, and may ne'er see thee again; and I am wae to let thee gang, for though thou was ay o' a nature that had nae right reverence for me, a deevil's buckie, my heart has ay warm't to thee mair than to a' the lave o'my grandchildren; but it's no in my power to do for thee as thy uncle has done, though it's well known to every one that kens me, that I hae a most generous heart,—far mair than e'er he had,—and I would na part wi' thee without hanselling thy knapsack. Hegh, Sirs! little did I think when the pawkie laddie spoke o' my bit gathering wi' Robin Carrick, that it was in a sincerity; but thou's get a part. I'll no let thee gang without a solid benison, so tak the key, and gang into the scrutoire and bring out the pocket-book.'

Walkinshaw was petrified, but did as he was desired; and, having given her the pocket-book, sewed by his aunt, Mrs Milrookit, at the boarding school, she took several of Robin's promissory-notes out, and looking them over, presented him with one for fifty pounds.

'Now, Jamie Walkinshaw,' said she, 'if ye spend ae plack o' that like a prodigal son,—it's no to seek what I will say when ye come back,—but I doot I doot, lang before that day I'll be deep and dumb aneath the yird, and naither to see nor hear o' thy weel or thy woe.'

So extraordinary and unlooked-for an instance of liberality on the part of his grandmother, together with the unfeigned feeling by which she was actuated, quite overwhelmed Walkinshaw, and he stood holding the bill in his hand, unable to speak. In the meantime, she was putting up her other bills, and, in turning them over, seeing one for forty-nine pounds, she said, 'Jamie, forty-nine pounds is a' the same as fifty to ane that pays his debts by the roll of a drum, so tak this, and gie me that back.'

Chapter XIV

The time between the visit to Glasgow and the departure of Walkinshaw for Glengael was the busiest period that had occurred in the annals of Camrachle from the placing of Mr Eadie in the cure of the parish. To the young men belonging to the hamlet, who had grown up with Walkinshaw, it was an era of great importance; and some of them doubted whether he ought not to have beaten up for recruits in a neighbourhood where he was known, rather than in the Highlands. But the elder personages, particularly the matrons, were thankful that the Lord was pleased to order it differently.

His mother and sister, with the assistance of Ellen Frazer, were more thriftily engaged in getting his baggage ready; and although the sprightliness of Ellen never sparkled more brilliantly for the amusement of her friends, there were moments when her bosom echoed in a low soft murmur to the sigh of anxiety that frequently burst from his mother's breast.

Mr Eadie was not the least interested in the village. He seemed as if he could not give his pupil advice enough, and Walkinshaw thought he had never before been so tiresome. They took long walks together, and ever and anon the burden of the worthy minister's admonition was the sins and deceptions of the world, and the moral perils of a military life.

But no one—neither tutor, mother, nor amorosa—appeared so profoundly occupied with the event as Mrs Eadie, whose majestic intellect was evidently touched with the fine frenzy of a superstition at once awful and elevated. She had dreams of the most cheering augury, though all the incidents were wild and funereal; and she interpreted the voices of the birds and the chattering of the magpies in language more oriental and coherent than Macpherson's Ossian.

The moon had changed on the day on which Walkinshaw went into Glasgow, and she watched the appearance of its silver rim with the most mysterious solicitude. Soon after sun-set on the third evening, as she was sitting on a tombstone in the churchyard with Mr Eadie, she discovered it in the most favourable aspect of the Heavens, and in the very position which assured the most fortunate issues to all undertakings commenced at its change.

'So it appears,' said she, 'like a boat, and it is laden with the old moon—that betokens a storm.'

'But when?' said her husband with a sigh, mournfully disposed to humour the aberrations of her fancy.

'The power is not yet given to me to tell,' was her solemn response. 'But the sign is a witness that the winds of the skies shall perform some dreadful agency in the fortunes of all enterprises ruled by this lunar influence. Had the moon been first seen but as a portion of a broken ring, I would have veiled my face, and deplored the omen. She comes forth, however, in her brightness—a silver boat sailing the azure depths of the Heavens, and bearing a rich lading of destiny to the glorious portals of the sun.'

At that moment a cow looked over the churchyard wall, and lowed so close to Mr Eadie's ear, that it made him start and laugh. Instead, however, of disturbing the Pythian mood of his lady, it only served to deepen it; but she said nothing, though her look intimated that she was offended by his levity.

After a pause of several minutes she rose, and moved towards the gate without accepting his proffered arm.

'I am sorry,' said he, 'that you are displeased with me; but really the bathos of that cow was quite irresistible.'

'Do you think,' was her mystical reply, 'that an animal, which, for good reasons, the wise Egyptians hardly erred in worshipping, made to us but an inarticulate noise? It was to me a prophetic salutation. On the morning before my father left Glengael to join the royal standard, I heard the same sound. An ancient woman, my mother's nurse, and one of her own blood, told me that it was a fatal enunciation for then the moon was in the wane; but heard, she said, when the new moon is first seen, it is the hail of a victory or a bridal.'

'It is strange,' replied the minister, unguardedly attempting to reason with her, 'that the knowledge of these sort of occurrences should be almost exclusively confined to the inhabitants of the Highlands.'

'It is strange,' said she; 'but no one can expound the cause. The streamers of the northern light shine not in southern skies.'

At that moment she shuddered, and, grasping the minister wildly by the arm, she seemed to follow some object with her eye that was moving past them.

'What's the matter—what do you look at?' he exclaimed with anxiety and alarm.

'I thought it was Walkinshaw's uncle,' said she with a profound and heavy sigh, as if her very spirit was respiring from a trance.

'It was nobody,' replied the minister thoughtfully.

'It was his wraith,' said Mrs Eadie.

The tone in which this was expressed curdled his very blood, and he was obliged to own to himself, in despite of the convictions of his understanding, that there are more things in the heavens and the earth than philosophy can yet explain; and he repeated the quotation from Hamlet, partly to remove the impression which his levity had made.

'I am glad to hear you allow so much,' rejoined Mrs Eadie; 'and I think you must admit that of late I have given you many proofs in confirmation. Did I not tell you when the cock crowed on the roof of our friend's cottage, that we should soon hear of some cheerful change in the lot of the inmates? and next day came Walkinshaw from Glasgow with the news of the happy separation from his uncle. On the evening before I received my letter from Glengael, you may well remember the glittering star that announced it in the candle. As sure as the omen in the crowing of the cock, and the shining of that star, were fulfilled, will the auguries which I have noted be found the harbingers of events.'

Distressing as these shadows and gleams of lunacy were to those by whom Mrs Eadie was justly beloved and venerated, to herself they afforded a high and holy delight. Her mind, during the time the passion lasted, was to others obscure and oracular. It might be compared to the moon in the misty air when she is surrounded with a halo, and her light loses its silveryness, and invests the landscape with a shroudy paleness and solemnity. But Mrs Eadie felt herself as it were ensphered in the region of spirits, and moving amidst marvels and mysteries sublimer than the faculties of ordinary mortals could explore.

The minister conducted his wife to the house of Walkinshaw's mother, where she went to communicate the agreeable intelligence, as she thought, of the favourable aspect of the moon, as it had appeared to her Highland astrology. But he was so distressed by the evident increase of her malady, that he did not himself immediately go in. Indeed, it was impossible for him not to acknowledge, even to the most delicate suggestions of his own mind towards her, that she was daily becoming more and more fascinated by her visionary contemplations; and in consequence, after taking two or three turns in the village, he determined to advise her to go with Walkinshaw to Glengael, in the hope that the change of circumstances, and the interest that she might take once more in the scenes of her youth, would draw her mind from its wild and wonderful imaginings, and fix her attention again on objects calculated to inspire more sober, but not less affecting, feelings.

Chapter XV

The result of Mr Eadie's reflections was a proposition to Walkinshaw to delay his journey for a day or two, until Mrs Eadie could be prepared to accompany him; but, when the subject was mentioned to her, she declared the most decided determination not to trouble the tide of his fortune by any interposition of hers which had been full of disappointments and sorrows. From whatever sentiment this feeling arose, it was undoubtedly dictated by magnanimity; for it implied a sense of sacrifice on her part; nevertheless, it was arranged, that, although Walkinshaw should set out at the time originally fixed, Mrs Eadie, accompanied by Ellen Frazer, should follow him to Glengael as soon after as possible.

To the lovers this was no doubt delightful; but, when the Laird of Kittlestonheugh heard of it in Glasgow, it disturbed him exceedingly. The departure of Ellen Frazer from Camrachle to Glengael, where his nephew was for a time to fix his headquarters, was an occurrence that he had not contemplated, and still less, if any degree can exist in an absolute negative, that the minister's insane wife should accompany her.

A circumstance, however, occurred at the time, which tended materially to diminish his anxieties: A number of gentlemen belonging to the royal city had projected a sea excursion in Allan M'Lean's pilot boat, and one of the party proposed to Kittlestonheugh that he should be of their party—for they were all friends, and sympathised, of course, with the most heartfelt commiseration, for the loss he had sustained in his wife, who had been nearly twenty years almost as much dead as alive, and particularly in the grief he suffered by the injudicious marriage of his daughter. George, with his habitual suavity, accepted the invitation; and on the selfsame day that our friend and personal acquaintance Walkinshaw set off in the coach from the classical and manufacturing town (as we believe Gibbon the historian yclyped the royal city) for the soi-disant intellectual metropolis and modern Athens of Edinburgh, his uncle embarked at the stair of the west quay of Greenock.

What stores were laid in by those Glasgow Argonautics—what baskets of limes, what hampers of wine and rum, and loaves of sugar, and cheese and bacon hams, with a modicum of biscuit, we must leave for some more circumstantial historian to describe. Sufficient for us, and for all acquainted with the munificent consideration of the Glottiani for themselves, is the fact, that seven of the primest magnates of the royal city embarked together to enjoy the sea air, and the appetite consequent thereon, in one of the best sailing and best navigated schooners at that time on the west of Scotland. Whether any of them, in the course of the voyage, suffered the affliction of sea-sickness, we have never heard; but from our own opinion, believing the thing probable, we shall not enter into any controversy on the subject. There was, to be sure, some rumour shortly after, that, off Ailsa, they did suffer from one kind of malady or another; but whether from eating of that delicious encourager of appetite, solan goose—the most savoury product of the rocky pyramid—or from a stomatique inability to withstand the tossings of the sea, we have never received any satisfactory explanation. Be this, however, as it may, no jovial free-hearted, good kind of men, ever enjoyed themselves better than the party aboard the pilot boat.

They traversed the picturesque Kyles of Bute—coasted the shores of Cantyre—touched at the beautiful port of Campbelton—doubled the cliffy promontory—passed Gigha—left Isla on the left—navigated the sound of Jura—prudently kept along the romantic coast of Lorn and Appin—sailed through the sound of Mull—drank whisky at Rum—and, afraid of the beds and bowls of the hospitable Skye, cast anchor in Gareloch. What more they did, and where they farther navigated the iron shores and tusky rocks of the headlands, that grin in unsatiated hunger upon the waves and restless waters of the Minch, we shall not here pause to describe. Let it be enough that they were courageously resolved to double Cape Wrath, and to enjoy the midnight twilights, and the smuggled gin of Kirkwall;—the aurora borealis of the hyperborean region, with the fresh ling of Tamy Tomson's cobble boat at Hoy, and the silvery glimpses of Ursa Major; together with the tasty whilks and lampets that Widow Calder o' the Foul Anchor at Stromness, assured her customers in all her English—were pickled to a concupiscable state of excellence. Our immediate duty is to follow the steps of the Laird's nephew; and without entering upon any unnecessary details,—our readers, we trust, have remarked, that we entertain a most commendable abhorrence of all circumstantiality,—we shall allow Allan McLean and his passengers to go where it pleased themselves, while we return to Camrachle; not that we have much more to say respecting what passed there, than that Walkinshaw, as had been previously arranged, set out alone for Glengael Castle, in Inverness-shire; the parting from his mother and sister being considerably alleviated by the reflection, that Ellen Frazer, in attendance on Mrs Eadie, was soon to follow him. Why this should have given him any particular pleasure, we cannot understand; but, as the young man, to speak prosaically, was in love, possibly there are some juvenile persons capable of entering into his feelings. Not, however, knowing, of our own knowledge, what is meant by the phrase—we must just thus simply advert to the fact; expressing, at the same time, a most philosophical curiosity to be informed what it means, and why it is that young gentlemen and ladies, in their teens, should be more liable to the calamity than personages of greater erudition in the practices of the world.

Chapter XVI

In the summer of the year 1793, we have some reason to believe that the rugging and riving times of antiquity were so well over in the north of Scotland, that, not only might any one of his Majesty's subalterns travel there on the recruiting service, but even any spinster, not less than threescore, without let, hindrance, or molestation, to say nothing of personal violence; we shall not, therefore, attempt to seduce the tears of our fair readers, with a sentimental description of the incidents which befell our friend Walkinshaw, in his journey from Camrachle to Glengael, except to mention, in a parenthetical way, that, when he alighted from the Edinburgh coach at the canny twa and twae toun of Aberdeen awa, he had some doubt if the inhabitants spoke any Christian language.

Having remained there a night and part of a day, to see the place, and to make an arrangement with the host of an hostel, for a man and gig, to take him to Glengael Castle, he turned his face towards the north-west, and soon entered, what to him appeared, a new region. Mrs Eadie had supplied him with introductory letters to all her kith and kin, along the line of his route, and the recommendations of the daughter of the old Glengael were billets on the hospitality and kindness of the country. They were even received as the greatest favours by those who knew her least, so cherished and so honoured was the memory of the ill-fated chieftain, among the descendants of that brave and hardy race, who suffered in the desolation of the clans at Culloden.

The appearance and the natural joyous spirits of Walkinshaw endeared him to the families at the houses where he stopped on his way to Glengael, and his journey was, in consequence, longer and happier than he expected. On the afternoon of the ninth day after leaving Aberdeen, he arrived at the entrance of the rugged valley, in which the residence of Mr Frazer was situated.

During the morning, he had travelled along the foot of the mountains and patches of cultivation, and here and there small knots of larches, recently planted, served to vary the prospect and enliven his journey; but as he approached the entrance to Glengael, these marks of civilization and improvement gradually became rarer. When he entered on the land that had been forfeited, they entirely disappeared, for the green spots that chequered the heath there were as the graves of a race that had been rooted out or slaughtered. They consisted of the scites of cottages, which the soldiers of the Duke of Cumberland's army had plundered and burnt in the year Forty-five.

The reflections which these monuments of fidelity awakened in the breast of the young soldier, as the guide explained to him what they were, saddened his spirit, and the scene which opened, when he entered the cliffy pass that led into Glengael, darkened it more and more. It seemed to him as if he was quitting the habitable world, and passing into the realms, not merely of desolation, but of silence and herbless sterility. A few tufts of heath and fern among the rocks, in the bottom of the glen, showed that it was not absolutely the valley of death.

The appearance of the lowering steeps, that hung their loose crags over the road, was as if some elder mountains had been crushed into fragments, and the wreck thrown in torrents, to fill up that dreary, soundless, desolate solitude, where nature appeared a famished skeleton, pining amidst poverty and horror.

But, after travelling for two or three miles through this interdicted chasm, the cliffs began to recede, and on turning a lofty projecting rock, his ears were gladdened with the sound of a small torrent that was leaping in a hundred cascades down a ravine fringed with birch and hazel. From that point verdure began to reappear, and as the stream in its course was increased by other mountain rivulets, the scenery of the glen gradually assumed a more refreshing aspect. The rocks became again shaggy with intermingled heath and brambles, and the stately crimson foxglove, in full blossom, rose so thickly along the sides of the mountains, that Walkinshaw, unconscious that it was from the effect of their appearance, began to dream in his reverie of guarded passes, and bloody battles, and picquets of red-coated soldiers bivouacking on the hills.

But his attention was soon roused from these heroical imaginings by a sudden turn of the road, laying open before him the glassy expanse of an extensive lake, and on the summit of a lofty rocky peninsula, which projected far into its bosom, the walls and turrets of Glengael.

From the desolate contrast of the pass he had travelled, it seemed to him that he had never beheld a landscape so romantic and beautiful. The mountains, from the margin of the water, were green to their summits, and a few oaks and firs around the castle enriched the picturesque appearance of the little promontory on which it stood. Beyond a distant vista of the dark hills of Ross, the sun had retired, but the clouds, in glorious masses of golden fires, rose in a prodigality of splendid forms, in which the military imagination of the young enthusiast had no difficulty in discovering the towers, and domes, and pinnacles of some airy Babylon, with burnished chariots on the walls, and brazen warriors in clusters on the battlements.

This poetical enchantment, however, was soon dissolved. The road along the skirt of the lake, as it approached the castle, was rugged and steep, and where it turned off into the peninsula, towards the gate, it literally lay on the cornice of a precipice, which, with all his valour, made Walkinshaw more than once inclined to leap from the gig. Here and there a fragment of an old wall showed that it had once been fenced, and where the rains had scooped hollows on the edge of the cliff, a few stakes had recently been put up; but there was an air of decay and negligence around, that prepared the mind of the visitor for the ruinous aspect of the castle.

Mr Frazer, owing to his professional avocations, had seldom resided there, and he was too ambitious to raise the means to redeem the bonds he had granted for the purchase, to lay any thing out in improvements. The state and appearance of the place was, in consequence, lone and dismal. Not only were the outer walls mantled with ivy, but the arch of the gateway was broken. Many of the windows in the principal edifice were rudely filled up with stones. The slates in several places had fallen from the extinguisher-less desolate roofed turrets, and patches of new lime on different places of the habitable buildings, bore testimony to the stinted funds which the proprietor allowed for repairs.

Within the gate the scene was somewhat more alluring. The space inclosed by the walls had been converted into a garden, which Mrs Frazer and her daughters superintended, and had ornamented with evergreens and flowers. The apartments of the family were also neatly repaired, and showed, in the midst of an evident parsimony, a degree of taste that bespoke a favourable opinion of the inhabitants, which the reception given to Walkinshaw confirmed.

Mr Frazer, an elderly gentleman, of an acute and penetrating look, met him at the door, and, heartily shaking him by the hand, led him into a parlour, where Mrs Frazer, with two daughters, the sisters of Ellen, were sitting. The young ladies and their mother received him even with more frankness than the advocate. It was, indeed, not difficult to perceive, that they had previously formed an agreeable opinion of him, which they were pleased to find his prepossessing appearance confirm. But after the first congratulatory greetings were over, a slight cloud was cast on the spirits of the family by his account of the health of their relation Mrs Eadie. It, however, was not of very long duration, for the intelligence that she might be daily expected with Ellen soon chased it away.

Chapter XVII

As Mr Eadie found he could not conveniently get away from his parish, and the health of his lady requiring that she should travel by easy stages, it was arranged, after Walkinshaw's departure, that his sister should take the spare corner of the carriage. Accordingly, on the day following his arrival at Glengael, they all made their appearance at the castle.

Mrs Eadie's malady had, in the meantime, undergone no change. On the contrary, she was become more constantly mystical, and the mournful feelings, awakened by the sight of her early home, desolated by time and the ravages of war, rather served to increase her superstitious reveries. Every feature of the landscape recalled some ancient domestic tradition; and as often as she alluded to the ghostly stories that were blended with her ancestral tales, she expatiated in the loftiest and wildest flights of seeming inspiration and prophecy.

But still she enjoyed lucid intervals of a serene and tender melancholy.

On one occasion, while she was thus walking with the young ladies in the environs of the castle, she stopped abruptly, and, looking suddenly around, burst into tears.

'It was here,' said she—'on this spot, that the blossoms of my early hopes fell, and were scattered for ever.'

At that moment, a gentleman, some ten or twelve years older than Walkinshaw, dressed in the Highland garb, was seen coming towards the castle, and the majestic invalid uttered a terrific shriek, and fainted in the arms of her companions. The stranger, on hearing the scream, and seeing her fall, ran to the assistance of the ladies.

When Mrs Eadie was so far recovered as to be able to look up, the stranger happened to be standing behind Ellen, on whose lap her head was laid, and, not seeing him, she lay, for some time after the entire restoration of her faculties, in a state of profound solemnity and sorrow. 'O Frazer!' she exclaimed pathetically.

'I have seen him,' she added; 'and my time cannot now be long.'

At that instant her eye lighted on the stranger as he moved into another position. She looked at him for some time with startled amazement and awe; and, turning round to one of the young ladies, said, with an accent of indescribable grief, 'I have been mistaken.' She then rose, and the stranger introduced himself. He was the same person in whom, on his arrival from France, she had fourteen years before discovered the son of her early lover. Seeing him on the spot where she had parted from his father, and dressed in the garb and tartan of the clan which her lover wore on that occasion, she had, in her visionary mood, believed he was an apparition.

Saving these occasional hallucinations, her health certainly received new energy from her native air; and, by her presence at the castle, she was of essential service to the recruiting of her young friend.

In the meantime, Glengael being informed of the attachment between Walkinshaw and Ellen, had espoused his interests with great ardour; and French Frazer, as the stranger was called, also raising men for promotion, the castle became a scene of so much bustle as materially to disturb the shattered nerves of the invalid. With a view, therefore, to change the scene, and to enable Mrs Eadie to enjoy the benefit of sea-bathing, an excursion was proposed to Caithness and Sutherland, where Glengael was desirous of introducing the officers to certain political connections which he had in these counties, and it was proposed that, while the gentlemen went to pay their visits, the ladies should take up their residence at the little town of Wick.

The weather had, for some days before their departure from Glengael, been bright and calm, and the journey to Wick was performed with comparative ease and comfort. The party had, however, scarcely alighted at the house, which a servant sent on before had provided for their accommodation, when the wind changed, and the skies were overcast. For three days it raged a continual tempest; the rain fell in torrents, and the gentlemen, instead of being able to proceed on their visit, were confined to the house. At the end of the third day the storm subsided, and, though the weather was broken, there were intervals which allowed them to make little excursions in the neighbourhood.

The objects they visited, and the tales and traditions of the country, were alike new and interesting to the whole party; and it was agreed, that, before leaving Wick, the gentlemen should conduct the ladies to some of the remarkable spots which they had themselves visited;—among other places, Girnigo Castle, the ancient princely abode of the Earls of Caithness, the superb remains of which still obtain additional veneration in the opinion of the people, from the many guilty and gloomy traditions that fear and fancy have exaggerated in preserving the imperfect recollections of its early history.

Mrs Eadie had agreed to accompany them, the walk not exceeding three or four miles; but on the evening preceding the day which they had fixed for the excursion, when the weather had all the appearance of being settled, she saw, or imagined that she saw, at sunset, some awful prodigy which admonished her not to go.

'I beheld,' said she, 'between me and the setting-sun, a shadowy hand bearing an hour-glass, run out; and when I looked again, I saw the visionary semblance of Walkinshaw's uncle pass me with a pale countenance. Twice have I witnessed the same apparition of his wraith, and I know from the sign, that either his time is not to be long, or to-morrow we shall hear strange tidings.'

It was useless to reason or to argue with her sublime and incomprehensible pretensions; but as it was deemed not prudent to leave her alone, Glengael and Mrs Frazer agreed to remain at Wick, while French Frazer and the young ladies, with Walkinshaw and his sister, went to inspect the ruins of Girnigo, and the rocks, caverns, and precipices of Noss-head.

Of all places in the wild and withered region of Caithness, the promontory of Noss-head presents, alike to the marine voyager and the traveller by land, one of the most tremendous objects. The waves of the universal sea have, from the earliest epochs, raged against it. Huge rocks, torn from the cliffs, stand half hid in the waters, like the teeth and racks of destruction grinning for shipwrecks. No calm of the ocean is there without a swell, and no swell without horror. The sea-birds, that love to build on the wildest cliffs and precipices of that coast of ruins, shun Noss-head, for the ocean laves against it in everlasting cataracts, and the tides, whether in ebb or flow, hurl past in devouring whirlpools. To the pilots afar at sea it is a lofty landmark and a beacon,—but the vessel embayed either within its northern or its southern cliffs, may be known by the marks on her sails, or the name on the pieces of her stern,— but none of her crew ever escape to tell the circumstances of her fate. Even there the miserable native earns no spoils from the waves;—whatever reaches the shore consists of fragments, or splinters, or corses, or limbs,—all are but the crumbs and the surfeit-relics of destruction.

Chapter XVIII

Mr Donald Gunn, the worthy Dominie of Wick, who had agreed to act as a guide to Girnigo, was, soon after sunrise, at the door, summoning the party to make ready for the journey; for, although the morning was fair and bright, he had seen signs in the preceding evening, which made him apprehensive of another storm. 'The wind,' said he to Walkinshaw, who was the first that obeyed the call, 'often, at this time of the year, rises about noon, when the waves jump with such agility against the rocks, that the most periculous points of view cannot be seen in their proper elegance, without the risk of breaking your neck, or at least being washed away, and drowned forever.'

Walkinshaw, accordingly, upon Gunn's report, as he called it, roused the whole party, and they set out for Staxigo, preceded by the Dominie, who, at every turn of the road, 'indexed,' as he said, 'the most interesting places.'

During the walk to the village, the weather still continued propitious; but the schoolmaster observed, that a slight occasional breeze from the north-east, the wildest wind that blows on that coast, rippled the glassy sea, as it undulated among the rocks below their path; a sure indication, so early in the morning, of a tempestuous afternoon. His companions, however, unacquainted with the omens of that ravenous shore, heard his remark without anxiety.

After breakfasting at Elspeth Heddle's public in Staxigo on milk, and ham and eggs, a partan, and haddocks, they went on to the ruins of Girnigo. The occasional fetching of the wind's breath, which the Dominie had noticed in their morning walk, was now become a steady gale, and the waves began to break against the rugged cliffs and headlands to the southward, insomuch, that, when the party reached the peninsula on which the princely ruins of the united castles of Girnigo and Sinclair are situated, they found several fishermen, belonging to Wick, who had gone out to sea at day-break, busily drawing their boats on shore, in the little port, on the south side of the cliffs, under the walls. The visitors inquired why they were so careful in such bright and summer weather; but they directed the attention of the Dominie to long flakes of goat's beard in the skies, and to the sea-birds flying towards the upland.

By this time the billows were breaking white and high, on the extremities of Noss-head, and the long grass on the bartisans and window-sills of the ruins streamed and hissed in the wind. The sun was bright; but the streaks of hoary vapour that veined the pure azure of the heavens retained their position and menacing appearance. There was, however, nothing in the phenomena of the skies to occasion any apprehension; and the party, without thinking of the immediate horrors of a storm, sympathised with their guide, as he related to them the mournful legends of those solitary towers. But, although he dwelt, with particular emphasis, on the story of the Bishop, whom one of the Earls of Caithness had ordered his vassals to boil in a cauldron, on account of his extortions, their sympathy was more sorrowfully awakened by the woeful fate of the young Master of Caithness, who, in 1572, fell a victim to the jealousy of his father.

'George, the Earl at that time,' said the schoolmaster, 'with his son the Master of Caithness, was on the leet of the lovers of Euphemia, the only daughter of an ancestor of Lord Reay. The lady was young and beautiful, and naturally preferred the son to the father; but the Earl was a haughty baron, and, in revenge for his son proving a more thriving wooer, was desirous of putting him for a season out of the way—but not by the dirk, as the use and wont of that epoch of unrule might have justified. Accordingly, one afternoon, as they were sitting together in the hall at yonder architraved window in the second story, the wrathful Earl clapped his hands thrice, and in came three black-aviced kerns in rusted armour, who, by a signal harmonized between them and Earl George, seized the lawful heir, and dragged him to a dampish captivity in yon vault, of which you may see the yawning hungry throat in the chasm between the two principal lumps of the buildings.'

The learned Dominie then proceeded to relate the sequel of this strange story—
by which it appeared, that, soon after the imprisonment of his son, the Earl being
obliged to render his attendance at the court of Stirling, left his son in the custody of
Murdow Mackean Roy, who, soon after the departure of his master, was persuaded
by the prisoner to connive at a plan for his escape. But the plot was discovered by
William, the Earl's second son, who apprehended Murdow, and executed him in
the instant. Immediately after, he went down into the dungeon, and threatened his
brother also with immediate punishment, if he again attempted to corrupt his keepers.
The indignant young nobleman, though well ironed, sprung upon Lord William, and
bruised him with such violence, that he soon after died. David and Inghrame Sinclair
were then appointed custodiers of the prisoner; but, availing themselves of the absence
of the Earl, and the confusion occasioned by the death of William, they embezzled
the money in the castle, and fled, leaving their young lord in the dungeon, a prey to
the horrors of hunger, of which he died.

About seven years after, the Earl, while he lamented the fatal consequences of
his own rash rivalry, concealed his thirst for revenge. Having heard that Inghrame
Sinclair, who had retired with his booty to a distant part of the country, intended to
celebrate the marriage of his daughter by a great feast—resolved to make the festival
the scene of punishment. Accordingly, with a numerous retinue, he proceeded to hunt
in the neighbourhood of Inghrame Sinclair's residence; and, availing himself of the
hospitable courtesies of the time, he entered the banquet-hall, and slew the traitor in
the midst of his guests.—

While the visitors in the lee of the ruins were listening to the Dominie's legend,
the wind had continued to increase and the sea to rise, and the spray of the waves
was springing in stupendous water-spouts and spires of foam over all the headlands
in view to the south.

'Aye,' said the Dominie, pointing out to them the ruins of Clyth Castle, over which
the sea was breaking white in the distance, 'we may expect a dry storm, for Clyth has
got on its shroud. Look where it stands like a ghost on the shore. It is a haunted and
unhallowed monument.'

'In olden and ancient times the Laird of Clyth went over to Denmark, and, being
at the court of Elsineur, counterfeited, by the help of a handsome person, and a fine
elocution, the style and renown of the most prosperous gentleman in all Caithness, by
which he beguiled a Prince of Copenhagen to give him his daughter in marriage, a lady
of rare and surpassing beauty. After his marriage he returned to Scotland to prepare
for the reception of his gorgeous bride; but, when he beheld his own rude turret amidst
the spray of the ocean's sea, and thought of the golden palaces and sycamore gardens
of Denmark, he was shocked at the idea of a magnificent princess inhabiting such a
bleak abode, and overwhelmed with the dread of the indignation that his guilt would
excite among her friends. So when the Danish man-of-war, with the lady on board,
was approaching the coast, he ordered lights and fires along the cliffs of Ulbster, by
which the pilots were bewildered, and the ship was dashed in pieces. The princess and
her maids of honour, with many of the sailors, were drowned; but her body was found,
beautiful in death, with rings on her fingers, and gems in her ears; and she was interred,
as became a high-born lady of her breeding, in the vault where she now lies, among

the ancestors of Sir John Sinclair of Ulbster; and ever since that time, the Castle of Clyth has been untenanted, and as often as the wind blows from the north-east, it is covered with a shroud as if doing penance for the maiden of Denmark.'

Notwithstanding the pedantry in the Dominie's language in relating this tradition, the unaffected earnestness with which he expressed himself, moved the compassion of his auditors, and some of the ladies shed tears; which the gentlemen observing, Walkinshaw, to raise their spirits, proposed they should go forward towards Noss-head to view the dreadful turbulency of the breakers. But, before they had approached within half a mile of the promontory, the violence of the gale had increased to such a degree, that they found themselves several times obliged to take refuge in the hollows of the rocks, unable to withstand the fury of the wind, and the lavish showers of spray, that rose in sheets from the waves, and came heavier than rain on the blast.

Chapter XIX

In the meantime, the Glasgow party on board Allan McLean's pilot-boat was enjoying their sail and sosherie. Enticed by the beauty of the sunny weather, which had preceded the arrival of our Glengael friends at Wick, they had made a long stretch as far to the north as the Mainland of Shetland, and after enjoying fresh ling and stockfish in the highest perfection there, and laying in a capital assortment of worsted hose for winter, they again weighed anchor, with the intention of returning by the Pentland Firth. Being, however, overtaken by the boisterous weather, which obliged Mr Frazer and his two recruiting guests to stop at Wick, they went into Kirkwall Bay, where they were so long detained, that the thoughts of business and bills began to deteriorate their pleasure.

To none of the party was the detention so irksome as to Mr Walkinshaw, for, independent of the cares of his mercantile concerns, his fancy was running on Ellen Frazer, and he was resolved, as soon as he returned to the Clyde, to sound her father with a proposal, to solicit her for his second wife. Why a gentleman, so well advanced in life, should have thought of offering himself as a candidate for a lady's love, against his nephew, we must leave to be accounted for by those who are able to unravel the principles of the Earl of Caithness's enmity to his son, particularly as we are in possession of no reasonable theory, adequate to explain how he happened to prefer Ellen Frazer to the numerous beauties of the royal city. It is sufficient for us, as historians, simply to state the fact, and narrate the events to which it gave rise.

Mr Walkinshaw then being rendered weary of the Orkneys, and, perhaps, also of the joviality of his companions, by the mingled reflections of business, and the tender intention of speedily taking a second wife, resolved, rather than again incur the uncertainties of the winds and waves, to leave the pilot-boat at Kirkwall, and embark for Thurso, in order to return home over land; a vessel belonging to that port being then wind-bound in the bay. Accordingly, on the same morning that the party from Wick went to visit Girnigo Castle, and the magnificent horrors of Noss-head, he embarked.

For some time after leaving Kirkwall, light airs and summer breezes enabled the sloop in which he had taken his passage to work pleasantly round Moulhead. But before she had passed the spiky rocks and islets of Copinshaw, the master deemed it prudent to stand farther out to sea; for the breeze had freshened, and the waves were dashing themselves into foam on Roseness and the rugged shores of Barra.

The motion of the sloop, notwithstanding the experience which the passenger had gained in the pilot-boat, overwhelmed him with unutterable sickness, and he lay on the deck in such affliction, that, he once rashly wished he was drowned. The cabin-boy who attended him was so horror-struck at hearing so profane a wish at sea, while the wind was rising on a lee shore, that he left him to shift for himself.

For some time the master did not think it necessary to shorten sail, but only to stretch out towards the south-east; but, as the sun mounted towards the meridian, the gale so continued to increase, that he not only found it necessary to reef, but in the end to hand almost all his canvas save the foresail. Still, as there were no clouds, no rain, no thunder nor lightning, the seasick Glasgow merchant dreamt of no danger.

'May be,' said the cabin-boy in passing, as the Laird happened to look up from his prostrate situation on the deck, 'ye'll get your ugly wish oure soon.'

The regardless manner and serious tone in which this was said had an immediate and restorative effect. Mr Walkinshaw roused himself, and, looking round, was surprised to see the sails taken in; and, casting his eyes to leeward, beheld, with a strong emotion of consternation, the ocean boiling with tremendous violence, and the spindrift rising like steam.

'It blows a dreadful gale?' said he inquiringly to the master.

'It does,' was the emphatic reply.

'I hope there is no danger,' cried the merchant, alarmed, and drawing himself close under the larboard gunnel.

The master, who was looking anxiously towards Duncansby-head, which presented a stupendous tower of foaming spray, over the starboard bow, replied,—'I hope we shall be able to weather Noss-head.'

'And if we do not,' said Mr Walkinshaw, 'what's to be done?'

'You'll be drowned,' cried the cabin-boy, who had seated himself on the lea-side of the companion; and the bitterness of the reproachful accent with which this was said stung the proud merchant to the quick—but he said nothing; his fears were, however, now all awake, and he saw, with a feeling of inexpressible alarm, that the crew were looking eagerly and sorrowfully towards the roaring precipices of Caithness.

Still the vessel kept bravely to her helm, and was working slowly outward; but, as she gradually wore round, her broadside became more and more exposed to the sea, and once or twice her decks were washed fore and aft.

'This is terrible work, Captain,' said Mr Walkinshaw.

'It is,' was all the answer he received.

'Is there no port we can bear away for?'

'None.'

'Good Heavens! Captain, if this continues till night?'

The master eyed him for a moment, and said with a shudder,—'If it does, Sir, we shall never see night.'

'You'll be drowned,' added the little boy, casting an angry look from behind the companion.

'Almighty Powers!—surely we are not in such danger?' exclaimed the terrified merchant.

'Hold your tongue,' again cried the boy.

Mr Walkinshaw heard him, and for a moment was petrified, for the command was not given with insolence, but solemnity.

A cry of 'Hold fast,' in the same instant, came from the forecastle, and, after a momentary pause, a dreadful sea broke aboard, and swept the deck.

The master, who had himself taken the helm, was washed overboard, and the tiller was broken.

'We are gone!' said the little boy, as he shook the water from his jacket, and crawled on towards the mast, at the foot of which he, seated himself, for the loss of the tiller, and the damage the rudder had sustained, rendered the vessel unmanageable, and she drifted to her fate before the wind.

'Is there indeed no hope?' cried Mr Walkinshaw to one of the sailors, who was holding by the shrouds.

'If we get into Sinclair's Bay, there is a sandy beach,' replied the sailor.

'And if we do not?' exclaimed the passenger in the accent of despair.

'We'll a' be drowned,' replied the boy with a scowling glance, as he sat cowering with his head between his knees, at the foot of the mast.

'We shall not get into Sinclair's Bay,' said the sailor, firmly; 'but we may pass Noss-head.'

'Do you think so?' said Mr Walkinshaw, catching something like hope and fortitude from the sedate courage of the sailor.

Another cry of 'Hold fast' prepared him for a second breach of the sea, and he threw himself on the deck, and took hold of a ringbolt, in which situation he continued, though the vessel rose to the wave. In the meantime, the resolute sailor, after looking calmly and collectedly around for some time, went from the larboard to the starboard, and mounted several rattlings of the shrouds, against which he leant with his back, while the vessel was fast driving towards Noss-head.

Chapter XX

The party from Glengael, who had, as we have described, been obliged to take refuge from the wind in the lee of the rocks, stood contemplating the scene in silence. The sky was without a cloud—but the atmosphere was nevertheless almost like steam, through which the sun shone so sickly, that, even without hearing the hiss of the wind, or the rage of the ocean, no shelter could have prevented the spectator from being sensible that some extraordinary violence agitated and troubled the whole air. Every shrub and bramble not only bent before the wind, but it may be said their branches literally streamed in the blast. There was a torrent which ran towards the sea, near the spot where the party stood; but the wind caught its waters as they fell in a cataract, and blew them over the face of the hill like a wreath of 'mist. A few birch trees, that skirted the dell through which this stream ran, brushed the ground before the breeze; and the silver lining of their leaves was so upturned in the constant current of the storm, that they had the appearance of being covered with hoar frost. Not a bee was abroad on the heath, and the sea birds were fluttering and cowering in the lee of the rocks—a bernacle, that attempted to fly from behind a block of granite, was whirled screaming away in the wind, and flung with such resistless impetuosity against the precipice, behind a corner of which the party were sheltering, that it was killed on the spot. The landscape was bright in the hazy sunshine; but the sheep lay in the hollows of the ground, unable to withstand the deluge of the dry tempest that swept all before it, and a wild and lonely lifelessness reigned on the mountains.

The appearance of the sea was awful. It was not because the waves rolled in more tremendous volumes than any of the party had ever before seen, and burst against the iron precipices of Noss-head with the roar and the rage of the falls of Niagara—the whole expanse of the ocean was enveloped with spindrift, and, as it occasionally opened, a vessel was seen. At first it was thought she was steering for the bay of Wick, but it soon appeared that she drifted at random towards Sinclair's Bay, and could, by nothing less than some miraculous change of the wind, reach the anchorage opposite to Kiess Castle.

Ellen Frazer was the first who spoke of the sloop's inevitable fate.—' It is dreadful,' said she, 'for us to stand in safety here, like spectators at a tragedy, and see yon unfortunate bark rushing without hope to destruction. Let us make an attempt to reach the beach—she may be driven on the shore, and we may have it in our power to assist the poor wretches, if any should escape.'

They, accordingly, endeavoured to reach the strand; but before they could wrestle with the wind half-way towards it, they saw that the vessel could not attain Sinclair's Bay, and that her only chance of salvation was in weathering Noss-head, to which she was fast nearing. They, in consequence, changed their course, and went towards the promontory; but, by the time they had gained the height, they saw it was hopeless to think they could render any assistance, and they halted under the ledge of an overhanging rock, to see if she would be able to weather that dreadful headland.

The place where they took shelter was to the windward of the spray, which rose like a furious cataract against the promontory; and in pyramids of foam, that were seen many leagues off at sea, deluged the land to a great extent far beyond Castle Girnigo. It happened that Ellen Frazer had a small telescope in her hand, which they had brought with them, and, when they were under cover, she applied it to her eye.

'The sailors,' said she, 'seem to have abandoned themselves to despair—I see two prostrate on the deck. There is one standing on the shrouds, as if he hopes to be able to leap on the rocks when she strikes. The dog is on the end of the bowsprit—I can look at them no more.'

She then handed the telescope to Mary, and, retiring to a little distance, seated herself on a stone, and, covering her face with her handkerchief, could no longer control her tears. The vessel, in the mean time, was fast drifting towards the rocks, with her broadside to the wave.

'I think,' said Mary, 'that she must have lost her helm; nobody is near where it should be.—They have no hope.—One of the men, who had thrown himself on the deck, is risen. He is tying himself to the shrouds.—There is a boy at the foot of the mast, sitting cowering on the deck, holding his head between his hands.'

Walkinshaw, without speaking, took the telescope from his sister, who went and sat down in silence beside Ellen. By this time, the vessel had drifted so near, that every thing on her deck was distinct to the naked eye.

'The person on the deck,' said Walkinshaw, after looking through the glass about the space of a minute, 'is not a sailor—he has long clothes, and has the appearance of a gentleman, probably a passenger. That poor little boy!—he is evidently covering his ears, as if he could shut out the noise of the roaring death that awaits him. What a brave and noble fellow that is on the shrouds,—if coolness and courage can save, he is safe.'

At this moment, a shriek from Mary roused Ellen, and they both ran to the spot where Walkinshaw was standing. A tremendous wave had covered the vessel, as it were, with a winding-sheet of foam, and before it cleared away, she was among the breakers that raged against the headland.

'She is gone!' said Walkinshaw, and he took his sister and Ellen by the hands.—'Let us leave these horrors.' But the ladies trembled so much, that they were unable to walk; and Ellen became so faint, that she was obliged to sit down on the ground, while her lover ran with his hat to find, if possible, a little fresh water to revive her. He had not, however, been absent many minutes, when another shriek from his sister called him back, and, on returning, he found that a large dog, dripping wet, and whimpering and moaning, had laid himself at the feet of the ladies with a look of the most piteous and helpless expression. It was the dog they had seen on the bowsprit of the vessel, and they had no doubt her fate was consummated; but three successive enormous billows coming, with all the force of the German Ocean, from the Baltic, rolled into the bay. The roar with which they broke as they hurled by the cliff, where the party were standing, drew the attention of Walkinshaw even from Ellen; and, to his surprise, he saw that the waves had, in their sweep, drawn the vessel into the bay, and that she was coming driving along the side of the precipice, and, if not dashed in pieces before, would pass within a few yards of where they stood. Her bowsprit was carried away, which showed how narrowly she had already escaped destruction.

The ladies, roused again into eager and anxious sympathy by this new incident, approached with Walkinshaw as near as possible to the brink of the cliff—to the very edge of which the raging waters raised their foamy crests as they passed in their might and majesty from the headland into the bay. Another awful wave was soon after seen rising at a distance, and, as it came rolling onward nearer and nearer, it swallowed up every lesser billow. When it approached the vessel, it swept her along so closely to the rocks that Walkinshaw shouted unconsciously, and the dog ran barking to the edge of the precipice,—all on board were for a moment animated with fresh energy,—the little boy stood erect; and the sailor on the shrouds, seeing Walkinshaw and the ladies, cried bravely, as the vessel rose on the swell in passing, 'It will not do yet.' But the attention of his admiring spectators was suddenly drawn from him to the gentleman. 'Good Heavens!' exclaimed Ellen Frazer, 'it is your uncle!'

It was even so. Mr Walkinshaw, on raising his head to look up, saw and recognized them, and, wildly starting from the deck, shook his uplifted hands with a hideous and terrific frenzy. This scene was, however, but for an instant; the flank of the wave, as it bore the vessel along, broke against a projecting rock, and she was wheeled away by the revulsion to a great distance.

The sailor in the shrouds still stood firm; a second wave, more appalling than the former, brought the vessel again towards the cliff. The dog, anticipating what would happen, ran towards the spot where she was likely to strike. The surge swung her almost to the top of the precipice,—the sailor leapt from the shrouds, and caught hold of a projecting rock,—the dog seized him by the jacket to assist him up, but the ravenous sea was not to lose its prey.—In the same moment the wave broke, and the vessel was again tossed away from the rock, and a frightful dash of the breakers tore down the sailor and the faithful dog. Another tremendous revulsion, almost in the same moment, terminated the fate of the vessel. As it came roaring along it caught her by the broadside, and dashed her into ten thousand shivers against an angle of the promontory, scarcely more than two hundred yards from the spot where the horror-struck spectators stood. Had she been made of glass, her destruction and fragments could not have been greater. They floated like chaff on the waters; and, for the space of four or five seconds, the foam amidst which they weltered was coloured in several places with blood.

Chapter XXI

The same gale which proved so fatal on the coast of Caithness, carried the Glasgow party briskly home.

Before their arrival the news of the loss of Mr Walkinshaw had reached the city, and Dirdumwhamle and his son were as busy, as heirs and executors could well be, in taking possession of his fortune, which, besides the estate of Kittlestonheugh, greatly exceeded their most sanguine expectations.

They were, however, smitten with no little concern when, on applying to Mr Pitwinnoch, the lawyer, to receive infeftment of the lands, they heard from him, after he had perused the deed of entail, that Robina had no right to the inheritance; but that our friend Walkinshaw was the lawful heir.

It was, however, agreed, as the world, as well as themselves, had uniformly understood and believed that old Grippy had disinherited his eldest son, to say nothing about this important discovery. Walky and Robina accordingly took possession in due form of her father's mansion. Their succession was unquestioned, and they mourned in all the most fashionable pomp of woe for the loss they had sustained, receiving the congratulatory condolence of their friends with the most befitting decorum. To do the lady, however, justice, the tears which she shed were immediate from the heart; for, with all his hereditary propensity to gather and hold, her father had many respectable domestic virtues, and was accounted by the world a fair and honourable man. It is also due to her likewise to mention, that she was not informed, either by her husband or father-in-law, of the mistake they had been all in with regard to the entail; so that, whatever blame did attach to them for the part they played, she was innocent of the fraud.

To Walkinshaw's mother the loss of her brother-in-law was a severe misfortune, for with him perished her annuity of fifty pounds a-year. She entertained, however, a hope that Robina would still continue it; but the feelings arising from the consciousness of an unjust possession of the estate, operated on the mind of Milrookit in such a way, as to make him suddenly become wholly under the influence of avarice. Every necessary expence was grudged; his wife, notwithstanding the wealth she had brought him, was not allowed to enjoy a guinea; in a word, from the day in which Pitwinnoch informed him that she had no right to the property, he was devoured, in the most singular manner, with the most miserly passions and fears.

The old Leddy, for some time after the shock she had met with in the sudden death of her son, mourned with more unaffected sorrow than might have been expected from her character; and having, during that period, invited Mrs Charles to spend a few weeks with her, the loss of the annuity, and conjectures respecting the continuance of it, frequently formed the subject of their conversation.

'It's my notion,' the Leddy would say, 'that Beenie will see to a continuality o' the 'nuity—but Walky's sic a Nabal, that nae doot it maun be a task o' dexterity on her side to get him to agree. Howsever, when they're a' settled, I'll no be mealy-mouthed wi' them. My word! a bien bargain he has gotten wi' her, and I'm wae to think it did nae fa' to your Jamie's luck, who is a laddie o' a winsome temper—just as like his grandfather, my friend that was, as a kittling's like a cat—the only difference being a wee thought mair o' daffing and playrifety.'

Nor was it long after these observations that the Leddy had an opportunity of speaking to her grandchildren on the subject. One day soon after, when they happened to call, she took occasion to remind them how kind she had been at the time of their marriage, and also that, but for her agency, it might never have taken place.

'Noo,' said she, 'there is ae thing I would speak to you anent, though I was in the hope ye would hae spar't me the obligation, by making me a reasonable gratis gift for the cost and outlay I was at, forbye trouble on your account. But the compliment is like the chariot-wheels o' Pharaoh, sae dreigh o' drawing, that I canna afford to be blate wi' you ony langer.

Howsever, Walky and Beenie, I hae a projection in my head, the whilk is a thought o' wisdom for you to consider, and it's o' the nature o' a solemn league and covenant. If ye'll consent to alloo Bell Fatherlans her 'nuity of fifty pounds per annus, as it is called, according to law, I'll score you out o' my books for the bed, board, and washing due to me, and a heavy soom it is.'

'Where do you think we are to get fifty pounds a-year?' exclaimed Milrookit. 'Fifty pounds a-year!'

'Just in the same neuk, Walky, where ye found the Kittlestonheugh estate and the three and twenty thousand pounds o' lying siller, Beenie's braw tocher,' replied the Leddy; 'and I think ye're a very crunkly character, though your name's no Habakkuk, to gi'e me sic a constipation o' an answer.'

'I can assure you, Leddy,' said he, 'if it was a thing within the compass of my power, I would na need to be told to be liberal to Mrs Charles; but the burden o' a family's coming upon us, and it's necessary, nay, it's a duty, to consider that charity begins at hame.'

'And what's to become o' her and her dochter? Gude guide us! would the hard nigger let her gang on the session? for I canna help her.'

'All I can say at present,' was his reply, 'that we are in no circumstances to spare any thing like fifty pounds a-year.'

'Then I can tell thee, Walky, I will this very day mak out my count, and every farthing I can extortionate frae thee, meeserable penure pig that thou art, shall be pay't o'er to her to the last fraction, just to wring thy heart o' niggerality.'

'If you have any lawful claim against me, of course I am obliged to pay you.'

'If I hae ony lawful claim?—ye Goliah o' cheatrie—if I hae ony lawful claim?—But I'll say nothing—I'll mak out an account—and there's nae law in Christendom to stop me for charging what I like—my goose shall lay gouden eggs, if the life bide in my bodie.—Ye unicorn of oppression, to speak to me o' law, that was so kind to you—but law ye shall get, and law ye shall hae—and be made as lawful as it's possible for caption and horning, wi' clerk and signet to implement.'

'If you will make your little favours a debt, nobody can prevent you; but I will pay no more than is justly due.'

The Leddy made no reply, but her eyes looked unutterable things; and after sitting for some time in that energetic posture of displeasure, she turned round to Robina, and said, with an accent of the most touching sympathy,—

'Hegh, Beenie! poor lassie! but thou hast ta'en thy sheep to a silly market. A skelp-the-dub creature to upbraid me wi' his justly dues! But crocodile or croakindeil, as I should ca' him, he'll get his ain justly dues.—Mr Milrookit o' Kittlestonheugh, as it's no the fashion when folk hae recourse to the civil war o' a law-plea, to stand on a ceremony, maybe ye'll find some mair pleasant place than this room, an ye were to tak the pains to gang to the outside o' my door; and I'll send, through the instrumentality o' a man o' business, twa lines anent that bit sma' matter for bed, board, and washing due to me for and frae that time, when, ye ken, Mr Milrookit, ye had na ae stiver to keep yourself and your wife frae starvation.—So out o' my house, and daur no longer to pollute my presence, ye partan-handit, grip-and-haud smedy-vyce Mammon o' unrighteousness.'

After this gentle hint, as the Leddy afterwards called it, Milrookit and Robina hastily obeyed her commands, and returned to their carriage; but before driving home, he thought it necessary, under the menace he had received, to take the advice of his lawyer, Mr Pitwinnoch. Some trifling affairs, however, prevented him from driving immediately to his office, and the consequence was, that the Leddy, who never allowed the grass to grow in her path, was there before him.

Chapter XXII

'Mr Pitwinnoch,' said the Leddy, on being shown into what she called 'the bottomless pit o' his consulting-room,' where he wrote alone,—'ye'll be surprised to see me, and troth ye may think it's no sma' instancy that has brought me sae far afield the day; for I hae been sic a lamiter with the rheumateese, that, for a' the last week, I was little better than a nymph o' anguish; my banes were as sair as if I had been brayed in a mortar, and shot into Spain. But ye maun know and understand, that I hae a notion to try my luck and fortune in the rowley powley o' a law-plea.'

'Indeed!' said the lawyer. 'What has happened?'

'Aye! Mr Pitwinnoch, ye may weel speer; but my twa ungrateful grandchildren, that I did sae muckle for at their marriage, hae used me waur than I were a Papistical Jew o' Jericho. I just, in my civil and discreet manner was gi'en them a delicate memento mori concerning their unsettled count for bed, board, and washing; when up got Milrookit, as if he would hae flown out at the broad side o' the house, and threepit that he didna owe me the tenth part o' half a farthing; and threatened to tak me afore the Lords for a Cananitish woman, and an extortioner.—Noo, don't you think that's a nice point, as my worthy father used to say, and music to the ears of a' the Fifteen at Embrough?'

'Mr Milrookit, surely,' said the lawyer, 'can never resist so just a demand. How much is it?'

'But, first and forwards,' replied the Leddy, 'before we come to the condescendence, I should state the case; and, Mr Pitwinnoch, ye maun understand that I hae some knowledge o' what pertains to law, for my father was most extraordinare at it; and so I need not tell you, that it's weel for me the day to know what I know. For Milrookit, as I was saying, having refused, pointblank, Mr Pitwinnoch, to implement the 'nuity of fifty pounds per annus, that your client—(that's a legal word, Mr Pitwinnoch)—that your client settled on my gude-dochter, I told him he would—then and there refusing—be bound over to pay me for the bed, board, and washing. And what would ye think, Mr Pitwinnoch? he responded, with a justly due,—but I'll due him; and though, had he been calm and well-bred, I might have put up with ten pounds; yet, seeing what a ramping lion he made himsel, I'll no faik a farthing o' a thousand, which, at merchants' interest, will enable me to pay the 'nuity. So, when we get it, ye'll hae to find me somebody willing to borrow on an heritable bond.'

'I think you can hardly expect so much as a thousand pounds. If I recollect rightly, Mr and Mrs Milrookit staid but six weeks with you,' said the lawyer.

'Time,' replied the Leddy, 'ye ken, as I hae often heard my father say, was no item in law; and unless there's a statute of vagrancy in the Decisions, or the Raging Magistratom, there can be no doot that I hae't in my power to put what value I please on my house, servitude, and expence, which is the strong ground of the case. Therefore, you will write a letter forthwith to Mr Milrookit of Kittlestonheugh, charging him with a lawful debt, and a' justly due to me, of one thousand pounds, without condescending on particulars at present, as the damages can be afterwards assessed, when we hae gotten payment of the principal, which every body must allow is a most liberal offer on my part.'

It was with some difficulty that Mr Pitwinnoch could preserve himself in a proper state of solemnity to listen to the instructions of his client; but what lawyer would laugh, even in his own 'bottomless pit?' However, he said,—

'Undoubtedly, Mrs Walkinshaw, you have a good ground of action; but, perhaps, I may be able to effect an amicable arrangement, if you would submit the business to arbitration.'

'Arbitration, Mr Pitwinnoch!' exclaimed the Leddy; 'never propound such a thing to me; for often hae I heard my father say, that arbitration was the greatest cut-throat of legal proceedings that had been devised since the discovery of justice at Amalphi. Na, na—I hae mair sense than to virdict my case wi' any sic pannelling as arbitration. So, law being my only remede, I hope ye'll leave no stone unturned till you hae brought Mr Milrookit's nose to the grindstone; and to help you to haud it there, I hae brought a five pound note as hansel for good luck,—this being the first traffic in legalities that I hae had on my own bottom; for, in the concos mentos o' Watty, my son, ye ken I was keepit back, in order to be brought forward as a witness; but there is no need o' ony decreet o' Court for such an interlocutor on the present occasion.'

The Leddy having, in this clear and learned manner, delivered her instructions, she left the office, and soon after Milrookit was also shown into 'the bottomless pit,' where he gave an account of the transaction, somewhat different, but, perhaps, no nearer the truth. He was, however, not a little surprised to find the pursuer had been there before him, and that she had instructed proceedings. But what struck him with the greatest consternation was a suggestion from Mr Pitwinnoch to compromise the matter.

'Take my advice, Mr Milrookit,' said he, 'and settle this quietly—there is no saying what a law-suit may lead to; and, considering the circumstances under which you hold the estate, don't stir, lest the sleeping dog awake. Let us pacify the old Leddy with two or three hundred pounds.'

'Two or three hundred pounds, for six weeks of starvation! The thing, Mr Pitwinnoch, is ridiculous.'

'True, Sir,' replied the lawyer; 'but then the state of the Entail—you should consider that. Be thankful if she will take a couple of hundreds.'

'Nay, if you counsel me to do that, I have no alternative, and must submit.'

'You will do wisely in at once agreeing,' said Pitwinnoch; and, after some farther conversation to the same effect, Milrookit gave a cheque for two hundred pounds, and retired grumbling.

The lawyer, rejoicing in so speedy and fortunate a settlement, as soon as he left the office, went to the Leddy, exulting in his address.

'Twa hundred pounds!' said she,—'but the fifth part o' my thousand! I'll ne'er tak ony sic payment. Ye'll carry it back to Mr Milrookit, and tell him I'll no faik a plack o' my just debt; and what's mair, if he does na pay me the whole tot down at once, he shall be put to the horn without a moment's delay.'

'I assure you,' replied the lawyer, 'that this is a result far beyond hope—you ought not for a moment to make a word about it; for you must be quite aware that he owes you no such sum as this. You said yourself that ten pounds would have satisfied you.'

'And so it would—but that was before I gaed to law wi' him,' cried the Leddy; 'but seeing now how I hae the rights o' the plea, I'll hae my thousand pounds if the hide be on his snout. Whatna better proof could ye hae o' the justice o' my demand, than that he should hae come down in terror at once wi' two hundred pounds? I hae known my father law for seven years, and even when he won, he had money to pay out of his own pocket—so, wi' sic erls o' victory as ye hae gotten, I would be waur than mad no to stand out. Just gang till him, and come na back to me without the thousand pound— every farthing, Mr Pitwinnoch—and your own costs besides; or, if ye dinna, may be I'll get another man o' business that will do my turn better—for, in an extremity like a law-suit, folk maunna stand on friendships. Had Mr Keelevin been noo to the fore, I would na needed to be put to my peremptors; but, honest man, he's gone. Howsever, there's one Thomas Whitteret, that was his clerk when my friend that's awa made his deed o' settlement—and I hae heard he has a nerve o' ability; so, if ye bring na me the thousand pounds this very afternoon, I'll apply to him to be my agent.'

Mr Pitwinnoch said not a word to this, but left the house, and, running to the Black Bull Inn, ordered a post-chaise, and was at Kittlestonheugh almost as soon as his client. A short conversation settled the business—the very name of Thomas Whitteret, an old clerk of Keelevin, and probably acquainted with the whole affair, was worth five thousand pounds, and, in consequence, in much less time than the Leddy expected, she did receive full payment of her thousand pounds; but, instead of expressing any pleasure at her success, she regretted that she should have made a charge of such moderation, being persuaded, that, had she stood out, the law would have given her double the money.

Chapter XXIII

Mr Pitwinnoch was instructed to lay out the money at five per cent, interest to pay Mrs Charles the annuity; and one of his clerks mentioned the circumstance to a companion in Mr Whitteret's office. This led to an application from him for the loan, on account of a country gentleman in the neighbourhood, who, having obtained a considerable increase of his rental, was intending to enlarge his mansion, and extend his style of living,—a very common thing at that period, the effects of which are beginning to show themselves,—but, as the Leddy said on another occasion, that's none of our concern at present.

The security offered being unexceptionable, an arrangement was speedily concluded, and a heritable bond for the amount prepared. As the party borrowing the money lived at some distance from the town, Mr Whitteret sent one of his young men to get it signed, and to deliver it to the Leddy. It happened that the youth employed in this business was a little acquainted with the Leddy, and knowing her whimsical humour, when he carried it home he stopped, and fell into conversation with her about Walkinshaw, whom he knew.

'I maun gar his mother write to him,' said the Leddy, 'to tell him what a victory I hae gotten;—for ye maun ken, Willy Keckle, that I hae overcome principalities and powers in this controversy.—Wha ever heard o' thousands o' pounds gotten for sax weeks' bed, board, and washing, like mine? But it was a rightous judgment on the Nabal Milrookit,—whom I'll never speak to again in this world, and no in the next either, I doot, unless he mends his manners. He made an absolute refuse to gie a continuality o' Jamie's mother's 'nuity, which was the because o' my going to law with him for a thousand pounds, value received in bed, board, and washing, for six weeks.— And the case, Willy,—you that's breeding for a limb o' the law,—ye should ken, was sic an absolute fact, that he was obligated by a judicature to pay me down the money.'

Willy Keckle was so amused with her account of the speedy justice which she had obtained, as she said, by instructing Mr Pitwinnoch herself of the 'nice point,' and 'the strong ground,' that he could not refrain from relating the conversation to his master.

Mr Whitteret was diverted with the story; but it seemed so strange and unaccountable, that the amount of the demand, and the readiness with which it was paid, dwelt on his mind as extraordinary circumstances; and he having occasion next day to go into Edinburgh, where Mr Frazer had returned from Glengael, to attend his professional duties, he happened to be invited to dine with a party where that gentleman was, and the company consisting chiefly of lawyers,—as dinner parties unfortunately are in the modern Athens,—he amused them with the story of the Leddy's legal knowledge.

Glengael, from the interest which he took in his young friend, Walkinshaw, whom he had left at the castle, was led to inquire somewhat particularly into the history of the Kittlestonheugh family, expressing his surprise and suspicion, in common with the rest of the company, as to the motives which could have influenced a person of Milrookit's character to comply so readily with a demand so preposterous.

One thing led on to another, and Mr Whitteret recollected something of the deed which had been prepared when he was in Mr Keelevin's office, and how old Grippy died before it was executed. The object of this deed was then discussed, and the idea presenting itself to the mind of Glengael, that, possibly, it might have some connection with the Entail, inquired more particularly respecting the terms of that very extraordinary settlement, expressing his astonishment that it should not have contained a clause to oblige the person marrying the heiress to take the name of Walkinshaw, to which the old man, by all accounts, had been so much attached. The whole affair, the more it was considered, seemed the more mysterious; and the conclusion in the penetrating mind of Mr Frazer was, that Milrookit had undoubtedly some strong reason for so quietly hushing the old Leddy's claim.

His opinion at the moment was, that Robina's father had left a will, making some liberal provision for his sister-in-law's family; and that Milrookit was anxious to stand on such terms with his connections, as would prevent any of them, now that Walkinshaw had left Glasgow, from inquiring too anxiously into the state of his father-in-law's affairs. But, without expressing what was passing in his mind, he so managed the conversation as to draw out the several opinions of his legal brethren. Some of them coincided with his own. There was, however, one old pawkie and shrewd writer to the signet present, who remained silent, but whom Mr Frazer observed attending with an uncommon degree of earnest and eager watchfulness to what was said, practising, in fact, nearly the same sort of policy which prompted himself to lead the conversation.

Mr Pilledge,—for so this W. S. was called—had acquired a considerable fortune and reputation in the Parliament House, by the address with which he discovered dormant rights and legal heirs; and Mr Frazer had no doubt, from the evident interest which he had taken in the Kittlestonheugh story, that he would soon take some steps to ascertain the real motives which had led Milrookit to act in the Leddy's case so inconsistently with his general character. In so far he was, therefore, not displeased to observe his earnestness; but he had often heard it said, that Mr Pilledge was in the practice of making bargains with those clients whose dormant rights he undertook to establish, by which it was insinuated that he had chiefly built up his fortune—his general practice being very limited; and Mr Frazer resolved to watch his movements, in order to protect his young friend.

This opinion of Pilledge was not unfounded; for the same evening, after the party broke up, he accompanied Whitteret to the hotel where he staid, and, in the course of the walk, renewed the conversation respecting the singular entail of old Grippy. The Glasgow lawyer was shrewd enough to perceive, that such unusual interest in a case where he had no concern could not be dictated by the mere wonder and curiosity which the Writer to the Signet affected to express; but, being unacquainted with the general character of Pilledge, he ascribed his questions and conjectures to the effect of professional feelings perplexed by a remarkable case.

But it happened next morning that he had occasion to attend a consultation with Mr Frazer, who, taking an opportunity to revert to the subject, which had so occupied their attention on the preceding afternoon, gave him a hint to be on his guard with respect to Pilledge, suggesting, on Walkinshaw's account, that Whitteret might find it of advantage to himself, could he really ascertain the secret reasons and motives by which the possessor of the Kittlestonheugh estate was actuated.

'It would not give you much trouble,' said he, 'were you to step into the Register Office, and look at the terms of the original deed of entail; for although the disinheritance of the eldest son, as I have always understood, was final, there may be some flaw in the succession with respect to the daughter.'

This extrajudicial advice was not lost. As soon as the consultation was over, Whitteret went to the Register Office, where, not a little to his surprise, he found Pilledge, as Frazer had suspected, already in the act of reading the registered deed of the entail. A short conversation then ensued, in which Whitteret intimated that he had also come for the same purpose.

'Then,' said Pilledge, 'let us go together, for it appears to me that the heirs-female of the sons do not succeed before the heirs whatsoever of the daughters; and Milrookit's right would be preferable to that of his wife, if the eldest son has not left a son.'

'But the eldest son has left a son,' replied Whitteret.

'In that case,' said Pilledge, 'we may make a good thing of it with him. I'll propose to him to undertake his claim upon an agreement for half the rent, in the event of success, and we can divide the bakes.'

'You may save yourself the trouble,' replied Whitteret coolly; 'for I shall write to him by the first post—in the meantime, Mr Frazer has authorized me to act.'

'Frazer! how can he authorize you?' said Pilledge discontentedly.

'He knows that best himself; but the right of the son of the oldest son is so clear, that there will be no room for any proceedings.'

'You are mistaken there,' replied Pilledge, eagerly. 'I never saw a deed yet that I could not drive a horse and cart through, and I should think that Milrookit is not such a fool, as to part with the estate without a struggle.

But since you are agent for the heir of entail, I will offer to conduct the respondent's case. I think you said he is rich, independent of the heritable subject.'

This conscientious conversation was abruptly terminated on the part of Whitteret, who immediately went to Mr Frazer, and communicated the important discovery which had been made, with respect to Walkinshaw being the heir of entail. He also mentioned something of what had passed with Mr Pilledge, expressing his apprehensions, from what he knew of Pitwinnoch, Milrookit's man of business, in Glasgow, that Pilledge, with his assistance, might involve the heir in expensive litigation.

Mr Frazer knew enough of the metaphysical ingenuity of the Parliament House, to be aware that, however clear and evident any right might be, it was never beyond the possibility of dispute there, and he immediately suggested that some steps should be taken, to induce Milrookit at once to resign the possession of the property; but, while they were thus speaking Pilledge was already on the road to Glasgow, to apprise Milrookit of what was impending, and to counsel him to resist.

Chapter XXIV

From the circumstance of Milrookit and Robina staying with the Leddy at the time of their marriage, the porter at the inn, where Pilledge alighted on his arrival at Glasgow, supposed they lived in her house, and conducted him there. But, on reaching the door, seeing the name of Mrs Walkinshaw on a brass plate, not quite so large as the one that the Lord Provost of the royal city sported on the occasion of his Majesty's most gracious visit to the lawful and intellectual metropolis of his ancient kingdom, he resolved to address himself to her, for what purpose it would not be easy to say, further than he thought, perhaps, from what he had heard of her character, that she might be of use in the projected litigation. Accordingly, he applied his hand to the knocker, and was shown into the room where she was sitting alone, spinning.

'You are the lady,' said he, 'I presume, of the late much respected Mr Claud Walkinshaw, commonly styled of Grippy.'

'So they say, for want o' a better,' replied the Leddy, stopping at the same time her wheel and looking up to him; 'but wha are ye, and what's your will?'

'My name is Pilledge. I am a writer to the signet, and I have come to see Mr Milrookit of Kittlestonheugh, respecting an important piece of business; '—and he seated himself unbidden. As he said this, the Leddy pricked up her ears, for, exulting in her own knowledge of the law, by which she had recently so triumphed, as she thought, she became eager to know what the important piece of business could be, and replied,—

'Nae doot, it's anent the law-plea he has been brought into, on account of his property.'

Milrookit had been engaged in no suit whatever, but this was the way she took to trot the Edinburgh writer, and she added,—

'How do ye think it'ill gang wi' him? Is there ony prospect o' the Lord Ordinary coming to a decision on the pursuer's petition?'

This really looked so like the language of the Parliament House, considering it came from an old lady, that Pilledge was taken in, and his thoughts running on the entail, he immediately fancied that she alluded to something connected with it, and said,—

'I should think, Madam, that your evidence would be of the utmost importance to the case, and it was to advise with him chiefly as to the line of defence he ought to take that I came from Edinburgh.'

'Nae doot, Sir, I could gie an evidence, and instruct on the merits of the interdict,' said she learnedly; 'but I ne'er hae yet been able to come to a right understanding anent and concerning the different aforesaids set forth in the respondent's reclaiming petition. Noo, I would be greatly obliged if ye would expone to me the nice point, that I may be able to decern accordingly.'

The Writer to the Signet had never heard a clearer argument, either at the bar or on the bench, and he replied,—

'Indeed, Mem, it lies in a very small compass. It appears that the heir-male of your eldest son is the rightful heir of entail; but there are so many difficulties in the terms of the settlement, that I should not be surprised were the Court to set the deed aside, in which case, Mrs Milrookit would still retain the estate, as heir-at-law of her father.'

We must allow the reader to conceive with what feelings the Leddy heard this; but new and wonderful as it was felt to be, she still preserved her juridical gravity, and said,—

'It's vera true what ye say, Sir, that the heir-male of my eldest son,—is a son,—I can easily understand that point o' law;—but can ye tell me how the heir-at-law of her father, Mrs Milrookit that is, came to be a dochter, when it was ay the intent and purpose o' my friend that's awa, the testator, to make no provision but for heirs-male, which his heart, poor man, was overly set on. Howsever, I suppose that's to be considered in the precognition.'

'Certainly, Mem,' replied the Writer to the Signet; 'nothing is more clear than that your husband intended the estate to go, in the first instance, to the heirs-male of his sons; first to those of Walter, the second son; and failing them, to those of George, the third son; and failing them, then to go back to the heirs-male of Charles, the eldest son; and failing them, to the heirs-general of Margaret, your daughter. It is, therefore, perfectly clear, that Mrs Milrookit being, as you justly observe, a daughter, the estate, according to the terms of the settlement, passes her, and goes to the heir of entail, who is the son of your eldest son.'

'I understand that weel,' said the Leddy; 'it's as plain as a pikestaff, that my oe Jamie, the soldier-officer, is by right the heir; and I dinna see how Walky Milrookit, or his wife Beenie, that is, according to law, Robina, can, by any decreet o' Court, keep him out of his ain,—poor laddie.'

'It is very natural for you, Mem, to say so; but the case has other points, and especially as the heir of entail is in the army, I certainly would not advise Mr Milrookit to surrender.'

'But he'll be maybe counselled better,' rejoined the Leddy, inwardly rejoicing at the discovery she had made, and anxious to get rid of the visitor, in order that she might act at once, 'and if ye'll tak my advice, ye'll no sca'd your lips in other folks' kail. Mr Pitwinnoch is just as gude a Belzebub's baby for a law-plea, as ony Writer to the Signet in that bottomless pit, the House o' Parliament in Edinbrough; and since ye hae told me what ye hae done, it's but right to let you ken what I'll do. As yet I hae had but ae law-suit, and I trow it was soon brought, by my own mediation, to a victory; but it winna be lang till I hae another; for if Milrookit does na consent, the morn's morning, to gie up the Kittlestonheugh, he'll soon fin' again what it is to plea wi' a woman o' my experience.'

Pilledge was petrified; he saw that he was in the hands of the Leddy, and that she had completely overreached him. But still he was resolved that his journey should not be barren if he could possibly prevent it. He accordingly wished her good afternoon, and, returning to the inn, ordered a chaise, and proceeded to Kittlestonheugh.

The moment that he left the Leddy, her cloak and bonnet were put in requisition, and attended by her maid, on whose arm she leaned, being still lame with the rheumatism, she sallied forth to Pinwinnoch's office, resolved on action.

He had not, however, acted on what she called her great Bed and Board plea entirely to her satisfaction; for she thought, had he seen the rights of her case as well as she did herself, and had counselled her better, she might have got much more than a thousand pounds. She was, therefore, determined, if he showed the least hesitation in obeying her 'peremptors,' that she would immediately proceed to Mr Whitteret's office, and appoint him her agent. How she happened to imagine that she had any right to institute proceedings against Milrookit, for the restoration of the estate to Walkinshaw, will be best understood by our narrative of what passed at the Consultation.

Chapter XXV

'It was a happy thing for me, Mr Pitwinnoch,' said the Leddy, after being seated in his inner chamber,—'a happy thing, indeed, that I had a father, and sic a father as he was. Weel kent he the rights o' the law; so that I may say I was brought up at the feet o' Gamaliel. But the bed and board plea, Mr Pitwinnoch, that ye thought sae lightly o', and wanted me to mak a sacrifice o' wi' an arbitration, was bairn's play to the case I hae noo in hand. Ye maun ken, then, that I hae ta'en a suspektion in my head, that Milrookit—the de'il rook him for what he did to me—has nae right because to keep, in a wrongous manner, my gudeman's estate and property o' the Kittlestonheugh. 'Deed, Mr Pitwinnoch, ye may glower; but it's my intent and purpose to gar him surrender at discretion, in due course of law. So he'll see what it is to deal wi' a woman o' my legality. In short, Mr Pitwinnoch, I'll mak him fin' that I'm a statute at large; for, as I said before, the thousand pounds was but erls, and a foretaste, that I hae been oure lang, Mr Pitwinnoch, of going to law.'

'You surprise me, Madam,—I cannot understand what you mean,' replied the astonished lawyer.

'Your surprise, and having no understanding, Mr Pitwinnoch, is a symptom to me that ye're no qualified to conduct my case; but, before going to Thomas Whitteret, who, as I am creditably informed, is a man o' a most great capacity, I thought it was but right to sound the depth o' your judgment and learning o' the law; and if I found you o' a proper sufficiency, to gie you a preferment, 'cause ye were my agent in the last plea.'

'But, Madam,' said the astonished lawyer, 'how can you possibly have fancied that Mr Milrookit has not, in right of his wife, properly succeeded to the estate?'

'Because she's no a male-heir—being in terms of the act—but a woman. What say ye to that? Is na that baith a nice point and a ground of action? Na, ye need na look saw constipated, Mr Pitwinnoch, for the heirs-general o' Margaret, the dochter, hae a better right than the heir-at-law o' George, the third and last son, the same being an heir-female.'

'In the name of goodness, where have you, Madam, collected all this stuff?'

'Stuff! Mr Pitwinnoch, is that the way to speak o' my legality? Howsever, since ye're sae dumfoundert, I'll just be as plain's am pleasant wi' you. Stuff truly! I think Mr Whitteret's the man for me.'

'I beg your pardon, Mrs Walkinshaw; but I wish you would be a little more explicit, and come to the point.'

'Have na I come to ae point already, anent the male-heir?'

'True, Madam,' said the lawyer; 'but even, admitting all you have stated to be perfectly correct, Mr Milrookit then has the right in himself, for you know it is to the heirs-general of his mother, and not to herself, that the property goes.'

'Ye need na tell me that. Do you think I dinna ken that he's an heir-general to his mother, being her only child? Ye mak light, I canna but say, o' my understanding, Mr

Pitwinnoch.—Howsever, is't no plain that his wife, not being an heir-male, is debarred frae succeeding; and, he being an heir-general, cannot, according to the law of the case, succeed? Surely, Mr Pitwinnoch, that's no to be contested? Therefore, I maintain that he is lawfully bound to renounce the property, and that he shall do the morn's morning if there's a toun-officer in Glasgow.'

'But, Madam, you have no possible right to it,' exclaimed the lawyer, puzzled.

'Me! am I a male-heir? an aged woman, and a grandmother! Surely, Mr Pitwinnoch, your education maun hae been greatly neglekit, to ken so little o' the laws o' nature and nations. No: the heir-male is a young man, the eldest son's only son.'

The lawyer began to quake for his client as the Leddy proceeded,—

'For ye ken that the deed of entail was first on Walter, the second son; and, failing his heirs-male, then on George and his heirs-male; and, failing them, then it went back to Charles the eldest son, and to his heirs-male; if there's law in the land, his only son ought to be an heir-male, afore Milrookit's wife that's but an only dochter.'

'Has Mr Whitteret put this into your head?—he was bred wi' Keelevin, who drew up the deed,' said the lawyer seriously, struck with the knowledge which the Leddy seemed to have so miraculously acquired of the provisions of the entail.

'I dinna need Mr Whitteret, nor ony siclike, to instruct me in terms o' law—for I got an inkling and an instinct o' the whole nine points' frae my worthy father, that was himsel bred an advocate, and had more law-pleas on his hands when he died than ony ither three lairds in Carrick, Coil, and Cunningham. But no to be my own trumpeter—ye'll just, Mr Pitwinnoch, write a mandamus to Milrookit, in a civil manner—mind that; and tell him in the same, that I'll be greatly obligated if he'll gie up the house and property of Kittlestonheugh to the heir-male, James Walkinshaw, his cousin; or, failing therein, ye'll say that I hae implemented you to pronounce an interlocutor against him; and ye may gie him a bit hint frae yoursel—in a noty beny at the bottom—that you advise him to conform, because you are creditably informed that I mean to pursue him wi' a' the law o' my displeasure.'

'Does your grandson know any thing of this extraordinary business?' said Pitwinnoch; but the Leddy parried the question by saying,—

'That's no our present sederunt; but I would ask you, if ye do not think I hae the justice o' this plea?'

'Indeed, Madam, to say the truth, I shall not be surprised if you have; but there is no need to be so peremptory—the business may be as well settled by an amicable arrangement.'

'What's the use of an amicable arrangement? Is na the law the law? Surely I did na come to a lawyer for sic dowf and dowie proceedings as amicable arrangements— no, Mr Pitwinnoch, ye see yoursel that I hae decern't on the rights o' the case, and therefore (for I maun be short wi' you, for talking to me o' amicable arrangements) ye may save your breath to cool your porridge; my will and pleasure is, that Walkinshaw Milrookit shall do tomorrow morning—in manner of law—then and there—dispone and surrender unto the heir-male of the late Claud Walkinshaw of Kittlestonheugh, in the shire o' Lanark, and synod of Glasgow and Ayr—all and sundry the houses and lands aforesaid, according to the provisions of an act made and passed in the reign of our Sovereign Lord the King. Ye see, Mr Pitwinnoch, that I'm no a daw in barrow't feathers, to be picket and pooket in the way I was by sic trash as the Milrookits.'

The Leddy, having thus instructed her lawyer, bade him adieu, and returned home, leaning on her maid's arm, and on the best possible terms with herself, scarcely for a moment doubting a favourable result to a proceeding that in courtesy we must call her second law-suit.

Chapter XXVI

The shipwreck of the third Laird had left an awful impression on the minds of all the Glengael party, who, immediately after that disaster, returned to the castle. To Mrs Eadie it afforded the strongest confirmation that she had inherited the inspiring mantle of her maternal race; and her dreams and visions, which happily for herself were of the most encouraging augury, became more and more frequent, and her language increased in mystery and metaphor.

'Death,' said she, 'has performed his task—the winds of heaven and the ocean waves have obeyed the mandate, and the moon has verified her influence on the destinies of men. But the volume, with the brazen clasps, has not yet been opened—the chronicled wisdom of ages has not yet been unfolded—Antiquity and Learning are still silent in their niches, and their faces veiled.'

It was of no avail to argue with her, even in her soberest moods, against the fatal consequences of yielding so entirely to the somnambulism of her malady. Her friends listened to her with a solemn compassion, and only hoped that, in the course of the summer, some improvement might take place in her health, and allay that extreme occasional excitement of her nervous system which produced such mournful effects on a mind of rare and splendid endowments. In the hopes of this favourable change, it was agreed, when Mr Frazer was called to Edinburgh on professional business, as we have already mentioned, that the family should, on her account, remain till late in the year at Glengael.

Meanwhile Walkinshaw and French Frazer were proceeding with their recruiting; and it was soon evident to the whole party that the latter had attached himself in a particular manner to Mary. Mrs Eadie, if not the first who observed it, was the first who spoke of it; but, instead of using that sort of strain which ladies of a certain age commonly employ on such affairs, she boded of bridal banquets in the loftiest poetry of her prophetical phraseology. The fortunes of Walkinshaw and Ellen were lost sight of in the mystical presages of this new theme, till the letters arrived from Mr Frazer, announcing the discovery of the provisions in the deed of entail, and requesting his young friend to come immediately to Edinburgh. 'The clasped book of antiquity,' said Mrs Eadie, 'is now open. Who shall dispute the oracles of fate?'

But with all the perspicuity of her second sight, she saw nothing of what was passing at Kittlestonheugh on the same afternoon in which these letters reached the castle.

Mr Pilledge, it will be recollected, immediately after his interview with the Leddy, proceeded in a post-chaise to see Milrookit; and, as he was not embarrassed with much professional diffidence, the purpose of his visit was soon explained. The consternation with which Walky heard of the discovery will be easier imagined than described; but something like a ray of hope and pleasure glimmered in the prospect that Pilledge held out of being able either to break the entail, or to procrastinate the contest to an indefinite period at an expence of less than half the rental of the property.

While they were thus engaged in discussing the subject, and Milrookit was entering as cordially into the views of the Edinburgh writer, as could on so short a notice be reasonably expected, Mr Pitwinnoch was announced. The instinct of birds of a feather, as the proverb says, had often before brought him into contact with Pilledge, and a few words of explanation enabled the triumvirate to understand the feelings of each other thoroughly.

'But,' said Pitwinnoch, 'I am instructed to take immediate steps, to establish the rights of the heir of entail.'

'So much the better,' replied Pilledge; 'the business could not be in abler hands. You can act for your client in the most satisfactory manner, and as Mr Milrookit will authorize me to proceed for him, it will be hard if we cannot make a tough pull.'

Mr Pitwinnoch thought so too, and then amused them with a laughable account of the instructions he had received from the Leddy, to demand the surrender of the estate, and the acknowledgment of the heir, in the course of the following day. Pilledge, in like manner, recounted, in his dry and pawkie style, the interview which he had himself with the same ingenious and redoubtable matron; and that nothing might be wanting to the enjoyment of their jokes and funny recitals, Milrookit ordered in wine, and they were all as jocose as possible, when the servant brought a letter—it was from Mr Whitteret, written at the suggestion of Mr Frazer, to whom he had, immediately after parting from Pilledge in the Register Office, communicated the discovery. It simply announced, that steps were taken to serve Walkinshaw heir to the estate, and suggested on account of the relationship of the parties, that it might be as well to obviate, by an admission of the claim, the necessity of any exposure, or of the institution of unpleasant proceedings, for the fraud that had been practised.

Milrookit trembled as he read,—Pitwinnoch looked aghast, for he perceived that his own conduct in the transaction might be sifted; and Pilledge, foreseeing there would be no use for him, quietly took his hat and slipped away, leaving them to their own meditations.

'This is a dreadful calamity,' were the first words that Milrookit uttered, after a silence of several minutes.

'It is a most unlucky discovery,' said Pitwinnoch.

'And this threat of exposure,' responded his client.

'And my character brought into peril!' exclaimed the lawyer.

'Had you not rashly advised me,' said Milrookit, 'I should never for a moment have thought of retaining the property.'

'Both your father and yourself, Sir,' retorted the lawyer, 'thought if it could be done, it ought; I but did my duty as your lawyer, in recommending what you so evidently wished.'

'That is not the fact, Sir,' replied Milrookit, sharply, and the conversation proceeded to become more abrupt and vehement, till the anger of high words assumed the form of action, and the lawyer and his client rushed like two bull-dogs on each other. At that crisis, the door was suddenly opened, and the old Leddy looking in, said,—

'Shake him weel, Mr Pitwinnoch, and if he'll no conform, I redde ye gar him conform.'

The rage of the combatants was instantly extinguished, and they stood pale, and confounded, trembling in every limb.

It had happened, after the Leddy returned home from Pitwinnoch's, that Robina called, in the carriage, to effect, if possible, a reconciliation with her, which, for reasons we need not mention, her husband had engaged her that afternoon to do, and she had, in consequence, brought her, in the spirit of friendship, as she imagined, out to Kittlestonheugh. The Leddy, however, prided herself on being almost as dexterous a diplomatician as she was learned in the law, and she affected to receive her grand-daughter in the spirit of a total oblivion of all injuries.

'Ye ken, Beenie, my dear,' said she, 'that I'm an aged person, and for a' the few and evil days I hae before me in this howling wilderness, it's vera natural that I should like to make a conciliation wi' my grand-childer, who, I hope, will a' live in comfort wi' one another—every one getting his own right, for it's a sore thing to go to law, although I hae some reason to know that there are folks in our family that ken mair o' the nine points than they let wit—so I'm cordial glad to see you, Beenie, and I take it so kind, that if ye'll gie me a hurl in the carriage, and send me hame at night, I'll no object to gang wi' you and speer for your gudeman, for whom I hae a' manner o' respek, even though he was a thought unreasonable anent my charge o' moderation for the bed and board.'

But the truth is, that the Leddy, from the moment Robina entered the room, was seized with the thirst of curiosity to know how Milrookit would receive the claim, and had, in this eccentric manner, contrived to get herself taken to the scene of action.

Chapter XXVII

Recalled to their senses by the interruption, both Milrookit and his lawyer saw that their interests and characters were too intimately linked in the consequences of the discovery to allow them to incur the hazards of a public disclosure. Pitwinnoch was the first who recovered his presence of mind, and, with great cleverness, he suddenly turned round, and addressed himself to the Leddy:—

'Though we have had a few words, Mr Milrookit is quite sensible that he has not a shadow of reason to withhold the estate from the heir of entail. He will give it up the moment that it is demanded.'

'Then, I demand it this moment,' exclaimed the Leddy; 'and out of this house, that was my ain, I'll no depart till Jamie Walkinshaw, the righteous male-heir, comes to tak possession. It was a most jewdical habit and repute like action o'you, Walky Milrookit, to reset and keep this fine property on a point of law; and I canna see how ye'll clear your character o' the coom ye hae brought on't by sic a diminishment of the grounds of the case between an heir-male and an heir-female.'

Milrookit, seeing his wife coming into the room, and eager to get the business closed as happily as possible, requested Pitwinnoch to follow him into another apartment; to which they immediately retired, leaving the ladies together.

'Beenie,' said the Leddy, with the most ineffable self-satisfied equanimity, 'I hope ye'll prepare yoursel to hear wi' composity the sore affliction that I'm ordain't to gie you. Eh, Beenie! honesty's a braw thing; and I'll no say that your gudeman, my ain oe, has na been a deevil that should get his dues—what they are, the laws and lawyers as weel as me ken are little short o' the halter. But, for a' that, our ain kith and kin,

Beenie— we maun jook and let the jawp gae bye. So I counsel you to pack up your ends and your awls, and flit your camp wi' a' the speed ye dow; for there's no saying what a rampageous soldier-officer, whose trade is to shoot folk, may say or do, when Jamie Walkinshaw comes to ken the battle that I hae fought wi' sic triumphing.'

Mrs Milrookit, who was totally uninformed either of the circumstances of her situation, or of what had taken place, scarcely felt more amazement than terror at this speech, and in perceiving that her grandmother was acquainted with the business which had brought her husband and Pitwinnoch to such high words, that their voices were heard before the carriage reached the door.

'What has happened?' was the anxious exclamation of her alarm.

'Only a discovery that has been made among the Faculty o'Advocates, that a dochter's no a male-heir. So you being but the heir-female of George, the third son, by course o' nature the property goes back to the son of Charles the eldest son—he being, in the words of the act, an heir-male, and your husband, Walkinshaw Milrookit, being an heir-general of Margaret, the daughter, is, in a sense o' law, no heir at all, which is the reason that your cousin Jamie comes in for the estate, and that you and Milrookit must take up your bed, and walk to some other dwelling-place; for here, at Kittlestonheugh, ye hae no continued city, Beenie, my dear, and I'm very sorry for you. It's wi' a very heavy heart, and an e'e o' pity, that I'm obligated not to be beautiful on the mountains, but to tell you thir sore news.'

'Then I'm to understand,' replied Robina, with a degree of composure that surprised the Leddy, 'it has been discovered that my uncle Charles' family were not entirely disinherited, but that James succeeds to the estate? It is only to be regretted that this was not known sooner, before we took up our residence here.'

'It's an auld saying, Beenie, and a true saying, as I know from my own experience, that the law is a tether o' length and durability; so ye need be nane surprised, considering the short time bygane since your father's death, that the pannel was na brought to judgment sooner. Indeed, if it had na been by my instrumentality, and the implementing o' the case that I gied to Pitwinnoch, there's no saying how long it would hae been pending afore the Lords.'

While the Leddy was thus delivering what she called her dark sentence o' legality, Pitwinnoch and Milrookit returned into the room, and the former said to the Leddy,—

'I'm happy to inform you, Madam, that Mr Milrookit acts in the handsomest manner. He is quite satisfied that his cousin, Mr Walkinshaw, is the true heir of entail, and is prepared to resign the estate at once.'

'Did na I prove to you, Mr Pitwinnoch, that wi' baith his feet he had na ae leg in law to stand on; but ye misdootit my judgment,' replied the Leddy, exultingly.

'But,' continued the lawyer, 'in consideration of this most honourable acquiescence at once on his part, I have undertaken that ye'll repay the thousand pounds, which, you must be sensible, was a most ridiculous sum for six weeks' bed and board in your house.'

'Truly, and ye're no far wrang, Mr Pitwinnoch. It was a vera ridiculous soom; for, if I had stood out, I might hae got twa thousand, if no mair. But I canna understand how it is possible you can think I'll part wi' my lawful won money for naething.—What's the gieing up o' the estate to the male heir to me? I'll get neither plack nor bawbee by't, unless it please Jamie to gie me a bit present, by way o' a fee, for counselling you how to set about the precognition that's gotten him his right.—Na, na, no ae farthing will I faik.'

'Then, Madam, I shall feel it my duty to advise Mr Milrookit to revive the question, and take the matter into Court upon a ground of error,' said the lawyer.

'Tak it, tak it, pleasure yoursel in that way; ye can do naething mair cordial to me;—but I think ye ought to know, and Milrookit to understand, baith by bed, board, and washing, and heirs-male, what, it is to try the law wi' me.'

The lawyer and his client exchanged looks: the Leddy, however, continued her address,—

'Howsever, Mr Pitwinnoch, sure am I there was no mistake in the business; for ye'll bear in mind that ye made me an offer of twa hundred, the whilk I refused, and then ye brought me my justly due. That settles the point o' law,—tak my word for't.'

'I am afraid,' said Pitwinnoch to his rueful client, 'that there is no chance'—

' 'Deed no, Mr Pitwinnoch,' replied the Leddy; 'neither pursuer nor respondent has ony chance wi' me in that plea; so just shake your lugs and lie down again. A' your barking would prove afore the Lords but as water spilt on the ground; for the money is in an heritable bond, and the whilk bond is in my hands; that's the strong ground o' the case,—touch it whan ye may.'

Pitwinnoch could with difficulty keep his gravity, and poor Milrookit, finding he had so overreached himself, said,—

'Well, but when you make your will, I trust and hope you will then consider how simply I gave you the money.'

'Mak my will!—that's a delicate hint to an aged woman. I'll no forget that,—and as to your simplicity in paying the justly due for bed, board, and washing,—was na every pound got as if it had been a tooth out o' your head, howkit out by course and force o' law?'

'In truth, Leddy,' said Pitwinnoch, 'we are all friends here, and it's just as well to speak freely. I advised Mr Milrookit to pay you the money, rather than hazard any question that might possibly attract attention to the provisions of the entail; but now since the whole has been brought to an issue, you must be sensible that he suffers enough in losing the estate, and that you ought to give him back the money.'

The Leddy sat for several minutes silent, evidently cogitating an answer, at the end of which she raised her eyes, and said to Pitwinnoch,—

'I can see as far through a milstane as ye can do through a fir deal, and maybe I may tak it in my head to raise a plea wi' you in an action of damages, for plotting and libelling in the way that it's vera visible ye hae done, jointly and severally, in a plea of the crown; and aiblins I'll no tak less than a thousand pounds;—so, Mr Pitwinnoch, keep your neck out o' the woody o' a law plea wi' me, if ye can; for, in the way of business, I hae done wi' you; and, as soon as Mr Whitteret comes hame, I'll see whether I ought not to instruct in a case against you for the art and part conspiracy of the thousand pounds.'

Milrookit himself was obliged to laugh at the look of consternation with which this thunder clap broke over the lawyer, who, unable to withstand the absurdity of the threat, and yet alarmed for the consequences to his reputation, which such an attempt would entail, hastily retired.

Chapter XXVIII

The Leddy having so happily brought her second law-suit to a victorious issue, and already menacing a third, did not feel that her triumph would be complete, until she had obtained the plaudits of the world; and the first person on whom she resolved to levy her exactions of applause was naturally enough the mother of Walkinshaw.

As soon as Pitwinnoch had left the house, she persuaded Milrookit to send the carriage for Mrs Charles, with injunctions to the coachman not to say a word of what had passed, as she intended herself to have the pleasure of communicating the glad tidings. This he very readily agreed to; for, notwithstanding the grudge which he felt at having been so simply mulcted of so large a sum, he really felt his mind relieved by the result of the discovery; perhaps, in complying, he had some sinister view towards the Leddy's good will—some distant vista of his thousand pounds.

Mrs Charles was a good deal surprised at the message to come immediately to Kittlestonheugh; and her timid and gentle spirit, in consequence of learning from the coachman that the old lady was there, anticipated some disaster to her son. Her fears fluttered as she drove on alone. The broad dark shadows that had crossed the path of her past pilgrimage were remembered with melancholy forebodings, and the twilight of the evening having almost faded into night, she caught gloomy presentiments from the time, and sighed that there was no end to her sorrows.

The season was now advanced into September; and though the air was clear, the darkness of the road, the silence of the fields, and the occasional glimmers of the fire that the horses' hoofs struck from the stones, awakened associations of doubt, anxiety, and danger; but the serene magnificence of the starry heavens inspired hope, and the all-encompassing sky seemed to her the universal wings of Providence, vigilant and protecting with innumerable millions of eyes.

Still the devotional enthusiasm of that fancy was but a transient glow on the habitual pale cast of her thoughts; and she saw before her, in the remainder of her mortal journey, only a continuance of the same road which she had long travelled—a narrow and a difficult track across a sterile waste, harsh with brambles, and bleak and lonely.

So is it often, under the eclipse of fortune, even with the bravest spirits; forgetting how suddenly before, in the darkest hour the views of life have changed, they yield to the aspect of the moment, and breathe the mean and peevish complaints of faithlessness and despondency. Let it not, therefore, be imputed as an unworthy weakness, that a delicate and lowly widow, whose constant experience had been an unbroken succession of disappointments and humiliations, should, in such an hour, and shrinking with the sensibilities of a mother, wonder almost to sinning why she had been made to suffer such a constancy of griefs. But the midnight of her fate was now past, and the dawn was soon to open upon her with all its festal attributes of a bright and joyous morning—though our friend the Leddy was not so brisk in communicating the change as we could have wished.

She was sitting alone in the parlour when the carriage returned; and as the trembling mother was shown into the room, she received her with the most lugubrious face that her features could assume.

'Come awa, Bell Fatherlans,' said she, 'come away, and sit down. O this is a most uncertain world—nothing in it has stability;—the winds blow—the waters run—the grass grows—the snow falls—the day flieth away unto the uttermost parts of the sea, and the night hideth her head in the morning cloud, and perisheth for evermore. Many a lesson we get—many a warning to set our thoughts on things above; but we're ay sinking, sinking, sinking, as the sparks fly upward.—Bell, Bell, we're a' like thorns crackling under a kail-pot.'

'What has occurred?' exclaimed Mrs Charles; 'I beg you'll tell me at once.'

'So I will, when I hae solaced you into a religious frame o' mind to hear me wi' a Christian composity o' temper; for what I maun tell is, though I say't mysel, a something.'

'For goodness and mercy, I entreat you to proceed.—Where is Mr Milrookit? where is Robina?'

'Ye need na hope to see muckle o' them the night,' replied the Leddy. 'Poor folk, they hae gotten their hands filled wi' cares. O Bell, Bell—when I think o't—it's a judgment—it's a judgment, Bell Fatherlans, aboon the capacity o' man! Really, when I consider how I hae been directit—and a' by my own skill, knowledge, wisdom, and understanding—it's past a' comprehension. What would my worthy father hae said had he lived to see the day that his dochter won sic a braw estate by her ain interlocutors?—and what would your gudefather hae said, when he was ay brag bragging o' the conquest he had made o' the Kittlestonheugh o' his ancestors—the whilk took him a lifetime to do—had he seen me, just wi' a single whisk o' dexterity, a bit touch of the law, make the vera same conquest for your son Jamie Walkinshaw in less than twa hours?'

'You astonish me! to what do you allude? I am amazed, and beginning to be confounded,' said Mrs Charles.

'Indeed it is no wonder,' replied the Leddy; 'for wha would hae thought it, that I, an aged illiterate grandmother, would hae bamboozlet an Embrough Writer to the Signet on a nice point, and found out the ground of an action for damages against that tod o' a bodie Pitwinnoch, for intromitting wi' ane of the four pleas o' the Crown? Had I kent what I ken now, uncle Watty might still hae been to the fore, and in the full possession of his seven lawful senses—for, woman as I am, I would hae been my own man o' business, counsel, and executioner, in the concos mentos sederunt—whereby I was so 'frauded o' my rightful hope and expectation. But Pitwinnoch will soon fin' the weight o' the lion's paw that his doobileecity has roused in me.'

Mrs Charles, who was much amused by the exultation with which the Leddy had recounted her exploits in the bed and board plea, perceiving that some new triumph equally improbable had occurred, felt her anxieties subside into curiosity; and being now tolerably mistress of her feelings, she again inquired what had happened.

'I'll tell you,' said the Leddy; 'and surely it's right and proper you his mother should know, that, through my implementing, it has been discovered that your son is an heir-male according to law!'

'No possible!' exclaimed the delighted mother, the whole truth flashing at once on her mind.

'Aye, that's just as I might hae expectit—a prophet ne'er got honour in his own country; and so a' the thank I'm to get for my pains is a no possible!' said the Leddy offended, mistaking the meaning of the interjection. 'But it is a true possible; and

Milrookit has consentit to adjudicate the estate—so ye see how ye're raised to pride and affluence by my instrumentality. Firstly, by the bed and board plea, I found a mean to revisidend your 'nuity; and secondly, I hae found the libel proven, that Beenie, being a dochter, is an heir-female, and is, by course of law, obligated to renounce the estate.'

'This is most extraordinary news, indeed,' rejoined Mrs Charles, 'after for so many years believing my poor children so destitute; 'and a flood of tears happily came to her relief.

'But, Bell Fatherlans,' resumed the Leddy, I'll tak you wi' the tear in your ee, as both you and Jamie maun be sensible, that, but for my discerning, this great thing never could hae been brought to a come-to-pass. I hope ye'll confabble thegither anent the loss I sustained by what happened to uncle Watty, and mak me a reasonable compensation out o' the rents; the whilk are noo, as I am creditably informed, better than fifteen hundred pounds per anno Domini, that's the legality for the year o' our Lord;—a sma'matter will be a great satisfaction.'

'Indeed,' said Mrs Charles, 'James owes you much; and your kindness in giving him the bill so generously, I know, has made a very deep impression on his heart.'

'He was ay a blithe and kindly creature,' exclaimed the Leddy, wiping her eye, as if a tear had actually shot into it—'and may be it winna fare the waur wi' him when I'm dead and gone. For I'll let you into a secret—it's my purpose to make a last will and testament, and cut off Milrookit wi' a shilling, for his horridable niggerality about the bed and board concern. Na, for that matter, as ye'll can fen noo without ony 'nuity, but your ain son's affection, I hae a great mind, and I'll do't too—that's what I will—for fear I should be wheedled into an adversary by my dochter Meg for the Milrookits,—I'll gie the thousand pound heritable bond to your Mary for a tocher; is not that most genteel of me? I doot few families hae had a grandmother for their ancestor like yours.'

Some farther conversation to the same effect was continued, and the injustice which Milrookit had attempted seemed to Mrs Charles considerably extenuated by the readiness with which he had acknowledged the rights of her son. For, notwithstanding all the Leddy's triumphant oratory and legal phraseology, she had no difficulty in perceiving the true circumstances of the case.

Chapter XXIX

In the opinion of all the most judicious critics, the Iliad terminated with the death of Hector; but, as Homer has entertained us with the mourning of the Trojans, and the funeral of the hero, we cannot, in our present circumstances, do better than adopt the rule of that great example. For although it must be evident to all our readers that the success of the Leddy in her second law-suit, by placing the heir, in despite of all the devices and stratagem of parchments and Pitwinnoch, in possession of the patrimony of his ancestors, naturally closes the Entail, a work that will, no doubt, outlive the Iliad, still there were so many things immediately consequent on that event, that our story would be imperfect without some account of them.

In the first place, then, Walkinshaw, immediately after the receipt of Frazer's letter, acquainting him with the discovery of the provisions of the deed, returned to Edinburgh, where he arrived on the third day after his friend had heard from Whitteret, the Glasgow writer, that Milrookit, without objection, agreed to surrender the estate. The result of which communication was an immediate and formal declaration from Walkinshaw of his attachment to Ellen, and a cheerful consent from her father, that their marriage, as soon as the necessary preparations could be made, should be celebrated at Glengael.

Upon French Frazer the good fortune of his brother officer was no less decisive, for any scruple that he might have felt in his attachment to Mary, on account of his own circumstances, was removed by an assurance from Walkinshaw that he would, as soon as possible, make a liberal provision both for her and his mother; and in the same letter which Walkinshaw wrote home on his return to Edinburgh, and in which he spoke of his own marriage, he entreated his mother's consent that Mary should accept the hand of Frazer.

On Mrs Eadie, the fulfilment, as she called it, of her visions and predictions, had the most lamentable effect. Her whole spirit became engrossed with the most vague and mystical conceptions; and it was soon evident that an irreparable ruin had fallen upon one of the noblest of minds. Over her latter days we shall, therefore, draw a veil, and conclude her little part in our eventful history with simply mentioning that she never returned to Camrachle; but sunk into rest in the visionary beatitude of her parental solitudes.

Her husband, now a venerable old man, still resides as contentedly as ever in his parish; and, when we last visited him, in his modest mansion, he informed us that he had acquiesced in the wishes of his elders by consenting to receive a helper and successor in the ministry. So far, therefore, as the best, the most constant, and the kindest friends of the disinherited family are concerned, our task is finished: but we have a world of things to tell of the Leddy and the Milrookits, many of which we must reserve till we shall have leisure to write a certain story of incomparable humour and pathos.

In the meantime, we must proceed to mention, that the Leddy, finding it was quite unnecessary to institute any further proceedings, to eject the Milrookits from Kittlestonheugh, as they of their own accord removed, as soon as they found a suitable house, returned to her residence in the royal city, where she resumed her domestic thrift at the spinning-wheel, having resolved not to go on with her action of damages against Pitwinnoch, till she had seen her grandson, who, prior to his marriage, was daily expected.

'For,' as she said to his mother, after consulting with Mr Whitteret, and stating her grounds of action, 'it is not so clear a case as my great bed and board plea—and Mr Whitteret is in some doubt, whether Pitwinnoch should be sent to trial by my instrumentality, or that of Jamie—very sensibly observing—for he's really a man o' the heighth o' discretion yon—that it would be hard for an aged gentlewoman like me, with a straitened jointure, to take up a cause that would, to a moral certainty, be defendit, especially when her grandson is so much better able to afford the expence. The which opinion of counsel has made me sit down with an arrest of judgment for the present, as the only reason I hae for going to law at all is to mak money by it. Howsever, if ye can persuade Jamie to bequeath and dispone to me his right to the damage, which I mean to assess at a thousand pounds, I'll implement Mr Whitteret to pursue.'

'I dare say,' replied Mrs Charles, 'that James will very readily give up to you all his claim; but Mr Pitwinnoch having rectified the mistake he was in, we should forgive and forget.'

'A'weel I wat, Bell Fatherlans, I needna cast my pearls o' great price before swine, by waring my words o' wisdom wi' the like o' you. In truth, it's an awfu' story when I come to think how ye hae been sitting like an effigy on a tomb, wi' your hands baith alike syde, and mento mori written on your vesture and your thigh, instead o' stirring your stumps, as ye ought to hae done—no to let your bairns be rookit o' their right by yon Cain and Abel, the twa cheatrie Milrookits. For sure am I, had no I ta'en the case in hand, ye might hae continued singing Wally, wally, up yon bank, and wally, wally, down yon brae, a' the days o' your tarrying in the tabernacles o' men.'

Her daughter-in-law admitted, that she was, indeed, with all her family, under the greatest obligations to her,—and that, in all probability, but for her happy discovery of the errand on which the writer to the signet had come to Glasgow, they might still have had their rights withheld.

In conversations of this description the time passed at Glasgow, while the preparations for the marriage of Walkinshaw and Ellen were proceeding with all expedient speed at Glengael. Immediately after the ceremony, the happy pair, accompanied by Mary, returned to Edinburgh, where it was determined the marriage of Mary with French Frazer should be celebrated, Mrs Charles and the old lady being equally desirous of being present.

We should not, however, be doing justice to ourselves, as faithful historians, were we to leave the reader under an impression that the Leddy's visit to the lawful metropolis was entirely dictated by affectionate consideration for her grandchildren. She had higher and more public objects, worthy, indeed, of the spirit with which she had so triumphantly conducted her causes. But with that remarkable prudence, so conspicuous in her character, she made no one acquainted with the real motives by which she was actuated,—namely, to acquire some knowledge of the criminal law, her father not having, as she said, 'paid attention to that Court of Justice, his geni being, like her own, more addicted to the civilities of the Court o' Session.'

She was led to think of embarking in this course of study, by the necessity she was often under of making, as she said, her servants 'walk the carpet;' or, in other words, submit to receive those kind of benedictions to which servants are, in the opinion of all good administrators of householdry, so often and so justly entitled. It had occurred to her that, some time or another, occasion might require that she should carry a delinquent handmaid before the Magistrates, or even before the Lords; indeed, she was determined to do so on the very first occurrence of transgression, and, therefore, she was naturally anxious to obtain a little insight of the best practice in the Parliament House, that she might, as she said herself, be made capable of implementing her man of business how to proceed.

Walkinshaw, by promising to take every legal step that she herself could take against Pitwinnoch, had evinced, as she considered it, such a commendable respect for her judgment, that he endeared himself to her more than ever. He was, in consequence, employed to conduct her to the Parliament House, that she might hear the pleadings; but by some mistake he took her to that sink of sin the Theatre, when Othello was performing, where, as she declared, she had received all the knowledge of the criminal law she could require, it having been manifestly shown, that any woman stealing a napkin ought to be prosecuted with the utmost rigour. But her legal studies were soon interrupted by the wedding festivities; and when she returned to Glasgow, alas! she was not long permitted to indulge her legal pursuits; for various causes combined to deprive the world of our incomparable heroine. Her doleful exit from the tents of Time, Law, and Physic, it is now our melancholy duty to relate, which we shall endeavour to do with all that good-humoured pathos for which we are so greatly and so deservedly celebrated. If nobody says we are so distinguished, we must modestly do it ourselves, never having been able to understand why a candidate for parliament or popularity should be allowed to boast of his virtues more than any other dealer in tales and fictions.

Chapter XXX

Marriage feasts, we are creditably informed, as the Leddy would have said, are of greater antiquity than funerals; and those with which the weddings of Walkinshaw and his sister were celebrated, lacked nothing of the customary festivities. The dinners which took place in Edinburgh were, of course, served with all the refinements of taste and dissertations on character, which render the entertainments in the metropolis of Mind occasionally so racy and peculiar. But the cut-and-come-again banquets of Glasgow, as the Leddy called them, following on the return of the Laird and his bride to his patrimonial seat, were, in her opinion, far superior, and she enjoyed them with equal glee and zest.

'Thanks be, and praise,'said she, after returning home from one of those costly piles of food, 'I hae lived to see, at last, something like wedding doings in my family. Charlie's and Bell Fatherlans's was a cauldrife commodity, boding scant and want, and so cam o't—Watty's was a walloping galravitch o' idiocety, and so cam o't—Geordie's was little better than a burial formality, trying to gie a smirk, and so cam o't—as for Meg's and Dirdumwhamle's, theirs was a third marriage—a cauld-kail-het-again affair—and Beenie and Walky's Gretna Green, play-actoring,— Bed, Board, and Washing, bore witness and testimony to whatna kind o'bridal they had. But thir jocose gavaulings are worthy o' the occasion. Let naebody tell me, noo, that the three P's o' Glasgow mean Packages, Puncheons, and Pigtail, for I have seen and known that they may be read in a marginal note Pomp, Punch, and Plenty. To be sure, the Embroshers are no without a genteelity—that maun be condescended to them. But I jealouse they're pinched to get gude wine, poor folk—they try sae mony different bottles: naething hae they like a gausie bowl. Therefore, commend me to our ain countryside,—Fatted calves, and feasting Belshazers,—and let the Embroshers cerimoneez wi' their Pharaoh's lean kine and Grants and Frazers.'

But often when the heart exults, when the 'bosom's Lord sits light upon his throne,' it is an omen of sorrow. On the very night after this happy revel of the spirits, the Leddy caught a fatal cold, in consequence of standing in the current of a door while the provost's wife, putting on her pattens, stopped the way, and she was next morning so indisposed that it was found necessary to call in Dr Sinney to attend her; who was of opinion, considering she was upwards of seventy-six, that it might go hard with her if she did not recover; and, this being communicated to her friends, they began to prepare themselves for the worst.

Her daughter, the Lady of Dirdumwhamle, came in from the country, and paid her every mark of attention. At the suggestion of her husband, she, once or twice, intimated a little anxiety to know if her mother had made a will; but the Leddy cut her short, by saying,—

'What's t'at to thee, Meg? I'm sure I'm no dead yet, that t'ou should be groping about my bit gathering?'

Dirdumwhamle himself rode daily into Glasgow in the most dutiful manner; but, receiving no satisfaction from the accounts of his wife respecting the Leddy's affairs, he was, of course, deeply concerned at her situation; and, on one occasion, when he was sitting in the most sympathising manner at her bedside, he said, with an affectionate and tender voice,—

'That he hoped she would soon be well again; but, if it was ordain't to be otherwise, he trusted she would give her daughter some small memorial over and by what she might hae alloo't her in will.'

''Deed,' replied the Leddy, as she sat supported by pillows, and breathing heavily, 'I'll no forget that—for ye may be sure, when I intend to dee, that I'll mak my ain hands my executioners.'

'Aye, aye,' rejoined the pathetic Laird, 'I was ay o' that opinion, and that ye would act a mother's part in your latter end.'

To this the Leddy made no reply; but by accident coughed rather a little too moistly in his face, which made him shift his seat, and soon after retire.

He had not long taken his leave, when Milrookit and Robina came in, both in the most affectionate manner; and, after the kindest inquiries, they too hoped that she had made her departure clear with this world, and that, when she was removed to a better, no disputes would arise among surviving friends.

'I'm sure,' said Robina, 'we shall all greatly miss you; and I would be very glad if you would give me some little keepsake out of your own hands, if it were no more than the silver teapot.'

'I canna do that yet, Beenie, my Leddy, for ye ken I'm obligated to gie the Laird and Nell Frizel a tea banquet, as soon's I'm able. But when I'm dead and gone, for we're a' lifelike and a' deathlike, if ye outlive me, ye'll fin' that I was a grandmother.'

'It's pleasant to hear,' said Milrookit, 'that ye hae sic an inward satisfaction of health; but I hope ye'll no tak it ill at my wishing for a token o' my grandfather. I would like if ye would gie me from yourself the old-fashioned gold watch, just because it was my grandfather's, and sae lang in his aught.'

'Aye, Walky, I won'er thou doesna wis for me, for I was longer in his aught. Bairns, bairns, I purpose to outlive my last will and testament, so I redde ye keep a calm sough.'

This they thought implied that she had made some provision for them in her last will and testament; and although disappointed in their immediate object, they retired in as complete peace of mind as any affectionate grandchildren like them could retire from a deathbed.

To them succeeded the mother of Walkinshaw.

'Come away, Bell Fatherlans,' said the Leddy—'sit down beside me;' and she took her kindly by the hand. 'The Milrookits, auld and young, hae been here mair ravenous than the worms and cloks of the tomb, for they but devour the dead body; but yon greedy caterpillars would strip me o' leaf and branch afore my time. There was Dirdumwhamle sympathising for a something over and aboon what Meg's to get by the will. Then came Beenie, another of the same, as the Psalmist says, simpering, like a yird tead, for my silver teapot, and syne naething less would serve her gudeman but a solemneesing wheedlie for the auld gold watch. But I'll sympathise, and I'll simper, and I'll wheedle them.—Hae, tak my keys, and gang into the desk-head, and ye'll fin' a bonny sewt pocket-book in the doocot hole next the window, bring't to me.'

Mrs Charles did as she was desired; and when the pocketbook was brought, the old Leddy opened it, and, taking out one of her Robin Carricks, as she called her bills, she said,—

'Bring me a pen that can spell, and I'll indoss this bit hundred pound to thee, Bell, as an over and aboon; and when ye hae gotten't, gang and bid Jamie and Mary come to see me, and I'll gie him the auld gold watch, and her the silver teapot, just as a reward to the sympathising, simpering, and wheedling Milrookits. For between ourselves, Bell, my time is no to be lang noo amang you. I feel the clay-cold fingers o' Death handling my feet; so when I hae settled my worldly concernments, ye'll send for Dr De'il fear, for I would na like to mount into the chariots o' glory without the help o' an orthodox.'

All that the Leddy required was duly performed. She lingered for several days; but, at the end of a week from the commencement of her illness, she closed her eyes, and her death was, after the funeral, according to the Scottish practice, announced in that loyal and well-conducted old paper, the Glasgow Courier, as having taken place, 'to the great regret of all surviving friends'.

Chapter XXXI

We have often lamented that so many worthy people should be at the expence and trouble of making last wills and testaments, and yet never enjoy what passes at the reading of them. On all the different occasions where we have been present at such affecting ceremonies, it was quite edifying to see how justly the sorrow was apportioned to the legacies; those enjoying the greatest being always the most profoundly distressed; their tears, by some sort of sympathy, flowing exactly in accordance with the amount of the sums of money, or the value of the chattels which they were appointed to receive:

But on no other occasion have we ever been so much struck with the truth of this discovery as on that when, after attending the Leddy's remains to the family sepulchre, our acquaintance, Dirdumwhamle, invited us to return to the Leddy's house, in order to be present at the solemnity. Considering the tenderness of our feelings, and how much we respect the professed sincerity of mankind, we ought, perhaps, in justice to ourselves, knowing how incapable we are of withstanding the mournful melancholy of such posthumous rites, to have eschewed the invitation of our sighing and mourning friend.

We were, however, enticed, by a little curiosity, to walk with him arm in arm from the interment, suggesting to him, on the way, every topic of Christian consolation suitable on such occasions, perceiving how much he stood in need of them all.

When we entered the parlour, which had been so often blithened with the jocose spirit of its defunct mistress, we confess that our emotions were almost too great for our fortitude, and that, as we assured the Laird of Dirdumwhamle, our sensibility was so affected that we could, with the utmost difficulty, repress our hysterical sobbings, which he professed with no less sincerity entirely to believe. Alas! such scenes are too common in this transitory scene of things.

Seeing how much we were all in need of a glass of wine, Dirdumwhamle, with that free thought which forms so prominent a feature of his character, suggested to his lady that she should order in the decanters, and, with a bit of the shortbread, enable us to fortify our hearts for the doleful task and duty we had yet to perform.

The decanters were, accordingly, ordered in; the wine poured into the glasses; and all present to each other sighed, as in silence, the reciprocity of good wishes.

After which a pause ensued—a very syncope of sadness—a dwam of woe, as the Leddy herself would have called it, had she been spared, to witness how much we all felt.—But she was gone—she had paid the debt of nature, and done, as Dirdumwhamle said, what we are all in this life ordained to do. It is, therefore, of no consequence to imagine how she could either have acted or felt had she been present at the reading of her last will and testament. In a word, after that hiatus in the essay of mourning, it was proposed, by young Milrookit, that the Leddy's scrutoire should be opened, and the contents thereof examined.

No objection was made on the part of any of the sorrowful and assembled friends,—quite the contrary. They all evinced the most natural solicitude, that every thing proper and lawful should be done. 'It is but showing our respect to the memory of her that is gone,' said Dirdumwhamle, 'to see in what situation she has left her affairs—not that I have any particular interest in the business, but only, considering the near connection between her and my family, it is due to all the relations that the distribution which she has made of her property should be published among them.—It would have been a happy and a comfortable thing to every one who knew her worth had her days been prolonged; but, alas! that was not in her own power. Her time o' this world was brought, by course of nature, to an end, and no man ought to gainsay the ordinances of Providence.—Gudewife, hae ye the key o' the desk-head?'

Mrs Milrookit, his wife, who, during this highly sympathetic conversation, had kept her handkerchief to her eyes, without removing it, put her hand into her pocket, and, bringing forth a bunch of keys, looked for one aside, which, having found, she presented it to her husband, saying, with a sigh, 'That's it.'

He took it in his hand, and, approaching the scrutoire, found, to his surprise, that it was sealed.

'How is this?' cried Dirdumwhamle, in an accent somewhat discordant with the key in which the performers to the concert of woe were attuned.

'I thought,' replied Walkinshaw the Laird, 'that it was but regular, when my grandmother died, that, until we all met, as we are now met, her desk and drawers should be sealed for fear....'

'For fear of what?' Dirdumwhamle was on the point of saying as we thought; but, suddenly checking himself, and, again striking the note of woe, in perfect harmony, he replied,—

'Perfectly right, Laird,—when all things are done in order, no one can have any reason to complain.'

Dirdumwhamle then took off the seal, and applying the key to the lock, opened the desk head, and therein, among other things, found the embroidered pocketbook, so well known to our readers. At the sight of it, the tears of his lady began to flow, and they flowed the faster when, on examining its contents, it was discovered that the hundred pound Robin Carrick was not forthcoming—She having acquired some previous knowledge of its existence, and had, indeed, with her most dutiful husband, made a dead set at it in their last affectionate conversation with the Leddy, with what success the reader is already informed.

A search was then made for the heritable bond for a thousand pounds, but Mrs Charles Walkinshaw surprised us all into extreme sorrow, when, on understanding the object of the search, she informed us that the said bond had been most unaccountably given, as the Milrookits thought, to her daughter for a dowry.

An inventory of the contents of the desk being duly and properly made,—indeed we ourselves took down the particulars in the most complete manner,—an inquest was instituted with respect to the contents of drawers, papers, boxes, trunks, and even into the last pouches that the Leddy had worn; but neither the silver teapot nor the old gold watch were forthcoming. Mrs Charles Walkinshaw, however, again explained, and the explanation was attended by the happiest effects, in so much as to us it served to lessen in a great degree the profound sorrow in which all the Milrookits had been plunged.

But yet no will was found, and Dirdumwhamle was on the point of declaring that the deceased having died intestate, his wife, her daughter, succeeded, of course, to all she had left. But while he was speaking, young Mrs Milrookit happened to cast her eyes into one of the pigeon-holes in the scrutoire head, where, tied with a red tape in the most business-like manner, a will was found,—we shall not say that Dirdumwhamle had previously seen it, but undoubtedly he appeared surprised that it should have been so near his sight and touch, so long unobserved,—which gave us a hint to suggest, that when people make their wills and testaments, they should always tie them with red tape, that none of their heirs, executors, or assigns, may fall into the mistake of not noticing them at the time of the funeral examination, and afterwards, when by themselves, tear or burn them by mistake.

Chapter XXXII

It appeared by this will that the Leddy had, with the exception of a few inconsiderable legacies to the rest of her family, and a trifling memorial of her affection to our friend Walkinshaw, bequeathed all to her daughter, at which that lady, with the greatest propriety, burst out into the most audible lament for her affectionate mother, and Dirdumwhamle, her husband, became himself so agitated with grief, that he was almost unable to proceed with the reading of the affecting document. Having gradually mastered his feelings, he was soon, however, able to condole with Mrs Charles Walkinshaw upon the disappointment she had, no doubt, suffered; observing, by way of consolation, that it was, after all, only what was to have been expected; for the Leddy, the most kind of parents, naturally enough considered her own daughter as the nearest and dearest of all her kith and kin.

During this part of the scene we happened inadvertently to look towards Walkinshaw, and were not a little shocked to observe a degree of levity sparkling in his eyes, quite unbecoming such a sorrowful occasion; and still more distressed were we at the irreverence with which, almost in actual and evident laughter, he inquired at Dirdumwhamle the date of the paper.

It was found to have been made several years before, soon after the decease of poor Walter.

'Indeed!' said Walkinshaw pawkily; 'that's a very important circumstance, for I happen to have another will in my pocket, made at Edinburgh, while the Leddy was there at my marriage, and the contents run somewhat differently.'

The tears of the Lady of Dirdumwhamle were instantaneously dried up, and the most sensitive of Lairds himself appeared very much surprised; while, with some vibrating accent in his voice, he requested that this new last will and testament might be read.

Sorry are we to say it, that, in doing so, Walkinshaw was so little affected, that he even chuckled while he read. This was, no doubt, owing to the little cause he had to grieve, a legacy of five guineas, to buy a ring, being all that the Leddy had bequeathed to him.

This second will, though clearly and distinctly framed, was evidently dictated by the Leddy herself. For it began by declaring, that, having taken it into her most serious consideration, by and with the advice of her private counsel, Mr Frazer of Glengael, whom she appointed executor, she had resolved to make her last will and testament; and after other formalities, couched somewhat in the same strain, she bequeathed sundry legacies to her different grandchildren,—first, as we have said, five guineas, as a token of her particular love, to Walkinshaw, he standing in no need of any farther legacy, and being, over and moreover, indebted to her sagacity for the recovery of his estate. Then followed the enumeration of certain trinkets and Robin Carricks, which were to be delivered over to, and to be held and enjoyed by, Mary, his sister. To this succeeded a declaration, that her daughter Margaret, the wife of Dirdumwhamle, should enjoy the main part of her gathering, in life rent, but not until the Laird, her husband, had paid his debt of nature, and departed out of this world; and if the said legatee did not survive her husband, then the legacy was to go to Mrs Charles Walkinshaw, the testatrix's daughter-in-law. 'As for my two grateful grandchildren, Walkinshaw Milrookit, and Robina his wife,' continued the spirit of the Leddy to speak in the will, 'I bequeath to them, and their heirs for ever, all and haill that large sum of money which they still stand indebted to me, for and on account of bed, board, and washing, of which debt only the inconsiderable trifle of one thousand pounds was ever paid.'

The testing clause was all that followed this important provision, but the will was in every respect complete, and so complete also was the effect intended, that young Milrookit and his wife Robina immediately rose and retired, without speaking, and Dirdumwhamle and his lady also prepared to go away, neither of them being seemingly in a condition to make any remark on the subject.

Such is the natural conclusion of our story; but perhaps it is expected that we should say something of the subsequent history of Walkinshaw, especially as his wife has brought him nine sons,—'all male heirs,' as Dirdumwhamle often says with a sigh, when he thinks of his son and Robina having only added daughters to the increasing population of the kingdom. But Walkinshaw's career as a soldier belongs to a more splendid theme, which, as soon as ever we receive a proper hint to do so, with ten thousand pounds to account, we propose to undertake, for he was present at the most splendid achievements of the late universal war. His early campaigns were not, however, brilliant; but, in common with all his companions in arms during the first years of that mighty contest, he still felt, under the repulses of many disasters, that the indisputable heroism of the British spirit was never impaired, and that they were still destined to vindicate their ancient superiority over France.

These heroic breathings do not, however, belong to our domestic story; and, therefore, all we have to add is, that, as often as he revisited his patrimonial home on leave of absence, he found the dinnering of his friends in the royal city almost as hard work as the dragooning of his foes. Since the peace, now that he is finally settled at Kittlestonheugh with all his blushing honours thick upon him, the Lord Provost and Magistrates have never omitted any opportunity in their power of treating him with all that distinction for which, as a corporation, they are so deservedly celebrated. Indeed, there are few communities where there is less of the spirit of ostracism, or where a man of public merit is more honoured by his fellow-citizens, than in Glasgow. Therefore say we in fine,—

LET GLASGOW FLOURISH!

www.ingramcontent.com/pod-product-compliance
Lightning Source LLC
Chambersburg PA
CBHW081226020726
47503CB00011B/2920